Fates and Furies

The Collection

Also by
Melissa Haag

The Judgement World
(swoony wolf shifters!)

Judgement of the Six

Hope(less) *(Mis)fortune* *(Un)wise*
(Un)bidden *(Dis)content* *(Sur)real*

Judgement of the Six Companions

Clay's Hope *Emmitt's Treasure* *Luke's Dream*
Thomas' Heart *Carlos' Peace*

The Mantirum World
(hot shifters of all kinds!)

Of Fates and Furies

Fury Frayed *Fury Focused* *Fury Freed*

By Kiss and Claw

The Howl *The Hunt* *The Hunger*

In Fire and Ash

Going to Hell *Raising Hell* *Hell on Earth*

THE COLLECTION

FURY FRAYED

FURY FOCUSED

FURY FREED

MELISSA HAAG

Shattered Glass
PUBLISHING

The characters and events in this book are fictitious. Any similarities to real persons, living or dead, are coincidental and not intended by the author.

Published by Shattered Glass Publishing.
Cover art by Joy Author Design Studio
Print Cover design by Shattered Glass Publishing
© Depositphotos.com
Proofread by The Proof Posse (Jackie, Dawn, Heather, Mirjam, and Roxanne)

ISBN 978-1-63869-043-6 (eBook Edition)
ISBN 978-1-63869-044-3 (Paperback Edition)

Version 2023.12.04

OF FATES AND FURIES

BOOKS 1 - 3

Fury Frayed

Megan's temper lands her in a town of misfit supernatural creatures. It's the one place she should be able to fit in, but she can't. Instead, she itches to punch the smug sheriff in his face, pull the hair from a pack of territorial blondes, and kiss the smile off the shy boy's face. Unfortunately, she can't do any of that, either, because humans are dying and all clues point to her.

With Megan's temper flaring, time to find the real killer and clear her name is running out. As much as she wants to return to her old life, she needs to embrace who and what she is. It's the only way to find and punish the creature responsible.

Fury Focused

Life in Uttira isn't easy for Megan. Knowing what she is hasn't helped her control her temper. Her mood swings don't bother her as much as the weird side effects that come with them. When things start to go up in flames around her, she knows she needs help controlling her abilities. But, the only person with the answers abandoned Megan in Uttira months ago.

Megan knows she must find her mother in the real world. However, the only way out of the magical barrier surrounding Uttira is with the mark of Mantirum. A mark she will only receive if she can manage to control her temper…or die trying.

Fury Freed

While preparing to leave Uttira after graduation, Megan finds the Book of Fury. The answers she's needed about who she is, her purpose, and her powers have been there the whole time, along with a shocking revelation.

Now, it's not just a matter of finding Megan's mother. Megan must find the two preceding generations as well, because the book is clear on one thing: there can only be three furies.

FURY FRAYED

CHAPTER ONE

THE RAPID THUMP OF MY FEET AGAINST THE CEMENT SENT STUDENTS scattering from the sidewalk as I sprinted from school. I needed to get home before Mom did.

"It wasn't my fault this time," I said under my breath. I raced around the corner, navigating the route home at high speed. "She pushed me into the locker. What was I supposed to do?"

I knew what I was supposed to do. Not fight. Yet, my temper never listened. Why couldn't I just be like other people my age? Moody but not irrationally angry?

I shook my head while neatly jumping over a kid on a tricycle. His mother squawked from her place on their porch. The look she shot me sent my temper flaring again.

"He's fine!" I shouted. "Maybe you should get off your ass and stand by him if you don't want people jumping over him." However, I was already four houses away when I finished my rant, so I doubted she'd heard more than "he's fine."

Focusing once more on what I planned to tell my mother, I rejected my first approach.

"Come on, Megan. You can do better," I said to myself. "I

was upholding the school's anti-bullying policy. I saw that girl shaking down people for their lunch money and used my words to ask her to stop." I nodded. That sounded good. I'd point out that I'd used my words, and not my fists, first. "She didn't like me sticking up for her victims and tried pushing me into my locker."

That sounded like a winner. But, enough to keep me from being locked up in the house for a week while suspended? Probably not. I ran harder. If I could make it home before Mom, I could delete the messages the secretary had left on the answering machine.

She was yet another person I'd like to punch in the face, and not just because of her condescending tone when she'd spoken to me today. Something about her had rubbed me wrong from day one, and it had only gotten worse during the month I'd attended Parkerville High.

Not even winded from the sprint, I stopped in front of my house, only seven blocks from school. Like the omen of ill fortune it was, Mom's shiny red sports car sat at the curb. I swore and touched the hood. Cold.

I was so screwed.

Rubbing a hand over my face in frustration, I stared at my reflection in the glossy paint. Wisps of brown hair, escaped from my ponytail, framed my angry face. I took a deep breath and tried to relax my expression into something that could pass as pleasant. My brown eyes softened just enough to not look like I wanted to rip someone's head off, which I totally did. I hated that I couldn't shake that feeling.

Working hard to keep my relaxed expression, I turned to the house and slowly started up the walk.

"I was upholding the school's anti-bullying policy," I repeated under my breath before opening the door.

My ready excuse fled my mind at the sight of boxes lining the hallway and stacked on the dining room table.

"Come on, Mom! Seriously?" I threw my bag off to the side and stalked toward the kitchen where I could hear the clink of dishes.

"Is that how you address me?" she asked calmly as soon as I entered.

My temper snapped. I needed a Mom, but she'd been fighting that role for years now.

"Okay, Paxton, pain-in-my-ass birth giver. Two little fights in one week don't warrant another move." Hopefully, she wouldn't point out that it was only Tuesday.

She set the coffee cup down slowly. I swallowed the curse I wanted to mutter. I'd pushed her too far. Again. I stood still, waiting for her to lash out at me. Instead, she stood there, gripping the cup as if it were my head and she wanted to smoosh it. A red flush crept over her flawless and naturally tanned skin. My imagination spiked because I could swear I actually felt the heat of her rage radiating off of her. Sweat beaded my brow.

"Paxton, I'm sor—"

The cup shattered.

"You think you know so much, but you don't. I've given you everything, and you throw the few rules I have back at me. Go to your room. Pack. When you're done, come help me. We leave in the morning."

I wanted to say something more, but the cold blue in her eyes when she finally looked up at me sent me scurrying to my room like a good little girl.

Not that I was little anymore. At seventeen, I stood only a few inches shorter than Mom. Paxton. I rolled my eyes in the safety of my room. She'd had no problem with me calling her Mom until I turned fourteen and started sprouting boobs. Then, suddenly, I had to call her Paxton because she didn't want her boyfriends to know she was old enough to have a kid my age. I didn't see why it mattered. She didn't look old. Not in the slightest. We looked more like sisters than mother and daughter. As long as she looked good, why did she care about her age? Vain.

I started shoving clothes into one of the boxes on my bed and hoped I didn't warp into a vain middle-aged woman like Mom.

After an hour of packing up my room, I went back to the kitchen. A note waited on the table along with a plate of food.

Went to deal with Darren. Eat and finish up the packing. We leave at 2.

I looked around the house. Most everything was already packed. We lived light because we moved often. Sometimes due to my fighting, but mostly due to Paxton's failed relationships. Although, lately, that balance had been tipping more in my favor. I didn't know what was wrong with me. Why did I have to be angry all the time?

I didn't use to be like this. The last therapist I had thought it might be due to a hormone imbalance brought on by puberty. Given my age, I had a hard time believing his prognosis. But my belief, or lack of it, didn't change the fact that I had anger issues and no one could figure out why.

Sighing, I sat and ate my plate of spaghetti then packed what remained. When I finished, I went straight to bed. Two in the morning would come early, and my temper got worse when I didn't get enough sleep.

The soothing vibrations of tires over pavement stopped, waking me. I opened my eyes and blinked at the dimly lit semi-rural road in confusion. Waist-high grass occupied the space around the house in front of which we'd parked.

"Why'd we stop?" I asked, trying to clear the fog in my head. Even with going to bed early, waking up to Mom's "let's go" had been rough.

"We're here."

"It's still dark? Why did we have to leave at two in the morning?" Even as I asked it, I knew why. A quieter road meant less reason for me to lose my temper.

She opened her door and got out without answering. Not yet done questioning her, I fumbled with my door to follow. Outside the car, my disbelieving gaze locked on the faded, white two-story house hiding in the overgrowth. Paint flaked off the wide boards in not so tiny peels. Within cloudy windows, half-torn curtains dangled, giving the house a creepy, abandoned vibe.

"What do you mean we're here?" I asked. "Where is here?"

"Home," she said, wading through the grass to the front porch. The boards held her weight and didn't send her plummeting straight to hell like I'd hoped.

This had to be a joke. Mom preferred furnished, trendy places, which she always talked her boyfriends into renting for her.

"This isn't a home. This is a fire waiting to happen."

"Hurry up and get inside, Megan," Mom said softly, unlocking the door. "I'll bring the boxes in myself."

Torn between anger and frustration, I stomped through the grass to the wide front porch while Mom disappeared inside. A light came on, then another, so I wasn't walking into the seventh ring of hell blind.

The musty stink of neglect filled my nose, and a sneeze ripped through me a moment later.

"Seriously, this place is a dump," I said, looking around.

The old bulb cast a weak glow in the living room that Mom had lit up. Old furniture coated with dust sparsely decorated the space. The next room, a small kitchen, didn't look much better. The larger room off to one side looked like it wanted to be a library when it grew up. Barren bookshelves and a fireplace played host to long-vacated spider webs.

"I am so not sleeping here," I said under my breath.

"Don't be a baby," Mom said from right behind me, making me jump. "There's a decent room to the right at the top of the stairs. Go back to bed. When you wake up in the morning, things will be different."

I shook my head.

"Yeah, daylight is going to make this all look way worse."

"Go!" Mom's angry yell sent me scurrying up the dark stairs.

A light at the top led the way to a bedroom that didn't look quite as bad as the rest of the place. A full-sized bed with a white, dust-free quilt tempted me. Ignoring the pull to go back to sleep and pretend this was all still a dream, I looked around the rest of the room. Dresser? Check. Creepy, empty closet decorated with more spider webs? Check. A good view from the room's single large window? Nope. Just a crap ton of towering pines.

"Lovely." I turned and face-dove into the mattress. No plume of dust greeted me, so I closed my eyes and let myself pretend.

However, when I opened them again hours later to way too much daylight, I knew I couldn't pretend any longer and trudged down the now dust free stairs. I frowned and poked my head into the library. That looked cleaner now, too, and it had a few more books.

"Come eat," Mom said from the kitchen.

I turned and saw a plate of food for me on the table. Eggs, bacon, toast with jelly. The works.

"Wow. Thanks. Did you sleep at all?"

"No. There's a lot I need to do yet. I went to the store and stocked the cupboards. It was too early for the bank or school so I'll need to leave again in a bit."

"Where are we?"

"Maine."

"I figured that since we didn't drive very long. Where in Maine?"

"This house is on the outskirts of the village of Uttira. Population of about one thousand, but most people only live here part-time."

"Are you trying to say this is a vacation home?" I couldn't keep the disbelief from my voice.

"Don't be smart. While I'm running errands, I want you to try to mow the lawn in back." She turned to look me in the eye. "Only in the back."

"Fine. Geez. You might want to power nap before you go."

She took a long, slow breath and continued her study of the backyard.

"I'll sleep later, once you're settled. Behave and stay inside once you're done with the lawn." She turned and left the room. A minute later, I heard the front door open and close.

I rolled my eyes and quickly finished my breakfast. She'd been trying to keep me inside and away from people for as long as I could remember. Couldn't blame her. I rubbed people wrong because they rubbed me wrong. Yet, I loved being outdoors.

After I washed my plate and put everything away, I strolled outside. The back deck was sad in comparison to the front and looked out over a sea of waist-high grass gone to seed. I didn't know of a lawn mower on earth that would tackle this job.

Parting the grass, I made my way to the weather-worn shed.

The right door opened easily. The left tried to give me a hard time, but I was stronger than I looked.

With the doors gaping wide, I studied the variety of rusted lawn care implements. The mower sat off to one side, the pull-start rotted and hanging in two pieces. Even if I could have gotten it to start, it would have done little good.

From the wall, I grabbed a golf club looking thing with a serrated edge at the bottom and gave it an experimental swing over the grass. It neatly sheared the top of the blades from the bottom on the first swing and the return.

Grinning, I stepped out further and set to work. By the time Mom returned, I was in the kitchen, sipping some iced tea. The backyard looked like a farmer had cut hay.

She placed a bundle of papers and a plastic bag with several boxes in it on the table and went to the back door.

"The mower didn't work?"

"The pull cord's broken, and there's no gas. I used that thingy against the door. It worked okay."

"Feel better?" she asked, her voice actually motherly for a change.

"Yeah. I do."

"Exercise always helps with moods. Don't forget that."

How could I? She raised me saying it. I used to jog to help with my moods. But, when the people I passed started pissing me off by just existing, I'd had to stop. After that, Mom suggested I try getting a boyfriend. She'd claimed the right one could help with moods, too. At fourteen, I'd gagged and locked myself in my room, trying not to visualize how she and her boyfriends exercised to help her stay calmer.

"I'll set up a service to cut the front yard."

"What's the point? It'll maybe need to be cut twice before it stops growing for the season. I can do it."

"People will want to stop you to talk."

I sighed and quit arguing. I didn't talk to people; I snarked at them.

"I'll see if someone can deliver a new lawn mower or fix the old one so you can do the back," she said.

"Okay."

She turned and nodded toward the stack of papers and the bag.

"That's for you. The school system here is a little different than what you're used to. They cater to the needs of the students. Because of your issues with fighting, you'll learn on your own at home with required weekly check-ins. If you ever reach the point where you can go to classes without wanting to remove someone's teeth, their doors will be open for you."

I indifferently picked up the first folder. It read Girderon Academy. These people had vacation homes and private academies that catered to individual students? That screamed money. We didn't have money. The men in Mom's life usually did, though. Maybe we were here so she could hook up with a new guy.

"Are we in some low-income part of an elitist community?"

"Something like that. I'm going to go upstairs and sleep. Don't answer the door, and stay out of trouble."

As she went upstairs, I reached for the bag. She'd bought me a new laptop, phone, cable modem and wireless router. I started setting everything up, made myself lunch, then picked up the phone. I wasn't sure why she'd gotten it. Friends weren't my strong suit. Who did she think I had to call?

Setting it aside, I went outside and started weeding around the base of the pine trees. By dinner, Mom was up and had a plate of food on the table for me.

She sat next to me with her own plate.

"There's no TV in this place. I ordered one, as well as cable hook up, so you won't go stir crazy."

All this outpouring of niceness was making me suspicious. For once, though, I kept my snark to myself and just said thanks.

"You're welcome, Megan." She reached out and gave my hand a squeeze.

That was the last time I saw my mom.

CHAPTER TWO

MY OPINION OF OUR NEW HOUSE HADN'T IMPROVED ANY BY THE time I opened my eyes on the second morning.

"Still looks like hell."

I peeled back the covers and made my way downstairs. Expecting to see Mom in the kitchen, I frowned at the note waiting on the table and looked around for my plate instead. She always made me breakfast.

"Dammit, Mom. You can't train me like Pavlov's dog and then not deliver."

With a scowl, I snatched up the note and started reading. After the first sentence, I sat down heavily and started again.

This is your home, now, but never again mine. You're more special than you know. Learn what Girderon Academy can teach you. You'll need it. There's a checkbook in the kitchen drawer to the right of the sink. The account has enough to start you out with whatever life you choose. I'm sure you'll catch on quickly how to make your own money before you run out.

I loved you, Megan. Never doubt that. Leaving was the best thing I

could do for both of us. I already held on too long, and I'm sorry for that.
Take care,
Mom

She left me? That didn't make any sense. If she was tired of dealing with me, why go through all the trouble of moving us here? Why not just take off from the last place? And why sign the note as Mom? She hadn't acted like a real Mom for a long time.

Her words from the day we'd left echoed in my head. *I've given you everything, and you throw the few rules I have back at me.*

"What bullshit," I said to the kitchen. "She's still pissed because of the fight. You know what? I don't care. I can make my own dumb breakfast."

I tossed the note on the table and went to the cupboards. Mom hadn't lied when she said she'd gone shopping. Food crammed each inch of storage space in the kitchen. There was enough food to last me weeks. I tried to ignore the tiny ball of dread building inside of me.

Box of cereal under one arm and a bowl and spoon in hand, I went back to the table and sat down. The note captured my attention again.

I could easily believe that Mom was still pissed at me for what had happened at school. Actually, for what had been happening with increasing frequency over the last few months if I were being honest with myself. My head was telling me that she was just taking off for a few days to teach me a lesson about respect or some other load of crap. But, my gut continued to tug my thoughts in a different direction. What if the note wasn't a way to get back at me?

Instead of pouring milk, I looked around. This wasn't Mom's normal style of house. I'd thought that right away. Mom liked fashion, attention, and town-living. Nothing we'd packed from the prior place was here, only the boxes full of my things, which now sat in my room. Yesterday, I'd figured a moving company would show up. Now? I wasn't as sure.

Looking around, I only saw more evidence that she'd moved me, not us. I didn't know what to do or believe. I couldn't call her to ask what was going on or when she'd be back. She never had a cell phone that I knew of. Men would always just stop by when they wanted her attention, or she would go to whomever she was seeing at the time to get his. I didn't know more about the last boyfriend than his first name. She never let any of them hang around me too much.

Numb with the realization that I had no way to contact my mom, I poured my milk and clung to the belief that this was just a punishment. She'd show up again after a few days. This would be just like those weekender trips she'd been taking with Darren. She'd come home, exhausted and wanting to sleep for a day.

After I cleaned up breakfast, I went to the second bedroom upstairs and opened the window after removing the tattered curtain. Fresh air circulated the dust-clogged room. If I were Mom, I wouldn't want to live here either if this were my room. I got to work dusting, cleaning, washing, and de-webbing the entire space. Since it wasn't big, it didn't take long.

Satisfied that when Mom came back she'd have a place to crash, I went to shower in the house's single, first-floor bathroom tucked into the tiny space between the living room and the kitchen. Like the rest of the place, the bathroom needed updating. And more room. Every time I reached up to wash or rinse my hair, I hit my elbow on the wall or knocked something off the narrow ledge near my shoulders.

"Vacation home from hell," I said under my breath. If I were lucky, Mom would be ready to move again in another month.

Just when I thought the place couldn't get any worse, the faint, off-key melody of "My Darling Clementine" reached my ears.

"That's seriously messed up." I switched off the water and wrapped a towel around myself as I left the shower. The sound grew in volume when I opened the bathroom door. The source of the noise, a newish white box mounted just above the front entry, was hard to miss. I needed a chair and a hammer.

First, though, I needed to tell off the person still pressing the damn doorbell.

I yanked the door open and startled two uniformed men having a discussion on the front porch. Instant anger flared up inside of me, and I tried to slam the door shut.

The police officer moved too quickly and stopped my attempt with his foot.

"Is there a reason you're trying to run?" he asked.

I quit trying to close the door and let him swing it wide again.

"Are you kidding? I'm standing here in a towel. Of course there's a reason."

His eyes narrowed at me slightly.

He's a cop, Megan, I reminded myself. You don't want to piss him off when you're only seventeen and have no way to reach your mom.

"Were you expecting someone else?" he asked with a smirk.

The instant need to punch him in the face had me curling my fingers, around my towel and the doorknob, in a death grip.

"Obviously, I wasn't expecting anyone or I would have been dressed already."

My gaze shifted to the delivery man.

"Can I help you?"

The man's eyes swept over my towel-clad torso and wet hair

while a light blush crept into his cheeks. My temper cooled a little, and I gave him a small, encouraging smile.

"I have a scheduled delivery for Megan Smith," he said. "A TV, and it looks like the cable company is here to hook you up as well." He motioned over his shoulder to the three vehicles parked on the gravel shoulder in front of my house.

"Yeah, sure, bring in whatever."

The man fled the porch, leaving me alone with the cop. I itched to do or say something to piss him off as much as he had me.

"You know the rules; all outside visits need to be approved before you can schedule anything."

"Sorry. I didn't know that. My mom and I just moved in yesterday. She set all this stuff up. Not me."

"I know. That's why I'll let it slide this time. But, I'd like to talk to her."

"Yeah, me too. She left this morning on a business trip and was a little vague on when she'd be back."

"I bet." There was that damn smirk again.

"You'll need to get used to how things work around here real fast or you and I will have problems. Welcome to Uttira, Megan." His voice seemed anything but welcoming as he handed me a pamphlet with the words "Welcome to Uttira," printed in bold yellow on a blue background.

When I looked up, the officer was already walking off the porch, and the delivery guy was wheeling a large TV box through the tall grass.

Leaving the front door open, I jogged upstairs and pulled on some clean clothes. Dressed in a pair of jeans and a t-shirt, I felt better equipped to deal with whatever new hell Mom had brought down on my head. Not the TV and cable install, which the guys wrapped up quickly, but the town in which she'd temporarily left me.

Barely an hour after the interruption to my day, I closed the front door on the installation guy and went to the kitchen. As soon as the sound of the delivery engine faded, I walked outside and took in a lungful of late summer air. The second week of a new school year never smelled so good. If Mom wanted to take off, so could I.

Grinning to myself, I started around the house and down the overgrown gravel driveway.

A vast field occupied the space directly across from the house. Beyond that, trees stretched as far as I could see. The twisty road to the right didn't look much different from the road to the left. Nothing interesting either way except distant mailboxes marking the presence of a few scattered houses.

Listening to my gut, I turned to the right and started walking. However, it soon became apparent that we lived nowhere close to town. Trees began to hug both sides of the narrow, twisty street, and roads split off at frequent intervals, creating a web in which I quickly became lost.

When the bird noise around me quieted, my steps slowed.

The hair on the back of my neck lifted with the sensation of being watched a moment before something darted through the trees to my right. The flash of light color low to the ground disappeared too quickly for me to see it clearly.

A soft growl came from behind me, and I twisted to look that direction. Another flash of movement, there and gone. A logical part of my brain said I should have been terrified. The growl had belonged to an animal. With trees this thick, who knew what roamed. Yet, I didn't feel fear, only impatience that whatever hid in the trees seemed to want to toy with me before attacking.

I waited.

A howl rose from within the trees, followed by another, and a third, until five voices blended into one mournful call.

"Just hurry up already," I said. "I have to get to Grandma's house."

A choked laugh came from behind me. I turned and found myself looking into an incredible pair of brown eyes that belonged to a tall boy close to my age. His longish shag of light brown hair fell around his amused face.

Surprisingly, he didn't annoy me at first glance. Not in the slightest.

"Wolves are howling, and the first thing you can think to say is that you need to get to Grandma's house?" A teasing smile played around his lips.

"I slipped into the role," I said with a shrug of my red hoodie-clad shoulder.

He laughed and held out his hand.

"I'm Fenris."

I shook his hand with ease.

"Megan."

"And behind you are my bitches," he said with a glance over my shoulder.

I looked back and found four wolves standing on the other side of the road. Something about the lead dog poked my temper. Probably because it had its teeth pulled back in a silent snarl. I returned the favor. The wolf added volume and started crouching. It was strange. I usually didn't mind animals, but something about that one made me want to kick her in the teeth.

"Aubrey," Fenris said. "That's enough."

The wolf immediately quieted.

"Wow. She's well trained. You probably should still have her on a leash, though."

He burst out laughing.

"Yeah. That'd be quite the fight. Based on the direction you're walking, you're coming from town. You staying at the inn?"

"From town? No. I thought I was walking toward town. I just moved here yesterday."

"And you're already lost. Come on, I'll walk you home."

The lead dog behind us growled low. Fenris might like me, but his dog sure didn't.

"If you just point me in the right direction, I'll be fine."

He continued to grin at me.

"The way you smell, I doubt you'd be fine. It won't take long for every male within a mile to track you down. I'll walk you. You girls can go home," he said looking at his dogs. "We're done running for the day."

The first one snarled and barked then pivoted and raced off into the trees. The other three followed her lead. This guy was crazy to have pet wolves.

"I think someday they're going to turn on you."

"Nah, they love me. They're just moody sometimes. Especially when a pretty girl distracts me."

I rolled my eyes.

"So, which way is home?"

He tilted his head the direction from which I'd come, the obvious first step. I wasn't sure we'd find our way back once we left the current road, though. I'd been walking for almost an hour, and I'd taken too many forks that led to other narrow roads within the trees.

"Tell me a little about yourself, Megan. Any heroic acts of bravery, life missions, or prophesized destinies hiding behind those pretty brown eyes?"

"Nope. Not really."

"Then what brings you to Uttira?"

"My flighty mother, who changes boyfriends as frequently as she does her favorite brand of mascara."

He made a sound between a laugh and consolation.

"What about you? How long have you lived here?"

"All my life. Born and raised in the overprotective circle of my smothering family. Unlike you, my parents have hammered my life's mission into my head since birth."

"Oh? And what's your life's mission?"

I glanced at him as he looked right then left at the T in the road. He inhaled deeply and looked at me.

"To help damsels in distress. We need to go right."

I grinned and walked beside him as we veered the direction he'd indicated.

"That's quite the life mission."

The sound of an engine from ahead had us stepping off the road just as a cop cruiser came around the bend. It turned on its lights without sound and stopped beside us. The man from earlier today rolled down his window.

"Afternoon, Trammer," Fenris said. "Something wrong?"

"Depends. Why are you two all the way out here?"

"The girls and I were out for a run. We found Megan headed the wrong direction, and I offered to walk her home."

"Wrong direction? Right."

The sarcasm in his voice made my skin tingle with the need to hurt him.

"They were out of hicksville roadmaps at the gas station," I said.

He narrowed his eyes at me for the second time that day. But, his obvious dislike didn't bother me like it probably should have.

"Get in. I'll take you back to where you belong."

"We'd love a ride. Thanks, Trammer," Fenris said, opening the door and sliding in.

I hesitated. I did not want to get into the car, but without an idea of where I was and my guide already in the backseat, I didn't have much of a choice. I got in and closed the door. The locks engaged, and I met Trammer's eyes in the mirror before his gaze shifted to Fenris.

"What would your parents say about this?"

"Good job, son. We're so proud you're finally helping out the community." Fenris shrugged. "There might be a few joyful tears with that, too. It's hard to tell sometimes."

Trammer's face flushed, and he turned the car around. The drive back to the house only took a few minutes, which annoyed the hell out of me. I had to have been walking in circles.

When Trammer stopped the car in front of the house, we had to wait for him to let us out of the back. He frowned at me the entire time, making my efforts to control my temper a real struggle.

As soon as we stood in my overgrown front yard, he took off.

"What is his deal?" I asked.

"The usual. Underpaid. Underappreciated. Has a very small —," he held his forefinger and thumb an inch apart near his waist, "—amount of self-esteem."

I snorted a laugh, enjoying myself and surprised that I'd found someone who didn't make me angry for a change.

"He's not too bad when you take all that into consideration," Fenris said with a shrug. He then looked over my house. "Huh. I don't think I've ever known of anyone living here."

"From the looks of it on the inside, I'm not sure anyone ever has."

A car came whipping around the bend and screeched to a halt in front of my house. The three female passengers in the convertible and waved our direction. The driver, a blonde, didn't release her tight grip on the wheel as she glared at me. From the corner of my eye, I noticed Fenris wave toward the car.

"The girls and I are going to the Roost for a party tonight. Want to come? It's a good way to get to know everyone."

I tore my gaze from the blonde to look up at Fenris.

"I'll pass. Thanks for the invitation, though."

"If you change your mind, just take a left out of your driveway. The road will take you right into town. You can't miss the Roost."

"I won't change my mind."

He grinned, leaned close like he was going to kiss me, but instead inhaled deeply by my face.

"Too bad." He licked the tip of my nose, and while I stared at him in shock, he turned and walked toward the waiting car where he jumped into the backseat and slid down between the two girls already there.

"See you Monday," he called as he waved.

Without a doubt, Fenris was a player. Not in a cocky way, though. A fun one.

Unable to help myself, I lifted my hand in return.

The blonde gave me another glare, pressed down on the gas, and cranked the wheel to send a spray of gravel my way.

CHAPTER THREE

I LET MYSELF IN THROUGH THE BACK DOOR AND WANDERED AROUND the house. Other than the TV, there wasn't much to do. So I binge-watched shows through the rest of the day, made myself dinner, and went to bed early.

The next morning, no plate waited for me on the table. I didn't let that bother me as I poured myself a bowl of cereal and moseyed to the living room for more TV time. Another day of no responsibilities and no school sounded like heaven. However, knowing that sitting around for too long would start to get under my skin, I eventually got off the couch and went in search of a more physical activity.

By dinner, I'd washed all the windows in the house in my desperation for something to do. The layer of grime that had kept a good portion of the daylight out had taken a fair amount of work to remove. Work that I'd needed. The results made the house feel less depressing. However, the clear view of nothing but towering pines outside my bedroom window didn't really inspire any happy thoughts. I was still alone and wondering how long it would take my mom to get over her anger.

Through the branches of the pines, a distant glow on the

horizon caught my attention before I left the room. Town. I stared at the light like a moth to a bug zapper, drawn but knowing it would only cause pain. That's where my similarities with the moth ended. Going to town wouldn't result in my pain but someone else's.

After running into Dudley Do Right twice, I knew I should avoid any situation that might lead me to trouble. My tendency to get into trouble was the whole reason Mom moved us here and took off, after all. Getting into more wouldn't bring her back any quicker. But, I couldn't hide in this house, waiting forever, could I?

Not giving myself time to second guess my decision, I changed out of my dusty clothes, washed my face, and put on my jacket. Outside, I tipped my face to the light of the full moon and breathed deeply. The cool night air kissed my skin and eased some of the tension that had taken hold of my heart the moment I'd read Mom's note.

"She'll be back, right?" I asked, softly.

The moon didn't answer.

Before I looked away, something large and dark flew across the sky. I shivered and blinked. What I'd thought I'd seen was already gone.

"Country living is making me crazy," I said to myself since I was sure I'd just seen something that couldn't possibly exist. Something with wings large enough to block out the light of the moon. Something with four legs, not two.

The shape appeared in the sky again then dove into the pines to my right. Branches snapped as it landed.

Not a minute later, a naked man, close to my age, walked out of the trees. Blonde hair and dark eyes glinted in the moonlight, along with a whole hell of a lot of beautifully tanned skin. I forced my gaze to stay above the shoulders no matter how much my curiosity was demanding it dip below the waist.

As he strode toward me, the remnants of his wings disappeared behind his back.

This was, by far, the weirdest and best dream I'd ever had. I just wished I could remember falling asleep. I'd probably passed out because of the fumes from cleaning the windows and boredom.

"You're not real," I breathed. Yet, despite the fact that he stood there naked as a baby and had only minutes ago sported massive wings, talons, and a beak, something about him seemed very real.

"Fenris said you seemed naive. Aubrey thought it was an act." His gaze swept over my face. "Which is it?"

The mocking curiosity in his eyes annoyed me as much as the fact that he actually seemed to be waiting for an answer. Instead of replying, I balled up my fist and slammed it into his face. He grunted, his head moving slightly with the impact, and he caught my wrist before I could fully pull back.

"What was that for?" he asked. Anger had wiped out any hint of mocking curiosity from his tone.

I could also feel the throb in my fist. He had a hard nose.

"To see if you were real."

"Most people pinch." He sounded a bit more nasally than he had before.

My imagination was sure good at adding the little details needed to make this all feel real. I didn't let it distract me from the moment, though.

"Most people don't walk around in someone else's backyard while butt naked." Not that I actually minded that part. His biceps were clearly defined, and his thighs were thicker than my head. Realizing where my gaze had wandered, I quickly looked up again.

He shook his head and released my wrist.

"Where were you going?" he asked.

"To town. Do you own pants?"

"It would be better if you stayed here."

"For who?"

"You."

"Stay in a house where a guy shows up naked in the backyard? Yeah, that's not sounding like a good option."

"It's the safest one."

"Of course you would think that. But since this is my dream, I'm going to see how many more naked men are frolicking around this place."

He stayed quiet for a moment, studying me. I was just about to turn and walk to the front of the house when he spoke again.

"The people in this town are going to eat you up and spit you out."

Without warning, he scooped me up and walked into the house with me. In the light of the kitchen, I studied his face. He looked mad, his jaw hard and a frown tugging his lips. Very nice lips. High cheekbones and a strong nose. His gaze flicked down to me just before he started up the stairs. Deep blue eyes. I had amazing taste in dream men.

When he turned to my room, my heart skipped a beat. Was I really going to dream this? A naked man carrying me to bed? I knew where this was headed.

"I think this needs to stop here," I said.

"Oh, it will."

He tossed me so hard, I landed on the mattress with a double bounce.

"If you're smart, you'll stay. You've been warned."

By the time I looked up, I only caught a glimpse of his bare backside. Flopping back down onto the mattress, I closed my eyes and forced myself to relax, the only way I could think of to wake up from a dream.

I woke up, not in a pile of used paper towels and high on cleaner, but in my bed, dressed as I'd been to go to town. Frowning, I sat up, rubbed my face and looked at the daylight pouring in through my window.

There was no way that had been real. Obviously, I'd finished the windows and changed with the intent to go to town, but I'd laid down, instead, and just couldn't remember that part. The stress of the idea that my mom actually abandoned me had probably caused some kind of weird mental snap where my dream had replaced those real events.

But to dream a griffin, of all things? I could totally understand why the dream man had mentioned Fenris. In the little bit of time I'd spent with him, I'd actually liked Fenris. No doubt, that's the same reason his dog's name had made a cameo in my dream, too.

Yet, I couldn't shake just how real the dream had felt. The way the dream man had looked at me when he'd carried me upstairs…

My stomach churned with that same "oh-oh" sensation I got whenever I had to tell Mom I'd gotten into yet another fight. I didn't think it was because I'd punched the dream man, though. He'd been annoyed by it but not really hurt.

Thinking of Mom, I got out of bed and checked the other bedroom upstairs. Nothing looked changed, and my anger with her started to outweigh the hurt. So I'd gotten into a fight. She'd raised me. I always got into fights. Taking off like she had wasn't cool.

I turned away and went downstairs. A nice, long shower helped the weirdness of the dream fade.

Feeling a little better, I made a breakfast of eggs, bacon, and toast and sat down at the table. Alone. Before I could stop myself, I wondered what Mom was doing. Did she miss me? Probably not. I wasn't the easiest person to get along with. Even though she'd ditched me, I missed her. How messed up was that?

Suddenly the eggs didn't look as good. I sat there and wondered why I was playing along. Why stay here? I was almost eighteen. Okay, not really. I still had six months. But still, why stay?

I stood, went to the kitchen drawer, and grabbed the checkbook the note had mentioned. The register showed fifty thousand dollars. I snorted and rolled my eyes, doubting the number was real. Hopefully, there'd be at least five hundred in there, or at least enough for a night in a motel while I hoofed it back to our old place. I didn't doubt for a second that Mom was either still there packing or having alone-time with Darren.

Tucking the checkbook into my back pocket, I quickly devoured my breakfast then took care of the house. Once I had the trash out and everything put away or closed up, I shrugged into my jacket and stepped outside.

Early morning light shifted through the trees as I walked down the road heading out of town. After paying better attention during the car ride home yesterday, I knew where to turn. Before long the twisty roads opened up to a long stretch of nearly treeless pavement ahead.

Smiling to myself, I imagined Mom's reaction when I showed up at her front door. I'd tell her that I was done playing her stupid game and that she'd need to Mom up for a few months before I'd be out of her life for good, like she obviously wanted.

Lost in my thoughts, I didn't notice the waver that looked like ripples of heat rising off a summer-baked blacktop. I did notice, though, when the hair on my arms stood at attention. My pace slowed. Not because I wanted it to but because my legs grew so heavy that each step took a considerable amount of effort.

"What the hell?" I muttered, looking down at my feet.

Due to the direction of my gaze, I didn't see how close I'd gotten to the weird waves until a bright light flared and sent me flying backward. I landed hard on the pavement, my head connecting with a hollow thud.

I didn't know how long I laid there, but the bitter smell of burnt hair and the taste of blood in my mouth roused me. I opened my eyes and blinked up at the clear blue sky above. It took a second to recall why I lay on my back in the middle of the road.

Given the stench filling my nose, I sat up and patted my head in panic then exhaled heavily when I felt a full head of hair.

"It doesn't actually burn anything," a voice said from beside me. "Just smells like it."

I turned my head and found the man from my dreams squatted down nearby. This time, he wore jeans. My eyes still feasted on his broad bare chest, though, as my scattered thoughts tried to form an explanation for what was happening.

How could I have dreamed an actual person? I doubted I had psychic abilities. If I did, I would have seen myself getting knocked on my ass. And, I doubted I'd seen him somewhere around town because I hadn't left my house. Even as I thought it, I recalled stepping out the back door in my dream and how he, a winged creature, had swooped down and stepped out of the shadows as a man.

There was only one answer. He still didn't exist. The fall had caused me to hit my head harder than I thought, and he was now the result of a concussion.

Sunlight glinted off his blond hair, clearly defining strands in vivid detail. Detail I couldn't possibly dream up.

"This isn't real," I whispered with growing desperation.

"Not that again." He stood and leaned down to offer me a hand, which I ignored. As soon as I got to my feet, he took a step back.

"If you feel the need to test reality, pinch your arm," he said.

I shook my head, not to answer him but in denial of the whole thing. However, the strength of my denial faltered when I looked down the road and saw the shimmering waves.

"I wouldn't try it again. In fact, if you were smart, you would start running through the trees to get home before Trammer reaches the barrier." I tore my gaze from the waves in time to see my dream man nod toward the woods to the left.

I understood what he was telling me. Run before I get caught. But caught for what?

"Barrier?" I asked.

"Yeah. You really have no clue, do you?" He sighed. "Parents do that sometimes. Keep us in the dark then ditch us. Do yourself a favor and run home. Don't try to leave again. No one leaves until they prove they can handle themselves around the humans."

I opened my mouth to ask what the hell he was talking about when I caught the sound of an engine. His warning about Trammer echoed in my mind. I couldn't afford another run-in with the police. Without waiting, I sprinted into the trees.

"Smart girl," he called from behind.

His high-handed superiority was starting to annoy me.

The thought had barely formed when I heard a huge whoosh behind me. The heavy beat of wings had me looking up as I ran further into the trees. Through the multi-colored canopy, I saw the creature soaring above. It flew in the direction I was headed, its speed quickly making it disappear from sight.

He was real? It was real?

The sound of the engine quickly faded. I didn't slow. I was freaking out too much. As I wove through the trees, my mind raced. What was really real? All of it? Where had my mom brought me? As much as I wanted to think the hit to my head was the cause of the big griffin flying above, doubt kept me from believing it. I hadn't hit my head last night.

Not more than a minute after the thing disappeared, it circled into view again and repeated the path as if pointing the direction. I veered slightly to the left. It made a deep sound like a rumble of thunder and swooped lower toward the trees before turning again. It circled back around and repeated the move until I corrected my course.

Yep. Definitely leading the way. I was so preoccupied watching the sky that I didn't at first know where I was when I burst through the trees into a clearing. The hacked-up lawn gave it away before the house or leaning shed. While I looked around, wondering where to run next, the griffin circled once then took off toward town. Staying where I was became the safer option.

I quickly let myself in and locked the door. The back of my skull throbbed, and I still tasted blood.

"What the hell is this place?"

I had no answer and no one I trusted to ask. At that moment, I hated my mom. But, I hated myself more. If I could have just learned to control my temper, none of this would have happened. I would still be back home, where I belonged, not in this crazy town.

The computer on the table caught my eye. I sat down and booted it up before tapping out a quick search of Uttira, Maine. A page of the town's activities, which included an upcoming Fall Festival and a reminder to be neat and orderly citizens, pretty much summed up the message on the town's pathetic website. It wasn't any more helpful than the stupid pamphlet I'd gotten the day before.

Giving in to the growing headache, I kicked off my shoes, shed my jacket, and went to the bathroom cabinet to take two pain relievers. Thinking to add to the numbing effects, I ambled to the living room and turned on the TV.

Before I could even get comfortable on the couch, the doorbell rang. I cursed myself for forgetting to rip it from the siding. It rang a second time just as I reached the entry.

I yanked the door open, already scowling. My temper frayed further at the sight of Trammer.

"Going somewhere, Megan?"

I looked pointedly at my bare feet before meeting his gaze.

"Yeah, the beach."

He narrowed his eyes.

"Stay where you belong or we're going to have problems. Do you understand?"

"That you like harassing minors for no apparent reason? Yeah. I understand. If that's all, I'd like to get back to my nineties re-runs."

I slammed the door in his face, too angry to care about the consequences. I didn't belong here, and we both knew it.

CHAPTER FOUR

Despite my certainty that I did not belong in Uttira, I had no clue how to leave. Every time I thought about trying to walk beyond the township's limits again, the smell of burnt hair surrounded me so intensely that I struggled to breathe. However, as soon as I stopped thinking about leaving, the smell would immediately disappear.

I could no longer delude myself that what I'd seen, felt, and smelled was a dream. Yet, admitting that there was a magical barrier being used to keep people and creatures inside Uttira sounded completely crazy.

So, I spent the rest of my weekend on the internet, researching plausible explanations. Nothing more turned up on the town than what I'd already discovered. A search on griffins was a joke. Not a single bit of information matched what I'd seen. Magical barriers proved mildly entertaining. People had videos of themselves doing incantations or spells that didn't prove anything. Yet, their complete certainty that they'd performed and documented an act of magic had me looking for medical conditions that would make a person smell burnt hair.

By Monday morning, I hadn't found anything to support

that what I'd experienced was even possible, and my non-life in Uttira once again felt like one long bad dream, which worried the hell out of me. Last time I thought events were a bad dream, reality bitch-slapped me. I had the bruise on the back of my head to prove it.

Frustrated and lost, I considered my options. Reaching out for help from anyone official was impractical. What would I say? Help me; I can't leave Uttira because of a magical barrier. At best, it would land me in foster care and at worst, a padded room. I had no one to turn to but myself. And the only way I'd understand what to do was to leave the house again and learn more about this place I now unwillingly called home.

So I showered, dressed, and ate breakfast like a normal person while my mind came up with a ton of weird possibilities regarding what I'd find when I reached town.

A sudden, loud pounding on my front door brought me to my feet. Any triumph I should have felt at disabling the doorbell over the weekend sunk to my toes at the sight of Trammer on my porch. Since he was staring at me through the now clean glass of the door's side windows, I had no choice but to answer.

"Good morning, Trammer." I tried for pleasant. I really did. But, it came out more sneer than anything. What was wrong with me?

"Let's go," he said, motioning to his car.

"Go where?"

"Girderon."

The name sounded familiar, and I quickly recalled how I knew it. It was the name for the preppy Academy here. The school that Mom had given me the paperwork for. The very one she said wouldn't require my actual attendance.

"Why do I need to go there?"

"It's Monday check-in. If you refuse, they gave me

permission to arrest you. Are you refusing?" He set his hand on the device hanging from his duty belt.

"Check-in? I have no idea what you're talking about."

"Get in the car or I'm taking your procrastination as refusal and arresting you."

I focused on breathing and not the increasing need to cause him physical harm.

"I'd like to grab my jacket if that's all right with you."

"Hurry up, and keep the door open."

I turned and went to the kitchen where I grabbed my phone and the Academy paperwork, all of it untouched since the day Mom left. Trammer stood in the same spot when I returned, and he waited as I locked up.

The ride in the back of his cruiser gave me a few minutes to thumb through some of the Academy papers. The welcome letter gave instructions on how to get to their special website to review the courses offered. They stressed that Girderon specific courses would not be available online for security reasons. Instead, they would be covered during the required attendance Mondays. The dress code, code of conduct, and internet safety policies seemed pretty standard at a glance.

Wondering what I was in for, I neatly stacked the papers once more and watched out the window. The curvy road on which I lived led straight into town. The place had a lot of buildings but seemed dead. No one walked along the street or moved from shop to shop. A bad feeling settled in the pit of my stomach. Where were all the people?

Trammer turned onto a boulevard lined with stately trees. Not far down the drive, he stopped the car at a gate and pushed the button beside a mounted speaker box.

"Yes?" a voice asked from the speaker box.

"I'm delivering Megan Smith as requested," Trammer said.

"Enter."

A buzzer sounded, and the gate rolled open.

He drove around a slight curve that revealed a huge stone building at least a mile ahead. The thing rose three stories high and sprawled out to the right and left, consuming more space than any one building should.

The cream stone shone pale in the morning light, giving the whole place a clean, new appearance. Yet, the date beside the grand, double-doored entry clearly stated the building had existed for over two hundred years.

Some part of me registered Trammer stopping the car and coming around to open the door.

"Thanks, Jeeves," I said, not looking at him as I continued to stare at the building. Preppy didn't begin to accurately describe the grandness of Uttira's school.

I walked straight up the steps toward the woman waiting there.

"Megan Smith?"

"Yeah."

She gave me a kind smile before she looked over my shoulder.

"You should leave, Trammer. Thank you for your service."

She didn't look at me again until the sound of the car faded, which gave me a moment to study her. Her long, dark hair fell loosely down her back. A plain grey business suit, white top, and grey pumps gave an air of authority. I waited for my infamous irrational anger to grip me and drive me to do something that would ultimately get me kicked out on my first day. Instead, I didn't feel anything but curiosity for the school, the locked gate, and the personal greeting.

"Welcome to Girderon Academy. Allow me to give you a brief tour and an explanation." She held out her arm, indicating I should lead the way inside.

The grand entry rose the full three stories. Glass windows on the roof domed the ceiling and provided light. Potted plants filled the space and created imaginative walkways to the dual staircases leading up.

"My name is Adira Grenald. I'm the studies coordinator for all the students at Girderon."

I tore my gaze from the impressive entry to look at her.

"What's a studies coordinator?"

"The person who tells you what sessions you need to take to graduate, follows your progress, and makes recommendations based on your performance and skills."

"So you're a guidance counselor?"

"Something like that." She flashed me another kind smile and started down the hallway to the left. I followed.

"We strive to make Girderon a safe place to learn for all of our students. As you can imagine, it's not a simple task. Certain safeguards are in place to prevent death on Academy grounds, but you can still be hurt."

I'd been trying to see through the narrow windows set into the classroom doors we'd been passing when her words registered. My steps faltered. The recent blow to my head must have messed with my ears. There was no way she'd said what I thought she had.

"Did you just say death?"

She stopped walking and met my worried gaze.

"I did. Like you, not all of the students have yet learned to control their impulses." She turned and continued down the hallway. "Most of the general studies are located along this corridor. If you test sufficiently in the core requirements, you will likely spend little time in this area."

She turned a corner to a wider hallway with fewer doors.

"Time between assigned sessions can be spent in this section doing independent, voluntary studies. Each room has an occupancy schedule, which I manage. If you would like to book a time, come see me. The rooms are warded so no one can come to harm and nothing inside can be destroyed."

"Right," I said, drawing out the word.

At the end of the hall, she turned again.

"These are the administrative offices. We'll pause the tour here so I can become more acquainted with your aptitudes." She opened the door to a spacious room with an executive desk and a chair set before it.

"Have a seat." She waved me toward the chair as she moved behind the desk. A maroon folder on the surface caught my eye. She noted the direction of my gaze and set her hand on the folder.

"I'll update your file after each aptitude review, which we will conduct every Monday. Now, Megan, tell me what you know about yourself."

"There's not much to tell except that I'm pretty sure I don't belong here."

She sat back in her chair and considered me for a moment.

"Why do you think that?"

What could I say that wouldn't make me sound as crazy as she'd sounded on the way here?

"Look. You said this place is warded. What does that even mean?"

"That magic protects the Academy and the students within it."

"Exactly. Magic. Something I don't believe in."

"Even after your run-in with the barrier?"

My eyes rounded.

"Yes. I know you tried to leave. I wouldn't have expected anything less, but I do discourage you from trying it again. Without the mark of Mantirum, the barrier will repel you."

"And the mark of Mantirum is…?"

"The mark you receive upon graduation to signify you are a full member of the Mantirum, the world of magic."

I snorted and grinned. "Right."

"I see," she said. "Doubt will not help you learn what you must."

She stood and held out her arms. As I watched, her clothes changed to wisps of material and her skin lost its pinkish hue, turning pale and almost translucent. Light moved just under the surface. Instead of looking creepy, I found it beautifully mesmerizing.

"Do you see me, daughter of Paxton? Do you see the magic pulsing in my veins? Magic is real. The world you knew has been kept blind to this fact. It's time for you to see our world for what it really is. It's time for you to see yourself for what you really are."

"And what am I?"

She dropped her arms, and her clothes and skin returned to normal. Well, what I considered normal.

"What you are is for you to discover in your own time," she said. "Now, tell me about yourself."

"Besides questioning my sanity for even considering to believe any of this, I have a problem keeping my mouth shut and my fists to myself."

She smiled slightly. "You're sane, Megan. And, with time, you will find the truth about this place and yourself. I think, for now, letting you acclimate would be wiser than continuing with your assessments."

She stood and motioned for me to join her. Not sure what else to do, I did as she wanted and followed her out of the room and up a flight of stairs to the second floor. At the third door, she paused.

"I will talk to you again soon."

She opened the door and stepped in. Through the opening, I

saw a room full of desks like school back home. In the sea of faces, one winked at me. My gaze stayed locked on Fenris as Ms. Grenald spoke.

"Good morning, Lucas. This is Megan Smith. Please make her feel welcome."

"Hello, Megan.

I tore my gaze from Fenris' grinning face and looked at the older man at the front of the room.

"Good morning."

"Please take a seat."

I looked back at Fenris and the body of occupied desks. The her-herd from Friday surrounded him, including the bitchy blonde driver. Ignoring her glare and the itch of annoyance creeping just under my skin, I moved further back in the room toward the only open desk. The teacher started speaking again as soon as I sat.

"Your very natures will tempt you. The Gods created you and gave all of you purposes that center around the humans. Whether to defend or devour them, you must learn to blend and avoid exposing your true selves."

I didn't care if I was being mentally redundant, but this couldn't be real. Who were these people? Magic? Gods? Devouring people? No, thank you.

Before I could fully form the thought to stand, the person to my left moved. I glanced over and met the calm gaze of the guy from my not-dreams. He was wearing clothes this time. A whole outfit, not just pants.

His deep blue eyes held mine for a moment while I struggled to believe he was actually real.

Ever so slightly, he shook his head then returned his focus to the teacher.

He was telling me not to leave? Why? Was something going to knock me on my butt again? Frustrated, I stayed in my seat through the duration of a lecture about keeping who we were secret while fulfilling our purposes.

When the bell rang forty minutes later, everyone stood.

"Megan," the teacher called before I could do the same. "If you wait a moment, I can explain your schedule."

I stayed in my seat and watched the rest of the students file out. Fenris' girls gathered around him, touching him on the shoulder or arm, all vying for his attention. He glanced back and winked at me while responding to a comment about someone's new hairstyle.

If all the kids in here were some kind of creatures that needed to blend, I had no idea what Fenris was supposed to be. Other than a girl magnet, of course. When I glanced to the left, that seat was already empty, too.

Lucas grabbed a stack of papers from his desk and came to me.

"Your mother indicated that you've been in the human public schools until this year, which should mean that you've already met the general requirements needed for Girderon. However, you'll need to complete the assessment tests in the core classes to verify that. Since you're choosing to homeschool, I've included a packet for English, Math, Social Studies, and Biology that you can use as a study reference if you feel the need. When you log into your Girderon account, you'll see an assessment test link. Whenever you're ready, you can take the tests."

Overwhelmed by everything that had been happening to me so far, I automatically took the papers when he handed over the packet.

"Until then, you will be required to attend History of the Gods, Human Studies, which is this class, and Self Discovery. Standard curriculum for your age."

He handed me another sheet. This one had a schedule with

the names of the classes he'd just mentioned. It took a few seconds of silence to understand he was done speaking and waiting for a reply.

I had no idea what to say, though. I'd already tried to tell Adira I didn't belong here, and it hadn't helped me any.

He set a hand on my shoulder and gave me an understanding look.

"I know you must feel lost right now. Living out in the human world without knowing who and what you are for as long as you have might make this seem unreal. I promise it is very real, and you do belong here. The sooner you accept that, the easier your transition will be."

"Transition?"

"Yes. To the life you were really meant to live. Welcome to Girderon, Megan. If you ever need someone to listen, you can knock on my door or seek out any other instructor here."

"Uh. Thanks."

"You're welcome. You better hurry. Self-Discovery's on the first floor."

CHAPTER FIVE

I LEFT THE CLASSROOM AND STEPPED INTO A SURREAL CHAOS IN THE hall. It wasn't the level of noise, but the crowd of students, that stunned me. Slowing to a stop, I yet again questioned my sanity and tried to make sense of what I was seeing.

Like any school between classes, the majority of students hurried to some unknown location while a few lingered in small groups, talking and creating congestion. However, unlike any normal school, less than half the student body appeared human.

Dwarves, whom I could easily mistake for normal short people if not for their excessive display of jeweled rings and necklaces, mingled with giants. Where their diminutive counterparts moved briskly with each step, the giants languidly made their way through the crowd. Some stood so tall, the tops of their heads almost brushed the ten-foot ceilings. They weren't the most impressive sight, however. Elves walked gracefully beside minotaurs, centaurs, and cyclopes.

I took a moment to watch a centaur prance past, the clop of his hooves rising above the sound of so many voices. He caught my gaze and nodded at me, the movement slightly terse. Probably because I was staring at him with my mouth open.

Closing it, my sweeping gaze made another pass over the creatures in the hall.

My disbelieving heart stuttered in my chest. There were even more creatures, but I didn't have a clue what they were. While most of them seemed human, a few looked anything but. This had to be real. I didn't have the kind of imagination, awake or sleeping, to make this sort of stuff up.

"Hey, newbie," a girl said, stopping in front of me. "Come to the pool with me, and I'll sing for you." She tilted her head slightly, exposing thin lines just behind her ears.

Gills? Were those gills?

"Ah, no thanks."

"Some other time, then." She shrugged playfully and walked away.

I should have been freaking out and running for the door. Instead, I found I couldn't tear my gaze from the bizarreness of the individuals around me. Across the hall, a group of girls wore skimpy tops made to showcase their green-hued skin. They preened at whoever would look at them, and one went so far as to grab a guy's butt as he walked past.

What was this place really? Sticking to the side of the hall, I began to make my way toward the stairs.

"Oh, new meat!" a high-pitched voice squealed.

Turning toward the main body, I briefly met eyes with the source of the squeal, a cute little redhead with fangs. She smiled at me hungrily. Before I could decide how to react, someone stepped in front of me. I looked up at the back of a shaggy head of dark hair.

"No you don't, Belemina," Fenris said. "You promised I'd be the only boy you'd put under your spell."

"She's not a boy," the girl said with a laugh. "But I'm sure I could be persuaded to look the other way if you walk me to my next class."

"If I walk you to class, Mina, you'll never look anywhere but at me ever again," he said, smoothly offering his arm. A slim pale hand looped through it, and they started away.

He glanced back at me and mouthed, "You owe me."

I wasn't sure what, exactly, he'd just saved me from, but I nodded, relieved. A boyish smile played around his lips before he turned his attention back to his companion.

Released from the fixation that had gripped me the moment I stepped from the door, I glanced down at my schedule. It was easier to think about getting to the next class than the strange world I found myself in.

Unsure how long I had, I turned toward the stairs once more only to be blocked by Fenris' her-herd.

A surge of irritation rose up inside me as I locked eyes with the blonde driver. It wasn't because she was tall, curvy, or insanely gorgeous. Half the females in the hall met that criteria. And my reaction to her had nothing to do with the sneer on her face, although it probably should have. Most people set my temper off for no good reason whatsoever.

"Aubrey, let's just go," the blonde to her right said, tugging Aubrey's sleeve.

"Aubrey," I said, recalling the wolf and the way Fenris had commanded it. I looked at the rest of them. They didn't all glare at me like Aubrey did and weren't nearly as irritating.

"Man, Fenris really has a thing for blondes, doesn't he?" I said, meeting Aubrey's gaze.

"He does. So stay away from him."

I rolled my eyes.

"He doesn't seem like a guy who can be stolen. He seems more like the guy who does the stealing."

In a rare show of restraint, I tried to step around her, but she shadowed my move.

"Seriously, furball? Go pee on someone else's tree."

One of the girls groaned as Aubrey snarled at me.

I grinned and made a fist. If she wanted a fight, I'd give it to her.

"Bring it, bitch," I said, embracing my anger.

As soon as she launched herself at me, I swung hard toward her face. My fist connected with a satisfying thwaump that encouraged my temper.

Aubrey screeched as she flew backward. Unfortunately, the crush of bodies still coming up the stairs stopped her from toppling down. I launched myself at her, more than ready to pummel her face so she wouldn't be able to snarl for a week.

Mid-swing, I found myself lifted up and away from Aubrey. Unable to stop the punch in progress, my fist bounced off the cheek of the largest man I'd ever seen. At least eleven feet tall to my five foot six, he dwarfed me. His peeved gaze pinned me as I dangled from his fingers by the back of my shirt. I tried to quell the anger boiling under my skin.

"I call Mulligan on that last one," I said, softly.

The giant lifted his free hand and made as if to flick me in the face. Since his fingernail was the size of my nose, I knew it was going to hurt and braced myself.

A voice cut through the commotion around us.

"That's enough."

I turned my head a bit to see Dream Guy standing behind me, his head nearly level with my stomach.

"Put her down, Finnegan. I saw the whole thing, and we both know hitting you was an accident."

"Hitting me was. But what about hitting Aubrey? New girls shouldn't hit people they don't know," the giant said, in a deep voice.

"You're right. And, people they don't know shouldn't try to pick fights with them on their first day either."

The giant nodded and set me on my feet just as a bell rang.

The hall around us immediately cleared, and the giant ambled away, ducking slightly to enter the room I'd just left.

Aubrey continued to glare at me. The increasingly red mark on her cheek and the slight swelling of her upper lip let me know I landed a solid hit with the first punch. I wondered if a second one would knock the glare from her face.

"Aubrey, we both know that Fenris flirted with her, not the other way around. It wasn't necessary to try to establish your claim with her. You need to establish it with Fenris. Do you want someone to look at your face?"

"I'll look at it for her," I said before I could stop myself.

"Why are you so angry?" Dream Guy asked, studying me.

"Mommy issues because she left you here?" Aubrey's attempt at a snide smile ended with a wince. It didn't make me want to hit her any less.

I clenched my fist and stepped forward. Dream Guy blocked me.

"Class or home?" he asked.

He'd better not be toying with me.

"If I seriously have a choice, home."

"I'll take you. Jenna, let Adira know."

The blonde beside Aubrey nodded, and the quad walked off. Dream Guy motioned me down the stairs.

"You going to fly me home?" I asked.

He glanced at me but kept walking.

"Was she right?" he asked.

"About my mom? Yeah, she left. So what?"

"Is that why you're angry?"

"Pft. I was angry long before that," I said.

We reached the first floor and started down a long hall that looked just like the one we'd left.

"Why?"

"How am I supposed to know? What about you? Why are you always so bossy?"

"Daddy issues," he said.

His comment didn't make me angry. In fact, it defused the lingering tension under my skin.

We reached the main atrium, but he didn't head toward the main door. He passed through the space toward the right wing.

The smell of salt water tickled my nose before the lilting sound of singing reached my ears. Instead of keeping straight on the main hall, I turned left, following the sound. I didn't walk far before I reached a section of windows set into the hallway to view two giant swimming pools.

Girls and boys swam in the water or sat on the edges. Some sang. Some played with the next person's hair. All of them had tails. None of them wore clothes. Thankfully, the girls had very long hair.

"How does that make you feel?" Dream Guy asked quietly.

"Watching them play with each other? Slightly pervy."

"I meant their music."

I shrugged and focused on listening.

"A little calmer maybe. Why?"

"A siren's song can be very alluring."

"Alluring? Who are you? Are you really my age?"

"I am. Come on."

We trekked back to the main hall and out through a side door to a parking lot.

"Please tell me you have a car here."

"I do."

He led me to a red sporty thing in a line of sporty cars.

"Way to be unique."

He shrugged and opened my door for me. I slid in, more than a little jealous of his car. Not because it was red or sporty but because it was a car.

When he got in, he caught me petting the leather seat.

"I thought you weren't a fan," he said.

"I'm a fan of anything that will get me to where I want to go without walking."

He started the engine and eased out of the parking spot. I looked out the window and stared up at the towering height of the school.

"I'm still not sure I believe any of this is real," I said. "Giants. Sirens." I looked at him. "Griffins."

His expression remained neutral, as it had been every time I saw him. Except for when I hit him.

"It's real," he said.

"How is it real? And why doesn't anyone know?"

"You were in Lucas's class. We blend. Look at you. You lived in the human world for how many years?"

"Seventeen, and I wasn't blending. I'm human." A thought occurred to me. "What's going to happen to me when they figure that out?"

He glanced at me and tapped the wheel for a moment as he slowed by the gate. It swung open without him needing to use the button.

"If you're here and enrolled in Girderon, you're not human, Megan. They don't make those kinds of mistakes."

"They?"

"The Council. The governing body that oversees the Academy, the town, and our community."

I shook my head slightly, realizing I was actually believing everything. It was hard not to believe after almost being flicked by a giant.

"Okay. I'll bite. What is this community really?"

"A home for the children and creations of the gods."

"Gods?" I couldn't keep the disbelief from my voice.

He glanced at me once more, his expression still neutral, then focused on the road. We drove the rest of the way to my house in silence. If I'd offended him by not buying into his beliefs, he was good at hiding it.

When he pulled over in front of my house, I caught a subtle, judgmental change in his expression after a glance at my front yard.

"The lawnmower's broke," I said, feeling the need to defend myself since the responsibility of the place fell on me now. That thought triggered the memory of what Aubrey had said in the hall. She'd known my mom had abandoned me. Did they all know?

"Thanks for the ride." I quickly got out and started toward the rear of the house. I didn't look back at the sound of his car slowly pulling away.

The idea that he'd stepped in to help me at school and gave me a ride home because I was the town's charity case sat like lead in my stomach and increased my hatred for this place. Yet, I knew it wasn't Uttira's fault. It was my mom's. She'd brought me here with the sole purpose of ditching me. If what everyone kept telling me was true, she had to have known what this place was and had withheld so much information from me. Why hide the truth from me? Why bring me here? Was it because I actually was something more than human? If so, what was I?

I let myself in through the back door and placed the Girderon papers on the table. After fixing myself a snack, I sat down and logged into the Academy's website. A list of interactive sessions and tests waited on my student home page.

More curious about the school itself than my course list, I clicked around and read what little there was. A page simply titled "Origins" caught my eye. The article, written by Lucas Flavian, contained a fair number of links to Greek and Norse mythology sites. While I munched on some veggie chips, I read how Mr. Flavian proposed "we" were descendants from the gods, some of us direct offspring between human and immortal, and some creations of those godly immortals. He went on to outline the ebb and flow of each god's reign.

To me, the article didn't have a point. It wasn't announcing, reviewing, or summarizing. It lacked persuasion of any kind. It was more a bunch of speculative opinions or the start of a lecture that might eventually lead to a point if it were ever finished.

I continued my random clicking through the website but didn't unearth anything useful to help explain what the school truly was. Deciding to look at the assessments that Lucas had mentioned, I went back to the main page and opened the first interactive session. It followed the standard "watch a short video then answer some questions" format.

The sound of a lawnmower starting up in my yard pulled me from my aptitude review of high school English. Frowning, I went to the front door and looked through the window. There was indeed someone trying to push a lawnmower through the waist-high grass.

Dream Guy.

I yanked open the door.

"Hey!" I called from the porch.

He didn't look up.

I jogged down the steps and waited for him to turn and see me. When he did, he cut the engine.

"What's your name?" I asked.

"Oanen."

"What are you doing, Oanen?"

"Cutting your lawn. Your mom made arrangements for it to be cut on Wednesdays. When I saw it, I figured waiting wouldn't help."

"You're the lawn service?" I asked in disbelief.

He shrugged and continued to look at me.

"Is there something else you want to ask?" he said after a moment.

"No. Nothing."

Confused and frustrated, I turned and went back inside. Outside, the lawnmower started up again.

I wished more than ever I understood Mom's motivation for leaving me here.

With each passing day, it was getting harder and harder to tell myself that she'd be back.

CHAPTER SIX

"BIG, HAIRY MONKEY BALLS," I MUMBLED UNDER MY BREATH.

Sitting at home with nothing but internet and cable TV to entertain me when I didn't feel like doing any online work sucked.

I idly flipped through channels, trying not to acknowledge that my outside-of-school pastimes were no different in Uttira than back home. Once a recluse because of anger issues, always a recluse.

A fight on the first day at the Academy had only reaffirmed my need to keep my crazy to myself. Granted, the incident hadn't been completely unprovoked. That didn't change the fact that I'd almost gotten face-flicked by a giant, though. Fighting at the Academy would be more dangerous than fighting in real school. It had been better to stay home the rest of the week and just do my school work online. Yet, after so much time sitting home with no outside contact at all, I was going stir-crazy.

Turning off the TV, I went to the kitchen and opened the fridge to stare blindly at the dwindling contents. I wasn't hungry. I was bored. No amount of snacking would cure that. Outside, the sound of the wind caressing the trees called to me. I closed the fridge and moved toward the door. My jacket hung on a peg just to the side, but I didn't grab it or move any further.

Staring into the darkness, I listened. For whatever reason, Oanen told me to stay put that second night. And, deep down, that warning still kept me inside. Why? Was I honestly afraid of anything that might be out there after seeing the possibilities at the Academy? I thought about it for a second and knew I wasn't. So why hadn't I already gone outside and found something to do? Because a bossy, shape-shifting boy my age told me not to.

"What the hell was I thinking?"

I grabbed my jacket and went outside. The heavy sound of Oanen's wings remained absent from the other night sounds as I locked the door. I breathed in deeply, savoring the taste of fresh air and freedom, and set off.

The uneventful walk to town took a considerable amount of time in the dark. The infrequent street lights liked playing peek-a-boo with rural mailboxes on the shoulder of the road. After the second run-in, I walked on the pavement where I felt safer.

Before long, the country shadows faded away with the brighter lights of town living. If you could call it living. Once again, not many people moved about on the sidewalks or from shop to shop. To be fair, most of the shops had closed signs turned in the windows already.

I checked my phone. It was only 7:30 p.m. This town seemed overly dead given the time.

The sound of an engine coming up from behind had me stepping onto the sidewalk. Instead of zipping past me, it slowed. I looked over my shoulder and tried to suppress the spike of anger knifing through me. The her-herd pulled up beside me in the shiny convertible. Their lead bitch grinned at me from behind the wheel.

"Look, Jenna, the Council decided we needed to add a vagrant to keep the town looking authentic."

"Wow, Aubrey. I'm impressed you know what the word vagrant means. Dogs usually only understand like fifty words, tops."

Her face turned red.

"Enjoy the walk, Orphan."

She peeled away with a screech of tires and a cloud of acrid smoke. Resuming my apparent vagrant shamble, I watched their taillights as I continued on. Of course, they stopped at the only lit up, interesting looking building in town. Sighing, I debated turning around and going back home. However, the idea of walking this far just to give up right at the end didn't sit right with me, even if I knew going home was the smarter choice.

As I drew closer, I noticed the sign on top of the two-story building. The big, bold letters of "The Roost," outlined in neon tubing, took up the front section of the roofline and cast the back half in shadow. This was the place that Fenris had invited me to go hang out, which explained Aubrey's presence.

While I was still looking at the sign, something on the roof moved. Given my experience so far with Uttira, something probably was up there.

The door opened as someone went inside, and the soft thump of music drew my attention. How could an almost dead town like this have a club?

It didn't take too long for me to reach the unguarded entrance. Some might think I didn't have a ton of experience with clubs, being a self-imposed recluse and all, but my temper had led me into one in New York. That had been two years ago. The last big city Mom and I had lived in. At fifteen, I'd ripped into the bouncer, beating him bad enough to put him in the hospital. I'd never reached my original target, some guy I hadn't even known who I'd spotted walking in.

That no bouncer stood by the red double-doors to prevent underage entrance, and the fact that the her-herd's car sat at the curb, meant this place welcomed underage derelicts of all kinds. I grinned to myself.

"Perfect."

Grabbing the long gold handle, I let myself in.

High school aged kids filled the open space of the dimly lit main floor. No one turned to look as the door closed behind me. They continued to talk in groups while unusual music played in the background. I couldn't exactly call it pop rock, even though it had that thumping beat, because of the soft, lilting voice that sang a song without apparent words. It had a slightly soothing quality, much like the singing I'd heard at the Academy by the pool.

Moving away from the door, I studied my surroundings. A wide loft wrapped around three of the four sides of the building and created a second floor that overlooked the first floor. Some kids hung around up there, sitting on stools along the red, iron rails and sipping drinks. Since couches and chairs outlined the open space of the main floor and a large, empty stage covered the back, the source of the drinks had to be up the stairs to my right.

I didn't make it more than a step in that direction when a small, dark-blonde almost ran into me. The look of panic in her eyes robbed me of any annoyance. I grabbed her by the arms to steady her.

"Is everything okay?" I asked.

"Not really. I need to get out of here."

I looked around at the people behind her. No one seemed to be paying us any attention.

"Is someone bothering you?" Please say Aubrey, I thought.

"No. I'm just really, really hungry." She leaned into me and inhaled deeply. That a girl two inches shorter and about twenty pounds lighter thought she'd make a meal out of me had me grinning.

She caught sight of my smile, pulled back, and blushed scarlet.

"I'm so sorry." I could barely hear her soft apology over the music. "I shouldn't have come here, but Adira said I needed the practice. I'm Eliana, by the way."

"I'm Megan."

"I know. New girl."

Her gaze shifted from my face to something just over my shoulder.

"Oh, we get to watch the mating rituals of the unwanted and pathetic," Aubrey said from behind me.

I curled my fist, ready to turn, but Eliana's hand on my arm stopped me. Some of the anger that had welled up at the sound of Aubrey's voice seeped away. I frowned at Eliana, and she immediately removed her hand.

The anger boiled forward again. Interesting.

I turned to Aubrey and cringed.

"This lighting is not kind to you at all," I said. "I bet the boys you're with have a lights off rule."

Eliana made a choked sound behind me while Aubrey's eyes narrowed.

"You know what I don't like?" she said. Her low, threatening tone, likely meant to intimidate me, just egged me on.

"Wow," I said with a laugh. "You must really like it when I piss you off."

"What are you talking about?"

"Offering to tell me what you don't like. Go ahead. Tell me. I'll be sure to write it down so I know what to do next time we meet like this."

She glared at me with so much malice, I thought she'd sprout claws then and there to rip my face off.

"I don't like you." Her clipped words were little more than growls.

I smiled sweetly.

"Perfect. I'll be sure to stick around then."

The door opened behind her, and she looked back. Her expression of anger changed to simpering desperation at the sight of Fenris. She rushed toward him to cling to his arm. She wasn't the only one. The other girls quickly surrounded him as well.

"Hey, Megan," he called with a wink.

Aubrey glared at me. I ignored her and smiled back at Fenris.

"Glad you finally found your way here," he said, he and his group moving closer to us.

Aubrey bared her teeth at me in silent warning. That girl needed another punch, or seven, to the face, and I itched to deliver them.

Eliana reached forward and wrapped her hand around my fist. Unclenching my fingers, I held her hand, relieved when some of the anger once again melted away.

"Oh, you two are so pathetic," Aubrey said, missing nothing.

Even Eliana's presence couldn't totally smother my desire to pummel Aubrey at that moment.

"Be nice, Aubrey," Fenris scolded.

Aubrey's haughty look turned to hurt. I didn't feel an ounce of pity for her, though. In fact, the inexplicable dislike I'd had since meeting her only intensified with her next words.

"Fenris, there's no need to give either of them social charity tonight. Let's go dance."

At the sound of heavy footfalls on the stairs behind us, I glanced over my shoulder, not ready to discover how it felt to be flicked by a giant. However, no giant descended the stairs. Just Oanen, putting a shirt on. Even in the dim lighting, I could clearly see each ridge of his six-pack. A very nice six-pack that I wouldn't have minded staring at for just a few seconds longer.

When his head cleared his shirt, he looked right at me before shifting his gaze to Fenris' group.

"Hey, Fenris," he said after he reached the bottom.

"Oanen," Fenris said in acknowledgment, his welcoming smile steady.

Oanen glanced at Eliana's hand holding mine. I thought he might try to give us crap, too. Instead, his expression infinitesimally softened.

"You should have gotten me if you were hungry," he said, focusing on Eliana.

"I'm not hungry." Her quick reply made him scowl slightly. His deep blue gaze flicked to me.

"Can we go dance now?" Aubrey part whined and part cooed, drawing his attention and probably making glass shatter all the way in China. She needed to work on the cooing.

"Yeah," Fenris agreed with his usual smile. "See you later, Oanen, Megan."

Oanen waited until they walked away before speaking again.

"Do you want me to take you home?" His gaze stayed locked on Eliana.

"No. I'm okay. Really. I thought, maybe, I'd hang out with Megan for a bit?" Her fingers lightly squeezed mine, and I realized she wanted me to support the idea.

"Yeah. Sure."

Oanen glanced at me before addressing Eliana again.

"Okay. Come get me when you're ready to go home."

What was with the boys here? Were they only allowed one facial expression? I liked Fenris' easygoing smile better than Oanen's deadpan.

Eliana tugged me across the room to a couch tucked in the shadows. Since I'd only been headed up the stairs to explore, I didn't mind the change of destination. As we passed people, I could feel my bitchometer twitch, but nothing compared to what I felt for Aubrey.

"Let's sit here," Eliana said, releasing my hand and plopping on a couch.

The bitchometer immediately started climbing. I sat next to her and looked out at the groups.

"It's a lot like human school," she said. "There are cliques and groups. Fenris and his girls are kind of in their own group, but they get along with most others."

"Most?"

"Yeah. Aubrey," she said with a shrug. "Once you start looking at the groups, they're pretty easy to figure out. Oanen would be part of the jocks. Aubrey is the leader of the mean girls' club. There are those who are serious about excelling at the Academy, and those who are just there, riding it out while looking for a good time."

"Why are you telling me all this?"

"Because I know what it feels like to know absolutely nothing about them or yourself. But it doesn't last long. The mentors at the Academy really will help guide you to the answers."

I looked at her, trying to believe she was telling me the truth because I had so many questions. Like why she'd tried running out of here then changed her mind.

"Are you still hungry?"

She blushed slightly.

"Not as much. You helped when you looked at Oanen."

"Huh?"

She blushed darker.

"Never mind."

"So who is Oanen to you?" I asked since she brought him up. The way he'd seemed concerned about her hinted that she meant something to him.

Eliana scrunched up her cute, pixie-like face before answering.

"Keeper? Pretend brother?"

"Pretend?"

"We're not the same kind," she said with another blush. "Can we change the subject?"

"Sure."

"How old are you?" she asked.

"Seventeen. You?"

"Sixteen. My mom brought me here when I was twelve. And immediately took off. I know it probably doesn't feel like it, but it's cool yours at least left you with a place to stay. I can't wait to graduate and get back out into the human world. I miss gyros. What was your favorite food?"

And just like that, I knew I had a friend. It wasn't because both our moms ditched us or because we had a similar love of gyros. It was because, when she'd mentioned her mom taking off, she'd noticed my hand curling into a fist and had changed the subject.

"Gyros are up there," I said, answering her question, "but so are tacos and Hawaiian pizza."

She groaned. "Why is it so impossible for the Academy to serve that kind of food?"

"What do they serve?"

"Nothing processed. They don't understand that's where all the flavor is. And it's not like we can get sick from it like the humans." She grinned at me, but the grin faded quickly when her gaze shifted to the right.

I turned my head, following the direction of her gaze, and found Aubrey glaring at us.

"What is her deal?" I asked.

"She's territorial." Eliana slapped her hands over her mouth and looked at me with wide eyes.

"I'm guessing that's not nice to say because she's a dog?"

Eliana snorted laughter behind her hands.

"I won't judge," I promised. "I think I've said worse to her."

Eliana folded her hands in her lap and smiled at me.

"Yeah, I heard about what happened at school. I kind of wish I would have been there to see it."

"It wasn't that impressive. Now, had that giant actually head-flicked me, it might have turned into something more."

"Finnegan is really nice. He just has a small crush on Aubrey."

"I don't know that there's anything small about him. Even his crushes."

She grinned.

"So tell me about Uttira. Is this the only place that's open after seven?"

She laughed and shook her head.

"You just caught Uttira at the wrong time. Everyone's prepping for the Fall Festival."

"I read about it online. Is it fun?"

She shrugged and made a face that said it was anything but fun.

Someone walked over to our couch. I looked up and found Oanen standing over us.

"We gotta go," he said, looking at Eliana.

"Okay." She looked at me. "Do you need a ride?"

CHAPTER SEVEN

If it had been Oanen asking, I would have said no.

"Sure," I said instead. "The walk here was a little long."

"You walked all the way from your house?" Disbelief laced her words as we stood. "You should request a car. The Council will bring in something for you to use since you're outside of town."

"That's okay. It's safer if I walk."

Oanen led the way out of the front door, nodding to people and saying goodbye as he went. A few waved to Eliana. She shyly waved back without pausing. No one seemed to notice me. And I was okay with that.

When we got outside, I saw Fenris leaning over Aubrey's car, his hands braced on the passenger door. It wasn't a she-lost-her-purse-and-I'm-looking-for-it kind of pose. It was an I-want-to-hit-something pose. A pose I knew too well.

"Keeping it together?" Oanen asked.

Fenris straightened, saw us, and smiled his flirty boyish smile.

"Yeah. I'm good. Better get back inside." He walked toward the door but stopped a moment to look back at me. "Maybe I'll see you tomorrow, Megan." He disappeared inside before I could respond.

Eliana cleared her throat slightly. I quickly pulled my gaze from the closed door to find her watching me. Oanen was already halfway down the block.

"We'd better catch up," she said quietly.

We jogged.

When she and I reached the car, Oanen silently held out his hand without looking at either of us. Eliana saved me from any confusion by dropping a set of keys into his open palm.

"You can have the front," she said, already opening the back door as he walked around to the driver's side.

Since Oanen seemed in a rush, I got in without arguing about the seating arrangement. He started the engine and told us to buckle up as he pulled out from his spot.

As soon as I buckled my seatbelt, Eliana passed me her phone.

"Send yourself a text from my phone so we have each other's numbers."

I took her phone and opened the text app. Her message list consisted of four conversations. Oanen, Adira, her mom, and Mom2. I didn't ask, just started a new conversation thread with my number and updated the contact information to Megan before handing it back.

"Maybe when you're done with Fenris tomorrow, we can hang out some more," she said.

"Sure."

The rest of the ride home passed in silence. Instead of stopping in front, Oanen pulled into the driveway and drove around to the back of the house.

"Thanks for the ride," I said, getting out.

"See you tomorrow," Eliana called.

I'd only managed two bites of my breakfast when someone knocked on the front door. I looked down at my milk stained t-shirt and shorts, shrugged, and stood. It wasn't like I was out to impress anyone.

Tugging open the door, I interrupted Fenris mid-knock. He grinned at me, his gaze sweeping over my body from head to toe.

"Wow. You look amazing."

"Shut up and come in," I said stepping aside. "When you said you might see me tomorrow, I didn't think it would be before eight."

"That's when a woman shows her natural beauty," he said smoothly.

"If you're attracted to this look, I really don't understand your fascination with the bitch brigade."

While he laughed, I closed the door and led the way to the kitchen.

"I'm going to use that. They'll love it."

"Will they really?" I asked, sitting down to resume my breakfast. "Because if they do, they have issues."

"No thank you. I already ate," he said as if I'd offered him something.

I rolled my eyes.

"Apparently, I'm an orphan. That means I'm not equipped to feed guests."

He sat beside me, a small smile still playing about his mouth.

"Then this is your lucky day. I wanted to take you to town so you could see what Uttira's like when all the shops are open. Including the grocery store, Moonlight Market. It's open twenty-four seven."

I drank the milk remaining in my bowl and took everything to the sink to wash it.

"I'd like that. But, I need to shower first," I said over my shoulder.

"Please tell me that's an invitation."

I shook my head and laughed. As soon as I set the dishes in the drying rack, I ran upstairs to grab some clean clothes.

Fenris still sat in the kitchen, looking completely at ease, when I returned.

"The bathroom door doesn't have a lock. And, that's not an invite but a warning. Stay out."

He pretended to pout as I closed myself in the bathroom. After quickly showering and dressing, I threw a load of my laundry into the washer just off the kitchen.

"Does it bother you?" he asked. "Being independent already?"

"Not really. I mean, I did a lot of this stuff before Mom left me here."

I turned and found him leaning against the counter, studying me. He wasn't smiling for a change, and I didn't like it.

"Don't pity me."

"Not possible when I envy you so much."

"How so?"

"There's no one telling you what to do, where to go, who to hang out with. That's freedom."

I snorted and grabbed my jacket.

"I'm still getting told all that stuff, just not by a parent."

He waited while I locked up the house, then we walked together to the front where an older car was parked.

"Wow. I thought everyone under the age of eighteen owned a sports car in this town."

"I do." He grinned. "I just thought I'd treat you special."

He opened the door for me, and it groaned in protest. That

sound should have forewarned me. Instead, I clapped my hands over my ears at the noise the engine made when he started it.

"Holy crap," I yelled to be heard.

"She gets all the stares. Just wait and see," he yelled back.

We didn't talk on the way to town.

As he'd predicted, actual people moved about on the sidewalks when we reached the shopping district. Most of the early risers looked our way as Fenris pulled over into a parking spot and cut the engine. My ears rang.

"This is Uttira," he said with a sweeping gesture. "Come on. I'll take you on a walking tour."

After considerable effort opening and closing the ancient door, I joined him on the sidewalk. We walked down the length of the street then back up the other side. The unique little shops offered a diversity of items from handcrafted jewelry to paints to custom clothing. Tucked in with the boutiques, casual shoppers had their choice of three cafes in which to sit and rest their feet.

"Come the festival, the road will be blocked for stalls with food, beverages, and games. The streets will be packed with humans."

"When is that happening?"

"It sounds fun, right?"

"No. It sounds awful. I need to know when to avoid town."

"No chance for that. It's mandatory attendance."

I stopped walking and looked at him.

"The town mayor is going to try to make me have fun?"

He chuckled.

"No. Adira and the rest of the Uttira Council. Our attendance is required in order for us to be considered for graduation. Remember Lucas's lecture about blending? That's what they're going to be watching for. That we can blend."

"I go to the weirdest school ever."

He opened the passenger door for me this time.

"I've heard there are a few weirder," he said with a grin.

I got in and waited for him to join me and start the car.

"Where to now?" I yelled.

He pointed down the road then, with a burst of grey smoke from the exhaust, eased out of the parking spot. We didn't talk for the short ride from the touristy downtown area to the commercial retail area.

Fenris parked in the grocery store parking lot and turned off the car again.

"There's the bank," he said, nodding toward the brown building. "The hardware store, post office, and bakery. The place next to it is where a lot of locals go for lunch."

"We have people who aren't local?"

"A few. Some human spouses who know the truth and chose to live here."

"And they aren't considered local?"

"Nope. Ready to shop?"

"I need to run to the bank first." He didn't question why and hung back when I quietly spoke to the freakishly goblin-looking teller to verify the checkbook and associated account were real. The woman assured me the account was real and the listed amount accurate. I couldn't believe Mom had left so much money for me. The guilt over ditching her child had probably helped her generosity.

After withdrawing some cash, Fenris and I went to the grocery store. I'd run out of the fresh food but still had plenty of dry goods. So, I shopped light. Fenris marveled at the idea I could pick my own food and, on the way home, begged me to make him something for dinner one night soon.

"What about Aubrey?" I asked.

"What about her?"

"I'm not sure she'd like me making you dinner. She's pretty into you, like she's already staked a claim."

"That's just part of who Aubrey is."

"And what is that?"

He glanced at me and grinned.

"That's like asking humans their sexual orientation. It's personal. Some might even consider it rude."

"Are you telling me this so I don't ask you questions or so I do?"

"I'm telling you this so you'll know not to ask someone you just meet this question, but to also let you know I'll try to answer any questions about anyone if I know the answer."

There were two people I really wanted to ask about, but I debated if I should.

"I'm straight, by the way," he said. "All into females, in case you were wondering."

I grinned.

"I'll keep that in mind."

"If you don't want to ask, that's fine too. If you pay attention, you'll figure out what most of us are. I just wanted you to know you have someone you can trust if you need me."

Someone to trust sounded kind of nice. Along with someone who seemed to calm me with a touch.

"Do you know what Eliana is?" I asked.

His smile slipped just a little before recovering.

"A succubus. But before you go grouping her with the rest of her kind, she's different. She's not a threat."

"Um, keep in mind that I don't know anything about anyone's kind. Are succubuses normally a threat?"

"Succubi. And some can be. They typically feed off of human sexual energy. If they can't control their hunger, feeding can kill their partner."

For whatever reason, he'd lost his smile with that explanation.

"Why do all topics lead back to sex with you?" I asked, trying to tease him into a better mood.

He grinned once more.

"Because it's the most interesting topic on your mind? Because I'm a male and you're insanely attracted to me?"

I laughed.

"I can see why you have your own following, now. So, what about me?" I asked, changing the subject. "Do you know what I am?"

He shook his head. "Not yet."

"Will you tell me if you figure it out?"

He nodded.

"All right. Then, I guess my last questions are what would you like me to make you for dinner, and when do you want it?"

He grinned widely.

"Something you ate a lot of in the human world."

I thought back to the dinners Mom had made.

"Spaghetti?"

"Yes. That."

He pulled into the driveway of my house and went to the back. After he parked, he helped me carry in the groceries and set them on the table. It wasn't even ten yet.

"Thank you for letting me take you to town," he said. He held out his hand, and I automatically offered mine, thinking he meant a handshake. Instead, his fingers closed around mine and brought my knuckles to his lips. The feel of his warm mouth against my skin sent a zing through me.

Before I could decide if it was pleasant or not, he released me.

"I'll see you soon, Megan."

With a wink and a flash of his boyish smile, he left.

I took my time putting away groceries then sat down at the table, wondering what to do next. TV didn't sound appealing at the moment, and it seemed too early to check in with Eliana. So, I opened my laptop and logged into my homeschooling page.

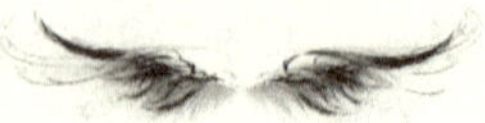

Leaning on the pole saw, I surveyed my work and grinned, glad I'd given up on schoolwork hours ago. Several of the pines boxing in the yard had died. Thanks to the handy pole saw I'd found in the shed, I'd trimmed back all of the dead lower branches. It didn't make the yard look any better. In fact, it left gaping holes in what had been a natural fence. However, I felt better after doing something physical.

With the sun touching the treetops, I put the saw away and stacked the last tree's branches on the large pile I'd created before going inside. Although the activity had cured some of the growing restlessness crawling under my skin, it hadn't purged all of it.

After I showered to remove old, dried pine bits from my hair, I listlessly walked to the kitchen for my phone and sent Eliana a text.

I'm home and bored. Have any plans?

Her reply was immediate.

I'm on my way!

Less than fifteen minutes later, I heard a car pull up outside and went to the front door.

Eliana parked the car Oanen had driven last night to drop me off. She saw me, waved, and got out. Instead of heading my way once she rounded the car, she went to open the passenger door, and I watched her grab several bags from the front seat. She turned to me with a wide smile.

"What is all that?" I asked, returning her grin.

"Snacks. I didn't want to come empty-handed."

I stepped aside to let her in. She kicked her shoes off by the door then followed me to the kitchen where she began emptying the snack bags onto the table.

"Where'd you find all this stuff? I was at the grocery store and didn't see this much variety."

"I asked someone to bring it in. That's the only way to get anything good here. I heard you have cable. There's a new movie I've been dying to see. Should we watch it?"

In short order, we popped some extra buttery popcorn and got comfy on the couches. Fenris' explanation of what Eliana was had me looking at her in a new light. Not judging, just more curious. Thanks to his little talk, though, I knew not to ask about it.

We watched the first movie in companionable silence until the credits began to roll.

"So what do you do out here all by yourself?" she asked.

"Not much. It's kind of boring. If not for you and Fenris, I might have died of boredom already."

"You can tell me to shut up if you don't want to talk about this...but you and Fenris. Are you really interested?"

I smiled and nibbled on my popcorn for a second.

"Fenris is nice. I like his smile and his easy-going personality. If I were in the market for a boyfriend, he could be an option, minus Aubrey."

She laughed and nodded. "Minus Aubrey is a given. But, you're not in the market? Why? Do you have a human boyfriend?" Excitement lit her eyes, and she leaned forward, eager for details.

"No. I had one once. Almost two years ago. I learned my lesson after that failed attempt at a relationship. It's fine to look at the opposite sex, but that's it."

"Why? What happened?"

"It ended abruptly when I punched him in the face for no apparent reason."

"Like Oanen?"

I made a face. "No. I thought I was dreaming when I did that. When I hit the other guy, I was pissed. Beyond pissed. I felt so horrible afterward. Then, the next day, I found out he'd cheated on me the night before anyway. I didn't feel so bad after that."

"That's actually really good," she said encouragingly.

"How so?"

"You lost your temper when you were wronged, even if you didn't know you were wronged at the time. It might be a trait, like how a banshee cries to announce a death."

"I thought we weren't supposed to talk about what we are."

Her face fell a little. "It's not polite to talk like this to people you don't know well. But, with friends, it's different. I'm sorry if I overstepped."

I reached over and clasped her hand. A subtle calm crawled its way under my skin, spreading out soothingly.

"We are friends," I said. "And, since we are, can I ask why I sometimes feel calmer when touching you?"

She tugged her hand from mine and blushed hard.

"I'm sorry."

"No, it's okay. I like it. I'm just wondering what it is. If you don't want to talk about it, that's fine."

"Well, I'm supposed to feed on sexual energy. But the idea of what I need to do to feed that way freaks me out. I end up getting so hungry that I'll feed on just about any emotion."

"Is it bad for you to feed on other emotions?"

"No, not really. It just doesn't give me what I need. It's like a human going on one of those weird diets where they only eat one low-calorie food. All lettuce or all watermelon or something like that."

"Are you telling me you're the succubus version of an anorexic?"

"Yeah, I guess. Adira is trying to help me overcome my hang-ups." She shrugged. "It's not easy."

"Well, any time you need an anger snack, you let me know. I'm more than willing and have plenty to go around."

CHAPTER EIGHT

I ROLLED OVER WITH A GROAN AND TUCKED MY HEAD UNDER THE pillow to hide from the sunlight. At the second beep from somewhere in the direction of the nightstand, I re-emerged in search of my phone.

It took four blinks to focus on the text from Eliana thanking me for last night. I shook my head and put the phone back on the nightstand without responding.

Hanging out with someone who didn't piss me off by just existing had been nice. That she hadn't left until after two hadn't bothered me until now. Whatever type of creature I was, I liked my sleep. However, the sun and my brain had other ideas. Within fifteen minutes, I gave in and got out of bed.

Another long day stretched before me. Out of the blue, I wondered what my mom was doing. It felt weird thinking about her, now. Even though she'd only been gone a week, so much had changed in my head since she'd left. I didn't miss her like I probably should have. It was hard to miss someone who had lied to me and didn't want to be around me anymore. Mom was so unlike Eliana.

Thinking of Eliana, I picked up my phone and sent her a quick text back.

It was nice having the company.

Her reply came almost right away again.

Do you want a ride to the Academy tomorrow for check-in?

That'd be great.

I'll see you at seven, then.

Sighing, I grabbed some clean clothes and went downstairs to shower before breakfast. Not that I needed to bother. No one came knocking on my door, and I spent the day focusing on assessments again.

By the time I finished, I was looking forward to going to the Academy in the morning. Anything was better than sitting at home, studying alone.

Heading upstairs for the night, I changed into my pajamas and turned off the lights. The brightness of the waxing moon lit my room as I made my way to the bed and curled under my blankets. I really needed to get curtains. Shutting my eyes on that thought and how I'd get to town to buy said curtains, it didn't take me long to fall asleep.

Anger woke me. I opened my eyes, my gaze sweeping the room. The moon's light had moved from my bed to my floor, letting me know I'd been asleep for a while.

My temper was a pain in my ass during the day, but this was the first time it ever bothered me while I slept. I exhaled slowly, trying to relax, and closed my eyes again.

A noise reached my ears. The soft brush of footsteps. I held my breath, trying to hear more. The sound came again. Downstairs. In the kitchen. Someone was in my house.

"Hell no," I said, flipping back the covers.

I flew down the stairs, the thump of my steps loud in my rush. Not loud enough to block out the sound of my quarry escaping out the kitchen door, though. I almost swore as I rounded the corner and mashed my hand on the light switch. The sudden burst of light illuminated the room just in time to catch the screen slamming shut. I raced out onto the porch but saw nothing. Whoever had been in my house had neatly fled.

Going back inside and flicking on lights, I went from room to room, checking everything. Nothing looked out of place. Who had been in my house and why?

I studied the kitchen again. A tuft of white hair on the latch of the screen door caught my eye. I plucked off the fur and held it between my fingers, my anger flaring. Since arriving at Uttira, I'd only seen one pale canine.

"Bitch," I breathed.

Aubrey was a dead dog walking.

While I listened for the sound of Eliana's car, I paced the entry and continued to plan what I would do or say to Aubrey when I found her. Currently, I was leaning toward the doing rather than the saying. But, I would need to be smarter about exacting my revenge within Girderon's halls. I couldn't just attack the moment I saw her.

Controlling my temper wasn't my strong suit, though. Not even for the few seconds it would take to look around for giants who might take offense at me punching Aubrey in the face. Chances were I'd end up face-flicked before the day ended.

The sound I'd been waiting for cut my plotting short. If you could call seven hours of plotting short. I hurried to the kitchen to grab my jacket and my bag before returning to the entry. I yanked the door open just as Eliana got out of her car.

"Let's go," I said, rushing toward her.

"You don't need to bring a school bag," she said. "I promise. There's never any notes to take and everything's online homework-wise. It's an either-you-know-it-or-you-don't kind of system."

I opened the front passenger door and got in. A large shadow moved across the hood, and I leaned forward to look out of the windshield at the sky. A griffin circled high above.

Eliana got in and noticed what held my attention.

"Yeah, sorry. He's following," she said with a shrug.

"Whatever. Let's just go."

She started the engine and gave me a hurt look as she pulled away from the house.

"Are you mad at me?"

I took a calming breath.

"Nope. Aubrey broke into my house last night, and I need to get to school so I can punch her face in."

"What? Are you serious?"

"Yeah. I did it once already. I just need to make sure there's no giants around to stop me this time."

"Not that. About her breaking in. Did you see her?"

I snorted. "I found white dog hair on the door after I came running downstairs, and the chicken fled."

Reading doubt in Eliana's lack of response, I launched into a defensive explanation of what I considered a logical and foregone conclusion.

"Think about it, Eliana. Aubrey's the only one who's had an attitude toward me since the moment she saw me. I mean, who else would sneak into my house in the middle of the night and snoop around my kitchen?"

The shadow passed over the car hood again.

"Megan, maybe we should talk about this later," she said hesitantly.

"Why? There's nothing to talk about. I missed seeing who was in my house by half a second because I wasn't sure what had woken me up, and it made me a little slow getting downstairs. But when we get to school and I confront her, you'll see."

A scream, very much like an eagle's, cut through the sound of the engine before the griffin sped off in the direction of the school.

"What's his deal? Does he follow you everywhere?"

Eliana made a face.

"Pretty much. Um, you should probably know his hearing is crazy sharp."

"What? You mean he was listening to us?"

"Yeah. And, I don't think he liked what he heard."

"Big deal," I said. I wasn't letting Oanen stop me this time.

"What do you do when you don't like something?"

"Punch it in the face."

"Exactly."

"Wait, are you saying he's going to punch me in the face?"

"Of course not. I'm saying he's going to react like he typically does."

I frowned and thought of the time Oanen did more than just impassively watch me.

"He's going to throw me on my bed?" I guessed.

"What?" Eliana squealed, half in shock and half giggling.

"I don't know. How does he normally react?"

"When did he throw you on a bed?" she demanded, grinning like a crazy lady.

"When I first met him. I thought I was dreaming and punched him."

"In the face?" she asked in disbelief.

"As you just pointed out, it's my typical reaction."

She shook her head and slowed down, having reached town.

Even though she wasn't scolding me or wearing a judgmental expression, I felt the need to defend what had occurred.

"He was fine. Maybe a little annoyed with me. He picked me up, carried me inside, tossed me on my bed, and told me to stay where I belonged."

"And you did?"

"Again, I thought it was a dream. I went to sleep and figured out it wasn't a dream the next day when I saw him again by the magical barrier that sent me flying."

"Ouch," she said sympathetically.

"Yeah, it wasn't fun. Now, about his reaction?" I asked as she turned into the Academy drive. The gates opened as soon as she approached.

"Lectures. Long, boring lectures about safety, responsibility, you name it. He likes to lecture."

"And I like to ignore, so it'll be fine," I said with a grin.

Eliana turned to the right, pulling around to the side of the Academy. Not many students had arrived yet, so it was easy to spot Oanen in the mostly vacant parking lot. With his arms crossed and a scowl on his face, he stood waiting for us in Eliana's chosen parking spot.

"Told you," she whispered.

He stepped back as she pulled forward and turned off the car. Through the windshield, his gaze remained locked with mine. Did he honestly think he had any right to lecture me on anything? He unfolded his arms, the material of his shirt pulling tight across his chiseled chest for just a moment, and moved toward my side of the car.

As soon as I opened my door, he was there, crowding me.

"You heard someone in your house, and you went running downstairs? Where's your common sense?"

I shouldered my bag, mildly annoyed.

"Hold on. I never claimed to have any common sense. I have anger issues. The two usually don't work well together. And what difference does it make to you?" Gravel crunched behind us as another car arrived. "Now, if you'll excuse me."

His gaze flicked behind me a second before he clasped my arms.

"Keep your hands to yourself," he said with a low warning.

"I was about to say the same thing." I threw off his hold moments before my anger reared its head. Not at Oanen, though. I turned and faced Fenris and his group of girls.

"Why'd you break into my house last night?" I demanded.

Fenris scowled. Jenna and the other girls' gazes darted to Aubrey.

"I don't know what you're talking about," Aubrey said. She reached for Fenris' arm and snuggled close to his side.

"How did you know I was talking to you, Aubrey? I was looking at Fenris."

The girl's face flushed scarlet, and her lips curled back to show her teeth.

"Stay away from him. He's mine," she snarled.

A hand slipped over my clenched fist, calling attention to the fact that two strong arms gripped me, and I was struggling to get to Aubrey. Eliana's small hand on mine did wonders to ease some of my anger. Enough to hear what Oanen said next, anyway.

"You need to take care of this."

Fenris sighed and pulled off his shirt. The view wasn't as nice as when Oanen removed his, but it still elicited a yearning whine from Jenna as she looked at Fenris. With a snarl, Aubrey turned on the girl and lashed out. Her claws left red welts on Jenna's cheek. Despite Eliana's hold, my temper surged again.

Fenris unzipped his pants, turned before showing anything interesting, and collapsed into a wolf. He sprinted away with a howl, leaving behind a pile of clothes and his girls.

Aubrey turned on the other girls, snarling as she slipped from her sundress and stood naked in the parking lot without an ounce of inhibition. I wasn't a prude, but I wasn't an exhibitionist either.

Collapsing into wolf form, Aubrey howled and ran after Fenris. A moment later, the other girls stripped where they stood and chased after the pair.

Oanen's hands released me.

"What the hell was that?" I asked, my anger fading to confusion.

"Desperation. Aubrey knows Fenris' mate run will happen soon and is doing everything she can to keep her scent foremost in his nose."

"Eliana, you know better," Oanen reprimanded her softly.

"If they don't want people to talk about it, they shouldn't make it so public."

"A mate run? What's that?" I asked Eliana.

"When his kind reaches a certain age, the urge to run out and mate hits hard. Overwhelmingly hard, I've heard. And, it's nothing like when the human boys get horny. Fenris can't just go out and have a good time. Fenris' kind mate for life. Whoever he picks in his moment of weakness is who he's stuck with forever."

"Ugh." The idea of him stuck with Aubrey for the rest of his life sent a surge of pity through me.

"Yeah," Eliana said in an equally sympathetic tone.

"Are you two done?" Oanen asked.

"Almost." I walked over to Aubrey's sundress and

thoroughly stomped it into the dirt. Adjusting the weight of my bag on my shoulder, I turned back to the pair waiting for me.

"Now I'm ready to go inside."

"Seriously, you don't need your bag," Eliana said, not commenting on the dress.

"I might." I took a step toward the school.

"What's in it?" Oanen asked.

"A change of clothes in case I get bloody."

He plucked my bag from my shoulder and tossed it back into the car.

"No fighting today." He stood, arms crossed and biceps bulging, before the door so I couldn't pull the bag back out.

"Who do you think you are? You can't tell me when not to fight. I fight all the time. Why do you think I'm here?" I said, exasperated.

"The clothes stay in the car," he said.

I narrowed my eyes at him.

"Fine, but if I end up needing them and don't have them, you're going to be on the receiving end of my temper next."

A howl cut through the air followed by four more.

"Come on. Let's get inside before they come back," Eliana said with a tug on my hand.

I gave Oanen one last glare and followed her inside. A few students already walked the hall, and I heard singing coming from the pool.

Adira waited for us in the main entry.

"Good morning, Megan. I was hoping I could talk to you before your first session."

I shrugged and said goodbye to Eliana before following Adira. It didn't escape my notice that Oanen stared after us a moment before following his ward.

As soon as we reached Adira's office, she went behind her desk, and I took a seat.

"I saw you completed all your assessments. I must say, I'm impressed. It usually takes more time for students in your situation to gain the focus needed to see what needs to be done."

"What's my situation?"

"Alone in a strange, new world."

"Ah. Yeah, well, I have no car to go anywhere and was bored." I shrugged.

"Regardless, you did very well. You've mastered the requirements to graduate from human high school. That means we can focus specifically on your Girderon requirements."

"Which are?"

"To master your control of yourself around humans."

"Perfect. Considering where I lived before coming here, that shouldn't be a problem."

"As you pointed out to Oanen in the parking lot, you have little self-control."

"Wait a minute. I pointed out I had a problem with common sense because of my temper. I never said anything about self-control."

We both knew it was a weak objection to the truth. When my temper flared, I didn't have control or common sense.

"Fine. What do I need to do? And if your answer contains the words 'visualize,' 'find your center,' or 'breathing technique' forget it. Been there. Done that. It doesn't work."

"The humans were trying to help you with something they couldn't begin to understand."

"I don't know, some of them gave my anger their best efforts."

"It's not just anger. It's part of your abilities."

"Hold up. My anger has something to do with what I am?" My mind raced, trying to think of any mythological creature known for anger issues or general grumpiness. Trolls, giants, brownies, dark elves...there were more grumpy ones than not. I'd need to do some research and compile a list.

"Stop trying to guess who you might be. It will distract you from who you are," Adira said, interrupting my thoughts.

"You're talking in circles."

She smiled serenely. Instead of calming me, it had the opposite effect.

"And, you're annoying me," I said flatly.

"I know. But, I'm not making you angry. Do you see the difference?"

"Not really. I still kinda want to wipe that smile off your face."

The natural abrasiveness I channeled when annoyed didn't faze her.

"Pay attention to your emotions. Break them down and ask yourself why you're feeling the way you do in any particular situation. By analyzing each feeling, you can start ruling your emotions instead of letting them rule you. Gaining that level of control, before your true form emerges, will—"

"True form? You mean this isn't what I really look like?"

I could feel panic welling up inside me. Everything else they'd thrown at me, I'd taken with a grain of salt. But this? Hearing that I would physically look different melted a sane portion of my brain.

"Breathe, Megan. I showed you my true form on your first day here. Yet, here I sit in the form you find the most familiar. The fact that you will have another form doesn't mean you must use it."

I stood and gripped the back of my chair.

"I don't want to be late for class."

Adira sighed. "Very well. Run away, Megan. It doesn't change a thing. I will see you at the Fall Festival."

"I'll pass. I don't do well in crowds."

"Attendance is required. Unless you're not interested in leaving Uttira. Ever."

"Why did I ever think you were nice?"

She smiled, not cruelly but as if she thought I was the funniest thing ever. We'd see how funny she thought me at the festival.

Turning on my heel, I stormed out the door and came to an abrupt halt at seeing Fenris leaning against the wall in the hallway.

CHAPTER NINE

When he saw me, Fenris straightened away from the wall and ran a hand through his already mussed hair, a look of guilt on his unusually serious face.

"I'm sorry about Aubrey," he said.

The door closed behind me. Apparently Adira didn't much care about our drama.

"Don't sweat it. Eliana told me about your mate run thingy. Are you considering Aubrey?"

"Not if I can help it."

"Then, why don't you tell her that?" We stayed where we were in a quiet corridor without other students.

"I've tried. You saw how she treats the others. It's worse when she doesn't think she has a chance."

He'd just given me more reason not to like her. I hated bullies.

"Is that why she has a problem with me? She thinks I threaten that chance?"

"She knows I hung out with you and that I'd like to do it again."

As much as I liked the idea of continuing to piss Aubrey off by just existing, because it was nice to know someone else lived in my hell, I didn't want to lead Fenris on.

"Look, I like hanging out with you, Fenris, but—"

"Aubrey won't be a problem. I have a plan to keep her distracted this time."

"Um, that's not what I was going to say."

The bell rang.

"We'll talk about this tonight. Okay? I'll swing by your place after school. Eliana's taking you home, right?"

"Yeah."

"Perfect. I'll catch you later."

He turned on his heel and jogged down the hall to the stairs.

Wondering why I'd been crazy enough to want to come to school, I followed. Slowly. When I reached the end of the hall, Oanen stood there. His expression wasn't neutral this time. Disapproval tugged at his brow and lips.

"What'd I do now?"

"You're late for your first session."

"I know. I'm going." I grabbed the railing, intending to start up the stairs. His hand closed over mine. The heat of his skin distracted me.

"Do you even know where you're supposed to be?" he asked.

I pulled my hand out from under his.

"Second floor. First hall. Third door on the right."

"No. Principles of Human Integration is your second session. Introduction to Self-Discovery is your first session. I'll walk you there."

I rolled my eyes and gestured for him to lead the way. Instead of taking the steps up, he turned and went down the wide hall that Adira first showed me and stopped at the second door.

"This is it. I'll see you in Lucas's session."

"You mean you don't have this one?"

He studied me for a second.

"I already know what I am," he said quietly.

"So this class is about figuring out what I am?"

"I don't know. Never had to take it."

"Why do you know my schedule?"

"Because I knew you wouldn't." He turned and walked away, leaving me at the door.

I stared after him a moment, wondering what his deal was. Was he really like this with all the girls or was I getting special treatment because of my association with Eliana?

Pulling my gaze from the view of his retreating backside, I entered the room and interrupted a woman mid-sentence.

"Megan," she said. "I'm LuAnn. Come in and take a seat. Adira said you'd be joining us today."

I looked at the students and immediately saw Eliana's smiling face and the empty seat beside her.

After almost ninety minutes, I understood that Self-Discovery wouldn't give me a straight up answer about what I might be. Instead, it was just like it said. Meditative self-discovery crap.

With a promise to find me during our lunch break, Eliana said goodbye in the hall. In the crush of bodies, I kept my eyes on the floor and found my way to Lucas's Principles of Public Integration session without incident.

Most of the desks were empty, except the group at the front. I openly smirked at Aubrey's dirty sundress. She scowled at me. Ignoring her, I winked at Fenris. The soft rumble of her growl filled the room. Satisfied, I took my seat and waited for the bell to ring.

"Why must you purposely annoy her?" Oanen asked from beside me.

"According to Adira, pissing people off is my superpower."

"Don't you take anything seriously?"

I thought about it.

"Not really. That must be another superpower."

He exhaled slowly and sat back in his chair, not talking to me again until the bell rang ten minutes before eleven.

"I'll walk with you to the cafeteria," he said, standing.

It wasn't an offer; it was an order. Oddly, though, it didn't annoy me. I had no idea where the cafeteria was anyway.

"Ok. Eliana said she'd meet up with me there."

We stepped out into the chaos. Only, this time, I didn't have to hug the walls and avoid eye contact. With Oanen beside me, people moved out of the way. Even Finnegan nodded to Oanen and gave him wide berth.

I glanced at the guy beside me, wondering what hold he had over everyone. It couldn't just be his incredibly good looks because his hold wasn't only on the students. The faculty all treated him with respect, too. Instructors nodded to Oanen when they passed him in the halls. And, when we reached the cafeteria on the ground floor, the lunch lady gave Oanen a wider smile and an extra helping of grilled trout and fried greens. She offered me the same because I was with him, but I politely declined. I'd have enough trouble finishing what was already on my tray.

Turning away from the extremely bland but nutritionally packed lunch line, I spotted Eliana already at a table. She waved at me, and I quickly started across the crowded room.

Mid-way, my temper flared. I froze, the tray dropping from my stiff fingers. Sniggers erupted around me. I clenched my fists and started to turn, already feeling the location of the object of my rage.

Before even seeing the person, arms wrapped around me.

"I don't think so," Oanen said. He lifted me off my feet and strode toward the side door. As soon as the door closed, I felt fine.

"Was it Aubrey?" I asked. "I could have taken her."

Oanen set me on my feet, his head bent as he looked down at me disapprovingly.

"Sorry to disappoint you, but Fenris and his followers always go for a run at lunch."

"I liked you better when you were still trying to figure me out and didn't scowl at me all the time," I said.

The door opened, and Eliana rushed out.

"Are you okay? Do you want a hug?"

"I'm fine. A hug isn't necessary." Did she think I was embarrassed over dropping my tray?

"Because, I could, you know, take some of that anger, if you wanted."

"Oh! Sure. Hug away." I opened my arms, and she shyly wrapped her arms around my torso and laid her head on my shoulder.

Eliana's hugs rocked. The anger lingering inside me immediately melted away, leaving me with an uncommon mellowness. It felt weird but oh so nice. Knowing I had Eliana to thank for this new feeling, I hugged her in return. The embrace turned into more of a snuggle, but I didn't care.

"I think that's enough, Eliana. She's starting to smile," Oanen said from beside us.

I was, and realizing it made me smile more.

"You have my permission to hug me anytime I look like I'm going to lose my temper," I said before Oanen pried me off of her.

"Only if I'm not around to stop the fight myself," he said. "Stay here, and I'll get you a new lunch. We'll eat outside."

Again with the bossiness. I stared after him, noticing the way his shirt hugged his shoulders and the way his jeans rode low on the curve of his tight—

"Can I come over and talk to you tonight?" Eliana asked, interrupting my thoughts.

I wrinkled my nose.

"I'd say yes, but Fenris is coming over. He and I need to talk."

"Oh?" she said with a teasing grin.

"Not that kind of talk. Although I enjoy doing anything that will piss off Aubrey, I don't want to lead Fenris on. I'm not healthy for a relationship. Especially one of my own."

Her playful smile fell, and she looked at me rather sadly. Before she could say anything more, Oanen returned with two trays, and we finished our lunch period in relative quiet.

My second and third sessions, General Living Skills and Advanced Human Studies, were a joke. The fight that I almost caused during the free time between the two sessions was just as sad. I didn't land a single decent punch thanks to Oanen.

Eliana met me in the hall after Advanced Human Studies, which was on the third floor.

"Oanen's already on the roof. He told me to tell you, no fighting."

I rolled my eyes and followed her down the stairs. No one moved out of the way for us this time.

"What gives? When Oanen's with us, everyone moves. When he's gone, people try to push us into the walls."

One of the passersby snorted and kept going. Eliana didn't say anything, but I caught her smirky grin.

Outside, people mingled by their cars. Fenris stood near the sporty red car he'd arrived in while talking animatedly with Aubrey. She caught me looking, and I blew her a kiss. Before she could take a step in my direction, Fenris grabbed her arm and pulled her toward their car.

That same eagle cry we'd heard on the way to school echoed around the parking lot.

"We better get going," Eliana said.

I glanced at the top of the building and saw Oanen perched there. His golden gaze pinned me.

"No one likes a bully, Oanen," I said softly. "I should know."

I got into the car and buckled up. A shadow fell over the hood, circling.

"Is he always like this?" I asked. "How has he not smothered you, yet?"

Eliana shrugged as she backed out of her spot.

"Do you think you'll come in tomorrow?" she asked.

"Not if I can help it. I thought I missed people, but today reminded me why I'm better off at home, reading the notes and watching the videos. Why do you go?"

"I didn't, but Adira talked to Mr. and Mrs. Quill and told them it would be in my best interest to attend."

"Mr. and Mrs. Quill?"

"Oanen's mom and dad. My guardians."

"And has it helped?"

"Not really." She glanced up at the sky then took the turn out of the Academy.

For the rest of the drive, neither of us spoke. When Eliana pulled up in front of the house, I thanked her for the ride.

"Let me know if you want company tomorrow after school," she said before she drove away.

I waved then looked up at the sky for Oanen, but he'd disappeared.

A single day of school should have cured me of my boredom; yet, now that I was home, loneliness surged again. Probably because I'd found someone I actually liked. Not just Eliana, either. Oanen, too, even though he could lighten up a little. And

Fenris. I sighed, thinking of him and the upcoming talk. Usually I liked making people cry.

Shaking my head, I walked around to the back and let myself in.

Over an hour later, Fenris knocked on my front door. With a smile, I welcomed him and waved him to a seat in the living room.

"As promised, Aubrey is conveniently distracted," he said with a small bow.

I chuckled, unable to help myself.

"Good to know. Is that why she came here? Because she'd found out that you took me to town?"

"Yeah. Even over the stink of the exhaust from that old car, she caught your scent when she saw me. Our noses are a pain in the ass sometimes."

We sat on the couch, and I turned toward him. He continued to watch me with that open, attentive look he gave everyone.

"Fenris, I need to be straight with you. I'm not interested in being anyone's girlfriend. My life is too complicated." I shook my head. "My issues have issues. I'm more likely to spontaneously hit you than kiss you. Hanging out like this, although really awesome for me, is just going to cause you more trouble."

He grinned a smile that would have melted the coldest girl's heart.

"You're adorable, and that is my favorite rejection, by far."

I rolled my eyes. "Like anyone ever rejects you."

"You'd be surprised," he said with increasing seriousness. "What did Eliana tell you about the mate run?"

"Not much really. Just that, like most teenage boys, your hormones will get the best of you; but whatever willing girl you find yourself with, whenever that magical moment occurs, you're stuck with for life."

"Willing? She doesn't know as much as I'd thought."

"Willing was my addition. Would you actually force someone?"

"No. I hope not." He rubbed his hand over the back of his neck, his frustration clear. "For us males, when our biological clock goes off, we're a slave to our instincts. Or, so my father has told me. The first female we smell, we want, and we tend to chase her down. That's the mate run. Chasing her until she stops and gives in. My father says it's a playful chase." He exhaled slowly.

"So Aubrey is sticking to your side in hopes that your clock will go off when she's near, so you can playfully chase her down, have your way with her, and make her your wife for life." I gave him a sympathetic look. "That's rough."

"Not just Aubrey but all the rest of the girls in my pack who are around my age."

"Aren't there any other guys?"

He shrugged and sighed.

"Thank you for being honest about not being interested in me. I'd still like to hang out, though, if you don't mind the occasional evil eye from Aubrey."

"I think I can handle that."

He looked toward the foyer a second before someone pounded on the door.

"Be right back," I said, already moving to answer.

I opened the door to Oanen. Bare-chested with jeans riding low on his hips, he stood barefoot on my porch. Sweat glistened on his chest, right between his pectorals. I licked my lips and tried not to stare.

"Oanen?"

His gaze barely swept over me before settling on something over my shoulder. I glanced back at Fenris.

"She's on her way here," Oanen said. I knew he meant Aubrey when Fenris groaned.

Fenris looked at me apologetically.

"I'm sorry." He stepped in and hugged me, breathing deeply next to my hair.

It didn't quite feel like a platonic hug. Awkwardly, I hugged him back.

"You know she'll smell you on her," Oanen said. "Knock it off."

When Fenris pulled away, his pupils looked a little too dilated, like he was high or something.

"I'll see you soon," he said. He leaned in once more to smell my hair then slipped past Oanen and jogged to his car.

Fenris quickly peeled off down the road.

"Can I come in?" Oanen asked.

"Sure." I motioned to the kitchen and closed the door behind him.

Instead of going to the kitchen, he went to the living room and sat on the couch. A position he kept just long enough to eye the length of his chosen seat before he lay down on it. His feet rested on one arm and his head, the other.

"Okay. Make yourself at home."

He stood and strode toward me. Before I knew what he had planned, he pulled me into his arms and buried his nose in my hair. Having Oanen do what Fenris had just done shocked the hell out of me. Oanen's hands smoothed over my back, pulling me firmly against his front, and I shivered at the full body contact. This was nothing like what Fenris had done.

Just as soon as Oanen had hugged me, he released me.

While I still reeled from having that bare, chiseled chest pressed against me, he strode outside, leaving the door wide open. The sound of a car pulling up in front drew my attention.

Oanen stood on the shoulder of the road, shaking his head at the slowing, shiny red car.

Anger bubbled up inside me at the sight of Aubrey. I fisted my hands, ready for her to try something. She didn't stop, though. At seeing Oanen, she continued by.

Oanen waited until Aubrey was out of sight then looked back at me.

"Behave, Megan." He walked into the pines and took flight not long afterward.

I closed the door and leaned my head against the panel.

"Monday from hell," I whispered.

CHAPTER TEN

TUESDAY, THANKFULLY, GAVE ME A REPRIEVE FROM LIFE-DRAMA until Eliana called me after school.

"Please say I can come over," she said.

"Sure. You can save me from boredom. I finished Academy stuff before lunch."

She cheered and promised to "be there in just a few."

The sound of a car pulling into the driveway only seconds after we'd hung up made me smile as did Eliana's playful knock on the back door.

"I'm so glad you said yes," she said when I invited her in. "You're not going to believe what happened today."

She launched into her story before I managed to close the door.

"Aubrey went ballistic because Fenris didn't show up for first session. And since you weren't there either, Aubrey naturally assumed his absence was due to you, even after Adira told her that Fenris' father called to excuse him. Rumor is Fenris answered the call of the trees, which means he's on his mating run. Which made Aubrey even crazier. You should have seen it.

Adira barely stopped her from coming over here. So?" she said, looking at me expectantly.

"So, what?"

"Was he here today?"

I rolled my eyes. "No."

"Aubrey was telling everyone who would listen that she'd tracked his scent here yesterday but that Oanen stopped her from checking the house. She would have come straight here after school today, but Oanen made it very obvious that he was tailing her. So, she went to Mr. and Mrs. Quill to complain about Oanen's interference in pack matters. That's why I came here. I couldn't stand listening to her whiny, desperate voice anymore."

She barely breathed before continuing.

"What happened yesterday? With you and Fenris?"

I gently steered her toward the kitchen table as I answered.

"Nothing. I told him I wasn't girlfriend material and, as much as I liked annoying Aubrey, I didn't want to make his life any more difficult. He seemed okay with it, but said he still wanted to hang out anyway."

"Hmm. Hang out because he's desperate to get away from Aubrey? Or because he's interested and is subtly not taking no for an answer?" Eliana sat in a chair and tapped her chin in thought. "He's always struck me as a player because he seems to thrive on keeping his little group of women around him. And, every time I see him with his swarm, he always reeks of sexual energy. I think he's interested. Better watch out for him."

I grinned at her.

"Yes, ma'am." I went to open the fridge. "You staying for dinner?"

"Can I?"

"Of course."

While I started getting out ingredients, she filled in more details around the Aubrey drama.

"After Adira threatened to magic her into a two-week coma, Aubrey started sniffing everyone. Looking for even a hint of a trace of Fenris' scent. You should have seen her face when she smelled Fenris on Oanen. Get this, he looked at her all calm like and said, 'I'm a hugger,' and shrugged. Half the kids in the hall busted up with laughter. That's just another reason she's bitching at the Quills right now."

Hearing that clarified the reason behind yesterday's spontaneous hug. Oanen had done it to cover up Fenris' scent. I couldn't help but feel a little disappointed about that.

"I wouldn't be surprised if she comes straight here when she's done ranting at the Quills, though," Eliana continued. "She said she could smell you on Oanen, too."

Eliana grew suddenly quiet. When I looked at her, her hands were flat on the table and she was pale and shaking.

I tossed the ingredients for lasagna aside and quickly moved to her.

"What's wrong? Eliana?"

When she looked up at me, her eyes were black.

"Don't touch me," she whispered. "Go upstairs and lock your door."

"Not a chance. Tell me what's happening."

"I had a bad thought. I'm so hungry now."

I turned to the cupboard where I'd stashed a bag of double chocolate dipped cookies. Before I could grab it, the back door clicked, and I found myself alone in the kitchen. I ran out the door and took a running jump, neatly clearing the hood of the car and blocking Eliana's escape.

"I'm not letting you leave like this," I said, studying her still black eyes.

Eliana feinted to the right then left. I kept up, not letting her set more than a finger on the door handle. The sound of an engine and the sudden scream of tires braking on the pavement at the end of the driveway stopped our little dodge game.

A car door slammed

"Bitch!" Aubrey yelled.

The sound of her voice hit me hard. Rage ignited in my blood, and I turned away from Eliana, completely focused on a new objective: piss off Aubrey then punch her in the face.

She was making it easy on me by stomping her way up the driveway. Her blonde hair snaked around her head in a windblown mess from her drive here. It added to the crazed look in her eyes as she snarled at me.

"Heard you finally figured out Fenris isn't interested in you," I said. My hands ached with the need to hurt her, and I took a step closer.

Something slammed into my back, knocking me forward. The weight of whatever had hit me stuck tightly and wrapped around my arms and legs as I fell face first toward the ground. The anger that had flooded me vanished, replaced by a disgruntled calm and a mouth full of grass.

I turned my head and spat.

"Time to get off, spider monkey," I said.

Eliana made a hesitant sound near my ear, and I knew she wasn't going to let go just yet.

I lifted my head and found Aubrey towering over us, only a step away. Her lips twisted in a vicious, triumphant smile as she took a picture of us on the ground.

"Fenris is smart enough not to want succubus seconds." She flounced her tangle of hair, turned on her heel, and marched back to her car.

Eliana got off me as soon as she pulled away.

"You gave me permission," she said. "Any time you were mad, remember?"

I slowly got to my feet, brushing myself off. When I looked at Eliana, her eyes were back to normal.

"Inside, now," I said, sounding stern.

Her bottom lip protruded slightly, but she listened and began a sulky pace toward the house. I spat out some more dirt and followed. When we were back inside, I poured us both a drink of water and sat at the table with her.

"I'm not mad about the hug. But I am mad about you trying to leave. What happened? I thought we were trying to be the kind of friends that could," I shrugged uncomfortably, "talk about stuff."

Eliana sniffled and nodded. "We are. It's just hard. You know what I am. But you don't know who I am. I'm Eliana Magdalene Margarete Howland, daughter of a piously religious man. That was who my mom seduced.

"For a year, she kept him under her spell feeding on his passion for her. After she gave birth to me, she left. He raised me, believing my mom some form of demon who tempted him from his path. He was right. The moment she walked through the door again, he fell to his knees and begged her to let him 'worship at her temple.'"

"Oh, geez. I think I just threw up a little."

"I know. I was there, and I definitely threw up a little. The point is, what I am and who he raised me to be doesn't mesh together well. Sometimes, it feels like I'm being ripped in two." She looked down at her glass, turning it in slow circles.

"And that's why you're not feeding. Because you feel guilty?"

"No. Because the way I need to feed feels so wrong."

She sounded so guilty when she said it that I quickly changed the subject away from her feeding.

"Maybe my mom was like yours because she thought sleeping around was great, too."

Eliana smiled slightly and looked up from the glass.

"I don't think so. We can sense our own kind. It's weird. Like seeing someone on the street and somehow knowing they're your brother or sister."

"That would be cool."

She shook her head. "You're thinking Brady Bunch, but it's more like Cinderella."

"Oh."

"And I don't necessarily need to sleep around. Being near people who are making out works, too, but it's kind of awful. It's like I am a peeping Tom on their emotions."

"Okay. But what happened just before you tried to leave? Why'd your eyes go black?"

She went back to looking down at her glass before answering.

"Thoughts pop into my head. Sexual ones. And they make me so hungry. I don't know why I think them. It's not who I am."

"We all think things we might not want to think. It's nothing to run from."

"It might be," she said softly.

"Spit it out. What thought did you have?"

She took a deep breath.

"We were talking about how Oanen smelled like you and Fenris, and the image of the three of you on—"

"Okay, I get the picture. It's not that big of a deal. I bet loads of people our age have weird sexual thoughts. I mean, look at what Fenris is dealing with, right? It'll pass. But, you don't need to run. Not from me. I won't judge you if your eyes go all black."

She nodded, flashing me a watery smile.

"Thank you."

"No problem. Now, let's make some food and binge eat a package of cookies."

An insistent dream about a snoring beaver woke me to the sound of a lawnmower running in my front yard. I lifted my head and looked at my clock.

"Seven? He is not sane," I grumbled, tossing back my covers.

I stomped down the stairs, almost falling, and yanked open the front door. The bright light of the early morning sun blinded me, but it didn't stop me from speaking.

"Why do you hate me? Is it because I hit you? Because I'm friends with your sister from another mister? Or do you just hate everything that's good in this world?" I leaned limply against the doorframe, too tired for a righteously indignant stance as I tried to blink him into focus.

Oanen, who'd turned toward me at the first sound of my voice, turned off the mower.

"Too early?" he asked.

"Yes! Eliana didn't leave until two. Again."

I blinked him into focus and caught his lips twitching along with the fact that he wasn't wearing a shirt. The sight of his sun-kissed chest and the steam rolling off of it as he stalked toward the porch perked me up better than a cup of coffee. Where was his shirt? Wasn't it too cold to be mowing without one? Not that I was complaining. How could stoic, lecturing Oanen look so good? All the sexual-thought talk with Eliana must have messed with my head.

"Did you get in trouble?" I asked, mostly to distract myself from the way the light played on his abs.

He stepped onto the porch and gave me a puzzled look.

"For what?"

"For keeping me from tearing Aubrey a new one at school?

For stopping her from coming here and getting her butt kicked?"

He studied me.

"You're very sure of yourself."

"Yep. Aren't you going to be late for school?" I gave the truck parked on the street a meaningful glance. As good as he looked without a shirt, I wanted sleep more.

"Is sass a superpower, too?"

I couldn't help the smile that curled my lips. I liked his wit.

"Maybe. Can I bribe you with a toaster waffle to come back and finish this after school?"

"Maybe. If you let me keep my things here so I can fly."

"Deal. Come on in. Don't forget your shirt."

I turned and shambled to the kitchen. The freezer surrendered its lone box of organic waffles, the only kind the store in town had offered, with very little struggle.

When I closed the door, Oanen was already sitting at the table. He once again wore his shirt, which clung to his sweaty skin. I wasn't sure covering wet muscle with a thin shirt was any better than just skipping the shirt.

He leaned forward, bracing his forearms on the nicked wooden surface, as he watched me work my culinary magic with the toaster.

"Want syrup?" I asked.

"Yes, please."

I got out a plate and a fork and put them in front of him before going back to the fridge.

"You're not going to eat?" he asked, watching me.

"It's barely seven, and there's no one here to stop me from sleeping until noon. I'm not eating breakfast until I'm ready to face the day." I set the syrup on the table just as the waffles popped.

"Breakfast is in the toaster. See you after lunch, lawn boy," I said over my shoulder on my way out the door.

"Megan, wait."

I stopped and groaned, removing the one foot I'd managed to place on the stairs. When I stepped back into the kitchen, he already had two waffles gone and a quarter of another on his fork. Chewing, he held out my phone. The play of his jaw muscles mesmerized me, and it took until he swallowed for me to take the phone from him.

"Text me if Aubrey shows up again, like she did last night. I already put my number in there."

"Uh, okay."

I quickly fled upstairs. Not long after I flopped on my mattress, I heard the water run then the door close.

"My life is so weird," I said to the ceiling. I thought of my estranged mother, wondered if that was why she'd left, and closed my eyes.

I crashed hard. When I woke up again and went downstairs to fix my own waffles, I found Oanen's dishes washed and in the drainer and his pants neatly folded on a chair. A note lay on top.

I'll be back for these this afternoon. Try not to kick them in the dirt.

I grinned then frowned. Was he planning on walking inside naked again? My pulse picked up at the thought. Setting his pants down, I ran back upstairs for my phone and a clean set of clothes.

Before getting into the shower, I sent Oanen a quick text.

Your pants are on the back porch.

I tossed them onto the old wood planks then went back inside to get ready for the day. By lunch, I was eating my cereal and feeling pretty all right.

CHAPTER ELEVEN

"Is there any chance I can sleep over tomorrow night?" Eliana asked.

I held the phone to my ear while muting the T.V., the current device to fend off boredom.

"Sure. Why? What's up?"

"Humans are going to start coming into town for the Fall Festival first thing in the morning. I'd rather not be anywhere near that mess until the last minute. Plus, if I stay over, we can drive together. We need to show up around three."

"Ah. Yeah, it's fine if you come over. I'm running low on food, though. Would you mind taking me to the grocery store for some food after you get here?"

"No problem. Talk to you after sessions tomorrow."

I set the phone next to me and blindly stared at the TV. Nothing about the festival appealed to me. I knew myself well enough to know I'd end up getting into trouble somehow. Yet, the restless boredom that kept crawling under my skin had me almost looking forward to it, trouble and all.

"Obviously, I have issues," I said before turning up the TV volume.

After I finished watching the current show, I shut everything off and went to bed. Just as I started to drift off, I heard something. It sounded like it came from above rather than below. I waited for it to come again, but the house remained quiet, and I eventually drifted off to sleep.

In the morning, I dusted the spare room, removed webs from the corners in the upstairs hallway, and washed the steps. Everyone thought having their own place was glamorous because no adult told them what to do. They didn't stop to think that meant there would be no adult taking care of the crap jobs like cleaning, laundry, yard work, and paying bills. The reality was…adulting sucked.

When I had the upstairs clean enough for Eliana to stay over, I started in on the downstairs. The kitchen didn't take much time because I kept up with it daily. Nothing had really been deep-cleaned in the living room, though. I pulled the couch into the entry along with the two chairs, the old oil lamp, and side tables. With the room mostly clear, I wiped the baseboards and mopped the wood floors. For the first time, the house took on a completely fresh scent. Rolling with it, I opened the windows.

Doing all that work helped cure a little of the restlessness and brought back Mom's words about exercise. I needed some kind of daily activity. A routine that would help keep me from going crazy. The money Mom had left could easily buy a treadmill, but I hesitated to use any of it for more than the basics. I had no idea if there were house payments I'd need to make or what other bills might come with this place. Which was also why purchasing a car seemed like a bad idea. Not only would it be a chunk of money, it would also take me to places where there were people. Hitching rides with Eliana seemed smarter, for now.

Finishing the task at hand, I moved the furniture back into

the room and went to read lecture notes for the current week's sessions.

The restlessness was back by the time Eliana pulled into the driveway, and I had my coat on before she reached the door.

"Ready?" she asked when I met her.

"Yep. I'm going crazy here and have come to the realization that, as much as I seem to hate people, I need them, too."

She smiled as she walked back to the car with me.

"It's almost the same for me. As much as I fear what I want to do to people, I need them, too."

"And, what do you want to do with people."

Her blush answered me.

"Oh, you sassy girl," I teased. "I can't wait until you take the plunge and actually make out with someone."

Her flushed face immediately paled.

"Hey, kidding. It will be fine. You'll see."

She nodded, and we both got in. She didn't make any move to start the car, though.

"I'm sorry," I said, feeling guilty that she still looked pale.

"It's not that." She exhaled heavily. "It's this weekend. If I want any chance of leaving this place ever, I need to show some progress. I need to kiss a human."

"Seriously?"

"Yeah. I'm so scared. What if I can't stop at a kiss? What if I jump them and take everything?"

"You won't. I won't let you. I'll tackle hug you to the ground like you did for me."

She turned her big brown eyes on me.

"Do you swear?"

"I promise. And in return for interrupting any possibility of a booty call, I'm hoping you'll do the same for me. Not the booty call part. There's no chance of that. The fighting. Someone's going to piss me off big time, and I don't want to go to jail for kicking some grandma's ass."

Eliana snorted a laugh and started the car.

"I swear to keep you from kicking granny booty."

We waited until the last possible minute to leave for the festival. Even the weather seemed to know it wasn't a day for fun. The overcast sky and cool damp air hinted at storms before nightfall. None of it would stop the festival from taking place, though.

Eliana took her time on the country roads, unlike the day before when we went to town for groceries. I knew she was still terrified of what she needed to do today.

"What happens if we don't go?" I asked.

"We'd fail our human relations sessions. You're in Principles of Human Integration, right? I think they put you there because you've lived outside of Uttira for seventeen years. I had to start with the beginner course, and I'm still there. Trust me when I say you don't want to hear the same lectures for more than one semester."

"Got it. Not showing up is an automatic fail."

"And for me, not kissing a human is an automatic fail." Nervous energy rolled off her with those words.

"Don't think about it," I said. "We have all afternoon. When we get there, let's just check out the booths and not worry about the humans. Okay?"

"Okay."

The town was crawling with people. We had to park seven blocks from the actual downtown area.

Eliana looked pale again.

"It'll be okay," I said. "We'll stick together."

She nodded shakily, and we got out and started walking. The wind toyed with my hair, using the ponytail like a whip.

We'd barely reached the edge of the festival when Adira found us.

"Good afternoon, Megan and Eliana. I wish you luck. Eliana, the kiss isn't as important as much as the way you control your feeding. Do you understand? You must feed the way every succubus is meant to feed. No more denying yourself."

Adira's gaze turned to me.

"Today is about control for you, too, Megan. Remember what we discussed in my office. Examine your anger before you give in to it. Ask yourself why, and see if you can discover a reasonable justification for your reaction."

"And if I can't?"

"We'll try again. I need to find Fenris now. Excuse me." With that, she walked away.

I turned to Eliana, the snarky comment dying before it reached my lips. Not a trace of color remained in her ashen face, and tears welled in her eyes.

Grabbing her hand, I tugged her behind the nearest vendor booth.

"Breathe, El. You got this. Don't let what Adira said get in your head."

"How? She wants me to feed. I've never even kissed someone without feeding, and she wants me to do it with feeding?"

Color returned, but not the right kind. Her skin took on a greenish hue.

I grabbed her arms before her knees gave out.

"Look at me, El. Look. You know what you are. You know what to watch for. I know, too. I won't let you do anything bad. Okay? Do you trust me?"

She nodded weakly.

"Then pucker up buttercup."

Before she could guess what I intended, I pressed my lips to hers. She immediately stiffened but didn't jerk away. Since I'd only ever had the one boyfriend, and not for very long, my little pool of experience didn't give me much to go on. I relaxed my hold on her arms and lifted one hand to gently cup her cheek. She exhaled softly against me and tilted her head. I felt the moment she started to feed. The ever so subtle stirring of lust in my belly caught me off guard.

"I've died and gone to heaven," a familiar voice said. Fenris. The sound of his voice acted like a bucket of ice water, breaking the spell of her kiss and the lust snaking its way through my blood.

"Shut up," Oanen said.

"How can you not think that's hot? I'm not even sure I can walk right now without breaking something," Fenris said.

I gently pulled back and looked at Eliana. Based on the expression on her scarlet face, she looked ready to bolt. But not sick or ready to hurl. Mostly just embarrassed.

"Are you mad at me?" I asked.

Eliana shook her head.

"Do you feel like jumping me and taking the rest?"

"Please say yes," Fenris said under his breath.

I shot him a look, but he only held his hands up pleadingly. Beside him, Oanen watched me, the intensity of his gaze a contradiction to his impassive expression.

"No, I'm okay," Eliana said, almost sounding impressed.

Focusing on her, and not our unwanted audience, I grinned at her.

"Then go try that with a human."

"Boo," Fenris pouted.

"Adira was looking for you. Why don't you go find her instead of tormenting us?" I asked, arching a brow.

"Tormenting? No way. I'm encouraging. I think it's great that Eliana's embracing what she is."

I glanced at Eliana. She didn't look like she believed him; she looked like she wanted to fall into a hole. I wrapped my arms around her and hugged her close, letting her hide against my shoulder.

"Adira sent us to keep an eye on you," Oanen said.

"She'll be fine," I said. "I'll keep an eye on her."

"Not Eliana. You."

"Me?" I looked at both of them over Eliana's head.

Fenris nodded.

"Why me?"

"Aubrey," Fenris said.

"You like to fight," Oanen said at the same time.

"She'll be fine," Eliana said, pulling away from me. "We're going to stick together. I'll make sure Megan doesn't fight."

Oanen shook his head and glanced at our joined hands.

"That's not going to help you do what you need to do, Eliana. You need to focus on yourself."

An adult poked his head behind the booth. His forehead went from smooth skin to a third, scowling eye in a blink.

"You guys need to find somewhere else to talk. Get going."

Too stunned to protest, I followed Eliana's insistent tug until we found ourselves on the main thoroughfare, weaving our way through the clusters of people. With her hand wrapped around mine, I barely felt the brief flares of anger. Being free of it meant that my other senses actually had a chance to work.

"Do you smell that?" I said, tugging her in a different direction.

"Pumpkin pie?" she asked.

"Is that what that is? It smells so good." I found the vendor booth where the ladies were taking slices of hot pie and putting them into to-go cups topped with a generous amount of whipped cream.

"Oh, I need some of that," I said.

Eliana's chuckle died almost as quickly as it started. When I looked to see why, I found her staring hungrily at a guy around our age. The sheer look of torture on his face as he walked behind his parents begged for rescue. However, in a single glance, I knew he wouldn't be a good candidate for Eliana's first feeding.

I tugged her to my side and whispered in her ear.

"Not him. He'd fall hopelessly in love with you and follow you everywhere. You need a player. Someone who'll kiss you and walk away."

She took a slow breath and tore her gaze from him with effort.

"Let's get some pie and walk around. We'll find you someone."

"Here," Oanen said from beside me. I looked down at the pie-filled cups he held out.

"Thank you." I didn't hesitate to snatch mine and take a huge bite. The cup warmed my cool hand, and the pie tasted even better than it smelled. I groaned.

"You've never had pie?" Oanen asked.

"Not that I remember. Mom cooked, but she didn't bake," I answered absently, doing my best to ignore our babysitters.

The crowd flowed around us as I took my second bite. Although there seemed to be a good number of families strolling around, I still spotted plenty of people our age wandering on their own. Eliana would have no problem finding someone with all these people. But, would she be able to feed with our shadows around.

The sudden urge to hit something sent my cup of pumpkin pie slipping from my fingers. Oanen deftly caught it, but I barely noticed. My gaze shifted to the man passing beside us, the source of my anger.

As I clenched my fists, Adira's words came back to me. What about him made me angry?

It took every ounce of control that I didn't think I had to study him instead of fly at him. Older. Physically fit. Neatly dressed. Alone. There wasn't anything that stood out as wrong. He walked far enough away that the anger faded. Instead of letting him leave and taking the non-encounter as a win, I started to follow him.

He made his way to the center square, where people lounged on the benches, and took a seat. Then he people-watched. That was it. I leaned on a pole not far away and scrutinized him.

"Are you okay?" Eliana asked softly beside me.

"No. I want to make that man over there bleed, and asking myself why, like Adira said to do, isn't helping anything. There's no logical reason that I can see. He's just a guy sitting there watching—"

His gaze met mine. He gave me a slight smile, stood, then headed our way.

"Hi, girls. This is something, isn't it?"

I wanted to hurt him so badly my hands shook. Eliana's hand slipped under my shirt, and her fingers touched the skin of my back.

"Is this your first time here?" Eliana asked.

"It is. You two from around here?"

"We are," I said, feeling more in control. "Don't let this fool you. Uttira is boring as hell."

His grin widened. "There's nothing for two, pretty girls like yourselves to do around here for fun? That's no good." He took his wallet out and gave Eliana a card. It had a number on it. That was it.

"If you're ever bored enough and want to have some fun while earning some serious money, give that number a call."

He moved like he was going to go back to his previous spot. Something told me not to let him walk away.

"I don't think we want to wait. Let's have some fun now," I said, thinking quickly. "My friend and I were taking bets on you."

"Oh?" He looked amused and completely interested in hearing what I had to say.

"We thought you were the kind of man willing to give a girl a kiss in public."

"Megan," Eliana whispered. That single word held so much worry. Her fingers twitched on my skin as I continued.

"Obviously, I thought yes. She thinks no. I know of a quiet spot."

"A quiet spot would be perfect."

"Then follow us. At a distance." I grabbed Eliana's supporting hand and started walking.

"What are you doing?" she whispered harshly. "I can't kiss him. That's so gross."

"Can you feed without kissing?" I asked.

"I don't know. Maybe. I've never done this before. But the sexual energy coming off of him is so disgusting. Please don't make me do this."

"You don't have to. I just figured you could get a hit off someone who didn't really matter before I kicked his ass."

"Why are you kicking his ass?"

"Mostly because I feel like it and partly because he's a pervy old guy."

"He didn't do anything wrong, though. Just talked to us."

"And gave us a card with a number and a promise of good work. Come on, Eliana. Nice people don't do that."

We ducked behind one of the closed shops. Cars lined the back alley but remained empty of people except us.

"What happened to Fenris and Oanen," I asked, for the first time realizing they weren't with us.

"They're close. Watching but staying out of it unless it looks like you need them."

The man walked around the corner.

"Well, girls. What did you have in mind?"

My rage knocked me blind for a moment. I breathed through my nose and fisted my hands.

"What's wrong, Megan? You look upset." He still sounded so calm. "I hope you're not going to try to change your mind now. Guys don't like girls who go back on their word."

Someone stepped in front of me, blocking my view.

"She's mad because I get to go first."

Before I could push Eliana aside, she moved close to him and brought her hand to his cheek.

"What's your name?" she asked. Her voice didn't sound like Eliana anymore, and that broke through the haze of anger.

His gaze heated as he stared down at her.

"Jesse. What's yours?"

"Doesn't matter." She trailed her fingers over his skin. He groaned and closed his eyes. "What matters is what you want to do to me, Jesse. Tell me."

He proceeded to tell her in great detail how he would use her body then sell her to the highest bidder. Gently used young women were in high demand. He couldn't promise gentle though because he ached for her.

"That's okay. I'll help with that ache." She pulled him down to her mouth. Instead of kissing him, she inhaled. From my standpoint, it looked like a backward attempt at mouth to mouth without the contact, until I saw her eyes.

They'd turned black again. The guy she'd held didn't seem to notice, though. His eyes were rolled back in his head.

"Eliana? I think you might need to stop," I said. "Not that I really care, but he doesn't look so good, and I don't want you to be upset by that."

She immediately pulled away with an "eep!" Like a puppet without its puppeteer, Jesse fell to the ground with a thud.

CHAPTER TWELVE

ELIANA AND I BOTH STARED AT THE UNMOVING MAN. HE LAY IN AN awkward sprawled position, his legs slightly folded under him. His head lolled slightly to the side, showing his eyes closed and lips slack. A bit of drool started to run from the corner of his mouth.

"Please tell me I didn't kill him," Eliana said in a panicked voice.

I squatted down beside him and felt for a pulse. The wind gusted through the alley, ruffling his hair.

"He's alive." I lightly slapped his cheek, but he didn't respond.

"You don't still want to hit him, do you?" she asked.

"No. Not really." Most of my anger had faded the moment his eyes had rolled back into his head. I wedged my hands under him and gave him a shove to roll him over to his side.

"You don't want to jump him, do you?" I asked.

"Ugh! No. I'm feeling a little sick, honestly. That was the most disgusting thing I've ever done."

"So sexual energy doesn't taste like chicken?" I asked, smirking as I pulled out his wallet.

"Not even close. It'll be easy to stop feeding if it always tastes like moldy cheeseburgers. Although, I'm not sure how I'll ever again be able to start in the first place. Are you robbing him?"

I grinned at her and opened his wallet.

"No. Not robbing him. Though, I'd make a fortune. There's at least a grand in here."

Continuing to look through the contents, I found his pictures. Polaroid's of girls and boys too young to be of age.

"Now, I'm going to be sick," I said. "We need to get Trammer."

"He's on his way," Oanen said. I looked up and saw him standing by the entry to the alley. He had his phone in one hand, and my cup of pie in the other.

"How much trouble are we in?" I asked, standing.

"None. You didn't hurt him, and Eliana did what Adira wanted. Fed without killing."

"I hope I never have to do that again," she said with a shudder.

"Feeding, my dear, is a part of your life," Adira said from behind me.

I yipped and spun around. Adira stood a few steps away, her grey pantsuit matching the stormy sky above.

"When did you get here?"

"Just now. Well done on your first feeding, Eliana. You're free to spend the rest of the day as you'd like."

"What about me?"

"Did you do as I asked?"

"He's not bleeding, is he?"

"Then you are free to do as you'd like, as well."

"That's it? You're not going to tell me what the point of this was?"

"No."

"Seriously? Everyone else knows what they are? So what's the big deal? Why keep what I am a secret from me?"

"We'll talk more Monday."

With a wave of her hand, a portal opened and Adira disappeared through it.

"Way less than helpful," I said.

"Eliana, can you go watch for Fenris and Trammer?" Oanen asked.

She gave me a quick, sympathetic look then left me alone with Oanen and the knocked-out man.

Oanen walked toward me and handed over the cup of pie. However, he didn't release his hold when I gripped the cup.

"Your ignorance is a gift. By not knowing what you are, you don't have to conform. You don't need to be what everyone thinks you should be. You decide for yourself who you want to be. So stop whining about what you don't know and focus on what you do."

Eliana was right. He did like to lecture.

"And what do I know?" I asked.

"That you're not human. So stop trying to act like one."

"What the hell is that supposed to mean?" I dropped my hand from the cup, too annoyed to take it now.

Before he could answer, I heard Fenris' voice.

"Trammer, you might want to lay off the extra portions. The sound of your heavy breathing is going to let everyone know there's something wrong."

The tittering laugh that followed Fenris' remark spiked my already simmering temper.

"Behave, Megan," Oanen warned softly just before Fenris rounded the corner.

Only a few steps behind Fenris, Aubrey looked at me with narrowed eyes as she walked into the alley but said nothing.

Instead, she focused on the man laid out on the ground nearby. Moving closer, she studied Jesse's face.

Behind her, a red-faced Trammer joined us. His irritated gaze swept over me and Oanen as a pale and shaky Eliana entered the alley last.

"Well, that's one less human to worry about," Aubrey said with a laugh.

Because she was facing me, she missed Trammer's angry glare. I didn't care so much about his opinion, but I did care about Eliana's. When she paled further and tears gathered in her eyes at Aubrey's insensitive words, my anger surged.

Without consciously deciding to do so, I balled up my fist and slugged Aubrey in the face. The satisfying sound of flesh hitting flesh brought a smile to my lips as her head snapped to the side. Her growl filled the air, and her face went from human valley-girl to freakishly fur-faced monster from a bad Hollywood movie.

As she changed, Fenris stepped between us.

"Enough, Aubrey." His growl cut hers short. Her face immediately reverted back to valley-girl.

"I don't have time for this," Trammer said. "Just show me the human you think did something wrong."

"We think?" I said, turning the remnants of my temper on him. "We know. Look at his wallet, Trammer. He has kiddie porn pictures in there. And he described in detail how he would sell Eliana after he was done raping her."

He bent down, tapped the guy's face, then looked at his wallet like I had.

"Well, we'll see what the Council wants to do with him after they wipe his memory."

"What do you mean?"

He stood and crossed his arms.

"I can't press charges against him for the photographs

because he'd need to go to court. Uttira doesn't have court. That means the two of you would be witnesses out there in the real world. And, what would you tell any law enforcement out there, anyway? My succubus friend was feeling a little munchy, and we decided to go for a pedophile?"

"Trammer," Oanen said, sharply.

The sheriff looked at Oanen, no trace of guilt or remorse on his face.

"It's the truth."

"Seriously?" I said. "A man who admitted to human trafficking is going to be let loose?"

Trammer shook his head at me as if he was disappointed.

"Because the secrets of Uttira could be jeopardized if the Council chose to pursue charges? Yes. Now, get out of here. Fenris and I will get him to the Council for the memory wipe."

I glanced at Fenris in time to catch his look of distaste before he stepped forward and helped hoist the man to his feet.

I couldn't believe that man would just go free. Rage boiled under my skin. I wanted to hurt him. I wanted to hurt Trammer, too, as if he were the one responsible. But based on Oanen's firm scolding, Trammer wasn't to blame. The fault lay with Eliana and me. My actions let this happen, and I wanted to yell my frustration.

Eliana grabbed my hand and some of the emotion slipped away. Her hand shook just as badly as mine, though. Together, we watched Fenris and Trammer haul Jesse away. Aubrey shot me a look that promised retribution as she followed.

"I need to go home," I said, my voice tight.

"I'll take you both," Oanen said.

I started down the alley, Eliana gripping my hand. Neither of us spoke once we reached the main thoroughfare. She took over and led me in the direction of where we'd parked. The distant car became a beacon of escape from the press of bodies.

Eliana handed the keys to Oanen and insisted I sit in front. Closing the door on the noise of the festival crowd, I buckled my seatbelt as Oanen slid in behind the wheel.

"It's not your fault, Eliana," Oanen said firmly once he'd pulled away from the curb. We weren't the only ones leaving. The dark clouds that looked like impending rain were sending the humans scurrying for their vehicles, too.

I glanced back at Eliana and saw her guilt-stricken face.

"It's not," I agreed.

She gave me a small nod.

"The Council will make sure to manipulate that man's mind in a way that he'll get caught so he can pay for his past crimes," Oanen assured us both.

"How quickly, though?" I asked.

"It'll most likely depend on the man and what he confesses to them," he answered.

"Not good enough. If we'd been anything other than what we are, he would have raped Eliana and had us in his trunk or something."

Oanen turned into a more spacious neighborhood with well-cared for lawns and took the columned driveway at the end of the street. The pristine tree-lined lane led to a sprawling stone house that looked as old as the Academy.

"Do you want to come in?" Eliana asked.

I gave the house a long look and shook my head.

"I'll see you Monday," I said.

"Okay. I'll pick you up at seven again."

Eliana got out and closed her door, heading toward the front entry as Oanen turned around. I waited until he was on the road again before picking up our conversation from before Trammer's interruption.

"What did you mean when you said I'm acting like a human? What other way is there to act?"

"You aren't human, so neither are your emotions. Stop treating your anger like it's normal. Adira is telling you to pay attention to it because it might be more than just a part of what you are."

"And the part about not conforming, where you called me a whiner?"

"Right now, you can be anything you want to be. Embrace it. Because once you know, they're going to treat you like a tiny gear in a large machine and nudge you into the right place for our world."

"Is that what they did to you?"

His non-answer confirmed the question.

"If you were me, what would you do?"

"Not worry so much about what I am and just learn everything I can about the new world I just discovered."

"Oh, like what?"

"The history of it. The creatures you'll likely encounter. Their strengths and weaknesses. Why they exist."

I had to admit, the topic of conversation piqued my interest.

"And where would a girl learn about all of that? Apparently, it's impolite to just ask people, and I didn't see that topic in any of the lecture notes."

"I'll teach you."

The offer made me immediately suspicious.

"Why?"

"Because of Eliana. Because I understand what it's like to come into this life and not know anything. Because…just because."

Oanen finally left the festival crowds behind and made his way toward the outskirts of town.

"Okay. Fine. Where should we start?" I asked.

"The most important thing for you to know is that the gods are real."

"Which ones?" I asked, humoring him.

"Zeus, Oden, Hera, Frigg, Thor, Loki, Hades. All of them. And, just like an overpaid CEO of a global corporation, they've each had their time in the spotlight. The waning adoration of the humans they so obsessed over brought an end to each reign. While knowledge of them faded into myth, the mementos of their reign, creatures like us that they left behind, have struggled to remain myth as well."

I thought about what he was saying for a moment.

"Why does it matter if I was created or just popped into existence by natural evolution?"

"If something created you, don't you want to know why?"

"Yeah. I guess so. But doesn't that start tying into what I am? I thought my whiner self wasn't supposed to focus on that?"

"You don't let things go easily, do you?"

"Nope."

He sighed.

"The 'why' ties into our purpose and our abilities, which is where you should focus. The gods had their own reasons for creating whatever they left behind. Most wanted to protect the humans. Some grew jealous of the humans' quick, passionate lives and created creatures to hurt them."

Hurting others sure seemed to be another one of my superpowers.

"Ah, crap. Does that mean I'm playing for Team Jackass?"

He snorted.

"It doesn't have to be that black and white. Look at Eliana. Her kind is supposed to feed on humans, use them and leave them in thrall. She won't do that. She can but won't. Even if we have no control over what we are, we can still try to choose who we want to be."

Instead of stopping in front of the house, he pulled into the driveway.

"Try?" I asked, opening my door.

He shut off the car and got out as well.

"Sometimes, like Eliana, it's a fight against your nature. It's a conscious choice every moment." He followed me to the back door. "I've seen you angry. I've seen you attack Aubrey for very little reason."

"Says you. She's a bitch. I consider that a huge reason." I opened the door and went inside, going to the fridge since I hadn't really eaten anything at the festival.

"My point is, I've seen you let your anger take over, and now I've seen you hold back. That means you have a choice. You can resist your instincts if you want. You can try to be who you want."

"I didn't resist my instincts at all. It was just about how I got what I wanted. I wanted that man hurt and figured out a way that wouldn't get me in trouble so I could still help Eliana." I pulled out the leftover lasagna and showed it to him.

"Want some?" I asked.

"Yes, please." He sat at the table and studied me while I got out the plates and heated two pieces.

"Why not hit him right away like you did with Aubrey?"

While I thought about it for a minute, the microwave beeped, and I gave Oanen his food before warming up some more for myself.

"Aubrey's my age. I knew I'd get in less trouble fighting with her because we mutually antagonize each other. Maybe, I've just gotten smarter about targeting adults with my superpowers after my last run-in, which landed me in anger management counseling for three months."

"Sounds less than fun," he commented.

"Yep. It was." But had twenty-four of those hour-long sessions really been enough to bore me out of impulsive fighting? No. I'd gone right back to it. Oanen was right. Why had I acted differently today?

"So what else should I know?"

"The Council was created out of necessity after the last of the gods disappeared. We police ourselves to prevent anything that may expose our existence to the general population."

"Like killing humans." I sat beside him, surprised he hadn't consumed one of the pieces already. He'd waited for me to begin eating.

"This is really good," he said, after his first bite. "And try not to assume anything about Uttira or its residents. We were all created for different purposes. For some, that purpose is to kill humans. We just ensure it's done in a way that doesn't create risk."

I swallowed quickly while he took a bite.

"Wait a minute. You're telling me it's okay to kill humans in this place? Why would any human want to live here?"

"No. It's not okay to kill here or in any other Mantirum town. Killing close to home would be a risk the Council wouldn't ignore."

"Mantirum. That sounds familiar."

"Did Adira maybe mention the mark of Mantirum?"

I nodded, the conversation with her coming back to me.

"Yeah. The mark I'd receive after graduation in order to leave this place."

He nodded, letting me know I had it right.

"That mark doesn't just let you come and go from here. It lets you into any Mantirum location because it signifies you belong to the gods and the world of magic. However, it also signifies you understand the rules of our world and the consequences of breaking them."

Thunder rolled outside and the first patter of raindrops hit the kitchen window.

"And will I learn those rules at the Academy?"

"No. A member of the Uttira Council will schedule a series of meetings with you once Adira believes you're ready."

"They could keep me here forever based on Adira's recommendation?"

"They could, but Adira wouldn't recommend that. Like I said, we all have our purposes. There's no point in trying to keep you from yours."

We finished our meal and worked together to clean up the dishes.

"I don't like you out here on your own," he said when we were done.

"Why?" I set the dish towel aside and met his gaze, waiting for his answer.

Instead of answering, he just looked at me. It normally took a lot to make me uncomfortable. However, his neutral, assessing expression managed to make me squirm in just under a minute.

"You know, it really annoys me when you do that," I said.

"Do what?"

"Look at me like I'm a bug in a jar. On display for detached clinical study."

His lips twitched slightly.

"That's not how I'm looking at you."

CHAPTER THIRTEEN

I opened my mouth to ask what he meant by that but never got the chance. His head jerked toward the hall.

"We have company," he said softly a moment before someone pounded on the front door.

I hurried to answer it, wondering what magic-world drama I was in for now.

As soon as I turned the knob, the door thrust inward. I flailed back at the same time my temper exploded. Oanen caught me mid-fall and pulled me against him, his hands remaining firmly locked around my biceps as Aubrey pushed her way inside.

"Where is he?" Aubrey demanded.

The anger that had welled up at her presence, faded at the press of Oanen's muscled chest against my back, and I struggled to concentrate on Aubrey's words.

"I know he's here," she said, looking around wildly.

"Who?" I asked.

"Fenris."

Oanen's hands slid up to my shoulders until his fingertips brushed my collarbones, and his thumbs rested on each side of my spine. The heat of his touch bled into my skin, and I shivered subtly.

"Fenris is with Trammer," I managed to answer.

"No, Fenris left with Trammer, the Council wiped the meat bag's memory, and then Fenris went for a run."

Oanen's right thumb smoothed upward, skimming over my shirt to the skin of my neck. My pulse jumped, and I realized what he was doing. He didn't have Eliana's ability to syphon my anger to prevent me from fighting, so he was distracting the hell out of me instead.

"Oanen, cut it out. Aubrey, Fenris isn't here. So why are you?"

Her gaze drifted to Oanen for the first time.

"Aubrey," he said lightly.

"Oanen." She focused on me once more. "I hope this means you've moved on."

"Psycho obsession is a huge turn off. Might want to try to medicate that."

Aubrey bared her teeth, and I fisted my hands, ready to give her the beating she was begging for. Oanen's hands tightened on my shoulders in warning.

"Stay away from Fenris," she said before turning on her heel and marching back to her car. The downpour robbed her exit of any dignity.

"Wonder if she smells like wet dog even when on two legs," I said.

Oanen sighed, reached around me, and closed the door.

"Her hearing works as well as mine."

"I know." I looked over my shoulder and grinned at him.

"I'd better get going and keep an eye on her," he said. "Thank you for dinner."

I rolled over in bed and wrinkled my nose at the weak light of a new day. Sleep hadn't come easily and had fled too readily. Why? Because my dumb head wouldn't stop replaying those few moments by the door with Oanen. What had been up with his hands?

Grabbing me to stop my fall, I understood and appreciated. Moving his hold to my shoulders might have been to give him a better means to control me in Aubrey's presence. Given my previous issues with her, I again understood and appreciated the gesture. But that swipe of his thumbs on the back of my neck? Completely unnecessary and in no way understandable. My skin still itched and tingled there, and I couldn't stop thinking about it.

He'd never shown signs of interest. Had he? No, I didn't think so. Although I may have been too busy drooling over his chiseled abs to notice. I had two options. I could pretend it hadn't happened and carry on as usual. Or, I could confront him about it and probably make a fool of myself.

"Pretending it is," I said to myself.

Sitting up, I looked out the window at the still overcast sky. The droplets on my window didn't invoke hope for sunshine anytime soon, which meant another boring day inside.

I decided to entertain myself by making an omelet. Cooking had been Mom's thing not mine. However, since Mom left, I'd managed a few basic meals. Stuff I'd helped Mom make over the years or I'd learned on my own on the occasions she stayed over somewhere. Now, I used the internet to search out a recipe for a broccoli and cheddar concoction that made my mouth water.

Heating the pan, I whisked my eggs and set about making myself some happy food while listening to the birds. I hummed over the caws and poured the eggs into the pan. While they sizzled, I went to the fridge for the cheese. A crow zipped past the kitchen window just as I turned. It looked way too big up close.

Shaking my head, I added my leftover broccoli bits and cheese. A sudden flurry of crows cawed loudly then quieted.

I frowned and turned off the burner before standing on my tiptoes to look out the window over the kitchen sink. They'd sounded like they were right outside, but I couldn't see anything.

With my face inches from the glass, I almost screamed when another crow flew up, flapping its wings right in front of me before it drifted back out of sight.

"What the hell is going on out there?"

I slipped on my shoes and went out the kitchen door. As soon as the screen slammed shut behind me, a chorus of caws rose from the back corner of the house.

Wrapping my arms around my middle, I shuffled forward slowly, a sense of something bad building inside me. Not so much dread as much as aw-crap-I'm-not-going-to-get-to-eat-my-omelet-anytime-soon.

A half dozen crows took flight when I rounded the corner. With their cries ringing in my ears, I stared down at the very dead body on which they'd been feeding. I'd beaten people to the point of hospitalization, but seeing the waxy color of the man's skin did something to me. I started to shake.

He had been partially eaten by something much bigger than a crow, however. And, although bits were missing, and blood stained much of his clothes, and he lay face down, I still recognized him.

"Shit."

Heart hammering, I turned and ran for the house. When the

door slammed closed behind me, I already had my feet on the stairs, racing to get my phone.

My hands shook as I dialed 911. I couldn't unsee the body. Every time I blinked, the image refreshed in my mind.

"Moonlight Market, how can I help you?"

I jerked the phone from my ear and looked at what I'd dialed. Yep. 9-1-1. I put the phone back to my ear.

"I dialed 911," I said

"Oh, honey, Uttira doesn't use that. Tell me what's happened."

I hesitated a moment. Who in the hell decided it would be a great idea to route 911 calls to a damn grocery store?

"There's a dead body outside my house. Crows and something else have been eating him."

"Oh my. I'll send Trammer right away."

The line disconnected, and I dialed my only lifeline.

"Hey, Megan," Eliana chirped. "Want some company?"

"Yes. This town is fucked up."

"What's wrong? You don't sound like you."

"There's a dead body outside my house, and I called 911 and got the grocery store. The grocery, Eliana. Do you know how crazy that is?"

"Holy Mary and Joseph." I could hear her running down some stairs. "I'm on my way. Don't hang up." She covered the mouthpiece, but I could still hear her.

"Megan Smith just found a body outside her house. Yes. I'm going there now."

The muffled sound left the phone.

"Tell me what happened," she said.

"Beyond discovering a chewed-on body being pecked at by crows? Nothing."

"Chewed on? By what?"

"I don't know. Do I strike you as a walking Animal Planet reference guide?"

"No. Sorry," she said quickly. "Any idea how it got there?"

"I'm about three seconds from hanging up on you. Of course, I don't know how it got there."

"I'm so sorry. I'm not good at this. What should we talk about?"

"My omelet."

"Uh, okay. What's your omelet's name?"

"Cold and soggy. Damn body interrupted my breakfast. But that's not the worst of it, Eliana. I know who it is."

"Who?"

"That guy from yesterday. Jesse."

She gasped.

"Yeah. I know."

After that, we didn't really talk about much. I listened to the sound of the car engine and her soft, erratic breathing until she pulled up in front of the house.

"Bye," I said a moment before racing downstairs and pulling the door open.

Instead of Eliana on the porch, I found Oanen. He filled the opening as he looked down at me with concern.

"Are you all right?" he asked. A siren wailed in the distance, the sound growing louder by the moment.

"I don't know. Am I? I don't know." The shaking hadn't stopped. That probably wasn't a good thing. But why was I shaking? I honestly didn't care that Jesse was dead. I think I was more pissed that someone had killed the guy and eaten him.

Oanen took me by the elbow and led me to the couch. The simple warmth of his hold helped calm me. When I sat, I saw Eliana hovering just behind him.

"Where is he?" Oanen asked, drawing my attention.

I shook my head and instead of telling him, stood up to show them. His hand wrapped around my arm to stop me.

"You can stay here. You don't need to see that again."

"No, I can't stay here. I need answers. Why is he dead? And why is he at my house? He was alive when he left that alley yesterday, Oanen. Who killed him?"

Outside, the siren silenced. Instead of moving toward the back of the house, I went to the front door again. The two walked with me so I wasn't alone to greet Trammer. Together, we watched him leave his car and give his duty belt a tug before walking our way.

"Why am I not surprised?" he said. "Trouble seems to like you. Or maybe you like it?"

I didn't respond. Eliana's small hand around mine was the only thing keeping my temper from igniting out of control.

"Well, show me what you found," he said impatiently. I could hear in his tone that he didn't believe I'd actually discovered a body in my yard.

Turning around, I led the way out the back door. When I reached the corner, just enough to see the body, I stopped and pointed with my free hand. Eliana gasped, and her fingers twitched against mine.

"Sweet mother of mercy," Trammer said under his breath.

He stepped around us and looked at what remained of Jesse.

Between the side of the house and the pines, I caught a flash of silver as a car pulled up in front. Trammer exhaled heavily and crossed his arms. Car doors closed. A soft murmur of voices floated to us from around the house.

I turned toward the driveway. A moment later, two well-dressed adults and Adira appeared.

"How are you, Megan?" Adira asked.

"Uh, not good. There's a body in my yard."

"How does that make you feel?"

"Are you serious right now?"

"Not just any body," Trammer said from behind me. I turned and saw he'd rolled over Jesse.

Trammer's hard gaze met mine. "You expect me to believe you had nothing to do with this after yesterday?"

"What? You think I killed him?" I snorted. "This is not what comes to mind when I think home-cooked meal. He's been gnawed on. Who eats people?"

Trammer opened his mouth to say more, but someone cut him off.

"We don't think you did it, Megan. But, we are interested in how it makes you feel."

When I looked at the other adults, Adira was now missing, but a simmering circle remained where she'd stood. Before I could ask why my feelings on the subject mattered, a wolf appeared through the portal. Adira emerged just behind the creature. No one spoke as the wolf trotted forward and sniffed around the body.

One moment I stared at a mottle-colored canine, the next a naked older man. I quickly averted my eyes. That was not the age bracket of nudity I wanted stuck in my retinal memory.

"Based on the feeding, it's one of ours," the man said in a deep somber voice. "But, the rain washed away any hint of scent. I'll start asking around to find out who was on their own last night."

"Might want to check with your boy first," Trammer said.

The man turned his steely gaze on Trammer, who paled slightly. Even I wanted to cower from that look.

"You believe Fenris did this?" the man asked.

"You said you would ask who was on their own. Per the Council's request, Fenris rode with me to return this guy. I left him on this side of the barrier, where he'd wait for a ride back to town, but he wasn't there when I returned."

"Aubrey was out last night, too," Oanen said. "She stopped here looking for Fenris."

The man exhaled slowly, his gaze going to Adira.

"We know that neither of them killed this human."

"We do?" I asked.

His hard, silver gaze turned to me. Eliana's fingers twitched in mine.

"No one without a mark could have left the barrier to kill this man and bring him here. I'll start questioning the pack."

"Thank you for coming, Raiden," the well-dressed man said. "Please let us know what you learn."

"Shouldn't I be there to question them, too?" Trammer said, frustration lacing his words. "It's my job, after all."

"No, Trammer. It would be best if you left this to the Council. Thank you for your services, but all we require is that you burn the body and remove all evidence of the man's return."

Trammer's face flushed.

"I'll go get a body bag from the car then." He stalked off.

"I will return you, Raiden," Adira said before looking at me. "Megan, I'll see you tomorrow."

She and Raiden disappeared into a shimmering hole that vanished quickly behind them.

"Will the two of you stay for a while?" the woman asked.

"If that's all right with you," Eliana said.

I glanced between Eliana and the woman, and the woman caught my look.

"I apologize, Megan. We know so much about you and have forgotten you know very little about us. I'm Anwen Quill, and this is Lander, my husband."

Holy crap. Those were Oanen's parents?

"Hi. Sorry we're meeting because of a dead body in my yard."

Anwen smiled slightly.

"It happens occasionally. Don't worry about it. We'll get it sorted out." She turned her gaze to Oanen. "We'll see you for dinner."

"Yes, Mother."

The pair of them walked away, passing Trammer with his arms full of body bag.

"Let's go inside," Eliana whispered.

I readily agreed, and we escaped into the kitchen.

CHAPTER FOURTEEN

I TOOK MY TIME IN THE SHOWER AND THOUGHT ABOUT THE DAY before.

A dead body.

A weird conversation where adults hadn't seemed overly concerned about who'd made the body dead.

And Oanen.

He'd managed to weird me out again. After Eliana had ditched me in the living room to warm my breakfast, Oanen had sat next to me on the couch and watched TV. Simple. No big deal. Except he'd put his arm behind me on the back of the couch. Still not that big of a deal. Until I'd felt his fingers on the back of my neck again. The soft stroke, up and down, had spread a tingle of something racing under my skin.

I'd bolted. Me. I didn't bolt. I decked people.

I groaned and stuck my face in the spray of hot water, wishing I didn't have to go to the Academy. The idea of skipping Monday check-in bounced around in my head until I remembered how Trammer had come for me the last time. If I wanted to avoid a ride in his dead-body car, I needed to go with Eliana.

Turning off the water, I mentally prepared myself for another Monday.

By the time Eliana pulled up in front of the house, I'd talked myself up enough to greet her with an enthusiastic smile.

"Hey, Megan," she said when I got in. "You look much better than yesterday. Headache gone?"

I only felt a tiny bit of guilt that I'd lied about having a headache to get her and Oanen to leave.

"Yep. All better." I leaned forward and eyed the skies. "No Oanen?"

She shook her head slightly. "He's running late, but he'll be there."

I settled back in my seat as she took off and debated asking her about him. He was like her brother. Did that make him a closed topic?

"Can I ask you about Oanen?"

"Sure. But you better make it quick. I'm not sure how long it'll be before he catches up."

"Does he have a girlfriend?"

Instead of the yes I was hoping for, she let out a crazed shriek that nearly gave me a heart attack.

"Oh my gosh! I can't believe I was right. I mean, I saw you checking him out that first day we rode together, but I wasn't sure if it was check-checking him out. He's going to go crazy when—"

"Whoa, whoa, whoa. Timeout. I wasn't asking because I'm interested."

"Right." She drew out the word in obvious disbelief. "I'm a succubus. I know you're interested every time I get a whiff of your l-lust when you look at him."

I ignored her stumble on the word and her beginning blush.

"What? No way."

Her peal of laughter filled the car.

"It doesn't mean anything," I said quickly, denying the possibility of me with Oanen. "It's like window shopping. I might like looking, but I have no intention to buy."

"Too bad," she said. "Because I'm pretty sure he has his eye on you. And he really wants to buy."

"I'm not for sale. Ever. We talked about this. I have way too many issues to be someone's other half. I'm barely my own half. I just need to know what to do."

"Do? What do you mean? Did something happen?"

A distant cry cut through the air.

"Never mind," I said quickly.

She said no more but grinned the entire way to school.

As usual, our flying escort zoomed ahead as soon as we reached the gates.

"Can you let me off at the front?" I asked her.

She did as I requested, and I quickly closed the door on her knowing smile. Once again, Adira waited for me in the main lobby.

"Good morning, Megan."

"Morning."

I followed her to her office, took my seat, and released a slow, calming breath, relieved that I'd managed to escape face to face time with Oanen.

"Is everything all right?" Adira asked.

"Yeah. Sure. I mean, except for finding that body over the weekend, everything's great." I might have been more convincing if I'd managed something other than a sarcastic tone.

"Yes. The body. A man named Jesse who was into human trafficking. Would you like to talk about him?"

"Not really. He was a scumbag. That much was clear when he detailed how he wanted to rape Eliana then sell her. I can't say I'm overly bothered that he's dead. I am bothered by how none of you seem too concerned about who did it, though."

She smiled slightly. "Good. That should bother you. I'd like to change things up for you, Megan. I think you're ready, and very able, to start attending sessions daily."

Disbelief coursed through me.

"What?" I fisted my hands, already knowing how this would end for me. "I don't think that's a good idea at all."

"Whenever you start feeling angry, I want you to let me know who triggered your anger."

"Before or after I beat them bloody? I mean, that's why I'm in Uttira, right? Because I don't have much control over my temper. Because I want to hurt everyone and everything ninety-eight percent of the time. Adira, I don't have many people in my life the way it is. The few friends I have managed to make, despite my amazing personality, are going to bail when I start getting into fight after fight."

"You're not among humans anymore. You might be surprised by how your friends here react when you do fight. However, I encourage you to come to me before you beat someone bloody. If you can manage."

I sat back in my chair and considered what she was asking of me. Try to control my temper? My gut reaction demanded that I laugh in her face. But I couldn't because, as Oanen had pointed out, I had managed to control my temper with Jesse. However, I'd had Eliana right there. It wouldn't be that way here, though. I doubted Adira would be too impressed with my efforts on my own. I'd probably get into so many fights that she'd kick me out of school. Maybe even Uttira. Two weeks ago, I wouldn't have cared. Now, though, I had a friend. Maybe more than one if I counted Fenris and Oanen. Although I did want to be able to leave town, I wasn't sure I wanted to be banished from it or whatever their punishment would be.

"What happens when I fight here?" I asked.

"You will not be expelled if that is your hope. If it proves too much for you on your own, I will assign someone to stay with you at all times while you're at the Academy. I believe Oanen is already in most of your classes."

The idea of Oanen with me every minute of the day made my insides go funny.

"No, I think I can manage on my own with minimal carnage."

"Good." She stood, and I knew we were done.

Leaving the room, I wandered toward the main halls, lost in thought. Although I had issues here, they were far less than at a human school. I'd get small flashes of irritation, but not full bursts of my true temper. Unless Aubrey was around.

"Hey, Megan," Eliana said when I reached the main hall. She straightened from the spot where she had been leaning against the wall.

"How'd it go?" We started toward our first session together.

"Okay, I guess. Adira wants me to start attending daily."

Eliana's face lit up with excitement.

"That's great. I can pick you up and drop you off every day. There's this new show I've been dying to watch but not alone."

I grinned knowing where this was headed.

"Yes, you can hang out with me after school."

Her smile widened, showing perfect, white teeth.

Further down the hall, a voice rose above the rest and ignited my temper. As my steps faltered, the back of Eliana's hand touched mine. The contact was enough to calm the heat of my anger so I didn't charge forward.

"I don't care what you need to do, just keep her away," Aubrey seethed, glaring at Oanen who didn't look the least bit upset.

"I didn't do it, you know," Fenris said softly beside me, making me jump.

"What?" I turned my head to meet his earnest brown gaze.

"Kill that guy. I couldn't care less what everyone else thinks, but I want you both to know I didn't do it."

For whatever reason, I believed him.

"Okay," I said.

"Good." He gave me his best boyish smile. "You still owe me a spaghetti dinner. What about this Wednesday?"

I glanced at Aubrey, who still spoke in a barely hushed, vehement tone to Oanen.

"I don't know, Fenris. Aubrey already has it out for me the way it is."

"That's exactly why you're going to say yes."

I sighed and playfully grinned back at Fenris.

"I'll see you Wednesday at five."

The bell rang, and Eliana and I headed to our first session.

As the minutes dragged into hours, I couldn't say I looked forward to a whole week of Academy time. Sure, I liked hanging out with Eliana, but as Adira had pointed out, the rest of my sessions were with Oanen.

When I saw him after the first session, he didn't ask about my headache and acted completely normal. He quietly sat beside me in class; and in the hallways, he kept me from losing my cool whenever my temper spiked. I only had to report to Adira twice that day for two separate girls. I didn't bother going to her every time Aubrey set me off, though.

By the end of the day, I was more than ready to escape and beat Eliana to her car by less than a minute.

"How'd you do after lunch?" she asked, backing out of her spot.

"Not too bad. Thanks for making me something, by the way. It was way better than having to wait in line. I'll need to remember to pack a lunch tomorrow."

"I didn't do it; Oanen did. He thought you might want to

avoid the crowd in the cafeteria. What's up with you and Fenris? I thought that was just a friend thing."

"It is."

"I don't know. Remember what I said about sensing emotions? There's a whole heck of a lot of lust coming off of him. Although, to be fair, he's always sending off waves of the stuff."

"He knows where I stand. I can't do relationships. I'd be bad for any boyfriend's health."

Overhead, a griffin cried out, reminding me our conversation wasn't exactly private. Neither Eliana nor I said anything else the rest of the way home.

"I don't understand why Adira and the Quills are forcing it so hard," Eliana said, gripping the steering wheel tightly in frustration. "I proved that I could feed. Why can't that be enough?"

"I think they're afraid that if you get hungry enough with a ready, willing food source nearby, you'll snap."

"I haven't snapped on you."

"That's because you're not pulling lust or passion from me. I'm the wrong food group."

She sighed and shook her head.

"I don't know what I'm going to do."

"You have time. You said it yourself. Adira's telling you now so you can wrap your head around it. The end of term is a long way off, and you get a break before the new term and your deadline. Plenty of time."

"What about you and Fenris? Ready for tonight?"

"There's nothing to be ready for."

She snorted.

"Every time he's near you, he's sending off waves of sexual energy. I'm betting he's going to make a move tonight."

This time I snorted.

"I'm betting he shows up at school with a black eye tomorrow, then."

She laughed and parked in front of the house.

"We can watch a few episodes of our show before I have to start dinner," I said.

She killed the engine and came inside to keep me company until four. Granted, she teased me the entire time and bailed as soon as I pulled out the pot to start browning the meat.

"Good luck," she said, giving me a tight hug.

"Don't need it. I don't plan on doing anything you wouldn't do."

She laughed and left me to get dinner ready on my own.

I only enjoyed about thirty minutes of quiet before Fenris knocked on the front door. Since I was in the middle of draining noodles, I just called for him to come in.

"It smells amazing in here," he said, walking into the kitchen.

"Thanks. I wasn't sure how much to make and think I overdid it. Hope you're hungry."

"Starving." The husky note in his voice was the only warning I had before his arms wrapped around me, and he hugged me tightly from behind. His hands didn't grip anywhere inappropriate. In fact, other than his arms, and his nose sniffing in my hair, he didn't touch me. Still…

"Er, Fenris? This doesn't feel like just friends."

"Sorry." He pulled away. "I was just really looking forward to this."

I put the noodles in a bowl and drizzled them with oil before setting the dish on the table.

"I bet you were. More Aubrey avoidance time?"

He gave me a sheepish smile.

"Something like that."

"Well, sit down. I think I have everything just about ready."

After his hug, I thought things might get awkward. Instead, dinner progressed in a relaxing stream of conversation. I learned a bit more about the Council's weak investigation into the body I'd found, and Fenris got to hear all about the shows Eliana and I were watching because I didn't have much of a life beyond that. He didn't seem to mind, though. He listened attentively and asked questions as if he was actually interested.

It didn't seem like an hour had passed until he sighed and looked at the clock.

"I better get going."

"An hour is all she gives you?"

He chuckled. "If I'm lucky. Hopefully, she'll leave you alone. It helped that Oanen was here last time she showed up."

I said nothing as I walked him to the door. He surprised me again with a tight hug and his face buried in my hair.

"Thank you, Megan. This meant more than you know."

He turned and left before I could respond. Watching him get into his junkie car, I hoped that this dinner with him didn't mean more than I wanted it to.

"So," Eliana said when I got in the car, "how was dinner?"

"Nice."

"Well? Was I right? Did he try to put any moves on you?"

"I don't think so. He hugged me when he got there and hugged me goodbye, but I think it was mostly just friendly. I don't hug many werewolves so I'm not sure. He sniffed my hair."

She snorted a laugh.

"Are you serious? That's funny stuff."

"It was a little weird; but other than that, he was a gentleman. It doesn't sound like his father is any closer to ferreting out who might have killed Jesse. All the adults are accounted for, and none of the underage wolves had left the barrier that night, not even with adult supervision."

"Honestly, I don't think the Council's too worried about it," Eliana said. "They sent a few guardians to affirm the guy's disappearance wouldn't be questioned. I guess he was into bad enough stuff that no one will really care if he just goes missing. And because of what he meant to do here, he apparently had been pretty quiet about where he was going when anyone last saw him."

"Doesn't it bother you that no one seems to care that there's a human-eating creature here?"

She laughed.

"The gods made us all differently. Some feed off of humans without killing them, like I do. Or like I would do if I wasn't so hung up on feeding. Some creatures, like Oanen, are just here to protect. And some others? Well, they like flesh. They have found ways to satisfy their hunger for it without killing every human they come into contact with. It was hard for me to come to terms with all the different ways we use humans. Obviously, I'm still hung up on a few. But, I keep reminding myself, no matter how one of us feeds, we all still need to eat. It's not any of our faults we were made the way we were."

"So you're okay with the occasional dead body?"

"If it's humans like Jesse? Yes. His death prevents the death of innocent humans."

She had a point.

When we got to school, Oanen was waiting in the parking lot. His steady gaze swept over me and settled on the bag I clutched in my hands. On Tuesday, he'd packed another lunch for me. I had assured him he didn't need to keep making meals for me, and even though his expression hadn't changed at the time, I'd felt that telling him so had somehow disappointed him. Now, I felt the same thing as he stared at the bag hiding my leftover spaghetti and garlic bread.

"I can smell it!" Aubrey screeched.

I looked to where Fenris and Aubrey stood near their car. He had her arm firmly clasped in his hand to keep her from running this way.

"Calm down," he said.

"You said you had spaghetti at home. Why do I smell it here?"

Something tugged the bag from my fingers. I turned my head forward again and blinked at the up-close view of Oanen's snuggly fitted shirt. He didn't say anything as he looked down at me and slipped a paper lunch bag into my hand.

My pulse increased the longer he stood so close. I opened my mouth to ask what he was doing, but the moment his gaze dipped to my lips, I forgot what I meant to say.

"I should have known it was you," Aubrey said from behind me.

Oanen broke his gaze away first and looked at Aubrey. I turned, ready to confront her, but Oanen quickly anchored me to his side by the weight of his arm settling over my shoulder. My confiscated lunch dangled against my arm.

"Morning, Aubrey," Oanen said.

Her gaze shifted to the bag that hung from his fingers to the brown paper bag that I clutched in my hands. Oanen had once again covered for Fenris. Or maybe me. I still wasn't sure who he was actually helping.

"Hey, Oanen," Fenris said. "I forgot to ask. You guys going to be at the Roost on Friday?"

"Of course," Oanen said.

Fenris looked at me and Eliana for confirmation, too.

"Sure," Eliana said.

Aubrey glared at me. I grinned.

"I wouldn't miss it," I said.

CHAPTER FIFTEEN

"SESSIONS WERE BORING WITHOUT YOU THERE TODAY," ELIANA complained. "How did you get Adira to allow you to stay home?"

We both sat at my kitchen table and munched on some afterschool snacks while I listened to how her day had gone. I'd only woken up and showered a few hours ago. However, I felt zero guilt over sleeping in after putting up with a week of regular anger.

"I told her if she said I had to come in, I'd run for the barrier and keep trying to get out until my hair really did fry off." Grinning, I recalled the brief pause before Adira had surprisingly agreed.

Eliana chuckled and ate another chip.

"I wish I was as brash as you."

"Brash?"

"Yep. And don't even try to deny it. You're passionate about what you think and feel—when you do think, that is—and you don't let anyone stop you from anything."

And that kind of stuff always landed me in trouble, but I didn't point that out to her.

"And if you were more brash, what would you be doing right now?"

"Probably eating something more satisfying than potato chips."

She sighed.

"So do it," I said, stealing a chip.

"Right." She rolled her eyes at me. "We both know it's not that easy."

"Why not?"

She gave me an impatient look.

"Okay. Walk up to Oanen and give him the kiss you know you want to plant on him."

"What? You're crazy. I don't want to kiss Oanen."

She snorted.

"Succubus, remember? I know you're trying not to have dirty thoughts about him. Why fight it?"

"Because I don't want to punch him in the face again. Guys tend not to like that."

"Exactly. Being with someone I don't really know just so I can feed feels morally wrong. And, I don't want to feed off someone I do know because I wouldn't be able to stand their false devotion to me. It'd be like I'd made a slave out of a friend."

"Fine. No boyfriends for either of us. Just the crappy excuse for junk food we can find at the grocery store."

We munched for a minute in silence, wasting time until we needed to get ready for the Roost.

"I think he missed you," she said.

"Who?" I asked. But, I already knew who.

"Oanen."

"Closed topic or I rescind your afterschool invitation."

"Fine. Let's go get ready."

"Get ready?" I looked down at my jeans and t-shirt and brushed off a few chip crumbs.

"Yeah. I promised Anwen I'd wear the dress she bought me, so we need to look at your closet and figure out what dress you'll wear."

I jerked my head up to frown at her.

"I'm not wearing a dress."

"Please?"

It only took three seconds of staring at her pleading gaze to cave.

"If I end up getting in a fight and exposing myself because of my attire, I'm not going to be very forgiving."

Eliana grinned widely.

"It'll be fine. You're with me. I won't let you get angry, remember?"

Thirty minutes later, I sat in her car and tugged at my skirt, a gift from my mother from ages ago.

"I look like a hooker."

"Yep, you do. Maybe this will teach you to do your own shopping."

As Eliana drove, I glared at the cute little sundress outfit she wore, complete with a tiny jacket. Compared to my black miniskirt and flashy top thingy that looked like a giant mouse had nibbled holes in the stomach and chewed off the shoulder, Eliana looked ready to go to church. I looked ready to be branded with the letter A.

"I still think we should switch," I said. "This outfit screams succubus."

"Oh, it screams all right. I can't wait to see everyone's reaction. This is going to be fun." She laughed.

"Yeah, for you."

I zipped up my winter coat and silently swore she'd need to pry it off my cold, dead body.

Eliana pulled up in front of the Roost and parked.

"Why are we here again?" I asked.

"Because you like pissing off Aubrey."

"Oh, yeah."

Suddenly the skirt and top didn't seem as revealing. Getting out of the car, I changed my mind again when a cool breeze brushed way too far up my thighs. We walked toward the door, which Eliana held for me.

"You owe me," I mumbled under my breath.

I walked inside, head held high and legs exposed from mid-thigh down. The crystals on the strappy sandals on my feet caught the flashing lights on the stage. Tonight they had live singers. The sultry melody tugged at my insides, and I knew they weren't human.

"Sirens," Eliana said, answering my questioning look.

"Great."

I glanced up and caught sight of Oanen and Fenris, talking on the second floor. They stood by one of the tables lining the rail. They already had drinks and company. Aubrey, dressed in a skimpy red tight dress, clung to Fenris's arm and played with his hair. It didn't appear that he was enjoying the attention as much as putting up with it. How could Aubrey not see the difference?

"I don't know how he can stand her," Eliana whispered.

Behind them, the rest of Fenris' girls stood in a cluster. None of them approached the trio, but looked at Fenris with longing. After seeing how Aubrey had run them off in the parking lot, I knew she was the one behind their distance.

"She is such a bitch," I agreed, feeling my anger burst forth even at this distance.

Aubrey stiffened and slowly looked in our direction. Her attention drew the notice of the rest of her group. Her eyes narrowed on us when she realized we'd gained Fenris' attention when she hadn't. I grinned and unzipped my coat.

Fenris' lips moved; and based on Aubrey's fierce scowl, whatever he'd said had been complimentary to me. Beside me, Eliana let out a small sound of amusement. I ignored her and shrugged out of my outerwear before blowing Aubrey a kiss. She bared her teeth at me and gripped the railing.

"Tonight's going to be amazing," I said, glancing at Eliana with a smile.

"Should we dance?"

"Yes. We should."

Before we turned away from the group above, Oanen's gaze captured mine. He wasn't grinning in amusement like Fenris. He watched me with a singular focus that made me wonder if I was in for another one of his "behave, Megan" warnings. Probably. However, I chose to carry on as if I didn't care. Which I didn't.

Eliana and I set our things on an unclaimed couch near the dance floor then swayed to the sultry siren songs. Eliana had crazy sexy moves when she let go, which she did in short, infrequent bursts.

"I kinda want to hump your leg when you do that," I teased.

She blushed red but did it again. We laughed and had a good time until she called it quits because she needed a drink.

"You go on upstairs. I think I'll avoid that area for a while," I said.

I sat on our couch and watched her disappear up the stairs. After that, I people watched. Everyone seemed pretty chill; but between one moment and the next, my bitchometer started to spike. It wasn't the level of anger I got around Aubrey, but it still called my attention.

I looked around the room, zeroing in on the source.

In the back corner, a girl sat alone at a dimly lit table. Her strawberry-blonde hair hung loosely around her face as she stared at the open book before her. She reminded me a bit of Fenris because she was doing her best to ignore the girl standing nearby, talking to her. No. Not talking. Based on the look on the other girl's face, the girl at the table was being bullied.

I got up and moved closer in an effort to hear what was being said. It sounded like the one standing was trying to get the one sitting to buy her something to eat.

"Hey, guys," I said. Irritation didn't require a fist before words, but I wouldn't be opposed to dishing it out if I thought it warranted.

The hungry girl looked at me, her eyes sweeping me from head to toe.

"Do you mind? It's my turn with the science project."

I glanced at the girl who hadn't looked up at my approach. Her unmoving gaze remained glued to the book.

"Science project?" I asked.

The hungry one sighed. "The human. You must be the new girl. You can have a turn practicing with her when I'm done."

There were so many levels of "what the hell?" going on in my head I didn't know how to respond.

"It's okay," the girl with the book said, speaking for the first time. "It's my assigned night. It doesn't bother me."

The other girl made a sound of disbelief.

"Of course it doesn't bother you. It's the only reason you're here, human. Now, go order some food so I can try to steal it."

"I have no money," the girl pretending to read said without looking up.

"I'm telling Adira you were being uncooperative."

"Okay." The reader's even, uncaring answer made me grin.

While the angry girl stomped off, I sat at the girl's table.

"Are you going to get in trouble for that?" I asked.

"No. The whole point is that they're supposed to get me to do what they want. She failed, not me."

She sounded bored and relaxed, but I knew better. She hunched forward slightly, her shoulders rounded protectively, and she'd yet to move her eyes from the page she'd focused on since I'd arrived.

"You don't like it here," I said. "Why don't you leave?"

"I'm assigned the Roost until eight. My uncle will pick me up then."

"How does a human get picked for something like this? I thought the only humans in town were the ones married to a non-human."

"Non-human." Her lips twitched, but she still didn't look up. "I like that."

"Is there something else to call them?"

"Them?" She glanced up at me, her hazel eyes full of amusement and confusion. "You're one of them."

I sighed.

"So I'm told."

"I didn't get picked. I was—"

"Megan, what are you doing?" Eliana asked, rushing up to the table with two drinks in her hands.

"Talking to—" I glanced toward the girl. "What's your name?"

"Ashlyn."

"There you go. I'm talking to Ashlyn."

"Unless you were assigned a task by Adira, we really shouldn't be over here," Eliana said.

A girl, who'd been singing on stage when we walked in, strode by and paused to look at the three of us before her gaze settled on Eliana.

"You can't really be so desperate that you need to feed from the science project. That's like sleeping with your pet." The snide tone of voice and the arched brow the girl gave Eliana had me opening my mouth.

"Wonder what you'll sound like after I throat punch you."

She tossed her hair in a huff and moved away from us.

I grinned at Eliana and pointed to the other side of the table. She sighed and took a seat, sliding one of the drinks toward me.

"Sitting here is going to draw attention and trouble," she warned.

"We both know I'd draw attention and trouble no matter where I sit, but why is this such a big deal?"

"Because any human in the Roost is here for testing. Adira assigns students tasks to complete on the human."

"Ashlyn," I said, not liking that Eliana wasn't using her name.

"No. Not just Ashlyn," Eliana said. "The humans take shifts. It's like an afterschool job."

"The pay sucks," Ashlyn mumbled.

Eliana looked at Ashlyn, sympathy in her gaze.

"Can I get you anything?" Eliana offered. "Something to eat or drink?"

"Nah, Uncle Trammer will be here soon enough. He'll have something in the car for me."

"Trammer is your uncle?" I asked, surprised.

"Yes. That's why I'm here."

"All humans are vetted by the human liaison officer to ensure they can be trusted with their assignment," Eliana said.

"That they can be trusted? What about the people in here? And, are you saying Trammer recruits humans so the upstanding youth of Uttira can test their skills?" I had a hard time believing he would actually do that.

"Pretty much."

"How many are there?" I asked.

"Five. Three girls and two boys. The other four are the last liaison's recruits," Eliana said.

The way she said it rose a red flag for me.

"Last liaison?" I asked.

"My father," Ashlyn said. "He was killed over a year ago. Uncle Trammer took over his position and brought me along so I wouldn't be alone."

"I'm sorry," I said softly.

"It's okay. It was an accident. A bar fight between giants. One tripped. My dad didn't have a chance."

Our moment of silence was disturbed by the pounding of angry high heels on the wood floor. Eliana reached across the table for my hand before I could look up. It didn't matter if I saw Aubrey or not. I knew it was her approaching by the feel of my mounting anger, which Eliana did her best to subdue.

"Quit hogging the science experiment's time," Aubrey said, stopping at our table. "Those of us who actually have a chance at graduating need the practice."

I chuckled.

"Oh, Aubrey, we both know your focus isn't on graduating."

She leaned in. If not for Eliana's hand lightly covering both of mine, I would have snapped and laid into Aubrey. As it was, I just sat there, pretending to be calm.

"I know it was you," she said. "I could smell you on him under the scent of garlic and tomato sauce. He's mine."

I glanced beyond her at the red entrance door before meeting her gaze.

"Are you sure? Fenris just slid out the front door with Jenna. Better run."

She snarled at me before pivoting on her heel and sprinting for the door.

"She's going to be so pissed when she realizes you lied to her," Eliana said after the door closed.

"Yeah. Too bad I won't be there when she realizes it."

With us at Ashlyn's table, no one else bugged her. Eliana and I sipped our drinks over the next hour and talked about Aubrey's obsession with Fenris, my obsession with pissing off Aubrey, and my choice of clothes.

"Those incubi have been watching you for the last fifteen minutes," Eliana said.

"Me? No. Probably Ashlyn. She's the primary practice target."

Ashlyn gave a short laugh.

"I'm not the one showing enough skin to tempt a saint."

"Speaking of saints, here comes Oanen," Eliana said.

I turned my head and saw him striding across the room, his gaze locked on me. The long-sleeved pale shirt he wore stood out in the crowd of jewel-toned colors as did the dark jeans hugging his hips. Something in the way he moved and the way he held my gaze made my stomach do a weird dip, and I recalled Eliana's goading that I should just kiss him already. Now, I couldn't stop thinking about it.

Eliana inhaled audibly, and I knew she could taste what was on my mind.

"I'm going to punch you if you open your mouth," I said softly, without looking at her.

"Ladies," Oanen said in greeting when he reached us. He focused on me.

"You look nice, Megan."

"Thanks." The word didn't sound thankful though. It carried more of a "shut your face" tone.

He looked at Eliana.

"When you're ready to leave, can you let me know? A storm's coming, and I'd rather have a ride tonight."

"Sure thing, Oanen. We'll let you know."

He nodded and walked off again.

"He is so hot," Ashlyn said. "Too bad griffins never go for humans."

"They don't?" I asked, surprised.

"Nope. They watch over humans, but it's nothing like the protective dedication they give their mates."

Something thumped under the table, and Ashlyn winced. I looked at Eliana who was giving me a way too innocent look.

"Did you just kick her?"

"Maybe. Wanna dance again?"

I narrowed my eyes at Eliana then looked at Ashlyn, who'd once again picked up her book.

"Fine. Let's dance."

But I couldn't enjoy myself like before. Eliana's reaction to Ashlyn's information spill and the way Oanen and Fenris watched us from the second story made me edgy. When my phone beeped, I quickly used it as an excuse to leave the dance floor, alone, and find a quiet corner.

Under the balcony, out of sight of Oanen's watchful gaze, I read the message from an unknown number.

Meet me out back in ten. Alone. Mom.

CHAPTER SIXTEEN

All sound bled away with the rapid beat of my heart. After abandoning me for three weeks, my mom was back. Excitement coursed through me. Annoyance immediately followed. How could I be excited to see the person who left me without a word? Correction. With the note that didn't explain jack. She had better have a damn good reason for ditching me like she had. And for not telling me about what this place was. Or what I was.

Looking at the message again, part of me wondered if she even deserved my time. She'd hurt me over the years with her insistence to call her Paxton and her increasing distance. But, I also remembered who she'd been before that. She'd been my everything. When no one else in the world had liked me, she had. She'd hugged me and told me she'd always love me.

My chest ached with the memory and with the realization that she'd abandoned me long before leaving me in Uttira. The one person who should have been able to love me unconditionally hadn't been able to.

As much as I wanted to tell her to leave like she'd proven she could do so well, I knew I couldn't pass up the chance to find out what I was. And, to see her one more time.

I tore my gaze from the phone and waited until I caught Eliana's attention on the dance floor. Wiping any trace of trouble from my expression, I motioned that I was going to the bathroom. She nodded and kept swaying to the sultry music, oblivious to the incubus trying to gain her notice.

Ducking into the bathroom, I took a moment to check myself in the mirror. The curls Eliana had coaxed into my hair still framed my lightly made up face. If I just focused on my head, I looked good. Like I'd managed just fine without any parental presence. However, from the neck down made me want to cringe.

"One month without supervision, and suddenly I'm a hooker," I said under my breath. Knowing Mom, she'd celebrate my choice of clothes instead of scolding me for it.

After waiting a few minutes, I slipped out of the bathroom. No one noticed as I made my way to the back door because everyone was focused on Trammer, who was glaring down an incubus at Ashlyn's table.

Closing the door on the music, I took a moment to let my eyes adjust to the dim light that cast shadows in the alley behind the Roost. The rank air from a dumpster that desperately needed to be emptied had me covering my nose as I looked around. Why in the hell would Mom want to meet me out here? I glanced toward the entrance. No one. I checked the time on my phone. One minute early.

Something buzzed to my left. I glanced toward the dark dumpster and caught sight of a faint outline of light on the ground. Someone's phone? I went to pick up the buzzing device, and my fingers touched something wet. I cringed in disgust but didn't drop it.

"Can this get any grosser?" I said to myself, turning the phone over.

A missed call from a private number showed on the screen.

Frowning, I looked at the mouth of the alley again. Was this Mom's phone? Had I already missed her? Why had she dropped it?

Looking back at the phone, I caught sight of the dark stain on my fingers. At first, I thought oil. Then, I brought my hand closer to my face.

Blood.

Fear wormed its way into my stomach, the feeling unfamiliar and unwelcome.

I turned the phone over and used its weak light to illuminate the ground. A puddle of blood pooled near where the phone had lain. More blood dripped onto the ground near the dumpster. Images of mom the last time I saw her filled my head. Slowly, I lifted the light of the phone.

Lifeless eyes of the corpse lying on top of the mounded garbage stared back at me. It wasn't my mom but a girl not much older than me. Exhaling in relief, I took in the dull brown hair that partially covered her neck, but not enough to hide the unmarred skin.

This body hadn't been eaten. I turned the light, trying to figure out how she'd died. When I got to her middle, I struggled to breathe evenly. She'd been gutted.

Trammer's loud voice shattered my fragile control.

"Drop what's in your hands," he barked.

I turned on him, rage heating the blood in my veins.

"Shit," he breathed, fumbling for something at his side.

While he struggled, I flew toward him. Everything inside me screamed to give the man a beating he wouldn't easily walk away from.

Before I reached him, he freed an object from his belt. An instant later, something invisible punched me in the chest. I flew back and landed hard on the ground, convulsing. My anger didn't seize with my muscles, though.

While I lay locked in convulsions, Trammer used his foot to turn me over. I barely felt the cool metal of the cuffs as they clicked into place.

"Not so tough now, are you?" he said.

A moment later the convulsions stopped, and Trammer pulled me to my feet. The probes of his Taser stayed embedded in my flesh just inside my right shoulder and below my collarbone. I rolled my shoulders, feeling the ache.

"Take them out," I said.

"I don't think so. Try anything, and I'm juicing you again."

He gripped my arm and led me toward the front of the building where his car and niece waited.

"Ashlyn, you'll need to ride in front," he said. He opened the door and proceeded to shove me into the backseat.

I met Ashlyn's wide-eyed gaze as he yanked the probes from my chest.

"It's okay. I'll walk home," she said.

Trammer grunted an acknowledgment and shut the door. Ashlyn stayed by the entrance of the Roost as her uncle got in and started the car.

With lights flashing but siren silent, he pulled away from the curb. Ashlyn's pale expression made more sense when I caught my reflection in the glass of the back window. Blood matted my hair and smeared my ear and cheek from when Trammer had rolled me over. Asshat.

When I looked back, Ashlyn had already disappeared. Facing forward, I looked at the guy I wanted to hit.

"Why am I in handcuffs?"

"You tried to attack an officer after being found at the scene of a crime."

"Speaking of the scene of a crime. Don't you think another dead body is a bigger concern than a teenager with anger issues?"

"Yep. That's the other reason you're in the back seat."

"What? You can't be serious. I didn't kill that girl."

"Then why were you in that alley?"

"Because I got a text from my mom."

He laughed. "Nice try. We both know she's not coming back. They never do here."

"I didn't kill that girl," I reiterated. "Do I look like a killer?"

"For all I know, you're just another flesh-hungry monster disguised as a human."

"Nice. Don't be afraid to tell me how you really feel," I said.

"We'll see how smart-mouthed you are after the Council deals with you. Human killing inside Uttira is forbidden."

"I didn't kill her."

"Right. You were just taking in the night air in a dark, back alley that happened to have a dead body in it? Nice try."

He didn't say anything more as he navigated the streets for several minutes. I stared out the window and wondered how long I would need to sit in jail before he actually went back to the scene of the crime and looked at my phone.

The idiot needed to do his job. Although, to be fair, I had tried to attack him. And I still wanted to. In fact, I was pretty sure he'd be feeling some pain as soon as these cuffs came off.

The car started to slow, but I barely noticed the pathetically small building labeled "police station" that he pulled in front of. Instead, my entire focus fixated on the partially clothed Oanen, who stood before the place. With his arms crossed and a frown pulling at his normally stoic expression, he looked wildly fierce.

When his gaze met mine, some of that fierceness softened for a brief moment before Trammer made a sound of annoyance and opened his door. Oanen looked up at the man.

"What do you think you're doing, Trammer? Let her out."

"Not happening. I found her in the alley right next to

another dead body. When I told her to drop what she had in her hand, she tried to attack me."

Oanen glanced at me and exhaled in obvious frustration when I gave a slight shrug.

"She can sit in a cell until the Council gets here." Trammer opened the back door. But before I could lurch toward him, Oanen was there, offering me a hand.

"Oanen," Trammer said from somewhere behind the wall of protective muscle helping me from the car.

Oanen's gaze missed nothing, including the two bleeding spots just above my right boob. He turned away from me but kept a hand around my upper arm as he spoke to Trammer. The cocky cop was looking far too pleased with himself.

"Did you call them?" Oanen asked.

"Of course not. My first priority is to secure her. Then, I need to go back and secure the scene."

"Good thing I called for you. They should be here shortly. Would you like to wait inside?"

Trammer's face flushed.

"I'm not waiting. I have a suspect and a crime scene to secure."

Trammer reached for me; but before his hand could close over my arm, Oanen once again stood in front of me.

"I'll help her inside."

With Oanen's hampering hold keeping me from Trammer, we moved as a group toward the tiny building, which looked more like a small-town post office than a police station. A desk sat in the tight space just inside the door. Beyond that, a single cell beckoned.

"She goes in the cell," Trammer said, moving past us to slide open the narrow-barred opening.

Oanen led me forward but stopped just before we reached

the cell. I looked up at him, trying to ignore the gentle swipe of his thumb on my upper arm.

"I'm sorry, Megan."

"For what?"

His lips twitched slightly.

"That you're here."

"Don't worry about it. As soon as Captain Duffus checks my phone, which I dropped in the alley when he zapped me, he'll see I was telling the truth."

"Get in the damn cell," Trammer said angrily.

I stepped in and listened to Trammer shove the door closed behind me. The lock clicking into place admittedly worried me. What the hell was going on? Who had texted me to meet in the alley? I no longer believed it was my mom. Trammer at least got that right. She wasn't coming back, and I'd been stupid to think that for even a minute. My stupidity only added to my anger.

Someone had set me up. Who and why?

"I thought you couldn't wait," Oanen said. I turned and found him staring down Trammer just outside my cell.

"You need to leave."

"No. I'll stay and keep an eye on things here while you go bag the body. The Council will want to know what happened to Camil."

"Who?" I asked, unable to help myself.

"Are you sure it was Camil?" Trammer asked, going pale.

"Yes. I looked before flying here. There were no bites like the last time, but pieces were missing. Heart. Liver."

Trammer swallowed hard, and his eyes widened.

"Ashlyn," he said. With that he disappeared out the door, taking a good portion of my anger with him.

I gripped the bars and looked at Oanen.

"Why is he worried about Ashlyn?"

"Camil was human. Just like Jesse. Someone in Uttira seems to have developed a taste for them."

A shimmering hole appeared inside the cell.

"Yes," Adira said, stepping through. "And that someone is very bold leaving a body at the Roost." She looked at me. "How are you, Megan?"

Was she serious?

"Not good. I'm covered in a dead girl's blood, and Trammer thinks I killed her."

"Unlikely or he wouldn't have left in such a concern for his niece." She set her hand on the lock. It clicked softly, and Oanen reached out to slide it open.

"Are my parents here?"

"No. They sent me to release Megan. They're at the Roost. I need to find Raiden before it rains."

A soft rumble from outside punctuated her words.

"You'll see Megan home?" Adira asked Oanen.

"I will."

Another circle opened and Adira disappeared through, leaving us alone. Oanen stepped close and gently moved part of my torn shirt to look at the two holes in my chest. I glanced down at them, too. Stupid Trammer wrecked my shirt.

"Eliana liked this top," I said, annoyed.

The tip of Oanen's finger brushed over the unmarred skin, just above the marks. A tingle of awareness coursed through me and set my pulse racing. However, when I looked up, his expression was once again closed off, making it hard to know what the touch meant.

"If it's okay with you, I'd like to leave before Trammer comes back," I said.

Oanen nodded and moved to hold the office door open for me. I quickly stepped out, desperate to leave before someone changed their mind about keeping me locked up.

Outside, the wind had picked up, and I shivered slightly.

"Eliana is coming from the Roost," Oanen said as we started walking in that direction. "She'll have your coat."

"Thanks."

"Are you all right?" he asked after a moment of silence.

"Not really. Trammer's convinced I'm capable of murder. And you know what? I have no idea if I am or not. I'm covered in blood and more annoyed about it than grossed out. I've seen two dead bodies in less than a week. Shouldn't I be upset? Shouldn't I be having some sort of an emotional breakdown? If I were normal, I would be. But, as everyone here has made very clear, I'm not normal. I'm not human. So, how can anyone be sure I didn't do it when I'm not even sure what I'm capable of?"

Thunder rolled through the skies, and Oanen paused his barefooted stroll to look down at me. Silent, serious Oanen. The streetlights cast shadows on his bare chest, and I didn't know how he wasn't freezing.

I shivered again.

He stepped closer, his gaze holding mine.

"I think you do know what you're capable of," he said softly. "You're just afraid of facing it."

CHAPTER SEVENTEEN

THE RAIN LET LOOSE, NOT IN A LIGHT SPRINKLE THAT INCREASED IN ferocity, but in a downpour accompanied by a flash of lightning and boom of thunder. Frigid water soaked my hair in seconds. I didn't care.

Grateful for a reason to look away from the intensity of Oanen's gaze and to wash away the girl's blood, I closed my eyes, tipped my head to the sky, and ignored my shivers.

I let the rain wash away more than Camil's death. I let it take the remnants of my anger, guilt, and self-pity. Trammer might piss me off to hell and back, but he cared about his niece, which meant he wasn't all bad. And, from the sounds of things, he was the only family she now had. I would need to remember that the next time I saw him. There was nothing I could have done for the girl in the alley. Discovering her body might mean she'd get justice if Adira found Raiden in time. And, who cared if my mom never came back. She had made her choice. It had nothing to do with me. Or my anger issues.

Yeah, right. What mom wanted a daughter who got into fistfights almost daily, swore like a drunk when mad, and—

The rain suddenly stopped touching my face. I opened my

eyes and blinked at the canopy of feathers over my head. Slowly, I traced them to their source. Oanen. He watched me closely, his wings curved overhead, a protective shield from the rain.

He lifted his hand and gently moved a wet strand of hair from my cheek. His fingers stayed there a moment, lightly caressing my skin as our gazes held.

"A thousand lifetimes and a thousand dreams could never conjure this," he said.

"What?"

"I should have asked you to dance."

My chest ached as I understood what he was getting at, and this time there was no denying or misunderstanding his meaning.

"Don't." The word came out a hoarse whisper.

"Don't what?" he asked.

"Don't want me. It's not safe."

I recalled the look of hate my last boyfriend had given me as he'd bled from his nose, and I knew I wasn't talking about Oanen's safety but my own. It would hurt more than I cared to admit to have him look at me like that.

Unaware of my thoughts, Oanen smiled slightly, a drop of water falling from his wet hair to his chest. I swallowed hard and followed its trail, wishing more than anything that it was safe for him to want me. Because, I wanted him like I'd never wanted a boy before.

"It's too late," he said.

I looked up again, my questioning gaze meeting his.

"I'll never stop wanting you."

He leaned toward me.

My heart started to hammer in earnest. I should have stepped back. I should have said no. But in the shelter of his wings, I did neither. Instead, I tipped my head up, wondering what it would feel like to finally kiss Oanen.

A blinding light made us both cringe. The honk of a nearby horn shattered the fragile moment and brought back a measure of sense.

"I'm serious, Oanen. Don't." With that, I ducked out from under the protective cover of his wings and raced for the car.

Eliana's worried gaze greeted me as soon as I opened the door.

"Get in quick," she said.

I did as she asked and slammed the door.

"Whoa," she said with a sharp inhale.

"Sorry. Didn't mean to slam it. The rain's cold though."

"I didn't mean the door. I think I just got a contact buzz." She leaned forward and peered out the windshield into the rain a moment before a pair of wet jeans hit the glass.

"Interesting," she said. "I guess he's flying. Reach out and grab his pants then start explaining what happened."

She didn't pull away from the curb until the saturated pants were on the floor of the backseat.

"Well?" she prompted.

"I got a text from someone claiming to be my mom. She said to meet her out in the alley. When I got out there—"

"Not that. I don't want to hear about another dead body popping up around you. Here's your phone, by the way." She grabbed it from the center console and handed it to me. "I want to know what just happened on the sidewalk back there. Oanen doesn't fly in the rain. It's dangerous. Especially when it's gusting like this. What happened? Did he try to kiss you and you hit him?"

"How'd you get my phone?"

"Mr. Quill gave it to me. Now, what happened?"

I sighed and struggled not to recall the moment just before she'd pulled up or she'd know exactly what had almost happened.

"I didn't hit Oanen. We were talking. Speaking of just talking, what was up with you kicking Ashlyn under the table?" I asked, neatly changing the subject.

"Nothing."

"Don't lie to me, succubus. I will slap this hooker outfit on you and drop you off at the nearest high school dance."

She rolled her eyes at me.

"We're trapped in Uttira, remember?"

"Talk."

"I can't. I promised this was one topic I wouldn't discuss with you. Please, Megan. I take my promises very seriously."

"Who made you promise that?" I asked.

She hesitated then looked up toward the roof of the car, giving me my answer.

I sighed and lay my head back against the seat.

"Sorry for getting your car wet."

"Don't worry about it. It's not mine. It's Oanen's."

The ride home was quiet. When Eliana pulled into the driveway, she got as close to the back door as possible.

"Want me to stay?" she asked.

"Nah, it's okay. I want a hot shower and an early bedtime. I'll call you in the morning. Be careful out there."

She gave me a sad smile.

"I don't think I need to worry. I'm not human."

I nodded and bailed, racing toward the house. As soon as I was inside, I flicked on the lights in the kitchen. Our chips still waited on the table. Opening the bag, I munched a few while I kicked off my stupid sandals.

"Shoulda known the night would end this way for a girl dressed like a hooker." I smirked at my wit and padded upstairs for a change of clothes so I could shower.

A little over twenty minutes later, I lay snuggled under my quilt while listening to the rain pound down on the roof.

Thoughts of Oanen and our almost kiss filled my head. Try as I might, I struggled to fall asleep.

I yawned and cracked an egg into the pan. Weak sunlight shone through the kitchen window. Mostly because of the clouds but partly because of the early hour. After a long night with little sleep due to noises I kept hearing around the house, I'd decided I had enough and got out of bed two hours before dawn.

My phone buzzed on the table. I shuffled over to it with another yawn and read the text notification.

Call me when you're up. Worried about you.

I dialed Eliana's number and wasn't surprised when she picked up before the first ring.

"Are you okay?" she asked.

"Peachy. Tired as hell because the storm kept me up. It sounded like someone pacing on my roof."

"Oh…that's weird."

"No, what's weird is the way you just said that."

She laughed.

"Want me to come over? We can spend the day watching our shows."

"Sure."

"I'll be right there." She hung up before I could say okay. Shaking my head, I set the phone down and went back to making a mess of my egg.

Eliana pulled into the driveway not long after I finished my last bite.

"That was fast," I said when she walked in.

"I was ready, hoping you'd say yes. You do look like you didn't get any sleep."

"Yeah, I might doze off during the first episode."

I didn't just sleep through the first one; I slept through the first two.

While Eliana looked in my fridge for lunch, I showered and dressed. We spent the rest of the day talking and watching TV. When the sun went down, she asked to stay over. I readily agreed, liking her company more than the thought of another lonely weekend.

Even with Eliana there and the storms long gone, I woke twice to what sounded like someone pacing on my roof. Eliana dismissed the idea with a laugh when I told her about it the next morning.

"Are we late or something?" I asked when Eliana pulled around the side of the Academy on Monday morning. More cars than usual already crowded the parking lot.

"We're not late, but something's up. Oanen looks mad."

He stood waiting near Eliana's spot. A heavy scowl pulled at his features. Between that and his firmly crossed arms and braced stance, "mad" seemed a bit of an understatement. The sight of his current mood made my rushed breakfast churn queasily in my stomach. It was probably because I hadn't seen him since I'd ducked out from under his wings on Friday, even though I'd thought about him plenty. We needed to talk, but now was definitely not the time.

His gaze locked with mine as Eliana pulled in between the two neighboring cars. He backed up a few steps, making room for her. Dark shadows smudged under his eyes like he hadn't been sleeping well. Because of Friday? Because of the almost kiss? Because I'd run? Crap. We really needed to talk. And, I definitely wanted to avoid that talk.

Before Eliana even cut the engine, he was moving toward my door.

"Why do I feel like I'm in trouble?" I whispered.

"Because you usually are," Eliana answered with a snigger.

Anxiously, I opened the door and stood.

"Morning," I said, forcing myself to meet his eyes.

"Good morning."

I didn't miss the way his gaze swept over my face then landed on my shoulder.

"It's fine," I said. "Well on its way to being healed."

He nodded but didn't step aside.

"Uh, everything okay?" I asked.

"No." He stared down at me for another moment. "But it's getting better."

My stomach went into acrobatic overtime. Ignoring it, I leaned to peek around him at the group of people waiting by the door.

"What's going on?"

His gaze flicked to Eliana, who listened from the other side of the car.

"Nothing much. Just rumors about Camil's death."

I rolled my eyes. "I bet. Are there any leads on who did it?"

"Not yet."

"Okay. Then, maybe we should go inside?"

He nodded and finally stepped aside.

A group of boys and one girl stood near the door. They all looked like they'd had unfortunate run-ins with an ugly stick. The girl's ugly stick must have been smeared with makeup. All of them watched me with a keen interest that gave me the willies. No anger, though.

One of the boys stepped forward as we neared. As soon as he

did, the ugly boy morphed into a hideous large…troll? Ogre? I'd need to ask Eliana later. The no-longer-a-boy smiled at me, a show of jagged, broken yellowed teeth.

"Megan," he rumbled. "We should meet up by the rocks some time."

Before I could process his invitation, Oanen stepped in front of me. His wings exploded from his shirt, fanning out in a crazy huge display of feathers.

"Whatever you heard, you heard wrong. She's not meeting you anywhere." While Oanen delivered his warning, Eliana gripped my hand. I didn't understand either of their reactions.

I shook off Eliana's hold, poked Oanen in his bare side, and ducked under his wing.

"You seem to know me, but I don't know you," I said addressing the big man.

"I'm Epsid."

"I'm curious. What did you hear about me, Epsid?"

"That you've killed twice and have gotten away with it both times. No evidence to point to you. We could use some tips. If you have time."

Feeling more than a mild level of disgust, which had nothing to do with his looks, I considered the creature before me.

"Why do you want to know how to kill?"

"We know how to kill. We need to learn how to do it without leaving evidence."

"Why?"

He frowned, looking confused.

"Because the humans can't know we exist."

"So you want to kill humans?"

"Of course." He glanced back at the rest of his group then lowered his voice further. "Not the nice ones like Camil, though. I liked her." The look he gave me was almost censoring. Almost, but not quite.

"I'm sorry to disappoint you, but I haven't killed anyone. Nice or not. Good luck at your rock meeting, though."

Shaking my head, I turned and walked toward the door.

The troll-giant people weren't the only ones waiting for me. The girls with green skin and leaves in their hair swore at me and flicked acorns my way. The mermaids at the pool slapped the water with their tails when I passed. Not sure if that was the equivalent of applause or boos, though.

It seemed the students of Girderon Academy were equally split in support or rejection of me. However, they remained unanimous in their belief that I'd actually killed two people.

By the time I reached Adira in the main lobby, I'd gained quite the following. However, she barely paid any attention to it as she focused on me.

"How are you this morning, Megan?"

"Pissed. Can you please set everyone straight?"

She glanced at the people behind me.

"They have the facts. A body was found at your house a week ago Saturday. You were found near another body this past Friday. Someone fed on both bodies but used two different methods."

"And did I do it?"

"We have no leads at this time to indicate any suspects."

"Why won't you say I didn't do it?"

"Perhaps we can discuss this further in my office."

"Discuss what? I didn't kill anyone." She was starting to annoy me, and she seemed to know it too because one second, we stood in the hall and the next, we stood in her office.

"I understand that, but we would like to let the other students believe you have."

"What? Why?"

"It's better for everyone if those reasons are unknown for now." She moved around her desk, sat, and opened my folder. "I understand that you tried hitting Trammer when he discovered you near Camil. Why were you angry with him?"

I rolled my eyes and sat with a sigh.

"I have no idea. I never have an idea. Why do you keep asking how I'm feeling?"

"Because it matters. This week, I need you to focus on the specifics of your emotions. When you get angry, try to determine why you might feel angry with that person. Before you confront them, come to me. Tell me who made you angry and anything you might have discovered about them or your anger."

What point was there to doing any of that? It felt like a useless task designed to try to keep me out of trouble. Annoyed, I stared at Adira. She sat there so calm, her hand open and loosely set over my folder.

"What's in that folder?"

"Your transcripts from the prior human schools you've attended, the student assessments you've completed online, and my notes on your progress."

"Progress on what?"

Instead of answering, she smiled and stood.

"Remember what I said. Come to me when you feel angry. I want the names of the people who are upsetting you. And think more about why you wanted to attack Trammer. Your main task this week is to gain a better understanding of your anger."

She picked up the folder and walked me to the door. One of the papers inside slipped as she moved, tipping just enough so I could read the hand-written note in the margin.

Current fourth generation.

Fourth generation what? Even as I shuffled out the door, my mind wouldn't let go of that question.

I needed to know what was in that folder.

CHAPTER EIGHTEEN

I WAVED GOODBYE TO ELIANA, TRYING NOT TO LET MY IMPATIENCE show, and let myself inside the house with a relieved sigh.

"School day from hell," I said under my breath.

My assessment of the Girderon's student body hadn't changed throughout the day. They either saw me as some human-killing hero or as the devil herself. A few switched camps, but they all consistently remained convinced I'd killed Camil, at the very least.

The whispers and stares hadn't bothered me. But, Adira sure had. As she'd requested, I went to her every time someone ticked me off. She quizzed me endlessly on the level of pissery I felt each time, until I made her a happy-to-mad face chart and gave each face a scale of 0 to stop-asking-these-stupid-ass-questions. After that, I just pointed to the correct, corresponding face. And, each time, she made a note in my damn folder as I left.

While I had tried not to look overly interested in the folder, I had started paying attention. The first few times I went to her occurred after some altercation that either Eliana or Oanen had to pry me out of. Well, Oanen did the prying; Eliana just kept hugging me. Each time, the folder waited on the desk as soon as I opened Adira's door.

Near the end of the day, I'd felt a mild surge of annoyance for a succubus. Other than wearing clothes similar to those I'd worn Friday night, no logical reason had presented itself to explain my anger. Determined to try one last time to discover where Adira kept my folder, I'd gone to her office.

Knocking on her door, I'd received the typical, "Enter."

However, that time, she hadn't been ready for me. She'd greeted me and motioned to the chair as she'd leaned over to open a filing drawer on her desk. I'd ignored the maroon folder she'd withdrawn and launched into an explanation of what I'd felt. To keep it real, I'd laid on the attitude.

During that session, a plan had been born.

I needed to break into the school and read my file after hours. And, I didn't want to wait. I intended on going there tonight.

I cautiously left the trees and skirted around the parking lot. The Academy lay in quiet darkness. I still had no idea how I'd get inside and hoped I wouldn't need to break a window or anything. Creeping closer to the door we used every day, I scanned the area. Quiet night sounds continued as normal. Good.

Covering the last few feet in silence, I grabbed the door's handle and gave a light tug. As I'd expected, it didn't open. Following the building around to the back, I began checking each window.

Near the pool, I got a break. Curls of steam drifted from one of the windows that someone had left open. I only had to pop out the screen to provide a way in.

Quietly, I hoisted myself up and eased through the opening. Warm air enveloped me as I carefully stood on my feet and looked around the dark space. Water lapped at the edges of the pool, making a soothing background sound.

I'd only taken two steps when a louder splash echoed in the cavernous space. Halting, I shifted my gaze to the water and saw, to my horror, a shape floating in the center of the main pool. I waited for whoever it was to say something, but as I watched, the body sank to the bottom.

Please don't be another dead person, I thought, squinting in an effort to see more clearly.

The shape stayed at the bottom for almost a minute before slowly rising again. Another louder splash echoed as it surfaced, then it started to sink again. I exhaled in relief. Not dead.

Taking care to stick to the deep shadows, I moved slowly to the door and exited the pool to the main hall. From there, I hurried toward the atrium. A tiny, blinking green light above the doors caught my attention. I stopped at the edge of the hall and briefly wondered if it was a motion detector before dismissing the idea. A blinking light would give away the detector's presence.

I hurried through the space and down the hall toward Adira's office. The door was closed but not locked. Shutting it softly behind me, I used my penlight to look at the drawer in her desk. It had a tumbler lock on it. Just one tumbler showing the letter J. I left it on J and tested the drawer. It opened with ease, and I stared at a space crammed full of maroon folders for all the students with the last name beginning with J.

I closed the drawer and frowned at the tumbler. It couldn't really be controlling the contents, could it? I turned it to S and opened the drawer again. The contents appeared the same, only this time with all the folders for students with the last name beginning with S. I fingered through the files, looking for Smith. When I found it, I quickly marked the spot and withdrew the folder.

There wasn't much inside. As Adira stated, I found my printed assessments, my transcripts from prior schools, and a single additional piece of paper.

Smith, Megan

Fury

Notes:

Week 1 - Beginning emergence of powers, which she believes to be anger issues.

Week 2 - No knowledge of true self or true form.

Week 3 - No apparent interest in humans, yet. Complete apathy when exposed to their deaths.

Week 4 -

That was it? The sum of my existence? The underlined note, "Current fourth generation," was written in the margin near the word, "fury." What the hell did that mean? What was a fury?

I replaced the contents of the folder and tucked it back into its spot in the files.

The whole breaking and entering thing hadn't gotten me much information. I closed the drawer and slipped out of the office. While my mind tried to solve how I would learn about the different creatures that existed, including furies, my feet started the trek back to the main lobby.

The reflection of red and blue lights on the hallway wall stopped me in my tracks. That stupid blinking light had to have been a motion sensor. I wanted to swear.

I focused on the small burgeoning thread of anger inside of me. Trammer. If I kept walking, I'd run into him. The large, raging part of me wanted that. He needed to be hurt. I shook my head and backed away. Was that really who I wanted to be? Was that a fury? All anger and fight? No thanks. What Oanen had said to me at the festival made more sense now. I had a choice, and I refused to choose that.

I retraced my steps to the back stairs. Just as I started up, a beam of light swept the hall behind me.

"Stop!" Trammer yelled.

I ran, taking the steps two at a time. His huffing breaths fell further behind as I passed the second landing. I raced to the third, wondering where I could hide when I saw a slim set of stairs leading up. The roof. Arms pumping, I sprinted for the door. It opened without a sound and closed just as silently.

Gravel crunched under my feet as I moved away from the door. How the hell was I going to get down from here? I leaned over the nearest side, and my stomach dipped at the sight of the very distant ground. Jumping was out.

I straightened just as a shadow passed over me. Oanen landed several feet away in a spray of gravel. Before the dust settled, he morphed into his very naked human self. My cheeks heated. I really needed to leave. Now.

"I've been looking for you for hours," he said, stalking toward me.

Don't look down. Don't look down.

"And you found me," I said in a rush. I hurried past him toward the student parking lot side of the building and looked over the edge. No gutters.

"And today's word of the day is 'screwed' spelled m-e-g-a-n," I mumbled to myself.

A hand circled my upper arm. I looked up and met Oanen's frustrated gaze.

"What did you do?" he asked.

"I broke into the Academy and read my file in Adira's office."

He glanced at the red and blue light show still going on toward the front of the building then released me.

"I'll help you, but we need to talk afterward."

The very naked Oanen disappeared, replaced by a familiar, large griffin. He dipped his wing, an obvious invitation to climb aboard.

The whole talking thing sounded a bit ominous. Especially when that meant Oanen would need to ditch his feathers. Yet, I didn't see that I had any other option unless I wanted to chance getting caught and potentially attacking Trammer.

"Fine. But you better not let me fall." I scrambled onto his wide back and settled a leg just behind each wing.

His hard muscles bunched between my thighs, and he leapt into the air. My stomach jolted, and I leaned forward, pressing myself against the space between his wings and gripping his neck to stay on. Wind buffeted my face as nothing but night sky and stars filled my view. He leveled out, and I felt each breath expand and contract the massive torso between my legs.

Exhilaration like I'd never felt before filled me. I lifted my head, not wanting to miss a thing. Wind buffeted and cooled my heated cheeks and stung my eyes. I didn't close them, though. I looked around in awe as Oanen soared away from the roof, passing over the parking lot and skimming the tops of the trees. Everything looked dark and peaceful.

With only the soft thwrump of his wings to mark his passing, Oanen moved silently through the night. As soon as he cleared town, he rose higher, and miles passed quickly below us.

In no time, I spotted my house ahead. He started his descent, heading right for it. I squinted at the roof. It looked like something was stuck by the chimney. He flew closer. It looked like a chair. He flew closer, still. I started to panic that he'd crash into the house, but he pulled back at the last moment and landed on the roof with his back feet first.

The feathers under my hands disappeared, and I found myself clinging to Oanen's bare back. He gripped my hands before I could let go and turned in my arms so he was facing me. With little space between us, I stared up at him. His eyes glinted in the weak light.

"Are you going to hit me again, Megan?"

"No. I know this isn't a dream."

His lips twitched, and his hold loosened on my wrists. Instead of stepping away, he reached up with his left hand and brushed his fingertips along my hairline from temple to jaw. The touch made my heart race. I moved my foot to step back, but he grabbed my arms quickly.

"There's no retreating here. You'll fall." He lifted me, pivoted, and deposited me on the chair wedged against the chimney. The view of his waistline, which was now eye level, made me squeak and scrunch my eyes shut.

"Breaking in was foolish," he said. "What happens when they bring Raiden in to check for scents?"

"Then, I own what I did and tell them they're all assholes for trying to keep stuff from me. You really need pants."

He chuckled, and I listened to the rustle of fabric. When I peeked through one eye, he was just zipping. I opened my eyes and looked up at him.

"Why do you have pants up here? For that matter, why is there a chair?"

"I got tired of standing."

"You've been standing on my roof? Why?"

He sighed and looked out over the trees. I followed his gaze and discovered he had a healthy view of the area surrounding my house.

"I started spending the nights up here after the first body was found. I didn't want you to go through that again, and I wanted to know who did it."

I thought back to all the weird noises I'd heard. Even during the rain. Too many emotions hit me at once. The sweet ache from his willingness to sit up here and lose sleep, in any weather, just for me. The fear over what that indicated. The annoyance that he'd done it all without me knowing. The trepidation for the conversation that still needed to happen.

He moved to the peak of the roof beside me and squatted down on his heels. His expression wasn't so closed off this time. His deep blue gaze held mine, and I could see his interest in me. Megan. The swearing, people puncher.

"Oanen..." My tone held warning, but my stomach twisted when his gaze dipped to my lips. That glance began to erode my resistance.

"Megan..."

He leaned toward me. Everything inside of me went cold then warm.

"I'm a fury," I blurted. "I have anger issues. Well, not issues. Superpowers. They have something to do with what I am."

He stopped his forward progress. I kept talking, panicked.

"That's what the file said anyway. What is a fury? Am I part of the human-eating food chain, too? Honestly, they don't look the least bit tasty. I'd rather hit most of them."

He pulled back and studied me.

"Furies don't eat humans. But, they punish the wicked."

"So, being a fury isn't going to clear my name," I said, disappointed in his answer but relieved we seemed to be respecting personal bubbles again.

"It might help, though," he said.

For a split second, I thought he meant getting back into my

personal bubble, and my insides went crazy happy at the idea. His next words set me back on the correct topic.

"Furies can sense the wicked, and I imagine anyone who would kill Camil would need to be pretty wicked."

"You're saying I might be able to sense the killer? How?"

Oanen shrugged lightly.

"I think you'd need to use your superpowers. Why else would Adira keep asking why you thought you were angry with someone?"

Stunned, I sat on my roof in the dark for another moment before the problem with our current location sank in.

"How are we getting down from here?"

He scooped me up in his arms and jumped. I nearly screamed but managed to bury my face against his bare chest instead. The rumble of his laugh and the impact of our touchdown had me lifting my head.

"Not funny," I said.

"No. Cute, though," he said, setting me on my feet.

I swallowed hard and met his gaze as I waged an internal battle. Invite him in or let him go back to the roof?

CHAPTER NINETEEN

THE HINT OF HUMOR IN HIS GAZE ONLY GREW THE LONGER I LOOKED up at him. Oanen had to know what he was doing to me, how conflicted he made me feel.

No, it was how I felt that conflicted me. Why was it so difficult to be near him, yet twice as hard to walk away?

"Have you eaten dinner yet?" I asked.

"No."

"Would you like to? With me? In the house?"

I wanted to smack myself in the head. What was wrong with me?

He smiled widely.

"I'd really like to have dinner with you, Megan."

"Okay." I stepped around him, needing to escape quickly. He didn't allow much distance, though. I heard him following closely behind as I strode to the house.

In the kitchen, I focused on pulling the makings for sandwiches out of the fridge. Like the last time, he sat at the table and watched me move around.

"Something's changed," he said.

"What do you mean?" I asked, not looking up from the plates I'd put on the counter.

"You seem nervous now. Why?"

"Because life is complicated. Because I have no one to talk to about any of it."

"You can talk to me."

His simple words made my heart pound so loudly in my ears that I struggled to think straight. I knew this was the moment to tell him that we wouldn't work. That I was too unpredictable to ever be anyone's girlfriend.

"It's just…I just…"

It felt like I'd swallowed my tongue for a choked moment. Now that the time for the talk was at hand, I wanted to run. With every ounce of willpower I had, I stood my ground and struggled with the words that would make him understand.

"I don't know you, Oanen, and I definitely don't know myself. I feel like I don't know anything. You told me to focus on what I do know, and I'm trying. But anything more than that is—"

"Too much right now. I get it."

I released a slow breath, grateful.

"Good." I turned and brought the sandwiches I'd made to the table. "As long as we're clear, you can stay in the spare room or on the couch tonight. Your pacing on the roof has been keeping me up."

He considered me as I sat then nodded and bit into his sandwich, consuming a quarter of it in one mouthful. I ate my dinner in silence, still unsure if I was making the right choices. Not just with Oanen, but my life.

I was a fury. Now what? Use my anger like a water diviner and seek out the murderer?

"Since I plan on keeping an eye on things," Oanen said, interrupting my thoughts, "I'll clean up down here."

I realized I was playing with the bread crumbs on my plate and took it to the sink.

"Thanks."

"No problem. And, Megan?"

I stopped at the kitchen door and looked back.

"Thanks for letting me stay. Next time, I hope you let me in."

I nodded and, uncertain of his meaning, fled upstairs.

Singing woke me. Female singing.

I sat up in bed and turned my head toward the door, not believing my ears. Unless Oanen had a third form, there shouldn't have been a sweet female voice singing a current pop hit from within my kitchen.

Easing from bed, I moved to the door. Was that the shower running? I crept down the stairs and caught Eliana busting a dance move in front of my stove.

"Good morning," I said from the kitchen doorway.

She jumped a little but turned with a smile.

"Morning! I'm making you breakfast while Oanen showers. He asked me to bring him a change of clothes for school." Her open smile changed to a knowing smirk. "So...sleepovers, hey?"

"Shut it. He's been standing on my roof like some gargoyle protector."

"Oh come on. He's nothing like a gargoyle. They scare the daylights out of me at night when they take their true forms."

"Wait, gargoyles are real, too?"

She sighed and shook her head at me. "Haven't you figured it out yet? Just about all of the myths are real. Some creatures are misrepresented or exaggerated, but most exist."

The bathroom door opened, and I automatically glanced that

direction. My lungs seized, and my brain crashed at the sight of Oanen with a towel wrapped low around his waist. He saw me, and his lips twitched in an almost smile. My heart joined the list of my other malfunctioning organs.

He looked devastating straight out of the shower. Wet strands of his lighter hair hung in short waves around his head. Early morning sunlight reflected off of each damp ridge he possessed. And, the way he moved when he stalked toward me had nothing on the clean, damp smell of him.

"Morning, Megan. Hope you don't mind that I used the shower."

"Oh, she doesn't mind at all," Eliana said, her voice sounding oddly distant.

I glanced over my shoulder at the kitchen and found it empty.

"Put your clothes on already!" she called from outside.

Oanen chuckled, the sound sending a shiver to my belly.

"I'll be back," he said. He grabbed the clothes from the kitchen chair then went upstairs.

Numbly, I walked to the kitchen door. Eliana stood by her car, her arms crossed and a frown on her face as she looked at me.

"You should take a shower, too," she said. "A cold one."

Instead of listening to her, I went outside and sat on the step. The cool air raised gooseflesh on my exposed arms and legs.

"How do you do it?" I asked.

"Do what?"

"Fight your instincts."

"I don't fight them. I fear them."

She rubbed her arms then walked past me to go inside.

"Breakfast is almost ready," she said.

I nodded but stayed on the step. Instead of dwelling on my

non-relationship with Oanen, I turned my thoughts to the instincts I possessed as a fury.

If I could sense the wicked through my anger, as Oanen suggested, I might be able to find the killer. But, so many people made me angry on a daily basis. How would I ever know which was the right one? I couldn't go around trying to beat the truth out of all of them, could I? I shook my head. No. No matter how satisfying it might feel, I didn't want to do that. To become that. Like Eliana, I feared where it might lead. I knew what rejected and alone felt like. I had friends now and didn't want to risk losing them.

After a quick shower of my own, I joined Oanen and Eliana for breakfast then rode with Eliana to school. All the while, my mind remained fixated on the residents of Uttira rather than the students of Girderon Academy. Jesse's death had proven the killer wasn't an unmarked member of Uttira, so I doubted I'd find the killer within the halls of the Academy. However, my time there wouldn't go to waste. I planned to test my fury power of identifying the wicked.

I stuck with Eliana as much as I could throughout the day. Instead of running to Adira every time someone ticked me off, I asked Eliana questions about the person. I paid attention to what she knew, which wasn't much, and the level of anger I felt. Aubrey still reigned as the top contender for who I'd like to punch in the face when it came to the students. And that made me all the more determined to figure out why. Not an easy task while at the Academy and under Oanen's watchful eye.

By the end of the day, I had a plan.

I waited until we were in the car to involve Eliana.

"Are you up for hanging out tonight?" I asked.

Oanen took flight from the roof and circled above our car as Eliana backed out from her spot.

"Sure. Dinner, too?" she asked. She merged with the flow of cars leaving the Academy grounds.

"Maybe. If there's time."

She glanced at me. "What do you mean?"

"Remember that siren in the hall after our first session?" I asked.

"Yep. Marla."

"And that guy at lunch?"

"Devian."

"Yeah, those two. I want to follow them around tonight and see if I can figure out why they annoy me so much."

Eliana made a face that was a cross between a frown and an "oh-oh".

"Oh, come on. Please?" I begged.

"Yeah, I'll do it. I just hope tonight doesn't result in another dead body. Especially one of ours."

"We'll be fine. We're the perfect team. I kick ass, and you stop me from going too crazy."

"If you had said, 'What could go wrong?' at the end of that little speech, I would have made you walk home. Remember, sirens don't just lure humans with their songs. And, I don't even know what Devian is. We're messing with the unknown."

And that didn't worry me. Not even a little.

Eliana took a right out of the Academy drive.

"So who are we bugging first?" I asked.

"That's Marla's car ahead. I have no idea where she lives. So, we'll need to follow her."

Marla headed out of town going north. After about fifteen minutes, she pulled into a nicer subdivision nestled on the shore of an enormous lake.

"Wow. How far does the barrier go?"

"Around the whole lake. Uttira is larger than it seems because it's sprawled out."

Eliana turned into the subdivision well behind Marla, and we watched the girl's compact yellow car pull into a driveway near the shore. Eliana pulled over and parked on the street.

"You know we're going to get caught, right?"

"That's why you're going to stay in the car, and I'm going on my own. If I'm not back in five minutes, leave without me."

Eliana sighed, which I took as her agreement, and I quickly left the car. Hopefully, my stroll down the sidewalk toward Marla's house looked casual to any observers. The way I pushed through the yard's towering shrub barrier probably didn't, though.

On the other side of the cedars, the soft lilting sound of a sweet voice drew me around to the side of the house. I couldn't make out the words until I was a few feet from the third window. Something about a naughty school girl undressing.

Like some pervy voyeur, I peeked through her window to see what she might be up to. What I saw confused me. She wasn't undressing but sitting on the edge of her bed, filing her nails while singing. She glanced up at the computer on her desk and smirked slightly at the split images of four older men. All of them had their sweaty, flushed faces way too close to their cameras. The sight of their heavy breathing and the expressions on their faces gave away what they were up to.

"Gross," I said under my breath.

I focused on Marla. She looked almost bored as she sang about taking off her underwear, which was damp from all her longing while at school. My anger warred with my need to gag. An alarm went off, and she quickly stood and wrapped herself in a robe.

"You know what this means," she said, ending the song. "My parents will be home soon. If you want to watch me again tomorrow, deposit the money in my account."

She turned off the cameras and went to sit at her computer to bring up a different screen. A list of deposits ranging from fifty dollars to three hundred filled the window. She smiled as two new deposits came in, then stood and removed the robe over her clothes. Using a remote, she reset an alarm on her desk, turned on her camera, and started her song again. This time it was a bit dirtier. Instead of singing about undressing, she sang about undressing and touching herself.

What the men thought they were watching was a lie, an illusion cast by her siren's song. She was cheating them. Definitely something I'd define as wicked. Yet, these were all older men who shouldn't have been watching her in the first place. I didn't really feel too badly for them.

I ducked away from the window and retraced my steps back to the car.

"That was seven minutes," Eliana said as soon as I opened the door.

"Good thing you didn't leave. Now, we need to find Devian."

She rolled her eyes at me and turned around, heading out of the subdivision.

"How are we supposed to do that? I don't know where he lives."

"Who would?"

"Oanen, but I don't think we should ask him. He's probably already freaking out and looking for us because we aren't at your house."

I chose to ignore all Oanen conversation for the moment.

"What's plan B? There's always a plan B."

"We go to the Roost and see who's there who might know. Anyone born and raised here is a likely candidate." She started the car and turned around. "Getting that person to tell us what we want to know will be a problem, though. If you haven't noticed, people in Uttira like to keep to themselves."

The Roost was livelier than I'd thought it would be for a Monday afternoon. Music thumped inside like always, and bodies filled the dance floor.

I immediately saw who we needed. Fenris danced in the middle of his swarm of females.

"Stay here," I said to Eliana.

Without hesitation, I strode into the crowd. Aubrey saw me first and stiffened. Fenris noticed and turned. As soon as he saw me, he smiled warmly.

"Hey, Megan."

"Hey, Fenris. Can I talk to you for a minute?"

"Sure."

Aubrey immediately grabbed his arm in a cloyingly possessive way.

"Alone, Aubrey," I said. "You can keep your jealousy in check for five minutes, can't you?" My anger begged for her to lunge at me.

Her face flushed scarlet, and I waited, anticipating her next move.

"Keep dancing," Fenris said, patting her hand. "I'll be right back."

Fenris extracted himself, and we moved off to the side without incident. I tried not to look disappointed.

"What's up?" he asked.

"I'm wondering if you know anything about Devian, a kid from school. Where does he go when sessions let out? Where does he live?"

Fenris thought about it for a moment then looked at the people on the dance floor.

"His girlfriend's out there. Give me a minute, and I can probably find out for you."

"Thank you."

He disappeared into the crowd of dancers, and Eliana joined me.

"Did he know?"

"No. He's going to ask Devian's girlfriend."

"Nice."

Aubrey chose that moment to stride toward us. I grinned widely and fisted my hands. Before I could take a step forward, Eliana pushed me back into the nearby couch and sat on my lap, wrapping her arms around me.

All the anger I felt left in an instant.

"Oh, don't you two look cute," Aubrey said with a sneer. "I've warned you, Megan. You keep messing with what's mine, and I'm going to start messing with what's yours."

"Oanen would kick your butt," Eliana said, her words loud in my ear since she was hugging me so close.

"Not Oanen, you dumb box. You."

Her head popped up from my shoulder.

"You think I'm Megan's?"

Eliana's peel of laughter turned several heads before she smothered her giggles in my hair. I couldn't help but grin, too. Aubrey's face grew redder.

"Aubrey, what are you doing over here?" Fenris said, re-emerging from the dancers.

"Talking to Megan."

"I see. Well, while you were talking to Megan, Nala and Brin left with Jenna."

"What?" Aubrey turned on her heel and marched out the door.

Eliana released her tight hold on me and climbed off my lap. A wisp of anger poked at me, but faded as Aubrey moved further from the Roost.

Fenris offered his hand, a polite but unnecessary gesture that I accepted. His warm fingers wrapped around mine, and he gave a tug, helping me to my feet. Instead of releasing me when I stood, he pulled me into his arms and hugged me close.

Eliana wiggled her eyebrows at me over his shoulder while he inhaled deeply then whispered Devian's address in my ear. Just as quickly as he'd hugged me, he released me and walked away.

"I'm starting to think you're at least half succubus," she teased.

"Shut up. Let's go."

We left the Roost and made our way to the address Fenris had obtained for us. Eliana gave me knowing looks the entire ride to the non-descript white house that sat in a rural area just outside of town.

She slowed down to pull over until we saw the front door open. She quickly resumed speed and passed by but not before I caught sight of Devian French kissing a girl on his front step. Since Fenris had obtained the address from Devian's girlfriend, I was pretty sure I'd just witnessed him cheating on her. I'd definitely classify that as wicked.

"Should I turn around and go back?" Eliana asked.

"No. I think I have my answers now."

"What answers? To what questions?"

"The answer to how a fury finds the wicked."

"Fury?" She glanced at me. "That's what you are?"

"Yeah. You mean Oanen didn't tell you this morning?"

"No. He just called and told me to bring some clean clothes for him to your house. How did you find out?"

"I broke into Adira's office."

"No way."

"Yeah. Oanen found me before Trammer did. And by the way, mermaids are creepy as hell when they sleep."

"I don't even know where to start. What did following Marla

and Devian answer? How did Oanen find you? Were you ever going to tell me? Does this mean you have to hate me now?"

Her eyes started to water with the last question.

"Whoa, what? Why would I hate you?"

"Furies punish the wicked. I can't think of any creature more wicked than a succubus."

"Seriously, if you weren't driving and I wasn't afraid of crashing, I'd power hug you right now. I don't know much about being a fury, but I do know that I won't let what I am change how I feel about my best friend. Ever."

She sniffled lightly. "Stop. You're making me even more emotional; I get hungrier when I'm emotional."

"Okay. Subject change. We were following Marla and Devian as a test. Oanen theorized that I can sense the wicked through my temper. Those two mildly upset me today."

Eliana snorted.

"If I hadn't held your hand, you would have tried to hit Devian."

"Well, that's because he's cheating on his girlfriend. I don't like cheaters."

"Why don't you get mad at Fenris, then?"

"He's very open with his interest, and he's not committed to Aubrey, despite what she believes."

"So every time you're angry at someone there's a wicked reason?"

"Based on tonight, that seems to be the case. I'm not done testing it yet."

"What do you mean? What more do you still need to do?"

"I need to follow my temper to Camil's killer."

CHAPTER TWENTY

OANEN STOOD ON THE FRONT PORCH OF MY HOUSE WHEN WE PULLED into the driveway. His gaze locked onto me. Arms crossed and looking more stoic than usual, he stepped off the porch and followed the car.

"You are in so much trouble," Eliana said.

"Me? Why just me?"

She just shook her head as she parked behind the house.

When I opened the door, he was there, crowding my space.

"What did you do?" he asked softly.

"Do? Why do you think I did something?"

"Because you're an hour late. Because I circled town looking for you, and you weren't there. That means you went somewhere else. For a girl who likes staying away from people, it seems odd that you'd suddenly want to roam around Uttira. Unless it wasn't idle roaming. Unless you had a specific goal. Like looking for a killer."

"Ha!" I said with a triumphant grin. "I was not looking for the killer."

He continued to stare down at me, and I rolled my eyes.

"I had to test what you said to see if it was true. Does my

anger indicate a wicked person? I believe it does. I also believe the level of anger hints at the level of wickedness."

"I repeat…what did you do?"

"I followed a siren home and watched her scam some rather nasty older men out of their money. I also saw a guy cheating on his girlfriend. That's it."

He exhaled slowly.

"Megan, when I suggested using your abilities to find the killer, I didn't mean alone."

I frowned. "I wasn't. I had Eliana."

He leaned forward, placing each hand on the roof of the car and caging me in. My chest grew tight and a flutter started in my belly. Vaguely, I heard the kitchen door slam shut as I stared up into his deep blue eyes.

"With me, Megan. You go with me."

His gaze held mine until I nodded. Then, it dipped to my lips. My heart beat painfully in my chest, and I forgot to keep breathing.

He closed his eyes and sighed.

"What do you want to do next?" he asked.

My brain hiccupped on that question. What did I want? I wanted him to do something about that longing look, didn't I? No. I didn't. It was too dangerous. Just standing like this was too dangerous. It felt like a fire was starting inside my stomach. That couldn't be good for either of us. He was already too far under my skin.

"Do you have any idea who the murderer might be?"

That froze the flames that had been licking at my insides.

"What?"

He leaned away from me and released his hold on the car.

"What did you plan to do once you verified that you could use your powers like I said?"

I tried not to blush that I'd misunderstood his first question so thoroughly. He'd been asking what I'd wanted to do next to find the killer.

"I thought I'd spend more time in town around the adults."

"And when you got angry at one?"

"Eliana has my back with her ninja hugging skills."

"You need to take this seriously."

"I am."

"You're talking about adults. People who've had years to hone their skills, not the fledglings in the Academy. Do you know what to do if you piss off a Gorgon? A Sphinx? How about a Minator?"

"Yeah, I hit them."

His hands suddenly cupped my head.

"You are killing me."

I jerked my head from his gentle grasp.

"Don't even joke about that." I pushed past him and stomped into the house.

Eliana, who sat at the table while looking out the window with an unfocused gaze, jumped at the sound of the door. She looked at me then over my shoulder. I didn't miss the hint of black in her eyes.

"You okay?" I asked.

"Yep." Her smile didn't reach her eyes. "I'm not feeling up for company, though, so I think I'll head home." She stood and escaped the kitchen before I could blink.

"I'll see you in the morning," she called from outside.

She'd left me alone with Oanen. Again.

I looked away from the door to where he leaned against the counter. He watched me with that same careful study he had since the moment I'd punched him in the face weeks ago.

"I have some things I need to do." He straightened away from the counter. "Do you promise to wait for me before going to town?"

"I don't plan on going tonight."

"Whenever you plan to go, do you promise to wait?"

"Yeah. Sure."

He didn't look like he believed me and took a step in my direction.

"I promise. Geez."

He gave me a long look then moved toward the door.

"Am I camping on the roof again, or is your spare room still available?"

Part of me seriously considered saying he could camp. But, despite my irrational temper, I wasn't that mean.

"The spare room is yours until the killer's found."

"Thank you."

He walked out the door, and I focused on pulling out dinner from the fridge rather than watching him strip for take-off. It didn't matter where I looked, though. My imagination gave me all the imagery I needed to match each wisp of sound before his wings beat loudly in the air.

Once he was gone, I brought his folded clothes inside and set to work preparing all the ingredients for tacos. The activity kept my hands busy but not my mind.

Adira wanted me at the Academy, attending sessions, which meant not being in town when most of the adults were out and about. If I couldn't be in town when the adults were, how could I ever hope to find the killer? A thought brought my head up. I stared out the window and grinned at my genius.

Maybe I didn't need to wander. Two deaths. Both human. Maybe I just needed to stay around the humans.

Eliana and Oanen had different plans the next morning.

"What do you mean we're not going? I thought skipping school meant Trammer would come knocking on my door."

"We're not skipping," Eliana said. "We called in and said we couldn't attend today and possibly not tomorrow."

"And Adira was fine with 'hey, I don't feel like coming in today'?"

"We let her know that we're going to town to help you work on your anger," Oanen said. "She only asked that you email her a report with the names of the people who upset you along with a reason why you think they upset you."

An Academy sanctioned leave of absence? I could live with that.

"By the way, thanks for setting dinner aside for me last night," Oanen said. "I didn't think I was going to be gone that long."

"No problem," I said, quickly standing and taking my plate to the sink. I didn't miss Eliana's knowing smirk.

She had made us breakfast again. Only this time when I'd come downstairs, Oanen had already been showered and dressed. It didn't matter. Having him here in any form distracted me in a really weird way. Like I kept wanting to look at him and just stare. As soon as we found the killer, I'd need to tell him he had to stop stalking my roof and sleeping in my guest room. I'd never be able to focus enough to figure out what being a fury meant with him around.

"So where are we going to start?" I asked.

"To keep what we're doing a secret, I thought we could start with the shops and look for a new top since your old one has Taser holes in it," Eliana said.

"You want to actually shop?"

She nodded, grinning widely. I shrugged.

"Fine."

Twenty minutes later, I stood in a dressing room trying on a top that Eliana had picked out for me.

"It's too tight," I said, attempting to wiggle it into place.

"It's supposed to be tight," she said from the other side of the door.

"I don't like tight. I like breathing."

Another shirt appeared over the edge of the door. This one had a modest heart-shaped neckline with a hint of shimmer to the loose material. I wiggled out of the strangler and gave the new option a try. The darker color looked good on me.

Smiling, I opened the door. Oanen sat in the chair opposite the changing room. His relaxed, leaning position didn't change when I stepped out, but the look in his eyes did. Appreciation replaced bored disinterest.

"Megan," Eliana said from beside him, drawing my attention, "that looks amazing on you. It falls over your curves instead of hugging them." A blush colored her cheeks as she spoke.

"Talking about my curves embarrasses you?" I asked.

"That's the first time I've ever heard her use the word," Oanen said.

Eliana narrowed her eyes at him.

"You keep it up, and you're waiting outside each shop."

"Each shop?" I said. "There's no point. Look around. There's no one here. Where do all the mark bearers go every day?"

"A lot of them have day jobs outside of Uttira."

I groaned. "Why didn't you tell me that?" Before the festival, the market district had been teeming with people at this hour. When I'd planned to spend more time in town, it was because I'd thought it would be full of people again.

"How do these businesses stay open?"

"They make their money off the unmarked, like us."

Frustrated, I returned to the dressing room to change out of the shirt. If the adults weren't in town, then there was no point for us to stay, either.

I stepped out again and stopped at the sight of Eliana's large, pleading eyes.

"Please don't say we have to go home. I've never been able to shop like this. Adira will count this as progress."

I snorted. "Progress? You're not the one trying on the hootchy shirts."

"Picking them out counts. It's a baby step."

Sighing, I rolled my eyes and nodded. She clapped and took the shirt from my hands.

"We're getting this, right?"

"Sure."

We walked toward the register where the woman sat reading a novel. She looked up at us and smiled.

"Find what you needed?"

"Yes, thank you," Eliana said, sliding the shirt onto the counter.

The woman started to ring up the purchase. Everything was fine until I handed her a fifty, and she opened the cash drawer.

Anger slammed into me. I reached out for Eliana's hand. Instead of connecting with her small, cool fingers, strong warm ones clasped mine. The shock of holding Oanen's hand distracted me from my anger.

"Here's your change," the woman said, holding out a few bills.

When I didn't reach for them, Eliana did.

"Thank you," she said.

"Enjoy the shirt."

Oanen led me toward the door. I stared at our joined hands, my insides flaring hotter and hotter by the second. At the last minute, I recalled the anger and looked back in time to see the woman slip my fifty from the drawer.

As soon as we reached the sidewalk, I eased my hand from Oanen's. Heat had spread from my stomach to my face.

"Are you okay?" Eliana asked.

"Yeah. She stole money from the cash drawer as we were leaving. I didn't feel anything toward her until I handed over the fifty. As soon as I did, it's like I knew she would do something wicked the moment she thought of it."

"Wow. That's pretty nifty," Eliana said.

I grinned at her. "Nifty?"

"What? It is. We're still shopping some more, right?"

I sighed and ignored the fact Oanen was still watching me closely.

"Lead the way."

I rolled over in my bed, pretending to sleep. Pretending that I couldn't hear Eliana singing in the kitchen or Oanen moving around in the shower.

The routine of the last few days was getting under my skin. No, it wasn't the routine. It was Oanen. I didn't know what to do about him. No, that wasn't it, either. I knew what I needed to do, and I hated it. Pushing him away now was better than having him wash his hands of me later. It was safer for both of us if I walked away now. Wasn't it? My insides churned at the thought.

The internal conflict was tearing me apart, and since I didn't know how to resolve it, I planned to hide from it. Besides, there was no reason to get out of bed today.

After that first day's success, we'd gone to town every day that week with Adira's blessing. Sure, I'd identified a few people involved with petty crimes. And I now better understood how the degree of my anger corresponded with the level of the person's wickedness. But, during all that time, I hadn't come close to feeling the level of anger I would have thought could be associated with murder.

Downstairs, the singing stopped, and the kitchen door opened and closed. My eyes widened. Eliana wasn't leaving me alone again, was she?

A minute later, Eliana's voice, just outside my bedroom door, made me jump.

"Get out of bed already. He's gone."

I rolled over and looked at her.

"For how long?"

"Until tonight. I thought we could keep binge watching our shows."

Relieved, I got out of bed. We talked, snacked, watched our shows, and relaxed until after dinner when Eliana's phone beeped with a new message.

She made a face as she read it.

"What's up?"

"Oanen's parents are worried that I'm not socializing enough for a young succubus. They want me to go to the Roost tonight."

I made the same face she'd made a moment ago. I didn't want to spend the evening alone. Not when Oanen had an open invitation to stay over.

"Do you have to?" I asked.

"If I don't, they'll just bring up their concerns to Adira, who will push harder for me to do stuff I really don't want to do. The Quill's mean well. They really do worry that I'm not…eating right." Her face paled with the words, and I could see the dread in her eyes.

"Want me to go with you?" I offered.

"Would you? I know you're tired of town."

"Of course I'll go. Tired or not, it's more fun hanging out

with you at the Roost than watching TV alone." I stood and grinned at her. "Besides, I wanna be there when you wear that dress I picked out for you."

Her previously celebratory smile started to fade.

"Come on. Don't be a chicken. You wear your dress, and I'll wear mine."

She laughed and clapped. Of course she would. My dress was far worse than hers.

CHAPTER TWENTY-ONE

"Stop tugging," I said, slapping Eliana's hand away from her neckline.

"I feel sick," she said, staring at the Roost's red double doors.

"No, you don't. You feel nervous. There's a difference."

"Let's go back to your place."

"No way. I want to see the boys fall all over themselves when they see you in this."

"This" was a tube dress topped with capped sleeves. And, it was a far cry from the typical, prim mid-calf sundresses Eliana usually wore. We both knew the dress would cause every head inside to turn. The material clung to every curve that Eliana owned. And that fact was freaking Eliana out.

I met her nervous gaze. Her makeup looked flawless and natural. The quiver in her glossy lips didn't convey any sense of "I am succubus, hear me roar" but rather damsel in distress. I thought the latter would prove more potent in this crowd.

"You're going to knock the socks off of everyone in there. There's going to be fighting and mayhem because of you. If I'm lucky, I'll get to throw in a few punches in defense of your honor."

She snorted, my words erasing the look of fear in her eyes, as I'd hoped.

"You can't fight tonight. That dress wouldn't survive."

The dress I wore, a black tube that barely reached below the curve of my butt cheeks and the top of my boobs, didn't need to survive more than one night, anyway. I never planned to wear the dumb thing again.

"We'll see," I said, reaching for the door.

We walked into the Roost together, the beat of the music rattling my rib cage. No sultry singers swayed on the stage tonight. Everyone was crammed onto the dance floor.

As I expected, it didn't take long for people to start noticing us. Not that we dressed so seductively compared to the rest of the crowd. I was pretty sure the girl wearing the dress with the opaque panel over her boobs won the seductive, yet tacky, dress contest.

Eliana leaned in to talk so I could hear her.

"I see Ashlyn at the back table. Let's go talk to her."

I nodded and let her lead the way. It wasn't like we were at the Roost to actually socialize. It was about appearances. Eliana needed to look like she was socializing and trying to become more like a typical succubus.

Before we made it to Ashlyn's table, Fenris stepped out from the mob on the floor.

"Ladies," he said, holding his arms out wide. "What a spectacular sight. Come dance."

"Thank you, but we wanted to talk to Ashlyn before she has to go," Eliana said.

"Tell me you'll dance with us afterward, then."

Aubrey chose that moment to step from the crowd. The annoyance that had simmered in the back of my mind flared into full anger. I'd witnessed Aubrey's meanness and certainly thought her level of bullying and bitchery qualified as wicked.

But wicked enough for this much anger? No. There was more to Aubrey's story, and I really wanted to know what...after I punched her teeth in.

I stepped toward Fenris, who was unaware of Aubrey closing in behind him.

His arms wrapped around me. Aubrey's eyes widened. Deciding this a better punishment, I wrapped my arms around Fenris in return and ran my fingers through the hair on the back of his head. Chest to chest, I looked up into his amused gaze.

"Get rid of your dead weight, and we'll dance with you all night long," I said.

"Bitch!" Aubrey screeched.

I laughed, and Fenris made a sound that fell somewhere between a groan and a sigh.

"Troublemaker," he said softly before releasing me.

He turned to Aubrey, his hands up in a placating manner. She didn't even spare him a glance. She flew at me, knocking him to the side.

I grinned widely and widened my stance, ready for her. Her curled fingers, now tipped with vicious claws, swiped through the air at my face. I leaned back, avoiding the strike, and swung hard, connecting with Aubrey's left cheek. She snarled and snapped her teeth at me. Dancing out of the way, I waited for my next opening then planted my fist in her ribs. Instead of my anger being alleviated, it burned brighter.

"Come on, Aubrey, tell me your sins," I said softly. "Tell me what wicked things you have planned."

She growled and tried coming at me again. This time Fenris wrapped his arms around her and pulled her off her feet. Slim arms encircled me. I sighed and didn't try to struggle like Aubrey did. I didn't want to hurt Eliana or lose the meager coverage of my dress.

A shrill whistle pierced the air. I turned my head and looked at Trammer, who was glaring at all of us.

"Break it up or take your animalistic hides outside where you belong."

"Come on," Eliana said in my ear, tugging me toward the rear of the building.

While Trammer gave Aubrey's still struggling form a final disgusted glare, Eliana and I took a seat at the table near Ashlyn. The moment Eliana released my hand a flood of anger robbed me of breath. I froze in the act of sitting and looked up at Trammer, who moved toward us. No, not us, but Ashlyn. I tensed, liking that he would never see me coming.

Eliana gripped me with more strength than I thought she possessed and dragged me down beside her. We'd barely settled into our seats when Oanen strode through the crowd, straight toward us. My stomach dipped at the sight of him even as the sound of Trammer's voice needled at my insides. Eliana kept her arm wrapped around my bare shoulders, muting the shit storm of rage that wanted to break its way in.

"Five minutes alone and you managed to fight," Oanen said, looking down at me.

I shrugged like it was no big deal, which it wasn't. The move drew his gaze to my bare shoulders. The look in his eyes changed, and I recalled the time that I'd thought that look was a detached study of me. I couldn't have been more wrong.

He held out his hand, and my pulse jumped.

"Come."

I glanced at Trammer, who was waiting for his niece to gather her things, then shook my head at Oanen.

"I can't leave Eliana right now."

He cocked his head at me, and his hand slowly returned to his side. He stood there in silence as Trammer and Ashlyn moved toward the front door. As soon as it closed, he offered his hand again.

Eliana released me and gave me a shove.

"Go. I'll be fine alone for a bit. Good practice," she said.

I hesitated a moment then lifted my hand to Oanen's. The first touch of his warm fingers against mine made me shiver. He saw it but didn't comment as he helped me stand. Holding my hand in his, he turned and led the way toward the dancers. I really didn't want to dance.

He didn't stop in their midst but pushed his way toward the stairs to the second floor. The whole way up the stairs, I could barely concentrate on each step because his thumb kept moving over my knuckles. If he didn't quit it, I'd trip soon.

Passing the bar, he moved to a door at the far end. Cool night air brushed my face as soon as he pushed it open. We stepped out on a metal landing then went up the stairs that led to the roof. Gravel crunched under my heels, and I looked over at the neon sign for the Roost.

Oanen stopped walking and turned toward me.

"I was getting dressed right here. Even with the loud music and a layer of tar and gravel, I could hear your voice when you told Fenris to get rid of Aubrey." He swallowed and looked down at my hand, which he still held.

"Do you care for him?" he asked quietly.

"Fenris?"

"Yes."

With my insides going wild, I studied Oanen's tense face.

"Fenris is just a friend. Friends are all I can do."

He looked up, his intense gaze pinning me.

"Why? You've learned a lot this past week. You're no longer in the dark about who you are."

"Exactly. And that's why friends are all I can do. Because of what I am. What I've learned this last week has only made things clearer for me. Getting close to anyone is dangerous. Except for maybe Eliana."

"You're afraid of hurting someone."

"I'm afraid of hurting someone I like." More importantly, I was afraid of someone I liked hurting me.

"Maybe the person you like just needs to understand the rules and not do anything wrong."

His words made my chest ache worse. His thumb brushed over my knuckles again, and I realized he was only doing it to my right hand. The one I'd used to hit Aubrey. The soothing gesture swayed me further. Dangerous territory.

I turned my head away and looked at the building's sign, trying to gain some mental distance from my distracting physical reaction to Oanen.

"Would you be willing to fly me to Trammer's house?" I asked.

"Now?"

I took a long, slow breath and let go of my regret.

"Yeah. I think now would be best. Since the moment I arrived in Uttira, that man has pissed me off for no explainable reason. I need to find out why."

"Okay." Oanen released my hand and turned toward a low set of lockers just behind the sign. He opened one and took off his shirt, throwing it inside.

I took a moment to stare shamelessly at his muscled torso. Was I being stupid for saying no to that? Probably. But it was safer this way.

Turning my back to him, I listened to the soft rustle of clothing as he stripped for flight. At the soft scratch of his claws on the gravel, I faced him once more. He dipped his shoulder to me, an elegant gesture that drew me closer. At the last minute, I kicked off my heels.

"Eyes forward. My dress is way too short for this."

He made a quiet noise then turned his head toward the sign. I lifted my leg over his broad back and settled in behind his wings, his downy feathers caressing my thighs.

"All set," I said.

He turned his head and bumped my leg with his beak before beating his powerful wings. Within seconds, we were in the air, circling over the buildings.

It didn't take Oanen long to find Trammer's house. He set down not far from the driveway. I quickly climbed off and stepped back, but Oanen didn't return to his human form. Tucking his wings, he walked beside me as I crept up the driveway.

Like at the siren's house, I peeked through windows until I found the pair. Ashlyn sat in the living room, reading a book. Trammer moved around in the kitchen, preparing an obviously late dinner.

"What are you hungry for, Hun?" he asked, his muffled voice barely reaching me through the window.

"I'm not really hungry," she said absently and without looking up.

"Ashlyn, you need to eat."

"I did eat. I had fish sticks today."

He stopped moving around in the kitchen and ran a hand through his greying hair.

"That's not enough. You need to eat dinner, too."

"I know Uncle Tram. I will."

He came into the living room and sat across from her.

"I'm worried about you," he said gently.

She closed her book and looked up at him.

"Why? I'm fine."

He shook his head.

"I want you to stay away from Megan and Eliana. They're trouble."

She gave him a doubtful look.

"I like Eliana. She's nice."

"How can you say that after what those monsters did to your father?" Trammer asked, not unkindly.

"I thought that was an accident," I whispered to Oanen.

He bumped me lightly with his head, likely a warning to be quiet.

"You need to let go of your anger," Ashlyn said from inside. "I did. It was an accident. Human or other, we all make mistakes."

Again, Ashlyn struck me as a truly nice person. Like Eliana.

Trammer stood, his face flushed. He didn't yell at her, though. He patted her shoulder and went back to the kitchen. She watched him go with a sad look in her eyes then picked up her book once more.

I didn't understand how someone, who obviously cared so much for another person, could be making me so angry. Seeing that they were settling in for the night, I backed away from the window and turned toward Oanen.

He dipped his shoulder, an invitation to take flight again. I barely paid attention to the houses passing beneath us. My mind dwelled on the puzzle of Trammer until Oanen landed on the Roost's roof.

I quickly slid off Oanen's back, and feathers abruptly vanished as he shifted to his human form. I squeaked, and turned around again, his soft chuckle teasing me.

"What were you hoping to see back there?" he asked.

"I'm not sure. Something wicked? There has to be a reason Trammer makes me so angry," I said as I picked up my shoes. "I mean, sure he's carrying a grudge for anything non-human because of Ashlyn's father's death, but that doesn't scream wicked killer. If anything, it screams just the opposite because the people dying are human."

The muted thump of the music didn't cover up the sound of Oanen dressing again.

"I don't know, either," he said. "His dislike for us is why he made a good candidate for human liaison. He's less likely to be corrupted by any of us."

"How long ago did Ashlyn's father die?"

"About a year."

The music suddenly grew louder as the main entrance to the Roost opened below. A long, catcall-whistle pierced the air.

"You are looking fine tonight," a male voice said.

"Of course I am." Heels clicked on the sidewalk. "I'm surprised you haven't been run out of here already. You must be sneakier than most."

Oanen frowned and moved toward the edge of the building. I followed, and we stared down at a man dressed in jeans and a leather jacket who spoke to a girl wearing skintight black pants, hooker heels, and a revealing top. My temper flared looking at both of them.

As we watched, the man reached into his pocket and produced a small baggie.

"Since you're looking so fine tonight, how about I give you a free sample?" he asked.

"I have a better idea." She started singing about how he wanted to give her all his money then go slam a car door on his pecker. Oanen stepped back from the ledge as the guy began to hand over his money.

"I need to go tell my parents there's another drug dealer here. There's something about Uttira that seems to attract them."

A car door slammed, and Oanen flinched at the sound of the man's hoarse yell.

"Have Eliana take you home," he said a moment before he shifted, ripping his clothes right off.

Unable to help myself, I looked over the side of the building once more. The sobbing man clung to the side of the car, his pants loose around his waist.

The siren had done Uttira a favor, but I still wanted to punish her for stealing from the guy. How messed up was that?

CHAPTER TWENTY-TWO

THE MUSIC PULSED LOUDLY AND THE LIGHTS FLASHED ANNOYINGLY when I went back inside the Roost.

Moving to the second-floor railing, I looked down at the dancers. They were all having a great time, completely ignorant of the man screaming outside. Or maybe they had great hearing, like Oanen, but didn't care. Probably the latter. And that made life seem just a little too messed up, even for a seventeen-year-old fury. Granted, my life had never been "normal," but I longed to know what "normal" felt like now more than I ever had in the past.

My gaze locked on Fenris and his group of girls, who danced in the middle of the crowded floor. He looked bored and completely miserable. Maybe normal, or at least our version of normal, wasn't that great anyway. His would improve, though, if he would just walk away from his groupies.

Shaking off my reverie, I made my way down the stairs and skirted around the dancers. A few people nodded to me, but I didn't slow. I wanted to get outside and check for that siren.

Eliana waited for me at the back table right where I'd left her and stood as soon as she saw me.

"About time," she said. "What happened?

"We'll talk about it outside."

She slipped her hand into mine, and we both moved toward the door.

Fenris called my name, and I stopped to look back at him. He motioned for us to come join them. His gaze pleaded with me. I shook my head and nodded toward the front door. He gave a playful frown but waved us off. Behind him, Aubrey gave us her usual evil glare.

Ignoring her, I tugged Eliana out the door. The man who had tried giving drugs to the siren still leaned against the car, his face pressed to the roof as quiet sobs shook his shoulders. Eliana gave him a puzzled look.

I released her hand, letting my emotions flood me again, and motioned for her to stay there. The knowledge of the man's damage to himself didn't reduce the incredible amount of anger I felt for him. However, it did allow a very human amount of pity.

I walked toward the man, my bare feet not making a sound on the pavement.

"Do you want me to open the door for you?"

The sound of my voice made him jump, which made him groan and gasp while frantically nodding his head. I reached between him and the car and pulled on the handle. He cried out as he fell to the sidewalk, clutching at his groin.

Having freed him, I no longer felt pity, only disgust. I turned and walked back to Eliana.

"What the hell was that about?" she asked, still staring at the man.

"That was a drug deal gone wrong. A siren took his money and made him slam his dick in the car door."

Eliana winced.

"Yeah, that's what I thought. The guy's an asshole, but the

punishment seemed a bit cruel. Ready?"

"Shouldn't we tell someone about him?"

"Oanen flew to tell his parents. I'm sure someone's on their way, and that guy's not going anywhere."

She tore her pitying gaze from him and nodded at me. But, before we made it more than a step, a shimmering hole appeared before us. Adira stepped through and gave us both a warm smile.

"I'm very proud of you, Eliana. I think you dressed beautifully tonight. Any luck?" she asked.

"Luck?" Eliana said. Then a flush covered her cheeks. "Not really. I wasn't trying for that. Baby steps, right? I have a very succubus style dress on."

Adira reached out and gave Eliana's arm a gentle squeeze.

"You've done very well. Progress is good; just make sure to keep moving forward."

"What are you going to do to him?" I asked, tilting my head toward the man behind us.

She looked down at the man, and her expression hardened.

"He is going to have his memory wiped and be removed from Uttira. There are other human towns he can terrorize instead of ours."

"Do you need help with him?" I asked.

"No, you two are free to continue your evening. I will see you on Monday, Megan. We can talk about your report regarding your week-long break in town."

I nodded, hiding my disappointment. At the end of each day this week, I'd fulfilled her request and had sent an email with names and conjectured reasons about why those people might have ticked me off. Each email had ended with a request to do the same thing the next day. Adira hadn't answered today's email, and I'd already guessed she wanted me back in class before she'd just confirmed it.

Adira stepped past us, and Eliana and I quickly moved to her car. I got in with a sigh of relief.

"Well?" Eliana said as she started the car. "What happened? Why were you gone so long?"

"Adira's been telling me to evaluate why someone is making me angry, right? There are two people in this town who have made me angry since day one. The first is Aubrey. She's a bitch, and she's underage. So, she is obviously not the killer. The other person is Trammer.

"Oanen flew me to Trammer's house so I could try to get a sense of why I might be so angry with him, like Adira keeps suggesting I do. Only, we get there, and Trammer's super sweet to Ashlyn and making dinner and all concerned about her. Doesn't seem like someone who's wicked, does it?"

"Not really," she agrees.

"And not only is he super sweet to his niece, he's got a grudge against anyone not human, which according to Oanen makes Trammer a perfect liaison. Now, if the bodies that keep showing up were creatures like us, I could totally see Trammer as a suspect. But, they're human. Trammer has no reason to kill humans."

"Well, maybe Jesse but not Camil," Eliana said.

"What do you mean?"

"Jessie was a human trafficker, right? Human. But, he didn't know we weren't human."

"So you think Trammer would want to kill Jesse because of human trafficking?"

The light in the car dimmed as we left town.

"If you were a human adult trying to protect a human niece, wouldn't you?"

I frowned.

"You're right. Jesse's death makes more sense than Camil's. But, why kill Jesse if his mind was wiped, and Trammer had orders to remove him? Removing him from Uttira would have removed the threat from his niece."

"True."

Yeah. True, but something about Trammer still pissed me off. And, until I knew what, could I afford to make any assumptions of innocence when my anger was telling me otherwise?

I took my phone out and sent Oanen a text.

I think we need to follow Trammer when he takes the guy out of town.

I'll be at your place in 10.

"What are you thinking about?" Eliana asked.

"I'm not sure. I just think there's a reason I'm angry at Trammer, and I shouldn't give up on finding out why. I've asked Oanen to help me follow Trammer when he leaves town with the guy from tonight."

She slowed and pulled into my driveway.

"If Oanen's going to come to get you in a little while, I might as well go home." She parked by the back door. "Call me when you're done, though, okay?"

"I will."

I ran inside and up the stairs. Riding a griffin in a dress once had been enough for me. Stripping from my dress, I kicked it aside and quickly put on jeans and a dark, long-sleeved shirt, which I layered with a hoodie for warmth.

Jogging back downstairs, I pulled my hair into a ponytail and drank down a glass of water. When Oanen landed in my backyard, I was outside and ready.

"I hope you know where to go," I said, climbing on his back.

He launched himself into the air, his wings beating hard to gain altitude. Once we soared well above my house, he took off south toward the barrier.

"Just don't run into the thing," I shouted.

A booming cry answered me.

He circled over a section of road twice then started to descend. Just before we dipped below the trees, I caught a glimpse of approaching headlights. Oanen set down near the tree line beside the road. I quickly hopped off his back and ducked behind a tree. Oanen shifted to his skin and moved behind me.

"We should have brought you clothes," I said softly, not taking my eyes off the road.

"I don't feel the temperature unless it's really cold."

"I wasn't worried about you. I was worried about me."

He chuckled, and I blushed.

Trammer's police car sped past and kept going down the road through the barrier.

"I wish we could follow him through that," I said.

"Me, too."

The faint smell of burnt hair reminded me not to think too hard about leaving Uttira. With Oanen standing behind me, I didn't feel the least bit cold. I did, however, feel very nervous. Why hadn't I thought to grab the pants he'd left at my house?

"You looked nice tonight," Oanen said.

My fading blush re-ignited.

"Thank you."

"I wish I would have been there when you arrived. I would have liked to dance."

Heat flared in my middle.

"We need to focus," I said.

"I am focused."

"On watching for Trammer," I clarified.

"I don't think he'll be back anytime soon. The nearest town is a twenty-five minute drive from here. There and back? That's close to an hour. So we have time to pick up our conversation from the roof."

"Huh?"

"The conversation where you were trying to tell me you don't date."

My throat burned, and sweat beaded my forehead as my pulse jumped into hyper speed.

"Are you serious right now?" I asked.

The bark of the tree bit into my palms as I pressed harder against it.

Oanen's hand settled on my shoulders.

"I have excellent hearing, Megan. You need to calm down. We're talking. You're not angry, which means I'm not doing anything wrong."

The approach of headlights from the south saved me from saying anything. With increasing anger, I watched the maroon car speed through the barrier and blinked at the driver.

"Wasn't that—"

"Yeah. Trammer. Hop on." The fallen leaves rustled behind me. When I turned, Oanen dipped his feathered shoulder for me to climb onto his back.

I gripped him tightly as he took off in a rush. Why had Trammer switched cars?

Oanen coasted on the currents, following the car from high above. Trammer signaled on the last left before my house and followed the meandering backroad to its end, not more than two miles from my back door. There he pulled over and killed the engine.

"We need to get closer," I said softly.

Oanen started to descend. Landing quietly on the top of one of the towering pines, he gave us the perfect vantage point to watch Trammer. The man climbed out of his car and looked around as he walked to the trunk. The sight of him tormented me with the need to cause him pain. The intensity of my need to hurt him had increased since the last time I saw him. Why?

I had the answer when he opened his trunk. A long, lumpy

form wrapped in black garbage bags lay within the dark interior. Trammer bent forward and tugged the plastic encased body from the trunk, letting it drop right to the ground. He squatted down and cut away the black material. The moonlight cast a pale glow on the drug dealer's lifeless face.

"But why?" I said quietly.

Oanen turned his head and nipped at my jeans with his beak. Yeah, I'd be quiet. For now.

We watched Trammer stuff the plastic back into the trunk then turn toward a nearby tree. He pulled a knife from the bark and squatted by the body once more.

Pressing my face into Oanen's feathers, I didn't watch what he did next. I stayed like that until the car started again, and Trammer drove away.

Oanen's unexpected launch into the air startled a squeak from me. He beat his wings hard, gaining altitude enough that I could see Trammer's headlights. Oanen silently tailed him. At the end of the road, Trammer signaled right, retracing his route.

"Wait," I said when Oanen started to do the same.

"There's no point in following him. We need to go back to that clearing."

None of what we saw was making any sense. Why would Trammer kill a human for trying to deal drugs to a siren? He didn't like any of the creatures in Uttira. And why take the man out of Uttira only to bring him back in? Why not just kill the guy and leave him in a ditch outside the barrier?

Oanen landed not far from the body. I slid off his back and tried to understand Trammer's motive for gutting the guy. Blood and innards spilled out onto the grass. The scent of death tainted the air.

"Why are we here, Megan? We need to report this to the Council."

"This doesn't make sense," I said. I turned and looked at the tree where the knife was once again embedded. "Why have a knife here, waiting? How could Trammer have premeditated this when no one knew we'd report this guy?"

"Trammer and the Council always know when a human enters the barrier."

"They do?"

Oanen nodded.

"Most humans avoid Uttira. Well, the decent ones do. The Council keeps an eye on them all, though, to make sure that any human who happens to find their way into Uttira doesn't discover anything they're not supposed to."

I recalled the way Trammer had conveniently appeared at my front door the day the cable and TV delivery men had shown up.

"Okay. So the Council and Trammer knew about him. That would mean Trammer could have come out here and put a knife in the tree in anticipation of having to remove the guy. But why would Trammer kill him for trying to sell drugs to a siren? Trammer couldn't care less about any of us."

Oanen shrugged. "This guy had been delivering drugs to Camil every week for months. He'd never done more than stop at her house and leave again, though. Since the Council was aware of the deliveries and the man caused no trouble, Trammer's orders were to leave him alone."

"It's just not adding up for me. How many times has Trammer had to remove this level of scum from Uttira?"

"At least a dozen."

"But no deaths until I showed up, right?" I paced around the body, studying it. "Why kill this guy tonight then? Why slice him open like this but not remove anything like Camil in the alley?"

I stopped pacing.

"The other bodies were eaten. Trammer wouldn't eat them."

I looked down again at the way he'd cut the man open and let his insides spill out. The scent of blood filled my nose.

"This is bait," I said with shocked realization.

Oanen immediately shifted and dipped his shoulder.

"We need to know who or what Trammer's baiting," I said. "We need to watch."

He nipped at my jeans until I gave in and climbed on. Instead of taking me home, like I'd thought, he flew us back up to the tree.

"Good," I said, running a hand down the feathers of his neck. "I want answers."

We sat in the tree for the next several hours in silence. When my eyes started to stay closed between blinks, he nipped at my pants again.

"Yeah, yeah," I mumbled, holding tighter. "I won't fall off."

He tipped forward, falling out of the tree and catching an updraft with his wings. My heart thudded in my chest from the scare.

"You could have warned me," I said.

Laying my head against his back, I held on as he flew the short distance to my house and enjoyed the warmth radiating from his feathers. Even with my eyes closed, I could feel it the moment he started descending. He reared back slightly as he landed, and he began to shift beneath me. Startled, I grappled for a new hold on bare shoulders as I slid off his back. He twisted and pulled me up into his arms. I blinked up at him.

"You're not going to throw me on my bed again, are you?"

His lips tilted up at the corners.

"No. Not this time."

He set me on my feet but didn't release me. His thumbs moved over my shirt on my biceps.

"I'd like to stay again, tonight."

Warning bells went off in my head, but given what was

going on just a few miles from my house, I wasn't stupid enough to say no.

"Yeah, that's fine. I wouldn't want to be alone if Trammer showed up, anyway. I don't know that I'd be able to stop myself from going after him."

Oanen shook his head slightly and nodded toward the house.

I turned and led the way inside. While I opened the fridge to use the door as a shield to keep my gaze from wandering, he grabbed his clothes from the chair in the kitchen and ducked into the bathroom. I glanced at the clock. Just after midnight. Despite seeing a dead body, I considered making us a snack since I already had the fridge open.

Pounding on the front door interrupted my thoughts. I moved to answer it. Oanen stepped out of the bathroom and blocked my path.

"I'll get it," he said.

He turned away from me, and my gaze swept over the jeans riding low on his hips and the t-shirt hugging his back.

I made a little face of longing before shaking myself from my mental cloud. Maybe I needed to tell him to hit the roof.

He pulled open the door, and my temper flared at the sight of Aubrey.

"He's not here," Oanen said before she could speak. "And I've been with Megan since she left the club, so there's no need for threats, either."

She snarled and turned away, marching down the porch steps as he closed the door.

"That girl needs a leash," I said as tires squealed on the road.

"Or maybe Fenris does," he said, frowning. "How many times has Fenris been missing just before a body is found?"

CHAPTER TWENTY-THREE

"YOU THINK FENRIS HAS BEEN CHEWING ON THE BODIES? NO WAY," I said firmly.

"Why not?"

"Because he's not that kind of werewolf. He's nice to everyone. He likes hugging, not biting." Way too much hugging, I thought.

Oanen quietly studied me for a long minute.

"Is your opinion based on how you feel about him?" he asked quietly.

"Yes, it is. He doesn't make me angry. Besides Eliana, he's one of the easiest people for me to be around."

Oanen stepped around me and walked to the kitchen. I wasn't stupid. I knew why.

"You know what? It's after midnight on one of the longest days of my life. You don't get to have hurt feelings because you're reading something into words that have no deeper meaning than the surface."

He stopped walking and looked back at me.

"What are you saying?"

"That we already talked about this, and I don't want to

rehash it. If you didn't believe me the first time, saying it all again won't change your mind. So, the only feelings I want to discuss right now are how tired and hungry I am."

"I wasn't walking away because of what you said. I believe you and trust your instincts. Fenris isn't the one eating human flesh. But, with him missing, the females will be running around the woods looking for him. That means I need to go back and watch the body."

Females? There was only one who kept knocking on my damn door. A door not far from the dump site.

"You want to go alone?" I asked, unsure.

"I wouldn't mind company. Still want to snack?"

"No. I want to catch Aubrey red-handed," I said.

"It might not be Aubrey."

"What other reason is there for my anger every time she's around?"

"I'm not sure."

He motioned for me to follow him into the kitchen then held the back door for me.

"I'll leave my clothes in here, again."

I took the hint and stepped outside. Alone in the backyard, I watched the stars and listened for the door to open. He didn't take long. Not wanting to turn too soon, I stayed as I was until something nipped at my finger, startling me.

I turned and found Oanen already shifted. His feathers glinted in the moonlight, as did his beautiful golden eyes.

"Ready?" I asked.

He dipped his shoulder, and I climbed on his back. In no time, we once again soared the skies, flying toward the clearing. When we reached it, nothing looked different. Below us lay the remains of the drug dealer.

He circled, lazily spiraling downward. As he glided, a pale

shape slunk from the trees. The familiar rage that I associated with Aubrey flared up inside me.

"I knew it," I said softly. "That's Aubrey."

Yet part of me wondered why I needed to feel so much anger toward her. The man was already dead. She hadn't caused it. Not that I agreed with eating humans, but was it fair to want to beat her bloody for instincts she probably couldn't control? I thought of Eliana's struggle to contain what she didn't like about herself. She fought her instincts constantly.

Any pity I had for Aubrey disappeared as she dove for the man's open middle. I gagged as she dipped her head inside and started devouring his soft bits. She wasn't attempting to control anything. She was gorging herself.

"Oh, that's so gross."

Oanen screeched loudly and tipped forward, descending rapidly. I clung tightly to his feathers and watched Aubrey's head jerk up at the sound of his cry.

She snarled but didn't run or back away. Instead, she hunched over the drug dealer like she was guarding a treat.

Oanen landed with a hard thump that clacked my teeth together and almost jarred me from my seat. A nearby snarl had me looking up in time to see Aubrey launch herself at us. My heart thudded with adrenaline, and I embraced the rage that filled me. Before I could slide off to face her, Oanen reared back, almost unseating me again.

I gripped his feathers as he swiped at her with his front talons. She hopped back but didn't give up. Darting forward again, she went for his throat. Oanen moved to dodge her and used his talons once more. The vicious tips caught her hindquarters, ripping a swath of red into her fluffy white coat. She yelped and rolled away.

Oanen dipped his shoulder, indicating I could finally get off. The wrong shoulder, though. I didn't want to hide by the trees.

Ignoring the direction he wanted me to go, I tried to dismount toward Aubrey. However, Oanen tilted his shoulders so I slid off the opposite side.

Aubrey had regained her feet by the time I landed on mine. But instead of facing me, she twisted around to look at her wound. She gave it a tentative lick and whined before turning on Oanen with another snarl. Bloody saliva dripped from her stiff, angry mouth.

I took a step to the side, ready to go around Oanen, but he half-opened his wings, blocking me. Aubrey's gaze finally darted my way. Oanen's feathers ruffled, making him look bigger and scarier. The deep, threatening cry he emitted at her made me shiver.

Aubrey didn't try attacking again. With a stagger, her fur receded until she stood before us naked, bleeding, and filthy.

"Did you leave this here?" she demanded, glaring at me.

Oanen shifted quickly and lurched forward, grabbing Aubrey by the throat.

"Is this the first time you've fed on a human?" Rage filled his words.

Stunned, I did nothing as Aubrey pulled ineffectively at his hands and made a strangled sound in answer. He lifted her off her feet in response and gave her a little shake.

"Is this the first time?" he yelled at her.

Her eyes darted to me before a choked yes came out of her.

"I don't believe you." He dropped her.

Aubrey landed on the ground in a heap, favoring her wounded leg. Moonlight glinted off her pale hair and exposed breasts as she looked up at Oanen. A tiny part of my mind hated that they were seeing each other naked.

"Report to Raiden and tell him everything. He'll know if you lie. Go!" he yelled when she didn't immediately move.

She hopped to her feet and limped off into the trees. I stayed where I was, letting my anger fade slowly with her retreat.

Once I knew she was gone, I looked at Oanen's back. Wisps of steam rose from his skin, and his shoulders moved with each angry breath as he continued to watch the trees where she'd disappeared. I wasn't sure what to do. I hadn't expected such a violent reaction out of him. He'd always been so controlled.

"Are you okay?" I asked when he continued to face away from me.

"No."

That single word sent a bolt of panic through me, and I rushed around him.

"Did she hurt you?" My gaze swept over him from head to toe, more worried about a potential injury than modesty. However, seeing the unmarred perfection of everything Oanen erased my concern. It erased everything but yum-yum thoughts.

"Megan," he said with impatience, and I realized it wasn't the first time he'd had to say my name.

I tore my gaze from his abs and met his eyes.

"Yeah?"

"Are you okay?"

"Yeah. Sure. Fine. Why?"

"You look flushed."

"Nope." My gaze remained laser-focused on his. "Just confused. You were pretty aggressive with Aubrey."

"Shouldn't I have been?"

"I don't know. I mean, my anger says yes, but my brain is questioning why I'm so angry with her. She didn't kill this guy. We know that. Yeah, she ate him, but I think Trammer put the guy here to bait her or someone like her. I don't know much about werewolves, but I do know that if you leave out food around a dog, it's going to be eaten. We all have instincts we're fighting to control. I suck at controlling mine. Is it fair for me to condemn Aubrey when she can't control hers?"

"This is more than just punching someone in the face. This is about eating humans. We can feed on their energy, on their blood, even on their life force, but we cannot feed on their flesh. Seeing her, I snapped. What she did not only goes against my nature, but it's against our laws, too. We can no longer delay reporting this."

Without another word, he shifted back to his griffin form. I smoothed my hand over his neck feathers and climbed on. I hoped he didn't think I'd been justifying Aubrey's actions. I hadn't. I was empathizing with them.

The flight to Oanen's house took longer than I anticipated. My fingers were numb by the time he landed on the roof of the stone mansion. Dismounting, I paid more attention to the glass greenhouse that took up half the space than bare Oanen.

"Dad built this so Mom could watch me learn to fly."

"Your Mom doesn't fly?"

"There's no such thing as a female griffin," he said with an amused smile.

"Hey. How am I supposed to know?"

"Come on." He clasped my cold hand, and I enjoyed the warm contact as he led me inside the greenhouse. He stopped at the shelves near the back of it and quickly dressed before opening the door that led down a set of stairs.

I shivered slightly at the sudden change in temperature and rubbed my arms. At the bottom of the steps, Oanen tapped the digital display mounted on the wall.

"Mother. Father. Please meet me in the study," he said, his voice echoing from different locations around the house. He tapped the screen again and started walking.

"Your house has a freaking intercom?"

"Yes. Yelling for me wasn't cutting it. Mom wanted it installed. Dad made it happen."

He led the way down the hall, another set of stairs, turned

right, and opened a set of heavy double doors to a very manly, grand room that only vaguely looked study-ish because of a mahogany desk in the back corner near the balcony doors.

"This place is ridiculous," I said quietly, looking around.

"Yep. It is. Family homes usually are around here. Are you still hungry? I can get you something."

"No. I'm fine." I wandered to one of the overstuffed leather chairs and took a seat.

When I glanced at the door, I found Oanen's parents there, dressed as if it weren't close to two in the morning but mid-afternoon. Neither one said anything as they studied me. Crap. I stood again. How much had they heard?

"Hello," I said, unsure.

"Megan. Oanen. What's going on?" his mom asked.

"Quite a bit. You might want to contact Adira as we explain." His father pulled his phone from his pocket and sent off a quick text as Oanen recounted what we'd witnessed in the last few hours.

"Where is Aubrey now?" Mr. Quill asked.

"I sent her to report to Raiden."

Oanen's mom walked further into the room. She kissed Oanen on the cheek then turned to me.

"Megan, please sit. Can I get you anything while we wait for Adira?"

"No, thank you." I sat, feeling more than a little nervous. Oanen moved next to me, sitting on the arm of my chair. Surprisingly, the move made me feel better instead of more freaked out.

Oanen's father slowly joined us, his attention on the text message he was typing into his phone. When he looked up, he let out a heavy exhale.

"Adira is bringing Raiden."

"Raiden?" I asked. "Why not Trammer?" The guy was

running around killing people, and we'd witnessed it. What more proof did they need?

Oanen's mom reached out and put her hand on mine. A soothing calm filled me. Not quite like what Eliana did but close.

"All will be well. We will address Trammer's crimes. However, he is not the greatest threat at the moment."

"How is he not? Just because humans are his victims and not us?" I only barely managed to keep the resentment from my tone.

Eliana shuffled into the room, rubbing her eyes. "Trammer's killing people?"

"And Aubrey's eating them," Oanen added.

His mom didn't look away from me.

"There is a reason consuming flesh is against our laws. It changes the nature of the creature. Makes them more violent. Makes them crave more at any cost. Even at the risk of exposing our world to the humans. For most of us, ingesting flesh holds no appeal. No temptation.

"That is not true for some, though. We need to ensure Aubrey is the only one to have succumbed and is dealt with appropriately, so her actions do not tempt others to do the same."

I understood what Mrs. Quill was politely saying. They needed to get to Aubrey so she didn't spread her brand of crazy. It might be a little late for that, given how long ago the first body was found, but I kept that bit of criticism to myself.

Oanen's mom's eyes sparkled with amusement almost as if she knew what I'd just thought. I gently eased my hand out from hers, and she smiled.

Eliana came over and sat on the other arm of my chair. Oanen's mom reached out and ran a soothing hand down Eliana's bare arm.

"You should sleep, dear one," Mrs. Quill said.

They might not be mother and daughter by blood, but I could see the true affection Mrs. Quill had for her ward.

"I'm okay. I want to know what happens."

A shiny portal opened near the door, drawing our attention. Adira and Raiden stepped through. The older man's hard, silver gaze swept the room and landed on me.

"Are you sure it was Aubrey?" Raiden asked without preamble.

"Yes," I said before Oanen could. "I recognized her white fur when she was a wolf and saw her as a human, as well."

Raiden's shoulder seemed to sag just a bit.

"We need to know if this was her first time," Mr. Quill said. "Or if there are others responsible for the prior incidents."

"Agreed," Raiden said.

"How was she missed when you questioned the pack?" Mrs. Quill asked without censure.

"I didn't question the young without the mark since the human was killed outside Uttira. Now that we know what Trammer was doing, I will question them all."

"Good. Perhaps you should issue a ban on solo runs while this is unresolved. If any others have had a taste of flesh, we don't want them hunting for more of it," Mr. Quill said.

Raiden gave a curt nod, and Oanen's father looked at Adira.

"Given the number of deaths, I feel it's unwise to wait until morning to question Trammer."

"I agree," Adira said.

"Agreed," Raiden added. "I believe my presence isn't as necessary here as it is with the pack now. With your agreement, I will return and start seeking answers from my own while you direct the interview with the liaison."

Mr. Quill nodded to him, and Raiden stepped back through the portal.

"I will return shortly," Adira said then disappeared.

CHAPTER TWENTY-FOUR

THE SILENCE IN THE STUDY GREW TO DEAFENING PROPORTIONS IN MY mind. What was the council going to do with Trammer? No one seemed overly upset that he'd been killing his own kind. Why not? And, why was no one talking? Was it because of my presence or because their son was sitting right next to me with his thumb giving my back a discreet and occasional caress? I hoped they weren't noticing that. I hoped they were instead speculating about why Trammer had killed those humans. They had to be at least a little curious, right? I sure the hell was.

When the shimmer finally returned, Oanen's stroke paused and I exhaled in relief.

Trammer stepped through first, dressed in full uniform. The shirt was a bit wrinkled, and his hair wasn't as neat as usual. The sight of him made my blood boil, and only Oanen's restraining hand on my shoulder kept me in my seat.

Trammer's gaze swept over us all before settling on Oanen's father.

"Mr. Quill," he said. "What seems to be the problem?"

"Oanen and Megan witnessed what you did to Mr. Ryan tonight."

Trammer's whole demeanor changed. He didn't look worried; he looked pissed.

"Mr. Ryan? That shitbag gets a fancy 'Mr.' for selling drugs in your town while plain 'ol Trammer is burning bodies to clean up your messes? Your standards are screwed up. You treat me like I'm inferior, but I'm not a parasite that only exists to feed off of others."

His gaze went straight to Eliana. She made a small, hurt noise; and I glared at Trammer while reaching for her hand. Her fingers shook in mine.

"Do you admit to killing Mr. Ryan?" Mr. Quill asked.

"Unbelievable," Trammer said. "Yeah, I killed him."

"Why? He's your own kind."

Finally, I thought.

Trammer laughed angrily.

"Neither of those men I killed was my kind any more than I'm your kind, you ignorant prick."

"Those men? What about Camil?" I asked.

His accusatory gaze pinned me.

"Do you seriously still think I killed that girl? I had no reason to."

He gave me a dismissive glare before facing Mr. Quill.

"Camil died from an overdose. The very man who you wanted to let go is responsible for her death."

"Is that why you killed him?" Mr. Quill asked.

Trammer snorted angrily.

"You remove what you consider trash to keep Uttira safe, but you're looking at it all wrong. Those men feed on humans just like you do. Do you even know what happens when you return them to their depraved lives? You claim to exist to protect humanity. But by letting the scum live, you're condemning hundreds of innocents to death. You're not protectors of anything but your self-interests."

"Fine," I said. "You killed those men to keep others safe and had nothing to do with Camil's death. But why bring the bodies back here? Why put Camil in the dumpster?"

He barked out a laugh again.

"I brought the first guy back to prove you're all just animals waiting to kill us humans. I don't know who found the body, but they sure had a feast despite your no flesh law. Camil, I didn't touch. I saw her after you did, and I only realized what happened when Mr. Ryan got a glance at her file in my car on the way here. I don't know who cut her open and fed on her, but I hear, once a wolf gets a taste of human flesh, they can't stop craving it. Bringing Mr. Ryan back inside the barrier and leaving him in the clearing was to prove that. We all know I'm not the monster here. Or, at least, not the worst monster."

He was talking about all of them. Us, actually. But, in my mind, I only saw Aubrey's face the night I'd discovered Camil's body. Aubrey had tried to get me to leave Ashlyn's table, and I'd sent her on a wild goose chase looking for Fenris. She would have had the time and opportunity to discover Camil's body before I did. Aubrey also would have already had her first taste of flesh and the motive to try to set me up for the kill. All of that just because of jealousy?

My head was starting to hurt. When I tried to see past the fury-anger, I wasn't sure what to think. Aubrey lost to her jealousy and instincts. But, what about Trammer? Yes, Trammer had killed people but only ones who were hurting other people. He wasn't just some vigilante; he wore the town badge.

"Given your statement, we no longer believe you hold the best interest for all humans in your position. As such, we find you no longer suitable as human liaison."

Trammer snorted.

"We sentence you to a memory wipe and removal."

So they were going to make him forget about Uttira and just send him back out in the real world?

"Wait," I said. "What about Ashlyn?"

"Was she involved with your actions?" Mr. Quill asked.

"Of course not!" Trammer said angrily.

"That wasn't what I meant," I said. "What happens to her when his memory is wiped?"

"She continues with her responsibilities."

"She doesn't get a choice to go with him? He's her uncle. From what I understand, she has no parents. No one else."

"Haven't you been listening?" Trammer said. "They only pretend to care about humans. But they don't."

"That is untrue, Trammer. The council will continue to provide for her like it has always done," Adira said.

"So she has no choice?" I asked.

"If she would want to leave, her memory would need to be wiped as well," Adira explained. "Since she has been here for three years, that would be a traumatic experience."

"But shouldn't it be her decision? And if she does choose to stay, shouldn't you get her so she can talk to her uncle and at least say goodbye?"

Some of Trammer's anger faded from his expression.

"Megan, maybe living in the real world helped you become more human. Don't let them kill that part of you."

With speed I couldn't have anticipated, he grabbed his gun from his holster and put it to his temple.

"Keep an eye on her," he said.

The sudden explosion of noise and brain matter made me jump. Trammer crumpled to the ground. I stared at the heap as Eliana leaned into me and started to cry. Absently petting her hair, I looked at the adults. They shared a look, but none of them seemed overly upset that yet another human had met his end in their town.

Keep an eye on her.

He'd said it while looking at me. I knew he meant Ashlyn. How could he leave her like that? So much like my mom had left me.

"Children," Mrs. Quill said. "I think it's time for you to sleep. We will talk more in the morning."

I couldn't believe they were telling us to go to bed with Trammer still twitching on the floor.

"What about Aubrey?" I asked.

"We will let Raiden know Trammer's confession, and she will be dealt with accordingly. Now go. Help Eliana to bed."

Eliana shook against me. Maybe leaving was for the best. I pulled Eliana to her feet and looked at Mr. Quill.

"I think Aubrey sent me a text from Camil's phone to get me into the alley that night. Have Raiden ask her about that." In my heart, I knew my mom hadn't come back, but I needed it confirmed.

Mr. Quill nodded, and with Eliana's face buried in my shoulder, I led her past Trammer's fallen body.

"Let me take her," Oanen said.

He scooped Eliana up in his arms and headed out the door. I followed slowly, pausing in the doorway to look back. I couldn't stop thinking about Trammer's last words.

"What about Ashlyn?" I asked.

"I will tell her in the morning," Adira said. "She will be given a choice, as you suggested."

"Let us know what she decides. I'd like to say goodbye if she chooses to leave."

Adira nodded, and I left to catch up with Oanen.

They weren't more than a few steps from the door.

"Oanen, put me down," Eliana said. "I just didn't want to see him."

Oanen set Eliana on her feet. She looked at me with sad eyes.

"At least everyone will believe you, now, that you're not the killer."

"I couldn't care less about that. Well, maybe not being the center of everyone's attention will be nice. But, I'm more worried about Ashlyn now."

"What he said in there wasn't true. They do care," Oanen said. "But we don't understand humans the way the two of you do. Like he did. That's why a liaison is necessary." He gave a troubled exhale. "Why would he kill himself like that?"

"I don't know," I said. "Maybe shame. He was angry and defiant until I brought up Ashlyn. Maybe he didn't want her to know what he'd done. Whether justified or not, he was killing people in secret. That's not something rational humans do."

"And now Ashlyn's all alone," Eliana said.

"No. She'll have us if she wants. We'll keep an eye on her."

Eliana rubbed her brow.

"I'm never going to unsee that. I'm tired, but I know I won't be able to sleep."

"Want to come to my house? Maybe a change of scenery will help?"

"I don't think so. Let's watch a movie in our living room," she said, looking at Oanen.

"You guys have your own living room?"

She smiled slightly and grabbed my hand.

"Come see."

She led me to a spacious room on the third floor. It wasn't just a living room. It had a kitchenette with a full-sized fridge, a pool table, two large TVs at the back of the room attached to every gaming console known to man, and a TV toward the front surrounded by a full sofa and two loveseats.

"Holy crap. Why have we been hanging out at my house?"

I sat on the sofa while Eliana browsed the paid movie

selection. Oanen brought me a bottle of water and a bag of snacks before sitting next to me. Eliana sat on the other side of me.

The movie started to play. I munched on my chips and stared at the screen, not really seeing it. I was tired. So was Eliana, because she fell asleep on my shoulder within minutes. Oanen sat beside me, seemingly unbothered by the need for sleep.

As soon as I finished my last chip, he took the wrapper and empty bottle from me. I leaned back and closed my eyes as I listened to him throw away my trash. I was glad I wasn't alone because behind my closed eyes all I saw was red.

I felt hot. Way too hot. I wasn't sweaty, though. All the heat was inside me, building in size and making me uncomfortable. It had nothing to do with my temper and everything to do with using Oanen as the best body pillow ever.

His hand rested on the middle of my back as if holding me in place against his muscled chest. My cheek lay on his shirt, right over his heart. The steady beat skipped when I lifted my hand to brush some hair from my face. Knowing that he was awake made the heat worse. As did the sensation of his other hand smoothing over my hair.

I lifted my head and looked for Eliana but didn't see her. Oanen and I lay on the long couch together. Alone.

"How did this happen?" I asked, finally meeting Oanen's gaze.

"Mom would say Freya answered my prayers. Dad would say Hera."

His prayers? Heat spread to my cheeks.

"What would you say?" I asked.

"That I only care how you answer them. You know what your anger's for now, and you know I'm not afraid of it. Stop hiding from life and start living it."

His steady gaze held mine.

"Say yes to me," he said softly.

He was asking me to let him in. I knew I should get up. That I should make up some excuse for why this wouldn't work and just walk away. But I couldn't.

"And if I hurt you?"

"Then I'll have probably deserved it."

"What exactly would I be saying yes to? Dating? Being your girlfriend?"

"Sure. We can start with that."

The heat whirled inside me, creating an uncomfortable ache.

"I'll think about it," I said before scrambling off of him.

"Perfect timing," his mother said, walking into the room. "I was just about to wake you two. Eliana offered to make breakfast while we talk."

Oanen stood and walked beside me as we passed through the halls. Although I should have been wondering what Mrs. Quill wanted to talk about, my mind wouldn't let go of the conversation Oanen and I had been having. Was I truly going to date him? Was I ready to risk decking him again and see his eyes fill with hate or disgust? My insides went hot and cold just thinking about it. So I tried not to.

Adira and Oanen's father were already in the study, waiting for our arrival.

"Good morning, Megan. Did you sleep well?" Adira asked as Mrs. Quill joined Mr. Quill on the sofa.

"Well enough. How's Ashlyn?"

Oanen led me to a chair and perched on the arm after I took

the seat. His nearness made it a little hard to focus on Adira's answer.

"She is upset over the events that took place and her uncle's death but chose to remain in Uttira. She is considering possible guardianship but will remain in the home she knows for now. I did let her know you are concerned about her."

"Thank you. And what about Aubrey?"

I needed to know the Council had done something about her. She might not have killed any people yet, but her level of wicked probably meant she wasn't far from it.

"Aubrey was the one to text you from Camil's phone. She'd gotten your number from Fenris' phone. Because Aubrey does not have the mark and did not kill her victims, the council didn't sentence her to death. However, the pack did sentence her for reconditioning. She has been removed from Uttira and will not return until the pack deems her cured."

"Is that enough?" I asked. Not that I wanted her put down, but I sure as hell didn't want her back in Uttira being a pain in my ass, either.

"The pack believes so. The first incident was an accident. She was jealous and angry with you because of Fenris' interest and sought to drag the body to your house so you would be accused of his death. However, she couldn't resist the taste of human flesh after the first mile."

"Ew. I'm so not going to eat breakfast now."

"I apologize."

"Okay, so Ashlyn's good, and Aubrey's still bad but dealt with. What's next?"

"Next, we talk about this past week away from the Academy. You missed several sessions, but your online notes don't reflect a negative change."

"No offense, but all the sessions I'm in are pointless. I already know how to order a pizza and not kill the delivery guy.

Blending with the human world isn't going to be a problem for me. This world is. I don't know anything about the creatures that exist or what they might be capable of. If I'm in this world, shouldn't I know more about it?"

"I agree." She looked at the Quills. "I'd like Megan to be given access to the Academy Library."

"Granted," Mrs. Quill said.

"What's in the Academy Library?"

"The most extensive collection of written information on our creation and history. While the other students attend sessions, you may read whatever you choose in the library."

"Your access comes at a price, Megan," Mr. Quill said. "We want you to fill in as temporary human liaison until we can acquire a new one. The information you gain from the library will help you understand who you will be dealing with in your new role."

"You want me to liaison? Why? I thought that was a human's job?"

"It is, and it will be. However, after last night, you've proven that you also have the humans' best interests in mind. You have the qualifications to fill in for the short term."

"And, you will continue to report any flares in your temper to me," Adira said.

All three adults watched me, waiting for some kind of response.

"Sure," I said.

The Quills stood. "We hope you'll join us for breakfast, Adira."

"Thank you. I will."

They left the room, but Adira didn't move from her spot. Her gaze flicked between Oanen and me.

"Have you finally agreed to his protection?" she asked me.

"Protection?" I echoed, confused.

"Humans call it dating, Adira," Oanen said.

"Ah. That's good. None of us are meant to be solitary. Not even furies." She started for the door then paused and looked back. "Oh, and don't break into my office again. I will not forgive it a second time."

My mouth dropped open as she left.

"I told you she'd find out," Oanen said.

I closed my mouth and gave him a sour look.

"This relationship won't work if you say 'I told you so,' every time I'm wrong."

"Do you plan on being wrong often?" he asked with the corners of his mouth twitching.

"No."

"Then let me have my moment."

He tugged my hand, pulling me closer and threading his fingers through mine. My heart started to pound hard at the simple contact.

"You won't regret saying yes," he said.

"I didn't say yes; I said I'd think about it."

He smiled slightly.

"I'm optimistic."

I snorted. "That's not the word I'd use to describe you."

"What word would you use?"

"Persistent."

He laughed.

"Come on. Let's feed you and find out what your liaison duties are for the day."

"They're going to give me duties already? I thought it would just be harassing delinquents."

He grew slightly serious.

"Now that you know what you are, they're going to want to use you to fill the role you were meant to fill."

"What do you mean?"

"You're meant to find and punish the wicked. They're going to want you on the Council."

"What they want and what they get probably won't be the same. I haven't even graduated yet."

"We'll see."

FURY FOCUSED

CHAPTER ONE

In the complete silence of Girderon Academy's secret library, my brain wanted to explode. The text explaining the numerous different types of giants and how to distinguish them, although not helping, wasn't the sole reason for my imminent mental melt down. Too many thoughts whirled in my head. Too many to think straight.

Groaning, I absent-mindedly lifted my hands from the thick, old book and rubbed my face. The damn thing slammed shut and flew back to its place on the shelves.

"Are you kidding me?"

I stood to retrieve the book from its spot, yet again. The stupid return spell, which kept the library neat and prevented anyone from leaving with one of these precious, nonsensical tomes, was driving me as crazy as my thoughts about everything that had happened over the weekend.

Nothing had really changed since Trammer's death, except my thinking. The Council, which consisted of Adira, the Quills, Raiden, and a few others, had decided that, as a fury, I'd be the best candidate to watch over the remaining humans until a new liaison could be found. I hadn't considered the implications when I'd agreed, but after a weekend to think about it, the responsibility of being a liaison was starting to get to me. Look at how many had died since I'd gotten here. Everything in Uttira seemed to want a piece of humans. How was I going to stop that from happening?

On top of that weighing thought, I had Oanen and the promise he'd somehow twisted from me. What the hell had I been thinking? My previous, single attempt at a relationship had ended epically with my fist. The last thing I wanted to do was throat punch Oanen because of some weird fury fit of temper.

Fine, that wasn't even it. I knew, as a fury, I only punished the wicked, and Oanen was far from wicked. He was great. Perfect. And, I was terrified of screwing it up with him. How many guys really wanted to go out with a girl who had a flash temper and a tendency to hit first and ask questions later? Not counting Oanen, I felt pretty sure the answer would be none.

With the book once again in my hands, I returned to my uncomfortable seat at the old table and forced myself to focus as I started reading again. It wasn't easy. Because of the way the book had been added to by different people throughout the ages, it didn't read like a book but more like a recipe card with special notes.

Not all giants were giants by human standards. The term giant could describe the creature's size but also their birth place. Most giants mastered the ability to control their size by adolescence. Only a few had other gifts, in addition to having the magic to change their appearance. Most just trained as warriors in case the gods ever called upon them to once again fight in their wars over earth.

None of the information on the pages seemed particularly valuable. I sighed and scratched my forehead while keeping one hand firmly in the center of the book.

From my place in the middle of the moderately-sized room, I

looked up at the other volumes lining the shelves along the stone walls. Adira had suggested I pick a shelf and start reading the contents, in order, so I didn't miss anything. There were a lot of books. Over five hundred, at least. And if they all read like this one, I would just be wasting my time.

Rolling my shoulders, I got back to reading again and tried to ignore the doubts that kept poking at my mind.

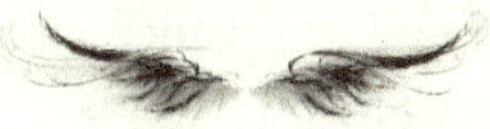

A sudden knock on the thick, old door echoed in the room and made me jump. Not that the book I currently read was that gripping. I was just that focused on trying to absorb the words.

Standing, I realized how badly my back ached. I worked out the kink as I moved toward the door and wondered how long I'd been reading. Adira had taken my phone when I'd arrived, saying that entering with any kind of technology would just destroy the device due to a spell that prevented classified information from being copied and shared. All of which made no sense to me. One, there wasn't anything important in here as far as I'd read. And two, what was to stop me from just telling someone what I learned? But, I hadn't argued with her. Giving up my phone to hang out in a library and avoid sessions and other people had seemed a fair enough trade.

I opened the door, expecting to see Adira checking up on me like she'd said she would. Instead, I found Oanen leaning against the frame, his muscled arms crossed and his close-cropped, golden hair glinting in the light of the hall. My pulse gave a sudden jump at the sight of him. I still couldn't believe I'd said yes to being his girlfriend.

His blue gaze held mine, and a hint of a smile tugged at his lips.

"You look surprised," he said. "Expecting someone else?"

"Yeah. Adira. She said she'd check in on me."

"She mentioned that she did when I saw her in the hall. Both times you were reading."

"What? She never came in here."

"She doesn't need to with her portals," he said. "Come on. I figured you'd forget lunch if I didn't come get you." He straightened away from the door so I could step out.

"It's only lunch time?" I groaned. It felt like I'd spent the whole day in the library already.

He wrapped his arm around my shoulders as we walked.

"Yep. Only lunch. Three more hours of reading."

I barely heard what he'd said. My heart pounded in my ears as the feel of his arm around me sent my internal temperature from I'm-fine to is-it-hot-in-here.

His fingers idly stroked down my arm as he continued to speak.

"Don't worry. We'll do something fun afterwards to make up for it."

All sorts of warning buzzers started going off in my head. Fun? What did he mean by fun? Was that code for kissing? It was too soon for that, right? Before I could completely send myself into a full-blown panic, I spoke up.

"You're freaking me out."

He sighed and dropped his arm.

"Yeah, I could tell by your pulse. I was wondering how long you'd let it go."

I turned on him and slugged him in the shoulder.

"That wasn't nice."

"No. It wasn't," he said. "And yet you didn't get fury angry, only girly mad."

I narrowed my eyes at him.

"Are you testing me?"

"No. I'm helping you see that I'm right and that there's nothing for you to worry about. You won't fly into a rage and hurt me."

He reached out and gently touched my cheek. My slowly calming pulse went right back to racing, and Oanen's lips quirked upward ever so slightly again.

"Not only do I make your heart race, I make you blush, too," he said softly. "I like it."

He wasn't making me just blush, he was turning my insides into molten lava. I stepped back, breaking the contact to gulp in some cooler air.

"You said slow. And I'm not even sure I'm ready for touching yet. So, keep your hands to yourself."

He tucked his hands into his front pockets and innocently arched a brow at me.

"That's a start." I resumed walking, and he stuck to my side as we navigated the busy halls toward the cafeteria.

"What did you bring for lunch?" he asked.

"Nothing. I figured I'd grab a tray."

Yet, even as I stepped into the cafeteria, I knew standing in line was a bad idea. At least one out of ten students was doing or thinking something to set off my fury to a mild degree. Individually, it wasn't enough to send me into a fit. Collectively, it was close.

"I packed an extra lunch if you'd rather skip the line," Oanen said when I hesitated.

"Yeah, that might be a better option."

We crossed the crowded cafeteria to get to the nearly vacant courtyard. Few students braved the cool fall air to lounge on the browning lawns and enjoy their lunches outdoors. Eliana already sat on a low wall near the trees.

As soon as she saw us, her face lit up with her usual shy smile, and she waved. I returned the wave, relieved she still seemed fine. Since she'd heard Trammer's insensitive remark about the creatures here being parasites that fed off of humans, I'd worried about her. She'd been sensitive about being a succubus before the man went on his hate rant.

"How'd the reading go?" she asked when I sat next to her. Oanen handed me one of the three insulated lunch bags she had nearby.

"It was okay. I was expecting some big secrets; instead, it's just—"

My lips kept moving but no sound came out.

"Part of the binding spell in the library," Oanen said. "You can't talk about what you read." He unwrapped his sandwich and took a large bite.

"Don't worry," Eliana said. "Anything that's common knowledge will loosen up inside you after a few days, and you'll be able to talk about it. It's a different sort of spell. Tricky. And not often used because of its quirks."

She noticed my surprised look and paused.

"What?" she asked.

"How do you know all this? Have you been in the library already?" Adira had made it sound like letting students in there was something they normally don't do.

"No. I was stuck in beginner's magic two years ago. All any of the druid-types could talk about was the binding spell. Getting it right shows a level of mastery that only a few like Adira have." Eliana pointedly opened my bag, which sat in my lap, and handed me my sandwich. "It was a really long year."

I unwrapped my lunch and glanced at Oanen, who'd already finished the majority of his. Taking a bite, I paused at the flavor and looked at the sandwich.

"Do you like it?" Oanen asked.

I finished chewing and swallowed as I studied the peanut butter and marshmallow fluff interior.

"Yeah. It's different but good. What is it?"

"A chocolate fluffernutter sandwich. My mom remembered them from the sixties. Well, the regular fluffernutters. They didn't have chocolate peanut butter back then."

I took another bite, enjoying the sugary goodness. It hit the sweet craving I'd been having for weeks now.

"Eliana mentioned that you missed some of the food from outside. I thought this might help."

I looked at his remaining bite of the healthier turkey club he held.

"You didn't want one of these, too?"

His lips did that small little twitch thing again like he'd almost smiled.

"I'm saving the peanut butter for you."

The way he looked at me and the remembered feel of his hand on my arm sent my heart racing again.

"I see Jenna. I'm going to go say hi," Eliana said, quickly moving to leave me alone with Oanen.

I grabbed her arm and turned to her, my eyes wide and, probably, panicked.

"Now? I thought we were having lunch together."

She rolled her eyes at me and tugged her arm from my grasp.

"Yes. Sandwiches. Not the stuff you two are throwing off. I'll be back when you're calmer."

She hurried away. Flushed red with embarrassment and guilt, I stared at my sandwich.

"She's not mad," Oanen said. "She's afraid." He paused for a moment. "Like you."

I looked up at him.

"This doesn't need to be awkward," he said. "I like you. Your smile. The way you think. Your temper. All of it. I think that saying we're together is scaring you because you think it means something more than it should."

"What does it mean?"

"That we're spending more time together to get to know each other better."

"That's it?"

"For now? Yes."

Why did he have to go and say, "for now?" I wanted to groan and cover my face.

He leaned closer.

"I can hear your heart beating faster. 'Now' doesn't worry you, does it?"

I shook my head.

"Good. Then, eat your sandwich, Megan, and stop worrying about what comes later."

Forcing my thoughts to something other than the large, muscled Oanen who smelled like summer and wind and everything I wanted to inhale, I thought about the library and managed to calm down after a few more bites.

"I haven't found anything talking about the history of the gods. What can you tell me about them? I mean, they were real, I get that. But, why did they create all of us and then just leave?"

He stuffed his lunch containers back into his bag.

"I'm not sure that they just left. No one really knows what happened to them. They just stopped directing us."

"All at once? Like, maybe they all died?"

He shook his head. "Gods don't die. And I don't think it happened all at once. But again, no one really knows. It happened a long time ago. Some of us live very long lives, but I don't think anyone is that old. All we have are stories passed down from those who were there during that time. Stories that are probably in those books."

I groaned.

"The writing in those books is awful. Old. Hard to read."

"And I'm guessing not all in English."

"Dunno. I haven't made it very far," I admitted.

"Why are you asking about the gods?"

"Something I read. Not all of the creatures seem to have strongly defined purposes without the gods here to tell them what to do."

"Yeah. That's part of why the Council and places like Uttira are necessary. It provides meaning for those without a purpose and accountability for those whose purposes don't align with the collective objective of remaining hidden from humans."

Eliana crossed the yard and rejoined us.

"You two all right now?" she asked, hesitating to sit.

"Yeah," I said quickly. Not wanting to think about what had sent her running, I continued the conversation with Oanen. "It still doesn't sit right with me, though. They created us, made us with these…instincts, then just bailed."

"That's the nature of things," Oanen said with a shrug.

I opened my bag of organic potato chips and munched, lost in thought while Eliana hurried to eat her lunch before the bell rang.

If we were keeping each other accountable, and creatures like me were keeping humans accountable, who was keeping the gods accountable?

CHAPTER TWO

"ALMOST DONE WITH THE FIRST BOOK OF GIANTS, I SEE."

I jumped slightly at the sound of Adira's voice and turned to give her a disgruntled look.

"First book? There's another book filled with useless giant information?"

She chuckled. "You might think it's useless now, but when you confront a giant for some misdeed you have discovered, what will your first thought be?"

"I'd wonder what race of giant it was. Mostly, if it's a magic using race that can manipulate time and space. The book makes those sound like the most dangerous."

"Or the most useful. What else would you consider?"

"If the giant is in its true form or if it gets bigger."

"And that information would help you decide how to deal with any wicked giant you encounter, yes?"

"I guess."

She set a hand on my shoulder.

"You're learning more than you know. Information and knowledge will only help you as you grow into your powers. And, in your role as temporary liaison. Which brings me to the reason why I've interrupted you before Oanen arrives. We're concerned about Ashlyn. Would you check on her after you leave here?"

"Sure."

A knock sounded on the door, and I glanced that direction, eager to escape the library. I looked back at Adira to see if she had anything else she needed me to do, but she was gone. Lifting my hand, I let the book fly back to its place on the shelf and hurried to make my escape.

"Ready?" Oanen asked when I opened the door.

"Yep. I've read more than I wanted to today."

I left the library, and the door shut softly behind me.

"Want to do something tonight?" he asked.

Why did I feel relieved that I had an excuse to say no?

"I can't. Adira asked me to go check on Ashlyn. Liaison duty, I guess." And, it was an official duty that I knew needed to be done. Since Ashlyn's uncle had killed himself, leaving her alone in Uttira, I'd wanted to talk to her. To make sure she was okay with her decision to stay.

"Okay. I'll drop you off there," Oanen said.

When we reached the student parking lot, Eliana's car was already gone.

"Are you sure Eliana isn't mad?" I asked, looking at Oanen.

"I told her not to wait. I drove a different car today."

"Oh, the hardships of your life. Not only do you need to decide what to wear each morning, you need to decide which car to drive." I rolled my eyes and followed him as he walked toward the back of the parking lot.

Amidst the gleaming reds, blues, and blacks sat a small orange car. Although new and shiny, it lacked the pompous display of the sports cars that dominated the lot. I grinned when he went right to it.

"Slumming?" I asked.

His lips twitched, and he opened the door for me without a word.

Alone with Oanen for the first time since I'd woken up half sprawled on him, I wasn't sure what to do or say. Why did liking him have to feel so damn awkward?

Thankfully, it didn't take long for us to get to Ashlyn's house.

"I'm not sure how long I'll be," I said as he parked.

"Doesn't matter." He turned off the car.

"Are you sure you want to wait?" I asked.

"I don't plan to. I'll fly from here, and you can take your car home." He opened the door and got out.

Frowning, I hurried to do the same. He met me on the sidewalk near the front of the car.

"Wait. What do you mean? You're loaning me this car?"

"Sure."

I narrowed my eyes at Oanen, real annoyance rising.

"Half-truths and pacifying answers are just as good as lies. I don't do lies," I said.

"Fair enough. I don't do lies either. I do, however, like to do things that will likely annoy you."

"Such as?"

"Such as asking my parents to get you a car so you're not stuck waiting for a ride from someone. Especially when you're so far out of town."

"So your parents bought me a car?"

He remained silent while just looking at me, his arms crossed.

"I'm about to hit you," I warned.

"I purchased the car; they retrieved it."

"Boyfriends don't buy girlfriends cars," I said.

"The good ones do."

I breathed deeply, trying not to get angry with him.

"Since I fly and you don't, you need a car. Unless you're saying you like riding me?"

My mouth dropped open, and my heart started hammering again.

This time he flashed a grin large enough to show teeth.

"You're adorable," he said. "I could stand here and watch you blush all day, but neither of us will get anything done then."

He whipped off his shirt and tossed it to me. I caught it by reflex.

"What are you doing?" I demanded when he reached for his pants.

"Flying home. Keep the clothes in the car. It never hurts to have spares handy." He unzipped his fly, and I glanced at the houses lining the street.

"You can't be serious right now. You're standing on the sidewalk in the middle of the afternoon about to drop your pants for the world so you can turn into a griffin and fly away. What happened to keeping our presence secret?" I would have asked what happened to his modesty, but he'd never really had any from the start.

"If there was anyone new in Uttira, we would know. Anyone watching already knows about us. They'll just have to close their eyes if they don't want to see something."

I wondered if I should close my eyes, too. The problem was that I wanted to see Oanen in all his glory again. Badly. But that would likely result in more blushing. So, I compromised with myself and averted my gaze to the side. I could tell he was stepping out of his pants but couldn't see the details.

"Call me when you finish with your visit if you want some company," he said as he folded his clothes and set them on the car.

I nodded but didn't look at him until I heard the sound of his wings beating the air. With a deep calming breath, I turned and went to the house. I couldn't believe it had only been a few days since I'd last been there.

Ashlyn opened the door after my third knock, her hazel eyes bloodshot and puffy. The mottled complexion of her pale skin made her neatly brushed, strawberry-blonde hair seem even more red.

"Ashlyn, I'm so sorry," I said. Anger and regret welled up inside me. The normal, non-fury kind. "I know we don't know each other well, but would you like some company for a while?"

She nodded. "Adira mentioned you'd probably stop by."

I stepped into her house. Her home seemed so oddly normal given what her uncle, Trammer, had done.

"Can I get you something to drink?" she asked politely as she closed the door.

"No, thank you."

She led the way to the living room and took a seat on the couch. I wasn't sure what to say or do, so I looked around the room while I gave myself a moment to think. The book I'd last seen her reading sat on the nearby coffee table.

"It's a good book," she said, catching the direction of my gaze. "You can borrow it if you want. I've already read it several times."

"I'm not much of a book person, especially after today. I was stuck in the Academy's super-secret library the whole day, reading stuff that made no sense."

"A library? I haven't been to a library in years."

The wistful way she said it gave me pause.

"Why years?"

She shot me an odd look. "Once a human says yes to Uttira, they don't leave."

"Trammer left all the time."

She looked away, swallowed hard, and nodded.

"He did. Only him, though, because of a spell that prevented him from saying anything once he left the barrier."

"So you're stuck here like me?"

She met my gaze again, frowning this time.

"Not like you. You can go wherever you want in Uttira. Attend school, make friends. Definitely not like you."

"Wait. You don't have to go to the Academy?"

"Have to? I'm not allowed to go to the Academy. I'm enrolled but complete all my work online. The groceries are delivered. With the exception of my other duties, I'm not supposed to leave the house."

My envy over her not needing to attend school disappeared as I understood what she was telling me. She was a prisoner in this house, locked in with her grief and as desperate to escape her confines as I was mine. Only, she'd chosen this.

"Why are you staying here then?" I asked.

"Because this is the only world I know. And, if I leave, I'll know nothing. Maybe not even my name. Adira explained how the spell works. It takes days from you. Years. It doesn't select which memories. It takes all of them. I've been here since I was a toddler. I'd lose who I am."

"Why can't they just put a spell on you so you can't say anything?"

"A binding spell? I'd accept it if that were an option. But, the Council ruled that no underage human shall be bound to Uttira. It prevents human parents from binding their kids without giving them a choice."

"When do you turn eighteen?"

"Another year and a half to go," she said. Her eyes welled up, and she blinked a few times. "I wish my uncle wouldn't have died."

I couldn't say the same. Her uncle had done bad things and had sounded like he would have done more if given the chance.

But, I did feel remorse at my part in his death because of how hurt Ashlyn was now.

"I know what it's like being stuck where you don't want to be. Do you want to come to my place? We can see if Eliana wants to watch a movie and have a girl's night."

Ashlyn was already shaking her head.

"I like Eliana. She's nice. But it's dangerous for me to leave the house. It's warded for my protection. I can't get hurt here."

The injustice of Ashlyn's situation poked at my temper and showed through in my tone when I spoke.

"Yet, the Council makes you sit in the Roost."

"It's warded, too."

"Okay, this is ridiculous," I said, standing. "I get why you're staying, but you're living like you're in prison with work release duties."

"What other choice do I have?" She sounded tired. Beaten.

"I don't know, but I'm going to find out. Do you have something I can write on? I want to give you my number. If you need anything, call me. And, that's not an empty offer. Call me."

She got up and found me a piece of paper and a pen, and I quickly wrote down my number.

"I'll be in touch soon, Ashlyn." I reached out and gently gripped her arm.

She set her hand over mine.

"My uncle told me you were raised in the human world. Thank you for not being one of them. For being different."

I wasn't sure how to respond to that, so I gave her a pathetic excuse for a smile then left. No matter how much I wanted to deny it, I was a creature of the gods. Yet, I hated the rules that came with what I was.

I parked in front of the Quills' and shoved my way out of the car. My anger had only built on the drive over. Not dangerously, but close. I didn't understand why, exactly, when there wasn't anyone even around me.

Pounding on the front door, I waited. Mrs. Quill didn't leave me standing outside for long.

"I need to speak to you, Mr. Quill, and Adira," I said.

"Come in. You look upset."

"I am," I said, stepping into the entry. She immediately led me to Mr. Quill's study where he sat at the desk.

He looked up as we entered.

"Megan would like to speak with us and Adira."

He stood and pulled his phone from his pocket. A quick call later and a portal appeared. Adira stepped out and gave me a kind smile. For some reason, that tweaked my anger further.

"There's nothing to smile about," I said. "I just came from Ashlyn's house. Some creatures are meant to be solitary. Not humans. Not Ashlyn. The situation you've created for her is cruel."

Adira frowned. "Cruel?"

"The rules of this place mean she's pretty much under house arrest. She's grieving and utterly alone."

"That's why we sent you to visit her."

"I'm not enough. If you value the humans who are here, then start treating them better. Definitely not like prisoners in their own homes. You say you're teaching the students of Girderon Academy to blend with humans, but you're not. You're teaching them to keep apart from humans with your segregation that forces the humans to remain in their special little locations. And, by doing that, you're also teaching your youths that humans have a certain place in life. That they are lesser than us. Trammer's crimes don't solely lay on his shoulders. He is a product of the treatment he and his family received here. If you don't want something like that to reoccur in the future, things need to change."

I felt a tiny bit better that they'd listened during my entire rant instead of trying to interrupt or defend their actions.

"What do you propose?" Adira asked.

"If you want to really teach about blending, give Ashlyn the choice to attend the Academy if she wants. You said no one can get hurt within those halls. And, she's starved for contact with people her own age."

"The contact may not be what she anticipates. Many of the students still do not have control over their instincts."

"Well, they're there to learn, right? And, when the students see the staff treat her with respect and kindness, they will be more likely to follow suit, not just here, but in the real world too."

"Is there anything else?" Adira asked.

"Yeah, this town should have a library. It's big enough by human standards."

"We have no use for a library," Mr. Quill said.

I struggled to control my annoyance.

"You're missing the point. The whole goal is to train the next generation how to blend, right? A library is normal. Most towns have them. Normal humans go to them all the time."

"You've been to a library?" Mrs. Quill asked.

"It's been pointed out to me that I'm not human or normal, but yes. I have been to a library." I looked at them, my frustration growing because they weren't understanding what they were doing to the humans in Uttira.

"Did any of you have pets while growing up?" I asked.

Adira and Mrs. Quill nodded.

"We had a fish," Adira said.

I blinked in understanding. Sisters? Wow.

"Okay. Tell me about your setup for the fish. Where did it live?"

"We had a beautiful pond, shaded on one side by trees and open to the lights of the sun and dual moons on the other. It was a tranquil place. Our fish loved it there."

"Of course it did. It had space to move and grow. Freedom enough to be happy. Uttira is that pond for the underage creatures here. Except for the humans. The humans are in a glass bowl with only an inch of water. Just enough to breathe. Not enough to move. Just enough to not die. Do you get it? You need to make Uttira a tranquil, beautiful place for all the creatures here."

Mr. Quill nodded slowly while Adira and Mrs. Quill looked truly upset.

"You've given us much to think about," he said, standing. "Oanen, would you see Megan out so we can discuss this further?"

Hearing Oanen's name made my pulse jump, and I looked over my shoulder toward the door where both he and Eliana stood. I wondered how long they'd been listening.

"Yes, Father." Oanen's gaze shifted to me, and he held out his hand, a silent invitation to leave the room.

"Since you've always wanted to know how people make me feel in the past, I'm telling you now that you're all frustrating me. A lot. And I think if you continue to mistreat the humans here, after having been told that there is mistreatment happening, it's going to piss me off."

Adira nodded, a regal acknowledgement.

"We understand, Fury."

I nodded and turned to leave the room before pausing once more.

"And, that wasn't a threat," I said, looking back.

Mrs. Quill smiled. "Furies never threaten, Megan. They act.

That's why we asked you to help Uttira. You've warned us and we, too, will act."

I nodded then continued to leave. When I reached Oanen, I glanced at the hand he still held out, and my pulse sped up. The thought of holding his hand heated my middle. Heck, the thought of touching him in any way sent jolts of naughty and nice through me.

"Come on," Eliana said, grabbing my arm and tugging me from the study. She led us down the hall to the living room she shared with Oanen.

"I hope they let Ashlyn attend the Academy," Eliana said the moment we entered.

"Me too. She's so lonely."

She nodded and sat on the couch.

"Are you staying for dinner?" she asked.

"Eliana, could you give us a minute alone?" Oanen asked.

Her eyes got wide, and she quickly hurried from the room.

"That was weird," I said, turning toward him.

"Not really. Instead of dinner here, let's go somewhere."

My stomach gave an excited flip then began to warm.

"Like a date?" I asked.

"Exactly like a date." I could hear the amusement in his voice.

"Okay." I could barely hear myself over the pounding of my heart.

He smiled slightly then reached for my hand. Warmth exploded inside me at the touch of his fingers against mine.

"You make it difficult to remember my promise when you look at me like that," he said.

"Like what?"

My breath caught when he leaned toward me. I knew what was coming. A kiss. And the thought jacked up the temperature already boiling me from the inside.

He stopped coming closer and just stared into my eyes, the heated look on his face blending with one of awe.

"You are so beautiful when your eyes glow."

He started closing the distance, and the thought of his lips touching mine delayed my reaction to his words. At the last second, I jerked back.

"What?" I said. Without waiting for an answer, I ran to the mirror above the sink in their kitchenette. I stared at myself then looked at him.

"My eyes aren't glowing," I said, seeing the normal brown.

"Not anymore. They were just a second ago. They stopped when you moved."

Panic settled in. Glowing eyes? Adira had mentioned a true form. Was I going through some kind of change? Right now? In front of Oanen?

I swallowed hard.

"I think I'll need to take a raincheck on dinner."

I raced out the door.

CHAPTER THREE

A GOOD NIGHT'S SLEEP AND NO REAPPEARANCE OF GLOWING EYES (or anything else even weirder) had muted some of my panic. But I couldn't let go of the incident. I kept envisioning Adira in her office, one moment human and the next, not. I needed to figure out what Oanen had seen and if it was an omen of something more to come.

After a quick text to Eliana to let her know I didn't need a ride, I drove to the Academy early, determined to scour the library for any reference to furies. Knowing what I was and the purpose behind my existence barely skimmed the surface of the questions I had. There had to be something more about furies. Which of the gods created us, and why had that god thought creating a female with severe anger issues a good idea? What the hell was up with glowing eyes? What else would happen to me?

Adira's comment about me having a true form kept coming back to haunt me. Why did the gods give us two forms? What kind of monster was I really?

Before I knew it, I was driving through Girderon's main gate. Only a few cars sat in the parking lot when I came to a stop, and I walked the quiet halls without interruption.

The library door swung open at my touch. Setting my phone in the basket outside the door, I stepped inside, determined not to leave until I had some answers.

My eagerness faded as I skimmed through book after book. There was plenty of information on other obscure creatures I'd never even heard of. Draugr. Scylla. Níöhöggr. Echidna. Fylgja. Cave dwelling creatures. Snake women. Shapeshifting giants. Yet, nothing on furies except a vague reference in a slim book outlining the beginning of a war between the gods.

I read the meager three pages twice, trying to make sense of the story. But, it wasn't just the reference to furies that was vague. The whole book read that way. Some argument or event had happened that brought even more unrest and conflict to the already discordant gods. The resulting war consumed not only the realms of those squabbling immortals, but also the realm of man. Deaths noted "too numerous to endure" flooded the underworld with souls so greatly that even the furies stopped punishing the living wicked in their need to deliver souls to their master. It didn't say how the war ended, who won, or anything further about the gods or master of the furies. It only described the destroyed world of man, the much beloved mortal world all the gods coveted.

My stomach began to growl loudly long before a knock sounded at the door. I released the book I currently skimmed and let it fly back to its shelf as I stood. This time when I opened the door, Oanen stood against the opposite wall of the hall, his ankles crossed as he leaned in a relaxed pose.

"Expecting to wait a while?" I asked.

"Since that was the third knock, yes."

"Really? Sorry. I didn't think I was that deep into what I was reading. Not when it completely didn't make any sense."

He stayed in his relaxed position and lifted a hand, offering me my phone. Curious why he had it, I stepped closer. It wasn't until he hooked his arms around me that I understood he'd used it as bait. Before I could protest, he tugged me close.

I tripped forward, colliding with his chest, and he grinned down at me. One arm weighing against my waist, he lifted a hand and brushed the backs of his fingers along my jaw.

"Have dinner with me tonight, Megan."

I stared up at him with wide eyes as I struggled to breathe normally and swallow past the sudden dryness in my throat.

"Why are you so afraid of a simple dinner?" His soft question sent a shiver of hunger through me. The way he'd said it, I knew that dinner with Oanen wouldn't be simple. It would be full of his heated looks and my increasingly harder to deny need to touch him. A date with Oanen would likely end with a lot more than the touching we were doing now.

My gaze dipped to his mouth as I imagined just how we would end our night.

"Megan, I will break every promise I made to behave if you give in to what you're thinking right now."

I lifted my gaze to his and braced my hands on his shoulders. He started closing the distance.

"You are so incredibly warm," he said.

His exhale tickled my lips.

"Megan. Oanen. May I interrupt for a moment?" Adira asked, her voice coming from right behind us.

I jumped and jerked back. Oanen sighed and released me. Turning with an embarrassed flush, I faced Adira. The woman smiled kindly and addressed Oanen.

"I apologize for the intrusion. I heard you ask about dinner and was wondering if you could postpone it. There are a few liaison duties that require Megan's attention tonight."

She focused on me.

"We would like you to meet us at the Quills' residence after you're finished here. There are a few human recruits we want you to meet."

Any remnants of the good feelings I had from touching Oanen fled in a hurry.

"You're bringing more humans to Uttira after the talk we had?"

"Yes. But, it is because of your talk. As you said, humans are not solitary creatures. We believe that bringing more here not only replaces those we've lost but will help the ones who remain. I will see you after sessions."

Before I could open my mouth to argue further, she disappeared. Just vanished.

"Argh! I want to hit her," I said, looking up at Oanen. "All of them. They didn't hear a single thing I said. Bringing more humans won't fix anything for the humans already here. Why can't they see that?"

He reached for my hand, threading his fingers through mine.

"They will see. You'll make sure of that. Come on. Let's get you something to eat before your stomach gets any louder."

He began to lead me down the hall. I gently tugged my hand from his before my heart exploded, then wrinkled my nose as I realized I'd forgotten to eat breakfast and hadn't brought a lunch.

"I'll need to get a tray today," I said.

"Why? I packed you a lunch," he said, not commenting on my withdrawal.

"Thank you. You really didn't need to do that though."

He looked at me. "Did you enjoy yesterday's lunch?"

"Yes. It tasted better than anything I could make for myself."

"Then I'll keep making them."

The butterflies those words sent flying in my stomach had nothing to do with hunger.

We joined Eliana on the lawn outside. I sat beside Eliana, and

Oanen sat on the opposite side of me, his thigh touching mine. Doing my best to ignore the contact, I handed him his lunch bag and opened the one he'd made for me.

"I can't find anything useful in that library," I said a moment before taking my first bite.

"I'm not surprised," Eliana said. "I mean, if you think about it, our kind was created before the written word was hugely popular. Most of our history would have been passed down verbally through the years. The stuff that's in there is likely from modern times when knowing how to read and write became more commonplace."

"Then why am I wasting my time in there?"

"Because some information is better than no information," Eliana said. "Adira doesn't do things that are a waste of time. If she wanted you to read the books, there's a reason."

"I wish she'd just tell me what that reason is."

"That's not how she works," Oanen said. "She's all about self-discovery and the importance of the struggle to gain knowledge. She says it gives the knowledge more meaning."

I sighed and kept eating my sandwich. How could struggling to learn the truth give the truth any more meaning than it had? It made no sense to me. However, as much as the library frustrated me, it was better than spending the day stuck in a classroom with other students.

The Quills were waiting for me at the door as soon as I came to a stop. Overhead, a familiar griffin soared, gliding on the currents and disappearing behind the large stone home. Oanen had followed me from the Academy. Likely, Eliana wasn't far behind. Although I wouldn't mind waiting for her, I knew that if I didn't hurry, I'd likely encounter a shirtless Oanen somewhere on the second floor. That motivated me to move. However, I wasn't sure if it was to meet up with him or avoid him.

The cold October wind whipped my hair around my head the moment I got out of the car and rushed for the house.

Mrs. Quill smiled as I approached, and she offered me something to drink while Mr. Quill shut the door behind me.

"We have cider we could warm," she said.

"I'm fine. Thank you, though."

She nodded and led the way to the study. I didn't catch any hint of Oanen prowling the hallways, and any chance of interruption or eavesdropping ended the minute Mr. Quill closed the study doors behind us.

"Adira will be here in a few minutes," he said. "We should have a seat."

I took the chair facing the sofa. It gave me a good view of the room so I'd know the moment Adira did her magic appearance portal. The shimmer appeared only moments after I took a seat.

Adira stepped through first, followed by a boy around my age. I tried to hold back my initial surge of anger and took a moment to study him. Adira directed him to sit on the couch across from me and moved to stand behind him as he hesitated. I paid her little attention while I continued my scrutiny.

His dark hair fell in disarray around his head as his equally dark eyes flitted around the room, landing briefly on each of us. He looked unwashed and angry.

"Have a seat Michael," Adira said.

The boy sat with a look of belligerence in his eyes.

"I don't know what the hell is going on, but I want my fifty bucks," he said.

"Nothing bad is going to happen to you here," Mrs. Quill said. "We just wanted to introduce you to Megan."

All three adults looked at me. I didn't take my eyes off the boy.

"Hello, Michael," I said.

He stared at me without any hint of fear, and I didn't like that. Not one bit.

"Megan, we were considering inviting Michael to live in Uttira," Adira said, "and we would like your opinion."

"Don't you think you should be asking me my opinion on that?" Michael asked. "I like living where I'm at."

I continued to gaze at the boy, my anger rising. Why?

"Where do you live, Michael?" I asked.

"Depends on the night. I live wherever I want."

"Where do you live, Michael?" I asked again. My voice had changed though. I could hear the anger in it this time.

"New York. What's it to you?"

"I found him alone, living on the streets," Adira said softly.

Homeless. That fact didn't change the anger I felt toward him. Fury anger.

"What did you do, Michael?" I asked, leaning forward, wishing the coffee table weren't separating us.

"I don't know what you're talking about," he said.

"You've done something. Something not good. Tell me what you've done." I waited, focused on him, wanting to know his crime. I could feel it in my blood. In my bones. The anger…the rage…boiling hotter with each passing second.

"Tell me," I said again. "Confess your crimes." The words felt so right on my lips. And the need to scream them at him rose, nearly choking me. I struggled to control the urge.

"Confess," I said angrily. "Tell me what you've done."

Michael leaned forward suddenly, his eyes blazing with hate.

"I don't know what level of crazy you are, bitch; but you need to get out of my face."

I opened my mouth, ready to give into the urge, when Adira

reached forward and set a hand on his shoulder, making them both disappear. The anger immediately vanished, but annoyance reared its head.

"That's who you want to bring here to keep Ashlyn company? That guy was—"

"Completely unsuitable," Mr. Quill said. "I hope you'll find the next one a better fit."

"The next one?"

"Yes, we have several candidates."

He'd barely finished speaking when the shimmer reappeared in the center of the room. This time Adira had two girls with her.

"Megan, this is Kelsey and Zoe. Sisters from Chicago."

The girls looked a little younger, maybe fourteen and fifteen years old. It wasn't their fearful expressions or ragged appearances that made my eyes water. It was the overwhelming odor.

"Hi," I said. "Not to be rude, but what is that smell?"

"Sewer," the older one said.

"Both you guys need a shower. The clothes need to be burned." I looked at the Quills. "I don't like what you're doing. Of course they'll say yes to whatever you offer them if you're pulling them from the sewers."

"No," one of the girls said. "We won't say yes to anything." She looked at Adira. "You said fifty dollars each to face a lie detector about how we ended up on the streets. We thought you were some kind of doctor. What was that glowing thing? Where are we?"

"You're in Uttira, a small town in northern Maine," Adira said. "The glowing thing was a portal. If you'd like to hear more, you're welcome to sit, and I'll answer whatever questions you have. If you'd rather leave, you only need to say so. I'll return you to your home and compensate you as promised."

The older sister glanced at the younger one.

"Let's just take the money, Kells. I don't like this place," the younger sister said.

"Most days, I don't either," I agreed.

Kelsey looked at me, frowning slightly.

"You might not like it, but you don't smell like someone else's crap, and you're not wearing the same clothes from a week ago." She turned to Adira. "We won't sit, but we'll listen."

"Uttira is a town for creatures created by gods long ago forgotten."

Zoe made a sound and said, "I told you," under her breath. I caught the word crazy too.

"It's easier to provide proof than to try to explain. Have you ever heard of a griffin?" Adira asked.

The doors to the study opened just then and Oanen strode in. His gaze met mine briefly then went to the two girls.

"Thank you for joining us, Oanen," his mother said.

He nodded and reached up for his shirt.

My chest cramped painfully as I understood that my newly acquired boyfriend planned to strip in front of these two girls.

"Since I already know griffins are real, I'll be going," I said.

I stood swiftly and started for the door.

"This is Oanen," Adira said, ignoring my exit. "He's a young griffin. He can choose to look like a human or—"

Just as I reached him, Oanen shifted with his pants still on, cutting off Adira's explanation. The metal button from his fly pinged off the wall by the door. Both girls screamed. The griffin paid them little attention. He moved quickly, stepping in front of me and blocking my exit.

I skidded to a halt, and he lifted his head. The feathers of his cheek brushed mine as he worried the hair by my right ear. Exhaling loudly, I reached up and smoothed my hand along his neck.

"You're lucky you sacrificed the pants," I whispered.

He clacked his beak twice then turned and left the room without shifting again. Realizing the girls had grown completely quiet, I faced the others. The girls gripped each other, their fear already having robbed them of color and voice. Adira and the Quills watched me with indecipherable expressions. Had Oanen told them we were together now? Or at least trying to be together?

Unsure and uncomfortable, I focused on the girls.

"It's real," I said. "The myths and legends we've heard are based on some very old truths. Werewolves exist. Griffins exist. Furies exist. That doesn't change the world you know, just your understanding of it. And you are as safe now as you were before you came here. Do you understand? Nothing's changed but your knowledge of the truth."

Kelsey nodded jerkily.

Mrs. Quill took over speaking.

"Adira brought you here to offer you a new opportunity. A new life. You could live here in Uttira. You would have your own home. All your bills would be paid. You would receive a human education and would want for nothing. In return, we ask that you help us teach the young of Uttira what it means to be human."

Kelsey met my gaze.

"What's the catch?" Her voice shook still.

"The catch is that you can't leave. Ever."

"Untrue," Adira said. "You can leave at any time. But we would remove any memory of your time here as a precaution to keep us, and you, safe."

"So we'd live here for the rest of our lives with everything paid for as long as we teach your young?" Kelsey hesitated over the last word, and her gaze flicked toward the door where Oanen had disappeared.

"Correct," Mrs. Quill said. "You would not teach all day,

every day. While you're underage, you will focus on school and be asked to spend eight hours a week helping us. Your free time would be your own. Once you graduate, we would ask that you work forty hours a week, choosing from the jobs available in Uttira. You would receive pay in addition to the housing and support to which you will have grown accustomed."

I could see in their eyes that they would say yes. My stomach soured, and I felt like I'd just lost an important battle.

CHAPTER FOUR

THE NEXT MORNING, ELIANA'S CAR ALREADY SAT IN THE OTHERWISE vacant parking lot. She leaned against her trunk, obviously waiting for me. I parked beside her and killed the engine.

"You shouldn't have taken off so fast last night," Eliana said as soon as I opened my car door.

"Eh, I'm pretty sure it was the safest choice for all of us."

I still felt pissy that the Council had trapped two more humans because of the desperation of their circumstances.

"Well, you missed the exciting news," Eliana said. "At dinner, Mr. and Mrs. Quill talked about Ashlyn and her need for more interaction. They've decided to let her attend the Academy if she wants. And not just Ashlyn. The new girls, too, once they're ready. And the Quills were asking me all sorts of questions about the things I remembered about the human world. I think they're considering building a library."

She grinned at me.

"Not bad liaising, Megan. You've started making some positive changes in just a few days."

"That's great." I returned her smile with one I didn't feel.

Although the changes truly sounded great, they didn't alter

the way I felt about this place. Like a fish in a bowl with too little water, Uttira was beginning to feel suffocating. Maybe it wasn't Uttira but my own skin. After Oanen's spontaneous change from human to griffin last night, I couldn't stop wondering when that would happen to me.

"I need to get to the library," I said.

"Yeah. I know. Oanen's waiting for you inside. Maybe we can hang out soon?"

"Sure," I said, already moving toward the doors.

My rush wasn't to reach Oanen faster but to get to the books. However, the need for answers vanished when I turned the corner to the hall for the library. Oanen paced before the door. As soon as he heard me, he stopped. His gaze swept over me before settling on my face.

"Are you angry?" he asked as I approached.

"Want to hit something angry? No. Feeling a little frustrated? Yes." I stopped in front of him and tried not to notice the way the sleeves of his t-shirt hugged his biceps.

"I'm sorry about last night," he said.

His sincerity made me smile.

"What part exactly? Where you started stripping in front of two other girls or when you bit my hair?"

He cocked his head and considered me for a moment.

"You're not frustrated with me," he said with certainty and just a hint of relief.

"No. I'm not. I'm frustrated with this town and this stupid library filled with useless books."

He reached out and pulled me into his arms without warning. I melted into the embrace and let myself lean against his hard chest. I might have even closed my eyes and inhaled the scent of him. I couldn't be sure exactly because I was drowning in pure Oanen. The way we fit together. The way he held me, so tender yet so firm. It felt like I'd found where I belonged. Like I finally had a reason to be in Uttira.

His hands drifted over my back in a soothing, non-groping way.

"Don't let frustration get to you. You won't be stuck here forever."

He pulled back slightly, and I reluctantly released my hold on him.

"We'll get our marks soon enough and be able to go anywhere."

I nodded, not voicing my doubts. Would they let me leave if I no longer looked like me?

"I'll come get you at lunch. And we'll talk about our dinner date. Tonight. I'm not taking no for an answer."

I threw the book in frustration. Before it could hit the wall, it changed course and slipped into its correct place on the shelf. I'd skimmed through over half the books in the library without seeing a single new reference to furies. There were more creatures than I thought possible. And if furies weren't mentioned in this collection, there was the very real possibility others weren't mentioned as well.

A knock sounded on the door. Ready to be finished with the day, I hurried to answer it.

"Any luck this afternoon?" Oanen asked.

During lunch, I'd vented about how my search for specific information was turning up nothing. Of course, I'd gone mute when trying to say what information. But, Oanen and Eliana had both encouraged me to keep trying before talk had turned to the impending date night and Eliana had fled.

"No. No luck." I stepped from the library and joined him in the hall. We started the walk to the parking lot exit.

"Don't give up. Talk to Adira. She might be able to point you in the right direction."

I rolled my eyes. To date, Adira hadn't been forthcoming with any information about me. Everything I'd learned, I'd learned on my own.

"Since you didn't say a time when you wanted dinner, I thought I'd come over at five," he said, changing the subject and creating a storm of nervousness that swirled in my stomach.

"Want me to bring anything?" he asked when I remained silent.

"No. I'll make everything."

Mostly just so I'd have less time to worry about what we'd do after dinner.

"Your heart's racing again," he said as he opened the door for me.

"Because the idea of having a dinner alone with you in my house is making me nervous," I said frankly.

"Would you rather go to a restaurant?"

"And risk someone ticking me off in the middle of our first date? No."

Oanen chuckled.

"I'll see you later then."

He didn't try to hug me goodbye, but he sure made it awkward by pulling off his shirt.

"I really don't like when you do that."

"I thought your issue was with someone else seeing." He handed me his shirt and cocked a brow, his hands hesitating at the fly of his jeans.

Many of the cars had already cleared the lot, including Eliana's.

"Just do whatever you're going to do, bird boy. I have a

dinner to make." I turned around, ready to get in my car and leave. A pair of jeans hit me in my back.

I shook my head at the sound of his beating wings and turned around to pick up his discarded clothes.

"I changed my mind," I called. "You bring the dessert. And make it good since I keep having to pick up after you."

His eagle scream answered me as he climbed higher. Taking his clothes to the car, I sent a quick text to Eliana, promising to hang out with her Friday night, then started the trip home.

The internet and a stocked fridge kept me busy for the next two hours as I put together the mozzarella-stuffed chicken parmesan and a Caesar salad.

When I finished, I debated changing what I wore, which reminded me that I still had Oanen's clothes in the car. Playing it safe, I fetched his things and left them on the porch before settling in the living room to watch some TV.

I clicked through the channels absently, tension robbing me of the ability to focus. Nervous was a new thing for me, and I hated it. But, there was just something about Oanen. The more we spent time together, the more I was drawn to him.

The knock on the back door made my pulse jump. Wiping my hands on my jeans, I went to answer it.

Barefoot and holding a foil-wrapped pan, Oanen waited on the porch.

"Thanks for leaving out the clothes," he said, a slight grin tugging the corner of his mouth.

"Thanks for putting them on."

I stepped aside and let him in.

"It smells amazing in here. Lasagna?" he asked.

"No." I closed the door and followed him to the table, which I'd already set. "I figured you had that once already, so I went with something different. Stuffed chicken parmesan. What did you bring?"

He set the pan down and removed the foil.

"Eliana swore that you meant something chocolate when you said bring dessert."

I hungrily eyed the powdered brownies.

"Eliana is very wise," I said. "Ready to eat?"

"Sure."

We sat and started with the salad. My stomach wouldn't stop freaking out. Neither would my racing pulse. Although I knew he could hear it, he didn't comment.

"Eliana mentioned you two might be going to the Roost Friday," he said after I served him some salad.

When I'd texted her, I'd said to let me know where and when she wanted to hang out. I'd rather hoped she would pick a movie night at my house.

"I guess. She wanted to hang out."

"You don't seem too enthused."

I sighed and played with my salad.

"It's not that. I do want to hang out with her. I'm just feeling off."

"Sick?"

"I've never been sick in my life."

"Me either. Just checking, though. So what is it?"

"I don't know. I'm just feeling…" I closed my eyes and tried to release the tension that had crept into my shoulders.

His hand closed over mine, trapping my idly moving fork. I opened my eyes and met his gaze.

"You can talk to me," he said. "About anything."

"Okay," I said, knowing he meant it. I took a deep calming breath and spilled my biggest worry.

"Adira said that how I look now isn't my true form, and I'm freaking out about what I might turn into. I don't know what I'll look like. When I'll change. Nothing."

"That's what you've been looking for in the library?" His thumb smoothed over the back of my hand.

"Yes, which really ticks me off for so many different reasons. What's the point of a super-secret library that almost no one can use if it barely contains any information? And, if I don't exist there, what else is missing? It's like I'm watching every other episode of a crime series. How can I piece everything together and see the full picture if I don't have all the clues?"

"Remember when I said Adira is big on struggling for knowledge? It's the same for self-discovery. You'll figure this out."

"Before or after I turn into some raving monster?"

He released my hand and sat back in his chair.

"Is that how you see my true form? As a monster?"

He didn't look or sound angry, but that didn't stop my guilt.

"No. I like your feathers and wings."

"And my beak?"

"It's growing on me," I said with a slight smile.

"Your true form won't be any more monstrous than mine. And, while it might be different and take some time for you to get used to, you'll accept it as part of who you are. So will I."

"You're so getting an extra brownie for that," I said, picking up my fork. "Have I been missing anything fun by hiding in the library?"

"Not really. We've moved on to practical demonstration for the second half of the semester. I've successfully mastered the art of ordering takeout food."

"I hope you understand how useless that is."

"Useless to you and me but there are some who do need the practice. Remember the troll, Epsid? He tried ordering bone dust as a pizza topping."

"Wow." I finished my salad and excused myself to remove the chicken parmesan from the oven.

"Why are the parents not teaching these skills to their children at a younger age? If they learn from really early on, this wouldn't be such a big deal now."

"Some kinds hide their young away from everyone until they reach eleven or twelve. By then, certain concepts are already set."

"Like eating human bones."

"Yeah."

I served Oanen one of the stuffed breasts along with a bed of angel hair pasta then served myself.

"I can't wait to see what you make for our next date," he said, cutting into his portion.

"Oh, I'm not cooking for the next one. You are."

He looked up at me, a grin pulling his lips.

"That's a deal. What kind of foods do you like?"

"Anything really. I've never been very picky."

We continued discussing favorite foods, books, movies, colors, and any other bit of information he could pull from me, or I from him, as we finished dinner. The conversation didn't stop at the table. It flowed through the clean-up and into the living room. There, it died a sudden death when he sat on the couch and patted the spot beside him.

"Do you want to watch a movie?" I asked, nervous once more.

"Yes."

Since I already knew he liked fantasy and science fiction because it amused him how wrong the movie industry got things, I picked out something that sounded interesting.

"Are you going to stand the rest of the night?" he asked when I hesitated to set the remote down and join him.

"Maybe."

"Megan." He stood and held out his hand over the coffee table. I clasped it and let him reel me toward his side. Without letting go, he sat then tugged my fingers until I sat beside him. Like the hug in the hallway, it felt right to lean into his side.

I turned my head and looked up at him. Our faces were close. Deliciously close. My pulse hitched higher.

"What are you so nervous about?" he asked, studying me.

I swallowed hard and went for brutal honesty, as usual.

"Kissing you."

"Why?"

"I don't know."

"Then, I think maybe we should just get it out of the way."

He closed the distance between us and lightly pressed his lips to mine. A bolt of heat shot through me at first contact. I inhaled deeply through my nose and reached for his shoulders, desperate for an anchor. He opened his mouth and licked the seam of my lips. I answered his silent plea and let him in. My senses flooded with the taste and feel of him, and I groaned. He changed the angle of the kiss a moment before his arms slid around me, pulling me into his lap.

A desperation crawled into my blood. A burning need to consume. To take. To release the wild thing I'd felt for Oanen since the moment he'd squatted beside me on the road.

I broke the kiss with a gasp for air.

He leaned forward and rested his forehead just over my pounding heart. His ragged breathing blended with mine for several long moments.

"Still nervous?" he asked.

"No. Now, I'm terrified."

And I mostly meant it. That out of control feeling now lingered just beneath the surface. It felt like I'd unlocked something, and despite his reassurances during dinner, I didn't want to know what.

"Me too," he said softly. He lifted his head and met my gaze. "I'm terrified of losing you."

He tucked me more firmly against his chest then nodded toward the TV.

It took some effort to pull my gaze from his perfect face and watch the show, but I managed. His fingers wove slow circles over the skin of my arm, relaxing me enough that my heart began to settle into its normal rhythm.

One moment I sat at the library table, frustrated with yet another book that told me nothing about what I would become; the next, I lay on the couch, pinned between Oanen and the back cushions.

A dream.

I snuggled into him, enjoying the cool feel of his chest against my hands. He made a sound in his sleep. Something between a moan and a groan. I slid my hand up over his shoulder, smoothing over the back of his neck, not stopping until my fingers touched his hair. Lifting my lips to his, I kissed him.

His tongue immediately danced with mine. Fire heated me, inside and out. This time, I let go of everything and lost myself to the feeling of being in Oanen's arms. Of his desperate kiss.

A sharp smell tickled my nose. Burned hair, like the day I'd tried to leave the barrier.

The remembered smell jerked me from my dream that wasn't a dream. I opened my eyes and saw we were on the couch, but it was daylight.

With a gasp, I pulled back from Oanen.

"Best way to wake up," he rumbled, a sleepy grin tugging his lips. He opened his eyes, and the hint of his grin faded.

"Your eyes are glowing again," he said softly.

I flew off the couch and ran for the bathroom. This time, I caught the glow before it faded. I clutched the sink, staring as the normal brown replaced the vibrant orange. Then I started to shake.

"Megan, it's okay," Oanen said from behind me. "Your eyes are amazing no matter what the color."

I faced him, my gaze falling on the scorch mark on his pale blue t-shirt. A handprint on his right shoulder.

"My eyes aren't the only thing changing, though, are they. Turn around and show me your back."

His expression, always so carefully guarded, changed ever so slightly. Worry.

"Megan, it's fine," he said.

My stomach cramped with fear and self-loathing.

"Turn around, Oanen, or leave."

He sighed and turned around. The skin on the back of his neck was red as if sun burned. That wasn't the worst of it. Some of his hair had melted all the way to his scalp. I could see the outline of three of my fingers.

"This can't be real," I said to myself. "This isn't happening."

He turned toward me.

"Megan, we all go through some awkward changes. This is no different. You'll be fine."

"Me? I could have hurt you."

"No. You can't. You'll see. By lunch, you won't even be able to tell anything happened."

My thoughts jumped, connecting what he said with what I needed to do. Lunch. The Academy. Talk to Adira.

"Yeah. Sure," I agreed, feeling sick. "You're right. It'll be fine. I need to—" I swallowed hard. "I need to get ready. I'll see you at school, okay?"

He stepped forward and pulled me into a hug, holding me tightly.

"I know you're panicking. I can hear it," he said against my temple.

"After what I just did, I'm allowed some panic time."

"Fine. But if you don't show up at the Academy, I will come, and I will find you. Because one little burn hasn't changed a thing. I still want you."

He pressed a kiss to my forehead then left.

CHAPTER FIVE

I STILL HADN'T STOPPED SHAKING BY THE TIME I PULLED INTO THE Academy parking lot. What the hell had I done? Although the practical, human-centric part of my brain wanted to dwell on the fact that I'd kissed Oanen first thing in the morning without brushing my teeth, the bigger non-human issue won.

"I almost cooked my damn boyfriend," I said under my breath. Who did that? What the hell was wrong with me?

Weeks ago, my mom had come to this place and registered me as a student. I'd seen the file Adira had on me. "Fury. Fourth Generation," it had read. Although additional information had been almost non-existent, the note had been there. Made by Adira. Likely, the very person my mom had talked to. Maybe Adira knew more. But, would she be willing to share what she knew? Probably not. And that really pissed me off.

I got out of the car and slammed the door, the early morning noise startling the few birds still in the skeletal, late-fall trees. Their flight brought my attention to the roof.

Oanen stood at the edge, looking down at me. My pulse jumped at the sight of him.

Crap.

Another car pulled into the lot as we studied each other. I needed a way to distract him for a few minutes so he wouldn't try to meet up with me in the hall. I really wanted to talk to Adira alone.

"I forgot my lunch again," I called. "I hope you had time to pack me something good. And a brownie. I really could go for another one of those."

"Yeah," a guy said with a laugh. "Now we're talking."

I glanced back at the guy and girl crossing the parking lot.

"Heathen," the girl said, giving me, then him, a glare.

"What?" he said. "Brownie wings are considered a delicacy by just about everyone. It's not like the brownie dies. Why do you think so many of them don't have wings?"

The guy winked as he passed me. The girl stomped ahead. I stood there in complete horrified shock. I would never be able to eat the chocolate dessert again.

Recalling Oanen and my request for the brownie, I looked up; but he was gone. Hopefully, on his way to get me lunch instead of wandering the halls.

Impatient to find Adira before Oanen found me, I jogged into school and headed toward her office. Oanen didn't appear in the halls, and I reached Adira's door without problem. Pausing for a moment, I took a deep breath to shake off some of my agitation before knocking.

"Come in," she called.

I opened the door, relieved she was in early, and quickly took the seat across from her desk.

"Good morning, Megan," she said, closing the folder in front of her. "You look upset. Is everything all right?"

"No."

Now that I sat in front of her, I realized the stupidity of my action. Did I really want to admit I had a dream about making out with Oanen then woke up to find out I'd actually been making out with him and burned him in the process? No. I one hundred percent did not want to talk to her about that.

"What happened?" she asked when I remained quiet.

"I, uh, think I almost started a fire in my sleep."

She smiled her usual, kind smile.

"There is absolutely nothing to worry about. Your house has been warded against fire, the same as the Academy, Roost, and any other public place. That means the structure and everything within it will never suffer any damage from flames created normally or magically."

"Oh." Her calm answer confirmed two things. She did know what I'd become because she hadn't denied the possibility that I could start a fire. And, whatever I would become did indeed have the ability to burn things.

"You see?" she said. "You have nothing to worry about."

Oh, I had plenty to worry about. If the house and everything inside of it was protected, then how had I managed to burn Oanen? Instead of demanding answers that I knew she'd be unlikely to give, I struggled to find a hole in her logic.

"How can I cook then? I mean, the stove is technically damaging everything I cook, isn't it?"

"The flames aren't damaging the food. They heat the pan which cooks the food. A loophole."

Maybe Oanen was a loophole, too, somehow. I needed to know how to make him not a loophole.

A piece of what she'd said finally registered. Why ward all the public places against fire along with my home? And why point that out to me? Because whatever was happening was going to get worse?

"I'm worried I might accidently hurt someone because I have no idea what's happening to me. But you do. And I'm struggling not to be completely pissed off that you're not telling me what I need to know." I met her steady gaze. "Not just what

I am now but what I'll become. My true form. And it must be pretty bad if you've warded most of the town against me."

She folded her hands on the desk and leaned toward me with worry in her gaze.

"Not against you. From accidental fire. Megan, right now, you're focusing on all the wrong things. You need to concentrate on what's important.

"Continue to study the information in the library and perform your tasks as temporary liaison, which does require your attention. Ashlyn is due to visit the lake later this evening. She needs you to accompany her. I suggest you spend your time focusing on water dwelling creatures rather than a fruitless search about your lineage's history."

"So there's nothing about furies in the Academy library?" I asked.

"No. Nothing useful. Shall I tell Ashlyn to expect you after the final bell?"

"Yeah. Sure," I said, standing and moving toward the door, seeking escape before I did something really stupid.

"Megan," she called before I could step out.

"Yeah?"

"Your hands are fisted. If you've sensed someone wicked, you need to tell me. We don't want any more incidents like Trammer."

"No. No one wicked," I said. Just a crap ton of people being narrow-minded and getting on my nerves.

I left her office and went straight to the library.

For the next three hours, I learned what I could about hippocamp, naiads, mermaids, sirens, and many other water dwelling creatures. The scant details on how to identify them, what they liked to eat, and their preferred habitats didn't amount to much. If it had all been in one book, it would have taken me thirty minutes to read.

By the time Oanen knocked, my frustration at the information in the library had pushed back thoughts of what had happened that morning. The way his intense gaze locked onto me the moment I opened the door, though, brought it all back. The skin along his neck didn't look red anymore, but he'd gotten his hair cut closer to his head, a sure sign the hair hadn't magically grown back. Guilt and fear kicked me in the gut. We were making a mistake pretending I could be what he wanted.

"Don't," he said, snagging the front of my shirt and tugging me the rest of the way from the room.

"Don't what?"

"Run and hide. That's not an option for either of us."

Maybe not for him, but it seemed like a decent option to me.

"Did you bring me lunch?" I asked, needing to change the subject.

"Of course."

We walked through the cafeteria and found two bags waiting in our normal spot.

"Brownies, as requested. The kind without wings," he said, handing me one of the lunch bags.

"Thanks. Where's Eliana?"

"Spending some time with Ashlyn, getting her ready to start attending school next week. Mom took them shopping outside Uttira. Eliana convinced Mom that humans skipped school all the time and a day away from Uttira would make Ashlyn feel better. How about you? Today going any better?"

The tension coiled inside me, along with the ever-present need to just hit something, made the answer pretty clear.

"Not really. Adira told me to quit trying to find anything about furies because it's not there. So I'm reading about—"

The stupid spell kicked in, and I lost my voice. Rolling my eyes, I took a bite of my sandwich.

Oanen chuckled and started eating, too.

My break from the infuriating monotony of the library ended too quickly. After Oanen walked me back, I struggled to focus on the words on the pages before me.

A restlessness crawled under my skin, much like it had back when I lived in the city with Mom, so I gave up and lifted my hand from the book. As it slid neatly back into place, I collected my phone on the way out. I didn't care that it was still the middle of the day.

I wanted to hurt something, and I didn't want that to happen here, not with Oanen around. I sent him a quick text to let him know I was leaving early then drove home.

However, being home didn't help my mood. I stood in the kitchen for one undecided moment then left again, on foot. While running in the city hadn't been smart for me, running here posed much less of a problem. Especially with so many of my peers occupied at the Academy. So, I let loose and sprinted toward the barrier, the only other place I knew that wasn't in town.

I didn't stop running until the winding road straightened out, and I felt the tingle of magic on my skin and could smell the lingering odor of burnt hair. Not even winded, I turned around and headed back the way I'd come.

When I arrived home for the second time, I felt a little better and went for a shower.

Ashlyn walked out of her house as soon as I pulled up. She didn't smile or wave as she walked toward my car and got in. Her eyes looked slightly red like she'd been crying. After a day of shopping, I would have thought she'd feel a little better.

"Is everything okay?" I asked.

"Yeah." She buckled her seatbelt and faced straight ahead.

"Um…try again because I'm not buying that answer."

She turned to look at me, tears welling in her eyes.

"I had fun today shopping with Eliana and Mrs. Quill."

She said it like she was confessing to a crime. Since I didn't want to punch her, I doubted any crimes were actually involved. So, I waited patiently for more information.

She sniffled and wiped at her eyes.

"My uncle just died, and I was eating at a mall and laughing. What kind of person am I?"

I considered her for a moment.

"A sane one," I said. "I don't know what death means for the people who are leaving us, but I know what it means for the people left behind. It means hurting. But, only at first. The pain starts to ease to let the memories in. The good ones. We're meant to remember. To smile and laugh. It honors the one who has left us.

"People aren't meant to live forever, Ashlyn. We will all die at some point. What we do in this life will influence how we're remembered by those we leave behind. We're supposed to keep living even as we say goodbye and remember those who have already departed. You did nothing wrong."

She nodded and wiped her eyes again. Seeing that she was pulling herself together, I eased from the curb.

"You've lost someone?" she asked.

I paused, wondering how I'd known to say what I'd said.

"No, I've never had anyone to lose," I said. "It must have been something I heard my mom say at some point."

But I knew it wasn't.

We drove in silence only interrupted by Ashlyn's quiet directions to whatever lake we were going to. The term "lake" did not correctly describe our destination. I saw it through the trees as I made the last turn. The enormous body of water shimmered in the evening sunlight.

The road ended with a gravel parking area, a portion of the space sloping directly into the lake's edge. A slim trail led to a pier that extended at least twenty feet into the water. A bench beckoned at the end of it.

"Wow. It's pretty out here," I said, pulling to a stop.

"Yeah. I guess."

Ashlyn got out and started walking. I followed, wondering at her tone.

At the end of the pier, a fishing pole and tackle box waited on the bench. She picked up the pole, added a fake lure, and gave an impressive cast. I wasn't sure what I'd expected her to do, but fishing hadn't even come close.

"I've never been fishing," I said, sitting on the bench. "Is it hard?"

"I don't think what I'm doing qualifies as fishing," Ashlyn said.

"What are you doing then?"

"Letting the lake people know I'm here, I guess."

I looked out over the still waters and thought of all the creatures likely in its depths.

"Why?"

"Some of them can't or won't come to the Roost for practice. So I come here. They learn how to avoid the hooks that fishermen cast out, and they attempt to lure me into the waters."

"How do they do that?"

"Sometimes they sing. Sometimes they try to trick me."

"Have they ever gotten you into the water?"

"If they had, I wouldn't be standing here. My uncle was good at keeping me safe."

A twinge of pity rose for Ashlyn. This was something the Council had forced her to do. Something she'd always done with her uncle. They hadn't even given her a week to grieve before sending her back out again. This time with me.

The restless feeling I'd thought I'd exercised away returned, and my mind raced to find a topic that would distract us both.

"What did you think of shopping with Eliana? Was she picking out crazy outfits for you to try on?"

Ashlyn snorted a laugh.

"Yep. It was pretty weird. She kept picking out little girl type clothes for herself but handing me clothes that would make a prostitute blush," she said.

I chuckled.

"She did the same to me. Did you find anything interesting?"

She glanced back at me with a smile.

"Lots of stuff. Wanna see a picture?"

With one hand, she held the pole. With the other, she reached for the phone in her pocket. The device caught on her shirt and tumbled from her fingers toward the water.

Time slowed as she grabbed for the falling phone.

I started to stand to tell her to leave it as a green-grey arm rose from the water. The webbed fingers clamped around Ashlyn's arm and tugged. Ashlyn, already leaning forward, lost her balance and crashed into the water with a splash.

Without a thought, I dove in after her.

In the murky depths of the lake, I saw Ashlyn's struggling form caught by a creature with a tail and a mass of green hair. I grabbed a fist full of the floating tendrils and pulled hard.

The creature screeched, the sound hurting my ears even under water. Releasing Ashlyn, it turned and swiped at me. Its nails raked over the skin covering my ribs, just below my left breast. Pain ignited, burning me from the inside.

As I choked on rage and water, an orange light grew before me, illuminating enough that I could vaguely see the shape of a face through the hair. I drew back my fist and hit hard, the water barely slowing me.

The creature's head snapped back. Her whipping tail stilled, and she slowly sank. Not taking a chance, I gave her face an extra kick.

Whirling toward the tug on my arm, I drew back, ready for more until I saw Ashlyn. As soon as I faced her, she started toward the surface. I followed, breaking through seconds after her.

"Get out, quick," I said, pushing her toward a ladder fixed to the end of the pier.

She scrambled up and flopped onto the deck, staring at the sky as she gasped, coughed, and sputtered.

"Are you all right?" I asked, kneeling beside her.

"Fine," she rasped. "Damn phone."

I stood.

"I want that phone found and returned now," I shouted at the lake.

A minute later the device came soaring out of the water, straight for my head. I caught it easily and glared at the placid surface. I wanted to jump back in and beat the shit out of anyone I could find.

"Does it still work?" Ashlyn asked, sounding a bit better.

I looked at the phone, saw the lit screen, and handed it to her.

Her expression grew a little wary as I held it out.

"What?"

She flinched a little at my tone. I hadn't been able to keep the anger out of it.

"I'm not mad at you," I said.

She nodded and tentatively accepted the phone.

"I figured. I've just never seen your eyes do that."

"Do what?"

"Glow with flames."

"That makes two of us. I think we're done here. I'll drive you home."

I helped her to her feet and, ignoring the pain in my ribs, returned her to town.

Once I was alone in the car, I lifted my shirt and looked at the three cuts marring my skin and oozing a dark green slime.

"Fucking mermaids."

CHAPTER SIX

LIGHTNING HIT ME REPEATEDLY, SCORCHING THE SKIN OF MY stomach and creating a funnel of agony that sank into my very bones. I lay on the ground, unable to move and struggling to breathe. The dark mists floating around me created a damp film on my skin, adding to my misery.

Another bolt hit. I opened my mouth and screamed long and loud, raging at the skies to leave me in peace. The sound of my ragged inhale changed my surroundings.

The mists dissolved, and I blinked up at my bedroom ceiling. Everything ached. Not just where the mermaid had scratched but all over. My sweat-soaked clothes clung to me as I untangled myself from the damp bedding and sat up.

The bedside clock showed that my alarm had gone off over an hour ago. I was late for school, not that I really cared.

With effort, I stood and thumped down the stairs, making my way to the bathroom. I'd expected my reflection to look like I felt. Instead, other than being sweaty, I appeared fine. I turned on the cold tap and took a long drink. It helped cool the heat that seemed to be burning me from the inside. It didn't help stop the sweating, though.

Needing to cool off and get clean, I started the shower then stripped.

Before I stepped into the spray, I checked my scratches in the mirror.

The long oozing gashes from the day before were completely gone. I ran my hand over the perfect skin and wondered what it meant. I'd never healed like that in the past. The few bruises I'd managed to gain throughout the years had healed normally enough, as far as I could remember. I hadn't bruised often, though, and had never broken a bone or scraped my skin. I'd always thought I'd been naturally tough.

I took my time washing and even more getting dressed. When I finally picked up my phone, it was well into mid-morning. I had seven texts from Eliana, wondering where I was and worried because she'd heard about the mermaid attack. And, I had one from Oanen that was less than five minutes old.

It simply said, "I'll find you."

That message sent a shot of warmth through me. Unable to stop my grin, I went out the back door and stood in the center of the lawn, watching the sky.

Oanen didn't disappoint. As soon as I spotted him, he seemed to spot me. He folded his wings and dove sharply, opening them at the last minute and landing as he shifted. The impressive display of power made my heart pound. The sight of the bare expanse of his...everything, made my knees weak. I could barely keep myself from drooling as he stalked toward me.

"Are you all right?" he asked.

"I am now."

He pulled me into his arms and hugged me close. The brief press of his lips against my temple began to heat my insides, and I tried not to think about what he so easily did to me.

"If you wanted to skip out today, you should have told me. I would have kept you company," he said.

"It wasn't an intentional skip out. I promise. I overslept and was a little slow to get ready. I just saw all your texts now."

"I only sent one."

He released me, and I quickly stepped back, creating enough space so I'd keep my hands to myself.

"Yeah, well, Eliana sent seven." I grinned. "I think there's a spare set of clothes in the guest room if you want to stay for lunch."

After he dressed, we ate a quick lunch I'd made while waiting, then he rode with me back to the school.

"So do we all heal quickly?" I asked just before we reached town.

"Not necessarily. Often it depends on the type of injury."

I made a noncommittal noise. First my eyes. Now freakish healing?

"What does 'hmm' mean, Megan? Did something happen when you went in the lake?"

"Yeah. A fish with an attitude scratched me with her claws. It hurt like a bitch and was oozing dark green slime. And, this morning, the gashes are gone. All of them."

"Pull over." His words were more clipped and stern than usual, and I spared him a quick glance. He looked pissed and barely in control.

"Please don't go griffin mode in the car," I said. "I really like being able to drive around."

I quickly slowed and parked on the shoulder. When I stopped, though, he didn't get out.

"Show me," he demanded.

"What?"

"Show me where you were scratched."

I couldn't stop the stupid grin that pulled at my lips as I tugged up my t-shirt.

"Did I really just pull over because you're worried about me?"

His gaze stayed locked on the unblemished skin of my stomach.

"Yes."

The clipped word made me grin bigger.

"I kinda like this."

He finally lifted his gaze to meet mine.

"I don't." He reached out and ran his fingers over my skin. My amusement fled, chased away by the heat of his touch and the intensity in his eyes.

"I don't like the position the Council has put you in."

"Your parents and Adira? It's no worse than the position they put Ashlyn in. What would have happened if I hadn't jumped in after her?"

"She'd probably be dead."

"Exactly." I tugged down my shirt, dislodging his touch. "I need you on my side in this, Oanen. Uttira's view of humans needs to change." I pulled back onto the road.

"I am on your side," Oanen said. "I'll always be on your side."

The three torturously boring hours in the library hadn't been enough to incite any level of excitement for meeting Eliana at the Roost. But, because I hadn't spent any real time with her all week, I forced myself into the dress she'd given me at school and brushed out my hair.

The dress seemed a step up from the last. The flowing skirt tastefully fell to just above the knee, and the modest neckline scooped to give just a hint of cleavage. The back packed all the wow. The see-through, stretch black lace panel of material started just below the neckline and ran to just above the swell of my butt. It was a dress that demanded no bra. I went with the flow and skipped the garment, knowing Eliana would be happy.

The drive to the Roost didn't take long. When I got out of the car, the music thumped as usual.

"This town needs some diversity in hang out spots," I mumbled, staring at the red doors.

I so did not want to go in. Based on the cars lining the street, the Roost was very busy. Busy meant more people. More people meant more of a chance that I'd flip my shit. And, odds were Oanen would show up at some point and probably witness me doing it, too. Seeing him get all upset and protective was cute. Seeing me bloody someone's face was not. Yet, despite openly acknowledging all of that, I reached out and opened the damn doors. I was obviously messed-up in the head.

Music blasted me as I stepped inside.

Tonight, the Roost seemed especially popular. Bodies clogged the dance area from tables to doors. It looked like the entire student body of Girderon had shown up. The bold ones were on the stage, publicly making out to the sultry voices of the sirens at the microphones.

"Perfect."

People bumped against me as I attempted to make my way around the crowded dance floor. The bumps I didn't mind. The grinds got old quickly.

Through the chaos, I spotted Fenris with his her-herd. His gaze met mine, and he grinned. I lifted a hand to wave in return, but my fingers never got higher than my head. Fenris' grin widened the moment someone's strong fingers wrapped around mine. Before I could elbow the person, an arm encircled my waist and anchored me to a familiarly hard chest.

I leaned my head back against Oanen's shoulder and looked up at his beautiful eyes.

His hold on my hand loosened and traced its way down my arm. I shivered at the sensation and closed my eyes. The room felt ten degrees warmer by the time he reached my ribs.

"Dance with me," he whispered in my ear.

I opened my eyes as he turned me in his arms and held me close. We swayed to the music, and I lost myself to the feel of him. The feel of his hands on my back. The feel of his shirt under my palms. The brush of his hips against mine.

Heat pooled inside of me, twisting and coiling. Oanen watched me closely as I stared at him.

Unable to resist any longer, I tipped my head up to him. The barest hint of a smile touched his mouth before he lowered his head. His breath teased my lips while his fingers traced the lace where my bra should have been. Anticipation boiled me from the inside as he moved his hand upward to cradle the back of my head.

The first touch of his lips to mine made my breath catch. He tasted like hope and home. Like air and freedom. He tasted like he was mine, and I was his.

I gripped his shoulder, pressing against him so not a speck of space remained. He groaned and swept his tongue inside, taking and demanding and billowing the flames of need that roared inside of me even higher.

The faint scent of smoke touched my nose, and I broke the kiss.

"Not yet," he said before claiming my lips again.

The second kiss stole my will to think or worry. Oanen controlled me with each stroke of his tongue. Like a marionette, I responded to each pull of my strings and continue to sway against him.

When he grunted and finally pulled back, it took several

blinks for reality to intrude. The sound of the music. The voices talking and laughing. The smell of something smoldering.

My gaze dropped to my hand where I still touched his shirt. When I lifted my palm, I saw the dark brown patch that outlined the shape of my hand.

Oanen gripped my chin and tilted my head up until I met his gaze.

"I'm fine," he said, his words almost nonexistent in the beat of the music.

"I'm not."

When I tried to pull out of his hold, he wouldn't let me escape. He wrapped his arms tightly around my waist and leaned in so his cheek rested against the side of my head. The position brought his lips close to my ear.

"You are fine," he said. "Just afraid. Don't be. Not when we're together."

That was exactly the root of my fears. Being together.

I reached up between us and pulled his shirt aside enough to look at the red hand print. This time, I'd blistered his skin right in the center of where my palm had rested. Being with him the way he wanted only seemed to cause him pain. We were both just kidding ourselves if either of us thought this would end in any way that didn't result in him lying on the floor, burnt to a crisp.

Tipping my head back, I looked up at him.

"I think this is a mistake."

His fingers pressed more firmly into my back.

"I know it's not."

I wanted to believe him. He seemed so confident, so sure that whatever was growing between us would work. I knew better. Life wouldn't give us what we wanted. Why should it? It hadn't ever cooperated yet.

"I appreciate your optimism, but I think we need to get real. I've burned you twice with just—"

Yelling and shouting broke out behind me. A tingle of annoyance raced up my spine, and I turned toward the back tables. An invisible string tugged me forward. I wedged my way through people, barely noticing when Oanen reached out to stop a few incubi from grabbing me as I passed.

Near the back, a group of bodies crowded around the booth where Ashlyn usually sat. Worried, I pushed forward harder.

"Move, dammit!" I yelled at a huge boy. He turned back to glare at me but stopped short when he glanced over my shoulder.

"Hey, Oanen," he said, stepping aside.

Ignoring the boy and Oanen, I focused on the cause of the commotion. Two boys held Kelsey back from attacking another boy who was kissing the hell out of her younger sister, Zoe. Zoe's fingers clenched the boy's hair. At first, I thought her hold was out of passion, then I saw her tears and pale cheeks. Had Zoe looked like she was enjoying herself, I would have turned around. Seeing her being forced into a kiss, though, ignited my temper, not only at the boy but at the Council. Kelsey and Zoe had no business being "on duty" at the Roost already.

I rushed forward, grabbed the incubus's shoulder, and pulled him away from his prize.

He grinned at me.

"You'll get your turn after I'm done with these two," he said.

I hit him square in his still glistening lips. His head jerked to the side at the contact, and his eyes turned black. Zoe tried to step away, but his hold tightened on her arm.

"I'm not done with you, human. Not until I drink every bit of that passion you're trying so desperately to hide."

"Oh, you're done," I said.

He hissed at me and reached out to caress Zoe's breast. The girl whimpered at the contact, and I snapped.

"Touch her again, and tip the balance. Become wicked. Become mine." My voice sounded strange to my own ears. Angry. Commanding.

The boy who gripped Zoe paled and released her. The ones holding Kelsey released her as well. Kelsey grabbed her sister and hugged her close. The pair shook together, their cheeks wet with tears.

"I'm not wicked," the incubus said, reclaiming my attention. "She agreed to kiss me."

"Asshole!" Kelsey yelled. "You tricked her."

"Darling, that's not my problem. She agreed. That's all that mattered."

"Are you sure?" I asked. "Because if that were true, I wouldn't be itching to punish you."

The boy narrowed his eyes.

"The fact that you haven't already, fury, means I'm right. I'm not wicked, and you have no fight with me."

"Maybe not as a fury, but as a pissed off girl, I sure do."

I laid into him, hitting his pretty face again and again. It took a lot more effort to make him bleed than it would have a human, but I didn't mind taking the time to do the job right. By the time I finished a few minutes later, he looked satisfactorily messed up.

"Next time, consider the consequence before messing with a human. There's always a bigger, badder monster out there; and that monster might take offense to what you do."

"The same applies to you, fury," the boy said, turning his head and spitting blood on the floor. When he looked at me again, there was retribution in his gaze. "There just might be more powerful creatures out there than you, who will take offense at what you just did."

"I look forward to hearing them complain." I turned my back

on the boy and looked at Kelsey and Zoe. "Can I give you two a ride home?"

"We have a car. We can't leave yet, though. Adira said until eight."

"And I'm saying now. If Adira has a problem with it, it'll be my fault, not yours."

Kelsey nodded and moved toward me, not releasing her hold on Zoe.

"We'll walk you out and follow you home," Oanen said from just behind me.

He led, and I followed the pair. No one messed with the girls, and everyone moved out of Oanen's way.

Outside, the cool night air brought my attention to my temperature. I hadn't realized how warm I'd grown inside.

"Thank you for your help, Megan," Kelsey said.

"Don't thank me. If I'd really been helpful, you wouldn't have been in there in the first place. You've only been in Uttira for a few days. Why did the Council have you working at the Roost already?"

"We wanted to know what we were getting into before too many days passed."

"You should have talked to Ashlyn, then. She would have been able to give you an honest view of life in Uttira for a human."

"Ashlyn? Is she human like us?"

I felt my temper twinge that the Council hadn't even introduced them.

"Human, and not a fan of this place. Hold on." I turned to Oanen. "Can I use your phone?"

"What happened to yours?" he asked as he handed it over.

"Where on this dress do you think I'd stash my phone? I left it in the car."

His gaze swept over my dress, and I knew he wasn't

thinking of my phone. Trying to ignore him, I sent a quick text to Ashlyn to see if she was home and had time for some company.

Oanen's phone immediately rang. Eliana's number.

"Hey, we're almost there. What's up?" she asked.

I felt a twinge of guilt. I hadn't even thought of Eliana since arriving, and it definitely hadn't occurred to me that Ashlyn would come to the Roost willingly for a night out.

"The new girls had a run-in with an incubus. I was thinking they should have a frank talk with Ashlyn before attempting any more assignments from the Council."

Eliana was quiet for a moment.

"Are they okay?" she asked.

"Yeah. Just shaken up."

"We're pulling up now." The call disconnected, and I saw the blinker go on for the set of headlights coming down the road.

A moment later, Eliana parked and got out. She and Ashlyn both wore cute, modest dresses and sad expressions.

"Kelsey, Zoe, this is Ashlyn and Eliana."

"Hi, Ashlyn. Nice to see you again, Eliana," Kelsey said.

"What happened?" Ashlyn asked.

"Some guy tricked Zoe into making out with him in front of everyone. Then a few more guys came up and said they were next. I tried to stop them, but every time I looked one of them in the eyes, I forgot what I was doing. He wouldn't even stop when Zoe started to cry. He said the salt of her tears gave the kiss more flavor.

"Then Megan showed up, eyes glowing, and kicked his ass."

The asskickery hadn't been nearly enough now that I'd heard the whole story. I wanted to go back inside and find the guy again.

"Eyes glowing?" Eliana said looking at me.

"It's nothing." I definitely did not want to talk about my freakish changes just then. "Kelsey and Zoe were here because they wanted to know what it would be like for them if they decide to live in Uttira."

The door behind us opened and the incubus who'd met my fist walked out with his two friends. His eye had swollen shut and his bottom lip had puffed up on the right side. Despite that, he grinned when he saw Eliana.

"About time you acted like what you are. I warmed the little one up for you. You're welcome."

Before I could take a step, Oanen's hands settled on my shoulders.

"Leave now, Eras."

The boy's eyes settled on Oanen and his hold on me.

"Your parents' influence doesn't matter to me," he said. "I'm not going to cower and bow like the other mindless idiots inside. There's three of us, and that fury can't do a thing if we haven't broken any rules."

The door had opened during his little speech, and a familiar chuckle reached my ears.

"It doesn't look like your opinion stopped her from doing something to your face a few minutes ago."

The incubi parted, and Fenris strolled toward us.

"It's always fun when you show up, Megan," he said with a grin.

"Not sure I'd call tonight fun," I said.

He winked and looked back at the other guys.

"You're in no position to continue this fight. Go home. I'm sure your mother will give you some love after she sees your face."

Eras's face grew red, and his eyes blackened. I fisted my hands, more than ready for him to make his move. Instead of giving me another reason to hit him, he pivoted and stalked away, taking his little followers with him.

"You coming back inside?" Fenris asked.

"If Megan wants to go back in, that's fine. But, maybe we should postpone our night out," Ashlyn said, her gaze flicking between Zoe, Kelsey, and Eliana.

Eliana nodded, a look of guilt on her face.

"I think we'll all pass tonight," I said to Fenris.

He sighed and nodded.

"Next time." He turned and went back inside.

"I'm really sorry that guy kissed you, Zoe," Eliana said softly after the door closed.

I suddenly understood Eliana's guilt and shrugged out of Oanen's light hold to wrap her in a hug.

"You didn't do this; they did. And, you are not them," I whispered in her ear.

She nodded against me.

"Let's take this back to my house," Ashlyn said. "We can all watch a movie and talk Uttira."

I released Eliana.

"You're invited too, Megan. Oanen," Ashlyn said.

"Thanks, but I think it would be better for everyone if I headed home. Take Eliana with you. If anyone can teach Kelsey and Zoe how to resist the creatures here, Eliana can."

Eliana tried to protest, but Ashlyn won her over quickly with a pleading look. The four of them walked away, leaving me alone with Oanen.

Sighing, I faced him. The fight had been a nice distraction, but it hadn't erased the issue of us. His shirt still hung open, and I could see the edge of the red handprint. I knew he wanted me to not worry about it. To go with the flow and pretend like it had never happened. But I couldn't. I'd hurt him just like I'd feared I would.

His gaze held mine, and he reached up to smooth back some of my hair.

"I know what you're thinking. You're wrong. This burn

doesn't matter just like the one before didn't matter. Just like all the future burns won't matter."

Panic hit me hard right in the sternum. Future burns? Hell no!

He exhaled heavily.

"I'll let you run and hide for now, but only for a little while."

He leaned in and kissed me tenderly, creating a familiar heat in my middle. This time I had the sense to keep my hands to myself. Barely.

When he pulled away, I almost followed him.

"Don't make me wait too long," he said.

He touched me one last time then went inside.

CHAPTER SEVEN

After ten hours of restless sleep, I once again woke sweaty. Only this time, I was irritable, too. How many times did I need to hurt Oanen to prove to myself I wasn't good for him? I had no answer. Not even after breakfast or a long shower or a marathon of science fiction shows.

Frustrated, I wandered to the kitchen. A knock on the back door interrupted my mindless staring contest with the inside of the fridge. I looked up and saw a familiar face that lifted my mood a bit. At least, enough to answer the door without a scowl.

"Hey, Fenris. Sorry about last night."

"No need to apologize. I was just wondering if you might want some company today?"

I stepped aside to let him in.

"Running from your her-herd again?"

He grinned.

"So what have you been up to? Other than last night, I haven't seen you all week," I said.

"Nothing special. Sessions and pack stuff. Aubrey's actions led to a pack-wide inquisition."

"Spanish style?" I closed the door behind him and went back to the fridge.

"No. No jailing or torture, other than Aubrey."

"Yeah, what happened to her?"

"She was moved to another pack where she's being kept in isolation, only speaking with that pack leader. It's like a retraining program." He grew quiet behind me. "So what are you hoping to find in there?"

"Some miracle food that will solve all my problems. Know of any?"

He chuckled. "Nope. But, I hear talking about problems helps. I have good ears."

"And teeth and eyes, I bet."

"Only for girls who like to wear red."

I closed the fridge door and rolled my eyes at him.

"Seriously, tell me what's going on," he said kindly.

"I hate not knowing what I really am or what I'm capable of. Sure, I'm a fury. But, what the hell's a fury? My mom could have at least given me some kind of heads-up before she took off. If I'd known something, anything, about myself maybe I wouldn't be so freaked out."

"Why are you freaked out?"

"I've burned Oanen twice now without meaning to, and my eyes are starting to glow when I'm angry or…well, never mind. No matter what, burning people can't be good."

"Is Oanen mad that you burned him?"

I snorted.

"No. He keeps telling me it's no big deal. I don't know what needs to happen for him to realize how dangerous I might be. Death by fire? He's insane for not seeing the risk."

Fenris studied me for a long moment before he wrapped me in a slow, comforting hug. I rested my head on his shoulder and released a long breath. I hadn't realized how much I'd needed a sympathetic hug until he gave it.

"Oanen's not insane," Fenris said quietly. "I don't think there's a guy alive who wouldn't suffer anything for the right girl."

"That's what I'm afraid of."

"I don't think you need to be. I'm touching you, and I'm just fine. You feel warm, but not hot enough to burn me. You'll learn control with Oanen, too."

I pulled back, and he released me, his gaze filled with compassion.

"Thank you."

"Any time. Now, how about we start making some dinner, and you tell me what else is bothering you?"

"Why do you think there's something else?"

"Because you said problems. Plural. So, spill it."

"You just want me to feed you."

He covered his heart with a hand and pretended to be wounded. Grinning, I opened the fridge again and pulled out what we'd need to make burgers.

"You're right. It's not just worrying about what might happen to Oanen. Uttira's getting to me. I can't stand the way the people here treat the humans."

I handed Fenris a tomato to slice and started forming patties.

"Maybe that's because you still see yourself as human," Fenris said.

"You're partly right. I know I'm different from them, but I don't feel like a completely different species. And I don't see how any other creature can view humans as so different when we all look like them. Why do we think our differences make us superior?"

"That's a good question."

I let the pan heat before putting two burgers in.

"See, that's what I'm talking about. There's no valid reason. The humans are treated the way they are because they've always been treated like that. You saw what happened to Zoe. If you had a younger sister, would you want some guy creeping on her?"

"No."

"Did you notice how I didn't say the species creeping on your pretend sister? You know why? Because I knew it wouldn't matter. No one wants to be treated like that."

"So what are you going to do about it?" he asked, taking two plates out of the cupboard.

"Uttira's attitude toward humans starts with the Council. Rules need to change in order to change perceptions."

"What rules?"

"The one where humans have to willingly be bait for all the creatures in Uttira. While I understand that the creatures here need to learn, it doesn't need to occur in a way that's threatening to the humans. Why not have them go to the Academy with the rest of us? They'd be in a more protected environment there. Ashlyn feels so segregated and fearful of her safety, she doesn't leave her house. And the Council encourages that behavior by having everything she needs delivered to her. Ashlyn should be able to run to the store if she wants, without worrying about someone trying to eat her."

I slid the two patties on the buns Fenris had waiting, and he carried the plates to the table. While we ate, I vented and he listened. He didn't agree or disagree with anything, just listened. When we finished, he helped me with the dishes.

"Thank you for listening," I said. "You're right. I do feel a little better."

He put the plate away and gave me his usual boyish grin.

"Any time. Just keep feeding me."

I hugged him, grateful to have a friend, and it made me

realize just how much I missed having Eliana around. I needed to call her today and—

The door opened behind me. I pulled back from Fenris and turned to see who'd come in.

Oanen stood just inside the kitchen. Shock briefly showed on his face before all expression vanished. The only tell at what he felt was his hard, twitching jaw muscle.

Before I could say anything, he turned around and walked out. I ran after him, reaching the porch as wings started to unfurl from his back.

"Don't you dare take off without listening to an explanation," I said.

The wings folded and absorbed back into his skin. He didn't turn to face me, though. Instead, I stared at his amazingly naked backside.

"I think what I saw was explanation enough."

"What you saw was a hug between two friends."

The front door opened and closed. I knew Oanen heard it, too, because he fisted his hands. I stepped off the porch, grateful that Fenris had left and given me the privacy I needed to talk to Oanen.

"Right. Friends."

"Friends, Oanen. Use your damn ears. Does Fenris make my heart race? Does he make me hot enough to burn him? No."

His hands remained fisted, fueling my already smoldering temper. I stalked forward until I stood just behind him.

"Given my disposition to most people, I know it's hard to believe that I might actually crave friendship. But I do. Finding someone who doesn't annoy the piss out of me is unbelievably rare. And, that's exactly why I need to keep the ones I have, no matter what the gender. Your jealousy isn't cute. It's infuriating. Either trust me or fly away."

He bowed his head for a moment then turned.

"Seeing you in someone else's arms hurt more than any burn you could ever give me."

"Because you're putting meaning into the gesture that just isn't there," I said. "I already feel so caged in this place. Don't cage me more because you're jealous."

"I can't change how I feel."

I briefly closed my eyes, struggling to control my temper.

"You can change it by trusting that what I feel for you I have never, and will never, feel for anyone else. You're choosing not to trust." I lifted my gaze to glare at him. The sight of his angry, red face pushed me too far.

When I opened my mouth, it wasn't my voice that echoed around us; it was my fury.

"Leave now, Oanen Allister Quill, before I pluck the wings from your back."

His wings erupted and wrapped around me at the same time as his arms.

"Take them," he said fiercely against my ear. "They're yours, like my heart."

His words penetrated the rage boiling in my mind.

"I'm sorry I doubted you, Megan. I won't make that mistake again."

I slowly exhaled in relief and hugged him in return. He winced slightly, and I immediately pulled back. It wasn't until that moment that I noticed the acrid smell of burnt feathers and scorched grass.

All the things I'd blocked out in my fit of temper hit me hard. I took a stumbling step back when I caught sight of his singed wings and the blisters on his chest and arms. His face wasn't angry red, just burnt red. Each retreating step crunched as I backed out of the blackened circle of grass around us. I'd done that. All of it.

"It's okay, Megan," he said, not trying to follow me. "I'm fine. Breathe. Just breathe."

I realized I was panting for air and stopped walking to brace my hands on my knees. I forced myself to take several slow, deep breaths. I started to shake. What the fuck was wrong with me? Who got that mad over a jealous boyfriend?

"I should have let you think that hug was something it wasn't," I said. "You would have been safe then."

A hand settled on my head.

"I'm glad you didn't."

I continued to just breathe as he ran his fingers over my hair. After a few minutes, the shaking stopped.

"I can't keep going like this," I said. "I need answers."

"Let me go inside and grab some pants, then we can go to my parents."

I nodded, not looking up.

A moment later, the porch door banged shut. I stood and stared at the damage I'd caused. Burned patches in the shape of footprints started near the back door and disappeared into the circle of blackened grass. The edges still smoldered, and wisps of smoke continued to rise up in the air. Inside the circle, twin patches of fall, brown-green grass in the shape of Oanen's feet remained untouched.

Turning away from the ravaged yard, I walked into the house. Water ran in the bathroom. While I waited for Oanen to reappear, I finished cleaning up the kitchen. By the time the bathroom door opened, I sat at the table.

When Oanen entered the kitchen, he wasn't wearing jeans but a pair of loose shorts I hadn't even known he'd left here. I understood the choice, though. All his exposed skin looked far too red. Some of it had blistered. Some of it had blackened and peeled.

I swallowed hard and averted my gaze, struggling with my guilt.

"All the burns in the world wouldn't come close to causing the pain I felt when I thought I'd lost you," he said.

I shook my head, unable to speak. He crossed the room and stood in front of me. Without a word, he held out his hand. I knew it was more than an offer to stand. He was asking for trust, just like I'd asked of him. I did trust him. But, could I trust myself? Both Oanen and Fenris thought I should. Yet, the blistered palm held out to me begged otherwise.

I looked up at him.

"Why me?"

He studied me for a long moment, then his lips twitched slightly.

"Because you got my attention when no other girl could."

"I hit you in the face."

"You did. And after that, I couldn't look away. It's you, Megan. Always."

He crooked his fingers to draw my attention to the hand he still held out. Heart aching, I clasped his hand gently and stood. I stared up into his beautiful blue eyes and felt myself start to cry. Our fascination with each other was going to get him killed.

"Don't," he said, stepping into my space. He released my hand and cupped my face, his thumb brushing away the tear that spilled over.

His lips gently settled over mine, a light caress of shared anguish.

"We'll get through this. I promise," he whispered against my lips.

I nodded and stepped back, too afraid that I'd accidentally hurt him more.

"I'll drive you home," I said.

He followed me out of the house. Instead of letting him open my car door for me, I opened his and watched him closely as he eased himself inside. He masked his pain well, but I knew it was there in the way he didn't fully relax into the seat and the way his expression didn't change at all.

I tried to emulate him as I got in behind the wheel and kept all my worry from my face. When he reached over and put his hand on my leg, I knew I wasn't doing as good of a job at hiding what I felt as he was.

"What are your parents going to think?" I asked once we were on the road.

"Hopefully, that it's time to tell us whatever they know about furies."

Unwilling to steal his hope with my doubt, I said nothing; and the rest of the car ride progressed in silence.

Mr. and Mrs. Quill both waited by the door when I pulled up before their home. I parked the car and got out quickly, meaning to help Oanen, but he opened his door and stood before I could reach him. His mother's face paled at the sight of him, and her gaze immediately flicked to me. I could feel myself growing warm with my climbing anger. None of this would have happened if Adira would have just explained what I was.

Oanen reached out and threaded his fingers through mine. With a gentle tug, he led me to his parents.

"You have blood on your cheek. Are you all right, Megan?" Mrs. Quill asked.

I frowned and wiped at my cheek while wondering why she was asking about me and not Oanen.

"She's okay, Mom. She was crying," Oanen said.

"Blood tears? Already?" she said, sounding worried.

My gaze pinned hers.

"You knew I'd cry blood? What else do you know?"

She was already slowly shaking her head.

"Please," I begged. "Look at Oanen. I don't want to hurt him like that again."

Her compassionate gaze held mine for a moment before she waved us in.

"Let's talk inside," Mr. Quill said.

Oanen waited for me to go first then hung back to walk with his father, who I heard ask, "How bad are the wings?" Oanen didn't answer.

"Let's go to the study while Oanen cleans himself up," Mrs. Quill said.

No steps echoed ours on the stairs, and when I glanced back, there was no sign of Oanen or his father.

"Oanen will be just fine," Mrs. Quill said softly.

"This time, maybe," I said, continuing up the stairs. "But what about next time?"

"Are you so sure there will be a next time?" she asked.

"Since I have no clue what's happening, that means I have no control. No hope of stopping it. And, Oanen refuses to stay away. So, yeah, I'm pretty sure there will be a next time."

I walked into the study first but stopped short at the sight of Adira.

"You are only partially correct," she said. "You do know what's happening. You're coming into your fury powers. You cry blood, and you can generate enough heat to burn things or people. And you're unable to control it. Yet. However, your lack of control has nothing to do with your lack of knowledge about what you will become. You lack control because you aren't spending the time to learn who you are now."

I stared at her for two heartbeats. Annoyance crawled under my skin, but no rage. Not yet.

"You know, for a guidance counselor, you do very little guiding. I don't need your bullshit answers right now. I need your help. And if you're not willing to give it, fine. Let me leave so I can find my mom. She owes me an explanation."

"I'm sorry, but that's just not possible. You cannot leave without your mark. And, you will not earn your mark until you learn to control your anger."

"You know what? This whole 'here to learn control and blend' thing is such a load of crap. I sure as hell do not feel like anyone is teaching me anything. All I see being taught is how to successfully hunt humans without getting caught. That's not control, and that's not blending. Take another look at your high and mighty Academy and see it for what it is. A training ground for the next generation of predators. You want peaceful coexistence? Start treating the humans like they have just as much right to exist as we do. And stop hiding the truth from everyone."

"What would you have us do?" Mrs. Quill asked.

"Start by giving me answers. Then, get rid of the humans' assigned duties. The duties degrade the humans in the Uttira residence's eyes. We need to stop thinking less of them, or you'll have another incident like Trammer on your hands."

"Without an opportunity to practice, how will our youth learn to control their urges?" Adira asked, completely ignoring my plea for information.

"Not my problem."

I turned to Oanen's mom. "Tell Oanen I'll call him later."

I took a step toward the door.

"You honestly feel you've learned no control since coming here?" Adira said.

"Yes. If I were in a crowded city, I'd be just as likely to punch someone in the face as I was before."

"Perhaps we should test that."

CHAPTER EIGHT

Good luck tonight. Call me when you're back.

I stared at Oanen's message for a second longer before turning off my phone and slipping on my jacket. Guilt continued to torment me. I needed to understand what was happening. The key to that was my mom. The key to reaching my mom was controlling my temper during an excursion with Adira. No problem. Right. I was so screwed.

Precisely on time, the shimmer of Adira's portal appeared off the back porch. I went outside just before she stepped through.

"Are you ready?" she asked.

"Yes."

"Let's see how well you can control your temper, then. Shall we?"

With the portal's shimmer still flickering behind her, she held out her hand. As soon as our fingers touched, my stomach twisted. The magic of the portal wrapped around us as she tugged me forward. One second, we stood in my backyard; the next, we stood on a city street.

I knew I was in trouble before I took my first breath. Waves of agitation crawled over my skin. Even though Adira and I stood alone, I could feel the people around us. Just the wicked ones. And these only felt mildly wicked.

"How do you feel, Megan?" Adira asked, watching me closely.

"Annoyed. What the hell happened to all the decent people in this world?"

Adira smiled slightly. "We happened. Many of the creatures made by the gods were created to corrupt the perfection of humanity."

"Bullshit. I'm not buying that. Why are the humans born all pure, but we aren't? Because that's what you're implying, right? That we are born to fulfill whatever purpose the gods set before us, but the humans get to frolic around like herds of goats, without any responsibility for their actions? No, Ashlyn has proven that humans have a choice. They can choose to ignore our corruptive influences."

"That would imply that we, too, can then choose to ignore our purpose and instincts."

Oh, she was good.

"I led myself right into that. Fine. I'll try to ignore mine."

"We shall see. Let's find the first candidate."

She started down the street at a brisk pace, and I hustled to keep up. She hadn't picked the nicest street. Dumpsters sat near the loading docks and back doors of businesses. The stink of rot overwhelmed the hint of fresh food being cooked somewhere else.

Movement by one of the dumpsters made me jump. Not Adira, though. She walked right up to the huddled form in the shadows.

"Eugene, I'd like you to meet Megan. She's from my hometown." Adira stayed several feet back from the boy.

"Hi, Megan." The voice was young but weak. Almost listless.

I stepped past Adira, trying to get a closer look. The shape seemed small, balled up in a fetal position.

"Are you all right?" I asked.

"I'm trying to sleep on the ground near a dumpster leaking fluid that no sane person would want to be near. I'm great."

Something got under my skin, but it was light and easily ignored compared to the signals coming from the other people hidden further down the alley.

"You don't belong here," I said.

"If not here, where?" he answered.

"Where are your parents? Family?"

"Dunno. I left when they were high. When I went back the next morning, there was an eviction notice on the door, and my upstanding parents were gone."

"I'd like to offer you a real home, Eugene," Adira said from behind me. "A real bed. Three meals a day. A chance to attend school again."

The boy uncurled himself enough to look up at me and then Adira, his dark brown eyes now alive with interest. Underfed and dirty, but with a light dusting of dark hair on his chin, he looked about my age.

I hated this. What kind of choice was Adira really giving him?

"What's the catch?" Eugene asked.

"You lose the life you know, and you're trapped forever in a world you'll wish you never knew existed," I said before Adira could try to gloss over the reality of what would happen.

"So, you're telling me to pick between the red pill and the blue one?" He snorted and stood up. "The truth seemed to work out okay for Neo."

"Um, he died at the end of the third movie, didn't he?" I said, thinking he was missing the point.

Eugene shrugged.

"If I stay here, I won't have a long life anyway. Give me the reality pill, lady."

"Any objections?" Adira asked as she glanced my way.

I sighed. "There's nothing majorly wicked about him. At worst, he probably stole something to eat at some point."

"Two bucks from another alley rat's pocket," the boy said, unashamed. "He would have just traded up for booze anyway."

"Then it's settled," Adira said. "Come with us. You'll be showered and in a clean, warm bed within an hour."

Anger slammed into me like a baseball bat to the back of the head. I grunted and took a step forward from the force of it. Head hanging, I struggled to control the urge to fight. To punish whoever carried so much wickedness.

"Megan?" Adira said softly. "Are you in control?"

A scuff of movement from behind us announced the source of my affliction. I lifted my head, fighting a losing battle.

Eugene took a step back when my gaze met his.

"Holy shit," he breathed.

"This is the truth," I said, my voice echoing oddly. "Watch. Then decide if a warm bed is worth the price of your ignorance."

"Eugene," a new voice said. "When did you start hanging with these high-class pieces of ass?"

The nails of my fingers bit into the skin of my palms as I clenched my fists tighter at the sound of the voice. I turned toward the newcomers. Three of them all dressed in dark clothing. Tattoos decorated the knuckles of one and the cheek of another. Their jewelry flashed in the distant dock light.

"Nice eyes," the first one said. "They contacts?"

"No." I walked toward them, my words coming from some hidden part of me. "Tell me your crimes. What sins will you confess?"

One of the guys burst out laughing. I hit him square in the mouth, the impact snapping his head back and sending blood flying onto one of his companions. He grunted and staggered. The friend with blood on his face pulled a gun from his pocket and aimed it at me.

"On your knees," I said, my voice scarier and more commanding than I'd ever heard it. Even as some part of me acknowledged something bad was happening, I couldn't stop it.

All three men fell to their knees.

"Confess."

That single word reduced the men to tears. They blubbered their way through stories of theft and attempted murder. The one with a broken nose barely made sense, but it didn't seem to matter. As they spoke, the need to make them pay for each crime increased until I felt bloated with it. I reached out and put my hand around the first one's throat, lifting him off his knees. I felt no strain.

"Randall Aaron Walker, your wicked confessions have guaranteed your place in—"

"Megan, stop," Adira said.

Rage boiled inside me at being interrupted. She touched my shoulder, and my stomach twisted. My hand slipped from around the man's throat, and I landed on my back. I blinked up at the stars, confused and no longer fury angry, just angry.

Eugene's face appeared above me.

"What are you?" he asked.

"Pissed off," I said, getting to my feet.

Adira stood on the sidewalk, not far from me.

"Some kind of angel?" Eugene asked, still watching me.

The complete absurdity of his guess distracted me from Adira. I stared at the filthy boy in disbelief.

"What? No way. What kind of angel has fiery eyes?" I asked.

"The one who beats the crap out of the guys who've been dealing to my parents for the last four months."

"That life is done now," Adira said.

Ignoring me, she nodded toward the house attached to the front lawn on which I stood.

"Everything in this house now belongs to you, Eugene." She handed him a key. "Clean yourself up. Sleep. Megan will be here in the morning to pick you up for your first day at Girderon Academy."

"Not a chance in hell," I said.

First, I was still mad at her for talking this kid into coming. Second, I was still mad at her for stopping me mid-asskicking. Third, I would not let her continue to mistreat the humans in Uttira.

"You wanted the humans to attend the Academy."

"Yeah, but not on the first day here. You need to give Eugene time to understand what this place is. First, he meets Ashlyn. If he decides to stay, he then decides when he's ready to attend the Academy, or if he'd rather homeschool for a while."

"I really don't mind," Eugene said. "I like school. Saying it's an Academy makes it sound fancy. Fancy wouldn't be bad after the last few weeks I've had."

"I get it," I said, turning to him. "I really do. But you need to talk to Ashlyn first. I won't throw you to the wolves—literally—by sending you to Girderon without you understanding the most disturbing truth about this place."

"And what's that?" he asked.

"All those legends you thought weren't real? Well, they are. Werewolves. Mermaids. Giants. Magic. It's all here. And it's not rainbows and pixie dust. The Council brings humans here so those very same creatures of myth can learn to control their impulses."

"Impulses," he said slowly. "Like making bad guys confess? That doesn't sound so bad. Personally, I think you should do more of it."

"We're not all the same. Some have impulses to eat you."

He paled slightly, but I didn't regret telling him the truth. He needed to understand that he'd only traded the type of danger he was in; he hadn't left it behind. And, I thought he was beginning to get it based on the way he looked down at the key in his palm.

"Yeah. If you think talking to this Ashlyn is a good idea, I'm okay with that," he said after a moment.

"All right. I'll ask her to come over tomorrow night. It'll give you some time to settle in and really think about what you saw tonight."

"That'd be good."

He started toward the house then looked back at us.

"I think I'm dreaming. I'm not sure if it's good or bad yet." He glanced at the house then back at us. "Am I going to die if I walk into that house?"

"That house is probably the safest place in Uttira for you," I said.

"Megan is correct," Adira said. "Nothing can harm you in that house."

He nodded and started toward the door. Without a word, he unlocked it and slipped inside. Adira and I watched the lights go on one by one.

"I controlled myself in that alley. Well, before those three men showed up. There were at least twenty other people I could feel, and I didn't do a thing about it."

"But you did for Randall Walker."

"You heard them. He and his friends were way more wicked. There was no way I could have just let them walk away. I mean, that's my purpose, right? To punish the truly wicked."

"It is. However, a fully developed fury doesn't need to strike the wicked for a confession."

"Well, I didn't know that. Maybe if you'd told me, I wouldn't have hit him."

"Did I have to tell you how to use your mind and your eyes to pull a confession from them? No. Yet, you somehow managed to do that." She gave me an understanding look that made me want to throat punch her.

"I know this is frustrating for you," she continued. "But, to keep the world safe, you need to remain in Uttira until you learn who and what you are, and you are able to control your instincts."

She reached out again and put her hand on my shoulder. A second later, we stood outside my house.

"Good night, Megan."

Then she was gone again. I stood there stunned.

"I don't believe this shit. That wasn't even a test. She just wanted to know if Eugene would work. Fucking unreal."

The renewed scent of smoldering grass sent me inside where I wouldn't start things on fire.

Are you avoiding me?

I groaned after reading Oanen's latest text and flopped back on the couch.

"Why must you keep texting me?" I mumbled, already tapping out my next message.

If I'm avoiding you, I'm doing a poor job of it. Aren't you supposed to be paying attention or something?

I can't when you're not here. I worry about you.

You need more interesting hobbies. Now, pay attention to whatever session you're in.

I'd rather you tell me why you didn't come in today.

I already told you. I hate people.

Adira asked if I saw you.

Adira can go pet a honey badger.

Seriously, that woman could go sit on a pole. I refused to listen to her and her dumb rules anymore. The Academy was a joke and a complete waste of my time. I wasn't learning anything there. Nothing I'd actually use once I left this place. I was tired of playing games and planned to stay on this couch until I rotted. No more recruiting new humans. No more babysitting existing ones. They could all suck it.

I set my phone on top of the small pile of papers on the end table, not wanting to see Oanen's reply. Nothing was going the way it should, and I wasn't in the mood for anyone, not even him.

After waking up feeling just as angry as when I'd gone to bed, I'd resolved to find my mom myself. Since coming to Uttira, well over a month ago, I hadn't received a single bill in the mail. Not one. Yet, I still had power, cable, and a working cell phone. Those bills had to be going somewhere. So, I'd done a little research and started calling around to look for information that might lead to my mom's current address or phone number.

However, my super sleuth skills had nothing on Uttira's impenetrable closed network. Calling the cable company had redirected me to the grocery store. Calling the power company had redirected me to the grocery store. And, calling the cell phone carrier number within the app on my phone had... redirected me to the grocery store. The woman working the day shift there probably hated her life now after that third call. She hadn't been able to tell me anything other than the Council takes care of all the orphans in Uttira. Fat lot of good that did me. If I couldn't track down my mom from inside Uttira to call her and couldn't leave Uttira to find her in person, I was royally screwed. Without her help, I had no chance of controlling whatever the hell was going on with me.

I stared at the TV, not really seeing the rerun so much as just attempting to let my mind go blank. What more was there to do than wallow? Nothing.

However, each passing minute only increased the resentment and anger crawling under my skin. One show changed to another, but I barely noticed. I wanted to break the TV. Burn the sofa. Destroy the stupid house in which my mother had caged me.

The knock on the back door only fueled the anger skulking inside of me.

"There's no one home. Go away," I said without moving.

The door opened, and the faint scuff of footsteps announced the approach of my would-be visitor.

"I should have locked it," I mumbled to myself.

"No, you shouldn't have, or I would have broken it," Oanen said.

I lifted my head to look up at him and wished I hadn't. Scabs still clung to his face in a few places, yet another reminder of my failings. Setting my head back on the couch, I resumed my TV stare.

Oanen moved closer and squatted down beside me, blocking my view. It didn't matter. I kept my eyes trained on the blur of his bare chest.

"Talk to me, Megan," he said softly. "Tell me what you're thinking right now."

"That I suck at girlfriending, and the only thing I do well is hurt people."

"That's not true."

"Careful. I'm pretty sure lying is wicked."

"What happened last night?"

"Exactly what Adira wanted to happen. I verified the new human wasn't wicked then lost it when a group of drug-dealing thugs came over. My actions validated Adira's point that I'm a danger out in the human world and allowed her to refuse my request to leave to find my mom so I could get some fucking answers, which everyone in this seventh-ring-of-hell, shit-place likes to hide."

I took a calming breath and closed my eyes against the orange glow that reflected off Oanen's golden skin.

"You need to leave," I said.

"I've never needed to stay more."

"You're annoying me."

"Good. Then maybe you'll open those beautiful, glowing eyes and look at me."

I did, but it was for a full out glare.

His lips twitched slightly as I met his gaze.

"What are you most afraid of?" he asked.

"Hurting you."

"I don't think so. You've already hurt me. You feel guilty for it, but fear? No."

I thought about it for a second.

"You're right. I'm afraid of screwing this up."

"Technically, you already screwed this up."

"Is this supposed to be a pep talk? Because you're sucking at it. How did I already screw up?"

"You punched me in the face during our first meeting."

"I'm thinking about doing it again."

He grinned at me.

"How can you be so okay with all of this?" I asked. "I burn things when I'm angry. I can make people tell me all the horrible things they've done. My freaking eyes glow when I'm really upset. It's not okay. I'm getting worse. What's going to be next?"

He reached out and traced a fingertip down the bridge of my nose.

"Your eyes are glowing now, and they're breathtaking. I could look at you for hours if you'd let me. Do you understand? There's nothing about you that I don't like."

"You're crazy."

"Probably." He frowned slightly and removed his touch. "Do my eyes bother you when I change?"

"No." Dark blue or golden, his eyes did the same thing to my insides whenever he looked at me. But, I wasn't about to admit that aloud.

"I get what you're doing," I said, sitting up. "You want me to face my fears and make them seem less scary. It's not working. I fear myself. I fear that, whatever I become, will hurt you so badly that you won't heal. That you'll be dead because that's exactly what I think I was about to do to one of the men last night if Adira hadn't teleported me back here. Not only do I have no idea why I'm doing what I do, I have no control over it."

He considered me quietly for a moment.

"You might know more about yourself than you realize. Tell me about your mom."

"She dated a lot. Never really got attached to any of the men, though. Despite leaving me here, I know she loved me. At least a little. I remember hugs and kisses when I was small. I remember birthday parties before I started losing my temper and hitting other kids."

"Do you remember your mom burning things or having flaming eyes?"

"No. That's exactly why I need to find her. She knows what I'll become, and she knows how to control it."

"Her control means you will be able to control it, too."

"Before or after I fry the rest of the hair from your head?"

He sighed slightly.

"It's just hair. It will grow back."

"Speaking of going back," Adira said, stepping from a portal that spontaneously appeared in my living room. "I suggest you start where you left off."

She set her hand on my shoulder and sent me tumbling backward. I landed hard on my ass and grunted in pain.

"He said grow," I mumbled.

A bell rang, calling my attention to my surroundings. In disbelief, I glanced down the hall as several doors opened.

Adira had sent me to school in my damn pajamas.

CHAPTER NINE

ANNOYANCE EXPLODED INTO ANGER AS STUDENTS POURED FROM opening doors.

"Someone kick you out of bed?" a giggling voice asked from nearby.

What the hell had Adira been thinking?

I jumped to my feet and started toward the library, storming down the hall in my socks. Students moved out of my way as if I had Oanen at my side. Only, this time, it wasn't fear of him. They were finally seeing me for what I really was.

"Hell hath no fury like me," I said under my breath, trying to ignore the way some of the students called to me.

Adira had pushed me too far this time. I'd stayed home for several very valid reasons. One, the curriculum at Girderon Academy was a joke. This wasn't an institution for learning but endurance. And, two, I was running too short on any form of tolerance for anything. The students crowding the hall didn't help.

A boy left a classroom, stepping into my path at the last minute. Had his wickedness been on par with Oanen or Eliana, I would have walked around him. Instead, I body-checked him without hesitation and smiled at his outraged yell as he fell. His backside barely hit the floor before I reached down and grabbed the front of his shirt to hoist him to his feet.

"Who do you think you are?" the boy demanded. I changed my grip from his shirt to his throat. He made a strangled noise, and his face began to turn red.

Another student tried to move in front of me. I backhanded him with my free hand, pushing him away, and focused on the wickedness coming from my victim.

"Francis Moss." My voice once again had that booming echo from the alley. "Conf—"

Something hit me from the right. The impact jarred me enough to loosen my hold. Thin arms wrapped around my waist, and a hand snaked up under my shirt. All the anger left me as I fell to the side.

My head hit the cement floor with a hollow thump. My ears rang for only a second, though.

"Don't let go of me," I said.

"I won't," Eliana promised in my ear.

"We have her," Ashlyn said from nearby. She continued talking, and I realized she was on the phone.

"She didn't hurt anyone...yeah, she's okay...Eliana, Oanen wants to know how warm Megan feels."

I just lay there and kept my eyes closed as if it would protect me from the reality of my life.

"Hot, but not burning me. She's cooling down already," Eliana said.

Ashlyn relayed the message to Oanen.

"He says he's on his way," she said after a moment.

A small groan escaped me.

"No. Tell him we're doing a girl's night," Eliana said quickly.

Snickering filled the hallway, reminding me that we weren't alone.

"Help me up," I said.

It felt like the entire student body of Girderon was trying to get a good look at the drama I'd caused. The kid I'd backhanded lay on the floor not far from me, shaking his head and blinking up at the ceiling. The boy I'd tried to strangle stood nearby, glaring but silent.

"Stop doing shit you shouldn't be doing, and I'll stop attacking you in hallways," I said. I pivoted and started walking, Eliana's hand still plastered to my back.

I'd only managed to clear the ring of gawkers when I realized I had no idea where to go.

"Which session is starting?" I asked.

"None. That was the final bell," Eliana said.

Adira had sent me here just to expose me to the students. Anger lit me from the inside again only to quickly disappear.

"Adira is such a bitch."

"Do you want to go home?" Eliana asked.

I immediately shook my head. I wasn't ready to face Oanen, who was likely still there with Adira.

"Want to come with us to Eugene's?" Ashlyn asked.

"Yeah, I'll ride along."

We took the back halls to the pool area before using the main hall to the parking lot. By then, most of the students had already left. Still, Eliana kept her hand on me, and Ashlyn gripped her phone, most likely ready to speed dial Oanen.

The trip to Eugene's was short. Ashlyn pulled up in front of the house then looked back at me and Eliana.

"You two waiting out here?"

"Yep," Eliana answered.

As soon as the car door closed, Eliana removed her hand and turned to me.

"What's going on?"

It wasn't an accusatory question, only a concerned one.

"I don't know. Sometimes I'm fine. Sometimes I'm not. That guy in the hallway? His wickedness was way less than Trammer's, but I was still ready to kill him."

"I noticed," she said.

I exhaled heavily.

"Oanen thinks I can control whatever this is because my mom obviously did. But, it's getting worse. You saw his face."

"Oanen's right. If furies couldn't control themselves, they would be on the human news. There's got to be a trick to it."

"I'm sure there is. And I'm sure my mom knows. Too bad Adira has zero interest in allowing me to ask her."

Eliana set her head on my shoulder.

"I know you probably don't want to hear this, but I have faith in you. You'll figure it out without the help of your mom. Just like I'll figure out what kind of succubus I want to be without my mom's help."

I wrapped an arm around her shoulders and gave her a squeeze. It was so easy to get caught up in my own problems and forget Eliana had problems of her own.

"I'm sure you're right."

She lifted her head and gave me an understanding smile.

"I think this calls for some chocolate," she said.

"Good luck with that. Unless you have a stash at home, you won't find any at the store. I've been checking."

Her grin widened.

"You up for some more people time?"

The idea of going to her house made my stomach turn.

"Not really. Especially not anyone associated with the Council."

"That's perfect because where we're going, the Council avoids. Let's move to the front."

We did a seat switch, and she sent a quick text to Ashlyn, letting her know our plans.

"She'll text when she's ready for a pickup," Eliana said, handing me the phone.

She drove through town then stopped in front of a shop near the bakery.

"You should know that the lady running this shop is bringing in non-Council approved goods from the human world and selling it at crazy high prices to teens like us."

"Are you telling me she's wicked?"

"I'm telling you she's breaking Council rules. Personally, I think anyone who's willing to sell chocolate to a craving teen is as close to a saint as this place gets."

"The Council's rules are stupid. I've broken several, myself. I hope that isn't enough to make a person wicked."

"Let's find out," she said with a smile on her face as she got out of the car.

I did the same but with a frown. Fall's chilled breeze swept over me. Now that my temper had cooled a bit, I felt every digit of the low temperature. Especially in my feet. Given the time of year, it wouldn't be long before snow covered the ground.

"I'm still pissed Adira didn't even let me put on shoes," I said.

Eliana glanced at my stockinged feet and grinned before entering the shop.

As soon as I stepped through the door, I could smell the chocolate. I inhaled deeply in appreciation and looked around at the homespun mittens, stockings, and hats hung on the walls.

"Can I help you?" the woman behind the counter asked.

"Hi, Mags," Eliana said. "I'm interested in the usual."

The woman glanced at me before answering Eliana.

"More mittens?" the woman asked.

"Gods, no!" Eliana said. "This is Megan. She's fine. We're interested in cocoa powder if you have it. If not, anything milk chocolate will do."

"Sounds like you have a craving," Mags said. As she spoke, anger threaded its way under my skin; and I reached out to hold Eliana's hand.

"Whatever you're thinking of doing, don't," I said. "Being wicked isn't healthy around me."

Mags grinned. "So, you're the new fury? I have some cocoa powder in back. Stock's low so I was going to charge double. But I'll give it to you at the regular price."

She shuffled to the back room, and almost thirty minutes later, we left the shop with not only cocoa powder but five pounds of sugar, too.

"Ready for some brownies?" Eliana asked.

"As long as we're talking the chocolate kind, yes."

We got into her car and drove to Eugene's to pick up Ashlyn.

"Please tell me that you convinced him there are better options," I said as soon as Ashlyn got in.

"I know you don't like it here, but for a lot of us, it's not a bad deal."

"You were almost drowned by a mermaid."

"And Eugene will escape gang rape if he stays in Uttira. He said he saw it happen to another boy his age. That's why he was sleeping in the cold by the dumpster in that alley. The men you saw, they only beat the boys."

"You know what frustrates me the most?" I said. "That there are people here who have the money and influence to make a difference, but they aren't. They're too caught up in their own petty problems."

"To them, controlling the creatures here is making a difference to the people out there," Eliana said.

Her phone beeped.

"Can you check that for me?" she asked.

I turned it over and found a new message from Oanen.

Where did you take Megan? I'm home and you're not.

"It's Oanen stalking me," I said.

"You better answer him," Eliana said. "You don't want him worrying and hunting you down."

"Unless you do," Ashlyn chimed in.

I rolled my eyes and started a text back.

"What are you saying?" Eliana asked.

"That you've tied me up and stuffed me in the trunk but were stupid enough not to notice I grabbed your phone. And that I'm running out of air."

"Don't send that!" Ashlyn said at the same time Eliana tried taking the phone from me.

I laughed at their reactions.

"Relax. I'm telling him to calm down his stalkerie, that we're on our way to my place to make brownies, and that he's not invited."

"You're making this hard on him, aren't you?" Ashlyn said with a grin.

"Making what hard on him?"

"Nothing," Eliana said.

I hit send and stared at her. When she didn't cave under my scrutiny, I turned to Ashlyn. She held up her hands and shook her head.

"She's my ride to school," she said.

"I'll drive you. Start talking."

"She means you're playing hard to get," Eliana said.

"What's to get? I already agreed to be his girlfriend."

Ashlyn snorted.

"Griffins don't do girlfriends."

Eliana slowed and signaled for my driveway.

"What does that mean?" I asked.

"Sweet mother Mary," Eliana said softly.

At first, I thought she was frustrated with Ashlyn saying something about griffins. Then, I noticed her attention focused on my car in the driveway. Through the back window, I saw the spidering cracks in the windshield. It looked like someone had hit the glass repeatedly with a baseball bat.

"What the hell?" I said, opening the door as Eliana parked.

The three of us walked to my car, all staring at the mess.

"We should call Oanen," Eliana said.

"No, we shouldn't. There's nothing he can do about this. Someone else might be able to help, though."

I went inside the house and picked up my phone from the coffee table where I'd left it. There was a message from Oanen telling me to text him when I got home. I ignored that and sent a text to Fenris.

Up for a favor? I need someone with a good nose to come over and tell me who bashed in my windshield.

I didn't have to wait long for a reply.

Will I be paid in spaghetti?

How about brownies? (The chocolate kind; not the ones with the wings.) We're making them now.

We?

Eliana and Ashlyn are over, I sent back.

Be there in 15. Can't wait for a taste.

"Um, who are you texting?" Eliana asked.

"Fenris. The Council's always getting his dad to sniff things out. So, I asked Fenris to come over and give my windshield a sniff. I promised to return the favor in baked goods, so we better get started."

"Oanen is not going to like that you called Fenris," Ashlyn predicted.

I waved off her concern. "I didn't call Fenris. I texted him. And Oanen will be fine with it. He knows that Fenris and I are just friends."

Eliana and Ashlyn shared a look before I strode to the kitchen. Having my car abused didn't put me in a good mood.

Feeling like my friends were keeping secrets from me didn't help improve it.

"If you have something to say, just say it. All the looks you're giving each other isn't helping the situation," I said, setting the mixing bowl on the table a little harder than intended. "Keeping secrets about presents or the Easter bunny is one thing. This feels like you're not telling me something really important."

Eliana shrugged sheepishly, and I knew she wasn't ready to admit what was going on. So, I looked at Ashlyn.

"I saved you. Don't make me regret it."

"Griffins don't date. They mate for life," she blurted.

I stared at her blankly for a moment. So they mated for life. Big deal. Why were they acting so weird about it? Then, it clicked into place. Oanen wasn't dating me.

Almost robotically, I sat in a chair.

"Do you think she's mad?" Ashlyn whispered.

Eliana bent in front of me so we were eye to eye.

"You're pale, which I'll guess means you understand. He made me promise not to talk to you about it. He didn't want you to worry."

"Why?" The word came out more of a croak.

"Griffin males are very protective of their mates. They care for them with a singular focus that's almost…"

"Scary?" I asked.

"I was going to say enviable. Succubi invoke complete adoration in their partners but rarely care for anyone more than they do themselves. Griffins aren't bespelled. Their adoration is their own. To be loved so completely by someone for what you are rather than some unnatural pull sounds like what love is supposed to be."

"I meant, why me," I said. "I was willing to give being a girlfriend a chance, but mate? I can't. My head feels like it's going to explode just thinking about it. How do I tell him no? I have to be the worst possible person for him to even consider spending forever with."

"Megan, just breathe."

I looked up at Eliana, who now stood by the kitchen door with Ashlyn. Both of their faces were flushed.

"Breathe?" I said. "You just told me Oanen already has me in a white dress in his head, and you want me to breathe?"

She swore under her breath, and Ashlyn fled outside.

"Megan, the heat coming off of you would be enough to cook an egg. If you don't want to hurt me, you need to calm down," she said slowly. "Focus on your breathing and nothing else."

I closed my eyes and tried. I really did. Only, once my eyes were closed, all I saw was Oanen's burned face.

The sound of the door let me know I was alone. I felt the first tear fall and wiped at my face, knowing it would be blood. It just made me more upset. What was wrong with me? Why was I so out of control? What the hell was Oanen thinking picking me?

The screen door creaked, and I opened my eyes to tell Eliana to leave. Instead, I saw Fenris.

He strode right up to me and wrapped me in a hug. I could smell his hair burning.

"Stop. You're going to get hurt."

"For the right girl, I'd do anything. Even risk my life for her best friend," he whispered in my ear. I jerked back and looked at him in surprise. His face was red and his hair a bit singed. However, no pain showed in his gaze.

"Feel better?" he asked.

I didn't know what to say or think.

Just beyond him, Eliana stepped up on the porch. Worry reflected in her gaze.

"I don't need brownies, just your silence," Fenris said softly before hugging me close again. He buried his nose in my hair and breathed in deeply. "Mmm. Her scent is all over you."

Eliana grinned big and wiggled her eyebrows.

"I told you so," she mouthed.

She didn't know. Like me, she had no clue. I wished I could go back to having no clue.

"You're getting warm again," Fenris said. "You're going to hurt my feelings if you keep thinking about him while I'm holding you."

I snorted.

"That's better. Now, do I have your word? She's not ready, and I don't want to upset her."

Since I wished I could go back to not knowing, I readily agreed with a nod.

"Good." He took one last, long inhale then stepped back from me. "The scent on your car is familiar. Someone from Girderon. I'll be able to give you a name tomorrow."

He leaned forward and, with a playful smile, licked the bridge of my nose.

"See you later, my sweet-tempered fury."

He turned and walked out the door with a polite nod to Eliana and Ashlyn.

"Is it safe to come in?" Eliana asked.

I nodded. Fenris had done his job and calmed me down by distracting me from my own drama. He was right. Eliana wasn't ready to know about his interest in her. Was it just interest, though? That thought led back to thoughts of Oanen as my friends joined me in the kitchen.

"Still want to make brownies?" Eliana asked.

"Yes. I'm sorry for losing it. Yet again."

"Don't worry about it," she said with a wave of her hand. "What are you going to do about Fenris?"

"Nothing. There's nothing to do. He's just a friend."

She rolled her eyes. "That's a lot of friendly hugging."

"I've kissed you. Do you see me as more than a friend?"

"Fair enough."

I sat in the chair and let Ashlyn and Eliana do most of the batter prep while I considered my situation with Oanen.

"I just don't see how this will end well for him," I said.

"Him who?" Ashlyn asked before licking some chocolate off her finger.

"Oanen."

"It'll be fine because you know you're meant to punish the wicked," Eliana said. "Just like I know I'm supposed to turn into a raving sex-addict and feed off the sexual energy of the thousands of poor souls I'll enslave in my lifetime. Who says I have to start now? Who says when you see wickedness you need to punish the person right on the spot. There's no timer for any of it, except these urges we get. So, next time, ask yourself why you need to rush it. Tell yourself you're taking your time to discover what the person did and even more time to weigh a suitable punishment. Be creative. Why let the gods have so much control even after they're long gone?"

What she said made sense. The gods had far too much control when they weren't even around.

CHAPTER TEN

I LIFTED MY HAND OFF THE BOOK AND LET IT FLY BACK TO ITS HOME on the shelf. My stomach growled as I stood and went to fetch the next one. Breakfast had been hours ago, long before sunrise.

Arriving at the Academy early had served two purposes. I'd avoided Oanen and given myself more time to look through the books. Fenris' revelation had opened my eyes to the value of knowing more about all the creatures here. So, while I hoped to stumble across a book that would tell me something useful about griffins, I no longer skimmed everything not related to my current topic of interest.

I still found most of what I read useless, though.

Taking the new book back to my chair, I opened the thin volume to the first page and started reading about harpies.

When I felt a cool breeze on my neck along with a mild tingle of annoyance that shivered over my skin, I remained focused on the book. When a heavy hand knocked on the door moments later, I ignored that, too. I wasn't in the mood to acknowledge Adira or face Oanen.

The breeze vanished, and the knocking stopped.

I glanced at the high window above the shelves. Plenty of

daylight still remained. That meant it was lunchtime. Although my stomach voted for food, I voted for more seclusion. I needed time to just be me. Time to calm down so when I saw Oanen next, I wouldn't melt the rest of his hair.

Focusing on the book once more, I spent the next hour reading.

"Yet another race screwed over by the gods," I said, taking my hand from the book.

I stood with a stretch and grabbed the next one as I glanced at the window. Lunch would be over by now, and the next session in progress. I decided to stay another hour then bail.

My intentions flew from my mind when I opened the book and read the first line.

Like most creatures of the gods, griffins do not reveal the secrets of their existence lightly. The information contained within these pages has been documented at great personal risk. Make no mistake; if any griffin finds this book, any person known to have read these pages will be brought before the Council to have their memories wiped. Read on at your own peril.

James Whitenmore ~ 1927

Since Adira knew what was in the library, I knew I'd suffer little peril. However, as I turned the page and began reading again, I did wonder what had happened to the author since the book now resided here.

Griffins were created for a single purpose: to guard and protect humanity against those creatures who would destroy us humans. However, there are not many griffins in existence. Their low population is perhaps due to all griffins being male. Based on my research, they are able to compatibly mate with any race. However, they only produce one male offspring with their chosen life-mate. Offspring are typically conceived not long after the bonding flight, the first flight for both the griffin and his life-mate, which they take together. A bonded pair…

I turned the page, eager for more, and found a blank sheet. Close to the spine, I spotted the jagged remnants of missing pages.

"Come on! Isn't censorship against the constitution?"

Releasing the book, I let it fly back to the shelf. I'd discovered enough to know I wanted to leave before the next session break.

I quietly left the library, collecting my things from the basket in the hall before scurrying down the empty corridors.

Outside, I went to where I'd parked my smashed car and found an empty spot.

"Smashing and now stealing?" I mumbled.

I lifted my phone, ready to message Fenris for another sniff-check, and found several missed texts from three of my four contacts. I read Eliana's first.

I told Oanen you know. Please don't hate me forever. He made me promise weeks ago. Please call me soon.

My stomach twisted with anxiety. Yet, I knew that Oanen knowing that I knew about the whole mate thing was probably for the best.

Closing her message, I opened the one from Oanen.

Saw your windshield and had someone pick up the car to fix it. I'll give you a ride home. We need to talk.

I growled and set off at a jog through the trees. Yes, we obviously had to talk. I just needed to postpone it for a while and give him more time to heal because I didn't trust myself to stay in control during that discussion.

More than twenty minutes later, I sat down on my kitchen chair with a relieved sigh and opened Fenris' message.

I know who it is. He won't bother you again.

The fury in me wanted to demand a name. I went for a brownie to shut her up.

For the next several minutes, I relaxed and composed a

carefully worded text to Oanen so he wouldn't come looking for me when the final session ended.

No longer need a ride. Don't call me. I'll call you.

I hit send and leaned back into the couch.

"That wasn't so bad."

My phone immediately started ringing.

"Crap." I didn't touch the thing until the call went to voicemail.

A new text came through from Oanen.

I'm coming over.

The air around me started to smell like an overheated dryer. I quickly stood from the couch and sent him a reply.

Back off, fly-boy, or I'll rip your wings off.

I stared at the phone. Just when I thought Oanen wouldn't respond, a new message came through.

I'll see you tomorrow.

"So how long exactly do you plan to avoid him?" Eliana asked.

I propped the phone up with my shoulder and turned off the TV.

"It's only been an hour since I texted him. I wouldn't call that avoidance."

"You threatened to rip his wings off."

"He threatened to come over."

"That wasn't a threat," she said. "He's worried about you."

"Well, I'm worried about me, too. I almost toasted my couch."

"Seriously. It's only going to get more awkward. Just talk to him."

I stared at the dark TV screen. There was no denying how

much I wanted to talk to Oanen. My insides went hot just at the idea of seeing him, of being near him. I wanted it so much. And that worried me.

"I can't," I admitted. "Not until his face is healed."

"You don't have to talk to him in person, you know. You do have a phone."

There was something about her tone and her persistence that gave her away, and I sighed in understanding.

"He's standing right there, isn't he?" I asked.

"He is," she said, sounding only a smidge guilty.

The phone became muffled as it switched hands, and my chest tightened in anticipation. How pathetic was I? I'd burnt Oanen so badly he was still sporting scabs, and guilt ate at my insides every time I pictured his face. Yet, I couldn't wait to talk to him or see him. Why couldn't I stop wanting him so much?

"I just need to know you're all right."

The low sound of his voice broke me as much as his words.

"I'm not," I admitted softly. "I don't know what to think, and what I feel is all over the place. I feel crazy and out of control. Why didn't you tell me that helping me off the roof would bond us? What if I don't want to be bonded? I'm not even sure I am ready for dating."

The one thing I did feel certain about was that I'd trapped Oanen into a relationship just like Aubrey had tried trapping Fenris. I angrily wiped away the moisture from my cheek, smearing blood across my fingers.

"Please don't cry," Oanen said. "The sound of your tears hurts more than any burn you could give me."

"Well, they aren't making me happy, either."

"Let me come over."

"No. Don't. I just need some time."

"You're saying no with your words, but I can feel your pain. Your need for me."

"You can feel me?" I said, freaking out even more. "There has to be a way to undo this, right?"

"This is why I didn't want Eliana to say anything. There's so much I need to tell you. Talking like this isn't helping. Please let me come over. If not tonight, tomorrow. You won't hurt me. I promise."

"No. I need more time. I'll call you when I'm ready."

I listened to his slow exhale, wishing he were right beside me instead of across town. I imagined his arms around me and another quiet tear fell.

"Don't make me wait too long."

Tuesday, I woke early to the sound of my phone, which had remained quiet after last night's call. I lifted it and read the message from Eliana asking if I wanted a ride to the Academy since I had no car. I wanted to beat whoever had broken my window. That one act of pissiness put me in an uncomfortable position. If I said yes to a ride, Oanen would come with Eliana. I wasn't ready for that. However, if I said no to a ride and stayed home, Adira might zap my ass to the Academy. And, although I wanted to see if I could find anything more in the library about griffins, I didn't trust myself to keep my distance from Oanen.

I sent a quick text saying no to Eliana then another to Ashlyn, asking for Eugene, Kelsey, and Zoe's numbers. While waiting for a reply, I showered and dressed to ensure I wouldn't end up in the halls unprepared again.

When I checked my phone, I had a reply from Ashlyn, an acknowledgement from Eliana, and a new message from Oanen. I read Oanen's first.

I'll let Adira know you won't be in today.

That was it. There was no ranting or begging. Just Oanen taking care of me like he always did. Could he be any more perfect? I doubted it.

I sighed and sent quick texts asking each of the three new residents of Uttira if they needed anything and if they planned on attending the Academy. Kelsey and Zoe both answered that they were doing well but taking things slowly and didn't plan on attending until next term. Eugene said he'd be there Friday after he received his new clothes because he didn't want to look like a homeless drifter anymore.

Making a mental note that I would need to go in Friday, I looked around for something else to keep me busy.

I cleaned the house with a vengeance. Floors, that weren't really dirty, got swept and scrubbed, including the stairs. I dusted the bedrooms, washed the bedding, and de-webbed ceiling corners. In the kitchen, I washed cabinets and removed everything from the fridge before washing the inside of that, too.

By the time I reached the library, I only opened the door I'd shut long ago, gave the room a glance, and closed the door again. The sun had set, and I was exhausted.

I made myself a quick dinner then went to bed. I thought of Oanen as I closed my eyes and wondered if his day had been as boring without me as my day had been without him.

Thinking of him just before sleeping proved unwise. I dreamt of him flying around endlessly in a storm, searching for me. Lightning hit him repeatedly, burning his feathers and scorching his skin, but he refused to land and stop his search. When I woke drenched in my own sweat, it was because I'd witnessed him die from a lightning strike straight to his heart. It hadn't come from the sky, but from my hands when he'd finally found me.

I wiped my face and sat up, shaking. Sunlight already lit the room, not that the brightness helped ease the fear I felt. I'd killed Oanen. With fire.

I picked up my phone and hesitated. Sending him a message to ask him to let Adira know I wouldn't be in again felt mean. Yet, after that dream, I couldn't ignore the warning.

I won't be in again today. Maybe tomorrow, I sent.

A moment later, he replied.

I'll let Adira know.

How could four words convey so much sadness? Maybe because of my own misery.

I set the phone aside and went back to sleep.

After several hours, I woke again and got ready for another boring day. Since I'd cleaned yesterday, I decided to make a mess in the kitchen. Using the internet, I found a recipe for chocolate mousse layer cake and spent the next three hours baking then eating my creation. Chocolate had to have soul-healing powers because, after a few bites, life didn't feel as bad.

Before I finished washing the mess of dishes I'd made, the rumble of an engine reached my ears. Frowning, I grabbed a towel for my hands and went toward the door just in time to see my car come to a stop. A sheen of familiar golden hair flashed through the newly repaired windshield. My heart thumped heavily, and I stepped closer to the door.

Oanen got out. He didn't look up at the house, instead he kept his eyes trained on the car. He set his hand on the roof and closed his eyes, a look of anguish crossing his features.

An aching need twisted in my chest. I couldn't stand seeing him hurt like that. Even burned, he hadn't looked so tormented.

I opened the door. His expression immediately closed off before his gaze met mine through the screen.

"Adira says that I can't really hurt anything in this house," I said, my heart beating faster. "It'd be better if you came inside."

He lifted his hand from the car and slowly stalked toward me. My pulse raced in anticipation and concern.

He didn't hesitate on the steps but took the door from my fingers and let himself in. I slowly backed away, keeping our personal bubbles intact.

His deep blue eyes studied me for a long moment.

"I never meant to hurt you," he said softly.

"You didn't. I understand why you didn't want me to know. I mean, I freaked out just like you'd anticipated, right?"

"Are you still freaking out?"

"Yes. My heart feels like it's trying to pound its way out of my chest."

"I know." He looked away for a moment. "But, I don't know how to make this easier, Megan. How to ease your fears."

"I don't think you can. Without knowing what I can do and how to control it, I'm going to keep being terrified that I'm going to hurt you."

"You won't," he said, stepping closer.

I immediately retreated a step.

"Your face is already red. I can feel my own heat, like there's a fire inside of me growing each second I'm with you. It's not anger. It's need. I'm so desperate for you it's insane. I want you to hold me, but I know what will happen if—"

He moved fast, closing the distance between us and wrapping his arms around me.

"Oanen," I whispered in warning.

"Don't push me away. I need this just as badly."

I couldn't push him away if I wanted to. We fit perfectly, and I melted against him, laying my head on his chest against my better judgement.

"You're going to get burned again," I said.

"Your burns hurt less than your silence."

His hands rubbed small circles on my back, soothing and comforting me. I lifted my head to look up at him.

"We need to talk about what's going on, though."

"What do you mean?" he asked.

I wanted to say "bonding flights" but could only manage to mouth the words.

"Stupid library," I mumbled. I set my head back on his chest and felt him swallow hard before holding me tighter.

"I'd ask what else you learned in the library but know you wouldn't be able to answer." His hand stroked all the way down my back. I liked how he touched me.

"How about you just tell me everything then?" I said.

"I don't want to upset you more."

I didn't see how he could.

"I'm not ready for kids, by the way."

His hands stopped moving.

"I know you're not. We're taking this at our own pace, no matter what you read in the library."

"Good. That makes me a little less freaked out. So what are we exactly?"

"Bonded."

"And what does being bonded to a griffin mean? You said you could feel me. Were you serious?"

"Yes. Just the strong emotions. When you're happy, sad, angry, hurting."

"What am I now?"

"Still upset."

"Probably because you're starting to smell like burnt toast," I said, lifting my head.

He let me go, and I took several steps back. His face looked sunburned, and I was willing to bet he had new blisters on his chest where I'd set my head.

"Don't apologize," he said. "Those aren't the words I want to hear."

"What do you want to hear, then?"

"That you're not giving up."

I knew what he was saying. He wanted me to tell him that I wasn't giving up on us and on learning to control whatever was going on inside me. That kind of promise was too dangerous to give lightly. So, I gave him what I could.

"As long as you're safe, I'll keep trying."

CHAPTER ELEVEN

LIFTING MY HAND, I STARED BLANKLY AT THE TABLE WHILE THE BOOK I'd just finished returned to its place. Knowing about the magic of light and dark elves was interesting since I was now certain Adira was a light elf, but I didn't see how the knowledge could help me.

Eliana's words floated around in my mind. Adira had given me access to the library for a reason. Sure, she made it sound like it was for my liaison duties, but other than checking the wickedness of new recruits, I hadn't done much of anything. Adira had also admitted there was nothing useful about furies in the library. Why, then, give me access? What was I supposed to learn in here? That I was just one of the many creatures that the gods had created? That the gods created us on a whim to fulfil a myriad of purposes to fit whatever agendas had filled their minds? All I was doing was questioning the validity of our existence. If the gods were no longer here to fight over the humans, why were any of us needed?

Someone knocked on the door. Shaking my head to clear the questions, I stood and answered the knock. Eliana grinned at me from out in the hall.

"Where's Oanen?" I asked. Since we'd agreed on taking things slow without me avoiding him, I'd assumed he wouldn't avoid me either.

"Flying already. We're meeting up at the Roost in thirty. That includes you."

I groaned.

"None of that," she said. "I know how you get when you're cooped up in that house too long. Being cooped up in this library is no different. You're my ride. Let's go."

Most of the cars were already gone by the time we reached the lot.

"How long ago did the bell ring?" I asked, getting in.

"Not long," she said, joining me. "I figured I'd wait a few extra minutes so you didn't have to deal with the crowds and me at the same time."

"Getting tired of tackling me?" I asked with a grin as I backed out.

"Not at all. Those moments are always the highlight of my day. I just thought you might be a little mad with me after..." She shrugged and looked down at her hands.

"I get why you didn't tell me, Eliana. It was the smart thing to do. I wasn't ready, and you were protecting me."

She snorted.

"No way. I wasn't protecting you; I was protecting my soul. I'd made a promise before I knew you and couldn't break it. Especially now that I know hell's real. For what it's worth, I think Oanen should have told you from the beginning. Keeping that kind of secret can ruin a relationship before it starts. I hope it doesn't ruin yours, though. I want you both to be happy."

Her words only made me feel a smidge of guilt about the secret I was keeping from her. No matter what she said, Fenris was right. Eliana wasn't ready to know about his interest in her.

"Me too," I said, staying on topic. "But I don't see how that will be possible if I keep cooking Oanen every time he's around me."

"Have you asked yourself why it's just him? I mean, you're fine around Fenris."

"Probably because I have zero interest in Fenris romantically."

She made a non-committal sound.

"I'm serious. And I'm positive he has no real interest in me." Before she asked how I knew that, I quickly changed the subject.

"Now, is it really necessary to go to the Roost? Given my instability, and how easy it is for my temper to go off lately, wouldn't a girl's night at home be better?"

"No. This is Oanen's idea. You're going to practice control. Oh, and he wants you to wear the dress."

I opened my mouth to tell her that wouldn't happen, but she spoke first.

"He thinks wearing it will be a helpful distraction. You'll be too aware of the dress to be overly aware of any wickedness." She shrugged as I pulled into my driveway. "He might be on to something. You were okay last time."

"Do you not remember the incubus I punched in the face? I was far from okay last time. No. No dress tonight. It'll put me more on edge, and I don't need that."

However, twenty minutes later, I tugged at my hemline as I sat in the car and wondered what the hell had happened to my determination.

"Thank you so much, Megan. It's a lot easier to dress like this when you're dressed the same."

I glanced at her dress, glad we weren't. She wore a floor-length lavender number with a side slit up to the top of her thigh and a v-neckline that exposed the valley between her breasts.

"I would trip if I ever had to wear that thing," I said, pulling out of the driveway.

"It's making me nervous that Adira's picking out my dresses now. This one isn't bad, but what about the next one?"

"Most girls would kill to have someone delivering dresses like that to their door."

"Not if the gifts were from Adira. There's always strings attached."

"What do you have to do tonight?"

"Just dance. I pulled a page out of your book and threw down an ultimatum when she told me she wanted me to feed on the crowd's sexual energy."

"Oh? What was the ultimatum?"

She gave me a sheepish grin.

"If they don't stop pushing, I'd call my mom and take her up on her offer."

"What offer? I didn't know you were still talking to your mom."

"Yeah. That's the only thing keeping her out of Uttira."

"Hold up. I thought she left you here. Abandoned you."

"Yes and no. Succubi don't have maternal instincts by nature. That's why she left me with my dad. When she came for me, it was to bring me here where I wouldn't hurt anyone while she taught me how to fend for myself."

"Weren't you twelve when you got here?"

"You see the problem. She didn't. The Quills didn't, at first either. Twelve is old enough for most succubi. But it wasn't for me. Oanen saw that right away. He's the one who stepped in when my mom brought me to the Roost and told me to pick a boy to give my virginity to. Because of him, she let me stay with the Quills. Because of my phone calls and updates from Adira regarding my progress, my mom's staying away. If I ask, she'll come back and show me how a Succubus is meant to live, using every man, woman, and child in Uttira as her teaching instruments."

"I can see why the Council would want to keep her away."

"Exactly. I guess Mom's one of the best. She doesn't understand that I don't want to have a horde of willing servants to satisfy my every whim. Her words not mine."

"So instead of feeding on horny teenage boys since you were twelve, you've been starving yourself?"

"No. My mom wouldn't have stayed away if I'd done that. I do feed when I have to."

"How?"

"I'd rather not talk about it," she said, blushing.

Since we were almost to the Roost anyway, I didn't press for more.

"So how are you going to monkey-tackle me with that dress on?" I asked instead.

"With grace, hopefully," she said as I parked.

I grinned at her, and we got out of the car. The cold air had us hurrying toward the door and the familiar thump of music.

Inside, people danced as usual while others congregated in conversation around the couches or on the second-floor balcony around the bar. Familiar faces glanced our way as the gust of cold air swept in behind us. Thankfully, I didn't feel any strong threads of wickedness in the crowd. I did, however, spot Fenris with his her-herd in the center of the floor. He winked at me and kept dancing.

"I see Ashlyn, Kelsey, and Zoe. Let's go say hi," Eliana said. She grabbed my hand and tugged me toward the back of the room. I didn't mind skipping the dance floor for now.

"Hey, guys," Eliana chirped happily. "Any problems?"

All three sat at the table. Each appeared to be reading a book. I knew better.

"None," Kelsey said without looking up. "Ashlyn's coaching has made a world of difference."

Ashlyn snorted.

"Coaching? What coaching? All I told you was to ignore everyone. And that it works better if you have something to pretend you're distracted."

"There was more than that," Zoe said with a roll of her eyes. "But she made us promise not to tell."

"Fair enough," I said. "Whatever keeps you guys safe."

Zoe's gaze shifted from me to someone over my shoulder. I turned and found Jenna standing there, looking much better than she had the last time I'd seen her.

"I just wanted to say thank you, Megan."

"For what?"

"Aubrey was a bitch. Not the good kind. Stopping her was the best thing you could have done for us girls and for the pack. And, having her away makes life much nicer. I just wanted to let you know we think you're great, even if Fenris spends way too much time watching you."

I smiled as Fenris came up behind her just then.

"Hey, Fenris. We were just talking about you," I said.

Jenna's eyes went wide, and she gave Fenris a sheepish look.

"All good things, I hope." His gaze slid over my dress before briefly flicking to Eliana and the rest of our group. "You girls look lovely tonight," he said, once again looking at me. "Any chance that you'll dance with me?"

"You know what? Dancing sounds like a great idea," I said. I held out my hand for Eliana.

"I think I'm going to sit this one out," she said.

"What? Why? We came here to dance."

"I don't think I had enough for dinner." Her gaze pleaded with me to understand. And I did. When she blinked at me, I could see a brief flash of inky blackness creeping into her gaze.

She warned me once before that Fenris had way too much lust oozing off of him. I kept my shock inside as I realized all the lust was because of her.

"Fine, I'll do this one solo." I turned to Fenris. "Looks like you're stuck with just Jenna and me."

"I don't mind." He took my hand, and Jenna's and led us on to the dance floor. Jenna grinned before busting a move in front of me. I smiled and started dancing until Fenris' arms circled me from behind. He pressed close and inhaled deeply with his nose buried in my hair. Now that I knew what he was doing, I didn't mind it. However, I was pretty sure Jenna did, based on her expression.

I mouthed "sorry" to her, and she shrugged lightly.

A shiver of awareness ran down my spine as if I were being watched. I looked around the crowded room while still dancing with Jenna and Fenris. A t-shirt, like the ones that Oanen usually wore, fell from above. I looked up, and my gaze collided with Oanen's as he gripped the balcony rail with one hand. The blue lights reflected off his chest. It was an amazing view that I couldn't really enjoy because his eyes were golden and very angry.

I stopped dancing.

With a small jump, Oanen launched himself over the railing. His gaze never left mine as he fell, and his wings burst forth to slow his descent. He landed in a crouch, and his gaze shifted to Fenris, who stopped dancing behind me but still had his arm hooked around my waist.

"Looks like you're not the only one with anger issues," Fenris said, much too close to my ear. "Because of what you're doing for me, I won't hit back."

Before I could tell him to cut it out and let go, he pushed me into Jenna's arms. I turned in time to see Oanen's fist connect with Fenris' face.

"Oanen, stop," I yelled. He didn't. Neither did most of the dancers or the music.

I grabbed Jenna's wrist and pulled her off of me just as Oanen hit Fenris again. Jenna whined in protest but didn't try to stop me once I was free. Stalking up to my irate boyfriend, I lifted my hand and caught his next swing with my palm.

His furious gaze shifted to mine.

"Outside, now," I said.

He jerked away from me, grabbed his shirt from the floor and stalked outside. I followed close on his heels. As soon as the door closed behind us and the music muted to the point we could talk, he stopped. He didn't turn toward me, though.

"We need to understand each other's rules so you don't go around trying to beat up my friends all the time. I mean, are you going to hit Eliana the next time I kiss her?"

"You plan to kiss her again?"

"If she needs me to, yes." I stared at his tense back in frustration. "Oanen, this isn't going to work if you have so little trust in me. I was dancing with friends, not having sex with them."

"You sure? Because it looked like that was where it was headed."

I lost it. My insides flashed so hot I thought I'd boil alive. Instead, the car right in front of Oanen exploded into flames.

I didn't care that a piece of metal flew from the car and hit him or that the fire would probably burn him. He could fry for all I cared. I wanted him to hurt like he'd just hurt me.

I took a step forward, ready to spin him around and give him a five-digit present when something hit me from behind.

"Are you kidding me?" I screeched as I went down.

The anger didn't disappear all at once but in slow degrees. As soon as I was in my right mind enough to know who I was struggling to get off my back, I stopped and just lay there, cheek against the cement.

I closed my eyes, hating myself. Could I get any lower? No. I'd managed to get every one of my friends hurt tonight. I could smell Eliana's melted dress. Guilt and shame clawed at my insides and ate away at whatever remaining hope I had for controlling the fury growing inside of me.

Eliana pressed tighter against me, and her hand brushed over my head.

"Shh," she said softly in my ear. "I have you, Megan. You won't hurt anyone else."

The last of my anger left me as did every other emotion. I lay there languid in the nothingness I felt.

"Are you okay, Oanen?" she asked.

"Fine. Megan?"

"She's not injured on the outside. Inside, she's not okay. We better get Adira."

Something moved inside of me. I wanted to feel anger toward Adira but couldn't. It kept slipping away from me. I felt stifled and raw.

"Get off me, Eliana."

"I can't. I promised I wouldn't let you hurt anyone. If I let go, you will. And, I won't break my promise."

Again, any hint of the anger or frustration I wanted to feel slipped away, along with my will to shake her off and stand. I continued to lay there as someone called Adira.

I never felt the portal open; it was already too cold on the ground to feel a temperature difference. But I knew the moment she arrived anyway.

"Your parents are on their way, Oanen," Adira said. "You can get up now, Eliana."

"It'll be okay, Megan," Eliana whispered in my ear.

Her weight lifted off of me. Before I could move, a hand

settled on my shoulder. My stomach twisted as Adira's portal shifted me from the cement to my bed. Suddenly laying face up, I was too disoriented to do anything as Adira leaned over me and kissed my forehead.

Darkness closed over my consciousness, smothering the rage that had once again been trying to consume me from the inside.

"Rest."

That word followed me into the void.

CHAPTER TWELVE

I WOKE AT FOUR IN THE MORNING WITH AN INSTANT AWARENESS OF what I'd done the evening before. The vision of that piece of metal flying toward Oanen's torso filled my mind along with the smell of Eliana's burned dress. Guilt threatened to suffocate me.

"Please let it not be that bad," I said as I reached for my phone.

I had a message typed and ready to send when I hesitated. If Oanen was hurt and recovering, I didn't want to wake him. Yet, if he was awake, he'd likely be worrying about me. That was his normal mode of operation. I frowned and looked at the phone. If he was awake, though, why didn't I have a text from him already? Worried, I sent my first text followed quickly by a second.

Are you okay? Please tell me you're okay.

Please don't give up.

When there was no immediate reply, I told myself he was still sleeping and sent a text to Eliana.

I'm sorry about last night. Are you and Oanen all right?

Instead of hovering near the phone until she answered, I went downstairs to make myself something to eat.

Two hours later, dressed and ready for the Academy, my self-delusion had evaporated. Neither Oanen nor Eliana had answered me. That could only mean one of two things. I'd either hurt them both so badly that they couldn't answer me. Or, they'd both given up on me. I doubted the latter. While Oanen might want to give up because of jealousy, I couldn't see Eliana giving up on me for what I'd done.

After a twenty-minute internal debate over just going to their house, I drove to Girderon early and continued to worry about both of them. Ashlyn arrived not long after with Eugene in the passenger seat of her car.

"Hey, Megan," she said as soon as she opened the door. "I'm glad you're here. I was a little nervous about bringing Eugene on my own."

It clicked that Ashlyn had been at the Roost last night, and I hurried toward her.

"Have you heard from Eliana? I'm worried that I hurt her last night."

Surprise flitted over Ashlyn's features.

"Hurt her? How?"

"You didn't hear the car explode after I went outside?"

"No. After Oanen hit Fenris, Eliana saw you and Oanen head outside and followed you. She sent a text later, saying that you guys were all heading home and that Adira would make sure that we got home okay."

"I missed a fight?" Eugene asked.

I turned my attention to him. Not only did he now wear clean clothes that complemented his jet-black hair and dark brown eyes, he also looked happy.

"Don't worry. You're bound to see a lot more if you decide to stay here."

He laughed.

"It's already decided. I love it here."

Ashlyn rolled her eyes but looked amused.

"You haven't even had your first day of school," I said.

"Doesn't matter. Look at how clean I am. They can do what they want to me in there, and I would die happy because I never thought I'd be clean and warm again."

Another car pulled in. Red and glossy with three blonde heads mixed in with one dark one, I knew right away who'd arrived.

Fenris waved as he held the door for Jenna. I noted that he looked completely unharmed by the two hits he'd taken last night. The girls looked over Eugene with keen interest as their group joined us.

"Everyone, this is Eugene. He's new to Uttira." I looked at Jenna and the other girls. "Would you mind keeping an eye on him while I talk to Fenris a minute about last night?"

Jenna nodded easily.

"Sure thing. We'll make sure nothing eats him."

The other girls grinned and wrapped their arms through his. Eugene smiled widely and gave me a thumbs-up before allowing them to lead him inside. Ashlyn followed with a shake of her head.

Alone, I faced Fenris. He watched me closely, his normal, easy smile absent.

"I'm worried that I hurt Oanen and Eliana last night. Please tell me you saw them after we went outside."

A look of relief crossed his features.

"I thought you were going to tell me I needed to stop touching you," he said, his boyish grin returning.

"I'm getting to that part, too. First, tell me what happened after I left."

He shrugged his shoulders and sighed slightly.

"I didn't want to make things worse, so I stayed inside. I heard the explosion a few seconds after Eliana followed you two out. I tried to get outside along with half of everyone else in the Roost. By the time I pushed my way to the front, I caught a glimpse of Mrs. Quill stepping through a portal before it closed. You, Eliana, and Oanen were gone."

That didn't help ease my worry at all.

"You need to tell Oanen the truth," I said, ignoring the cars parking behind him. "He's jealous of you."

Fenris snorted. "If I told him the truth, he wouldn't just punch me in the face; he'd try to kill me. Griffins are protective, if you haven't noticed. The only reason he's not angrier at me for the attention I've been giving you is because he knows he has your heart. No, I'd like to leave things the way they are for a while."

"Fine. Then, no more hugs for you."

He made a face.

"Now you're just being mean. But, that's all right. I'll love you anyway."

One of the people walking past us started walking faster, no doubt looking to spread that bit of gossip.

"And to prove my love," Fenris continued, "I've been considering your problems and think I found a way to help you. How do you put out a fire?"

"It depends on the kind of fire. Why are you asking?"

He chuckled.

"I've seen the flames in your eyes and Oanen's burns. There's a fire inside of you. You're trying to control the burn, right? Try putting it out."

He winked at me and merged with the flow of students going into the building. I stood there, thinking about what he'd said and waiting for any sign of Eliana's car or Oanen's shadow in the sky. When the first session bell rang, I gave up and went inside in search of Adira. Her door was tightly closed as usual, but there was no answer when I knocked. Frustrated, I checked rooms until I found Eugene with Ashlyn. Seeing them safe, I went to the library.

Words drifted before my eyes but none of them stuck in my mind. Hours passed. No one knocked on the door, and the growl of my stomach grew louder. Giving up, I went outside and waited in my car until the final session bell rang.

The cars cleared the parking lot in droves. While I waited to find out how Eugene's first day went, I sent the same text to both Oanen and Eliana.

I'm trying not to freak out, but your silence is scaring me. Please call as soon as you can.

Not long after I hit send, Ashlyn and Eugene emerged from the building along with Fenris and his girls. They all were talking and smiling. A part of me hated them for their good moods. Why couldn't I be like that?

Eugene spotted me and jogged over to my car. Fenris and his girls kept going to their vehicle, but he gave me a small nod of acknowledgement.

"Hey, Megan," Eugene said. "I just wanted to let you know I haven't changed my mind. Thanks for introducing me to Jenna. She and her friends are great."

"I'm glad you like it here. Just don't forget what this place is, and be careful."

He nodded and went to catch up with Ashlyn, who gave me a wave as she got into her car. Feeling defeated and alone, I started to back out of my spot. My phone chirped. I slammed on the brakes and picked it up.

My eyes devoured Eliana's message.

I'm coming over as soon as I can. Don't freak out.

I read the last line twice. What did she mean by that? Why did she think I would freak out when I saw her?

Checking behind me, I finished backing out and sped home. Once there, I paced in the kitchen, freaking out despite her warning not to.

When I finally heard Eliana's car, I had the door opened before she even parked. I focused on her face as she got out. She looked okay. Sort of. She was wearing more makeup than I'd ever seen her wear before.

"You had to use makeup to cover the burns?" I asked. Fear laced my words.

"No," she said, hurrying toward me. "I didn't. Look closely. The skin's all good. Let's go inside before you set something out here on fire."

I nodded and went inside with her. She held out a hand, which I clasped before hugging her tightly.

"I was worried I hurt you guys so badly you couldn't even text me," I said against her hair.

"I swear I'm fine," she said.

"Oanen?" I asked as I pulled back to look at her.

"Hurt, but not badly. All stuff that will heal."

"What happened? Why didn't you guys call me?"

"A lot's happened. Let's sit down. I've got an hour before I need to be back home."

I sat across from her and noticed how beautiful her eyes looked with dark mascara and eyeshadow.

"If you're not wearing makeup to cover something up, why are you wearing it? I mean, it looks great; it's just very different from what you usually do."

"The makeup ties in to my visit." She reached across the table and held my hand again. "After the car exploded last night and Adira returned you, she and the Quills decided Oanen and I were hindering your progress."

"They what?" My anger wanted to rear its ugly head but couldn't, thanks to Eliana.

"We're not supposed to see you for a while. Especially Oanen. They took away his phone and have forbidden him from leaving the house for five days. Once they know he can control his urges to see you, they will allow him to leave the house, but he's done attending the Academy until you receive your mark."

Here and there, heat caressed me from the inside only to disappear. The Council was taking everything from me. My friends. The only family I had now. Even though I couldn't feel my anger, I could feel the overwhelming sensation of being alone and trapped.

I tried to stay focused on Eliana as she continued her story.

"The Quills were supposed to take my phone away, but I promised them I wouldn't text you without permission. When I got your last message, I knew someone needed to tell you what was going on before you lost control completely. I used heavy makeup as a bargaining chip. A week of makeup for an hour to talk to you."

My hands shook. I lived alone in the house where my mom had abandoned me; yet, my life had never before felt so controlled and managed by others.

"I know you're angry, Megan. Oanen is too. So am I. We just need to prove to the Council that he and I have nothing to do with the speed of your progress. Honestly, they should know that already. Look at me, right?"

"You're walking proof that they're right. Because of me, you're wearing makeup. Don't you see? We're all pawns on a chessboard to them. They move us around to manipulate our actions and reactions to each other. Now, the Council is taking you and Oanen out of the equation. Since we know you two aren't hindering anything—I mean, look at how fast these new abilities appeared—we have to ask ourselves why. Why are they separating us? Do they want a certain reaction out of one of us? What do they hope to accomplish?"

I took a deep, slow breath and let go of her hand.

"You should go. Let Oanen know I'm thinking of him."

She stood and gave me another hug.

"I will. I'd tell you to behave but..." She lifted a shoulder and gave me a knowing grin.

"I'll give 'em hell when I'm ready."

She nodded and left.

For the rest of the night, I dwelled on the possible reasons behind the Quills' and Adira's decision.

I looked at the phone number and hesitated to answer. Last time an unknown number had contacted me, I'd found a dead body in the alley of the Roost. While discovering that body had, ultimately, helped catch the murderer, I wasn't up for any super sleuthing today. After waking up to a yard full of snow, I wasn't in the mood for anything more than a day binge-watching TV.

The phone stopped ringing, but a moment later a text message came through.

We require your assistance. Please meet me at the Quills' in twenty minutes. Adira.

I tapped out a quick reply.

I thought I wasn't allowed anywhere near Oanen or Eliana. You wouldn't want to keep me from reaching my true potential, would you?

Her reply was immediate.

Of course not. That's why we'll keep the meeting brief. See you soon.

I growled, turned off the TV, and got ready. In less than five minutes, I was on the road.

"Maybe this is a test," I told myself. "If I do well, they'll let me spend time with Oanen and Eliana. If I don't do well, maybe they'll kick me out of their crap town." I grinned at that thought. Outside of Uttira, I'd finally have a chance at gaining the answers I needed.

"So, I either need to play this really cool or lose my shit completely. There can be no middle ground," I warned myself. And since the likelihood of them kicking me out was low, I knew I'd need to try to play nice.

When I reached the Quills' house, I parked in the neatly plowed driveway. As usual, Mrs. Quill opened the door well before I reached it.

"Hello, Megan," she said with a welcoming smile.

"I can't decide what's real or not with you," I said instead of a polite greeting. "I mean, do you honestly like me? It's hard to say when I'm not welcome in your home unless I can serve some menial purpose. Speaking of...what can I do for you today?"

I couldn't believe I'd managed to get all those words out while keeping a smile on my face. Oanen's mother's smile, however, had faded.

"We never meant for you to feel used or unwelcome. We're only trying to do what's best for both of you."

"Right," I said. "Because actually giving answers and guidance doesn't do anyone any good. Got it. Now, what was it I could do for you?"

"We have someone in the study we would like you to meet."

"Lead the way," I said, fighting to keep my cheery smile.

I followed her up the stairs to the familiar study where Adira and Mr. Quill already sat with another woman. She was petite, blonde, and only a blip in my wicked radar. She was also much older than any of the other recruits.

"Megan," Adira said. "I'd like you to meet Uttira's new liaison officer, Anne Regan."

I stood there for a moment, unsure what to feel. I hadn't ever really wanted to be a liaison. Yet, the idea of someone else keeping an eye on the kids I'd okayed to live here felt wrong. Mostly, I felt set up, again. It felt like they were trying to control me in some way. Or maybe my reaction.

"Anne Regan, did the Council tell you what I am?"

"I'm sorry, no."

"Don't be sorry. Be aware. I'm a fury. I've been told I'm supposed to punish the wicked."

"You are, Megan," Adira said.

"And yet, you stopped me, Adira." I focused on Anne again. "They say they have our best interests at heart. And those of the humans. I can't say I've seen much proof of that, though. Watch those in the Council closely. Stand up for the humans. And, don't ever let me find out you're doing otherwise."

I turned and started out of the room.

"Aren't you going to ask about Oanen?" Adira said.

"Don't toy with me, Adira. I'm young and inexperienced now, but I won't always be."

I walked out of the study and almost collided with a wide-eyed Eliana. She grabbed my hand and led me down the stairs.

"I heard," she whispered when we reached the front door. "I'm sorry they took that away from you."

"It's no big deal. They said it would be temporary. I better go. I don't want to get you in trouble."

She grinned slightly.

"After your parting comment, I don't think they're going to do anything to upset you for a while." She hugged me tightly. "I'll see you tomorrow."

I left the house with a heavier heart than when I'd entered. When I reached my car, I looked back and caught sight of Oanen in a third-floor window. He stood there with his hands in his front pockets as he watched me. I couldn't tell what he was thinking or feeling in that moment, but I knew what he needed from me.

"I'll see you tomorrow," I said.

A hint of a smile curved his lips, and I knew he'd heard me.

CHAPTER THIRTEEN

"Mr. and Mrs. Quill, I've come for your son," I said to myself, grinning widely as I put on my jacket. "I mean to do right by him and won't take no for an answer."

Obviously, I'd been watching too many reruns in the last twenty-four hours.

Last night, I had decided to wait until after lunch today before I returned to the Quills' home. My decision had been less about the time of day and more about the amount of time I would need to mentally prepare myself for the unannounced visit. All morning, I'd tried to come up with something clever to say when I got there. Something persuasive that might reverse their decision to keep me from Oanen and Eliana. However, I wasn't any closer to being prepared now than I'd been last night. It didn't matter. I refused to put off my visit. I needed Oanen.

I locked up the house and got serious as I moved toward the car. Mr. and Mrs. Quill would likely tell me to get lost. However, I hoped my comments to Mrs. Quill yesterday would at least get them to hear me out. It frustrated me that I didn't even know the real reason they were trying to keep Oanen and me apart.

"Why is honesty such a hard concept for so many people?" I mumbled to myself.

I pulled out onto the road and hoped I wouldn't come to regret what I was about to do.

Fifteen minutes later, I parked in front of Oanen's house. He was at the window and watched me get out of the car.

"You could make this easier by coming out," I said.

He shook his head slightly then stepped back.

"Playing hard to get isn't attractive for any gender," I said under my breath.

There was no one waiting to open the door. This time, I had to knock and wait in the cold.

When Mrs. Quill answered, surprise showed on her face.

"Hello, Megan. I didn't think we'd be seeing you for a while," she said, inviting me inside with a wave.

"Yeah, about that," I said when I was out of the cold. "This whole forced separation thing isn't working for me. I'm here to see Oanen."

"I'm sorry, Megan, but I can't allow that."

"Oh, you can; you're just choosing not to. Perhaps, if you could tell me the real reason why?"

"We're concerned that your time together is hindering your progress."

"Progress toward what?"

"Control."

"See, I disagree. What's hindering my progress is any lack of guidance, like I said last night. And I would like to believe that you, Mr. Quill, and Adira are unable to guide me because you lack the knowledge. However, I've seen Adira's files and the Academy's censored library and feel pretty confident that you three are purposely keeping information from me. Do you know what some people believe?" I asked, already feeling my inner fury stir as it had done at home when I'd thought this through.

"Some people believe that omission is as great a sin as an outright lie. And, in my book, sinner means wicked."

I embraced the change this time and knew the moment my eyes started to glow.

"I'm tired of being a pawn. Of being lied to. The gods control enough of my life already. I'm not giving more control of it over to anyone else. The Council has two choices. Let me leave Uttira or keep me but leave me in peace."

A cold chill crossed my back, and I turned just in time to catch Adira's wrist before her hand could touch me.

She winced and pulled back quickly, cradling her burned skin.

"You should know not to touch a fury when she's angry," I said, my voice already taking on a deeper echo.

"Megan, you need to control yourself," she said calmly.

I smiled, and it wasn't nice.

"I don't think so. Controlling myself would benefit you, not me. I think I need to let go."

Adira paled, and Mrs. Quill quickly stepped around me to stand beside her sister.

"We were wrong to try to keep Oanen from you. He's upstairs," she said as she reached out to press a speaker button near the door.

"Oanen, you have a visitor."

I briefly wondered why they were giving me what I wanted so easily.

"I expected more from you," Adira said. "And far less attitude."

"Why would you think I would have less attitude given the way you've treated me?"

"Because you were raised as a human."

I snorted.

"Human teenagers have enough attitude that most parents

wish there were late-life adoption options. Don't judge all humans based on what you see in Uttira. Don't expect far less attitude from a teenage fury. Expect more."

Mrs. Quill reached out and touched her sister's arm, and they both disappeared in a portal.

I looked up at the sound of footsteps on the stairs. Oanen walked down, his gaze never leaving mine. I crossed my arms and studied him. He looked burned, again, but not as badly as I had imagined. Just a red face and singed eyebrows. Nothing that would have kept him in bed.

My anger continued to rise. Not at Oanen, but at Adira and the rest of the Council.

"I have to ask. What hold did the Council have over you that kept you from coming to me?"

"My mark," he said after a moment.

Although I'd figured they'd been blackmailing him with something, I hadn't thought that. He'd never mentioned wanting his mark so much that he'd give me up for it. Hurt speared me.

"Why is your mark so important?"

He didn't answer until he reached the bottom step where he stayed at least fifteen feet away from me.

"Because of you. Your house is almost always vacant. Furies don't live in Uttira. At least, not if they can help it. And, from what I've gathered, no one else wants furies living in Uttira either. That means, at some point, you're going to get your mark."

I considered him for a moment, letting his words and his meaning sink in.

"And without your mark, you think I'd just leave you behind when I got mine?"

"Something like that."

"I don't think this bonding thing works like that. Less than twenty-four hours without hearing from you, and I was going crazy."

"How crazy?" he asked, his lips twitching.

"Like level-cities-to-find-you crazy or at least rip-off-Adira's-hidden-fairy-wings-to-find-you crazy."

He chuckled.

"You seem to have a thing with ripping off wings."

"Apparently. Must be in my blood."

"She doesn't really have wings, you know."

"Whatever. Am I cool enough to approach yet?"

He glanced down at my feet. "Floor's still trying to burn."

I looked down and saw the spreading scorch marks around me.

"If I go outside to try to cool off, will I need to come back in to save you again?"

"No. I think you've made your point, and they'll leave us alone."

"For now." I sighed and moved for the door. "I'll be back."

Outside, I walked around, having fun melting the snow and blackening the grass underneath. After I finished writing "Furies should not play with fire" on the Quills' front lawn, I knew I could go back inside. It had taken me three passes to get the word fire dark enough.

Smiling to myself, I jumped a little when I turned around and saw Oanen right there.

"My mom sent me out to tell you she feels you've suitably learned your lesson about playing with fire and can stop writing."

"She doesn't really believe I was doing this to punish myself, does she?"

"No."

I glanced at the house.

"I don't know much about this boyfriend-girlfriend thing,

but I do know I'm supposed to get your parents to want to like me. I completely went the opposite way in there."

"Don't worry. They do like you." He glanced at my creation on the lawn. "Feel better?"

"Are we talking temperature or vengeance?"

"Both."

"Then, yes."

"Good." He closed the distance between us and wrapped his arms around me. I hugged him in return, relishing the feel of his hold. It seemed like forever since we'd touched, and I hadn't realized how much I missed it and craved it until now.

He brushed back a bit of my hair and pressed a kiss to my temple. The fire that had gone mostly dormant flared, and I quickly stepped out of his hold.

Fenris' question about how I would put out a fire echoed in my head again. I hated that I needed Oanen so much but couldn't touch him or be touched like I wanted.

"Are you free to leave the house again?" I asked.

"Yes."

"Good because I want to go somewhere and try something."

"That sounds scarily vague."

I grinned and led the way to the car. Once we were inside, I opened all the windows before starting the engine. I didn't trust myself to stay calm.

"Are you going to give me any hints?" he asked when we reached the main road.

"Not yet. If I think about it too much, it'll get hot in here."

"I'm intrigued."

His tone was making my insides warmer by the second.

"Cut it out."

I forced my thoughts away from what I was going to propose. When I'd come up with the idea at home this morning, I'd almost melted the fridge handle.

It only took us a few minutes to reach the Academy.

"Are we breaking in again?" he asked.

"If we have to but not to get into Adira's office. The pool this time."

We got out and tried the student door. It was locked. I led the way around to the side where I'd found the open window before, and we climbed through. This time no one floated on the surface of the pool.

"All right," Oanen said once he stood beside me. "Now what?"

"Now, you get in the pool."

I took off my jacket and put it on a chair. When I bent and started to take my shoes off, a huge splash echoed in the room. I glanced at Oanen's pile of clothes then his wickedly handsome smirk as he treaded water.

"I think I see where this is going," he said.

"Really? Because I'm not even sure where it's going to go." I unzipped my jeans and put them on the growing stack of my clothes. Oanen didn't say anything as I tugged my shirt over my head and set it aside. I couldn't talk if I wanted to. My hands shook. I was nervous about standing in front of him in my bra and underwear. But, more than that, I was nervous about everything going wrong.

I walked toward the pool and sat on the edge, sticking one leg at a time in the water. Steam hissed up around me at first contact. The cold water started pulling away the heat curling inside my limbs and the steam slowed.

"In theory, the pool should keep me from overheating because of the temperature control for the water creatures who normally use it. If it doesn't, as soon as you feel the water starting to warm, you have to get out so I don't slow boil you like a lobster. Deal?"

"Deal," he said. "Now get in so we can test your theory."

I took a deep breath to steady my nerves then eased myself the rest of the way into the pool. Oanen swam closer, an almost predatory glint reflected in his eyes.

"Relax, Megan," he said with a slight grin. "I won't hurt you."

He wrapped one arm around my waist and pulled me against his chest while he gripped the edge of the pool with his other hand. The feel of his skin against mine escalated the heat inside me. Steam rose around us in the barest wisps while the water of the pool worked to keep me cool.

"Are you okay?" I asked.

"No. You're killing me. Kiss me already."

I grinned and set my hands on his bare chest before closing the distance between us. I touched my lips to his hesitantly, paying more attention to how the contact was affecting me and the temperature of the water than the actual experience. Oanen didn't allow that for long. He licked my upper lip then gripped me tighter and demanded more.

Holding tight, I groaned at the touch of his tongue against mine. His hand moved over my back, a cool stroke over my heated skin. We parted and looked at each other.

"Still good?" I asked.

"The best."

His mouth claimed mine once more. The passion of it robbed me of breath and cautious thought. I clung to him, losing myself to the kiss. To the taste of him. To the feel of him. The water rose over my shoulders and climbed up my throat as he let go of the pool and wrapped my legs around his waist. The feel of his erection firmly pressed against my underwear brought in enough awareness that I broke the contact once more.

Oanen reached up to move a piece of wet hair from my temple as he treaded water with his legs and watched me with golden eyes.

"You are the most beautiful thing in my life. A perfection I never thought the gods could achieve," he said.

"You're not just saying that to get in my panties, are you," I said, already knowing the answer.

"No. It's not the truth because I want you; I want you because it's the truth."

I looked at him for a long moment, embracing what I felt for him.

"How have you become my everything?"

I kissed him softly, a gentle touch of my lips to his.

The soft melody of a song about love and acceptance wrapped around my heart and encouraged me to give myself over to the handsome, exceptional creature who wanted me for his own. I smoothed my hands over his shoulders and around his back, pressing my chest against his. He groaned into my mouth. The song threaded around us, coaxing us both to let our passion for each other free.

Oanen gripped my legs and arched his hips against mine. Pleasure tingled through me. The need to give and receive even more rose higher as we sank under the water, our mouths melded in a hot kiss that threatened to consume my soul. I felt his need for me. His desire to call me his other half. All that I felt for him collided and gelled together inside my chest, a ball of emotion so intense it burned to be shared.

I loosened my hold on everything I'd been too afraid to let myself feel and sent it straight toward Oanen.

Water exploded around us. I opened my eyes in shock as his lips were ripped from mine and, through the bubbles, watched him fly backwards. He hit the other side of the pool with so much force that I could hear the tile crack even under water.

I surfaced, not even close to out of breath, and frantically swam toward him. He wasn't moving, his body floating face down near a ladder. I hooked one arm around him, just under his arms, and pulled him toward the edge, ignoring the ladder and heaving him out of the pool and onto the cement ledge.

The moment I was on my knees beside him, I pressed my ear to his chest. The beat of his heart and the rise and fall of his chest reassured me.

Sitting back on my heels, I brushed back his hair.

"Oanen?" I called.

His face was once again blistered. Most of his skin had some degree of burn. His hair hadn't melted, but likely only because of the water.

"Oanen, can you hear me?"

He groaned slightly.

"Ooh. Looks bad," a voice said from behind me.

I glanced over my shoulder in surprise at a green-faced girl swimming in the water.

"I think I hurt him," I said, trying to fight my panic. "He's not answering."

"Oh, that's too bad. Enjoy that kick to the face," she said before diving under.

I didn't know who she was, but I wanted to kill her. Oanen gripped my hand, his hold stopping me from jumping into the water. I turned back to him and found his eyes open.

"Are you okay?" I asked.

"Yes and no. I'd like to go back in the water and try again, but I think I'll need a few minutes." He spoke slowly, taking small breaths after every third word. He would need far more than just a few minutes.

"You want to try again? Are you insane?" I asked.

"For you," he said with a smile followed closely by a wince.

I felt sick.

"How bad is it?" I asked softly.

"I think I might have cracked a rib or two. Help me up."

"I'm not sure you should stand. Let me call—"

"Megan, I'll be all right. I just need a hand up so I don't hurt myself more."

I hesitated until he tried rolling on his side on his own. The pain on his face had me getting down beside him so he could use me as a brace to stand. Each wince that pulled at his features tore at me. I'd done that. I'd hurt him. Again. How many times was it now? I'd lost count.

As soon as he stood, I helped him around the pool to his clothes. Helping him put on pants was awkward. Mostly because the green-faced bitch kept popping her head above the water and openly eyeing Oanen's ass.

Once he had pants on, I quickly dressed as well. When I turned to offer to be his crutch, I found him already halfway through the window.

"You're going to kill yourself," I said, not sure if I should help him climb out or pull him back in.

"I'll be fine," he said. He lifted his leg over the windowsill and disappeared from sight.

I leaned out the window, saw him lying in the snow, and quickly scrambled after him.

"We could have used the doors." I helped him to his feet and guided him toward the parking lot.

"We could have, but then the new liaison would have needed to come here, and I don't think she's ready for a second round with you just yet." Humor laced his words, an attempt to mask the strain in them.

"Second round?" I asked, playing along. "That's sounds like I attacked her or something."

"She's afraid of you after just one meeting," he said.

"Good. She should be afraid of everyone here. She'll pay more attention that way."

"Or become paranoid."

I opened the passenger door for him and watched as he

eased onto the seat. Either he was getting better at not wincing or he was hurting less. When he was settled, I closed the door and ran around to get in behind the steering wheel.

"I don't even know if this place has a hospital," I said.

"It doesn't. There's no need. We all heal fairly quickly." He reached over and set his hand on my leg. "I can feel your panic. I'll be fine. Please stop worrying. Give me a week, and we'll try again."

The fact that he'd gone from saying a few minutes to a week hit me hard.

"How?" I asked. "I don't know how to control the things happening to me or even know what will happen. I didn't even know I could explode fire like that. We're not getting into that pool again."

"It's not your fault."

"Isn't it? I took you to the pool. It was my idea to see if the water would work."

"It might have if the siren hadn't started singing."

"Siren?" I thought of the melody that had been in my head and the memory of the siren who'd tricked men into thinking she'd been stripping on line.

"I thought that didn't work on us."

"It normally doesn't because our minds are naturally more shielded when we're aware of the song. We were distracted."

"So the song worked? I want to kill her."

"It wasn't a her. It was a him. The mermaid in the pool probably talked him into helping her. I'm guessing she's the one who went after Ashlyn?" he asked.

"I don't know. I never saw her face. I only—" I swore.

"What?"

"I kicked it. Yep, that was her."

I pulled up before his house and parked the car. He put his hand over mine to stop me from turning off the car.

"I'll see you tomorrow." He brought my hand to his mouth and kissed my knuckles. "Thank you for an amazing afternoon."

He was breaking my heart with the devotion in his gaze. He could barely move without wincing and had blisters all over his chest and face. The skin around his waist, where my legs had been, looked like it had already started peeling. All the damage I'd done, and he was thanking me?

I swallowed hard.

"Bye, Oanen."

He let me go, and I bit my lip as he slowly worked himself out of the car. At the door, he stopped and leaned down just enough to see me.

"Say it," he said. "Say you'll see me tomorrow."

"I'll see you tomorrow."

His lips curved slightly, but the smile didn't touch his eyes as he closed the door. I watched him start toward the house. Before he reached the door, I rolled down my window. The cold air calmed my mind and helped me make a hard decision.

"Oanen," I called.

He turned to look back at me.

"I think we made a mistake. We both need to come to terms with the fact that, no matter how much our hearts are saying yes, our bodies are saying no. Try to stay away. I'll try to do the same."

CHAPTER FOURTEEN

THE IMAGE OF OANEN STANDING SHIRTLESS IN THE SNOW STAYED branded in my mind all the way home. He hadn't called my name or tried to stop me as I'd pulled away. Instead, he'd sent a text before I'd reached the road. A text I still hadn't read.

I turned into my driveway and parked in the back. Resisting the urge to pull the phone from my pocket, I got out and made my way into the house. Only after I'd hung up my jacket and put my shoes by the door, did I look at what he'd sent.

Playing hard to get isn't attractive for any gender.

I groaned. I'd known it wouldn't be easy as soon as I'd made the decision that we shouldn't be together like he wanted anymore. Taking a slow breath, I carefully composed a reply.

I'm not playing hard to get. I've tried to be the girlfriend you need. It hasn't worked. I'm sorry, but this is for the best.

His reply was immediate.

A few burns and broken bones change nothing. You're still mine. I'll see you tomorrow.

Why couldn't he just accept that we were done? I typed out another reply, hoping he'd understand.

I think it would be best if I take a few days off. Some distance will help us both come to terms with this being over.

I thought I'd get another text, but the phone remained quiet the rest of the day. Even Eliana didn't text. I kept telling myself it was for the best. However, the ache in my chest disagreed and continued to grow until I could barely breathe.

Once the sun set, I crawled into bed, hoping that sleep would mute the regret and denial I felt. However, sleep didn't come easily. I tossed and turned, the corrosive pain creating a misery I couldn't seem to escape.

Exhaustion finally pulled me under well after midnight.

Tormented by dark, wind-swept skies filled with lightning and an eagle's cry, I ran endlessly. There was no safety from the cold, pounding rain. No winged harbor in which to shelter. I was completely alone in a world that wanted to destroy me. Lightning struck me again and again, until the only forward progress I made was on my hands and knees, crawling through the mud.

Then, the rain stopped. A hand ran down my back and soothed the pain raging inside of me.

"You've suffered enough."

The mud between my fingers changed to sheets. The bed moved, and I turned to find the one person I'd been searching for. Oanen settled behind me and wrapped an arm around my waist to pull me close to his bare, wet chest. I relaxed against him and let my heartbeat slow.

"I refuse to believe what I feel for you is a mistake," he said softly, his breath brushing my neck. "We took the bonding flight. There will never be anyone else for me. You're mine, Megan. It's time you come to terms with that."

I sighed and snuggled in. The storm inside me settled and didn't return to torment me while I lay within the protection of the harbor I'd so desperately sought.

I woke slowly, remembering the feel of Oanen's arms around me. However, when I turned, I was alone in bed. Frowning, I got up and went downstairs. He wasn't in the kitchen and the bathroom door stood open.

"Oanen?" I called. There was no answer.

Making my way back upstairs, I recalled the vividness of my dream. Had Oanen been just my imagination, too?

My heart ached at the thought that he'd only been in my head. How was I ever going to keep my distance if I felt like this in less than a day? I wouldn't be able to stop myself from running right into his arms if I saw him in person. Which was exactly why I needed to get my ass moving and get to the Academy before he did.

When I reached my room, I stopped and stared at my bed, hoping he hadn't come. Streaks of blood painted my pillowcase and my sheets. I'd been crying in my sleep. A lot. I wiped at my face and felt traces of crusted blood around my eyes.

"So attractive," I mumbled as I started stripping the bed.

With the bedding in my arms along with a clean change of clothes, I returned downstairs to throw my sheets into the washer and take a shower.

Fifteen minutes later, I flew out the door with a lunch in hand and got into my car. It wasn't until I was at Girderon's gates that I realized my mistake. Monday check in. I'd need to face Adira. After the big scene I'd made about them not keeping me and Oanen apart, I'd gone and broken up with him. I hated eating crow.

The parking lot only had a few cars when I rolled to a stop. I got out and hurried inside, wanting to get the meeting over with.

Any hope of avoiding Adira died at the sight of her open door.

"Come in, Megan," she called before I could back away.

I went inside and stood by the chair.

"I'm here. What fruitless task in the guise of education would you like to set me on now?"

"You're welcome to continue using the library."

"What? You don't want the out of control fury mingling with the masses?" As soon as the sarcastic words left my mouth, I realized I'd spoken the truth and laughed.

"What happens when I read every sorry excuse for information in the library? What stall tactic will you use then?" I asked.

"I'm hoping you'll have discovered who you are before that happens."

"Why don't you just tell me?"

She sighed, her pleasant façade finally slipping.

"Fine, Megan. You're a fury, like your mother before you. Does hearing it from my lips help you understand who you are any better than you did before? No, it does not. Knowing who you are is about self-discovery. You need to learn who you are from the inside. When you do, you'll have all your answers about who you will become."

"Who I am on the inside?" I gripped the back of the chair. "I gave you a glimpse of the real me yesterday. I'm a burning ball of rage. A fire burning so hot I will destroy anyone and everyone around me. And, do you know why I'm so angry on the inside?" I leaned toward her. "Because my mom left me here. Because I have to deal with dumbass answers from adults who think they know so much. Because the gods made me this way."

The back of the chair disintegrated under my grip. I looked at the ash raining down on the floor then met Adira's gaze. A hint of worry now resided there.

"Stop playing games with me. It won't end well for you."

I left her office and closed myself in the library where I hoped I wouldn't hurt anything. With hours to waste, I set to work and searched for hints of anything that might help me break the bond with Oanen. He wouldn't like my solution, but it was the only one I had. I'd tried his way, and it hadn't worked.

The room brightened as the sun rose higher. However, each passing hour brought no new, useful information. I ignored the knock on the door and was relieved when no cool air appeared after it stopped. My stomach cramped, and I slowly ate my sandwich while I continued to read.

The light from the window dimmed, the first hint of just how long I'd spent pouring over these useless books. The current one outlined the lineage of several creatures. I was about to lift my hand and let it return to the shelves when something caught my eye.

Many creatures descended from Echidna, known by mortals as the mother of all monsters. She possessed the beautiful face of a maid with the body of a serpent. From her, a multitude of offspring were born.

Her offspring were gifted with an ability to appear exquisitely human to lure in their prey before devouring the flesh so many crave. However, one of her children, the Sphinx, did not crave the flesh of mortals but their minds instead. Only the smartest survived her presence. Those males she took to her bed; and from them, the first of the oracles came to the world of men.

These rare creatures were much like their goddess grandmother, Echidna, in appearance and their demi-goddess mother in knowledge. They could foresee the past, present, and future. So sought after was their counsel that many perished in the wars of men. Those who remained retreated from the world of men. Like the gods, their existence has turned to myth in the minds of mortals.

I lifted my hand when the book went on to outline another branch. I didn't care about minotaurs; I cared about oracles. If they'd all retreated from the world of men, that meant one could be here in Uttira. And, she could give me real answers about what I'll become and how to control my rage.

I quickly left the library and grabbed my things. There weren't any messages from either Oanen or Eliana, which I thought odd given that it was close to five. I couldn't believe I'd stayed in the library that late. Making my way through the dark halls, I sent a text to Fenris.

You wouldn't happen to know any oracles, would you?

His reply came through before I reached the exit.

No, but I'll ask around.

It was already dark outside when I left the building. Not dark enough to hide what someone had done to my car, though. This time, instead of breaking the windshield, my hater had scratched the paint to hell. First the smashed windshield, then the bullshit siren stunt at the pool, and now this? Everyone in Uttira seemed determine to test the expanse of my anger.

Pissed, I took a picture of the damage and sent it to Fenris without any words. Whoever he thought he'd dealt with hadn't listened, or I had more than one hater, which was a good possibility.

Lights shone through my windows when I got home. Frowning, I turned into the driveway and pulled around back. The lack of a parked car made me suspicious, and I quietly got out and made my way toward the backdoor.

Through the window, I caught sight of Oanen at the stove. My heart skipped a beat, and my chest tightened. Even with what I'd found at the library, I knew it would be smarter to stick to what I'd said and send him away until I could figure out a way to control the rage-storm always waiting to explode from inside of me.

He turned slightly. Although his moves were once more graceful and his expression free of winces, the view of his still red face helped firm my resolve. Those fearful moments beside the pool had almost killed me. I couldn't go through that again.

I opened the door and stepped inside.

"I hope you're hungry for burgers. That's about all I'm good at making," he said.

"A burger sounds good." I took a steadying breath. "I thought we agreed that we should try to stay away from one another."

"No. That's what you want to do. I never agreed to it." He turned the stovetop off and faced me. "We took the bonding flight. There's no going back. You need to stop running and accept what you already know."

"And that is?"

He walked toward me.

"We're meant to be together. I know you feel it. This need to be close to me. To see me, talk to me, touch me." He lifted his hand and cupped my cheek. "I know it hurts when you try to stay away. And I know you're afraid you'll hurt me more if you don't." He reeled me in until my chest brushed his. "Stop denying yourself what you really want."

His lips settled over mine in a kiss that stole my breath and made my heart race. I threaded my fingers in his hair and gave in like he wanted, even if only just a few seconds. His hips pressed against mine, a contact too close to what had happened at the pool, and I pulled away. He didn't let me go far.

"Tell me you're done fighting us," he said, resting his forehead against mine.

"Probably not. Each time I hurt you, I'm going to try to walk away. I care about you too much to risk you like that."

"And I care about you too much to let you go."

"We're at an impasse then."

"For now. Ready to eat?"

I nodded, and he released me. He fixed two plates, and we sat together at the table.

"What are your plans for tomorrow?" he asked.

"Not sure. I really don't think I can handle another long day in the library."

"I bet not. I'd ask what you found in there that kept you so long, but I know it wouldn't do any good."

I opened my mouth just to give it a try, and nothing came out. He chuckled then grew serious once more.

"What are the chances of you letting me spend the night again tonight? I won't be in tomorrow—my parents asked me to attend a Council meeting—and I'm not sure either of us would like another twenty-four hours alone."

"So last night wasn't a dream?"

"No. And I'm glad you didn't hit me to test it. Anyway, I couldn't have stayed away from you if I'd wanted to. You were in too much pain."

I couldn't deny what I'd felt then or now.

"Yes. You can spend the night. You can help me make my bed, too."

"Already done in hopes you'd say yes."

My insides went hot and cold at the insinuation.

"You mean you want to risk sleeping with me in my bed, don't you?" I asked.

"I do."

I couldn't stop the fear that raced through me. What if I hurt him again? I reminded myself he'd managed just fine the night before. Maybe everything would be okay.

"Changing your mind?" he asked, softly.

"No. You can still stay."

The rest of the meal passed in a blur. Oanen took a shower; and while he did, I quickly went upstairs and changed for the night. When I finished, I paced.

One bad dream, one little slip, and I'd crisp him.

"And I'm pretty sure fried griffin doesn't taste like fried chicken, Megan," I mumbled.

At the sound of Oanen's chuckle, I whirled to face the door.

"You talk to yourself a lot."

"All the sane people do."

"People talk to themselves about how much they want to taste their boyfriends?"

My insides exploded with heat.

"It's okay, Megan," he said with a slow smile. "I want to taste you again, too."

The heat grew worse, and I could smell the wood under my feet.

"New rule. You can't sleep in my bed unless I'm already sleeping." I lifted my arm and pointed to the hall. "You're in the guest room until you hear me snoring."

"You don't snore."

"Then you'll be waiting a long time."

He grinned, pulled me close to give me a quick kiss, then left the room.

"You're hot, Megan. But, nothing I can't handle," he called.

I shook my head and crawled under my covers. The smell of smoldering fabric surrounded me as I tried to calm my breathing.

"Sleeping yet?" Oanen asked from the other room.

"Go to sleep, Oanen."

CHAPTER FIFTEEN

A NOTE AND A PACKED LUNCH WAITED FOR ME ON THE TABLE WHEN I came downstairs. Although his thoughtfulness warmed me, I would have rather had him present. Waking up alone in the bed had been a relief and a disappointment at the same time. But, the dual dents in my pillow and lack of charred sheets had helped ease some of the disappointment.

Grabbing the lunch, I headed out the door. I had no plans to spend the day stuck inside the library like Adira wanted. The time for patience was done. I wanted answers, and I wanted them now. The school was full of people who had grown up in Uttira. One of them was bound to know something about oracles. I should have asked Oanen last night, but the drama of us had gotten in the way.

Eliana was waiting for me when I pulled into the parking lot.

"Just the girl I wanted to see," I said, opening the door.

"Me too. Oanen said that he wouldn't be here today. I'm excited he's finally giving me a turn."

"You know you can hang out with us, too, right?"

"No way. Eew." She scrunched up her nose at me.

"Why not?"

"With what you two are giving off each time you look at each other, do you really want me to turn into a black-eyed crush muncher and start feeding off my pseudo brother?"

"Point taken. Sorry I didn't think of that sooner. You should come over tonight. I'll tell Oanen to take a hike."

Eliana laughed.

"Like he'd ever listen. You're officially in bonded-male griffin territory. There's no way he's going to let you alone for any significant amount of time."

"He's gone now," I said with a wry grin.

"He is. And I'm betting you have something planned that will probably upset him when he's back."

"Not really. I just want to find an oracle."

Eliana shook her head.

"Do you even know what an oracle is?" she asked.

"Yes. Someone with answers. Who do you think would know anything about oracles? Like are oracles still alive? Where do they live? Is there one in Uttira?

"Well, Fenris was a good place to start last time," she said.

A thread of annoyance wormed its way up my spine a moment before a laugh interrupted our conversation.

"Like wolf boy would know anything about an oracle."

I turned to look at the girl. Her hair was a familiar mermaid green, which I tried not to hold against her.

"And you do?" I asked.

She smiled, showing a sharp row of small teeth.

"I do. I know a lot actually."

I let my doubt show on my face.

"Okay. What do you know?"

A hard light came into her eyes.

"Oh, it's not going to work like that, sweet fish. You want information; I want something in return."

Her attitude was starting to annoy me.

"You took what was mine," she said. "I want it back."

I frowned. Confused.

"I haven't taken anything."

Any hint of humor left her expression.

"You took my human and kicked me in the face."

Anger lit inside of me. This was the same mermaid? The one who'd tried to kill Ashlyn, and the one who'd watched Oanen and me at the pool? I fisted my hand.

Eliana's fingers immediately closed over mine, and some of the building rage left me.

"What exactly are you saying?" I asked. "That you want Ashlyn back in exchange for information that you may or may not have?"

"That's exactly what I'm saying."

"You're sick in the head. There's no way I'm handing over a human. Ever."

"Suit yourself." She smirked and continued on into the school.

I glanced at Eliana.

"Are you going to need to wear me like a backpack today?" she asked.

"Maybe. How much do you weigh?"

She grinned but didn't let go of my hand as we started toward the school.

The loud rev of an engine and the spray of gravel had us both turning in time to see Fenris pull up. He was missing his usual her-herd. He spotted us before he even turned off the car and waved for us to wait.

His easy jog in our direction caught the eye of just about every female still lingering in the parking lot.

"Ladies. This is a sight. Tell me there's more after the hand holding."

I rolled my eyes, and Eliana released my hand.

"There might be. Someone trashed my car again last night." I pointed at the long scratches.

Fenris frowned and went over to inspect the paint. He sniffed a few times and shook his head in disgust.

"It's not the same person. I'll find out who it is, though."

"Thanks. This time let me do some talking, will you?"

He grinned widely. "Only if I get a hug."

I opened my arms and wasn't surprised to find myself pressed chest to chest with him before I could blink. He stuck his nose in my hair, breathed deeply, and made a quiet sound of disappointment before pulling away.

I tried not to smirk as he took my hand and lifted it to his mouth for an old-fashioned back-of-the-hand knuckle kiss.

"You need to work on your hugging skills," he told me.

"Thanks for the tip. I'm sure Eliana will be happy to help me today, though. You just get me a name."

"I'm on it, my wrath goddess."

I grinned and watched him jog away. When I looked at Eliana, I found her watching me.

"What?" I asked.

"I think he's trying to cause trouble between you and Oanen. Oanen's going to smell him on you."

"As you pointed out, Oanen's not here today."

She shook her head, and we walked inside, joining the masses in the halls.

"So why do you need to know about oracles?" she asked.

"Because I'm tired of bullshit answers."

Eliana laughed.

"That's all everyone here does. Why do you think an oracle would be any different?"

She had me there. But that didn't change my plan. I asked everyone during our first session. Some gave me looks like I'd dropped a silent bomb in class. Some sniggered and smirked but said nothing. The second session wasn't much different. I even asked Professor Flavian.

"Megan, oracles are dangerous creatures. It would be a better use of your time here if you returned to your studies in the library."

"Nope. It wouldn't. Been there. Read that. I need answers, and no one here wants to give them."

"I'm sorry, Megan. I can't help you."

"You won't help me. There's a difference."

I walked out of the room and straight into Eliana.

"I heard," she said.

"It's really starting to piss me off. You want lunch?"

She gave me a startled look then quickly hugged me. I laughed and hugged her back. My frustration immediately faded.

"That's not what I meant, but I'll take it."

"Oh, you meant–"

"Now this is what I like to see," Fenris said from behind Eliana. "Can I get in on that?"

Eliana pulled away and gave Fenris a scolding look. "I think you've hugged Megan enough. She's with Oanen, and you know it. Stop trying to cause trouble."

He gave her his best boyish smile.

"Does that mean you'll give me a hug instead?"

Eliana shook her head and turned to me.

"Ready for lunch?"

Fenris winked at me over her head.

"I wanted to let you know that I haven't found the car scratcher, yet, and the word's spreading that you're looking for an oracle. I'm still keeping my nose and ears out for both."

"Thanks."

We left Fenris and merged with the flow of bodies heading

toward lunch. Instead of going outside, we sat in one of the free rooms to eat our meals in peace.

"Seriously, Megan. What are you hoping to learn? Why an oracle?"

"First, I want to know if there's an oracle even alive. Second, I want to find out where said oracle would live if said oracle is alive. Finally, I want the oracle to tell me what I will become or how I can control my temper. Both, if the oracle is willing."

"I don't know much about oracles, but I do know nothing's ever free. You'll need to give something to get something."

"Your hugs are free. Oanen's protection is free."

"Nope. I take something from you with each hug. And, the bond is the price of Oanen's protection."

"What about your friendship? Is that free?"

"Nope. There's a price there, too. You now carry the stigma of associating with the succubus who can't feed."

"My stigma doesn't seem to bother Fenris."

"That's because he wants something. I just haven't figured out what yet."

I took another bite of my Oanen-made sandwich so I couldn't answer if she asked me anything. She didn't, though.

"How am I going to find out what I need?" I asked after I swallowed my mouthful.

Eliana shrugged. "Keep asking people, I guess. Word is spreading. Someone's bound to know something."

After we finished our lunches, we tossed the bags in the recycling near the door. A tingle of irritation ran up my spine, and my head whipped in the direction of the hall. Eliana immediately grabbed my hand. Neither of us moved as voices filtered into the room.

"She's asking everyone."

"I bet she is. Don't tell her a thing. That bitch owes me a human. She has no idea what she stepped into."

I recognized the second voice. The merbitch I'd kicked in the face.

"Why not tell her?" the first voice asked. "She'd never make it to the island without help."

There was a moment of silence.

"You're brilliant. This is far better than getting people to trash her car or trying to get her to fry her boyfriend."

If not for Eliana's hold, I would have flown out the door. Instead, all of the rage trying to pump into me slipped away before I could embrace it. Eliana held my hand until their footsteps faded. As soon as she released me, I ran out into the hall but found it empty.

Eliana watched me closely, no doubt trying to decide if it was backpack time.

"Where's the island?" I asked.

"There's only one lake. I'm guessing it's there."

The same lake where I'd kicked the merbitch in the face. If there was an island somewhere on that large body of water, I needed to find it. There were two ways to do that. A search by water or by air. Either one would take some time if I didn't know a general idea of where to look. The lake was beyond huge.

"I need to go back to the library. I'll see you after school," I said absently, already thinking of what I would need to do.

"Behave," Eliana called as I hurried away.

I took my phone from my pocket and started dialing Oanen's number. Before I reached the second turn, I heard Adira's voice and stopped. She was the last person I wanted to run into. I was still pissed as hell at her.

"I trust you'll do well when you choose to leave," she said. "Your parents and I understand that it won't be until the bond is settled between the two of you. But when it is, there's some important work we need you to complete."

"I understand," Oanen said. "I'll do what's necessary."

I frowned and stepped around the corner. Both turned to look at me.

Adira smiled slightly.

"I'll let you share the news." She stepped back into her office and closed the door.

"News?" I asked.

"That meeting my parents wanted with the Council? It was for my mark. I didn't know."

A bubble of excitement burst inside of me.

"Let me see."

He turned his head, and I saw a large trinity knot on the column of his neck.

"My mom had that on the inside of her wrist," I said. I couldn't believe that was the mark that would let us in and out of Uttira.

"Yeah. Location and size don't matter. You can choose both when it's time."

"This is perfect, Oanen," I said, stepping close and grasping his forearm. "You can take me to see my mom."

His expression shifted slightly.

"I can't. It was the one oath I had to give before they gave the mark. I cannot take you from Uttira until you have a mark of your own."

I could feel my insides start to heat and quickly took two steps back from him.

He reached for me like he was going to close the space again, and I held up my hand.

"Don't. I'm not even sure this is far enough."

His expression changed to one of hurt.

"I'm not mad at you," I said. "I'm mad at the Council. Why are they such assholes?"

"They're trying to protect the humans. Without control, you could hurt a lot of them."

"No shit. I could hurt a lot of people in Uttira, too. That's why I need to figure out how to control this. I need the answers my mom can give me."

I clenched my hands in frustration and glared at Adira's door. Furls of smoke started to curl up from the wood door.

"I can try to find her," he said. "Your mom. The Council never said anything to prevent that. Do you know where she might be?"

My gaze flew to him, and all my anger left me.

"Yes. I do." I texted him our last address. "I think she's still there. Maybe."

"Good, and I'll go right now on one condition," he said.

"Sure. What is it?"

"You go home and stay there until I get back. Eliana will check up on you."

"Done."

He stepped closer and wrapped his arms around me.

"We'll figure this out, Megan. Together."

When he nudged my head up, I didn't think why.

His lips touched mine lightly, sending a zing of desire straight through me. Heat gathered in my middle once more. His tongue swept against the seam of my lips, and I opened with a small sound of need. The heat pooled under my skin. I gripped his shoulders and stretched taller, needing more contact.

He kissed me like he would never see me again, and I kissed him back just as desperately.

When we finally tore apart, his face was red, and he had two scorch marks on his shoulders.

I cringed.

"Don't," he said. "I loved every second of that. The fire of your kiss does more than burn me. It lets me know what you feel is real. That I really am the one you want to be with."

"Of course you are." I couldn't believe he would ever doubt it.

"It's sometimes hard to tell when you always smell like Fenris."

"About that. He's promised me to secrecy, but I swear to you there's a reason for it that has nothing to do with his interest in me."

Oanen studied me for a moment then nodded.

"Thank you. I trust you, Megan. And I trust him because you asked me to. But, it's still not easy smelling him on you."

"I know. I'm sorry. I'll ask him again if I can talk to you about it."

"After I'm back. Hopefully, it won't take long."

I smiled and shooed him down the hall.

"Go. The sooner you leave, the sooner you're back. And the sooner I can stop giving you second degree burns every time we're together."

He gave me one last kiss and strode away. Excitement coursed through me at the thought that all of our struggles might soon be over. I couldn't wait to just hug him without worrying about hurting him.

It wasn't until he turned the corner that reality pooped on my rainbow. My mom had moved us often, and there was no guarantee that she hadn't moved again. What if she wasn't where I'd left her?

I sent off a quick series of texts to Oanen with all the prior addresses I could remember then went to the library. Even if he did find her, there was still no guarantee that she'd talk to me. After all, she'd left me here with no clue in the first place. I was tired of waiting. The information about oracles was a solid lead to get answers. And now, I also knew one lived on an island in the lake. Wouldn't it be smarter for me to at least research what I could and know where she was if Oanen didn't find my mom?

Researching in the library proved to be helpful for a change. On one of the lower shelves, there was a large book that had a hand drawn map of Uttira. The massive lake had a spell on it that reduced its size in the human world while maintaining its size within Uttira. It was easily half the size of one of the Great Lakes.

In the center of the water, the mapmaker placed a dot and called it the Isle of Woe. There were no other details and no other dots.

I headed out the door with the information and didn't bother going to any of the other sessions. If I wanted to get to the island without Oanen's help, I'd need a boat and some supplies. And a lot of real, practical advice about mermaids that I wouldn't find in the books. I picked up my phone from the basket in the hall and sent a message to Ashlyn.

Do you have time to come over tonight? Or could I come to your place? I have some questions about the lake.

Sure. I'd rather you come to me.

I'll be there by five, I replied.

Oanen would understand.

CHAPTER SIXTEEN

ASHLYN SAT ON THE COUCH AFTER OFFERING ME SOMETHING TO drink. She looked less sad now. The dark circles that had shadowed under her eyes during the first week following her uncle's death were gone. Yet, I still saw hints of sorrow in her expression. It would likely linger for a long while. I couldn't imagine how it must feel to be still living in this place after losing her family twice.

I took a seat across from her.

"I'm sorry we haven't had time to talk much," I said. "How have you been?"

"Good. Well, not good. But better. I like having Eugene, Zoe, and Kelsey here. Camil and I didn't talk much even though we were close to the same age."

I recalled the girl who I'd found dead in the dumpster and felt a pang of regret that things hadn't changed in Uttira quickly enough to help her.

"How are they adjusting, in your opinion?" I asked.

"Eugene is embracing all of this. Kelsey and Zoe are taking it in. I think they're still deciding what to do."

"I wish the Council would just give them enough money to improve their lives and let them go."

Ashlyn snorted.

"Your heart's in the right place, but all the money in the world wouldn't stop what would happen to them. They have no parents. No guaranteed safety net. No one to protect them from all the harsh things out there. After living here, you should know the human world that you saw isn't what it really is. There are predators out there that will feed on the forgotten and unattached."

A shiver ran through me, a nudge of anger that didn't really have a source.

"Are you okay?" she asked. "Your eyes just flickered orange."

"You're safe; but no, I'm not okay. The talk of predators stoked the fires that have been kindling inside me since your uncle's death. There's an itch to do something about all of it. But, I'm stuck here." I leaned forward slightly. "Do you know anything about the Isle of Woe?" I asked.

"No. What is it?"

"It's an island in the center of the lake. There's an oracle that lives there, I guess."

Her expression changed to suspicion.

"Who told you that?"

"I overheard some mermaids talking."

She shook her head.

"Don't believe anything they tell you. They will do whatever they can to get you into their waters. It's probably a trap."

"That's why I wanted to talk to you. You're my best source of actual information when it comes to mermaids. What happens when they get you in the water?"

"I don't know. Previous humans, who've gone in, haven't come back. Ever."

It was the same thing that Oanen had said. My outrage poked my fury anger, but nothing happened.

"I need to get to the oracle. Do you have any tips for me?"

"Yeah, don't do it. As soon as you put a boat on the lake, the mermaids will try to tip it. You saw what happens when they get you in their water."

"And you saw what I do."

She studied me for a moment.

"You'll need some extra weight in the boat to make it harder to tip. Some weapons to deter them wouldn't hurt either. Probably a change of clothes. If it's any amount of distance, you're going to go in. More and more mermaids will swarm the boat, and they'll work together. The sheer number will eventually tip you over."

I thought about it and nodded. I wasn't human. Even though I'd been hurt the one time I went in, they couldn't seem to hurt me permanently. Was it a risk I was willing to take? I thought of Oanen's burnt face and missing eyebrows. Yes. It was.

"When are you thinking of going?" Ashlyn asked.

"Soon," I said. "Oanen's trying to find my mom. He already checked her old address, and she isn't there. Everything's gone. This is my backup plan. I need answers, Ashlyn."

"Whenever you do go, start out at dawn. They aren't as active. And, promise to text me before you leave. I won't try to stop you; but if something goes wrong, the Quills will need to know where to start looking."

"Fair enough. Just make sure to give me a full day before raising the alarm."

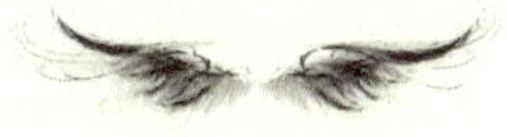

My phone beeped. I tossed aside the kitchen towel and checked the message. My heart thumped seeing it was another one from Oanen. He had been updating me on the progress of his search for my mom over the last three days, and none of it had been good so far. Being apart from him for this long might have been tolerable if he were at least finding clues about where my mom might have gone. But he wasn't.

Each day, the need for him grew stronger, and I worried about what would happen when I finally did see him again. I felt so unstable inside. I needed answers. I needed Oanen so much it hurt to breathe. And, that worried me.

Struggling to stay calm, I read the message. It didn't bring any better news than the last one.

Cali is another dead end.

I wanted to swear. Instead I typed out a relaxed message.

All right. Thank you for checking it.

How are you holding up? Want Eliana to take you to the Roost tonight?

I'd been stuck in the house for days. Truthfully, I was going stir crazy. But the last thing I wanted was a crowd of people and thumping music. I wanted to get the hell out of this damn town and strangle my mother. But I couldn't tell Oanen any of that, or he'd fly right back to me.

The thought of seeing him made my heart race in excitement, and for the briefest of moments, I considered telling him to come home. The memory of his burnt face stopped me. So, I lied.

I'm doing okay. Just finished the lunch dishes. Not really in the mood for the Roost. Fenris would probably be there in all of his hugging glory.

I felt bad using Fenris as an excuse, but I didn't want Oanen to make a call to Eliana despite my reassurances I was fine. Hopefully, his suggestion had nothing to do with what he might feel from me and had more to do with how well he knew me.

I miss you. I'll be home soon, he replied. A second later, another text came through.

We'll do some more research and try again in a few days.

My heart started to race in earnest. He was coming home? I squashed the panic and kept my reply cool.

Sounds good. I miss you, too.

And I did. So badly that I wasn't sleeping well at night. Mostly because of dreams where I was burning down the town. Sometimes Eliana was in the way. Sometimes Ashlyn or Fenris. Oanen was never in the way, though. Even in my dreams, I knew he was gone.

I grabbed my jacket and locked up as I left. I'd held off on my plans for the lake in hopes that Oanen would find my mom. That hope was now dead. With Oanen on his way home, the time had come for me to get serious about finding the Isle of Woe and the oracle.

First thing I needed to do was check the boat I saw at the lake.

The drive didn't take long. I managed to arrive just before dark. The boat I'd spotted on the previous trip to the lake still sat off to the side, buried under a few inches of snow. After I brushed it off, I walked around it, looking for holes. It appeared solid. There were oars and even a life vest under it.

I took a picture and sent it with a message to Ashlyn.

How sturdy is this boat?

Her reply only took a few moments.

It's sturdy. That's one of the rules. The mermaids can't sabotage the boat before it gets in the water. You're not leaving now, are you? It's too dangerous at night.

No. Not leaving now. I'm checking it for tomorrow. I'll let you know for sure when I leave.

She didn't answer.

I checked the boat one more time then got back in my car for the drive home. On my way through town, I picked up three times my weight in water softener salt. The clerk didn't say anything, but I could see the curiosity in her eyes.

When my house came into view and I saw a light, for a brief moment anticipation exploded inside of me. Oanen. He was home. The thought had barely formed before I realized how impossible that would be unless he'd suddenly developed the ability to open portals like Adira. Flying would take him a few days to get back.

Eliana sat at my kitchen table when I walked in. Her expression sent a bolt of fear through me. I stopped just inside the door, afraid that whatever news she had would upset me enough that I would hurt her.

"What's wrong? Did something happen to Oanen?"

She stood and put her hands on her hips, scowling at me.

"No, you idiot. Something's going to happen to you. What are you thinking, going out on that lake alone after what we heard in the hall?"

Relief coursed through me. The fire that had scorched in my middle didn't cool, though.

"You didn't tell Oanen, did you?"

"No, because I'm going to talk you out of it before he even gets here."

"That's why I need to do this, Eliana. I can see your face turning red and know it's not anger. It's the heat rolling off of me. What do you think is going to happen to Oanen when he comes back? He's going to want to see me; and no matter how much I'm trying not to be, I'm desperate to see him. Every time I think of him I get warmer. He won't stay away because he'll feel how much I need him. Do you see the problem? I'm going to cook him like a Thanksgiving turkey. I need to go to the lake. I need to try to get answers. I need Oanen to be okay when he sees me next."

She exhaled heavily and dropped her hands to her sides.

"I know. I just need you to be okay, too, and I don't trust those mermaids."

"Neither do I. I have a ton of salt in my trunk. Ashlyn said to weight the boat, and I figure I can throw it in their faces if they try to tip me."

"Good. We'll stop and pick up some vinegar tomorrow morning, too. It'll burn them like the salt."

"We?"

"You're not doing this alone."

The heat slowly eased up as I faced my friend.

"You're amazing, and I love you," I said.

She grinned and crossed the room to wrap me in a hug. All the build up from the week slowly faded away as I returned her embrace.

"You're going to make me fat," she said, her head resting on my shoulder.

I snorted.

"I thought I was empty calories."

She giggled. "You are."

When I was pleasantly drained, she pulled away.

"Did you eat dinner yet?" she asked.

"No."

While she and I made sandwiches, she asked questions.

"What time are we leaving? How long do you think it'll take us to get to the Isle? And what's the plan for when the mermaids get us in the water? Because, according to Ashlyn, that will happen."

I looked at Eliana.

"You're making my Grinch-size heart grow way too big. I love that you're willing to go with me, but you can't."

She started to frown, and I held up a hand.

"Hear me out."

"I'm listening," she said.

"Did Oanen tell you what happened at the pool?"

She shook her head.

"He didn't say where you guys went or anything when he came back. Just went up to his room." She gave me a sheepish look. "I could tell he was hurt and had new burns, though."

"Well, I took Oanen to the pool, thinking the water might be the answer to me not burning him when we touch."

"I'm sorry it didn't work."

"It might have if the merbitch hadn't talked a siren into singing for us. Needless to say, things got hot. Whatever's inside of me just exploded out. It sent Oanen flying. I could hear him hit the side of the pool even under water. I can't even imagine what would have happened to him if we hadn't been submerged." I held her gaze, silently pleading with her to understand. "I'm dangerous. I don't want to be, but I am. If they get me in the water, I'll get mad. I won't be able to control what happens, and anyone in the water with me will get hurt."

"So that's your plan? Boil the mermaids?"

"I don't think it's a plan as much as a foregone conclusion. It's not like I've ever made myself intentionally hot. It just happens with anger and passion."

She flushed at the word passion but nodded.

"It makes sense. The two emotions are very closely related." She smiled slightly. "It makes you taste good."

I laughed hard.

"You pervy little succubus. I'm your personal fury snack shack."

Her smile slowly faded as we brought our plates to the table.

"What if you go in and you don't get hot? They might get close enough to hurt you. What if your furnace doesn't work when you're hurt?"

I shook my head as she took her first bite.

"First, I think my furnace works harder when I'm hurt. Second, if I go in, it's going to piss me off. I hate lake water. It's gross. Once I'm in it, I don't think they'll be able to get close. At the pool, my heat dried me within seconds of getting out of the water. The merbitch was in the pool with us, but she never got close. I think it's because I made the water too hot around me. My heat will be my personal protection bubble."

She held out her hand.

"Phone please."

I gave my phone over and ate my sandwich as I watched her install an app.

"What's that for?" I asked when she gave it back.

"I'm still going with you to the lake. But I'll stay on the shore and watch your progress on my phone. That app will track you. You should probably put your phone in a baggie before you get into the boat."

She had a valid point.

"And we should probably pack you a lunch and something to drink," she added.

I lay in my bed, quietly contemplating the hairline cracks in my ceiling while trying to ignore the faint scent of scorch rising from my sheets.

After Eliana called the Quills to let them know she planned to spend the night, we'd packed my provisions and sealed up my phone. With nothing else to do, we'd gone to bed early so we could wake well before dawn and head into town for the vinegar Eliana wanted me to take.

Even though there was nothing left to do at the moment but sleep, I couldn't stop thinking.

What if there was no island? What if what we'd overheard and the map in the library was just some big prank to get me into the water, like Ashlyn said? Or, what if the island was real, but there was no oracle there?

The scent of scorch increased. If there was no oracle, there'd be no answers. Without answers, Oanen was as good as stuffed and served on a platter.

A scuff of noise preceded Eliana's entry. She wore a long, white virginal gown that made me grin.

"You need to sleep," she said, shooing me over.

I moved over for her and she laid down on top of the covers, facing me. She reached up and stroked my hair. It wasn't skin contact, but I could still feel her pull my worry.

"Just until you fall asleep," she said softly.

I closed my eyes and drifted off within minutes. My mind didn't stop its tormented thoughts, though.

I searched through storm swept seas, looking for an island. What I found was something that made my chest squeeze with fear. A mountain made of red jagged glass rose up from the water. Waves crashed upon the spiked shards, and the water turned to blood. Without a choice, I drifted to the shores.

When I woke, I was alone and there was blood on my pillow. Enough to leave it more red than the cream color it had been when I'd gone to sleep. I hated that I didn't know what I was becoming. It fed the rage that was building inside of me. Even alone, I wanted to strike out at something.

Staying quiet so as to not wake Eliana, I made my way downstairs and checked the time on my phone. Eliana's alarm wouldn't go off for another thirty minutes. Needing some time to myself, I went to the bathroom in hope that a shower would cool me off. However, I caught sight of my face in the mirror and only got hotter.

Dried blood flaked on my cheeks and crusted on the skin around my eyes.

"If I ever see my mom again, I'm going to throat punch her for taking off like she did. This is bullshit," I said to myself in the bathroom mirror.

After a shower, which only made me feel marginally better, I dressed and went to make us breakfast. I slid the second omelet onto the plate just as Eliana came downstairs.

She smiled at me, looking much too chipper first thing in the morning.

"Morning," she said.

I rolled my eyes at her and set our plates on the table.

"What? Didn't you sleep well after I left?"

"Not really."

"I'm sorry. I would have stayed longer, but it's not safe for me to feed after I get really tired."

"No, it's okay. It's just being away from Oanen. Sleeping is getting harder. My dreams are so weird. Last night, I was dreaming that I was already out on the water looking for the island. When I found it, it wasn't what I expected. I was thinking a small bit of green land with sandy shores. What I found in my dreams was a mountain of glass covered in blood. I knew I had to go there and sacrifice myself to get the answers."

Eliana paled. "I don't like this."

"It's fine. It was just a dream," I said.

"I've only been here a few years, but I've already caught on to something very important. Nothing is 'just' anything here. There's hidden meanings, hidden agendas, hidden everything."

"So you're saying I should wear boots?"

She shook her head slowly.

"Your dream, if it is something, won't be anything that obvious. Just be careful, and don't be afraid to come back without answers."

We finished up our breakfast and got to town to buy out their supply of vinegar with ten minutes to spare according to Eliana's timetable.

"We need to get that boat loaded with salt, yet," she said as she pulled out of the parking lot.

"The bags aren't heavy. We'll be fine."

She gave me a worried glance.

"It was just a dream," I said for the umpteenth time. "I shouldn't have told you."

"Yes, you should have. We're friends, and we don't keep things from each other, right?"

I thought of Fenris and felt a brief stab of guilt.

"Telling you only made you worry more. It didn't change anything else. And seeing you worry now is making me feel like a jerk."

"You aren't a jerk. I would have worried no matter what. And it did change plans, remember? If we get to the lake and the mermaids are already stirring, you're going to bail."

"Right. But Ashlyn said they are never up this early. When Trammer tried taking her fishing at dawn, the fish folk had complained that their kids weren't getting a fair chance. It'll be fine."

She exhaled hugely and nodded. However, she didn't look any less settled when we pulled into the parking lot.

We worked in silence to unload the car and carry the supplies to the dock. The moon barely lit our path, and the brisk wind had Eliana shivering within minutes. She didn't complain, and I didn't try to tell her to wait in the car. When we had everything ready, we team lifted the boat and carried it to the water's edge. The gentle waves lapped at the wood vessel, the sound seeming loud in the otherwise quiet, predawn light.

Eliana glanced at the water for a long moment. I did the same. Nothing moved.

Grabbing the first bag of salt, I carried it to the boat and ripped the top open. Bag by bag, we filled the bottom of the boat with almost four hundred pounds of salt.

"That doesn't seem like enough," Eliana said softly.

"It'll be fine."

She nodded and watched me put my bag with my clothes, food, water, and phone into the boat. When I finished, I turned to her. She was on me before I could blink, wrapping me in the tightest hug yet.

"Be safe and come back," she said.

"I will. I promise."

She released me and watched as I climbed into the boat. The salt crunched under my feet with each step, and the boat rocked slightly as I sat. The lapping noises of the water had us both looking out over the expanse.

We waited like that as orange slowly painted over the sky's pre-dawn blue. As soon as the sun broke the cusp of the horizon, Eliana stepped forward and put her hands on the bow.

"If you see anything, turn back," she reminded me softly.

I nodded and eased the oars into their holders. She nudged me out into the water, careful not to step into the lake with her last push.

Carefully dipping the oars in the water, I gave my first experimental stroke to direct the boat backward. It was a little awkward the first go and Eliana chewed on her bottom lip as she watched me. But, the second one went much smoother. The sounds of oars softly slapping the surface and the slight thunk of the things holding the oars in place were carried away by the wind.

Eliana lifted her phone and glanced at the screen before giving me a thumbs-up. She was tracking me, and I wasn't even ten feet from shore. I shook my head at her and glanced at the water around me.

The sight of a face just below the surface almost made me yip. The mermaid's green hair drifted around her face as she smiled at me. Beneath the surface, something zipped toward us from her right. From the corner of my eye, I caught more movement to her left.

Instead of focusing on what it was, I looked up at Eliana and gave her a quick wave and smile, doing my best impression of a girl in a boat not surrounded by mermaids.

In three more strokes, I passed the end of the pier and headed out into open water.

CHAPTER SEVENTEEN

My mind raced as I continued to place more distance between me and the shoreline. Eliana didn't retreat to the car but watched me with a sharp eye. As did the mermaid circling just beneath the gentle waves.

Were the mermaids going to wait for me to reach the point where I'd be unable to swim back? If that was the case, they'd be disappointed. I swam well, and like any other physical activity I performed, I didn't tire easily.

I glanced at the faces beneath the surface, again, then grinned at Eliana as if the waters were still clear. I didn't want her freaking out and calling the Quills, or worse, Oanen. The threat of a few mermaids didn't worry me. But the idea of Oanen finding out what I was up to and rushing back did. I couldn't face him like I was. I couldn't risk hurting him. No, this was better. I could face a few mermaids, no problem. I just wished I knew what they were waiting for.

Maybe, like me, they didn't want to involve anyone else and were waiting until I was out of Eliana's sight. Hoping that was the case, I kept rowing. My arms didn't tire as Eliana's form grew smaller and smaller, but I did get thirsty. Just before she became too small to see, I lifted the oars from the water and found my drink.

"Can she still see you?" a muffled voice asked.

I used the bottle to hide my mouth before I answered.

"Yep. She's looking right at me."

Laughing drifted up around the boat; and I took a long swallow, relieved that I'd guessed correctly. After a quick, final wave to Eliana, I picked up the oars once more and mentally prepared myself for what was to come.

As soon as Eliana disappeared from view, the first mermaid poked her head out of the water.

"That took you far too long. You have to have the weakest arms I've ever seen. Are you rowing or having mini seizures?"

I ignored her and kept my pace steady.

"Does she know she's rowing in circles?" a quieter voice asked. Several others hushed her.

This time I rolled my eyes. Did they think I was stupid? Not only could I still see the shore on the horizon, I could also see the sun. Since both had stayed pretty much in the same place, I knew I wasn't rowing in circles. However, the question did bring up a good point.

Rowing in a straight line was all well and good, but I needed to make sure I was rowing toward the general direction of the island. At least, as far as the map in the library was concerned. I pulled up the oars once more.

"Why is she always stopping?"

"She's going to drink so much that she'll need to pee. I don't want her pee in my lake."

The boat rocked slightly.

"Poseidon's trident! How much does this land whale weigh?"

Ignoring them, I checked my phone. My location dot on the map showed that I was barely off the shore. Leaving the app open, I resealed the phone in its baggy and set it on the seat in front of me.

This time when I went to stick the oar in the water, a hand reached for it. I jerked the oar and whacked the hand.

Laughing, along with some swearing, erupted around me.

I set to rowing again, watching the mermaids dart through the water. They made a game of swimming under the boat to bump it, making it rock continuously. I didn't have a light stomach so the motion didn't bother me. In fact, if that was the worst they had, I would have no problem reaching the island.

They entertained themselves like that for a time while I slowly made progress. Rowing might not have been tiring, but it sure was boring once the shoreline faded from sight.

No sooner did I have that thought than a set of hands grabbed the right edge of the boat and pulled down as the left side was lifted up. I immediately leaned to counterbalance and put the oars in the boat. As soon as my hands were free, I picked up my hard, reusable water bottle and hit the hands still gripping the edge.

A head came out of the water, and the mermaid with green-blue hair hissed at me, showing her tiny, sharp teeth. Her grip on the boat tightened as she started pulling herself out of the water. Reaching down to the bottom of the boat, I grabbed a fistful of coarse salt and threw it in her face.

She screamed and dove back into the water. All rocking stopped.

"Fun fact," I said, starting up my rowing once more, "although mermaids can live in ocean water, they can't tolerate direct contact with dried salt. And, wouldn't you know, I got a boat full of it."

"I hate her," a voice whispered from under the water.

"I told you," another said. "Don't worry. She'll get hers soon."

I checked the water on both sides but didn't see anything. That worried me more than when they were swimming around.

Focusing once more on the map on my phone, I rowed harder. The battery was doing well, but my progress made me worry that I'd run out of juice long before I reached the shores again. Or worse, that I'd be making the return trip in the dark.

The absence of mermaids didn't last long. Within an hour, the number of them swimming around me had doubled. Another hour doubled that number again.

However, during those next several hours, little else changed. According to my phone, I was only a quarter of the way toward the center of the lake. And, every new mermaid asked the same dumb questions.

"Where is she going?"

"She thinks there's an island."

"She thinks there's an oracle."

Laughter ensued the last comment.

"An oracle? She doesn't need one of those. I can see her future just fine. Dead at the bottom of our lake."

While rowing had initially worked well to exercise the tingle of anger that kept trying to worm its way up my spine, the activity was losing its effectiveness. However, my white-knuckled hold on the oars didn't just indicate my slipping control. It also kept the oars firmly in my grip. I easily powered through the hands attempting to steal the oars and even managed to connect with a few heads with every heave.

The cursing and hissing grew louder as the surrounding water churned with mermaid tails.

Was hitting them mean? Not based on the anger crawling

under my skin. They were planning something that wouldn't end well for me if they had their way.

"Don't you have anything better to do? Go comb your hair with a fork or something," I yelled, losing patience with yet another attempt to grab an oar.

"She did not just go there."

"Oh, yes, she did," I answered the unknown, underwater voice. "Take your chum ass out to deeper water and go sing to Sabastian or something. Just leave me alone."

A head popped up to my right, and I zeroed in on the girl's livid face. Seeing a real target fueled my temper.

"Did you just call us shark bait?" she demanded.

"I sure did." I jerked the oar and hit her in the side of the head. She went under like a stone, and I laughed.

Another head popped up near the end of the boat, killing my humor. Her hate-filled gaze locked with mine. The anger I'd been feeling now made more sense, and the smell of smoldering wood tickled my nose as I stared at the mermaid who'd made me blow up my boyfriend.

"You think you're so smart filling your boat with salt, don't you?" She smiled, flashing her tiny, sharp teeth. "Your boat's sitting heavy in the water. Too heavy to tip. Good job, orphan."

I wanted to launch myself at her but held my ground. She was baiting me. Why?

"What do you want?"

Her smile widened.

"You know what I want. I want that human. But I'll settle for you."

I snorted.

"You couldn't handle me."

"Alone? No. But I'm not alone."

She swam within arm's reach of the boat.

"Do you know what the problem is with your salt-filled boat that's sitting so heavy in the water?" she asked sweetly.

I narrowed my eyes at her.

"It's heavy enough to sink."

Something small jumped at the back of the boat a moment before water started gushing in. I pulled the oars out of the way of grabbing hands and rushed toward the back as the merbitch disappeared under water once more. Grabbing the plug, I swiped the salt away from the hole and jammed the rubber back into its place.

I looked around at all the faces staring at me from a healthy distance.

"Sink me and that means I'm in the water with you. Ever heard of a fish boil?"

They twittered with laughter and dove back under the surface.

Returning to my place, I picked up the oars and started rowing in the increasingly choppy waters with a ferocity that made them laugh harder. The scent of burning wood and hot salt grew stronger, and I struggled to control my temper. How did my mom do it? All those times I'd said something that I'd known would upset her, she'd never lost her cool. I frowned. Not true. When she'd broken her coffee cup that last day in our old house, I remembered feeling a flash of heat. Back then, I'd written it off as my imagination. But I now knew it hadn't been.

The memory was less than helpful in calming me down, so I thought of Eliana waiting for me on shore. I needed to focus on getting to the island and back before sunset. I didn't want to worry her. I needed to keep it together.

The plug at the back of the boat popped out, again.

"I swear to the gods I'm three seconds from jumping into that water," I yelled as I once again put up the oars and went for the plug.

The lake's surface lapped at the outside of the boat, only inches from the top now, and I had nothing to bail out the water-laden salt. They would sink the boat if they continued to push out the plug.

Something clunked behind me, and I turned just in time to see one of my oars disappear over the edge. Whichever bottom feeder had it, she tossed it away from the boat. It landed with a splash just out of reach.

I swore and lifted the other oar out of its holder. I knew they wanted me to lean over and try to grab for the floating one, but I wasn't stupid. I'd already witnessed what they would do in that scenario. Instead, I used the oar I had to maneuver myself closer to the oar.

The boat rocked precariously beneath me, and I widened my stance so the mermaids couldn't knock me over.

"The movies got it all wrong," I said. "Beautiful, kind creatures who long to be human, my ass. More like overgrown piranhas with the mentality of a goldfish."

A hand rose out of the water, gave me the finger, then closed over the oar. I watched the floating wood move away rapidly and bared my teeth in frustration. The boat jolted under me, almost offsetting my balance.

"Do it," I called. "See what happens when you knock me in."

They laughed again, and I continued to use my single oar in an effort to propel myself in the direction of the stolen one. The boat's movement in the water was slow and jerky. What little progress I made vanished each time the bitch with the oar swam further.

"Are your arms getting tired yet?" a singsong voice called.

"Hop in the boat and find out for yourself."

Silence greeted me and my hair whipped in my face as I stared at the surface. With all the rowing and anger, I hadn't noticed the wind until that moment. What I'd thought was churning water because of the mermaids was actually stronger waves. Tearing my gaze from the threat-filled lake, I looked up at the clear sky. Clouds hugged the horizon to the north, but the sun hadn't yet reached its zenith. Good. These mermaids were doing everything they could to slow me down, but I still had time.

The boat jerked under me. My eyes flew to the plug, but it was still in place. The boat jerked again then started forward so suddenly that I lost my balance and fell. My back hit the edge of the seat. I winced and rolled to my side to get to my knees.

The wind battered my face and made my eyes burn. Staying on my knees, I reached for my phone to figure out which direction they were taking me.

To my surprise, the mermaids weren't speeding me toward the shore. Just the opposite. As I watched, the dot on my GPS tracker crept closer to the middle of the lake. They were taking me right where I wanted to go. I grinned.

The boat stopped so suddenly that I flew forward and hit my head on the other seat. I swore and lifted my face to feel for splinters. I didn't find any, but my fingers did come away with blood. Heat pooled in my stomach and boiled over into my veins.

"That's the second time, Merbitch," I said under my breath.

I stood slowly, watching the water around the boat, looking for their laughing faces. I couldn't see any, though. However, in the distance, I saw something jutting out of the water. My heart gave a jump, and I wanted to shout with laughter. The island.

Something made a sound near my feet. I looked down at the water rushing in. They'd popped out the plug. Lake water closed over my shoes. I looked up at the island again then grabbed my phone, glancing at the dot through the baggy.

Lake water rushed over the back end of the boat. Weeds and

bits of who knew what floated in with it. I had no choice now; I was going into the lake.

I dove over the side, smoothly entering the water. It hissed and sputtered the moment it hit my skin. I could feel how terrifyingly cold it was for only that split second. Then, my heat took over.

Surfacing, I wiped a piece of lake debris from my face.

"I smell like fish!" I yelled, truly pissed.

The water steamed around me and nothing swam nearby. Further away, a few heads surfaced, just enough to see their eyes.

"You wanted me in the water. Now, come get me." None of them moved. I started swimming toward one, which happened to be in the direction of the island.

"Here, fishy, fishy, fishy," I called.

There was no laughing this time. The mermaid dove under the surface and did not reappear. I put the phone baggy in my mouth and started swimming toward the island. Within seconds, I knew holding the phone like that was a mistake. The taste of melted plastic clung to my lips as I emptied water out of the bag and tried to power on my phone. It didn't work. Giving up, I stuck the device in my pocket and set out once more.

Numerous times, I had to stop to make sure I was still on course. It wasn't easy. Without the phone, I had to tread water and bob in the waves, waiting to catch a glimpse of the island.

My anger didn't cool with the freezing lake water surrounding me. However, the amount of steam drifting around me did begin to decrease.

The closer I drew to the island, the bolder the mermaids became. They circled me, once again throwing out insults and taunts.

"Does she actually think that's swimming?"

"Mmm...can you taste her blood in the water? It's delicious."

"That's right, sinker. One arm in front of the other. Get yourself nice and tired for us."

"Do you feel that? The water's cooling."

They were right. As the island grew closer, I could feel the strain. I had never pushed myself this far before. Any activity I'd done, I'd only continued to do until I felt my anger ease. Even though my anger wasn't easing this time, my energy was flagging. Why?

It took a moment to realize the talking around me had stopped. When I paused to get my bearings again, I noticed the mermaids a distance behind me.

"You're almost there," Merbitch said. "Do you think you'll make it?"

Ignoring her, I turned and continued on. The sight of the rocky, barren island sent a shiver of disquiet through me. It was far larger than I'd anticipated, and its jutting rock formations created a towering skyline that didn't look so different from my dream. The island wasn't glass, though, or covered with blood. Maybe my apprehension was from all the dead fish skeletons I'd need to wade through to get to the shore. Could the place get any more disgusting?

My feet hit bottom, and I sagged with relief. Plodding through the waist high water, I purposely ignored all the floating fish corpses. Exhausted, I stumbled onto the rocky shore and sat heavily. I'd exerted myself more than I'd realized because as I sat there I shivered. I needed to get out of the wind, dry off, and maybe even powernap before starting my search for the oracle.

In the distance, a single head rose above the water. Merbitch watched me with a malicious smile. She was probably thinking the same thing I was. I'd safely made it to the island, but how was I going to get back?

The smile on her face fled, and she dove underwater, leaving me completely alone.

I thought of Eliana and sighed. She was going to be so worried.

"Well," a feminine voice said from nearby, "this is a surprise."

CHAPTER EIGHTEEN

Startled, I looked over my shoulder. A woman dressed in a white, flowing gown stood near a pile of boulders. She was beautiful with windswept golden hair and brilliant silver-blue eyes. A warm, welcoming smile spread over her features as I stared.

Another shiver ripped through me.

"Such a nice surprise," she said. "It's not every day I get such a lovely visitor. My name is Lucia. Can I offer you a drier place to sit and, perhaps, something to drink?"

I carefully stood and wiped off the seat of my pants. Sand and delicate fish bones fell away from my cold fingers.

"My name is Megan, and somewhere warm and dry sounds great."

"Warm," she said with a smile. "Yes. Warm is good."

She motioned for me to follow and disappeared into a space between two giant boulders.

My shoes squished wetly as I walked up the sloped beach to the boulder strewn plateau. The crevice between the rocks was tight, but I could feel the warm air flowing out and saw the soft flicker of firelight.

With some wiggling, I pushed my way through. The dim passage I found myself in wasn't much wider than the entrance.

"It helps keep the heat in," Lucia said from somewhere ahead, as if reading my mind.

I took a step forward and something crunched under my shoe. I squinted down at my feet but couldn't see anything in the icky darkness gathered around my legs.

"I apologize for the mess. It's not easy to keep a cave clean."

I continued forward, that feeling of disquiet growing. But, no anger.

The ground tilted down slightly for several yards before I came to a bend. The light flickered more strongly ahead. I stepped around the edge, thinking to see an end, but it was just more passage. I looked back, staring at the sliver of daylight I was leaving behind.

"We're almost there, Megan. A warm fire and some wine. If you're old enough, that is."

I turned toward the firelight once more, my shoes crunching on something with each step.

"Old enough? I didn't think those rules applied here."

Her gentle laughter floated back to me.

"I do try to respect all rules. Without them, our world would be complete chaos. No one wants that."

Something rolled under my foot when I placed my next step, throwing me off-balance. I spread my arms to keep myself from falling, and my palms connected with cold, slimy rock. A dank, damp smell heavy with bitter smoke filled my nose. Flinching away from both the smell and the rock, I removed my hand. The smell vanished.

The oracle's home was disgusting.

"Why do you live in a cave?" I asked, carefully moving toward the flickering light.

"There's nothing to build with on the Isle of Woe."

I frowned. She was right. There'd been nothing but rock and bones. How, then, was there a fire?

Another bend reflected in the light. Warmth wrapped around me, making steam rise from the cold, wet jeans clinging to my legs. I knew I was getting close. Instead of hurrying, I slowed.

My gut was telling me something wasn't right, but my fury temper was quiet. Not a whisper of anger. Sure, I was annoyed as hell that I was cold and wet and smelled like fish, but that had nothing to do with Lucia. Why, then, did I feel like continuing was the wrong thing to do?

"Are you coming, Megan? I just poured you some warmed wine."

Unsure why I was feeling weird about the place, I soldiered on and rounded the bend. Relief rushed through me that the space before me wasn't more narrow passage.

A fire burned in an open pit to one side of the large cavern. Thick smoke curled up toward the tiny hole in the ceiling. My eyes barely noted the flames that I'd followed there. Instead, my gaze was drawn to a large, wooden table that took up the center of the space. Its grain gleamed so palely in the firelight that it appeared almost white. Dark engravings decorated the surface, epic battle scenes showing men in loincloths and armor fighting on mountains and in valleys.

"It is beautiful, isn't it?"

Lucia's voice drew me from the mesmerizing images. She stood beside the table and pulled out the single, cushioned dining chair.

"Come. Sit. Rest yourself, and tell me why you're here."

I walked toward the table and the old-fashioned goblet blocking part of a scene that kept drawing my eye.

"I came to talk to you."

"Me? Why?"

I managed to look up at her.

"You're an oracle, right?"

She smiled softly and gestured to the table.

I sat with a heavy exhale. Until the moment when I eased the weight off my legs, I hadn't realized just how tired I was. It felt weird being so exhausted. I would need to remember swimming in hypothermic lakes the next time I felt angry.

"I am an oracle. The only one in Uttira at present," she said, motioning to the heavy goblet. I picked it up and felt her hand brush over my wet hair.

"You're so cold. I have another gown if you'd like to change."

I shook my head and brought the goblet to my lips. The metallic taste of the cup made me hesitate. A heavy feeling gripped my stomach, and I glanced at the fireplace just above the rim of the cup. The flames danced prettily from their source. Bones.

I set the cup down quickly but couldn't seem to focus on the source of the flames again.

"What's wrong? Don't you like wine? I can fetch you some water."

"No. It's okay." I blinked, trying to focus on what was feeding the fire. Had I really seen bones?

A jab of anger hit me right between my eyes. Before I could react, it was gone. I frowned and rubbed my eyes, having a hard time focusing on anything but the flames, themselves, and the table and the feel of her hand on my head.

This wasn't right. I looked at the walls but could only see a hazy darkness. Something was very wrong.

"Why are you living in the middle of the lake?" I asked.

"We are all meant to be somewhere, Megan. Where would you have me be?"

"In town. In a normal house."

"Easily accessible? No, my sweet treat. That's how wars start."

Sweet treat? I wanted to shiver at the words and decided it was time to start listening to my gut even if my fury temper was quiet. My gut yelled at me not to relax or rest, that I needed to hurry up. That I was taking too much time even though I'd just gotten there.

"So how does this work?" I asked. "My friend told me there's a price for everything. What's your price to answer my questions?"

Lucia laughed lightly.

"Your friend sounds very wise. Most people who come here think answering questions is my purpose."

"Isn't it?"

"Yes and no. Although I can see glimpses of the future, that's not the sum of my existence. We should be more than just our purpose, don't you agree, Megan?"

"I guess."

"Don't guess. Know."

"That's why I'm here. Because I don't know."

"Oh?" she said, her hand stroking over my hair again.

"I need answers. My mom left me, and I need to know why."

"Let the past stay in the past. Why she left doesn't matter. Your future is what you seek, is it not?"

"Fine. What do you see in my future?"

"I see you drinking your wine."

A tingle of frustration raced through me, and I knocked the goblet aside. A hiss resounded near my ear. I turned back to look at Lucia and caught a glimpse of something that wasn't Lucia. A wide mouth and scaled skin. Her face came back into focus, smiling kindly with golden hair falling prettily around her shoulders.

She touched my hair again, stroking the dried strands.

"What's your true form, Lucia?"

She jerked slightly.

"True form? What do you mean?"

"We all have true forms, don't we? That's why I'm here. I need to know mine. I need to know what I'll become."

"Become. You'll become nothing more than what you are, cod fish," she said. Her hand left my hair, and she moved toward the fire. "I have some bread warmed, if you'd like."

She reached for something from the darkness near the pot. As she walked toward me again, her eyes reflected silver, like they'd caught light. But, she had her back to the fire.

Rage ripped through me, so harsh it felt as if I was going to be torn in half. I stood suddenly, knocking over the chair and slammed my hands down on the table before me. The scent of fresh wood smoke teased my nose.

The oracle stopped walking, the form of her face flickering ever so briefly between snake and woman at the same time my rage vanished. We stared at each other for a long moment.

"You are not what you seem," I said. "And, this place isn't what it seems." As I spoke, I looked around the room again. This time, I saw more than I wanted to.

A waist high ledge made of bones ran the circumference of the room. The floor was covered with them as well. They weren't human, but they weren't fish either.

"Are you eating mermaids?" I asked, dragging my gaze back to her.

She smiled slightly.

"You've already noted that there's nothing on this island. What did you think I ate?"

"I don't understand," I said, frowning.

She laughed.

"Of course you don't. If you did, you wouldn't be here."

Another jolt of anger poked at me only to vanish again.

"What I don't understand is why I'm not hurting you. Killing is wrong."

"My sweet fledgling fury, what defines wrong but the rules we are taught?"

My skin warmed with my growing irritation. She was responding to my questions with half answers and vague counter-questions. Although the swim in the lake had worn me down for a bit, my general pissiness was more than ready to bounce back.

The scent of fresh wood smoke grew stronger, and her gaze dipped to her table.

"Stop," she commanded, rushing forward. "You'll destroy it."

Smoke curled up from the table. My hair tickled my cheek as I lifted my hands from the wood and looked down at the scorch marks. The carvings that had been under my palm were gone.

"Hateful, hell bird," she hissed.

"Lying snake," I said, looking up at her.

Her gaze narrowed on me.

"I don't lie."

"How do you explain these bones?" I asked. "You're killing people, and I think I even see a few human bones over there."

"I've already answered that. I must eat."

"And, why am I not angry? Consuming flesh is against the rules. Wicked."

"Because the past does not exist here. Nor the future. Only the present. And, in the present, I haven't killed anyone or consumed anything."

Her words worried me. Not the killing, but about the time. Something was wrong with what had been happening since I'd arrived. My hair had dried while she'd touched it. Only minutes had passed yet my hair, which took a good hour to air dry, was no longer wet. My gut told me again that I needed to hurry up and get my answers then leave.

"What is my true form, and how do I control my rage?" I asked.

She smiled and reached out to touch my hair. I batted her hand away. Now, the touch of her skin against mine sent a shudder of revulsion through me. She felt cold and damp, like the stones.

Impatience stoked the fire growing inside of me.

"Lucia, you have about ten seconds to start giving me some real answers before I get really mad."

She laughed.

"I've done nothing for you to label me wicked, my tidbit."

I shivered at the words. If she wasn't doing something wrong, now, she definitely had something wicked planned for me in the future. Since getting angry at her wasn't working well, I went another route.

I focused on the flames licking me from the inside and thought of Eliana waiting for me and her worry. Then, I thought of Oanen. Of all the times I'd burned him because I didn't know what I was doing. Finally, I thought of my mom and all the answers she hadn't shared.

My anger climbed higher, and I knew the moment the oracle understood the situation. Her silver eyes reflected the orange light glowing from mine.

"If you leave now," she said, "I'll give you the answers you seek."

"No." I set one of my hands on the table and smiled. "Smells like toasting marshmallows, don't you think?"

"Hateful hell brat. I'll answer one now and one when you're in the boat, rowing away."

"Fair enough. But, I will turn around and destroy everything on this desolate rock you call home if you go back on your word."

She nodded and looked pointedly at my hand. I lifted it from the table and arched a brow.

"Come." She turned and started toward the crack in the rocks. "Your true form is born of—"

She disappeared from view, and I rushed forward, slipping into the passage.

"Born of what?" I asked.

"Born of fire. Keep up. I won't repeat myself. That is not part of our bargain."

I hurried, slipping and sliding over the bone littered floor.

"Vague answers aren't part of the bargain, either. I already know I have fire. I want to know my true form. What will I look like? Am I going to be a snake woman like you? I want specifics."

She laughed from somewhere ahead, the howl of the wind almost carrying the sound away.

"You are nothing like me. That you are born of fire means you are made from the flames of hell. You are hell's messenger. You bring the souls of the damned to their final place of unrest."

"But what will I look like?"

I turned the second bend and could see a dim sliver of light ahead but no Lucia. Another shiver ripped through me as the first gust of cold air rushed into the passage and hit my slightly damp jeans. It wasn't until I stepped out of the opening, into a wind lashed early twilight, that I understood what had happened.

Time had passed while I'd been in the cave. More time than I'd anticipated. A storm had rolled in, blotting out the light of day and turning the lake into a sea of crashing waves.

Ahead, on the shore, Lucia stood near a boat. I stumbled forward, the wind battering me and whipping the strands of my hair into my face. It hadn't yet started to rain, but I could feel moisture in the heavy air.

"What will I look like?" I repeated as I neared.

Her gown billowed in the gale winds but her golden hair barely moved.

"You will look much like you do now. Hair flying and eyes burning bright. Only, you will be covered with giant flames."

That didn't sound so bad.

"And the rest?"

"In the boat." She motioned to the vessel the waves were trying their hardest to pull back out into open waters.

I stared at the boat that had carried me most of the way to the isle. The plug was once again in place, and both oars waited for me. My bag, which had held my change of clothes, lay ripped and empty in the bottom of the boat. There was no salt. No weapons. And, the oracle wanted me to head out into storm-tossed waters just before sunset.

Our eyes met, and she smiled slowly.

"In you go, Megan. Once you're in the water, we'll both get what we want."

"You want me dead." I said it without thinking, but I knew I was right when she smiled wider.

"Stay here with me and never learn the truth, or get in the boat and take your chances with the open waters."

"Not much of a choice," I said.

"But it's still a choice. And one only you can decide."

Pushing back my hair, I stepped into the boat. It rocked under me then jerked forward. I looked back at Lucia, who was pushing me into the crashing waves.

"The answer," I yelled over the noise.

"Row, Megan. And, I will keep my word."

I started rowing, getting drenched quickly with the first wave that hit the bow.

Lucia's voice carried to me as I put distance between the shore and the boat.

"Controlling your temper is like asking a fish not to swim. You were born to be angry. There is no controlling it. Those who've told you otherwise have been lying to you."

Adira. The Quills. The Council. They'd all lied to me. Everything I'd been told to do. All the tests. Lies. Why? They were keeping my mark from me based on my inability to control my rage. Did that mean I would never get my mark? That I would be forever trapped in Uttira?

I saw red. And through that color-stamped haze of emotion, I also saw Lucia change. Her beautiful face melted away to reveal the sleek flat head of a snake. Her body elongated, and her arms and legs disappeared.

Suddenly, I understood what she really meant when she said we'd both get what we wanted once I was in the water. She had given me my answer, and now she was going to get what she'd wanted all along. A meal.

I pulled hard on the oars and ignored the icy water hitting my back. Nothing mattered but rowing as fast as I could. My life depended on it.

CHAPTER NINETEEN

I WATCHED LUCIA SLITHER FORWARD ON HER BELLY AND ENTER THE foamy surf.

The intent to kill danced in the reflective silver of her eyes. So, why wasn't I angry? Where the hell was my fury temper?

"Of all the times to conveniently disappear, now isn't one of them. A make out session with Oanen? Yes. Two minutes from being sushi? No."

The oracle opened her mouth wide and tested the air with her forked tongue. Then, she ducked under an incoming wave and started in my direction, her body zigzagging smoothly through the turbulent water.

I shivered again and rowed harder, keeping my seat by bracing my feet against the next one. The oars groaned under the strain of my effort to move faster.

"I am not going to be eaten by a twenty-foot snake." Yet, the waves fought me, reducing the forward thrust of each stroke.

Lucia drew closer.

I lifted the oars out of the water and took one from its holder, ready to use it as a weapon. If beating her with it didn't work, I'd shove it down her throat.

At the last moment, her head dipped under the water. The boat lurched forward, away from the island with increasing speed. The swells grew bigger, nearly unseating me as the boat powered over them. I set the oar down and gripped the sides of the boat instead, wondering what Lucia was doing. Behind the boat, the island rapidly grew smaller.

Just before it vanished into the dark haze of the horizon, Lucia stopped pushing. I released my hold on the boat and scrambled to pick up the oar once more.

Lucia's large, wet body flew out of the water and landed in the boat with me. Her tail pinning the oar in place, she opened her mouth. I reacted without thought and punched her in her exposed throat. She jerked back and hissed at me.

"What's wrong?" I taunted. "Don't like it when your food fights back?"

She shifted to her human form, white gown in place and weirdly dry. With a hand covering her throat, she scowled at me.

"As much as I desire to discover the taste of young fury, I'm not yet ready for a journey to the underworld. So, I'll bait my trap like they baited theirs."

"What?" I asked.

"It was no accident you made it to my island, an island hidden by magic even from the land and air creatures here. You made a mermaid mad by stealing her sweet human, and she thought by sending you to me, I would take care of her problem. Usually, I would be inclined to help if it fills my belly. But, I'm not foolish enough to do anything that might gain the attention of the gods."

"What do you mean?" I asked. "Aren't they dead or sleeping or something?"

"Or something," Lucia answered, shifting her attention to the waves around us. She picked up the oar and put it back in its place. When she turned her eyes to me, the pupils were wide and reflective again.

"Row, Megan."

"Why?"

"As I've said, I'm inclined to do things that will help fill my belly. I do very much enjoy the taste of mermaid."

That Lucia wanted to use me as bait to catch another mermaid for dinner was now very clear. But, what would happen to me once she got her mermaid?

I stared at her for a moment, considering my options. Nothing had really changed. I still needed to get back before dark.

Exhaling slowly, I gripped the oars and struggled to make more progress away from the island. The further I got, the warmer I became. I should have felt relief because I was returning back to my version of normal, but there was still so much wrong with my current situation. That I was losing daylight and not gaining much distance didn't worry me as much as what would happen when I lost sight of the island. There was no sun, and I had no GPS to guide me.

As I rhythmically pulled at the water, the sky lightened briefly. Then, the first snowflake fell.

"Shit," I swore under my breath.

Lucia's gaze shifted from the water to the sky, and she smiled.

"Be a good girl and go for a swim," she said softly.

Before I could tell her to go to hell, she shifted forms again. Her tail lashed out and hit me hard across my back.

There was no stopping my graceless topple from the boat. The freezing water slammed into me face-first. Any heat that I generated was ripped from me just as quickly as it appeared. The choppy waves kept me under and rolled me several times, disorientating me. When I opened my eyes, it took a moment for me to focus in the murk. Churned up by the storm, bits of weed and debris floated here and there in an otherwise still, underwater world.

I kicked hard toward the frothing of motion above me, and my head finally broke through the surface. Gulping a breath, I looked around for the boat and spotted it several yards away. Lucia was nowhere in sight. I shuddered at the thought of her slithering in the water with me as I started toward the boat.

Waves washed over my head as I swam. I tried not to think about Lucia or how cold the water was or how to get back to the shore. Instead, I focused on my current goal. I just needed to get in the boat. Another wave hit me. It knocked me under water and rolled me once.

Again needing to find my way back to the surface, I opened my eyes and almost choked at the face staring back at me. The mermaid smiled. Lightning fast, she snagged my hair and started towing me deeper.

My temper flickered then ignited, and water bubbled off of me in a rush. The mermaid didn't notice until I grabbed her arm. She squealed, the sound hurting my ears even underwater. With her free hand, she swiped at me, just missing my face with her claws. I released her and watched her dart away into the surrounding darkness before I kicked my way to the surface.

I breathed in deeply and looked for the boat again. Any progress I'd made in my first attempt to reach it had been lost. Diving under the water this time, I swam hard. The heat from the run-in with the mermaid stayed with me until I surfaced again. I shivered slightly as I focused on the boat, which was much closer this time. Going under once more, I powered my way toward my reprieve from the stupid lake filled with asshole creatures that all wanted to eat me.

When I surfaced, the boat was right there. I closed my hand over the side in relief. Before I could pull myself up, though, something pried my fingers off. Unprepared for the loss of support, I went under again. This time, there were more faces around me. At least a dozen mermaids.

They darted my way, teeth flashing. Something fell into the water. The explosion of white bubbles made it impossible to see what, but I suddenly knew. Lucia hadn't left the boat. She'd been hiding, waiting for her bait to work.

I kicked for the surface, the need to get out of the water that very second overriding everything else. The mermaids not near the churning bubbles grabbed for me. I managed to kick one in the side, but another one bit my arm. My breath left me in a scream of rage. The water started bubbling off of me again, and the mermaids trying to keep me under darted away.

Kicking toward the surface, I grabbed for the boat but it moved just out of reach. I ducked under the next wave and looked around. Lucia bolted past me, hot on a mermaid's tail. Her abrupt appearance sent the mermaids who held the boat scattering. I swam hard for the vessel, staying under water until the last moment. Once more I took hold of the rim and tried to haul myself over the edge.

With a grunt I fell into the bottom of the boat. Laying there, I listened to the waves and caught my breath. My arm ached. I lifted it and studied the tiny punctures that formed a wide crescent. Dark green goo oozed from it already.

"We're not done yet," a voice yelled.

The boat tilted sharply to the side.

I snarled, sat up, and grabbed an oar ready to beat back the finned bitch trying to return me to the lake. The water erupted upward, dousing me yet again. Not that I paid much attention to that as I dropped the oar and wildly grabbed for the side of the boat to keep from falling out.

Lucia's body soared out of the water, sailing overhead. I tracked her progress, slack jawed at the sight of the mermaid she had by the tail. The mermaid squealed and thrashed as they slammed into the water on the other side of the boat.

A wave jostled the boat, snapping me from my stunned slouch against the seat. I grabbed up the oar, slammed it into place and started rowing. I no longer had any sense of where I was. It didn't matter. I just knew I needed to get away from the fighting before I went in again. My arms and legs ached; and outside of the water, away from the mermaids, my fury temper wasn't keeping me warm enough. I couldn't seem to stop shivering, and I doubted it had anything to do with the snow, now falling in earnest, or the fading light. Glancing at the bites on my arm, I forced myself to row harder.

My hair froze to my head as I strained.

Several times, I saw Lucia's body rise only to disappear again. When something burst from the surface near the end of the boat, I thought it was her. Instead, a mermaid landed on the seat in front of me. She immediately shifted from fins to legs, hissed at me, then stared out at the waves.

One minute the mermaid sat there, the next Lucia exploded out of the water, snatched up the girl, and swallowed her whole before plunging back into the depths of the lake.

I forgot to row as I stared at the space where the oracle had disappeared.

"That should have been you," a familiar voice said.

The boat tipped and, unprepared, I went over the side again. I barely felt the cold as the lake swallowed me whole. I kicked hard toward the surface, tired and pissed. My head bobbed through a wave, and I looked around for the boat. It rocked nearby.

Before I could start in that direction, Lucia's head surfaced near mine. She circled me twice, her oddly bulging body skimming the surface. I didn't miss the way her middle wiggled from the inside. Revulsion filled me but no anger. What was wrong with me? How could the mermaids be wicked, but not the mermaid-eating oracle?

Lucia stopped scanning the water and focused on me.

"Such a tasty looking bit, you are. So pale with pretty blue lips. You're getting tired." Her tongue flicked out.

"What happened to not angering the gods?" I asked.

She chuckled.

"Smart little fledgling. That hasn't changed. But there are a few mermaids who might be willing to risk that." She looked out over the water. I followed her gaze and saw several heads watching us.

"This has been fun, my sweet treats," Lucia said. "We'll need to do it again soon." The mermaids hissed at her. "If you happen to kill Megan before sunrise, bring her to me. I wouldn't mind a taste. In fact, I might even reward the one who brings her to me."

She dove under the water, disappearing from sight.

The mermaids and I stared at each other for a moment. They went under. I bolted for the boat.

Within seconds, someone grabbed my ankle and pulled me beneath the surface. I kicked hard and connected with a body part. A squeal rang out. A hand grabbed my bitten arm. Fingers caught my hair. Claws raked my side, setting paths of fire in the skin over my ribs.

I could barely think through the pain as another blazing trail ignited over my thigh. My struggles to get free lost their strength and slowed. I was angry. But, I was so tired too.

Hands gripped my head, turning me and forcing my attention to the wide eyes only inches away from mine. The familiar face smiled.

"You're mine," she said. Her grip tightened as she tugged me upward. The mermaids holding my arms and legs didn't let go but followed as Merbitch and I broke through to the surface.

"What's wrong, Megan?" she asked. "Where are your threats to boil us alive now?"

"Go to hell," I said. My tone lacked its usual bite, and I knew I was in serious trouble.

"You wish. I'm going to enjoy this."

"Spare me your villain monologue and just do what you need to do."

She hissed at me and slashed a claw down my neck. I grunted at the burn.

"Do you know what that venomous snake eats when we don't bring her a human? Us! Our brothers and sisters."

"Do you think I care or that I'll give you pity after you tried to feed me to her? Feed Ashlyn to her? You really are stupid."

She pulled her hand back, looking pissed enough to tear my face off as she swung forward. Before her claws could touch me, an eagle's cry split the air.

My pulse jumped in hope and fear. Before Merbitch could dive under, she was ripped out of the water. I looked up in time to see her dangling from Oanen's talons. She screamed and thrashed as he climbed higher into the sky.

A hand locked around my ankle.

"Oan—"

Water closed over my head once more. A second later, a very large and very pissed griffin plunged into the water. The mermaid holding me squealed and tried to flee, but Oanen's beak caught her fin and ripped it clean off.

I grinned slightly, feeling vindicated as I slowly drifted toward the surface. I bobbed there, my blinks becoming slower as I waited for Oanen to emerge. He did several moments later in a shower of water with a mermaid by her tail. He flung his head to the side, and I watched her go flying.

He turned toward me, his golden gaze sweeping my face. I

wrapped my arms around his neck and held him, my fear of hurting him gone. I had no heat left in me.

"I am so glad you're here," I said. "Rowing sucks."

His beak nuzzled my hair for a moment before he started to bump me. He didn't quit until I floated on my back.

"You could have just said, 'float' you know," I mumbled.

He jumped out of the water, hovering above me. His talons circled my torso, and with the heavy beat of his wings echoing around us, he pulled me from the waves. I wrapped my hand around his leg and closed my eyes.

Vaguely, I knew there were things I should have been doing, like wondering why I wasn't burning Oanen or asking how he'd found me; but my brain felt too fuzzy to focus. Instead of trying to force my mind to work, I focused on nothing.

Wind and pelting flakes of snow buffeted my face. That stinging burn was nothing compared to the agony growing inside of me. A shudder coursed through my body, and Oanen cried out.

"I'm fine," I said. "I'm just sick of smelling like fish. Take me home, bird boy."

I'd never felt so tired before in my life. As much as I wanted to blame it on all the swimming and rowing, I couldn't. Pain ate at me from the inside. Not wanting to worry Oanen, I forced myself to relax as much as I could in his hold. I focused on the steady thump of his wings, the howl of the wind, and the crash of the waves. It didn't help. Tracing the feathers under my fingers did. A little.

My heart ached with how much I'd missed him. I couldn't wait to get back home, shower, and snuggle under a tower of blankets with Oanen wrapped around me. The thought of being warm sent another shiver through me.

He made another sound, but I didn't have it in me to comfort him.

My fingers gave a final stroke to his ankle feathers then stilled. The oozing mermaid bites and cuts were sapping me of everything. Only, this time, I wasn't burning up. I was growing colder. So cold, in fact, that after a few minutes, my shivers stopped. I knew that wasn't good. But, sleep pulled at me, and the agony of my injuries began to fade. I sighed, ready to give into the exhaustion.

Oanen's eagle scream jolted through me, and I opened my eyes to see the shoreline and Eliana's car illuminated by the glow of her headlights. Home.

I exhaled heavily and closed my eyes again, dangling loosely in Oanen's grip. My back gently touched ground.

A moment later, Oanen's warm arms wrapped around me.

"Do you have a blanket?" he said. "Anything. She's so cold."

"Cold?" Eliana said, sounding worried. A hand brushed my forehead. "No. We didn't bring a blanket. Here. Take my jacket."

Material covered my torso. It didn't help.

"Megan, open your eyes," Oanen said.

I wanted to. I just didn't have the energy.

His lips pressed against my forehead then my temple, leaving little patches of heat that too quickly faded.

"You're scaring me," he said softly. "I can hear the beat of your heart. But, it's too slow, and I can't feel anything. Please, Megan. Open those pretty eyes." His hold on me tightened.

My heart ached for Oanen. I tried harder to open my eyes. To move my hand and stroke his hair. I had nothing left. What was wrong with me? I'd never felt sick in my life, but now…it felt like I was dying.

CHAPTER TWENTY

"PLEASE, MEGAN," OANEN WHISPERED AGAIN. "GET MAD. YOU need to warm up. Don't leave me." His voice broke on those last words.

Held tightly against his chest, I wished I could hold him in return. Touch him. Talk to him. Now was my chance. I was cold enough that I could actually do all the things I wanted to do without hurting him. Instead of moving though, I just lay there, trapped inside of myself.

He pulled away and touched his lips to mine. The light press of heat against my cold skin started a flutter in my belly.

When his lips left me a moment later, I wanted to beg for him to come back.

"Don't stop," Eliana said. I heard her shuffle closer.

"What?" Oanen asked.

"I could feel something from her. It was faint but there. Kiss her again."

His hand cupped my face.

"Come on, Megan," he said softly.

My fingers twitched at the feel of his mouth brushing gently over mine. The warmth of his exhale washed over my face as his fingers traced the curve of my cheek. Heat ignited in my stomach, hard and fast. It burned through me, setting each cut and bite ablaze. But there wasn't any pain, only the taste of Oanen.

Determined not to waste my chance, I lifted my hands and threaded my fingers through his hair. With a relief-torn sound, he deepened the kiss. The first touch of his tongue to mine felt like it set fire to my skin. I groaned and slid my hands from his hair to his bare chest. I'd been so hungry for him. For the feel of his arms around me. I wanted to hold on and never let go. I wanted him over me. In me.

A hand slapped down on the top of my head, cooling all my Oanen-centered thoughts.

I jerked back and looked up into his golden eyes. The heat I saw reflected in his gaze made my insides curl with delight. However, the sparks of passion that continued to pop and flare inside of me, couldn't seem to ignite again.

"Oanen," Eliana said, sounding strange, "your eyebrows just grew back. Go stand by the car."

He pulled away from me with obvious reluctance, and I hungrily watched his retreating backside.

"And put some clothes on," Eliana added.

I tilted my head up at her and noted her pure black eyes as she watched Oanen follow her orders.

"Miss me, monkey?" I asked.

Her gaze dipped to me.

"I'm so mad at you. Don't ever make me do this again." She gave my hair a slight tug, making it clear what she never wanted to do again, and lifted her hand.

"I thought you liked the taste of fury," I said, batting my lashes at her.

"Fury. Not lust."

"Liar," Oanen said from near the car.

I glanced his way, and all the passion I had for him slammed back into me. Only this time, it didn't feel so good. The heat flared to life in the wounds, burning them with molten pain. I made a sound, and Eliana reached for me.

"Don't," I managed to say. "Not this time."

Oanen took several steps in my direction, and I held up my hand.

"No. I'll be okay."

I wasn't sure I would be, though. I couldn't remember it hurting so much the last time I'd healed. Everything ached. Pain radiated through me. Anger swiftly followed. None of this needed to happen.

"Talk to me, Megan," Oanen said. "What's wrong?"

"I'm hurt, and I'm pissed," I said.

"Hurt? Where?"

I pulled back the sleeve of my steaming shirt to expose the mermaid bite. Green sludge dripped from my skin to the melting snow beneath me.

"None of this needed to happen," I said, echoing my earlier thought. "Oanen leaving to search for my mom. My trip to the damn lake for the oracle. Every single bite and scrape. It's all the result of adult bullshit."

Another intense stab of pain bolted through me. I clenched my teeth against the need to cry out and waited for it to pass.

"If my mom hadn't taken off," I said when I could speak, "or if anyone in this place would just tell the truth for once—"

The next piercing shard of agony tore a scream from me. The smell of something burning clogged my nose as I struggled to inhale.

"That's right. Breathe, Megan," Oanen said. "Focus on me. On the sound of my voice."

I opened my eyes, which I hadn't realized I'd closed, and found Oanen squatted down a few yards from me. His face was red and beaded with sweat. Just behind him, Eliana stood with wide eyes as she stared at me.

"Sweet Jesus," she said softly.

Panting with pain, I looked down at myself. Flames licked my skin around the bite, burning away my sleeve.

Was this how I healed?

Before that thought fully settled in my mind, the fire spread, racing up my arm. I looked at Oanen, panic coursing through me as quickly as the flames were consuming me.

"You're okay, Megan," he said. "It's not burning you."

"The hell it isn't! It hurts like a bitch."

"Look at your skin. You're fine."

I looked down again, seeing he was right. Why was it hurting then? I groaned again as the inferno inside of me burst outward. The roar of flames filled my ears, and my skin tightened to the point it felt like it would split.

Then it all stopped. I fell to my knees, panting and tired and wondering at what point I'd gotten to my feet.

"She's okay, Oanen. Why don't you get your shirt?"

I lifted my head to look at the pair. Eliana held Oanen's arm to keep him from coming toward me. His eyes met mine, and my heart melted at the worry I saw there.

"I'm okay," I said.

"Go get her your shirt," Eliana said, nudging him toward her car. "She needs a minute."

I frowned and looked down to see how much damage I'd caused my clothes. My mouth dropped open. I wasn't wearing a thing. Crossing an arm over my boobs and shielding my nethers with a hand, I looked up again. Oanen had already turned around on his way to the car.

Eliana gave me a sheepish smile.

"Looks like you might need to start stashing clothes, too," she said.

"I really hope that kind of thing will not be a regular occurrence," I said, carefully getting to my feet. The now exposed sand beneath me had melted into an irregular sheet of glass.

"It looked like it might be."

"What do you mean?"

She shrugged slightly and lifted the phone she held, turning it so I could see the picture she'd taken. I was floating in the air, arms flung wide, consumed in an inferno of flames. My mouth was open, and my head flung back. Everything about me was on fire. Even my hair. I squinted and stepped closer, trying to ignore the fact that I was completely exposed in the picture.

"What's that behind me?" I asked as I stared at the twin flames that extended from either side of me.

"It looks like small wings."

"Can my life get any worse? I'm going to kill that oracle."

"Why?"

Before I could answer, Oanen approached with a shirt held loosely in his hands. The heated look in his eyes made my insides flare with warmth again.

"Cool it, you two," Eliana said. "Oanen, turn around. Megan, keep talking."

Oanen winked at me as he tossed the shirt over then gave us his back. I quickly tugged the covering on over my head.

"The oracle didn't say a thing about wings. She also told me that there was no way to control my temper and that Adira and the Council have been lying to me."

"Hmm," Eliana said, looking off toward the lake.

Oanen turned around and tugged me into his arms while she was distracted.

"Don't ever scare me like that again," he said against my hair.

"Not sure I can promise that. I think Eliana's right, and flames might be another superpower for me."

"I wasn't talking about the flames. Why didn't you wait for me?"

"Because I wanted to be able to hug you without turning you into a piece of extra crispy when you got back. I don't want to hurt you anymore."

"I don't think you will. I'm holding you now, and I'm fine."

I looked up at his red face and made a sound of doubt.

"This is because I was too close when you exploded. You're not too hot now."

I lifted up to my toes and kissed him hard. He kissed me back. For several long moments, there was nothing but me and Oanen and what we felt for each other. I basked in the ability to kiss him and touch him like I wanted.

Distantly, I heard Eliana clear her throat.

"I think you can safely conclude you're in control of yourself now," Eliana called.

I pulled back to see Oanen's golden eyes. He still had all of his facial hair. I grinned. He threaded his fingers through mine and gave me a tender look.

"Since we know you won't hurt me anymore, how about we promise to stick together from now on?" he said. "No more trying to break up with me."

"I think I can manage that." My smile faded as my temper spiked. "What is up with everyone lying in this dump?"

"The Council?" Oanen asked.

"No, the oracle. She said that there was no controlling my temper. I just hugged you without setting you on fire."

"I think the oracle told you the truth, Megan," Eliana said, standing by the car. When I focused on her, I noticed the car's paint had bubbled.

"Holy shit," I said, looking at what I'd done.

"Yeah, no more monkey hugs for you when you're mad," Eliana said.

"No kidding. Now, why do you think she told the truth?"

"Because if there was someone wicked nearby, I don't think you'd be able to control your temper. That you're not burning Oanen or me accidentally means you're in control of your power. I think you can control your power, but not your anger. Your anger is what helps you identify the wicked."

"That's splitting hairs. I have no doubt she purposely misled me. You know what the most frustrating part is? By my definition, she was wicked, yet I didn't get fury angry at her."

"Why do you think she was wicked?" Eliana asked.

"She's been eating mermaids. A lot of them. And, I saw her do it."

"There's no rule that says she can't eat mermaids or other creatures," Oanen said. "Only that we can't consume human flesh."

"She did say she always tried to follow the rules," I said, thinking things through. "That whole trip was a complete waste then. She didn't tell me anything that would help me."

My temper jumped a bit, and I quickly looked down at our joined hands. His thumb stroked over my skin, no hint of red appearing. I wasn't generating any external heat.

"Not a waste," Oanen said, drawing my attention. "Not if you really can control your powers now."

"I think we should test it," Eliana said.

"How?"

She grinned widely.

"Let's go to the Roost."

"I don't like this," I said, looking at the Roost's red doors through the passenger window.

"Me, neither," Oanen said.

"Stop being babies," Eliana said from the back seat. "This is the best way to test if Megan's fixed, and you both know it."

I wanted to deny I was ever broken, but given the number of times I'd burned Oanen, I couldn't.

"Fine. Let's just get this done."

I opened my door and stood, wincing at the cold air whirling around my bare legs. Oanen's t-shirt extended past my butt by a meager three inches. While I'd wanted to go home and change first, Eliana had argued that showing up in nothing but a t-shirt would be more likely to illicit wicked ideas from the patrons.

"I swear, if anyone sees my butt, I'm going to be so mad."

"Good. That's the point," Eliana said as she got out to stand by me.

"Mad at you," I clarified.

She smiled, clearly not worried about my temper. The driver's side door opened, and I looked back at Oanen.

"Are you sure you don't want to wait in the car?" I asked.

"Together, remember?"

I nodded and started for the entrance. As usual, music already thumped from inside even though it was barely six.

The light dusting of new snow covering the sidewalk swirled around my feet as I opened the door. Warm air enveloped me, but I didn't get a chance to enjoy it.

A tingle of annoyance immediately traced down my spine. Without pausing, I strode in and pushed my way through the dancers toward the back of the room. A few of the guys on the floor paused to look at me. I could feel the nudge of their wickedness as they took in the sight of my breasts barely concealed by Oanen's thin t-shirt. That wickedness only inflated when they saw I wasn't wearing pants. However, their thoughts were pure in comparison to what I felt coming from the back of the club.

Instead of trying to calm down or run away, I opened myself to my temper. Details flooded my mind. Things I shouldn't know. Like my temper was flaring because Eras was harassing Kelsey and Zoe, again. But, that wasn't the sole cause. Something else was poking at me. Something he'd done in the past that I couldn't see for myself in the present.

I broke through the dancing crowd and found Eras and his friends sitting at the back table with Kelsey and Zoe, who were both clutching their books and keeping their heads down.

"Come on, girls," Eras said in a seductive voice. "You don't need to look at me. No one else needs to know. It'll be between us. Just nod. I'll reach under the table and have you shaking with need in seconds. It'll feel amazing. I promise."

"Not nearly as amazing as this," I said, my voice echoing with my fury power. "Eras Amadeus Aeccin, confess your sins."

Eras's mouth fell slack as he turned to look at me. The boys at the table with him quickly scrambled away.

Kelsey and Zoe's heads jerked up. They stared at me with wide eyes, both looking like they were about to cry. Eliana quickly stepped around me and slid into the booth to comfort them.

"Don't make me repeat myself, Eras," I said.

His mouth snapped shut.

"I wasn't breaking any rules, Fury. There's no reason for you to attack me."

"Oh, but there is. Something you did in your past. Something that did break the rules." The heat inside me intensified. I didn't fight it as I stepped closer to him and leaned down.

"Confess."

The soft word set off a blubbering confession about some petty theft, voyeurism (which I highly doubted was a crime), and vandalism. The last one made me scowl as he detailed how he'd smashed my window and seduced a mermaid into scratching my paint.

"You are guilty of wickedness," I said, grabbing Eras by the collar of his polo shirt and hauling him from the booth. The boy was a sobbing mess.

"Continue on this course, and you are guaranteed a spot in Hell's hall. Make amends and cleanse your slate."

"I'll make amends. I promise. Just tell me what to do."

His eagerness and complete sincerity calmed my temper.

"Uttira needs a library. Help build it."

He nodded frantically, and I let go of his shirt. He thumped to the ground and dashed for the door. Only after the fact, did I realize what I'd just done. I'd controlled my power by letting my temper go. I'd also just exposed the hell out of my backside.

I turned to face the room.

"Did anyone here see my butt just now?"

Every single head started to shake.

"Remember, lies are wicked," I said with a frown.

Half the people nervously raised their hands.

"Can you reach over the table again?" Fenris shouted from within the crowd. "I didn't get a good look. Oanen got in the way."

I glanced at Oanen, who looked mad enough to skin a dog.

"How about you and I head home," I said softly.

Before he could say anything, a portal appeared beside us and Adira stepped out.

"Oanen has other obligations tonight, Megan," she said. "As do you."

"Oh? And what might our obligations be?" I asked, arching a brow.

"The Council would like Oanen to fly to the Goose and

Gizzard in New York on official business, and I have two more recruits for you to verify."

I looked at Kelsey and Zoe, who were still pale. Although some of the color loss could be blamed on Eras, I knew most of it was due to me.

"I'm sorry, guys," I said.

"No, we're cool," Kelsey said. "We didn't see anything."

I started to grin, but my temper flared hot and fast, the only warning I had to turn and grab Adira's wrist before she could touch my shoulder. I let all the anger Adira and the Council had caused to burn in my eyes.

When she saw the flames there, she flinched and paled.

"I warned you not to toy with me, Adira. Don't ever try to teleport me without my permission again. Do we understand each other?"

"Yes. Perfectly. With your permission, I would like to teleport all three of us to the Quills' for an overdue meeting."

"No. Oanen has been gone for days. He's not doing anything tonight but spending time with me. And, I'm not verifying another recruit for you ever again. Uttira needs to fix its educational process before putting more fish in the fish bowl. Are we clear?"

"Yes. Please come see us first thing in the morning."

I rolled my eyes.

"I'll see you when it's convenient to me. Now, stop pushing."

She gave a single nod then disappeared.

Eliana's phone immediately buzzed. She looked at it with a frown.

"What?" I asked.

"It's from Adira, and it's for Oanen. She says to keep a close eye on Megan tonight."

I smiled widely. Adira had just confirmed what I'd suspected the moment she'd paled. The Council knew they could no longer control me. I was free. Almost.

Oanen stepped close and wrapped his arms around my waist. He pressed his lips to my temple in a brief kiss and looked at Eliana.

"I already planned to keep a very close eye on her. Tonight and every night after."

CHAPTER TWENTY-ONE

I SCRUBBED MY HAIR A SECOND TIME BEFORE ADDING CONDITIONER. At my feet, bits of seaweed swirled near the drain.

"I hate mermaids," I called loud enough for Oanen to hear. He probably would have heard without me yelling, but I wanted the volume to convey the loathing I felt.

"Lakes too!"

I finished up in the shower and quickly dressed. When I joined him in the kitchen, he was leaning against the counter, waiting for me.

"So a moonlit ride in a gondola is out?"

"Since gondolas are usually found in Italy, no. I'd suffer some water for that to happen. But more swimming in Lake Uttira? No way."

He pushed away from the counter and stalked toward me. My stomach fluttered wildly, but nothing started burning. I still couldn't believe that I was okay.

He snagged the edge of my shirt and slowly reeled me into his arms.

"Are we done fighting this, now?"

"You were never fighting it," I said with a small smile.

"Stubborn fury, just answer the question."

I grinned and stood on my toes to kiss him lightly.

"I'm done fighting what's happening between us."

"Good." He released me then tugged me toward the table where he had sandwiches waiting for us. A brownie sat on my plate, too.

"I'm so hungry," I said. I sat and took a huge bite, moaning at the taste of mayonnaise and turkey.

"Thought you might be." His lips twitched as he watched me swallow. "That brownie is from Michigan, which is where I was when Eliana called me."

I wrinkled my nose and squinted at him.

"Is this where you lecture me again?"

"Nope." He picked up his sandwich and took a bite.

I could see he wanted to say more and waited for him to finish chewing. He didn't leave me waiting long.

"I'm too smart to annoy a fury with lectures."

"I'm going to remember that."

"I bet you will. I'm sorry I didn't find your mom," he said, changing the subject. "I'll look again when I go to New York."

"We'll look," I said after finishing another bite.

He frowned at me.

"Did you already forget our promise?" I asked. "Together from now on. Remember?"

"That might be a problem when I need to leave for Council matters."

I grinned. "I don't think so. First, there's no longer any reason for the Council to keep me trapped here. I'm not burning you every time we touch now, and I didn't beat Eras tonight even though I was angry. That means I have control. I just have to tell Adira tomorrow. Second, the Council doesn't own you. You're the one who told me not to be a cog in their wheel of lies."

"I don't recall saying wheel of lies," he said, the corner of his mouth twitching.

"It was implied. Regardless, they don't own you, right? So, until I get my mark, we'll stick together. And once I have my mark, if you choose to continue to help the Council, I'll go also. If we're lucky, we'll run into my mom at some point."

"You still want to find her?" he asked.

"Yeah. I want to know why she couldn't have spent five minutes explaining things to me instead of just bailing."

After we finished up our late dinner, we went to the living room where we watched TV together. Oanen held me the whole time, his fingers traveling the length of my arm. I stopped watching several times to turn my head and kiss him. Each time ended with me breathless and wanting more. But, no fire. No burns.

I stared out at the Quills' large house, not looking forward to our meeting.

"We can go do something else," Oanen said.

I laughed lightly and shook my head.

"There's nothing else to do in this town at eight in the morning."

"We could go back to bed."

I turned to him and arched my brow. We spent the night comfortably sleeping in each other's arms. It'd been the best night's sleep I'd had in ages. The kisses he'd trailed along my neck to wake me had been amazing, too.

"I like this new you," he said. "I know when you're thinking about me. Your eyes start glowing light orange."

"How do you know I wasn't getting mad at you?"

"They start glowing a deeper orange when you're angry."

I rolled my eyes and shook my head at him.

"As much as I want to have a repeat of last night, I also want to get this done." I glanced at the house again. "You won't try to stop me, right?"

"No. I'll support whatever decisions you make in there. Even against my parents. I trust you, Megan."

"All right. Let's do this."

We got out and walked the snow-covered path. As usual, his mom opened the door before we reached it.

"Good morning you two," she said with a wide smile.

I frowned at her barely contained joy, not trusting it.

"I changed my mind. Let's leave," I said softly, threading my fingers through Oanen's.

A look of hurt crossed Mrs. Quill's face.

"I know these past few weeks have been a struggle for you —"

"No thanks to the Council and Adira," I said.

"—but I want you to know, I couldn't be happier with Oanen's choice in a mate."

Oh, sure. Now, she was happy.

Oanen's fingers squeezed mine lightly, and I knew I needed to be gracious for his sake.

"Thanks." That was as gracious as she was getting from me after trying to keep us apart.

She smiled and stepped aside to let us in.

"We're meeting in the study," she said.

Oanen and I walked the familiar path. When we entered, I was surprised to see several people already there. While I recognized Fenris' dad, Mr. Quill, and Adira, the rest were new to me.

"Thank you for coming, Megan," Adira said, turning toward

me. "With your permission, my sister and I would like to lay our hands on you."

I glanced at Oanen, wondering what the hell was going on. The amused glint in his eyes and encouraging nod had me agreeing. He released my hand and took a few steps back.

Mrs. Quill touched one shoulder and Adira the other. Both said several soft words I couldn't understand. A flare of pain scorched the inside of my wrist, and I jerked back from their hold. Lifting my arm, I saw the small, umber mark of Mantirum decorating my skin.

"Congratulations, Megan," Adira said.

"I don't understand. I thought there was a whole process to ensure I was ready. Questions that the Council needed to ask me."

"The process is different for each candidate. You proved your control last night. We saw no reason to delay giving you the mark. We do ask that you leave Uttira as soon as possible."

That got my attention.

"What? Are you serious? First you're hell-bent on keeping me here, and now you're kicking me out?"

"Yes," Adira said. "That's the condition of your mark. Having a mature fury inside Uttira is dangerous to the young still trying to learn the rules of our world. We want to ensure they have a chance to learn to do what's right before being punished for any mistakes made in ignorance. Oanen, you're welcome back any time, of course."

My temper flared, and the orange glow from my eyes reflected on Adira's skin.

"No," I said firmly. Everyone watched me, waiting. I could feel their fear. Of me.

"I will go, but I will return as I choose. And, I will punish the wicked as I see fit. If you truly want to protect your young, set better examples and start teaching them the rules from the moment they are born. Stop with the ridiculous classes in the Academy. Start teaching them their history and why they need to toe the line. And let them know, when they break the rules, there are bigger consequences than banishment from Uttira. I'll drag them to hell."

Raiden dipped his head.

"Yes, Fury."

All the rest followed suit and said the same.

Oanen took my hand again, reclaiming my attention.

"Want to hang around for a while, or are you ready to go to New York?"

"I'm ready," I said.

I was finally, truly free.

"It's not fair," Eliana said as she put another item from the fridge into the cooler. "I mean, it's fair you have your mark; it's not fair that they're making you leave town."

"They're making your mom stay away," I pointed out.

She gave a dry laugh.

"Mom is staying away because I asked her to. She doesn't care what they say. You have your mark; you can come and go as you please. Just stay."

I smiled at her. I would have never survived my time in Uttira without Eliana. I wasn't about to abandon my friend permanently.

"I'll be back," I said.

"Then why are we packing everything up?"

"Because I won't be back soon. It's going to take some time to find my mom."

"What am I supposed to do while you're gone? You are my only friend."

"Not true. You have Ashlyn, now. And Kelsey, Zoe, and Eugene."

She snorted.

"They're afraid of me. They know I'm something but just haven't figured out what yet. When they do, they'll start avoiding me like everyone else."

"Fine. What about Fenris? He knows what you are, and he doesn't ignore you."

She turned and rolled her eyes at me.

"Fenris is the last person I'd want to hang out with."

"I think that would hurt his feelings if he heard you say that," I said. "He's nice."

"He's way too into women. Look at all the trouble he caused because he wouldn't leave you alone."

I stopped trying to stick up for him. He'd need to figure out how to win over Eliana on his own.

"You'll be fine. And if you get bored, you can call me. Or better yet, get your mark so you can come hang out with me in the real world."

She groaned and continued loading things from the fridge to the cooler. My phone buzzed, and I read the text from Oanen.

Hope you're ready. I'll be there in twenty.

"If you got this covered, I'm going to go check over the rest of the house one more time. Oanen will be here in twenty minutes."

"Go for it," she called, her head buried in the fridge.

I walked upstairs and peeked into both rooms. I was leaving the place better than how I'd found it. Well, I was leaving it cleaner anyway. It was just as sad and empty as before, though. How many generations of furies had been dumped here?

"I got everything from the fridge," Eliana called from downstairs. "I'm going to take the cooler out to the car."

I returned to the first floor just as the porch door slammed shut. I checked the bathroom to ensure I had all my toiletries packed then turned around. The dismantled door chime caught my eye and made me smile. It hadn't been easy living here, but it had been an adventure. Several of them, in fact.

Turning, I started toward the kitchen then paused to open the library door. I didn't want the room to get musty if it took a while for me to return. Opening the door somehow knocked over one of the few books on the shelf.

Stepping into the room, I righted the thin tome. My fingers slid over the spine as I read the cover.

The Book of Fury.

Disbelief coursed through me as I plucked the book off the shelf and started to read. It was all there. Everything I needed to know. How to identify the signs of emerging power. How to embrace the anger to control the power. When it was time to leave my child behind so our powers didn't feed off of one another.

I paged through to the end where it talked about the final phase of a fury's growth and found a loose sheet of paper.

I know this probably isn't nearly enough information to answer all the questions you have right now. I'm sorry for that. Here's your great grandmother's address. She'll be waiting for you. Good luck. Call me when it's done.

Love Mom

She'd even written her phone number. I skimmed the letter again. Call when what was done? I looked at the last page of the book and read the words that made a ball form in my stomach.

By the laws of the gods there can be only three furies. Each new generation must tear the oldest generation from her position in order to fully embrace her power.

"Oh, hell no," I said, sitting heavily in the chair.

"Megan?" Eliana said from the doorway. "What's wrong?"

I looked up from the sheet of paper and met my best friend's eyes.

"I think I'm supposed to kill my great grandma."

FURY FREED

CHAPTER ONE

I STARED DOWN AT THE THIN *BOOK OF FURY* GRIPPED IN MY HANDS. Finally, I had the book containing all the answers I'd been seeking. However, the fact that it had been in my house all along stirred my rage. I wanted to throw it. I wanted to yell and scream. Instead, I stood shaking uncontrollably as I waited for Oanen.

Eliana said something behind me, but the sound of my heart pounding hard in my ears and my own thoughts drowned out her words. Her arms wrapped around me, and an immediate peaceful nothingness filled me.

"How are you going to survive out there without me?" Eliana asked, resting her head against my back. "Just because some dumb book says you need to kill your great-grandma, doesn't mean you have to. You have a choice. We always have a choice."

I exhaled heavily and set my hand on her forearm. She, better than anyone, knew the truth to those words.

"You're right. I do have a choice. It's just so infuriating, you know? All that time I was looking for answers, they were right in this house. Why didn't my mom just leave the dumb book on the table? No. That would have been too easy for her to do. She probably stood in the kitchen, looking around and wondering where I would be least likely to find it." Thanks to Eliana's touch, any rage I wanted to feel slipped away from me so my words were a mellow rant.

The crunch of tires over the snow announced Oanen's arrival, and Eliana released me with a final squeeze.

"It'll be okay," she said as Oanen got out of his car.

I opened the screen door and launched myself at him before he'd made it more than two steps toward the house. He caught me in his arms and held me tightly.

"You're shaking. What's wrong?"

Burying my face in the curve of his neck, I said nothing for a moment. The desperation to feel his arms around me faded as his fingers made little circles on my back.

"I hate my mom."

His fingers stilled.

"That's the first time I've heard you say that. Why now?"

I pulled back and showed him the book.

"*Book of Fury*?" His gaze met mine. "Where did you find it?"

"Here. In the library I never used. It has everything, Oanen. All the shit that I put up with these last few months…all the fear...none of it was necessary. She could have just handed me this damn book and told me to read it."

Ignoring the book, he wrapped me in his arms again and pressed his lips to my temple.

"I'm sorry for everything you've gone through. What your mom did wasn't right. But don't hate her. If you'd had all the answers, would you have needed to come here? Would you have tried leaving your house the night I met you? Because of her, I have you, Megan."

I pulled back and looked up into his beautiful blue eyes.

"You're really good at melting my heart," I said just before brushing my lips against his.

His hold on me tightened as he kissed me. When I pulled back, I was breathless and grinning like an idiot. His now golden eyes watched me closely.

"I love when they do that," I said, reaching up to gently trace the skin near his eye.

"And I love when yours glow, which they've been doing since you walked out the door. It makes me wonder if finding the book is the only thing upsetting you." His gaze briefly flicked to something behind me.

I turned to look at Eliana, who watched me with concern and a hint of black in her eyes.

"I know what she means to you," he said. "We don't have to leave today. You and Eliana can spend some more time together."

Giving Oanen another quick hug, I threaded my fingers through his and shook my head.

"I'll miss her, but I know I'll be back." I looked down at the book. "At least, I think I will be."

"It's the book that's upsetting her, Oanen," Eliana said from the back door. "The thing says she needs to kill her great-grandma. I told her it's bull pucky. No book should dictate her life."

"Bull pucky? Wow, Eliana. I didn't know you felt so strongly about it." I grinned widely as Oanen and I started toward the house.

"Shut up," she said with an answering smile.

Eliana opened the door for us, and I shivered slightly as I stepped into the heat. Since releasing my power on the beach the night before, my internal thermometer felt out of whack. I was never too warm anymore. If anything, I felt any chill much faster now. Not that I cared since I could finally touch Oanen without burning him.

"Can I see the book?" Oanen asked, kicking off his shoes, a sure sign we were staying for a while.

"Of course." I handed it over and took off my own shoes.

"I'm going to get going," Eliana said before I could move toward the table.

"Why?"

"Being sad makes me hungry, and you two are way more than I'll be able to resist."

I didn't bother trying to tell her I wouldn't mind if she took a little of the energy Oanen and I put off. She'd already made her stance on that very clear.

"Call me. Every day," she said, pulling me into a quick hug again. "I mean it. Or I'll worry."

"Yes, Mom," I teased. "I'll be back before you know it."

"You better be. This place is going to suck without you guys around."

"Suck? Like, what kind of suck are we talking here?"

Her mouth dropped open, and she blushed profusely.

"I changed my mind. I'm glad you're leaving."

"Whatever. You love me, and you know it. Besides, I'm helping. Every time you even get a little depressed, you're going to think about sucking. That'll motivate you to keep busy and happy so your mind doesn't go where you don't want it to."

"You're so twisted," she said, shaking her head at me.

"I know."

Despite my smile, I gloomily watched as Eliana walked out and quietly closed the door. I'd miss the hell out of her while we were gone.

Turning to Oanen, I found him frowning at the book.

"Most of the stuff in the middle is boring," I said. "Go to the last page."

He did, and I watched his eyes skim the words.

"Have you called her?" he asked, looking up.

"Call her?" My stomach churned at the thought. "What would I say? 'Hi, Paxton. Remember me? The kid you ditched a few months back. What the hell is up with this note you left in the book you hid?'"

"Yeah. Say exactly that. She owes you answers, and this book and note don't help."

I thought about what he said for a moment then reached for my phone. My stomach continued to twist as I paced the kitchen and listened to the call dial through.

Mom picked up on the second ring.

"Hello?"

It was hard to hear her over the heavy sound of traffic.

"Mom? It's Megan. I can barely hear you. Where are you?"

"New York. Hold on. Let me find somewhere quieter."

I waited a few moments, and the background noise became muffled.

"That's better," she said. "So, is it finally done?"

After over three months of not seeing me, no "Are you okay?" or anything else the least bit caring.

"Is what done?" I asked.

"Your great-grandmother, Irene. I left a note with the book. Didn't you read it yet, Megan?"

Her impatient tone poked at my temper. "Since I didn't know the book existed until twenty minutes ago, no, I haven't rushed out to kill my great-grandmother yet."

"Well, now you know. Hurry up and get it done. The longer you wait, the more you'll suffer."

"What do you mean? And why do you think she needs to die? And why do I have to do it?"

Silence greeted my questions. I looked at the phone and saw the call had ended. Scowling, I dialed again. It rang five times then just disconnected without the option to go to voicemail.

I tossed the phone on the table and sat across from Oanen. He reached out for my hand.

"You heard most of that?" I asked.

"All of it."

"She's in New York. What is that…maybe 8 hours away?"

"Don't dwell on it," Oanen said. "You can't change what she did, only what we do from here. What do you think she meant by you suffering?"

"Who knows with her? She's probably just making crap up, her way of making sure I'll do what she wants."

"I don't know. I read the part about gaining your powers. The book made it sound like the only way to gain them was by taking them from the oldest living fury."

"Bullshit. Look at what happened on the beach. I was in the air and on fire. I don't burn you anymore when we kiss. I've already freed my powers."

He considered me for a moment.

"I just don't want anything to happen to you," he said finally.

"I know. I don't want anything to happen to me, either. Since the Council wants you to go to New York anyway, we'll see if we can find mommy-dearest and get some clarification at the same time, okay?"

He nodded and stood.

"Everything packed up?" he asked.

"Yep. Eliana took all the crappy, healthy food with her so it wouldn't rot and stink up the place. Everything else is like I found it."

I grabbed my bag, which had some clothes and my wallet in it. Oanen took it from me and held the door. It felt weird to finally be leaving the place that kept me a prisoner for so long.

"I thought you'd be happier right now," Oanen said.

"I was just thinking about that, too, and I've realized my only drive to leave this place was to get answers." I held up the book. "I have them now. And I made friends here. There's really nothing for me out there. Except maybe some pizza." I grinned at the thought. "Oh, yeah. I'm totally going to pig out while we're in New York."

He chuckled and opened the door to his sporty red car. I looked at mine, parked near the shed.

"Don't worry. It'll be fine. Fenris promised to keep an eye on it," Oanen said.

"You talked to Fenris?"

"Yeah. He called to apologize for his comment last night. He only meant to defuse the situation so you wouldn't lose your temper with anyone else in the crowd."

"And?"

"And what?"

"Were you okay with his apology?"

"Of course. I knew what he was doing the moment he spoke. That didn't make hearing his words any easier."

I frowned slightly.

"I don't get it."

"I'm trying my hardest not to be jealous because you don't like it. Although I trust you completely, I still don't like other males even looking at you." He leaned down so he could set my bag in the back, putting us face to face. "You're mine, and I never could share well."

His lips brushed mine in a soft kiss. I closed my eyes and threaded my fingers in his hair.

Too quickly, he pulled away and shut the door. I watched him walk around the hood and took those few moments to gather my thoughts. When he opened his door, I was ready.

"So, your possessiveness isn't just a bonding thing?" I asked.

He started the car and gave me a look that started a fire smoldering in my stomach.

"Oh, it's definitely a bonding thing. But, because you asked, I'll keep it in check as best I can."

He backed out of my driveway, and I gave the house one last look. Paint still peeled off the boards, making it look old, but the clean windows and white blanket of snow over the cut grass made it feel less derelict and more cared for.

"We'll be back," Oanen said. "And in the spring, we're painting that thing."

I grinned and turned to watch the road. The familiar, winding path to the barrier only took a few minutes to travel. And when we reached the straight stretch, no scent of burnt hair tickled my nose. However, a tingle ran through my body as we crossed from Uttira into the real world.

I turned my wrist over and looked at the mark of Mantirum.

"It's weird how a little tattoo can make such a big difference."

Oanen chuckled.

"That's what I thought, too, the first time I flew outside."

"So, what's in New York? Other than pain in my ass Paxton?"

"A troll death. The Council wants me to ask around about it."

"Why?"

"Why what?"

"Why you? Why is a troll death a big deal? I mean, we die like humans, right? Well, at least species who don't have books saying the fourth generation needs to knock off the first generation."

"Yes. Most species have human equivalent lifespans. Trolls included. A troll showing up dead isn't a problem. How he died is."

"Well, don't leave me in suspense. Was he eaten? Mutated? Turned inside out? What?"

"You need to stop watching so much TV. The troll died smiling."

I stared at Oanen for a moment, confused. Oanen glanced at me and caught my look.

"You remember Epsid?" he asked.

"Yep."

"That's as happy as trolls get. And that only happens when they're young. As trolls age, they just get ornerier. The troll that died was old. They never smile. That he was still smiling in death is very off."

"Okay. So what would make a troll die with a smile?"

"No idea. That's why we need to check it out."

"And why you?"

He glanced at me.

"Because Uttira has the closest Council, and I'm a cog in training."

"Ugh. I have my mark now. Why not just tell them to shove it?"

"Honestly? I don't mind doing this. It beats getting a job at one of the shops in town to contribute to Uttira."

"Fair enough. What's the plan?"

"See what we can learn from the inglorious patrons of The Goose and Gizzard. According to Adira, it's the best place to gather information. If there is any to gather."

I ignored his mention of Adira, still too annoyed with the woman to even think about her.

"What kind of place is The Goose and Gizzard?"

"Don't know. This will be my first time there."

We passed our first car on the road, and my internal fury gauge only stirred a little, quickly settling with more distance.

"You all right?" Oanen asked. "You got quiet."

"Yeah. I'm okay. I could feel something from that car, but it went away already. Much better than the last time I was in a car in the outside world. The anger used to crawl under my skin and fester there until I wanted to beat someone."

"Let me know if it starts bothering you again, okay?"

"I will."

We talked for the next two hours about what Oanen suspected might have happened to the troll, how I planned to stuff the trunk with enough chocolate to keep Eliana supplied for the next year, and what color we wanted to paint the house.

"I'm still going with rainbow," I said, sticking to the house color of my choice.

"That sounds awful."

"Exactly. It'll work better than a 'keep away' sign on our front lawn," I said with a grin. A sign on the side of the road caught my attention.

"Can we stop at the next gas station? I'm craving some real potato chips."

"Sure." He glanced at me. "Just a snack break, or do you need a break from the traffic?"

The cars we passed so far were all right for the most part. A few made me clench my fists, but again, putting distance between us always brought it back down.

"Just the snack. We already left later than either of us wanted to. It'll be close to midnight by the time we get there the way it is."

"Later is better in this case. Too early, and no one will be at the Gizzard."

He took the next exit and turned into a small gas station.

"What town is this?" I asked as he parked.

"We're just outside of Brunswick, I think."

We both got out of the car, and a tug of tension drew my eyes to a woman at the pump.

"On second thought, fury fire and gas pumps probably aren't a good idea. I think I'm going to stay in the car. Pick something good for me."

I quickly got back inside the car and closed the door. But, sitting there didn't muffle the anger crawling under my skin in the least. So I distracted myself by ogling Oanen's backside as he jogged toward the entrance. The play of muscle under his form fitting t-shirt made me smile.

As soon as he disappeared, though, there was no distraction. How was I going to handle New York if I couldn't even get out of the car at a side-of-the-road gas station? I remembered the rage that consumed me the night Adira introduced me to Eugene in some back alley in the city. It hadn't been pretty. I'd wanted to kill those men. But, that was before I came into my power. Things would be different now. They had to be.

A blast of anger hit me hard. Not the woman who was paying at the pump. Someone else.

I turned my head to look at the car parking two spaces over from me. The driver, a man in his mid-twenties, glanced my way and smiled. The fire inside of me burned hotter. The need to punish clawed at me.

"Don't do it, Megan," I mumbled. "Keep your ass in your seat."

He opened his door.

My hand reached for the handle.

"Weak, Megan. Really weak."

I got out at the same time the man did. His smile widened as I walked his way.

"Hi. Can I help you with something?"

"Don't 'hi' me, asshole. What did you do to piss me off?"

His smile vanished, and he gave me a truly confused look.

"Excuse me?"

People could say the right words and give the right look to

make themselves appear good and innocent. But it didn't fool my fury-side. Ever.

"Nice try. Just confess what you did so we can both move on."

His eyes narrowed on me.

"Hot and crazy isn't my type," he said. "Beat it."

He moved to the side as if to walk around me.

"Will Yajlin," I said, stopping him with just my voice. "Confess."

The word brought him to his knees before me. Trembling where he knelt, words tumbled from his mouth. I listened to how he'd just beaten the crap out of his girlfriend before running out for a bag of beef jerky that she didn't want to get for him.

"Beef jerky?"

"I'm not even sure if she's still breathing," he admitted with a sob.

The fire inside of me roared with the truth behind his admission. I could see his girlfriend where she lay, her face bloody and pale. Her chest still.

"Elizabeth is not breathing. She died by your hands."

He mewled pathetically as I grabbed him by his throat and lifted. Fire danced up my arm, slowly consuming my sleeve.

"Will Yajlin, you've earned your place in hell."

With those words, I embraced my fury power. Fire exploded over my skin, and pain ripped through me from my stomach to the top of my head as if I were being split in half.

I opened my mouth and screamed, shattering the windows in Will's car.

The sound of Oanen calling my name was the last thing I heard before the agony of being burned alive swallowed me whole.

CHAPTER TWO

THE FAINT ECHO OF OANEN SAYING MY NAME AND THE PERSISTENT tapping on my cheek made my head throb. I groaned, turned my head, and heaved my guts out.

"Megan, tell me what's wrong?" Oanen said, holding back my hair.

"I'm throwing up," I said, weakly swiping my mouth with the back of my hand.

"Yeah, I can see that. Why, though?"

The gentle stroke of his fingers over my hair took away some of the ache drumming in my skull.

"How am I supposed to know? I just woke up."

The wrongness of that statement struck me as soon as the words left my mouth. I hadn't been sleeping. I'd been in the middle of punishing someone. A guy. No, a murderer.

From my position safely cradled in Oanen's lap, I lifted my head and looked around. We sat in the empty parking space next to our car. The man and his vehicle were gone.

I looked up at Oanen.

"What happened?" I asked.

The worry clouding his gaze intensified.

"I don't know. I came out with your snacks, found you on the ground, and some guy squealing tires out of the parking lot."

"That would have been Will, a guy who just killed his girlfriend. Can you help me up? I need to go to the bathroom and get this taste out of my mouth."

Oanen lifted me to my feet and walked with me to the bathroom. My legs felt a little shaky, and my stomach wasn't sure which way was up. However, none of that bothered me as much as the fact that I'd let a murderer get away.

Oanen said nothing as I closed myself into the dirty washroom. I used the toilet then cleaned up. Skull still pounding, I stared at myself in the mirror and tried to figure out what the hell had happened. I'd obviously done something wrong. But what?

I'd let go of my power just like I had on the beach. Only, the pain had been worse this time. And, instead of feeling better afterward, I hurt. My head. My stomach. Even my back.

Oanen knocked lightly on the door.

"Everything okay?"

"Yeah. Just a minute."

Not wanting to worry him further, I splashed some cool water on my face before opening the door. His concerned gaze swept over me.

"Feeling better?" he asked.

"As well as a girl can after heaving her guts out in front of her boyfriend."

His gaze warmed.

"I like the sound of that."

"You like the sound of me trying to see the inside of my stomach?" I asked in disbelief. "You have issues."

"I like the sound of boyfriend. Not you getting sick; our kind isn't supposed to get sick like that."

"I'd prefer to pretend it didn't happen," I said quickly, noting the pre-lecture look on his face. Which was completely unfair since I hadn't done anything to deserve it.

He lifted my bag. I hadn't noticed him holding it until then.

"In case you wanted to brush," he said.

"You're amazing." I accepted the bag. "And when I come back out, we won't mention my time kissing the pavement ever again."

He nodded, and I closed the door on him once more, relieved that I'd managed to hide just how much my head was hurting. Making a face at myself in the mirror, I slathered my toothbrush with paste and set to work erasing the last few minutes of my life.

While the minty freshness helped quell the remaining queasiness in my stomach, it did nothing to ease my mind. I didn't know what was supposed to happen when I condemned a wicked to hell, but I felt pretty certain that me passing out wasn't it.

I spit and rinsed and considered trying to call my mom again. She'd be able to tell me what went wrong. However, I disregarded that idea as quickly as it formed. Mom had made herself clear during our last call. She had no intention of talking to me until I offed granny dearest. It would be better to wait until I had Mom cornered in New York. Hopefully, she'd answer questions when we were face to face.

With my brush and paste back in the bag, I opened the door. Oanen turned, pocketing his phone, and I smiled at him.

"What kind of chips did you get me?" I asked, determined to stick to my word and pretend nothing had happened.

He took the bag and walked with me to the car.

"Three different kinds. Sour cream and onion. Cheddar. And vinegar."

"Vinegar?" I asked.

"Something to help balance how sweet you are."

I laughed and gave him a peck on the cheek. Oanen's arms wrapped around my waist, and he held me for a moment. The press of his chest against mine and the feel of his heat seeping through my clothes reminded me that we were going to be staying together tonight. My heart skipped a beat at the thought.

Easing away with a shy smile, I got into the car. The moment my back touched the seat, I winced. Oanen caught my expression and watched me closely as I shifted my position to take the pressure off the area that hurt.

"You're not okay, are you?" he asked.

Gold flecks appeared in his gaze.

"I got knocked into the boat yesterday and hit my back pretty hard. I think it's just bruised."

He frowned slightly.

"I thought you were healed after last night?"

I stared at him for a moment, confused. Although I knew for a fact that the bites on my arms and legs had disappeared after my pyrotechnics display the night before, I couldn't recall if my back had hurt afterward. So much had happened in such a short period of time. Testing my abilities at the Roost. Spending the night in the same bed with Oanen without melting his hair. Getting my mark this morning. So much, in fact, that I'd never stopped to take inventory.

"Yeah, I thought so, too. Maybe when I fell just now, I hurt it again."

"I thought we weren't going to talk about that," he said.

Before I could answer, he leaned in to toss my bag in the backseat and brushed his lips along my neck. I exhaled softly and relaxed against the seat, ignoring the part of my back that stung. When he was done kissing my neck, he lifted his head and studied me.

"I never want to see you on the ground like that again."

"And you think I wanted to be there?" I asked, arching a brow.

His I'll-be-patient-because-you're-not-well expression morphed into his famous pre-lecture expression. I quickly grabbed his head and kissed the hell out of him.

When he finally pulled back, his hair was messy; and I was struggling to breathe and remember my name.

"You won't get away with that every time," he said.

"I might."

His lips twitched.

"You might."

I exhaled in relief when he closed the door. I was crazy about Oanen, but I might threaten his wings again if he attempted to lecture me when I felt this crappy.

My yawn ended with a wince when I shifted sleepily on the seat. Sitting up, I opened my eyes and looked around. The daylight and light traffic had disappeared, replaced by buildings and streetlights as far as I could see.

"Where are we?" I asked.

"The city. We're almost there. How are you feeling?"

I rubbed my face, yawned again, and stretched carefully.

"Better."

"Really?"

He sounded surprised.

"Yes. Really. The headache's gone."

"You had a headache?"

"Just a little one. Sorry I slept so long. I didn't mean to stick you with all the driving."

"It's okay. I figured it would be easier on you if you slept through this part, anyway."

I looked around at all the buildings again and understood what he meant. The streets were crawling with people. However, I didn't even feel a tingle of irritation.

"I'm actually good. No overwhelming urges to hit anyone." I smiled. "See? Powers under control."

"In that case, I'd like to head to the Goose and Gizzard first."

"That's fine with me."

My stomach growled loudly, a reminder of just how empty it was.

"Did you stop somewhere to eat?"

"No. I wanted to wait to see how you felt."

He cast me a pensive side-glance.

"I'm fine. I swear. Whatever happened in the parking lot was because I have no clue what I'm doing. That little book my mom left me is far from an instruction manual. While you ask questions about your dead troll, I plan to ask about a fury."

"Good. I'm struggling not to be worried, and I'll feel a lot better if your mom can clarify her comment about you suffering the longer you wait."

He pulled over in front of one of the many tall buildings on the block.

"We're about eight blocks north of Central Park," he said. "We're staying near the park on the west side. My parents have a condo there with roof access. I texted you the address already."

"Okay," I said, drawing out the word. "Why are you telling me this?"

He shut off the engine and turned to look at me.

"We're in a city full of people, going into a bar full of creatures. The likelihood of you running into someone punishable for their wickedness isn't just high; it's definite. If you end up chasing someone down when I'm not looking, I want to know that you can find your way back to me."

I reached up and set my hand over his tense jaw muscle.

"I should tell you not to worry about me, but honestly, I like it. I haven't had someone worry like this in a very long time. Thank you."

He turned his head to kiss the palm of my hand.

"Let's get this done so we can go relax at the condo."

The way he said it made my stomach dip and spin in a mix of anticipation and nerves. I quickly exited the car so he wouldn't see either in my expression.

Looking at the plain building before me, I frowned. The brick and stone façade screamed apartment for rent, not supernatural bar.

"I thought we were going to the Goose and Gizzard."

"We are."

He threaded his fingers through mine as he joined me on the sidewalk. With a light tug on my hand, he led me up the stairs toward the door.

A tingle of something brushed my skin and made the hair on my arms stand up when we reached the landing.

"Magic," Oanen said softly. "Keeps the humans out."

He opened the door, and a low murmur of voices filled the air as we stepped into the large bar.

The Goose and Gizzard wasn't anything like the Roost. No music with a dancing beat blared from speakers. No nice couches waited for intimate moments. No color. No fun. Probably because the patrons of the Goose and Gizzard edged toward geriatric rather than teen.

A bar ran the back length of the place. Several pool tables lined the right side with booths toward the front. To the left, there were a couple of battered tables where a few creatures were eating their meals. The place looked like a complete dive.

Definitely not the kind of establishment I could see my mom frequenting. However, the troll snoring on the pool table to our right told me this was just the place Oanen needed to be.

He studied the troll for a moment then met my gaze.

"Good luck," he said.

"Yeah, you too. I'm going to go talk to the bartender."

He nodded and stepped toward the sleeping creature.

I strode to the bar. Behind me, the snoring stopped, and I glanced back at Oanen. With his arms crossed and his expression masked, he stood beside the irate troll.

"Go away," the troll rumbled.

"No. You and I need to talk."

The troll drew back his fist and made to hit Oanen. Oanen caught the extra-large, meaty fist in his own. The contact echoed in the room and quieted the low murmur of conversation.

"I have no quarrel with you," Oanen said clearly. "Just some questions that need to be answered."

Someone snorted behind me, drawing my attention back to the bar. The few patrons who sat there appeared older. Greying hair. Stooped shoulders. Expressions in varying degrees of life-bitterness.

"Just what we need," a craggy-faced man said.

I took the empty seat beside the man. With his leather jacket and weathered face, he looked like an old biker.

"What do you mean?" I asked.

"An enforcer. We have no freedom the way it is. What's left to suppress?"

"What's an enforcer?" I asked.

He gave me an incredulous look.

"The ones responsible for the current state of our world."

"You think that guy's going to suppress you in some way?" I asked, trying a different approach.

"They all do. First, it was don't eat humans. Now, it's don't kill humans. Stay hidden. Stay quiet. I miss the days when I could open my wings and soar high. If humans scurried below me like frightened cattle, I could scorch them or not. It was my choice back then."

The person on the biker's right said something I couldn't hear, and the biker chuckled.

"You are right, my friend. This world is no longer ours. The enforcers have made sure we have no place in it."

I looked in the mirror behind the bar and saw that the person on the biker's right was hidden by a deep hood. Only the bottom half of the man's face was visible, showing his whiskered chin wasn't salted with grey like the biker's.

"What can I get you?" the bartender asked, coming my way.

"A glass of water and a menu."

He belly-laughed and walked away.

"I don't get it," I said.

"Fledgling," the biker beside me said, "the stuff they make here isn't meant for a menu."

I frowned and glanced back at the other patrons who were quietly eating. Oanen had his back to me, in quiet conversation with the troll. If the scowl on the troll's face was any indication of their conversation, I didn't imagine things were going well for Oanen.

The bartender walked out of a side door and delivered a plate of mashed up food to one of the tables in the main room. I couldn't identify what exactly was on the plate. But, the chunks were a bit too large for stew.

I sniffed the air and watched the patron take his first enthusiastic bite. It smelled like normal food in the Goose and Gizzard, but I couldn't forget what kind of creatures this place catered to.

"It's not human, is it?" I asked, glancing at the biker. "The food."

The guy's hard gaze locked with mine.

"Are you a special kind of stupid to ask something like that with an enforcer in the same room?"

"Apparently."

"We don't serve human here," the bartender said, having returned with a glass of water and a plate of food. The glass he slammed in front of me, and the burger with fries he set down in front of the guy beside me.

"Sorry," I said holding up my hands. "I didn't know any of us existed until a few months ago. Blame my ignorance on my parenting."

"See?" the biker said, looking at the bartender. "This is what I'm talking about." He focused on me once more. "We need to return to the old ways. You would have known what you were from the moment you were born. You wouldn't have had your powers suppressed or grown in the shadows of a world you were made to dominate." He closed his eyes, and a shudder ran through him. When he opened his eyes again, I stared at the vertical slits of his pupils that reminded me far too much of Lucia.

The biker shrugged out of his jacket and something heavy fell from his back. He shook himself again, and the thick leather of his wings unfurled further. I'd read about his species in a book. Dragon.

"My kind used to rule the skies," he said. "Now, I hide in a hovel of broken buildings on a forgotten island. Where's the pride and majesty in that?"

I didn't know what to say.

"If you're smart, you'll stay away from enforcers," the dragon continued, tilting his head toward Oanen. "You might actually find a few moments in life where you can enjoy being what you were meant to be."

The cloaked figure stood and clapped the dragon on his

back.

"Only the lucky can fulfill their true purpose," he said before making his way toward the side door the bartender had used.

"Very true," the bartender said. He took the money from the guy's spot and started to move away.

"Wait. There's a fury here in the city. Do either of you know where I can find her?"

The bartender started to laugh, and the dragon swore.

"I'm done with this place." The dragon threw down some cash and stood. His gaze pinned me as he put on his jacket and hid his wings.

"If you had any brains, you wouldn't be in here asking for that kind of trouble."

He stalked out of the bar.

"You should listen to him," the bartender said. "Furies are nasty business. Not just for humans. Don't involve yourself with them, or you'll find yourself with a one-way ticket to hell."

He reached for the dragon's untouched plate of food.

"Hold on," I said, stopping him. "What is that?"

"A bacon cheeseburger. The best you'll find in Harlem."

"The dragon paid for it, right?"

"Yeah, so what?"

I grabbed the plate and pulled it toward me.

"He knew bacon cheeseburger was my favorite." I picked up the burger and took a large bite before the bartender could take it from me. The bacony goodness hit my taste buds with love, and I groaned.

"So good," I said around a mouthful of burger.

The bartender shook his head and walked away. I swallowed my first bite and took a second one. Burgers in Uttira had been okay. The lean meat and limited topping choices stunted the flavor possibilities, though. Unlike this burger. Grease and mayonnaise dripped onto the plate as I held the concoction, ready for my next mouthful.

I turned it slightly to look at the wadded stack of bacon, onion rings, lettuce and tomato on top of the inch and a half thick patty. There had to be seven pieces of bacon. I swallowed, grinned, and took another mouthful.

As I chewed, the room gave a weird spin.

Frowning, I shook my head slightly. My blink felt heavy, too. The background noise faded, and movement slowed. I breathed sluggishly. Something was wrong. Why wasn't I concerned? I knew I should be. It felt like when Eliana touched me to syphon my anger. Only, no one was touching me.

I swallowed my bite and looked down at the burger. A grey-green powder dusted the bacon.

A darkness swam into the room, rapidly tunneling my vision. I opened my mouth to call Oanen's name, but nothing came out. The bar and the people sitting beside me disappeared.

The last thing I saw was the burger falling to my plate.

CHAPTER THREE

"JUST GET RID OF HER BEFORE THE SPELL WEARS OFF."

The words poked at my mind in the persistently annoying way of a mosquito until the echo of fading footsteps took the place of the words.

My brain didn't want to work. Neither did my eyes.

I wanted to sink back into the fog shrouding my thoughts, but some small part of me insisted I resist the pull. I groaned, my head lolling to the side.

A small laugh teased my ears.

"The spell's already wearing off. You're in trouble."

The sharp rattle of metal and a high-pitched shriek annoyed me enough that I managed to open my eyes. Bits of my surroundings swam in and out of focus with each slow blink.

A cement floor. A table with a cage on it, not far away and to my right. A bald kid walking toward me. Sharp teeth.

I jerked back and tried to lift my hand to rub my eyes. My arm wouldn't move.

I opened my eyes again and stared at the glowing ropes tying me to a sturdy chair. The cloud of my exhale momentarily distracted me as I gave another tug. The ropes tightened around my forearms, biting into the skin. It should have hurt, but I was too cold to feel anything.

"Struggling only makes it worse."

Lifting my gaze, I found the child-sized creature standing within kicking distance, which I would have tried to do if my ankles hadn't been bound, too.

He studied me as I studied him. His size was the only thing he had in common with a human kid. The wizened wrinkles creasing his face and the tuft of hair sticking out from his pointed ears matched perfectly with his rough-spun shirt that looked a hundred years old.

"You're in a pickle, aren't you, my pretty plaything. Old Elbner will set things right. For a price."

"This is really not the way to make a good impression with me," I said, my voice surprisingly clear. "Untie me now."

"I can't. Once those bonds are on, only the buyer can untie you. Prevents backcrossing on deals struck."

"He's lying," a high-pitched voice chirped.

I looked beyond good 'ol Elbner to the cage on the table. A small creature with wings flitted around, shaking the bars as if testing their strength. When the thing saw I was looking at it, it flew at the bars and stared at me in return. A tiny shirt hung loosely from its bony shoulders, and the long pants it wore were held up with a string belt.

"You're pretty," it said.

"Thank you. What are you?"

"A brownie."

Elbner stepped in my line of sight.

"We can share his wings if you'd like." He licked his lips, the glisten making me feel sick.

The brownie squealed, and I scowled at Elbner.

"He looks pretty attached to his wings. Now, are you going to untie me or what?"

"I told you. Can't."

"He's lying," the brownie called again.

Elbner growled and pivoted to the cage, which made the brownie squeal and take off. It zoomed around it's prison in a panic, trying to find a way out.

"How is he lying?" I asked.

"His master told him to get rid of you. He's supposed to set you free."

Elbner stopped advancing toward the cage and cast a sly look over his shoulder at me.

"'Get rid of' doesn't mean set free," he said.

"Someone bigger than you briefly considered killing me," I said. "She decided not to risk it, though."

He turned toward me fully, a low chuckle rising from him.

"Oh? And what stopped her? Fear of you?"

He moved closer and reached out a bony finger, trailing it from my chin down my throat. The sharp edge of his nail scraped my skin, not quite breaking it but definitely leaving a mark.

A spark of anger lit inside of me. Small in comparison to what I'd felt in the past, but enough. I tugged hard on the bonds. They bit in painfully, and I pulled harder still. The fire inside me burned brighter with the pain.

"Fear of pissing off the gods," I said.

Elbner stopped touching me and stared at me with a puzzled frown.

"What are you?" he asked.

"You tell me, and I'll tell you."

"I'm a goblin."

I closed my eyes and focused on the fire burning inside of me. When I opened my eyes again, an orange glow reflected on Elbner's skin.

"I'm a fury."

The old creature's eyes rounded. He made a choked sound and stumbled back a few steps as the ropes binding me began to smolder. The glow faded, and the ropes fell away in seconds.

I stood, and the old guy fell to his knees in a shaking heap.

"Looks like you're in a pickle, aren't you?" the brownie chirped happily from his cage.

"I never meant to hurt you," the goblin said, his voice muffled. "It was only a prank. Just my nature. To trick and tease."

"And the brownie wings? Is that tempting offer still open?"

The brownie looked at me in horror as Elbner jumped up and raced over to the table.

"Yes. Of course. Two might be a bit filling, but I'd be happy to eat the second one for you." He pulled a rusted knife from the back of his ripped pants.

The fire, which had freed me, slowly died. How could wanting to cut the wings off that tiny creature not be wicked?

Annoyed, I reached Elbner before he could open the cage. The old goblin made an awful moaning sound when I grabbed his arm and spun him around. The useless knife went clattering to the floor.

"I'm not interested in his wings. I said that to see what kind of person you are. And, I have my answer. Not a good one."

He started to frantically shake his head.

"I'm no enforcer, but I'm not wicked. Just a few pranks. Harmless tricks."

"Right now, I don't care what you've done in the past; I'm interested in how I got here and why. Start talking."

"My master only wants—"

His words stopped, but his lips still moved. I wanted to swear.

"What *can* you tell me?" I asked, interrupting his silent confession.

He licked his lips nervously as his gaze shifted around the room. Suddenly, his expression brightened.

"I can serve you," he said. "You can be my master if you'll have me."

"Ew. No." The last thing I wanted was this creepy old goblin hanging around me.

"Say, yes," the brownie said. "The spell will fade once his ownership changes hands. He'll be able to give you answers eventually."

I looked at the brownie.

"You're just full of information. If I let you out, is something bad going to happen?"

The little creature giggled and pointed at Elbner.

"I'll pull out his ear hair."

Elbner growled. "Touch me, and I'll eat your wings."

"No, you won't," I said. I reached for the cage door. "What does being his master mean?" I asked.

"He has to listen to you," the brownie answered earnestly. "And, if you treat him well, he'll listen. If you don't treat him well, he'll make your life miserable then leave."

My hand hesitated on the latch.

"Treat him well? What's that mean, exactly?"

"Feed him. Goblins like milk. Milk soaked oats. Milk soaked oats with honey are their favorite."

"Not true," Elbner said. "Milk soaked oats with honey and brownie wings are my favorite."

"Why are you so willing to trade masters?" I asked, ignoring his obsession with the brownie's wings.

"His master forgot to feed him today."

The phone in my pocket buzzed.

"It's been doing that a lot," Elbner said. "I like the sound. Reminds me of wings beating."

I pulled out my phone and looked at a string of messages

from Oanen, the oldest from over three hours ago. The first one started out calm enough, asking where I'd gone. Then, each one after progressively showed his growing concern. The final one worried me.

If I don't hear from you in ten minutes, I'm calling Adira.

I typed out a quick message while keeping an eye on Elbner.

I'm okay. I'll call in a minute. Are brownies and goblins safe to be around?

His reply was immediate.

Safe enough. Where are you?

I looked at Elbner.

"Fine. I'll be your master. As soon as the spell wears off, you're going to tell me what's going on here. Got it?"

He nodded.

"And no eating brownie wings while I'm your master. I'll feed you everything else but that."

He scowled at me and gave a single nod.

I opened the brownie's cage and squealed when the thing flew straight at my face. Its tiny arms stuck to my neck as it hugged me.

"Thank you! Thank you! I thought I would die in that cage like my grandparents." He released me and flitted back to look me in the eyes.

"My name is Piepen. What's yours?"

"Pie Pen?"

He nodded.

"I'm Megan."

He flew forward and hugged me again. His little hand stroked the side of my neck.

"I love you, Megan." The tiny puff of his breath brushed my skin. Or was that his lips? Were his hips moving?

"Okay. I think I'm all hugged out."

He didn't let go. I carefully pinched his shirt and tugged him loose.

"You're free to go, now," I said.

His happy face fell.

"Go? I have nowhere to go. My grandparents are dead now, and I have no parents. Please don't leave me behind." His small cherub face scrunched up, and tears glistened in his eyes.

"Let's talk about this later. I really need to make a phone call."

With numb fingers, I dialed Oanen. He picked up immediately.

"Megan, where are you?"

"Oh, um…" I looked around at the empty room. "I think I'm in some kind of old warehouse."

The phone was quiet for a long moment.

"I want an address, not a description." The warning in his tone made me grin.

"Hold on." I looked at Elbner. "What's the address for this place?"

He opened his mouth, but nothing came out. I wished I was a lip reader.

"Fine. Where's the exit?"

Elbner led the way to a set of stairs. I clumsily jogged down the first flight with Piepen flitting alongside of me, his tiny wings buzzing.

"What's that noise?" Oanen asked as I started down the second flight.

"That's Piepen, a brownie I set free."

"And you won't regret it," Piepen said. "I'm good at making beds and washing dishes."

"You're going to regret it," Oanen said in my ear.

"Already am," I said softly.

I pushed through the door at the bottom of the stairwell and stepped into what looked like a shipping yard. Metal containers and boards poked through the snow and littered the space before the building.

"There's a sign to the right," Elbner said.

Glancing back, I caught the glint of his eyes as he hovered in the shadows. He pointed down the road.

"Just a second, Oanen. I need to run to the street corner."

He remained quiet as I jogged.

"26th and 4th street," I said, looking at the signs.

"There is no 26th and 4th street in Harlem, Megan. Open the map on your phone."

I put him on speaker, pulled the map up on my phone, and sent him my current location.

"You're not even in Manhattan. How did you get across the river?"

I looked around and saw the glimmer of lights reflecting on water further down the street. A shiver coursed through me. How in the hell had I crossed that?

"Not sure," I said. "I just woke up fifteen minutes ago."

"Woke up?"

"Yeah, I think the burger I ate was drugged."

A shiver of emotion tingled along the back of my neck. Anger. Fear. A lot of fear.

"Are you safe? Right now. Are you safe?" he demanded.

"Oanen? Did you just…" The idea that I'd just felt what he was feeling made my stomach dip and my heart flutter.

"Just what?" he asked.

"Nothing. I'm safe."

"I'm flying to you."

The call disconnected, and I frowned at the phone.

"I don't like him," Piepen said. "He didn't sound nice."

"He's really nice. And, I like him a lot."

A scruff of noise from behind us had Piepen diving for my

hair. I turned, trying to ignore the brownie shaking on my shoulder.

"Lost, honey?" a man asked, stepping from the shadows.

"No. Just waiting for my boyfriend."

"Want me to keep you company?"

"Thanks, but I don't think that'll help his mood."

A snarl came from behind the man a moment before a long piece of two by four lumber swung out of the dark. The chunk of wood hit the man in the head. His eyes rolled back, and he fell like a brick to reveal Elbner standing behind him.

"What the hell, Elbner? Why did you hit him?"

"He was going to hurt you."

"No, he wasn't. I'm a fury, remember? I would have felt his wickedness if he was going to do something."

Elbner cast the board aside and scowled at me.

"If you mistreat him, he'll make you miserable," Piepen said softly, right in my ear. "He'll want extra milk for protecting you." I was about to thank the brownie for the reminder when something touched my earlobe. Something tiny and wet. I shuddered and reached for Piepen.

"Okay. Ride's over. Get out of my hair."

The little guy flew out and went to investigate the fallen man.

My phone rang again, and I quickly lifted it, ready to ask Oanen to hurry up. Instead of Oanen's name, Eliana's flashed. I smiled and answered.

"You officially broke your promise," she said.

"Huh?"

"It's after midnight. You said you would check in daily, and I didn't get a call yesterday."

"The day I left doesn't count."

"Sure, start bending the rules already. So, what's it like having freedom?"

I watched Piepen lift the guy's eyelid.

"Knock it off," I said.

"Do I even want to know what Oanen's doing?" Eliana asked.

"Not Oanen. A brownie named Piepen is messing around with some guy's eye."

Piepen zipped over to me and flitted around my head, trying to listen. I waved my hand, shooing him away.

"A brownie?" Eliana asked.

"Yeah, long story."

"I've got time."

"I let him out of a cage, and now he's following me."

"I'm not following. I'm going to help you. I'll take care of your house."

"No, you won't," Elbner said from the shadows. "That's my job."

"No, you take care of everything outside. I take care of the inside."

Eliana started snickering.

"Two of them? What are you going to do with two?" she asked.

"One's a brownie and one's a goblin. And I have no idea." I paced to the corner and back toward the shadows where the man lay, still unconscious, before turning again. Moving wasn't warming me up like I'd hoped.

"They're not going to like the hotel or the car. They're much happier in real homes," Eliana said.

"She sounds nice," Piepen said. "I like her."

"Aw! Isn't he sweet," she said.

Piepen's face lit up with joy, and he started zipping around my head faster.

"Stop. He can hear you, and I think you're going to give him a heart attack. What's wrong with hotels?"

"What's a hotel?" Piepen asked, slowing to hover in front of me.

Elbner stepped from the shadows, a severe scowl on his face.

"A hotel? A hotel!" His ears quivered with his anger. "I will not lower myself to the upkeep of rented rooms."

"Told you," Eliana said in my ear.

"I have a house," I assured Elbner. "I'm just visiting the city for a while."

"Where's your house?" he demanded. "I'll wait for you there."

"Tell him," Eliana encouraged through the phone. "You'll be happier with him here. I'll feed them both for you."

"Are you sure?" I asked her.

"Yep. It'll be fine."

I looked at both of the creatures, hoping I wasn't about to make a mistake.

"I live in Uttira. N125 W837 Crooked Road."

"Hmm." Elbner looked north. "It'll take me a few days," he said after a moment. "It better not be a nice house."

"Oh, it's not," I assured him.

"Tell him I'll have a bowl of honey-soaked oats waiting for him," Eliana said.

Elbner's eyes gleamed, and I knew he'd heard her.

"Can I go, too? Can I?" Piepen begged.

A speculative look glazed over Elbner's eyes as the old goblin stared at Piepen's wings.

"Can I trust you to care for Piepen?" I asked Elbner. "That means protecting him and his wings, from yourself and everyone else."

Elbner grumped and grumbled before nodding. He waved for Piepen and started across the street. The brownie-boy flew at my head, kissed the tip of my nose, then took off into the dark after Elbner. Once they were far enough away, I gave Eliana the rundown about what had happened once we got to New York. Getting drugged. Waking in the warehouse. A goblin with answers but bound by a spell.

"I'll call you if he says anything about who his previous master was," Eliana said when I finished.

"Thank you. And watch yourself around both of them. Oanen said they wouldn't hurt me, but Elbner seems sketchy."

"Did he make you mad?" she asked.

"Surprisingly, no."

"Then I'm sure he'll be fine."

An eagle's cry split the air.

"I better go," I said. "Oanen's coming, and I need to check the guy Elbner knocked out."

"What guy?"

"I'll tell you later."

I hung up and hurried over to the man on the ground. When I tapped his cheek, he groaned, a sign he was close to coming to. At least, I hoped so.

Straightening, I stepped away from him and looked to the sky. The clouds and the nearby streetlights made it impossible to see Oanen until he fell from the sky. His graceful shift from griffin to human as he landed made my pulse quicken. I doubted I would ever tire of watching him do that.

He strode toward me, his golden gaze locked on my face. The tick of his jaw and the scowl on his face distracted me from the fact he was walking around naked in New York in the middle of winter as if it was no big deal.

Without a word, Oanen pulled me into his arms and held me tight. I could feel him shaking and tried to hold back my wince when his hand brushed over the sore spot on my back. Wrapping my arms around his waist, I just let him hold me.

"Furies aren't the only ones with a temper," he said against my hair. "Don't ever leave my side again, Megan. New York wouldn't survive what I would do to find you."

The man behind me groaned. Oanen lifted his head, and I pulled back in time to see his pupils dilate. I quickly cupped Oanen's face and forced his attention on me.

"I'm tired, cold, and a little sore. Feel like giving me a ride home, bird boy?"

The heated look he gave me sent a shiver all the way to my toes.

"I'm never letting you go again, Megan. I'm done playing nice."

CHAPTER FOUR

My stomach dipped to my toes.

"What do you mean?" I asked.

He stepped back and shifted to his feathers without answering. When I didn't immediately move, he swung his head toward me and snapped his beak.

With his words still ringing in my ears, I hustled to climb aboard the Oanen Express. Loose snow from the sidewalks swirled around us as he started to beat his wings. Steadily, he rose into the air. I leaned forward and wrapped my arms around his neck, snuggling into his heat. Even with my jacket on, I felt the sting of the occasional snow flake drifting in the air.

Looking below, I watched the expanse of the river pass by. Awe filled me when I lifted my eyes from the water to the skyline. Lights stretched as far as I could see.

"It's so pretty," I said, smoothing my hand over the feathers at his neck.

We passed over buildings, climbing higher and higher. I shivered slightly, and my fingers grew stiff. Not that I really noticed. I was staring at everything. The tiny cars moving far below. Our reflection in the glass of buildings so tall, I'd get bored trying to count the floors. When we hit the park, I knew we were getting close to the condo he'd mentioned.

Again, his words came back to me. How had he been playing nice, and what was going to change? Ugh. Did that mean I was in for lectures now?

I was still debating what he'd meant and how I might avoid any form of conflict that would tick me off when he started to descend toward a rooftop with a lit-up, glass sunroom. The balcony had been cleared of snow, so nothing swirled around us as he landed.

Sliding off his back, I looked at the cute table and chairs just inside the glass.

"Come on."

Oanen grabbed my hand and pulled me toward the door.

"Are you mad?" I asked, scrambling to follow him. "Because, if you are, I don't think we should go inside."

"You're freezing. We're going inside."

I let out a long, heavy exhale and said nothing as he dragged me through the sunroom into a modern kitchen. He didn't stop there. When I saw he was pulling me toward a living room with pale grey stained hardwood floors, I balked.

"At least, let me take off my shoes," I said, trying to tug my hand free.

Instead of letting go, he turned and scooped me into his arms.

"Shoes aren't a problem now."

With my eyes wide, I stared at his determined expression. The look on his face worried me. I set my hand on his chest and felt him flinch. My chest tightened with apprehension.

"I don't want to fight," I said quietly. "I don't want to lose my temper again. Not with you."

His gaze dipped to me before returning to the hall he walked.

"We're not going to fight because you're going to listen."

I struggled with the initial urge to bristle at those words by chanting, "I will not fry my boyfriend," in my head.

When he turned into a bedroom, my pulse spiked, and butterflies launched for flight in my stomach.

"Um, what are you doing?" I asked.

He set me on my feet and stared down at me, his eyes still amber.

"You can warm up two ways. Shower or me."

My mouth dropped open for a moment.

"Is that an invitation?" he asked.

I snapped my mouth shut and crossed my arms. He was right. He wasn't playing nice anymore. And I wasn't amused.

"Where's the bathroom?" I asked.

He pointed to the right.

Narrowing my eyes at him, I started to turn that direction. I didn't make it a step before he grabbed my arms and pulled me to his chest. My heart skipped a beat. Gazes locked, we stared at each other for a moment. Oh-so-slowly, he lowered his head. My breath caught, and the frantic beat of my heart echoed in my ears.

"I think you're choosing the wrong door," he whispered just before his lips settled onto mine.

He held me close, his mouth claiming me in a way that sent a buzz of need rushing through every limb. Desperate for an anchor, I gripped his arms and groaned at the onslaught. His hands moved from my arms to encircle my waist, the move pressing his hips to mine and making his need for me impossible to ignore.

The angle of the kiss changed, becoming all consuming. His hand slid under my shirt and up my side, his fingers skimming the sensitive skin over my ribs. All my focus was on that hand until his other hand touched the damaged spot on my back.

I pulled back with a gasp and blinked up at him, disoriented, and panting for air.

"Oanen, wait."

"I am. But, I don't need to do it patiently."

He grabbed the back of my head and kissed me hard. My lips tingled when he finally eased away.

"Get in the shower and start talking. I want to know what the hell happened tonight."

His bossy attitude cut through the haze of passion he'd created.

"I want 'playing nice' Oanen back."

"I want you in that bed. One of us might get what they want tonight."

I retreated a step toward the bathroom, and Oanen shadowed the move.

"Cut it out, Oanen," I warned, taking another step.

"You're mad," he said as he matched my movement. "And you're afraid."

"I am not."

He shook his head slowly, not closing the distance between us, not giving me any more space, either.

"You're not afraid of me but yourself. Of what you want."

Stepping into the bathroom, I gripped the door then slammed it shut.

"Talk, Megan," he said from just outside. "Or I come in."

"There's not much to say. I was sitting at the bar one minute, and the next, I was waking up and finding out I was tied to a chair. All I remember from the bar is a dragon who got upset when he heard there was a fury in town—not me, my mom—and left."

I turned on the water to warm.

"I was starving, so I stole the burger he didn't even touch.

There was this powder on the bacon. It didn't taste funny, and I didn't notice it until I was four bites in."

As I spoke, I stripped out of my clothes, taking care with my shirt. As much as I twisted in the mirror, I couldn't quite see the spot that hurt.

"When I came to, I realized I was inside that warehouse with a goblin who couldn't tell me anything about why I was there or how I'd arrived. He was spelled too, you know? Like the library prevented me from talking about anything."

I stepped into the shower.

"I called you as soon as I saw the messages. You hung up on me. The goblin knocked out the guy on the street for talking to me. Then Eliana called and said I should send the goblin and the brownie to Uttira and that she'd call when the spell wore off the goblin."

I spun under the water, wincing at the sting on my back. I must have scraped it when I fell in the parking lot.

"That's everything?" he asked, not sounding as muffled as he should.

Knowing that he was in the bathroom with me while I was completely naked had me flushing from head to toe.

"Everything I can remember. What about you? What happened with the troll?" I asked, hoping to distract him from hearing my racing pulse.

"I'll tell you when you're done." The door clicked shut.

I rolled my eyes and quickly washed. When I finished, I opened the curtain and found a tank top with matching character shorts and a clean pair of underwear waiting. My old clothes were gone.

I dried off, not sure how I felt about that. A guy who's willing to pick up? Not a bad thing. A guy who's laying out what I should wear next? Possibly more controlling than I could accept. Yet, those were the only pajamas I'd packed, so was it really controlling or just common sense that those would be the clothes I'd want?

With my hair wrapped in the towel, I dressed and opened the door. Oanen was waiting just outside. His steady gaze swept over me, and I was relieved to see blue instead of gold.

"The troll?" I said, taking the towel from my head and hanging it on the back of the door.

"The troll in the bar knew the one who'd died but had no idea who would have killed him or why."

"So, no leads?"

"No. The dead troll was old, his family already gone. Typical of his age, he had few friends and kept to himself. His only socialization was going to the Gizzard once a week for a beer and a burger."

I made a face when he said burger.

"We need to figure out what was on that bacon," I said.

"Agreed. But in the morning. You're pale, and you look tired."

He held out his hand. I looked at it, then the bed in the only bedroom in this place. My pulse picked up again.

"You know I won't force anything," he said softly.

"I know." But I wasn't sure I'd want to stop if he kissed me again like he had before.

Instead of taking his hand, I turned away and took a step toward the bed without him.

"Megan."

The anger in that word surprised me, and I looked back at him. His gaze wasn't on my face but on my back. He took two steps forward and pulled the back of my shirt up.

"Hey!"

"Is this what happened?" he demanded.

"What? I don't know what you're talking about."

His finger traced around the area that hurt.

"Is it bruised?" I asked.

"No. It's a raw sore. Like a burn."

"I wasn't near anything hot, so I doubt it's a burn. And it hurt before I was drugged, so I don't think anything happened when I was sleeping. Maybe I scraped myself when I fell," I said, repeating my earlier theory.

"Hold your shirt. Let me get something for it."

I held my shirt up while he dabbed a cooling ointment on the wound and bandaged it to keep my shirt from scabbing to it. I could feel his anger and agitation; I felt pretty certain it wasn't directed at me, though.

When he finished doctoring me, he led me to the bed and pulled back the covers.

"Go to sleep, Megan."

Once again, gold was filling his stoic gaze. I quickly got into bed.

Sunlight bathed my face and seared through my eyelids.

I groaned and pulled the covers over my head. Behind me, Oanen chuckled. The arm around my waist tightened, bringing my back flush with his warm, bare chest. His fingers moved under my shirt, stroking my belly, which growled.

"It's too early," I mumbled as if he'd just told me to get out of bed.

"It's almost noon." His lips brushed the back of my neck.

I shivered, and my eyes popped open when his fingers stroked my skin more firmly.

"All right, I'm up." I scrambled out of bed and raced for the bathroom.

He left me alone while I slowly went through my morning

routine. When I reemerged minty fresh, my bag waited on the made bed. The bedroom door was closed, and I was alone.

I quickly got dressed and found him waiting in the kitchen, talking on the phone. His serious expression and the way he tracked my progress made me nervous.

"That confirms the first death was part of something. We'll check it out."

He hung up and pocketed the phone.

"Another troll," he said without me asking. "He was found not far from where you were last night. Dead with a smile on his face, just like the first one. We need to identify him and ask around again."

"Does the Council have any ideas about what's happening?"

"No. That's why we're here."

"So, look at a dead troll then back to the Gizzard?"

"Yeah. Want to risk something to eat, first? I don't want another burger to tempt you."

I made a face.

"I doubt anything from the Gizzard will tempt me ever again."

I followed him to the double doors and stepped into a hallway where he pushed the button to call the elevator.

"No flying today?" I asked.

"No. You were too cold last night. We'll drive."

The trip down was quiet. When we stepped out into a modern, plush lobby area, I spotted Oanen's car through the glass doors.

I shivered when I stepped outside, and it had nothing to do with the temperature. In the daylight, I could feel wisps of mild wickedness around me.

"That's weird," I said as Oanen opened the passenger door for me.

"What is?"

"I feel more wickedness during the day than at night. I thought it would have been the other way around."

He frowned and looked around.

"Me too."

I shrugged and got in then started buckling my seatbelt while he closed the door and walked around the car.

"I asked Adira if she knew where we could find your mom," he said as he slid behind the wheel.

"Oh? How'd that work out for you?"

"As well as you're imagining. She said for your safety, we should not seek her out." Oanen didn't sound pleased with that answer.

"Yeah, I got the same reaction from the old dragon last night when I asked if he'd heard about a fury."

"Do you want to try calling her again?" he asked, merging into traffic.

"No. I'll find her. It just might take a while." My stomach growled again. "Think we can still find breakfast somewhere?"

"There's a diner not far from here that my dad recommended. They serve breakfast all day."

The diner, only a few blocks away, was tucked in the lower level of a large building, just like every other business in the area. The light scent of breakfast foods teased my nose as soon as I got out of the car. My mouth watered.

Within minutes, we were seated at a table, sipping juice and waiting for our food.

"While I was talking to the dragon last night, he called you an enforcer. What does that mean?"

"When you work for any of the councils, your role is technically to enforce the Mantirum laws."

"He also said you're suppressing their rights. Apparently, he wants to be able to toast some humans if it strikes his fancy."

"Some of the old-timers are still having a hard time adapting to the laws created over five hundred years ago."

"Holy crap. He was that old?"

"Probably a little older," Oanen said.

"Wow. How old is your dad?"

"In his sixties. Mom's a lot older."

His dad didn't look nearly that old. Late thirties, maybe. Just like his mom. I itched to ask more but didn't want to be overheard.

"I don't really know how old my mom is," I said.

He reached out and placed his hand over mine.

"It's nothing you need to worry about now. I talked to Eliana last night after you fell asleep. I let her know how important it is to find out what happened once your visitors arrive."

"Oh no. What did you tell her? I didn't go into detail because I didn't want her to worry."

"I told her the truth. Someone tried taking you from me."

I tugged my hand from his and scowled at him.

"Eliana's probably freaking out now, thinking I'm in danger."

"No. She's going to try to figure out if there's a way to get your friend to talk sooner."

The waitress came with our food, distracting me from my annoyance. The stack of pancakes on my "side" plate made my mouth water just as much as the over-easy eggs, hash browns, and sausage.

It wasn't until I stuffed the last bite of syrup-soaked pancakes into my mouth that my thoughts circled back to our conversation. No matter what Oanen said, Eliana would worry. That's just who she was. I needed to prove to her and Oanen that I was fine, and the only way to do that was to prove no one intentionally drugged me.

"The burger wasn't even meant for me."

Oanen studied me from across the table, an amused light in his eyes.

"Do you want more?" he asked.

I looked down at my empty plates.

"I don't think I could eat another bite."

"Then why are you talking about burgers?"

I leaned forward and lowered my voice.

"Last night. I took the burger the dragon ordered because he'd left without touching it. I don't think anyone was trying to drug me. I think someone was trying to drug the dragon. Whoever the—Elbner's friend was, he told Elbner to let me go. Why drug me and let me go if I was the intended target?"

"Why drug a dragon?" Oanen said with a thoughtful frown. He reached for his wallet. "We need to get back to the Gizzard."

"I thought we were going to check out the warehouse first."

"You sure your stomach's up for it?"

"Please. I never get sick."

He frowned at me.

"We agreed to pretend that never happened," I said.

He exhaled heavily, placed some money on the table, stood, then held out his hand. I slipped my fingers through his and followed him out the door. A new tingle of annoyance traced down my spine and pulled my attention to a man in a business suit, crossing the street.

I took a step in that direction, and Oanen's hold on my hand tightened. I turned back to him with a scowl, ready to tell him to let go.

The sight of his hard, golden gaze killed the words.

"You don't leave my side today," he said, leaning close. "Got it?"

"Yeah. Got it."

Oanen narrowed his eyes as if he didn't believe me then

started toward the car. When he reached the door, he released me.

"I know you're strong. But I also know you can be hurt. Your safety matters more than Eliana's feelings. More than dead trolls. More than anything else. Do you understand?"

"Yes, Oanen. I get it. I'm glued to you from now until the end of time."

Something flashed in his eyes before he shut them, and he took a slow, deep breath.

"Get in, Megan."

Annoyed and confused, I did as he asked only because arguing would just waste time. He shut the door and walked around toward his side.

"No one likes a bully, Oanen," I said, crossing my arms.

His gaze swung to me through the windshield.

"Stupid bird hearing," I mumbled.

He opened the door, slid behind the wheel, and turned to look at me.

"No," I said, firmly. "No lecture. I'm right next to you, so there's nothing you need to say except let's go look at a dead troll."

"I think there is something I need to say." He reached out and gently trailed his fingers along my hairline.

"I love you, Megan Smith. And, 'from now until the end of time' is exactly how long I want to be with you."

CHAPTER FIVE

All I could do was stare at Oanen. Love? That was big. I'd known how he felt about me, but I hadn't thought we were to the saying it stage. Saying it was one step closer to white picket fences and babies.

Swallowing hard, I fought the stomach bile rising at the thought of kids. I didn't have my own shit together yet. I couldn't be responsible for someone else. Not for years. And maybe even more years after that.

"Megan, it's getting warm in here," Oanen said. "Why does telling you that I love you make you panic?"

"Can we please not talk about this right now?"

He studied me for a moment.

"You're right. This isn't the place. We'll talk about it tonight."

That did not make me feel any better.

He started the car then carefully pulled into traffic. It took over thirty minutes to reach the warehouse and another ten to find the home of the second troll.

"Who found the body?" I asked, desperate to break the silence as we walked inside the run-down building. "And why just leave him here? Wasn't there a chance a human could stumble across him?"

"This troll had family who found him. They're with him now."

Oanen knocked and the door immediately opened.

"He's in the bedroom," the troll said, moving aside.

Given my knowledge of trolls, I expected one or two surly relatives. This guy had at least twenty glaring behemoths crammed into a very human-sized apartment.

Oanen took my hand and led the way through the room. I didn't mind his hold this time. My skin crawled with the need to ask the younger troll with the twin black eyes what he'd done.

Only the dead troll waited in the bedroom. He lay on the bed, the mattress bowing under his weight. The smile on his face seemed so out of place after passing through a living room full of scowls.

Oanen released my hand, and I wandered around the room, opening the closet, looking out the window, under the bed.

"I don't know what we're looking for, but I'm pretty sure it's not here," I said, straightening.

Oanen lifted his gaze from his study of the troll.

"You're right," he said.

A shadow filled the doorway behind him a moment before the boy who needed a beating stepped forward. I moved around the bed, but Oanen blocked me. Setting my head against his back, I closed my eyes and listened while trying to ignore my growing anger.

"He knew it was coming," the young troll said.

"Knew what was coming?" Oanen asked.

"His death."

"Why do you think that?"

"I got into some trouble a few weeks back. News spreads fast here. Especially with the old timers. Gramps caught wind and beat me for it. A fair punishment. Better than I'd get from you or the fury I hear is in town. I didn't hate him for it. But, he thought I did. He called me the night before last. Told me he loved me. Shocked me stupid."

"That seems to be a theme today," I mumbled.

Oanen reached back and set his hand on my thigh. Just a simple touch, but it let me know he wasn't mad about my reaction to his declaration.

"Gramps told me to use my head and follow the laws because he wouldn't always be around to watch out for me. Then he hung up. I came by this morning with some goat to let him know we were okay. I found him like this."

"I'm sorry for your loss," Oanen said. "Thank you for sharing what happened with us. You mentioned a fury in town. Any idea where we can find her?"

"No. You know how they work. They can be anywhere."

That made furies sound like the damn boogeyman for supernatural creatures.

Steps shuffled away, and I lifted my head from Oanen's back.

"You all right?" he asked as he faced me.

"Yeah. But, I'll need you to hold my hand on the way out. Whatever that kid did, I want to give him a second beating for it."

No one talked to us as we left, and Oanen didn't release my hand until we reached the car. Anger still poked at me, though. Not from the troll several stories up but from the man walking down the sidewalk.

Oanen's phone chirped as he opened the door for me. I quickly got in and clasped my hands in my lap as Oanen closed the door. The man looked at me through the window, his dark eyes assessing.

Oanen looked up from his phone.

"Keep moving."

I almost grinned at Oanen's possessive tone of voice. Almost. Until I remembered what he'd said last night and just after breakfast.

He waited until the man moved on then went around to his side of the car.

"Please tell me that text had an answer to the smiling troll riddle," I said as he got in.

"No. I had my dad check to see who owned the building you were in last night. The city. Which doesn't help."

"Seriously, Oanen. I don't think whatever was on that burger was meant for me."

"And I don't think it's a coincidence you were dosed with something at the same place that the two trolls, who are now dead, liked to frequent."

"Well, when you put it that way, no, it doesn't sound like a coincidence."

He started the engine and turned around to head back the way we'd come.

"Not to rock the boat, but if getting drugged at the Gizzard is the commonality here, why aren't I dead with a smile on my face?"

His grip on the steering wheel tightened.

"Think about it," I said. "We were there last night, and that troll wasn't."

"We don't know that."

"So we need to go back to the Gizzard and ask."

"Exactly."

We parked a block from the bar and walked the distance in silence. Once again, the atmosphere of downtrodden old people welcomed us when we opened the door. Only this time, the wickedness crawled under my skin as soon as I stepped inside.

With his hand on my back, Oanen steered me toward the bar. The same bartender from the night before came to ask us what we wanted. While I felt anger toward many of the patrons, I didn't feel much for him.

"I want to know what that grey-green powder was on the bacon last night," I said, taking a stool.

"There's no powder on any of the food. Just grease and salt," the man said.

"She ate a bacon cheeseburger here and woke up somewhere else. We need to know what happened," Oanen said.

The bartender studied us for a moment, then the creatures sipping their drinks at the bar, before waving us toward the side door. I glanced at Oanen, and he shrugged and took my hand.

No one paid us much attention as we went to the door. The bartender waited for us just inside the hall coming from the kitchen. Instead of turning that way, the man went to an office to the right.

"I have cameras," he said without preamble. "Five in the main bar, one in the hall, two in the kitchen, and one in this office." He pointed to the monitor on the desk showing nine frames. "The system keeps two months of live feed then purges every ten seconds of video, leaving still frames for six months beyond that. Help yourself."

Oanen sat in the chair and, within a few clicks, had rewound then paused the video to the point where I sat at the bar the night before.

"Has anyone new been coming around?" Oanen asked.

"The odd fellow in the cloak started showing up a few weeks back." The bartender tapped the screen on top of the guy who sat two stools from mine. "Comes every night. Has a drink or two. Talks to whoever's at the bar. Then, he leaves."

"Do you remember if he talked to either of these two trolls?" Oanen asked, pulling up the pictures of the dead, smiling trolls on his phone.

"I serve hundreds of drinks every night. Do you think I remember everyone?"

I had a hard time believing he sold that many drinks, given the meager crowd last night, but I managed to keep my doubt to myself.

Oanen diplomatically did the same and hit the play button. On screen, I watched the dragon turn toward me. Behind him, the cloaked man moved.

"Is there a different angle?" I asked, nudging Oanen.

He pulled up a different window synced at the same timeframe. We all watched the cloaked man reach over, lift the bun, and sprinkle something.

"Right on the damn bacon," I mumbled.

The cloaked man left. The dragon did the same shortly after. I watched the bartender speak with me briefly before I started to eat the burger. Four bites in, I put the burger down and just walked out through the side door.

"I don't remember doing that," I said.

Oanen switched views to the hall outside the office. I went straight out the emergency exit without stopping.

"Did I seriously walk myself to that warehouse?"

"You were gone over three hours," Oanen said. "It's possible. It would explain why you were so cold, too." He turned toward the bartender. "Any idea what he would have put on that burger or where we can find him?"

"I don't know his name, but I can ask around. As for the powder, you might learn more at the Tabernam. I've never heard of anything that trances us."

"Tabernam?" I asked.

"A place where any spell caster can find what they need," Oanen said. He stood and looked at the bartender. "Put the word out that I'm looking for information."

He gave the guy the address of our condo.

The smell of herbs, grass, and a hint of smoke filled the air as soon as we opened the door. I inhaled deeply and immediately felt more relaxed.

"I like this place," I said, stepping into the store room filled with aisles of racks. Little bottles and baggies lay in neat rows on each shelf. Some had labels with weird names. Some just said "ask sales associate."

"I'll like this place if we can get some answers," Oanen said.

"You go talk and do your thing, and I'll look for the powder."

"Not a chance. We stick together."

I rolled my eyes and followed him down the center aisle toward the back where a woman stood at a register. She smiled as she watched us with her dark eyes. The curve of her red lips reminded me of a snake. Anger pooled in my stomach. I reached for Oanen's hand to anchor myself. It didn't help much.

He glanced at me and gave my hand a squeeze before turning to the woman.

"Hi. We're looking for a grey-green powder that would put someone in a trance and possibly make them walk somewhere without remembering it."

"I don't sell spells. Only the ingredients to make them."

"What are the ingredients, then?"

She walked around the counter and led the way to the far-left corner. Everything there was labeled with "ask sales associate." A shiver of disquiet raced through me when I saw a bag half filled with deep green powder.

"It's not safe to dabble with things you don't understand," she said, looking at Oanen.

"Do you tell all your customers that?"

"Only the ones who don't look like they have a clue."

"I need a list of names. Everyone who purchased the ingredients needed to work the spell I mentioned."

One side of her mouth lifted in a wry smile.

"I don't ask names. Just for this reason. Anonymity keeps this place in business."

Oanen released my hand and crossed his arms.

"The Council allows a business to continue only through the cooperation of its owner when problems arise."

Her smile faded.

"I don't have any names to give you."

"What do you have?"

The bell above the door chimed. Through the aisles, I caught sight of a cloaked figure walking in.

"Excuse me," the woman said. She quickly headed toward the new arrival.

"Is that the person from the bar?" Oanen asked.

I shook my head. The vibrant red of this cloak couldn't have been further from the dark grey of the cloak from the night before. That, and boobs were filling out the front of it.

"No. It was a man with a dark beard. Not as old as the rest of the crowd in the Gizzard, though."

The saleswoman spoke softly to her new customer and led the woman to another area in the store, closer to us. The lower half of the woman's face felt familiar to me, and I frowned as I strained to hear what they were saying.

"I think I know her," I said softly to Oanen.

"You do?"

"I'm not sure."

I pretended to browse the contents of the racks so I could move closer to the pair. The woman noticed and looked toward us. From behind me, Oanen quietly groaned.

The woman's eyes rounded, and she pushed back her hood.

"Oanen?" she said. She walked to the end of the aisle. Oanen slowly did the same with me now trailing behind. Near the register, they both stopped.

I looked at Oanen, wondering how he knew the woman.

"Hello, Nicolette," he said.

"Darling! It's been too long. How is my baby?"

"Baby?" I said, fighting the strong stirring of jealousy that wanted me to rip her pretty blonde hair from her head.

"She means Eliana," Oanen said, wrapping an arm around me. "Megan, this is Nicolette Barchim, Eliana's mother."

I looked at the woman again, seeing the resemblance. In the hair, nose, and mouth. She didn't look old enough to be Eliana's mom, though. Older sister, maybe.

"Megan?" she said. "Eliana has told me so much about you. I'm happy you arrived in Uttira when you did and relieved you were able to help her make some progress. That girl's issues are enough to make a mother cry, which would destroy my complexion for at least an hour. Tell me how she is. How does she look? Are her curves coming in? Is she feeding enough?"

"I'll go wrap this for you," the saleswoman said, walking behind the counter.

Nicolette's gaze pinged back and forth between Oanen and me as she waited for a response.

"Eliana is well," Oanen said.

"Yeah. She's a good friend."

Nicolette smiled.

"I'm so glad to hear that. I thought that girl would never have a friend. Any lovers yet?"

I glanced at Oanen, unsure what to say. Eliana had told me enough about her mom to know that the woman had completely different methods for childrearing than I'd experienced with my mother.

"No lovers yet," Oanen said. "But as I'm sure Adira has

already reported, she has fed off a grown man and has been wearing more provocative dresses and makeup."

She waved her hand.

"Yes, yes. I know that. I was hoping, living with her, you might have inside information that the starchy Council does not." She stepped closer to Oanen, and he released me, gently nudging me behind him. The protective gesture made me smile.

However, all humor fled the moment she reached out and trailed a finger down his chest.

"If my bedroom were next to yours, there would be no question about whether we were lovers. Off limits always tastes the best."

Jealousy hit me hard right between the eyes and rage quickly followed. I stepped around Oanen and grabbed her wrist.

She yelped, and her eyes turned black.

"You're burning me," she said. "Back off, fledgling."

Oanen moved to stand behind me, our roles reversed. His arms wrapped around my waist, and he nuzzled the back of my head.

"I'm yours," he said softly. "Always."

Nicolette jerked her hand free and stared at me with her wide, black eyes. I let my anger show in mine, and her face lit with a soft orange glow.

"Don't ever touch him again," I said, my voice carrying a hint of the fury echo.

"This is interesting," she said, her cheeks flushing from the heat I knew I was putting off. "A griffin and a fury. Tell me, dear. Does your mother know?"

It pissed me off that she wasn't even showing a hint of fear or concern.

"I doubt it. My mom has been out of the picture since she left me in Uttira."

Nicolette tsked.

"It's a shame when our kind abandons their young. I would have never done that to Eliana if she hadn't fought so hard to be allowed to develop her skills on her own."

"Go, Nicolette," Oanen said from behind me. "Now."

Nicolette set some money on the counter, without looking away from us, and accepted her wrapped package from the shopkeeper.

"I'm sure I'll see you around, Fury," she said with a nod of her head. "Delicious to see you again, Oanen. Maybe next time I'll get a taste."

His arms tightened around me, keeping me from flying at her.

Her sultry laugh followed her out the door. I turned my angry gaze on the saleswoman. I could feel her nervousness and a hint of something wicked that wasn't there a few moments ago.

"Do all your customers wear cloaks?" I asked.

"Only the ones who want to keep their identities secret," she said.

I pulled Oanen's arms free of my waist and stepped up to the counter. The woman cringed when I leaned toward her.

"No more secrets. Start taking names or you'll be confessing whatever it is I'm sensing. Do you understand?"

"Yes, Fury."

Oanen said nothing as I turned and stormed out of the shop. The cool winter air caressed my cheeks as I stood on the sidewalk with my eyes closed for a few minutes.

"You okay?" he asked.

"Yeah. Eliana's mother is—"

"A succubus," he said. "And Eliana will be grateful you didn't hurt her."

I opened my eyes and looked at him.

"Are you sure about that?"

He shrugged and laced his fingers through mine, a hint of humor making his lips twitch.

"You hungry?"

"I could eat."

Forty minutes later, we were seated in a diner whose patrons made my skin crawl. Nothing overwhelming, individually, just a whole lot of messed up, collectively. Based on the tingle that had raced over my skin walking through the door of the café, I knew it was another Mantirum-only establishment, which explained the overall whisper of wickedness. Eating somewhere else might have been more pleasant, but at least here we could talk freely.

"How are we supposed to find out what's happening when no one seems to know anything?" I asked, opening a menu.

Oanen wasn't the least bit put off by my surly attitude.

"We'll find something soon. Word will spread that we're looking for information. Between the bar and Tabernam, someone will have something for us.

A waitress stopped at our table and set two glasses of water down.

"Griffins never could see what was right in front of their faces," she said. "The victims were all males and all trolls. What do you think would leave a troll with a smile on his face? And, I hear there's a pregnant one in the city. You know what that means."

She winked at me. Clueless, I looked at Oanen for an explanation as the waitress moved off.

"She's talking about a succubus," he said.

"You don't think—"

"Eliana's mom is responsible? I don't know, but we need to find out."

CHAPTER SIX

OANEN STOOD AND HELD OUT HIS HAND TO ME. I MADE A FACE, tossed down the menu, and joined him.

"I thought I'd be eating like a pig in New York. Instead, I'm going to starve," I grumbled.

He gave my hand a gentle squeeze and led me out to the street. On the sidewalk, he turned toward me and cupped my face.

"After this, it'll be just you, me, and an extra-large pizza."

"Don't toy with me, bird boy. You better deliver."

He tilted his head and studied my face for a moment.

"Are you okay?" he asked.

"I'm hungry, and we're leaving the place that could have fixed that. What do you think?"

"I think it's not food that's upsetting you. Your eyes have just a hint of orange to them."

His words brought my attention to the wickedness slowly coating my skin. I opened myself to the source.

"Who is it?" Oanen said softly.

The wickedness came from everywhere. From everyone to one degree or another.

"Crap," I said under my breath. "I just can't catch a break." I grabbed Oanen's hand again and hustled toward the car.

"What's going on?" he asked.

"Let's just hurry before I go after someone here on the street."

"It's more than one person?" he asked, opening my door.

"It's everyone."

He frowned at me as I got in but didn't say anything more.

The need to jump out of the car grew stronger on the drive to the Tabernam, and I didn't understand why. Well, I did. But given how I'd been fine the day before, I didn't understand why people on the street and in passing cars were suddenly adding to the anger coating me with each passing second.

"I think I should take you home," he said when we were only a block away.

"Why? We're almost there."

His hand covered my fist. I made a face and tried to relax my fingers. It wasn't easy. The need to do something, to punish someone, rode me hard.

"I'll be fine."

However, once inside the Tabernam, my mind went back to how Eliana's mom had hit on Oanen, and my anger only grew. Had the succubus still been there, I would have owed Eliana a sympathy card.

Oanen stopped my forward progress with an arm around my waist. Before I could tell him to let go, he turned me, grabbed my head and planted a kiss on me that made me forget the anger threading its way under my skin.

When he pulled back, the orange glow from my eyes reflected off his face. Only this time, it wasn't anger.

"You are the most beautiful creature in this world," he said softly. "And, it's hard to think straight when your eyes glow like that."

"Then maybe you should stop randomly kissing me," I said.

"Never."

I rolled my eyes at him, and his lips quirked at the corners.

"We're here for a reason," I reminded him.

"Hopefully it's to purchase something." The familiar voice killed the happy glow Oanen's lips had created.

Clenching my fists, I turned toward the clerk.

"Creatures are dying. I'm skipping meals to chase down answers. And, I'm fighting the urge to throat punch someone. Do you seriously think we're here to buy something?"

"Nicolette Barchim, the succubus," Oanen said, setting his hands on my shoulders. "What did she buy?"

I could see the hesitation in the woman's eyes.

"Do not make me pull out my Fury," I warned.

The woman blanched and quickly answered.

"Herbs."

"Not good enough. What herbs? What are they for?"

"They're harmless. Just a boost to her energy while she's pregnant."

"Thank you," Oanen said.

The next thing I knew, I was in his arms and on the way out of the shop.

"I can walk," I said scowling up at him.

"And, I can carry you. It was my turn."

"You're ridiculous."

"No. I'm in a hurry. I promised you pizza, and you were looking ready for a fight."

He set me down on the sidewalk and opened the car door for me.

"I'm sorry I didn't feed you first."

"You better be."

I got in and buckled up. On the drive back, he asked me to message what we'd learned to his dad.

"Don't you think you should let Eliana know first? I mean, it is her mom."

"And if it's her mom killing creatures because she's trying to feed Eliana's new sibling?"

Eliana already hated what she was. I couldn't imagine how much it would freak her out if she learned her mom was killing creatures because she was pregnant.

"Point taken. I didn't think their kind killed to feed." Although, I did remember Eliana's concern that she'd killed the guy in the alley.

"A succubus typically feeds off of sexual energy, not life energy. They can weaken their meal to the point of unconsciousness. Once unconscious, there's no sexual energy."

"These killings don't sound like a succubus, then?"

"They don't sound like anything we know."

I typed out a brief message—*Eliana's mom is preggers*—and hit send.

"Now, about this pizza."

"Anything you want," he said. "It's New York. Just about everywhere delivers."

"Pizza. Pepperoni is a must. Along with bacon, green olives, and onion."

He glanced at me.

"That's an unusual combination."

"Am I a usual person?"

We talked about other food quirks on the way to his parents' place. I tried to play it cool like his talk was distracting me but knew I'd failed when he covered my fist with his hand again. The anger, along with a familiar restlessness, was still building. If I were back home, I would go for a run. That wasn't an option here, though.

As soon as he parked, I opened my door and hurried for the entrance.

His hand smoothed down my back the moment we were inside.

"It'll be better in the condo. It's protected."

I hoped he was right. Using the stairs as an outlet, I sprinted upward, taking the steps two at a time.

"There's a treadmill in the living room closet," Oanen said as he reached around me to open the door. I liked that he always kept up with me.

"A treadmill in the closet?"

I looked at the double doors on the opposite wall.

"You're not the only person to get restless."

He closed the door then crossed the room to pull out the treadmill. As soon as he had the track down, he started it and motioned me forward.

"I'll order the pizza while you run."

"Thank you."

I cranked the speed up, testing myself and the machine as I went all out. I wasn't winded by the time I finished but managed to work up a bit of a sweat and purge some of the restlessness.

"Better?" Oanen asked when I shut the machine off.

"Much. How long until the pizza gets here?"

"Another fifteen minutes."

"Perfect."

I took a quick shower and put on last night's pajamas. Since there was still time before dinner arrived, I used it to call Eliana. She answered on the first ring.

"Any sign of the brownie or goblin yet?" I asked.

"Not yet." She didn't sound like herself.

"What's wrong?"

"Nothing."

"Are you trying to lie to me?"

"Yes. Because I want you to focus on getting the job done so you can get home sooner."

"Talk, succubus."

Eliana sighed.

"I didn't know how lonely I was until I made a friend and she left. And then, I find out someone is trying to kill her and my only friend might not come back."

"I miss you, too. And that burger wasn't meant for me. Oanen overreacted because of the whole bird bond thing. As for the smiling dead trolls, we have a few leads. It shouldn't be too much longer. I'm coming back. I promise. How did it go at the academy today?"

"Good. Eugene is loving classes and asking a ton of questions. It rubbed a few people wrong, but by the end of the day, I think they were catching on that Eugene is impressed and curious and not a threat. Oh, a siren almost got him into the pool at lunch, but Ashlyn was there to block him. And, Fenris was being pretty good about keeping an eye on the humans, too."

"Oh? So you and Fenris were hanging out?"

She snorted.

"No way. He keeps texting me annoying updates. I think he misses you."

"Then, I think you should be a friend and keep him company."

"Not me," she said, sounding completely panicked. "I think the new girls are stirring his wolfie hormones or something because he's getting worse."

"Worse? You mean he's flirting?"

"No. He hasn't changed at all in that way. It's his lust. I can barely be in the same room with him. When I spot him now, I just go the other way."

I felt bad for Fenris and wondered what kind of miracle it was going to take for Eliana to figure out that all Fenris' lust had everything to do with her. I could only imagine how desperate he was starting to feel if Eliana thought his lust was worse than before.

"How's your succubus training going? Adira still dressing you?"

"She set out clothes for me this morning. I got creative with them while still following the rules. I wish everyone around here would just leave me alone. I might be a little on the small side, but I don't think I'm unhealthy. Nothing to warrant this much unwanted attention."

In the living room, the doorbell rang. I opened the door and waved to Oanen as he left to get the pizza.

"So how is it staying in New York? Are you missing your backpack with all the wicked you're running into? Did you kill anyone yet?" Eliana asked.

"Not yet. It's weird here. Most of the time, it's not as provoking as I thought it would be. People I would have thought I'd want to beat the hell out of, like Elbner, don't bug me. Yet today, regular people were starting to get under my skin. I'm just glad it's not like it was the night I came here with Adira. That would have been hell. As it is, I think New York would be more fun if we weren't having to deal with dying trolls."

"I heard Adira and the Quills talking. While you're checking out the deaths in New York, the council near Flagstaff is investigating the deaths of three Nemean lions."

"What's a Nemean lion and did they die with smiles, too?"

She laughed.

"No. Nemean lions are a lot like regular lions. They're animals but a lot harder to kill. Their coats are impenetrable by mortal blades. Since they're a protected species by our laws, the word is going out, asking for information about their deaths."

"I'm not sure how this is supposed to make me feel better about dealing with troll deaths."

"It's not. I told you so you'd know the Council isn't giving Oanen all the poopy jobs. An enforcer has to look into any death that's questionable."

"Poopy?" I said with a laugh. "Adira should forget the succubus clothes and work on your language skills."

"Swearing isn't a language skill."

"Says the person who doesn't know how."

"I know how, I just choose not to."

I snorted at her as the door opened and Oanen strode in carrying the pizza. The smell of it hit me hard and made my stomach growl.

"I better go. Oanen just walked in with our pizza, and I'm starving."

"Tell him I said hi. Talk to you tomorrow."

I hung up and hurried to the pizza. Oanen's lips twitched as I hungrily watched him open the box.

"That smells amazing," I said, inhaling.

"I'll let you have some if you sit on the couch and watch a movie with me."

"You had me at 'I'll let you have some.'"

He chuckled and set a huge slice on a plate for me. The tip of the wedge hung off the edge. I sat on the couch and dug in while he started the movie.

I ate three slices the size of my head before I pushed my plate away with a groan.

"Best pizza ever."

"Feel better?" he asked.

"I do. Thank you."

He wrapped an arm around my shoulders, pulled me close, and pressed his lips against the top of my temple. I leaned into his side and exhaled contentedly, only partially focused on the movie. My mind continued to dwell on the troll deaths and Eliana's mom. It would devastate Eliana if her mom was responsible for them. Eliana already hated what she was and feared what she'd become.

That kind of fear was something with which I could empathize. As much as I'd pushed aside what I learned in the *Book of Fury,* I dreaded what gaining my full powers would mean for me. Without a doubt, Eliana and I were in the same boat, and I couldn't help but wonder what the future would hold for both of us.

Oanen's hand smoothed over my arm.

"That was a big sigh for an action movie," he said.

"Sorry. I didn't realize I sighed. I was just thinking about the future."

He paused the movie.

"You didn't need to do that. I'll stop talking."

"I paused it so you would keep talking. The future…our future…is something that very much interests me."

The low rumble of his voice and the way the flecks of gold in his blue eyes multiplied as I watched sent up warning flags. Our conversation from earlier, or rather, what he'd declared earlier, came back to me in a rush. He loved me and wanted forever.

I swallowed hard, wondering what I should say. I didn't want to talk relationship. Not now. Not this close to bedtime.

"What are you thinking that's making you blush?" he asked.

He leaned in slowly, and my pulse picked up speed. His lips quirked at the corners just before his mouth touched mine. The taste of him set off a storm, and fire and lightning exploded inside of me.

My head spun, and I gripped the front of his shirt tightly, anchoring myself and holding him in place. He leaned in further, causing me to slowly slide down into the cushions. The weight of him warmed me. The feel of his chest against mine made it hard to breathe as want consumed me. I wanted to feel all of him pressed against all of me. My body ached for that much contact.

I tore my mouth from his, struggling to remember why we needed to stop. Why I couldn't wrap a leg around his waist and pull him closer.

It wasn't easy to think clearly when his mouth was trailing kisses down my throat. Images of us tangled in sheets, his hands sliding over my bare skin, filled my mind and left me breathless.

I wanted him so much it hurt. My fingers itched to inch their way up his shirt. To remove his clothing. To make the images in my mind a reality.

The stroke of his tongue against the edge of my ear sent me flying off the couch. With that touch, the reason we shouldn't pushed its way forward.

He chuckled, his golden eyes pinning me.

"Not your thing?"

I stared at him for a moment, debating what to say. He caught my hesitation and grew serious.

"Talk to me," he said softly.

I let out a slow breath.

"When we kiss like that, it's hard to remember why I need to say no."

"Why do you need to say no?"

"We're eighteen. I don't want to start a family at eighteen. I'm not even sure I'll want to start a family at fifty. I mean, I'm barely holding my own shit together. There's no way I want the responsibility of caring for someone else."

He watched me for a moment, really considering my words.

"Sex doesn't need to mean kids. I'm not saying that to try to talk you into something you're not ready for. I'm saying it to let you know I'm okay with waiting for kids."

He stood and closed the distance between us.

"And, I'm okay waiting for you."

Even though he said the thing that should have soothed me, I was stuck on one word.

"Kids? Plural? Shoot me now."

He chuckled and pulled me close, kissing me gently.

"Baby griffins are adorable," he said, holding me. "Picture a chicken-sized griffin."

I groaned.

"I'm never going to look at you the same way, again," I said.

"What? You said you liked my beak."

"You should stop now."

"I'm hoping if I keep talking, you'll get desperate enough to kiss me like we both want."

"Remember you asked for this, bird boy," I said a moment before I lifted my head and claimed his lips. It was his turn to groan. He clutched me close as my tongue teased his. As my hands slipped under his shirt. As I stood on my toes and pressed my hips against his.

A moment later, he had me in his arms and was walking toward the bedroom.

"Wait," I said, breaking the kiss.

"Now who's the chicken?" he said. "We're just going to bed."

"While kissing. I'm not stupid."

"No sex tonight, Megan. I want to feel your lips against mine until we both pass out. I want it to be the last thing I remember before closing my eyes, and the first thing I think of when I open them again. I know you're not ready for more; just like I know you'll let me know when you are ready."

I looked up at him, tangling my fingers in his hair.

"Just a hella lot of kissing then?" I asked.

"And maybe some petting. I hear birds like that."

I grinned at his deadpan delivery.

"I think I can handle that," I said before kissing him again.

Anger flooded me with a suffocating fullness. I woke, breathing slowly and deeply. The smell of warm cotton tickled my nose, and I carefully slid from Oanen's arms, our heavy make out session barely a thought.

An invisible line pulled me from the bedroom. Barefoot, I padded across the living room toward the sunroom and balcony. Someone very wicked moved out there.

I smiled in anticipation and opened the door.

"Come to confess?" I asked the creature that straightened from the shadows.

His humorless black eyes found mine as I closed the distance between us. He reeked of blood, booze, and fear. I inhaled deeply and didn't stop walking until we stood toe to toe with his back against the metal and glass rail.

Even though I could smell his fear, it didn't reflect in his gaze or his words.

"Not in this life, little girl. You need to leave town. Now."

Lightning fast, I grabbed his throat and lifted him high.

"I'm not the one leaving town. You are. Hell's waiting for you."

"Hell's for humans, bitch," he rasped.

"We'll see about that. Elwood Rumlar, confess." The word brought him to his knees like all the others. He shook, and anger filled his gaze as he spoke of his crimes. He'd killed. Eaten human flesh. Broken the laws of humans and non-humans, alike.

The rage inside of me roared to life and fire danced up my arm.

"Elwood Rumlar, you've earned your place in hell."

I embraced my fury power as I reached for his throat. Before

I touched him, pain exploded inside of me from head to toe like I was being ripped in two.

I opened my mouth to scream, but no sound emerged as blackness consumed me.

My pulse thumped in my head. Opening my eyes, I blearily stared at the snow-dusted surface before me. The patio floor. I'd fallen. Again.

I tried to sit up and hissed at the pain searing my chest. I looked down at another burn mark.

"Fuck."

Oanen was going to notice this one.

Getting to my feet, I looked for the thing that had drawn me outside. I was alone. However the creature had gotten out there, it seemed it had left the same way.

Pre-dawn light reflected off the sunroom glass. I looked over my shoulder in surprise. How much time had passed since I'd gone outside? Obviously half the night. Suppressing a shiver, I used my cold, stiff fingers to open the door.

I went straight for the shower. Oanen would definitely notice how cold I was if I tried crawling into bed with him. The hot water felt good on everything but the burn. I gritted my teeth through washing and drying and put the same cream on the new burn as Oanen had put on the old one. When I finished, I wrapped the towel around my torso and crept out of the bathroom to grab myself some clean clothes. Escaping to the living room to dress, I noted the sun was just clearing the horizon.

"So much for going back to bed," I muttered to myself.

Despite having been passed out for hours, I was exhausted. I pulled on my clothes, careful of the new injury. Dressed and slowly toweling my hair, I stared out at the patio.

Other than wicked and not human, I didn't know what that thing had been or why it had come here in the first place.

I thought back to everything he'd said. He'd wanted me to leave town. Why? Was he trying to warn me away from the troll deaths? Were we getting close to finding the killer?

"You're up early," Oanen said from behind me, causing me to startle.

I looked back at him. He wore a pair of shorts, leaving his gloriously golden chest bare for my enjoyment. If only my head wasn't pounding.

"You're up early, too."

"It's not as fun sleeping late without you beside me. Your spot was cold. How long have you been up?"

"Not long," I said. It was the truth, but not what he meant.

I tossed my towel onto the couch and walked toward him, knowing I needed to distract him from his current line of questioning. There was no way I was going to admit I passed out on the patio for the past several hours.

"I thought the first thing you wanted to think about in the morning was a kiss."

His lips curved in a sexy half-smile, and he met me in the middle of the room.

"You would be correct." He wrapped his arms around me and pulled me close.

I almost winced at the sting from the heat of his chest on my burn.

"Do I detect a hint of minty freshness?" I asked instead.

"I heard you in the shower," he said.

"And you missed your chance to join me?"

Gold pooled in Oanen's eyes.

"Don't tease me, Fury."

CHAPTER SEVEN

Grinning, I stood on my toes to kiss Oanen lightly and pulled back before he could take things further.

"We're in food-central, and I'm starving. Something just isn't right about this."

He sighed and brushed his fingers along my jaw.

"I know you're nervous," he said.

My pulse jumped, and I reached up to the neckline of my shirt. There was no way he could see it, could he?

"I meant what I said. I'll wait for as long as it takes. Just don't stop kissing me."

Relief coursed through me. He'd meant sex, not the burns. I found it ironic that I found sex a safe topic this morning.

"If you want more kisses, feed me."

My stomach let out a growl.

He grinned, kissed my forehead, then left me so he could shower.

Less than twenty minutes later, we were seated in a familiar diner.

"Is one of everything an option?" I asked, studying the

choices and seeing too many things I'd want to try if my head didn't hurt so much.

"Are you sure you're feeling okay?"

"Hey, no judging a girl with a healthy appetite."

"Not that. You can get whatever you want. You just look a little pale today."

"I'm fine, Oanen." But, I was starting to think I wasn't. This was twice now that I'd been burned trying to use my powers. Once in the parking lot and now on the patio. Both times I tried to send someone to hell. Obviously, I was doing something wrong. But, the *Book of Fury* didn't exactly outline the steps to a successful trip to hell.

After the waitress took our order, he reached across the table and played with my fingers.

"I know we're not supposed to talk about this, but you're different. I think something's wrong."

I opened my mouth to say I was fine again, but he lifted his hand.

"Hear me out. Before the lake, you ran hot. Now, you get cold. You threw up. You're not sensing the wicked like you used to. And you have a burn that's not healing as quickly as it should. I'm worried."

His phone rang, but he didn't move to answer it.

"Adira, Mom, and Dad are worried too."

"You told them?"

He took his phone out of his pocket and met my gaze.

"There isn't anything I wouldn't do for you. Including risk your temper to keep you safe. I'll be right back."

He stood and strode toward the exit while my mouth was still hanging open. He would flip his shit if he found out I had another burn. My gaze tracked him as he walked outside and stood on the sidewalk to answer his phone.

Across from me, someone sat in his place.

I turned, and my jaw almost dropped for a second time.

"You're wasting time," Mom said.

She looked exactly the same. I struggled between wanting to hug her and wanting to punch her in the face because of ditching me. I surprised us both by partially standing and hugging her. She set her cheek against my head and stroked a hand down my hair. Too quickly, she pulled away.

"You need to get to your Grandma Irene."

"Why?" I asked, trying not to let my frustration show.

"I told you. You can't deliver the wicked to hell without your wings because without them, you're not a fury, and your power will consume you."

The straight forward answer stunned me. She took advantage of my silence to continue.

"Ditch the unnecessary baggage and get to St. Louis."

"Baggage?" I asked, confused.

Mom's gaze flicked to Oanen, who had his back to us.

"Oanen isn't baggage. He's my boyfriend."

A wave of heat came from across the table.

"Have you slept with him?" she demanded.

"We're staying at his parents' apartment. There's only one bed."

"Stop being thick. Have you had sex?"

I didn't like her tone or the anger in her expression.

"You ditched me, remember? I think that means my sex life is none of your business."

"Of course it is. Didn't you learn anything in that shit town? Griffins only have sons. Furies only have daughters. It will never work. You will destroy each other."

"It's a little late for that warning. We're already bonded."

Her expression changed, becoming more earnest.

"Learn from your succubus friend. The boy can love you, but you don't need to love him."

There was so much wrong in what she just said. How did she know about Eliana? And was her attitude the reason for the revolving door of her love life?

"You should have listened to the messenger. It's dangerous for us to keep meeting. I'm guessing you already have your first burn or you wouldn't be this calm."

"Hold up," I said. "Messenger? You mean you sent that guy last night?"

She exhaled slowly, a look of annoyance crossing her features before she suppressed it.

"You need to focus, Megan. Your power is free, uncontrolled and unpredictable, and it will burn you out if you don't get your ass to your great-grandma's place in St. Louis and kill her so you can claim your power as a fury in full. Do you understand? I didn't bring you into this world just to watch you die before your time."

A waitress walked over with my chocolate milk.

"Get it done," Mom said, sliding out of her seat.

"Wait."

She left without a backward glance. As much as I wanted to push the waitress out of the way and chase her down, I stayed in my seat.

"Your food will be out in a minute," the waitress said before walking away again.

I barely heard her. The gas station. The man on the balcony. If Mom was being honest, things were worse than I'd thought. And, they'd keep going downhill from here.

Heart sinking, I glanced out the window at Oanen. I couldn't tell him what Mom had said. He'd made the priority of my well-being pretty plain. And I couldn't—no, I wouldn't—kill my great-grandma just to save myself. There had to be another way. If it was my power burning me up because I was trying to send people to hell, then I'd stop trying to send them. How hard could it be?

Oanen pocketed his phone and headed for the door. I took a drink of chocolate milk and focused on trying to calm down. By the time he strode in, I was able to arch a brow at him.

"And what was so important that you needed to run away before I could unleash my anger?"

His lips twitched a little as he sat down.

"Your anger has never concerned me."

"Oh, you're begging for it now."

"I thought I've been begging for it since the moment we met," he said.

I frowned at the gold creeping into his gaze.

"We're not talking about the same thing anymore, are we?"

A small grin tugged at his lips before disappearing. He was breathtaking when mischievous and amused.

"That was Adira," he said, answering my original question.

The waitress interrupted with the delivery of our food. I dug into my pancakes and waited for Oanen to continue.

"The Council believes that Eliana's mom is tied to the murders."

"Why?"

"All the victims are males. The smiles in death. And the fact that pregnant succubi are ravenous enough to easily be one of the most dangerous creatures out there. The Council wants us to investigate Nicolette further."

I sighed and took another big, syrup and butter-soaked bite.

"So are you going to tell me what your mom wanted?" Oanen said.

My heart gave a hard thump as I swallowed.

"You saw?"

"After you disappeared from the Gizzard, I'll never fully take my eyes off you again."

I took a sip of my milk while I tried to think what to say. I didn't want to lie. He'd know if I did. Omission wasn't far from lying, either. But I told myself I wasn't going to hide what I knew forever. Just until I could figure out a way for me to live without someone else dying.

"She pulled her normal Paxton bullshit," I said finally. "She wanted to know if we've had sex. When I told her it was none of her business, she said that griffins only have male offspring and furies female. That we can't mix. She wants me to get rid of you."

Oanen's eyes darkened.

"There is no going back," he said. "We're bonded."

"I told her that. It didn't matter to her. It seems like babies are on everyone's brains."

He exhaled slowly.

"I'm not sure how much we can trust what she says. Like the Council, your mother seems to be withholding information."

"Exactly. The information that she gives is reliable enough, but there are too many holes and missing bits for us to clearly see the big picture."

"Maybe we should go to your great-grandmother."

My heart stopped before my anger started to surge. He held up a hand.

"Not to do what your mom wants but to ask questions. Maybe your Grandma Irene would be more willing to share some straight forward answers."

I considered what he was suggesting.

"Okay. We can try talking to her. Hopefully she's more mellow than Paxton."

We finished our meal and, with renewed determination, left the diner. Oanen wanted to re-check the places the trolls had died for any clues that might point to Nicolette.

In the kitchen space of the first apartment we went to, the ceiling was slowly giving up its hold and crumbling down to the floor in hand-sized chunks. Some of those chunks had been crushed to small mounds of dust that intermingled with other debris. Old food wrappers. Small bones. Shredded bits of material. Thankfully, the heat was off so the place didn't smell too bad.

"What type of clues are we looking for?" I asked as I studied the place.

"I'm not sure," Oanen admitted.

"If Nicolette is anything like Eliana, I can't see her setting foot in here, no matter how hungry she is. I mean, Eliana's too… clean."

He looked around the efficiency apartment, his eyes lingering on the tattered bare mattress, dark with who knew what kinds of stains, and shook his head.

"You're right. I don't see any succubus willingly coming in here."

"If I remember right, the other apartment was better than this one, and that one still was something I couldn't picture Nicolette willingly visiting. When we saw her in the Tabernam, she wore a nice cloak and her nails were a perfectly polished red that matched her lipstick. My point is that she was put together. High class, not streetwalker, put together."

"Maybe she didn't go home with them. Maybe they went to her home."

"And she carried them back to their places after feeding?" I asked. "It doesn't fit her upscale you're-beneath-me vibe. The way she acts, she expects guys to carry her, not the other way around."

"You were in Uttira for several months. We're taught to blend. To not leave a trail. It's possible she could have left her kill in a location where no one would suspect her. I think the proof we need won't be here but at the Goose and Gizzard on those tapes."

"Alright. Let's go." Although I didn't like the idea of going back there again, I was willing to do just about anything to get out of this apartment.

Oanen led the way and opened the car door for me. Across the street, a group of young men openly watched us with looks of hostility on their faces. Not a hint of wickedness touched me. Mom's words came back to me. *I'm guessing you already have your first burn or you wouldn't be this calm.*

"You're not feeling anything from them, are you?" Oanen asked, noting my hesitation.

"No. Nothing." I looked up at him and gave him a quick kiss. "Stay focused on the case," I said. "I'll be fine."

He didn't say anything as I got in, and he closed the door. But he was right. I should have been able to sense something from them. Their body language alone said they were up to no good.

When he pulled away from the curb, he didn't turn around and head back to the Gizzard.

"Aren't we going the wrong way?"

"Nope. The Gizzard won't be open for a while, and I promised to keep you fed."

"But we just had breakfast."

"We're going somewhere for fun then food."

He took 278 south to Ocean Parkway. I paid attention to the tree lined boulevard, feeling a sense of familiarity that I couldn't quite place. It'd been a long time since I'd been in New York. When we turned onto Surf Avenue, and I saw the red spire on the horizon, I knew where we were going.

"Coney Island?"

"Have you been there already?" he asked.

"Yeah, but a long time ago. I remember it was great, though."

The remnants of my headache faded as I leaned forward in my seat and waited for the first glimpse of the rollercoaster. My memories of the amusement park were of people, good food, games, and rides. So, it happened a long time before I started losing my temper. I frowned slightly and hoped I wouldn't ruin it this time, either.

Oanen found a place to park, and hand in hand, we strolled down the boardwalk. The sights, sounds, and smells filled me with excitement.

"What do you want to do first?" he asked.

"All of it."

We moved from ride to ride. He grinned at my enthusiasm and shook his head when I suggested the roller coaster be renamed to Soaring Griffin.

"It's pretty close to flying with you," I said.

"I doubt that."

"You weren't the one clinging to your back when you dove down at Aubrey in that clearing."

After we'd had enough of the rides, he humored me with a few games. Most of them would have been hard for a human to win. I delighted in making the booth attendees' jaws drop when I bested them.

"I think your stuffed animal collection is big enough," Oanen said, his voice muffled by a unicorn's fluffy pink tail.

I picked the animal off the pile and handed it to the nearest kid.

"Let's find some new owners for the rest of these then get something to eat," I said.

The toys were easy to get rid of. Deciding where to eat was

harder. We settled on hot dogs and went to sit shoulder to shoulder on the beach, listening to the waves as we ate.

It felt like a date. Not the secluded, come-to-my-house-and-have-a-quiet-dinner kind but a real date.

"Thank you for this," I said when we'd finished eating. "It felt so…normal."

"The first date of many that will be like this," he said, his gaze sweeping over my features in a way that made my pulse skip. When he leaned toward me, I met him eagerly.

His lips touched mine, and his arms wrapped around me, careful to avoid the burn on my back. I barely had time to note that before he deepened the kiss and stole my ability to reason or breathe. Oanen was my world. Then and always.

When he pulled back and broke the kiss moments later, the cool ocean breeze brought clarity as I tried to catch my breath.

I liked kissing Oanen. Talking to him. Sleeping beside him. Just being with him. No, it wasn't like. It was so much more than like. And, that still scared the hell out of me.

He watched me closely, his golden gaze missing nothing.

"I love the fire in your eyes and the way you look at me after we kiss. I see every bit of passion your fear is holding back, and it makes my heart race because, I know when you unleash it, not even the gods will be able to keep us apart."

"Oanen, I…"

His lips twitched as he watched me fumble with what to say.

"I know the time's not right for you to admit how much you can't live without me. Don't worry; I'm patient."

His teasing helped with the awkwardness.

"Patient? I would have gone with overconfident. Now, don't we have some tapes to look at?" I said, standing and brushing my butt off.

He chuckled and joined me.

"Here, let me help."

I hopped away before he could touch me.

"Hands to yourself. You've messed with my head enough for one day."

He studied my face for a long moment.

"I've meant everything I've said. Kids don't matter. Sex doesn't matter. You admitting how you feel about me doesn't matter. You're all that matters."

He was getting into the scary territory again. I thought of my burns and my great-grandma and needed to shift the topic.

"That's not what I meant. I meant all this talk about kissing and passion is distracting me from our focus."

"That is my focus, Megan. You."

"Dead trolls, Oanen. That's our focus. And Nicolette. Come on."

There was no handholding on the way back to the car. I was too rattled and worried. I loved Oanen loving me. Although the idea of kids still scared the hell out of me, I trusted him when he said having kids wasn't something we needed to do right away. I also trusted that he would wait and let me drive the pace of our physical and emotional relationship. It was his complete need to keep me safe that worried me. What would he do when he found out about the second burn? Or that these burns were signs of my powers eating me alive?

The car ride to the Gizzard was just as quiet.

As soon as we walked into the place, we had the bartender's attention. He nodded to the side door and moved to meet us in the short hall.

"No news, Enforcer. Words out, but no one's talking."

"I was wondering if we could look at your tapes for the past several weeks."

"Knock yourself out. Want me to bring you anything to eat or drink?"

"No, thank you," Oanen and I said at the same time.

The man left us alone in the back room for the next two hours. Oanen and I watched endless footage of patrons coming and going. Eating and drinking. We didn't see much conversation happening. And, there definitely were no signs of a put together succubus.

"There's nothing here to link Nicolette to the troll deaths. I'm going to call Eliana."

Oanen grabbed my hand before I could pull my phone free.

"You can't call her," he said.

I narrowed my eyes at him.

"She's my best friend, who I promised to call every day. If I don't call her, she'll be angry."

He removed his hand.

"Don't say anything about her mom."

"You've already said that."

I dialed Eliana. Like the last time, she picked up on the first ring.

"Where's the seventies porn background music?" I asked.

"What? Ew! Why would you say that?"

I laughed.

"I figured Adira would have converted you by now."

She snorted.

"No. She's been surprisingly quiet today."

And I knew why.

"So, I have some interesting news," I said.

Oanen turned in his chair and crossed his arms at me. I rolled my eyes at him.

"I saw my mom today," I said to Eliana.

"No way. Did she tell you what's going on?"

"Yep. Apparently Oanen and I can't be together because griffins have boy baby chickens and furies have girls with anger issues. According to her, we won't mix."

"While she might be right about the past, who's to say what

will happen? I don't think a griffin and fury pairing has ever been done before. At least not in written history."

"I just wish she didn't try so hard to be a pain in my ass, you know?"

"I'm sorry it wasn't a pleasant reunion."

"It wasn't as bad as it could have been, I guess. She looked exactly the same. But, this time when I saw her, I realized just how much I didn't know about her. Other than her taste in men. But back then, I thought she was just a regular, human gold digger, you know?"

"My mom's motto is usually the richer, the better."

I gave Oanen a triumphant look.

"Usually?"

"Apparently my dad was an exception." A morose note crept into Eliana's voice. "His devotion tasted sweeter because it had never been given to a mortal before. Only to one of the gods."

"Hey. I didn't mean to bring you down. Let's talk about something else. Anything interesting happen at the Academy today?"

"Not really. I better go. It's just about dinner time, and if I get down there first, I can be sitting before Adira arrives."

"Um?"

"She won't notice my dress enough to make me change."

"Ah. Okay. I'll talk to you tomorrow."

After I hung up, I gave Oanen a pointed look.

"And that confirms it. Nicolette would never go to a dive like this to pick up men. She'd go upscale."

The monitor behind Oanen caught my attention.

"Look," I said, pointing at the screen. "There he is again."

"It's the same cloak," Oanen agreed. He changed the angle to find a camera with a shot of the guy's face, but it was never a clear look.

"It's like he knows where the cameras are."

Oanen made a sound of agreement then froze the frame.

"That's him. The troll grandpa who beat his grandson."

He was sitting right next to the cloaked man.

"I need to call the Council. But not from here," he said, standing. "Let's pick up something to eat and head back to our place."

CHAPTER EIGHT

WARM WATER GENTLY TAPPED AGAINST MY BACK. THE SORE THERE had healed enough for a shower without pain. However, the sore on my front was another story. It still looked raw and red.

Thankfully, Oanen hadn't commented when I'd stolen one of his t-shirts to sleep in last night instead of my usual tank top. I smiled at the memory of how his eyes had heated when he'd seen me in his clothes. Nope, he hadn't minded a bit.

I finished rinsing my hair and turned off the water. Just as I stepped out of the shower, the bathroom door started to open. I grabbed the towel and managed to cover my chest before Oanen saw anything.

His heated gaze swept over me from head to toe as he leaned against the door frame.

"What happened to knocking?" I asked.

"I didn't want to miss my chance."

I shook my head at him.

"The water's already off, and you're already dressed. I'd say you missed it."

"I'm not so sure."

His gaze started to dip lower.

I quickly stepped toward him and lifted my lips for a kiss. He didn't disappoint. Before I lost all sense, I wrapped the towel around myself, freeing my hands and hiding the burn.

He groaned against my lips and gently pulled back.

"As much as I want to continue, there's another reason I came in here."

"Oh?"

"Adira just called. The Council met and discussed what we told them. The fact that there was nothing to link Nicolette to any of the murders and the fact that the hooded man spoke to both of the trolls changes nothing. The Council still wants us to continue to investigate Nicolette."

A tingle of anger ran through me.

"What did they say about the hooded man?" I asked.

"If we want to pursue that lead, we can. But Nicolette remains our priority."

"Why aren't they taking his connection to the deaths seriously?"

"Because they're more afraid of Nicolette."

"Why?"

"She's the most powerful succubus out there."

I recalled Eliana saying something along those lines as well.

"Fine. Let's clear Nicolette so we can go after the other guy."

"And then we head to St. Louis for answers," he said firmly.

"Agreed."

His gaze trailed over my face.

"Need any help getting dressed?"

"This whole waiting thing is going to be a real struggle for you, isn't it?" I said with a smirk.

"You have no idea."

He kissed me hard and left me breathless in the bathroom, wondering why we were waiting in the first place. Right. Baby chickens.

After closing the door, I quickly dressed and brushed out my hair while thinking of Eliana. What would she do when she found out the Council was after her mom? Probably freak out and think the Council's actions were an indication of how badly everyone viewed Eliana's species. That was not a good thing for someone already down about who she was.

I hung up my towel and went out to the living room where Oanen was waiting.

"We need to hurry up, find Nicolette, find the cloaked crusader, and get to grandma's house."

Worry filled his gaze and he strode toward me.

"What happened? Did you pass out again?" He gently touched my cheek. "You're less pale than yesterday. I thought you were better."

I reached up and closed my hand around his.

"It's not me. It's Eliana. What do you think is going to happen when she finds out her mom is a suspect? She's sad and misses us already. I just want to hurry up so we can be there for her when she needs us most."

His gaze warmed.

"I agree. Which is why I already made plans to track down Nicolette tonight."

"Tonight? Let's go now."

His lips twitched.

"Where we need to go, they won't let us in dressed like we are."

"Where do we need to go?"

"La Fatiata Torbeni's, a high-end restaurant that caters to humans and non-humans alike if they have the money."

"Um…do we have the money?"

"We do, courtesy of the Council. Enough for a nice dinner and the clothes necessary to get in. Ready for breakfast and a day of shopping?"

I made a face.

"I think you're confusing me with Eliana. I only buy new clothes when the ones I own are falling off of me."

A wicked gleam entered his gaze, and I held up my hand in a very Oanen-like move.

"Let's pretend I didn't say that last part. Feed me, and I'll go shopping."

I examined the price tag and almost gagged.

"Who pays this much for a dress?" I asked myself.

Lifting my head, I scanned the store for Oanen and found him sitting in the lounge on the other side of the room. One of the female attendants was offering him a drink. It had been the same when we'd stopped at the suit place. While Oanen was being measured, one of the male attendants had brought me a glass of champagne and offered a shoulder massage. For a moment, I'd thought the guy had been hitting on me. But he'd done the same for the next woman who'd walked in with her husband. Given the fact I'd been drugged by bacon and that Oanen had a hard time with me receiving any male attention, I'd declined both the drink and the massage.

However, Oanen seemed to have no problem accepting his champagne and shoulder rub.

Narrowing my eyes at the woman, I turned my back to them and continued browsing through dresses. I was out of my element. They all looked fancy to me. But so did the black lacy dress that I owned.

I took my phone out and dialed Eliana.

Since it was in the middle of school, I didn't expect her to pick up on the third ring.

"Hey, Megan," she said breathlessly.

"Hey. Are you okay?"

"Yeah, I just ran out of General Living Skills."

"You didn't need to do that. I could have left a voicemail."

"Are you kidding? It's General Living Skills. I know how to live with humans. The class is a waste of my time. What's up? Why'd you call?"

"I'm hoping you can help me pick out a dress. It's supposed to be for a super fancy restaurant. Think high class, not hooker."

Eliana sniggered.

"Turn on video chat and show me the options."

I did as she asked and panned the dresses.

"Grab the red one, the gold one, and that lavender one. Those colors will look good on you."

Each dress had a plunging neckline. I turned the phone around, already shaking my head.

"Those won't work. I have a bruise," I said vaguely, knowing Oanen could probably hear, "and need something with a higher neckline.

"Okay. Show me again."

She picked three different ones, which would cover the burns on my front and my back. I went to grab them from the racks, but Eliana stopped me.

"No, no, no. You wave one of the attendants over. They handle the dresses while showing you to a fitting room. Send me pics of each one front and back so I can tell you which works. I better get back to class."

"Thank you," I said quickly.

Pocketing my phone, I looked toward the attendant hovering around Oanen. When I caught her attention, I waved her over. The woman took the dresses and showed me to a changing room. I dutifully sent a picture of myself in each dress to Eliana.

She chose the one in rose gold and gave me the strict order to pair it with large diamond stud earrings and a soft updo because of the high neckline. I smirked as I typed up my response.

What exactly does an up do?

You're hopeless. When you get home, we're going shopping for a week so I can be assured you'll not go out looking like a frump.

Frump? When did my grandma get here?

I'm texting Oanen that I need a picture before you walk out the door.

Grinning, I stepped out of the changing room once again in my everyday clothes. A giggle across the store drew my attention. Both of the women were again hovering around Oanen, each rubbing a shoulder. I might not have bird hearing, but the way the one was leaning forward and trying to give Oanen a view of her cleavage hit me right between the eyes with the rage stick.

Oanen stood quickly and strode toward me, capturing my face between his hands and blocking my view of the two women I needed to kill.

"Let go," I said between clenched teeth.

"This wasn't intentional, but perhaps you now understand how I felt every time I saw Fenris touching you."

I scowled up at him.

"Fenris is a friend. One I trust not to push that boundary. Miss Hotstuff, here, is a ho who wants to ride your man-stick." He kept my face firmly between his hands, and I knew why when I saw a flicker of orange glow cast on his face.

"You're the only one who gets to ride me, Megan. Now and forever. And, unlike you, I love every ounce of jealousy you're displaying. However, we might want to make it a little less public."

I huffed out a breath.

"Would you like to purchase that dress?" a female voice asked.

My gaze narrowed.

Oanen bent his head and kissed me swiftly with so much passion that the room spun. I clutched at his shoulders and returned his kiss with every bit of need I felt for him. When he pulled away, I could only blink stupidly at his handsome face.

"Yes, we want the dress," Oanen said without looking away from me. He tugged it out of my arms and handed it off before returning to my lips.

"God, she is so lucky. What I wouldn't give for an hour alone with him."

The whisper snapped me out of the moment, and I jerked away from Oanen.

He didn't release me.

"I'm blinded by you, Megan" he said. "Struck senseless. There isn't a sunrise or sunset that can compare to the beauty of your eyes. Or any temptation that could lure me away from the chance of a moment in your welcoming arms. There is only you."

I sighed in defeat.

"You win. There will be no maiming today."

"I'd like to guarantee that."

"How?"

"Close your eyes and let me carry you out of here."

"I bought a ridiculously priced dress and need diamond stud earrings the size of my pinky nails to go with it. Since I'm dressing like a diva, I might as well act like one. Go ahead and carry me out to the car, bird boy."

He grinned, and I closed my eyes as he bent to pick me up.

"You bitches better not be looking at his backside," I called over my shoulder as he walked out the door.

He chuckled and paused long enough for two bags to be set on my stomach. Thankfully, they didn't touch my front burn.

I waited to speak until the sound of traffic indicated we were outside again.

"So where am I going to go buy earrings?" I asked.

"Nowhere. Eliana will pick something from her jewelry and have Adira leave it in the apartment before we get home."

I opened my eyes to peer up at him.

"She also demanded a picture, stating, and I quote, 'No friend of mine can show up at La Fatiata Torbeni's looking like a hobo.'"

"Jeans and t-shirts do not make me a hobo."

"This is not a battle I will ever win. Talk to Eliana."

"Chicken."

"Nope. Griffin. But I hear there's a close family resemblance when we're young."

I snorted and held the bags as he opened the door and deposited me inside. Despite the bustling sidewalks and busy shops, only a few wisps of wicked distracted me from my perusal of Oanen's backside as he walked around the car.

"It's not the same, you know," I said when he got in. "Your jealousy and mine."

"How is that?"

"I could see that woman wanted to get into your pants. Fenris didn't want to get into mine."

"I'm still not sure about that."

I snorted.

"Trust me, he has no interest in me that way. At all."

"He sure made it seem that way."

Annoyed, I lifted my phone and typed out a quick message to Fenris.

Enough's enough. I'm telling him.

I understand. But promise you'll keep him away from Uttira for at least 3 weeks afterward so he cools down.

Deal.

I turned slightly in my seat and faced Oanen.

"I'll tell you why Fenris acted the way he did, but you have to swear to me that once I tell you, you won't do anything to hurt Fenris physically, mentally, or emotionally."

Oanen's expression closed off.

"Tell me."

"Promise me."

"I promise I won't do anything until we're home."

"And you won't go home without me?"

"No. We stick together."

"Okay then. Fenris likes Eliana."

Oanen frowned a little and glanced at me.

"That doesn't deny the possibility of him having interest in you, too. You've seen how he is with females. He likes them all."

I made a face.

"I think it's a bigger deal than Fenris is letting on. Remember how he loved hugging me? He was doing it to smell Eliana on me. Like a lot. And when I found out that you were into me because of this whole mate and bonding thing and freaked out, Fenris came into the kitchen when I was boiling hot and burned himself to calm me down. And why did he risk himself like that? Because Eliana was worried. It had nothing to do with me. It was all about her. The level of interest he was showing..." I shrugged. "I don't know anything about this mate run. But, I know Fenris said something about once a werewolf catches a scent that he finds irresistible, he won't let up. I think Fenris' irresistible is Eliana."

Oanen's grip on the steering wheel tightened, and I heard the leather crackle.

I reached over and set my hand on his leg.

"I can't think of anyone better for Eliana than Fenris."

"In what world is that leg-humper good enough for Eliana?"

I grinned at his brotherly sentiment.

"In the world where a succubus is afraid of anything sexual. Fenris is waiting for her, Oanen. He's giving her space and time. He's fighting every single urge he has. If that doesn't mean he's good enough for her, I don't know what does."

Oanen let out a long breath, and his grip relaxed slightly.

"Does she know?"

"No. Just like you swore Eliana to secrecy, Fenris swore me to secrecy. He thinks if she knows, she'd freak out even more."

Oanen nodded.

"We need to resolve the troll deaths and your sickness then get back to Uttira."

"About that. I promised that I'd keep you out of Uttira for the next three weeks."

"I thought you said you wanted to hurry up and get back for Eliana."

"Yes, I do. You, however, need to stay out of her and Fenris' business, and I don't think you're going to if you're nearby. Maybe you'd be willing to let me stay in Uttira while you're out on enforcer business?"

He held up a hand to stall me from saying anything else. "Let's worry about that when we return to Uttira later. Right now, we have more important things to worry about."

"Like what?"

"Like our first real dinner date."

My stomach did a happy dance.

Several hours, multiple Eliana calls, and a dozen makeup tutorials later, I emerged from the apartment bathroom, dressed and ready for a late dinner at La Fatiata Torbeni's.

I nervously smoothed my hands down my skirt and gave myself one more sweeping glance. The high neckline of the floor-length dress circled my neck, covering my burns but leaving my shoulders bare. The strings of material that ran down my sides to connect the front and back didn't cover much at all. Between the delicate cross lacings, my skin showed from the side of my breast all the way to my hip.

Even with so much exposed, the dress had class. The earrings and softly upswept hair helped.

I looked amazing. But, for how long? Even though my temper had been quiet, I worried that tonight it would rear its ugly head.

"Don't screw this up, Megan. One busted lacing and you'll look like you're wearing a loincloth," I warned myself in the mirror before turning away to leave the bedroom.

At the sound of the door opening, Oanen stopped his pacing in the living room and turned to look at me.

He said nothing as I did a slow turn with my arms a little raised.

"Breathtaking," he finally said.

"You're not so bad yourself."

He was positively mouthwatering. The dark suit fit him to perfection, accentuating his golden good looks. The increasing amber flooding into his eyes created a warm pool in my middle.

If we kept staring hungrily at each other, I knew what would happen whether I thought myself ready or not.

"Ready to feed me?" I asked.

He offered his arm and escorted me from the apartment.

I wasn't going to lie to myself; I felt like a damn princess. But in a good way.

Oanen couldn't stop glancing at me all the way to the restaurant, which was a great distraction from the annoyance crawling under my skin.

When we arrived, more than one well-dressed patron

glanced my way. With all the flattering male attention, it was hard to remember why we were there.

The Maître D led us to the high-ceilinged dining room and pulled out my chair for me. Oanen waved him away. I smiled and let Oanen help me sit. Not that I needed it. When I was appropriately seated, his fingers brushed the back of my neck.

"I wish we would have stayed home," he said close to my ear.

I shivered, and he chuckled before taking his own seat.

A server brought us leather-bound portfolios; and another server appeared with a green bottle, which he opened with a flourish and poured into two glasses for us. All the while, the first one spoke in low tones about the chef's two menu options for the night.

"We'll need a few moments," I said when he stopped talking and looked at me expectantly.

He walked away, and I glanced at Oanen.

"What the hell kind of place is this?"

"The kind that requires a suit jacket, doesn't put prices on the menu, and caters to everyone."

I opened the menu and saw he was right. I also saw that I didn't understand half of what was on the fancy paper.

"Is this in English?"

"Yes. Most of it. Why?"

"The only English bits I understand are eel, sole, and tuna. I'm going to starve."

"The chef is amazing. Give the food a chance."

"You weren't almost eaten by an overgrown fish. Several of them. I don't think I'll ever be able to eat seafood again."

"There's a duckling with fig sauce."

"Perfect." I snapped my menu shut, and the server returned immediately.

A burst of sultry feminine laughter drew my attention to the other side of the room while Oanen ordered for us. A large table of seven men and one familiar female dined there. Nicolette leaned toward the man on her left and gave him a long kiss while the rest watched wistfully.

Our server moved away, and I looked at Oanen.

"Now what?"

"Now we enjoy our meal. As long as she's sitting there, there's nothing for us to do. When she leaves, we'll follow and see what we learn."

For the next hour and a half, we did just that. Course after artistically displayed tiny course, we consumed our meal and speculated about when Elbner and Piepen would arrive in Uttira, how long I'd enjoy a rainbow-colored house, where we'd travel when everything was done, and how I wouldn't try to kill the chef for tucking a chunk of raw tuna into an innocent looking ball of crumbs.

After all our plates were cleared, Oanen came around to help me stand again.

"Where are we going?" I asked, flicking my gaze at Nicolette's table. They were still drinking wine and eating their meal.

As I watched, a well-dressed older man approached their group from the bar area. Nicolette smiled seductively as he leaned down to say something to her.

Her sultry laugh rang out in the room again.

"I'm sure you would taste divine, but I enjoy youth over experience."

The comment only further confirmed that Nicolette wouldn't have gone after an old troll.

Oanen set my hand on his arm and guided me out of the restaurant into the cold winter evening and quickly helped me into his car. Positioned to watch the entrance, he started the engine but didn't pull away from the curb.

He reached into the back and wrapped a soft cream-colored blanket around me.

"Where did this come from?"

"The apartment. I wasn't sure how long we'd need to wait tonight," he said.

"You heard Nicolette when we left, right?" I said.

"Yes."

"There's zero link here. We need to call the Council."

"We can try." He dialed Adira's number and put her on speaker phone.

"Have you followed her home?" Adira asked.

"Not yet. She's still in the restaurant."

"Adira, I don't think she's the killer. She's into young men. There's nothing linking her to any of the troll deaths. And, I don't sense anything around her. If she were a killer, wouldn't my fury be going crazy?"

The line was quiet for a long moment.

"Have you passed out again?" she asked. "Since the gas station?"

I looked up at Oanen and gave him a dirty look.

"What does that have to do with anything?" I paused and frowned. "Do you know something I should know?"

"Fury," she said respectfully, "I know many things that you do not know. But I doubt any of it would help you. It is the belief of the Council that Nicolette is guilty regardless of what you currently sense. Notify me when you have her subdued, and I will retrieve her."

Adira disconnected the call.

"Subdued? What in the hell does that mean?"

"It means I need to fight Eliana's pregnant mom."

CHAPTER NINE

"The Council is so stupid. Why can't they see there's no proof that Nicolette is guilty?" I shifted in my seat, irritated.

"They see it," Oanen said, not looking away from the door, "but they don't care. My guess is that they're thinking if she's not guilty yet, she soon will be."

Before I could reply, one of the men from Nicolette's group stepped out of the restaurant. He paused on the sidewalk and reached into his pocket. From down the street, a set of headlights flashed and he headed that direction. An engine purred to life a few moments after I lost sight of him.

Nicolette strolled out of the restaurant, surrounded by her entourage, as the car pulled up in front of her. Her gaze swept over the street, and Oanen quickly turned his head toward me.

"Don't let her see your face," he said softly.

I shifted slightly so his head blocked me from Nicolette's view.

We waited as she got into the car, and the men disbursed to their own vehicles. It wasn't hard to follow her line of lovers to her place, a high-rise apartment in Manhattan with underground parking and a guard. Nicolette's car led the way underground. Each car after her stopped to speak to the guard.

Oanen hesitated then went around the line and parked on the street.

I looked at the building's front door where another man guarded the entrance.

"I can take him," I said with confidence.

"So could I, but we don't need to."

He shrugged out of his jacket and handed it to me. I groaned.

"I really don't like when you do this."

"Why? Because all the ladies will see my man-stick?"

"I regret ever saying that."

His lips twitched as he unbuttoned his shirt and kicked off his shoes.

"You'll need to carry my clothes," he said. "There's a bag in the back."

I twisted in my seat and grabbed a backpack laying on the backseat along with his winter jacket. His lips brushed my neck before I could straighten. My eyes closed, and I held still to enjoy the feel of him for a moment.

"What was that for?" I asked when he stopped.

"A reminder that what I feel for you is real."

"I already know that."

He exhaled slowly and looked up at the building.

"I just don't want you to forget it when we get inside Nicolette's apartment."

"I won't."

He handed me his jacket, shoes, and socks, then got out of the car. I had everything in the backpack by the time he opened my door and offered his hand.

I accepted his help and grinned when he held the bag so I could put his jacket on while he stood there barefoot in an unbuttoned shirt.

"Careful, you're only adding to my growing princess complex. I'm going to want peeled grapes next."

"I'll feed them to you tonight. Ready?" He held out his hand, and I threaded my fingers through his.

"Where are we going?" I asked as he started down the sidewalk away from the building.

"Somewhere less public."

We found a quiet place in a nearby park. Oanen led me into the trees and stepped back to strip out of the rest of his clothes. I caught everything and folded it into the backpack. When I once again had the bag on my shoulders, Oanen stood before me in his beak and feathers.

"Let's go, bird boy."

He bent a knee so I could climb on his back. The skirt of the dress didn't have enough room so I ended up bunching it around my waist. My legs prickled with the cold, and I frowned.

"Don't take too long in the air," I said as I ran my hand down his neck.

He clacked his beak and turned his head to nuzzle my bare leg. A moment later, he lunged into the air and broke free of the trees.

I would never tire of flying with Oanen. My heart soared, seeing the lights and cars below us and the stars above. I held tight as he made his way back toward Nicolette's building, circling it slowly.

"There," I said, pointing to a balcony at the top.

The French doors were open, and the apartment was filled with people in various stages of undress. Most of them were men. But there were a few couples doing things publicly that hinted at a succubus's playhouse.

Oanen went right for the balcony. His landing went unnoticed by the couple on the lounge.

Averting my gaze from the man's naked backside as he

rapidly thrust into his moaning partner, I slid off Oanen and dug in the bag for his pants.

He put them on quickly, while keeping his gaze on me.

"It's likely to get worse," he said quietly.

The sound of skin against skin almost drowned out his words.

"How can it get worse than this?"

The woman started yelling, "Yes, yes, yes!" at the top of her lungs then wailed in rapture. My cheeks heated, and my legs no longer felt so cold.

I waited for the couple to notice us as Oanen put on his shirt then socks. But they didn't. Instead, they started up again.

I stared at Oanen in shock.

"We can't feel it, but what they're doing is giving off sexual energy. It's what nourishes a succubus," he said softly. "With Nicolette being pregnant, she'll be hungrier than a typical succubus. Like I said, it'll be worse inside. Are you ready?"

Now fully dressed and with the empty bag over his shoulder, Oanen held out his hand to me.

I swallowed hard and nodded. Together, we walked inside.

A man holding a tray of champagne walked our way. He wasn't wearing a thing except a bow tie.

"These formal affairs are amazing, don't you agree?" he said, giving me a heated look.

Oanen's fingers tightened around mine.

"Incredible," I said with a smile. "Can you point us toward our hostess?"

The man nodded toward the center of the room and walked away with a wink.

"Do not leave my side," Oanen warned.

"I won't."

We moved in the direction the server had indicated, weaving our way through people, until we saw the pile of pillows in the center of the room. People lay on the cushions. While there was an obvious imbalance of men to women, the few women there didn't seem to mind that they were being petted by several men at once.

I tried to focus on Nicolette, who lounged in the center of it all, sipping a glass of green liquid. Her black gaze flicked from one pile of sweaty bodies to the next.

"I think Paulette would be more comfortable on all fours," she said to the group on her left.

The men immediately moved away from the woman so she could change position. A molten heat filled my face as one man knelt behind Paulette and another lay down under her.

"Much better," Nicolette said.

Even if Oanen wasn't in over his head in all of this, I sure was. I nudged him, desperate for him to do whatever he needed, so we could get the hell out of there.

The move caught Nicolette's attention, and her gaze flicked to us.

"Aren't you two just adorable," she said. "Are you here to have some fun?"

"No," I said quickly.

"We're here on behalf of the Council," Oanen said. "They would like to speak with you."

"Really?" Her amused tone was gone. "I think not."

She stood in one smooth move, her dress shimmering in the light.

"I think you're here to satisfy some urges, Oanen. Look at her." Nicolette's voice turned sultry. "Her pretty eyes. Deep pools pleading with you to end her longing."

Oanen turned to look at me, his eyes already a deep gold.

"Oanen?" I said, hesitantly as he dropped the bag.

"Megan." His voice was a rough rasp as he caressed my

cheek. "Be strong for both of us," he said a moment before his lips crashed upon mine.

I trembled under the intensity of his kiss.

"That's right," Nicolette cooed. "You have so much suppressed passion for each other. Let it free."

A heat pooled in my stomach and drifted lower. I threaded my hands in Oanen's hair and kissed him back with as much passion as he kissed me.

"Bring her to the cushions, my darling Oanen. And remove your shirt so she can touch you."

His lips didn't leave mine as he picked me up and moved us. But they did when he removed his shirt. Panting, I stared up at the golden expanse of his chest. I wanted to touch him. To run my tongue over every ridge and dip. I wanted to fill myself with Oanen and to be filled by him.

"Megan, my dear. I think that beautiful dress is in his way. Take it off."

The heat surged. I wanted to be under Oanen. Naked. Waiting. Exposed.

I blinked.

Exposed?

My gaze shifted from Oanen's loving face to those of the people around us. Even as part of me knew that what was happening was wrong, my fingers found the clasp at my neck.

"The Council wants you to go to Uttira," I said, unhooking the back.

"Focus, my love. Bare your breasts to him. Let him taste you."

My skin heated further, and a tingle started between my legs. But something changed. A spark ignited in my chest. Anger. My fury didn't like that it was being forced to do something that wasn't its own choice.

"Don't you understand?" I asked, fighting the urge to slip

the top of the dress over my arms. Oanen's gaze tracked the material as it started to lower. I swallowed hard.

"I understand that you're trying to fight this. Don't. You both want it."

Oanen's hand found my leg under my skirt. Slowly, he skimmed his way up to my knee.

"The Council has kept you out of Uttira. Away from Eliana. Now, they want you there."

Oanen paused, his hand on my inner thigh, his fingers skimming the line of my panties.

I began to burn. Two ends of a Megan candle. One passion. The other rage. Around us the couples continued with their public orgy in earnest. The gasps and groans of pleasure weren't helping me maintain my focus.

"Eliana won't have a say whether or not you stay this time," I said. "You'll finally be with your daughter."

The black in Nicolette's gaze faded.

"You're smart," she said. "And also very resistant. It could have been fun."

Nicolette snapped her fingers.

"Finish and leave."

The sex around us turned frenzied. I gazed up at Oanen. The look in his eyes was as tormented as it was hopeful. I gently withdrew his hand from under my skirt, gave it a pat, and righted my dress, doing my best to ignore the escalating, screaming pleasure.

Everything slowly quieted and people picked up their clothes on their way to the door. One man in particular drew my attention. Like most males here, he was young, lean, and naked. However, he was also wicked as hell. A new kind of tingle started under my skin.

"You like the naughty ones?" Nicolette asked, watching me.

"No. Not at all."

When I turned toward her, orange reflected on her skin, and black briefly consumed her eyes before disappearing.

"Be careful with displays of power, Fury. Some of us can't help but rise to a challenge." She looked at Oanen. "Call your parents. I'm ready."

His hands shook as he retrieved his phone from his pants and dialed a number.

"We have her," he said then hung up.

Nicolette laughed. "You don't have anything fledgling. But, you almost did."

She winked at me just as a portal appeared beside Oanen. Adira stepped through and held out her hand to Nicolette.

"See you soon, darlings," Nicolette said before she ignored Adira and stepped through the portal on her own.

Adira looked at us.

"You don't look well, Megan."

"Don't even try to say I look pale because I know my face is on fire after what I witnessed here."

"No. It's not that. It's in your eyes. They're missing their spark."

"Well, it's been an exhausting night. I think I'm allowed to be non-sparky."

She dipped her head in acknowledgment then disappeared.

Alone in Nicolette's plush apartment, I glanced at Oanen's flushed face as he finished buttoning his shirt. Guilt laced his expression.

"Your fighting skills need improvement," I said.

"Megan, I—"

"Your make-out skills are A plus, though."

His lips twitched, and he picked up the empty bag and reached for my hand. Threading my fingers through his, we left Nicolette's apartment and waited for the elevator together. I could still feel the tremble in his hand.

"Are you okay?" I asked.

"No. I'm still fighting the urge to carry you back to the cushions and slide that dress off of you."

"I'm sorry she did that to you."

He turned toward me, the dilated pupils in his golden eyes making my pulse skip.

"That was me, Megan. She barely nudged me to do what I've been dying to do…what I've been holding back. My fingers are desperate to feel the soft skin of your thighs again. Tell me you're ready, and I'll stop fighting this."

Hearing that didn't fill me with fear. But as much as I wanted to say yes, I couldn't.

"I want our first time together to be special, not on some well-used cushions in a succubus's playhouse. And not in the middle of a murder investigation."

He closed his eyes, taking a deep breath.

"Are you mad?" I asked.

"Never. You're right. Now isn't the time. This isn't what I want to remember, either."

When he opened his eyes, there was more blue than gold in them.

"Let's go home," he said.

The elevator finally dinged and opened for us.

"You mean back to the apartment, right? We both know that Nicolette isn't the killer. We need to find the hooded man."

He nodded and pushed the button for the first floor.

"Back to the apartment. We'll start again tomorrow."

He studied me for a long moment.

"Adira's right. Your eyes are different. There was something more to them before. A warmth. A hidden fire before they ever started glowing orange. I don't see it now."

Damn Adira for bringing it up.

"Maybe my eyes changed when my power did."

"Maybe. Maybe we should forget about this hooded man, since the Council doesn't care, and leave for St. Louis first thing in the morning."

"No way. We can't do that to Eliana. She's going to freak out when she finds out her mom is in Uttira because of me."

"No. Her mom is there because of the Council and will be under Council custody," Oanen said.

I shook my head and looked at the polished door.

"I don't know about that. The Council isn't stupid. Annoying, yes. Stubborn, yes. But not stupid. There's too much evidence to say Nicolette didn't do it. So why bring her back to Uttira? There's obviously something else going on there that they aren't telling us."

Another thought occurred to me.

"Text Adira and say that we're choosing not to pursue the hooded man and see what she says," I said.

The elevators opened up to the lobby, and we stepped out. The night man at the door opened it for us and said nothing as we left.

Oanen sent a quick text off after we were settled into the car then drove us home. There was a response by the time we reached our building.

"They want us to follow up on our lead," he said.

"That's what I thought."

We walked inside, and I veered for the elevator.

Oanen frowned at me. "Are you sure you're okay?"

"I'm wearing heels. All of me is fine, except my feet, at the thought of climbing all those stairs."

While standing by the elevator door, Oanen kissed my temple and wrapped an arm around my shoulders as we watched the floors count down. The doors opened, and Oanen stepped back, guiding me with him. If he hadn't, I wouldn't have moved.

My Fury reared its head. But it felt different this time. The compulsion to yell at the guys stepping out of the elevator was there as was the anger. However, the power felt unreachable, somehow. My lips ached with the need to call out a man's name. To demand his confession. My fingers twitched to grab his neck as he obliviously strode past me.

Oanen guided me forward. My steps were slow, each one harder than the last because it was taking me further away from the man.

"Are you okay?" Oanen asked, already reaching to press the button for our floor.

The urge to strike out and slap his hand away road me hard, creating a physical ache on my hip. I frowned as the ache turned into a burn.

The door closed, blocking the man from me and snapping the draw on my power. I almost wilted in relief.

"I'm fine. Just tired."

I was more than tired. I was ready to fall to the floor. More than that. I knew I was running out of time.

The weight of Oanen's arm pinned me to the mattress. Warm and comfortable, I could have slept forever. However, the phone ringing near my head insisted that wasn't an option.

I reached out and swatted in the direction of the sound. My fingers hit something, and I heard a thump on the floor a moment later. Everything went quiet.

Oanen's phone started to ring next.

"I think it's unavoidable," he said before kissing my covered shoulder and rolling out of bed.

Without opening my eyes, I listened to his rough "hello."

"Yeah. She's right here. Hold on."

The mattress moved as he leaned toward me.

"It's Eliana," he said. "She's upset."

I rubbed my hand over my face and opened my eyes but didn't move from my side-sleeping position. Everything hurt just like each time I woke up after trying to send someone to hell. Only this time, it was a little less intense. As much as I wanted to take that as a good sign, I had a feeling it was because I hadn't actually acted out what my fury wanted last night.

Taking the phone from Oanen, I set it against my ear.

"Hey, Eliana."

"My mom's here," she said. I could hear the panic and anger in her voice.

"I know. And I'm sorry for my part in that. Oanen and I have been telling the Council that we don't think she had anything to do with what's going on."

Eliana snorted.

"Of course she doesn't. She doesn't kill; she just destroys lives." She made a sound of annoyance. "Stop touching yourself when you're on my bed. I saw that smear on my pillow this morning, and you're lucky I didn't kill you in my sleep."

"Uh…Eliana?"

"Sorry. Piepen and Elbner arrived last night. Elbner's at your place with his honey-milk. Piepen's here."

"That's great."

"No. It's not."

I could hear a door close.

"He's in a horny, adolescent phase and keeps touching himself. While on my pillow. Brownie lust does not taste like you'd think. You need to get your butt home as soon as possible. The brownie and my mom both need to go. Mom's staying here, Megan. At the Quills'. She's already found my stash of chocolate and eaten half of it. Once the chocolate's gone, she's going to turn her attention on me. She already commented that I look underfed."

I could hear a tapping in the background.

"I told you, I need privacy while I'm in the bathroom," Eliana said. "If you can't respect that, we'll need to find you somewhere else to stay while Megan's away."

She lowered her voice.

"I caught him showering in the run off from my pubic hairs this morning. When I went to kick him, he thanked me for the view of my flower."

As much as I hurt, I couldn't stop my laughter.

"This isn't funny, Megan. It's traumatizing. Help me. No one sees my flower. Ever!"

I bit my lip and struggled for control as Oanen watched me.

"I am helping. I swear. We're going to follow up on a lead we have that links someone else to the trolls' deaths."

"Who?"

"We don't know his name. He's just a hooded man who talked to the victims at the Goose and Gizzard before they died."

"Piepen mentioned a nice man who helped his grandparents find peace. Maybe it's the same guy."

"Maybe. Talk to Piepen and see if you can get anything useful out of him. A name. An address. What the hell the guy looks like."

"I will. Just hurry."

I heard the door open on Eliana's end before she yelled.

"Put down my underwear!"

Then, the line disconnected.

CHAPTER TEN

I HANDED THE PHONE BACK TO OANEN AND CAREFULLY SAT UP.

"Eliana's freaking out just like I said she would. It's not bad enough that the Council wanted Nicolette in Uttira. They put her in your house with Eliana."

Oanen frowned.

"As if that's not stressful enough for her, the brownie I sent her way is masturbating on Eliana's pillow and sneaking into the shower with her. We need to figure out who this hooded guy is fast."

"All right. Let's get dressed."

I stood too quickly and had to reach for the nightstand to steady myself.

"What's wrong?" Oanen was at my side in an instant.

"Nothing. Just got a little dizzy from standing up too fast."

"You're pale." He reached out to touch my forehead, but I swatted his hand away.

"I'm also annoyed that people keep telling me that. You can change in the bathroom. I'll change out here."

He studied me for a long moment then grabbed some clothes and closed himself in the bathroom. I hurried to get dressed, glancing at the new burn on my hip. It wasn't as severe as the others but still served as a reminder that we needed answers. Today.

Ten minutes later, we stepped outside, and I looked up at the clear sky.

"How late is it?" I asked.

"Almost noon."

"Wow." It hadn't felt like we'd slept that long.

"Are you hungry?"

"Not really."

He gave me a considering look then opened the car door for me.

Neither of us spoke during the ride to the Goose and Gizzard. I didn't mind the quiet. I closed my eyes and drifted off. When the car slowed, though, I jerked awake.

Oanen parked and cut the engine but stopped me before I got out.

"I know you don't like me asking if you're all right. You probably hate hearing it as much as I hate asking it. I just wish you'd be honest with me and tell me what's going on. I know something isn't right."

"It's more than something. It's everything. Dead trolls. Nicolette. The Council. My mom. My great-grandma. I'm sorry I'm not myself lately."

He continued to study me.

"That's not it. Or at least not all of it. If you're not ready to confide in me, that's fine. But whether you tell me or not, it won't change what will happen if you get worse. You're mine, Megan. Mine to love. To care for. To protect. Even from your stubborn self."

"Got it."

He leaned toward me and gently stroked my cheek.

"And that's how I know whatever is happening is getting very serious. Megan Smith does not simply say, 'Got it.' Ever."

He had me there. But I was too tired to argue.

"Are we going inside, or do you plan to play with my face all day?" I asked.

He kissed me lightly then reached across me to open the door.

"After you."

I felt more than a little guilty as I got out then waited for him on the sidewalk. He did have my best interest at heart. Yet, if I told him what was happening, I was worried what his plan B would be if we talked to my great-grandma and she didn't have any answers. I needed my own plan B before I said anything. Besides, things weren't as bad as my mom made it sound like they were going to be. I'd successfully managed to avoid trying to condemn someone to hell and reduced the effects of the backlash. I could hold out long enough to find the troll killer and come up with a backup plan for saving myself.

No problem.

A little, pessimistic inner voice laughed its ass off at that thought.

Inside the Gizzard, a few patrons already sat at the bar.

"No eating anything," Oanen warned before moving off to talk to a very large, ugly woman sitting by herself in one of the booths.

I went to the bar and sat beside the man there. The bartender looked at me, shook his head, then approached.

"What can I get you?"

"A soda. Any human kind," I ordered even though I had no intention of consuming any of it.

The bartender made a noise that suggested he thought I was stupid and moved off.

The man beside me gave a longsuffering sigh.

"Human drinks. Bah. I miss drinking from them. Biting into their juicy flesh. The coppery taste of their blood coating my tongue."

I glanced at the weathered old man, wondering what type of creature he might be. No matter what kind, I should have felt some fury rage right then. He'd just admitted to eating humans. Perhaps I didn't feel anything because it had happened long ago. Before the laws even. Or, perhaps the aftereffects of the burns were causing an inability to sense anything. Maybe that was what Mom meant about me being calm.

"More than that, I miss the sky," he added.

His shoulder drooped a bit more.

"My wings are shriveled and shrunken. I can barely make it from the mainland to the island anymore. Four hundred years ago, I could have flown around the world in my true form."

That admission confirmed my long time ago theory. Yet, I couldn't help but feel my other theory fit as well.

"Why not go to somewhere secluded and fly?" I asked.

He snorted.

"The humans are everywhere."

"What about going to one of the towns like Uttira? I hear we can use our true forms openly there."

He turned his craggy face toward me and scowled.

"Exchanging the freedom to fly for my freedom to roam would solve nothing. My life, the lives of all dragons, mean nothing now. This world has no place for us."

The bartender came back with a burger, which he set in front of the old man. While the old guy lifted his bun to inspect the food, the bartender poured me a glass of white soda.

"Everything okay with the burger, Magroal?" the bartender asked.

The old guy set the bun down.

"As good as ground up, old-kill animal flesh can be."

The bartender nodded and took a half-full glass from the other side of the old man and went in the back. Magroal took a huge bite of his burger, chewed methodically, and swallowed. The thing smelled amazing. Had I been eating it, I would have been making moaning noises of appreciation. Well, not here, but anywhere else that served a bacon cheeseburger.

He finished the rest of the burger in three bites, threw down some cash, and left. His fries and drink were untouched. I looked around the rest of the bar.

Oanen was still talking to the ugly girl. There was another older guy in a booth, but something about his red eyes as he glanced at me kept me in my seat.

I really was losing my edge.

My stomach rumbled, and I looked back at the remnants of old guy's meal, tempted to take a fry. I reached out and turned the plate.

"Megan," came Oanen's warning voice from across the room.

I would have turned to grin at him, but my gaze was caught on the green flecks of powder on the edge of the plate.

"Oanen, there's more powder here."

He rushed to my side. Instead of looking where I pointed, he grabbed my shoulders.

"Did you eat any?" Worry filled his expression.

"Of course not."

His gaze searched mine before he released me and looked at the plate.

The bartender walked out from the kitchen. Oanen waved him over and pointed to the powder.

"It happened again. Do you have someone in back that we can borrow?"

"Borrow?" I asked.

"We need someone to eat that so we can follow them."

"Yeah," the bartender said. "I've got someone. He needs to come back, though. He's my nephew and does the dishes."

I couldn't tell which part was more important to him. The relation to the boy or having his dishes washed.

"Tek! Get out here!"

A young man close to our age appeared from the back.

"Eat that," the bartender said.

"The fries?"

"No. The powder on the plate."

"Why? It's not from me. I know that plate was clean when you grabbed it."

"It's not a punishment. Just eat the damn shit."

The boy licked his finger, dabbed up the few granules of powder, then swiped it on his tongue. We all watched him, waiting.

"Doesn't taste like anything," the boy said after a few long moments.

"How long does it take to work?" Oanen asked.

"The guy ate his whole burger. I only managed a few bites." I shrugged. "I have no idea."

We both watched Tek.

"Work?" he asked. "What was that stuff?"

"A spell that calls you to a location, I think," Oanen said.

"You had me eat a spell, and you don't even know what it does?" Tek asked, looking a little nervous now.

Oanen ignored him and focused on the bartender.

"Who was he? The guy sitting here?"

"Magroal. A dragon. He lives on one of the islands, but I'm not sure which one."

"The Council called Raiden to sniff out a killer," I said. "Can we call him to see if he can follow Magroal's trail?"

The bartender snorted.

"In New York? Good luck."

Oanen shook his head.

"There's too many smells here. We'd never find anyone that way."

"Okay. Well, how did the powder get on the burger? Maybe we can figure out something that way."

Oanen and I went back to review the camera footage. It didn't take long to rewind the thirty minutes since we had arrived. When we did, my jaw dropped.

I watched us walk in. Oanen went to the ugly chick. I went to the bar to join the two men sitting there. Two. Directly on the other side of the old dragon sat the hooded man.

"How?" I said. "We didn't see him."

"A powerful spell," Oanen said grimly. "He knows we're looking for him."

As we watched, the old dragon lifted his bun. The hooded man reached over and sprinkled the food while the old dragon talked to the bartender. Instead of getting up and leaving, the hooded man waited until the dragon finished the burger then got up with him and followed him out the exit.

"Wait," Oanen said, sifting through the camera angles. "There."

He paused the video frame. This time, one of the camera's had captured a clear image of the hooded man's face. He was younger, just a little older than Oanen and me. We finally had a picture of him.

I took my phone and snapped a picture.

"Time to visit the Tabernam," I said again.

We checked on Tek before leaving. He still seemed unaffected.

"Likely because of the low dose," Oanen said. "Keep an eye on him and call me if anything changes."

The bartender nodded.

Outside, Oanen hesitated on the sidewalk, glancing at me then the sky.

"I agree," I said. "You should fly and try to spot him. He can't have gotten too far."

"No, we stick together."

"I'll be fine, Oanen. I'll drive straight to the Tabernam."

"Until someone distracts you. No. We're together. Always."

I didn't argue as he continued toward the car. He was right. If my rage kicked in, I'd likely drive off the road, trying to get to whoever. But, given how I was feeling, I doubted it would happen. And that wasn't something I was going to mention to Oanen.

The drive to the Tabernam didn't take long, and when we entered the store, the woman came out from behind the counter to greet us.

"Enforcer. Fury," she said a bit too loudly. "How can I help you?"

I took out my phone and showed her a picture of the hooded man.

"Have you seen him?"

"Yes. He came in a few weeks ago. I haven't seen him since, though. And before you ask, I do not know his name or where he lives. All I can give you is a list of the ingredients he purchased."

"Good," Oanen said. "Send it to the Council. If you see him again, call the Council immediately."

"Yes, Enforcer."

Oanen nodded, and with his hand on my back, we left.

"You didn't buy that bull, did you?" I asked.

"Most of it. I think she told the truth about not knowing his name or address. But I also think she knew someone who would know it. And that someone was probably in the shop."

We sat in the car for over an hour, waiting for someone to emerge, but no one did.

"Should we go back in?"

"No. Whoever she was warning probably already left another way."

He started the car and merged with the light traffic.

"We have his picture and know he's part of the nonhuman community since he was in the Gizzard. And, he obviously knows we're looking for him already if he's using the cloaking spell. So, let's start visiting all the nonhuman secret places and asking around. Someone is bound to recognize him."

Oanen gave me a wry side glance.

"This is New York. Do you know how many places there are that cater to only non-humans? And how many more places cater to both? We'll be searching for weeks."

"Then we better get started."

Another early morning call woke me.

"We need to leave our phones in the kitchen on silent from now on," I mumbled into my pillow.

"That wouldn't help us leave here any faster." Oanen chuckled as he left the bed to answer the call.

"Hello," he said as he walked from the room.

As much as I wanted to go back to sleep, I knew that Oanen was right. We'd spent the previous day going from place to place, showing the picture of the hooded man. At most places, no one claimed to have seen him. At a select few of the establishments, he'd been noticed, but no one knew who he was. However, I'd noticed a pattern that might help narrow our search. The hooded man liked to slum it and seemed to only visit places the old and poor would go.

Thanks to that little bit of information, Oanen and I were looking at a few days more of searching instead of a few weeks.

I got out of bed and closed myself in the bathroom. Brushing my teeth was a chore. Dark circles ringed my eyes. We'd stayed out too late, and I looked like hell for it. But I shouldn't have. All-nighters shouldn't have been affecting me at all, physically.

As I stripped for a shower, I checked the burns. They weren't looking any better.

I slipped into the water with a sigh and started washing.

The door opened.

"Bad news," Oanen said. "There was another death. A dragon this time."

"Big surprise."

"It is. The death happened a few days ago, but the body was discovered this morning."

"So not the dragon from yesterday."

"Apparently not. Dress warm. We'll have to fly to this one."

The door closed, and I hurried through the rest of my shower. I was a little bummed it wasn't the dragon from the day before. Not that I wanted him to die, but if it had been him, it would have cleared Nicolette's name. I didn't trust the Council's reason for keeping Nicolette in Uttira.

However, clearing Eliana's mom's name wouldn't have solved my biggest problem. I needed to figure out how to not die or kill Grandma Irene before we went to talk to her.

Thankfully, my hope that we'd find the killer yesterday had been too lofty. The city was big and the non-human community too suspicious. That meant I had more time. It also meant, Oanen's worry would only grow.

Oanen hadn't mentioned it when I'd started yawning by eight

last night. He'd only stopped at a corner store, like I'd asked, to grab some breakfast food so we wouldn't need to keep going out. I didn't mind eating at restaurants, but I didn't want to waste any more time than necessary…more for Eliana's sake than my own.

Fifteen minutes and a bowl of cereal later, I stood on the balcony, Oanen's clothes already in the bag on my back. He shifted quickly and dipped a knee.

"You make me nervous when you skip breakfast," I said climbing on.

He twisted his head to look at me.

"I'm worried a random rabbit is going to distract you mid-flight." He clacked his beak at me and bit the cuff of my jeans. I grinned.

"Come on, bird boy, before you get any hungrier."

The feathers around his neck ruffled a bit before he leapt into the air with enough force to make me squeal.

The flight to the island didn't take long. Seated between two bodies of water, the place was big enough for a few buildings but was lush with greenery instead. Oanen circled, dropping lower with each pass. On the third one, we were low enough for me to see bits of cement and steel in the green. He landed on top of a building that had a large hole in its roof.

I hesitated to get off when Oanen bent his leg.

"I better not fall through," I said. "I have a feeling falling into this building would be as nasty as falling into a lake."

He tugged on my pant leg with his beak, and I slid off. He shifted to his skin and crossed his arms, giving me his pre-lecture look.

"You are not allowed to lecture naked. It's too distracting," I said tossing the bag at him and turning my back.

"You think I'd hunt a rabbit with you on my back?" he asked.

"Ew. You'd actually eat a raw rabbit," I teased as I listened to him zip his pants.

"A little bit of cereal in your belly," he said close to my ear, "and you're nothing but trouble."

I turned and lightly kissed him.

"You like me this way."

"I do." He wrapped his arms around me and kissed me more firmly before pulling away.

I shivered lightly, and it had nothing to do with his toe-curling kiss.

"Let's get you inside."

He led me to the roof exit and opened the door.

"The hole isn't real," he said. "You should have felt the tingle of magic when we landed."

I cringed, but he didn't say anything else, and that worried me more than any lecture.

Inside, the building looked fairly nice. Much better than either trolls' place.

We walked down the well-lit flight of stairs to the hall.

"Third door on the left," Oanen said.

I followed him to the open door and stopped short at the smell. Oanen frowned slightly and walked further into the room. I covered my nose and mouth with my hand and stepped in behind him.

The man lay on his couch, his prone pose peaceful. The serene smile on his face seemed out of place. Probably because of the scowl lines between his eyes.

"He's been dead several days for sure," Oanen said pulling back the man's sleeve and looking at the darkened underside of his arm.

I looked around the room while he continued to inspect the body. Every piece of furniture looked old. Really old. But all well cared for. I didn't know much about antiques, but the pieces seemed like they were from different eras.

"I don't get it," I said, my sleeve muffling my words. "Why go from killing trolls to killing a dragon? Other than being all males and dying with a smile, there's no pattern."

"No pattern that we're seeing," Oanen said.

My sleeve stopped working, and I gagged.

"I'll be on the roof," I said, backing up a step.

Oanen's gaze pinned me, and he opened his mouth. However, whatever he saw when he looked at me had his expression changing.

"I won't be long. Stay on the roof, and keep the door open so I can hear you. A little fresh air will do this place some good."

I nodded and fled before I threw up all over the crime scene.

CHAPTER ELEVEN

"ARE YOU SURE YOU'RE OKAY?" ELIANA ASKED, YET AGAIN.

"I'm fine. You would have sounded breathless and shaky, too, if you'd inhaled a whiff of four-day old dead dragon."

My stomach rolled sickeningly.

"It's a smell I'm never going to forget. I don't know how Oanen is still down there. He's going to need a shower after this."

"I like showers!" a high-pitched voice shouted in the background.

Eliana gave a long-suffering sigh.

"Please tell me you're getting closer to figuring out who really did this."

"I wish I could. It would have been great if this dragon was freshly dead."

"Uh?"

"It would have been clear evidence that your mom wasn't responsible."

"Oh, yeah. Well, not that I'm wishing for any fresh deaths, but you're right. It would have been convenient."

"How's it going? Is she being a good mom?"

"Absolutely. She's the perfect succubus mom. She brought me an assortment of toys yesterday. And I'm not talking teddy bears. Also, she assures me she'll get me a teddy immediately. Not the stuffed kind." She lowered her voice. "I'm afraid I..."

I angrily kicked at the roof's ledge when the silence grew. My hate for the Council only increased.

"I'm sure the Council would understand matricide in these circumstances," I joked, desperate to lighten her mood.

Eliana gave a weak laugh.

"I better go check on Elbner. The less I'm at home being showered by my mother's affection and sage advice, the better."

"Let me know if either he or Piepen has anything useful to say."

"I will."

When I hung up and turned around, Oanen was leaning against the door.

"Feeling better?" he asked.

"Yep."

He took a step toward me, and I held up a hand.

"You don't smell like him, do you?"

Oanen cocked his head and studied me, worry clouding his eyes.

"You were never this squeamish."

"Wrong. The sight of blood and gore, I can handle. Seeing Aubrey eat someone, while gross, was no problem. Watching Trammer blow his brains out was upsetting because of Ashlyn, but not because of the graphic display. Seeing the oracle gobble mermaids whole? Well, that was just fun. But, in every one of those situations, not once was I exposed to a smell like I was in there. I'm not visually squeamish. It's all about the nose. So stop worrying, and tell me you found something that will help us figure this out faster."

"I did. He's the dragon whose burger you ate the first day here."

I frowned.

"That means he had to have run into the hooded guy again after. It's a three-day window."

"Three days of footage we already covered at the Gizzard."

"Crap. How are we supposed to find this guy?" I paced the roof for a moment. "We know the victim, have a suspect, and know the timeframe. I say we keep asking around. Only this time, we have more details."

It shouldn't have been that hard. At least, not in my way of thinking.

However, a day later, we weren't any closer to finding the hooded man.

"You're getting edgy again," Oanen observed as I tossed my hairbrush to the vanity counter.

I gave him a so-what look.

"It's close to noon, and I'm hungry."

He shook his head, not buying my explanation.

"Since coming here, you get worse after you get edgy."

I exhaled slowly and tried to ignore the annoyance that had started crawling under my skin late last night. We'd managed to stay out until three a.m. before I'd said I needed sleep.

"I'm—"

"Fine. I know." He straightened away from the doorway. "Let's go out for breakfast. We can ask around while we eat."

I nodded and followed him out of the apartment.

On the street, I could feel wisps of wicked. Nothing to set me off but enough to make me think I'd been right the day before. Whenever I got a burn, my ability to sense wickedness seemed suppressed for a while. And Oanen had noticed the pattern before I had.

The ride to the restaurant was quiet except for the ping of Oanen's phone.

"Want me to check it?" I asked.

"Nah. It can wait until after we eat."

"You think it's another dead body, don't you?"

"I do."

I reached into his pocket and withdrew his phone. He didn't try to stop me from scanning the message.

"Another dragon," I said, sliding the phone back into his pocket. "Same building as the last one." I looked out the window. "And your mom wants to know if I'm feeling any better."

"Are you mad?" he asked after a moment.

"No. I get that I'm worrying you, and I'm sorry for it."

We didn't say anything else until he pulled in front of a familiar non-human diner. Oanen caught my hand before I could reach for the door.

"Don't be sorry, Megan. Just let me help."

"You are."

I leaned forward and kissed him lightly. Worry that bordered on fear consumed me then vanished.

In that moment, I knew I was in trouble. It had nothing to do with killing my grandma or my burns but everything to do with my heart. I loved Oanen. So much that it hurt to breathe.

"You just paled."

"I'm sure I did," I said, reaching up and gently running my fingers through his hair. "You were in my head."

He closed his eyes briefly.

"I'm sorry. I didn't mean to let it slip."

"Don't be sorry for caring, Oanen." I exhaled deeply and set my head on his shoulder. "I can't wait for all of this to be over. I want to go home and paint our house rainbow colors and make the Council twitchy just for fun."

He grunted a half laugh and stroked his hand over my hair. We took comfort in each other for a silent moment before I pulled away.

"Sitting here won't make my dreams come true any faster. Let's eat so we can get to the corpse before it starts to smell."

His lips twitched, and he got out to open the door for me.

"From any other person, that statement might worry me."

I stood on my toes and pressed a quick kiss to his cheek.

"That just means I'm your kind of warped," I said.

The wisps of annoyance intensified the moment Oanen opened the diner's door for me. Playing it cool, I didn't hesitate. I went straight to an open booth and plopped down. Oanen slid in across from me and grabbed a menu from the holder. He tried to offer the single, laminated sheet to me, but I shook my head.

"I already know what I want," I said. "You sure it's okay to eat first?"

"I learned my lesson the last time we left here without feeding you. Besides, it's not like the guy's going anywhere."

The same waitress as before came to our table and set two waters down.

"I know what I want," I said before she could leave.

"All right. What can I get you?"

"Two eggs, over-easy. Bacon. A double order. Hash browns with onions and cheese. And a side order of pancakes."

"You got it." She turned her attention to Oanen without writing anything down. "You know what you want?"

"The same, please."

She nodded and went back to the kitchen.

"I'm going to ask around while we wait for our food. Don't move from this table," Oanen said.

He took his phone out and brought up the camera app, using it to scan the room. It took a second to realize he was using it to check if the hooded man was in the diner with us.

"Smart and good-looking," I said. "I might just keep you."

He winked at me and left our booth. I kept an eye on him as he went around the diner, showing the picture to the patrons. I wasn't the only one keeping tabs on Oanen, however. The waitress watched him closely, too. Hopefully, she wasn't thinking of trying to kick us out for disturbing customers or something. I wanted my food.

The phone in my pocket buzzed, and I took it out, expecting a message from Eliana. Instead, I saw my mom's number.

Rumor is that you haven't left town yet. For your sake, those better be unfounded rumors.

My temper flared. The old me would have been slightly cowed by this kind of message. Not the new, abandoned-and-so-over-it me.

Your mom-card expired the day you ditched me in Uttira. Stop acting like you care now.

I watched the phone, waiting for a reply, but none came.

Oanen slid back into the booth.

"Eliana again?" he asked.

I was saved from answering by the arrival of the waitress.

She set down our plates, and my mouth watered with anticipation. I was so focused on the food, I almost didn't catch her reaching out to place a hand on Oanen's shoulder.

"The plate's hot. Be careful."

She walked away before I could decide if she was being handsy.

Oanen reached out and touched his plate. With a frown, he picked up his fork and started eating.

"What's the frown for?" I asked, picking up my own fork.

He chewed slowly and nodded toward my food. I took a bite and almost groaned. It was so good. Or, maybe, I was just that hungry.

"Here," Oanen said lifting a bite from his plate toward me. "You think the eggs are good? Try the hash browns."

I swallowed and opened my mouth, more than willing to eat some of his share. And, I almost spit out the ice-cold hash browns as soon as my mouth closed around his fork. Only the light press of Oanen's foot on top of mine stopped me. I chewed quickly and swallowed.

"You're an amazing man for sharing your food."

His lips twitched, and he continued to eat his cold meal. After a moment and another press to my foot, I dug into mine.

What the hell was up with our sucky waitress? There was no way his plate was hot. She'd probably stuck the damn thing in the freezer. It would explain why it took so long to bring the food out.

I chewed and watched Oanen turn his plate to get to his eggs. Then turn it again to get to his bacon. I'd never noticed that quirk before. When he cleared that plate, he slid the pancake plate toward him while shuffling the cold plate over.

"Are you almost finished?" I asked after he had taken one bite.

I didn't play with my food. Despite the weirdness of his meal, I'd quickly decimated mine.

"Yep. No rush, though. I like watching you eat."

His gaze flicked to mine, gold flooding into the blue.

"I don't even know where your mind went just now, but keep it to yourself."

His lips twitched, and he pulled out his wallet to leave money on the table.

"Let's go, troublemaker."

"Hey, I was a complete angel this time."

I followed him out of the restaurant and got into the car. He circled around the car and got in more quickly than usual.

"In a rush?" I asked.

"Maybe." He started the car and pulled out into traffic before reaching into his pocket and handing me a folded piece of paper.

"What does it say?" he asked. He tapped his fingers on the wheel showing his agitation.

I looked at the writing.

"It's an address. That's it. Where did this come from?"

"The waitress. It fell into my lap when I moved the cold plate."

"The waitress was watching you show the hooded man's picture," I said. "Do you think this is his address?"

"I do. She told us to be careful. It sure wasn't because of a hot plate."

"Dead body or mysterious address?" I said, mostly to myself. Looking at the body first meant less smell and clearing Nicolette faster if we could prove he died after Adira took her. Checking out the address meant finding the killer, clearing Nicolette, and getting to my great-grandma's place faster. Something I wasn't prepared for.

"Dead body," I said at the same time he said, "Mysterious address."

He glanced at me.

"You don't think we should check out the address first?" he asked.

"Nope. I don't trust the waitress. What if it's a setup, and someone's there waiting for us? Impatient people make mistakes. Better to let them wait and get restless."

He focused on the road and was silent for a moment.

"Is that the only reason?"

"No. I also want to clear Nicolette's name for Eliana. There's no saying that finding this hooded guy without proving the body was killed while Nicolette was in Uttira will result in Nicolette's freedom. We'd need the guy to confess. And, I'm honestly not sure I'm up for pulling a confession from anyone right now."

"You're right. We'll check out the body."

This time, instead of taking off from the condo, he drove to Port Morris and found a quiet spot to park.

"How are we going to do this? The clouds are higher today."

"We're going in low and fast. The island's right there."

He pointed to the island just off shore. I could see bits of a crumbling building from where we stood, and I wondered if it was another illusion.

A rustle of clothes was the only warning I had before Oanen's pants landed on my head.

"You're weird, you know that?" I said.

"Just be grateful I don't wear underwear."

"Ew. And under no circumstances should you start," I said.

"Because you'd miss the impressive views?" he asked close to my ear.

I shivered—this one had everything to do with proximity—as he reached around me and set the rest of his clothes in my arms.

"I don't know," I hedged. "I haven't really seen anything impressive."

He chuckled low in my ear.

"Now, you're just being mean. Ready to ride me, Fury?"

A flush erupted on my face and raced all the way to my toes. Need flooded my mind only to disappear a moment later when Oanen's feathered head nudged my back.

"Yeah. Hold on. That last comment robbed me of the ability to think, and I still need to put your clothes away." I took a moment to fan my face then filled the backpack.

The ride to the island was just as fast as he'd promised. And, the icy wind on my face actually felt good, this time.

When we landed on the same roof as before, I didn't hesitate to slide off, ditch the bag, and face the door. Oanen's low, knowing chuckle kept me flushed for an extra few moments while he dressed.

"I like this," he said, turning me in his arms.

I took a quick peek down and found all his views were covered.

"Disappointed?" he asked.

"Relieved. My face feels like it's about to burst into flames."

"It's almost as attractive as when your eyes glow."

He kissed the tip of my nose then led me toward the door.

"It won't be as bad this time," he promised.

"Does that mean the other body is gone?"

"Yes."

"Who took it?"

"We have our own version of funeral homes and morticians."

"Nope. Don't say any more. I don't want to know."

We walked down a single flight of stairs and went to another apartment on the same floor as the previous day. We didn't proceed past the first door in the hall this time.

"This is the one," he said.

He opened the door and went inside. Thankfully, there wasn't any odor. I looked around the barren apartment noting that, unlike the other guy, this one hadn't collected much. But, then I noticed dents in the carpet.

"Did someone clear this place out already?" I asked.

Oanen snapped a few pictures of the dents with his phone and spent a little time studying the patterns on the floor.

"I'll ask for more information."

He moved down the hall. Like a good little shadow, I stuck close.

We found the dragon in the bedroom. The bed was neatly

made beneath him, and a folded piece of paper waited on the nightstand.

Enforcer,

Stop looking for him. He's doing us all a favor.

Magroal

I looked at the smiling dragon's face, trying to reconcile him with the bitter dragon I'd met the day before.

"He's the one who ate the burger and left. Call the Council. With my eyewitness sighting of this guy after Nicolette was taken plus his note, they have to let Nicolette go."

Oanen nodded but continued his examination of the guy and the room. While I waited, I sent a text to Eliana.

Freedom is one phone call away. Get ready to say goodbye to mommy-dearest!

I waited for a reply, but none came. A ball of worry formed in my stomach. This was the girl who rushed out of class to answer my phone call.

Everything okay? I texted after three minutes went by.

Everything is fine. See you soon, hopefully.

Relieved, I tucked my phone away and went to stare out the window. Nicolette would be cleared today, and I still didn't have a plan. But, it didn't really matter. While I could already predict what Oanen's reaction would be, the final decision about what to do was up to me. And there was no way I was going to kill someone else just so I could live.

"That was a big sigh. Ready to go?" Oanen asked.

"Yeah. Did you call the Council?"

"Not yet. I was going to wait until we were back in the car."

There was no playful striptease on the roof, which made for a colder ride back to Port Morris.

Before we even landed, I felt a strand of wicked calling to me. It grew stronger with each beat of Oanen's massive wings. I braced myself for the pull.

As soon as Oanen landed, I slipped from his back and raced for the car. At the last minute, I tossed the backpack on the ground then slammed the door shut. Closing my eyes, I tried to focus.

"Hold it in. Just don't let go," I mumbled to myself.

The intensity of the wickedness crawled under my skin. It begged for my attention. It demanded my intervention.

"You can do this. You can hold it."

The car door creaked. My eyes popped open, and I stared at Oanen. The orange glow on his face said it all.

"Is everything all right?" he asked calmly, his face a careful blank mask.

"No, I have to go to the bathroom. Get in so we can go."

He cocked his head at me as he slowly got in.

"You just lied to me."

"Stupid lie detector. Just hurry up, Oanen. We have to go."

He started the car and turned around. I refused to look at the man who was slowly walking down the side-street towards us.

"I'm trying to be patient," Oanen said quietly. "I'm trying to be understanding. But, it's hard to do when you won't tell me what's going on. Or worse. When you lie to me."

The more distance we placed between the man walking down the road and the car, the easier it was to think clearly. It didn't mean I was out of danger. I could now feel the wisps of wicked crawling under my skin. How much longer did I have before I wouldn't be able to resist it?

"Talk to me, Megan. Now." The complete authority in Oanen's voice made my fury stir.

"This is one of those times that you don't want to push, Oanen."

"This is one of those times I think I need to push."

I partially growled and groaned.

"Fine. I wanted to whip out my fury card on that guy

walking down the street, okay? Given our current goals, I didn't think it was the right time to stop and punish someone. Better?"

In response, the steering wheel groaned under his white knuckled grip.

His fear hit me hard, and I mentally staggered under the weight of it.

"No. There's more you're not telling me."

"Tonight, Oanen. Whether we find anything at this address or not, we'll talk. I promise. Will you just give me until then so we can focus on helping Eliana and stopping this killer without distraction?"

"The distraction is there, Megan, whether we talk about it or not. But, yes. I'll drop it for now, and we'll talk tonight."

He turned his golden gaze on me.

"No exceptions. No more delays."

CHAPTER TWELVE

WE PARKED ACROSS THE STREET FROM A HOUSE THAT LOOKED exceptionally normal. The well-kept, three-story home was squished between two not so nice-looking houses. Those houses matched the rest of the neighborhood, which was why a tingle kept worming around under my skin. I itched to get out of the car and confront the sources. But, I knew better than to give in. Instead, I tried to focus on Oanen's half of the conversation with the Council.

"Megan spoke to him the day after Nicolette was taken into custody. It proves she's not responsible."

A long drawn out pause followed that statement. I tried to read Oanen's expression for clues, but he wasn't giving much away. Not since my promise to talk after we were done here.

"I disagree," he said, "and can confidently speak on Megan's behalf that she disagrees, too."

I frowned. I trusted Oanen. He knew me well enough to speak on my behalf if he thought it necessary. Why was it necessary, though? The evidence couldn't be any clearer.

"No. Nothing has changed. She seems more tired and not as quick to anger."

"She's sitting right next to you, too," I said, "and feeling plenty of anger. What's going on?"

"I understand," he said, just before hanging up.

Without me needing to threaten bodily harm, he turned toward me and started talking.

"They don't believe Nicolette is innocent and won't remove her house arrest."

"What? Are they deaf or blind? Or just stupid?" I clenched my fists and wished I was in Uttira.

"Neither. They believe she's working with someone or maybe several people. Adira wouldn't give me more information than that. She asked how you were doing and if you've run into any wicked."

That just pissed me off more. She knew something. I was sure of it.

"Fine. Adira and the Council are once again useless. No offense to your parents."

"None taken. I agree with you. They're up to something. We'll need to prove without a doubt that Nicolette is innocent by finding the real killer."

He looked at the house, again.

"I think it's time to say hello," I said, reaching for the door.

Sleeping in until noon meant that we hadn't had much daylight when we started out. After going to the island then heading to New Jersey, not much remained. As we let ourselves in the gate, a hint of twilight creeped into the sky.

"I want you to stay behind me," Oanen said softly, holding the gate so I could pass.

"Fine." I knew he was trying to watch out for me. But no matter where I stood, if the hooded guy was truly wicked, I wouldn't be able to hold myself back. Even if Oanen was in the way.

I followed him up the steps and waited on the small porch as he knocked.

A curtain to our right moved a few moments prior to the door opening. Instead of the guy from the bar, a young woman looked at us questioningly.

"Can I help you?"

"I hope so," Oanen said. "We're looking for someone." He pulled out his phone and showed her the picture of the hooded man.

I saw the flicker of recognition in her eyes before she looked up at us.

"Sorry. I can't help you."

"Can't or won't?" I asked.

"My name is Oanen Quill. This is Megan Smith. We're here on behalf of the Uttira Council," he said. "And, you know what that is because you knew not to lie just now. How do you know this man?"

She started to shut the door.

Oanen stepped forward to block it with his hand. As soon as his palm crossed the plane of the threshold, he flew backward. He hit the fence with a metal clatter and crashed to the ground.

Rage filled me, and I turned to the door.

"Elizabeth Sias, open the damn door."

"Megan, quiet," Oanen said. The strain in his words made my anger worse.

I fisted my hand, ready to beat down the puny panel keeping me from kicking the ass of the girl who just fried my boyfriend.

Oanen's fingers captured mine.

"I'm fine. And you just figured out her name," he said softly. "And, right now, she's talking on the phone. I'm trying to listen."

His explanation and a quick glance at him calmed some of my anger.

"It'll take more than a fence to hurt me. You know that." He kissed my temple gently then slowly tugged me away from the door.

"We're looking for a man named Zayn. Elizabeth knows him well. She told him not to come home."

"So a girlfriend, wife, or relative."

"Exactly what I'm thinking. And if that's the case, he's on his way here because he'll want to keep her safe."

"She's not in danger."

"He doesn't know that. And right now, she's watching us leave. When the car doesn't move, she'll let him know."

We got back into the car. Street lights came on, and the curtain in the window moved again.

"Stay here. No matter what," he said, reaching for his door.

"Where are you going?"

"To the roof. I'll be able to see more from up there." He paused and gave me a stern look. "Say it. Say you'll keep your butt in that seat no matter what."

My fury stirred again, and I couldn't keep my mouth shut.

"No. What you really want me to say is that you're cute when you're all domineering. Not going to happen, bird boy. Bossy isn't attractive."

His pupils dilated noticeably.

"Megan..."

"I will stay in the car. Now, stop being a bully and go fly away."

He exhaled slowly and left the car without kissing me, an indication of how far I'd pushed him.

Sulking, I watched the house.

What the hell was my problem? Everything was off. My temperature. My mood. My ability to sense any wickedness. My ability to send the wicked to hell. I was a broken fury. And if I wasn't careful, I was going to break one of the few things I still had going right.

Restless and feeling sorry for myself, I pulled out my phone and called Eliana.

"Yeah, what's up?" she answered, sounding annoyed.

"Everything okay?"

"Get off my pillow. I told you not to do that," she said in a strained and slightly muffled voice. Before I could ask what she was talking about, her words became clear again. "I need to find Piepen a better home."

A high-pitched squeal came from the background, followed by fervent begging.

"You do what you need to do," I said, feeling bad I'd made a mess for Eliana. It seemed I was on a roll for messing up relationships.

"Thanks. I gotta go."

The line went dead.

Sighing, I pocketed the phone and leaned back in my seat. Rather than focus on the wisps of wicked around me, I closed my eyes.

"You can do this, Megan."

"Wake."

The word echoed in my mind, pulling me from a deep sleep. If not for the ache in my shoulder and the chill penetrating my legs, I would have tried to ignore the command. Uncomfortable and more than a little cranky because of my discomfort, I opened my eyes to look for my pillow and blanket.

Instead of seeing familiar bedroom walls, I saw a face I knew well from the picture on my phone.

"You," I said, trying to sit up. I couldn't get my hands under myself.

"Here," he said, reaching for me. "Let me help you."

He helped me from my side-lying position to sitting up against a beam.

I frowned at my bound hands and feet, confused. I couldn't remember confronting him or trying to send him to hell. Nothing new hurt on me. No burns. So then, what had happened? How was I no longer in the car, and why wasn't I angry?

Giving my bonds an experimental tug, I studied the now unhooded-man.

"Zayn, right?"

"Correct. And those are magic bindings," he said. "Like last time." He tilted his hand and studied me. "How did you get out of the last ones?"

"Why don't I want to send you to hell?"

He smiled slightly.

"Because I've been good lately, not breaking any rules. Human or non-human."

A shimmer in the air just behind him caught my attention. I sat in the center of another large space. A table lit with a dangling overhead light lay just behind the guy squatting before me. However, between him and the table, a shimmer of something moved in the air, creating a bubble around us.

"More magic?" I asked.

"Yes. For your protection. I've invited a few people here and wasn't sure if you'd be ready to face them."

"What do you mean?"

He shifted slightly on the balls of his feet, pivoting just enough to expose the three older men sitting at the table. Their rough, weathered faces were turned in our direction. Their dark eyes were filled with a weary acceptance I'd seen before.

"They are dragons with more years than either of us can hope to see. And with those years come a lot of mistakes." He shrugged lightly. "Or, rather, choices a fury might not agree with."

That last statement drew my attention back to the hooded man.

"You know what I am and took me anyway?" I asked.

"I know what you are, and I know once you understand, you'll have no reason to come after me."

"I doubt that."

"You've said it yourself. You have no desire to punish me. That's because I've done nothing wrong."

My gaze flicked back to the dragons.

"Why do I need protection from them?"

His grin widened.

"This shield isn't to protect you from them but from yourself. You're a fourth-generation fury, and I don't want you burning yourself out. The last thing I want is for the other three to come after me because I wasn't careful."

I snorted.

"Right."

"What part do you doubt? My fear of you or my care?"

"Any of it. All of it."

"I know a lot of things I shouldn't. Trust me when I say I will take the utmost care of you. Now, be patient and listen. You'll understand what's going on soon enough."

He patted my stretched-out leg and stood, leaving the shield. As soon as he stepped through it, the shimmer turned into an opaque green like I was sitting in an upside-down glass bowl. My ears popped painfully, but I could suddenly hear things. Seagulls crying out. Distant traffic. The quiet murmur of deep voices coming from the table.

I could also feel.

One of those three dragons was not like the others. Oh, they all had a level of wicked that made my skin feel too tight. But, one of them had done things that begged me to send him straight to hell. My gaze locked on the one with longer, grey-streaked hair he kept back in a low ponytail.

I opened my mouth, the words to demand a confession from Rylee McGoan on the tip of my tongue. However, not a sound emerged.

Rage clawed at my middle, and I struggled with my bonds.

"We'll need to speak quickly," Zayn Sias said. "I don't know how long that spell will hold her."

"Why is she here? Why are we here?" the dragon closest to me asked. His dark eyes watched me instead of Zayn.

"She's here as a witness. You're here because each of you has spoken to me about your desire for the old ways to return. About your discontent with the way things are now.

"I cannot change your lives for you. I cannot miraculously fulfill your dreams of flying free or eating whatever you'd like. None of us can break those rules without consequence. And that's why she's here. To be a witness. So that she knows, and so that you know, what I'm saying is the truth and what I'm doing is within the bounds of what we are allowed to do."

While he spoke, my anger and the need to free myself intensified. Knowing what would happen, when I gave into the urge gripping me hard, didn't even give me pause.

My gaze remained focused on the furthest of the three men; and the intense, burning need to punish only grew stronger with each passing second. The space within my magic cage began to warm and reflect an orange glow. And, it wasn't just from my eyes.

I could feel the fire growing inside of me. I tried to hold it back. I knew what would happen if I completely gave in to it. I could feel my old burns starting to tingle with pain. Yet, I was helpless to completely stop what was happening or my need to punish.

"Get to the point, Druid," the middle dragon growled.

"Yes, of course. I'm here to offer you an opportunity to be free of your oppression. To make a stand against it. To give your life for it. I won't promise redemption. I won't promise you will go to a better place once you're gone. But I can promise your soul will be used to create something that will always stand against those who wish to oppress the unique and undesired."

A tingle of pain encircled my wrists, and I looked down at my bonds. Green sparks flew from the metal as flames engulfed my hands. Like the last few times my fire appeared, it seared my skin. And, like the last few times, I couldn't stop any of it.

I opened my mouth to cry out, but nothing came. In agony, I raged against my silence, the rage feeding my fury to the point where I stopped feeling.

"You want to kill us?" the first dragon asked. "Use us in some type of ritual sacrifice?"

"Yes," Zayn said with not an ounce of shame or remorse.

He'd just admitted to wanting to kill them; yet, I still felt not even a hint of wickedness from him and everything from the three dragons.

"You've all admitted to me that you're weary of this existence. That you're tired of what this world has to offer you. I'm offering to help you find a quick and peaceful end. An opportunity to use what's left of your existence in a way that strikes a small blow of retribution against those who oppressed you. That's all. If you're not interested, you are free to leave. There's no spell keeping you here. If you are interested, I will willingly accept the gift of your soul, and I will respect any dying wishes that you have."

The metal binding my wrists burst apart with a loud snap.

Zayn, who'd been focused on the dragons, glanced at me as I reached for the bindings on my ankles.

"We don't have much time," he said. "As soon as the fury is free, you will want to be gone."

I set my hands on my ankles and watched the flames burn through the shackles there. Free, I got to my feet and moved to the green surrounding me. It sizzled and sparked as I neared it.

All four of the men were watching me now. Zayn's eyes were filled with urgency. We both knew it wouldn't be long now.

"There's nothing else I can say that will convince you of my need," Zayn said rapidly. "Many others have already given their souls to my cause. They believed their willing sacrifice would earn them a place in whatever god's realm upon their death. I can't say I believe the same, but I swear you will live on because of your soul-sacrifice. Who among you is ready to be done with this world? Who among you is ready to commit one more act of defiance against those who oppressed you? Who among you will help me?"

I pressed both hands against the barrier. Light engulfed me to the point it was hard to see. Outside the magic bowl, the men squinted.

The dragon who had been quiet so far, the one pulling me with his wickedness, finally spoke.

"I will."

And with two words, he set my world on fire.

"He is mine!" I screamed.

Rage consumed me. Ablaze, I could feel my skin giving way to the fury. I struck the shield with my fists, raining blows on the druid's magic.

Two of the dragons fled seconds before I burned through the shield.

"No!" Zayn yelled as I stepped through the remnants of the shimmer. "Please, I need him."

Yet, he didn't try to stop me from reaching out for the dragon.

The old one stood as I stopped before him, his steady gaze on me. He didn't flinch as I reached out and grabbed him by the neck.

"Don't do this," Zayn begged. "How many burns do you have already? You can't condemn him to hell. You can only condemn yourself."

His words barely registered through the words ricocheting in my mind.

"Rylee McGoan, confess."

"Fury, I have done many things in my life. More than most. Confessing would take more time than either of us cares to give. Take me to hell. If you can." His gaze shifted to the druid who was mumbling something I couldn't understand.

"Maybe next time, Fury," the dragon said with a slight smile.

"No. This time, I'll get it right."

"Rylee McGoan, I condemn you to he—" A bone-shattering ache exploded in my core. My mouth opened in a silent scream as the flames finished engulfing me.

Darkness extinguished my vision, but not before I saw the fire spread to Rylee, who smiled serenely at me.

"Fury?"

A trickle of cold water splashed on my face. I turned my head and opened my mouth, taking a small drink and sputtering.

"Thank the useless gods," a familiar voice said. "I thought you'd gone too far and burned yourself out."

I wasn't so sure I hadn't. My skin felt raw and exposed. Like

I'd been burned all over. That thought created an avalanche of memories that dumped on me all at once.

Opening my eyes, I groaned.

"I think I can help you heal a bit if you'll allow me," Zayn said.

"Yes." I didn't care what he did. I just wanted the pain to stop. Even my eyelids hurt.

He held up a tin, twisted the top off, and dug out a finger full of salve.

"Open up and try to swallow as quickly as possible. Your gag reflex will only increase the longer it sits in your mouth."

I opened up, and he swiped the paste so far back, I almost gagged anyway.

"Swallow," he said.

I did, just as the taste hit me. The rancid tang had me gagging as an aftereffect.

"Sorry. There isn't a way to make that more pleasant tasting without ruining the spell."

He reached out and pulled back the blanket covering me. I wanted to grab it back and swear, but I couldn't move. Everything hurt.

"Why am I naked?" I rasped.

"You burned everything away."

Burned away my clothes? That hadn't happened before.

He continued to look down at me. I did, too, but had to turn my head away from the sight of my raw flesh. How close had I come to burning myself out like Zayn said?

My gaze caught on the crisp husk of a body not far from me, and I gasped. The dragon. He'd been burnt to almost nothing. Like me, his clothes were gone. Unlike me, his corpse was blackened from head to toe. A thin bone protruded from behind him, all that remained of his wings.

I closed my eyes against my impotent anger and frustration. I didn't even know what he'd done to deserve that kind of end.

The gods had done this. They'd made me this way by giving me a power that I couldn't control and didn't understand. All the anger I felt in that moment was directed at them for robbing me of the life I should have had.

Something wet trailed from the corner of my eye.

"I don't understand," Zayn said. "The paste should be helping."

CHAPTER THIRTEEN

THE DRUID'S CONCERN CUT THROUGH MY SELF-LOATHING. I TURNED my head away from what I'd done and opened my eyes. As I moved, I noticed there was less pain than before.

"The paste is helping. I don't hurt as much," I assured him.

"You're crying blood, though."

"Yeah, that's just something I do when I'm upset."

I wiped away the tears, careful of my tender skin.

"Or when you're in extreme pain," Zayn said.

I eased myself into a sitting position and tucked the edges of the blanket under my butt, a thin barrier against the cold cement.

"How do you know so much about furies?" I asked.

He gave me a wry smile.

"I'd prefer not to say. Why are you upset?"

I waved a hand at the dragon and exhaled heavily.

"I hate what I am. What I do. I don't even know what the dragon did to deserve that, but I couldn't stop it."

Zayn, who'd been hunkered down on the balls of his feet, sat and studied me. In turn, I did the same. This was the first time I really looked at him without his hood up. And, everything I'd noted before had been done in a fog of panic or anger. I hadn't noticed the green flecks in his kind, hazel eyes or how his hair was long enough it was showing a hint of wave as it fell around his head in disarray. Mostly, I hadn't noticed the crease lines marking his forehead. A sign of constant worry or constant surprise?

"In all the research I've done," he said slowly, "I've never heard of a fury who didn't embrace what she was."

"Yeah, well, I didn't know what I was until a few months ago. My mom ditched me in Uttira without a word of explanation. I thought I was human."

"That had to be a shock."

I shrugged lightly.

"Not as much as it should have been. I guess deep down, I knew something was wrong with me."

"Wrong?"

"I don't want to be who I am. I don't know what the hell is going on half the time. I hate the urges I have to hurt people when I don't even know why. The gods are assholes for making me this way."

"Not gods. Just one. You serve Hades."

"Awesome. Know where he is? I'd like to throat punch the asshole."

Zayn laughed.

"He'd probably find it amusing. You furies are like his daughters. I'm not sure there's much you could do wrong in his eyes."

"Lovely."

"You didn't kill him, by the way. The dragon, I mean."

I arched a brow and glanced at the burnt body.

"His current condition would beg to differ," I said.

"He was gone before the flames consumed him. I gave him

the peaceful, quick end he'd asked for. It wasn't murder. I had his consent."

"I'm too tired and hurt to care one way or another. As long as you're gone before I get my wicked radar back, we're good." I studied his hazel eyes for a moment. "Why are you doing this? Killing all these creatures?"

"Not killing," he said with a pacifying gesture. "I collect their life-energy, or soul, depending on whatever you believe, which they gave freely."

"Okay. But why?"

He grew serious and slightly sad.

"You saw my sister. She's a prisoner of her own home. Because of magic. Because the gods are cruel and made my twin mortal."

Twin? I wasn't expecting that.

Somewhere nearby, a phone buzzed.

"What's your name?" he asked.

"Megan Smith."

"I'm glad I met you. I hope you'll remember this conversation when you wake."

Insistent buzzing near my ear brought me back out of my magically induced sleep. There was no groggy disorientation this time. I knew right where I was and exactly what had happened. It was hard not to remember with the throbbing pain drumming inside my skull and the sickening dance going on in my stomach. I opened my eyes and managed to prop myself up enough so I could throw up.

When I finished heaving, I looked around.

Zayn was gone. He'd left behind his jacket, though, which

he'd laid over me for extra warmth. And my phone. He must have removed it from my coat before sticking me in his shield. I hadn't even thought to check for it after freeing my hands. I'd been too busy with the fury fire burning inside of me.

While I was grateful it hadn't burned up with the rest of my things, I was more grateful that I hadn't thrown up on it. I needed to call Oanen. He was probably worried as hell.

Sighing, I sat up and winced at the pain on my forearms. Zayn's paste had healed most of the burns I'd gained from my little stunt, but the deeper ones on both forearms remained. They throbbed in time with the older burns.

I hissed out a breath and wished I had more of Zayn's ass-paste to eat.

I frowned at that thought, knowing it hadn't come out right.

My phone buzzed again, distracting me, and I picked it up. Oanen's name showed brightly on the display.

"Hello?" I answered.

"Where are you?" His clipped, angry words made me smile. I'd never been so glad to hear his voice.

"I'm not sure. And no, I'm not going outside to check. I'm lying naked on the floor with a blanket and a jacket covering me."

Nothing but silence answered me for several, long heartbeats.

"Whose?"

"Whose what?"

"Whose jacket is covering you?"

"That doesn't matter. Just come get me. I'll turn on my GPS and text you the location."

The line went dead. That seemed a bit overdramatic. I wrinkled my nose at the phone but did as I said I would. Less than a second after I sent the location, he sent back that he was on his way.

With a sigh, I scooted away from my vomit pile and lay back down on the cold floor. It felt good on my head but was making the rest of me ache.

I dozed lightly until a door banged nearby.

"Megan?" Oanen's voice rang out.

"Here."

I didn't bother trying to sit up. I was too tired. Too cold.

Steps scraped against the floor, drawing closer.

When I blinked my eyes open, Oanen was there, already bending down toward me. His carefully blank mask never slipped, but the hold he had on what he was feeling did. Rage, something close to that of a fury's, filled my head along with a paralyzing fear.

"Please tell me you brought the car," I said softly. "I'm too cold to fly."

He made a pained sound and scooped me into his arms. Without a word, he turned on his heel and walked back the way he'd come.

I closed my eyes and leaned my head against his rapidly beating heart.

Moments came and went. Him buckling me in. The vibration of the tires on the road. The sound of cars. The feeling of being carried upstairs. The soft sheets rubbing against the raw places still remaining on my skin. Then, nothing for a while.

When I opened my eyes again, the pain in my head had been downgraded to a mild headache, and the sun had come up to light the bedroom.

I rolled from my side to my back and winced.

The bed beside me moved, and I looked up at Oanen, who was leaning against the headboard.

"How long have I been out?"

"Almost six hours."

I groaned and struggled to sit up, the jacket and blanket from Zayn hampering my movements.

"What happened, Megan? You promised not to leave the car."

His tone had me whipping my head in his direction mid-struggle.

"Are you serious right now? You know better than anyone else what I am. How little control I have over what I do. What the hell do you think happened?"

"I don't know. Where are your clothes? And who gave you this jacket?"

My fury lifted its head wearily.

"No," I said firmly. "I'm not doing this. I'm not going to get angry with you. And I'm not going to deal with your pouty possessiveness right now."

Ignoring the aches and pains, I threw off the jacket and blanket and rose naked from the bed.

"I burned away my clothes and a lot of my skin. Zayn Sias, the druid we've been looking for, covered me and gave me some paste to make the worst of it go away.

"When you're in your right mind, I'll keep my promise, and we'll talk."

I turned my back to him, ignored his soft curse, and marched my butt to the bathroom. After I used the toilet and brushed my teeth, I attempted a shower. It didn't last longer than a hurried hair wash to remove the puke smell. Instead of reaching for a towel to dry off, I just stood there, dripping.

On the other side of the iced-glass partition, the bathroom door opened.

"Did you send him to hell?" Oanen asked.

"No. I can't send anyone to hell. All I do is hurt myself every time I try."

"You hurt yourself trying to send him to hell?"

"No. He's innocent as far as my fury is concerned. I didn't do anything to him."

There was a long moment of silence.

"I'm trying to understand, Megan, but you're making it hard."

I knew he was trying to understand what had happened to me, but he was focusing on who I was with rather than what happened to me. I opened the door so he would get the full picture.

His gaze swept over me, lingering on the burn on my chest and the ones on my hip and arms.

"There's the burn on my back, too. Four times, Oanen. Since the lake, I've tried to send someone to hell four times. Each time, I pass out and wake up with a burn and the inability to feel wickedness."

Understanding started to light his eyes as he crossed his arms.

"The numbness doesn't last long. A day or two, at most. Then I start feeling the wickedness again. That's what I was feeling yesterday in the car. The wickedness was everywhere, but I was sitting there trying to resist the urge to get out and beat someone because I'd promised you I'd stay put. I don't know what happened next. I don't remember leaving, only waking up where you found me.

"Zayn was there along with three dragons. He's not what we thought he was."

"What's that?" Oanen asked softly.

"A killer. He isn't killing the people we're finding dead. He's asking them for their life-force. And some of them are so unhappy with their lives, they're willingly giving it." I looked at the burns on my arms. "These are because one of the dragons was wicked. Very, very wicked. I wanted to hurt him so badly that I couldn't stop myself." I closed my eyes and took a deep breath.

"I remember grabbing him by his throat and then feeling pain. So much pain. When I came to, the dragon was burnt to a crisp. But, Zayn was still there. He was worried I'd pushed myself too far and was trying to heal me. The paste he gave me helped take away some of the pain and heal some of the burns.

"I don't know what he's doing with the life forces he's collecting, but I don't think it's for anything bad. If it was, I would have sensed his wickedness last night before I tried punishing the dragon."

"I don't care about who's wicked or punished or any of that," Oanen said, slowly stalking toward me.

"What I care about is standing in front of me. Bruised. Battered. In pain. And I can't do a thing about it. You're killing me, Megan. Slowly. Methodically. And I can't walk away."

He stopped in front of me and gently put his forehead against mine. I felt every ounce of his anguish.

"I'm sorry," I whispered, hurting for both of us.

"Those aren't the words I want to hear."

I knew what words he wanted. And even though admitting it terrified me, I owed him the truth.

"I love you, Oanen. So much it hurts to breathe at the thought you might be ready to give up on me."

His hand cupped the back of my head.

"Never," he said just before his lips touched mine.

He stole my breath with each gentle taste and touch until I broke away, panting. He set his forehead on mine again.

"Thank you," he said softly.

"I didn't do anything."

"You did. You gave me your heart. It's mine. Now and always. It's all I've wanted since our first flight."

I smiled softly before reality intruded.

"We need to call the Council and tell them what happened."

He exhaled heavily and pulled back from me.

"I doubt they'll listen. They know there's something wrong with your abilities and aren't trusting your word."

My fury tried to lift her head again.

"Nope," I said firmly. "Not worth it. Save your strength."

Oanen gave me an odd look.

"I'm not going to let my fury get riled up over the Council. She needs a break, or my powers will kill me."

His expression grew serious, and as he moved away to grab some ointment, I continued to air dry and stare off into space.

"We can't sit here and do nothing. We know what Nicolette is like. How she gets in a person's head and makes them do things they might not want to do otherwise. If she does that to Eliana..."

"Eliana is stronger than you think," he said.

"She's also more fragile than you want to admit."

Oanen started spreading ointment on my burns, soothing the rest of my pain. It was nice having someone wait on me.

My eyes widened.

"Elbner," I said loud enough to make Oanen wince.

"Sorry. I just realized we have a witness. Elbner can tell the Council it was Zayn."

"Elbner is still spelled."

"Yes, but once it's out that we know it's Zayn, it's common knowledge; and he'll be able to speak it. Just like the library, right?"

Oanen's lips twitched.

"I love seeing the excitement in your eyes," he said.

"I gotta get my phone."

I moved to run from the bathroom at the same moment he reached forward to dab more salve on my front. Instead of touching the burn, his fingers brushed the top of my right breast. We both froze.

Gold exploded in his eyes, and his palm slowly closed over me, making my skin tingle with an expanding warmth.

"Please don't take this the wrong way," I said breathlessly, "but this really isn't the right time."

He nodded, but his fingers began stroking the sensitive skin. I pressed forward into his palm. His hand lightly tested the weight and shape of me. Then his thumb brushed over the peak.

I struggled to keep my head as heat licked its way from my middle upward. Need scorched me, and I knew it wasn't all my own when his pupils dilated.

"Oanen. We need to think of Eliana."

He made a pained noise and removed his hand.

"Go."

I fled the bathroom and grabbed my phone from the nightstand. It was hard to hear the dial tone over the beating of my heart.

"Eliana, you need to get to Elbner," I said as soon as she answered. "Tell him I know his master was Zayn Sias. I know Zayn was the one responsible for all the creatures who died with a smile. Tell Elbner I'm making it common knowledge. Once you do that, you should be able to take him to the Council as a witness. Got it?"

"Yes. Zayn Sias. Got it. Thank you."

She hung up without saying anything else. I could only imagine how stressed out she was with her mom there.

A gentle touch to my back had me looking over my shoulder. Oanen's gaze was locked on the burn there, but I could tell from his eyes that his mind was still focused on something else.

"I don't think there's anything else for us to do here," I said.

"Oh, I think there's plenty to do."

"I mean, now that we know the cause behind the deaths, we should probably leave. Track down my great-grandma." Even as I said it, I mentally cringed at the idea.

"There's no rush. We can wait a few days for you to heal."

I knew what he had in mind while we waited and turned fully to capture his hands.

"I don't think you understand."

"I'll admit it's been a little hard to focus with you walking around naked."

"You do it all the time."

He nodded slowly, letting his gaze drift downward, and sighed wistfully.

"But I don't look like you."

I snorted a laugh.

"Don't move."

He stayed where I left him while I went to his suitcase and grabbed one of his button-down shirts. It was soft and big and easier to put on than a t-shirt. With the sleeves rolled up and only a few middle buttons used, it didn't bother any of my burns, either.

He groaned as I walked toward him.

"You have no idea how sexy you are. Wearing my shirt just made it so much better."

"Focus, Oanen."

He heaved a sigh and sat on the edge of the bed.

"What don't I understand?"

"I'm stuck in a spiral of self-destruction. I feel someone wicked, try to send them to hell, burn myself in the process, and suppress my abilities for a few days just to do it all again. Only I'm not healing. Or regulating my temperature like I used to. I'm more tired every time."

The concern on his face grew the longer I spoke.

"What are you saying?"

"When I woke up on the floor with Zayn hovering over me, he said, 'I thought you burned yourself out.' And he's not the first one to say something like that."

I sat beside Oanen and took his hand in mine, already knowing how angry he was going to be.

"Stop saying his name," Oanen said. "I'm trying not to think about how he took you from right under my nose. I want to kill him for that."

"He didn't do anything bad."

"How can you say that? You said he put you to sleep."

"So has Adira."

"Exactly. I think it's safe to say you hate her."

"Different reasons. Adira is a pain in my ass and doesn't share information. It's hard to hate a guy who gives up his coat and doesn't cop a peek. At least, I don't think he did."

Oanen's expression hardened.

"You're not helping," he said.

"And you're keeping us off topic."

"Right. Just stop saying his name, and we'll be fine."

"As I was saying, the hooded-guy—"

"That's not any better."

"—isn't the only one to say I'll burn myself out. I didn't tell you everything my mom said that day in the diner."

Oanen waited for me to continue.

"Her exact words were, 'You can't deliver the wicked to hell without your wings because without your wings, you're not a fury, and your power will consume you.'"

His fingers twitched around mine.

"Why didn't you tell me?"

"I knew what you'd want me to do. And I can't, Oanen. If I kill my great-grandma just to claim my power, won't I become one of the wicked I'm here to punish? I can't kill her just so I can live. There has to be another way."

He said nothing, just looked down at our joined hands, his thumb slowly stroking the skin on the back of mine.

"What do you want to do?" he asked finally.

"I don't know. I didn't tell you all of this sooner because I thought I'd come up with something better than just going to St. Louis to talk to my grandma and seeing if she has any answers."

"Why isn't that an option?"

"It is an option. I'm just worried that when we get there, she won't have answers or won't give them. Then, you'll want me to do what my mom wants just to keep me from getting hurt more than I already am."

He nodded slowly, and when he looked up at me, his eyes were blue again.

"You're right. That's what I'd want because I'm selfish and desperate to keep you with me. But, if the last twenty-four hours has taught us anything, it's that I can't force you to do something you don't want to do. Or stop you from doing something that's in your nature to do. I don't want to change you, Megan. I want to love you just as you are."

I leaned over and set my head against his shoulder.

"Ditto, bird boy. I'm sorry I came down so hard on you for being jealous. If the roles were reversed, I probably would have acted the same."

"The difference is that I love it when you get jealous over me."

I grinned and nudged him.

"You're insane to provoke my fury like that. I don't think she'll share well once we're officially…"

"Mated?"

My face flushed.

"Yeah. That."

His phone rang, saving me from any further embarrassment.

"Hello?" He listened quietly for a minute. "No. You're going to need to send someone else for him. Megan needs to get to St. Louis. Her powers are killing her. And, I'll blame you if that happens."

He hung up and looked at me.

"Please tell me that wasn't your mom," I said.

CHAPTER FOURTEEN

Oanen's lips twitched, and he reached out to toy with the ends of my hair.

"No, that wasn't my mom. It was Adira."

"Oh, I bet being told 'No' made her real happy. Should we expect a portal?"

He shook his head.

"I doubt it. She won't admit this, but she's afraid of you. They all are."

"Good."

I rubbed my head and wished I could just take a nap.

"Are you hungry?" he asked.

"No. But I should eat."

While Oanen went to order food for us, I dug out the *Book of Fury* to read again. Gaining the little bit of understanding I had didn't help me grasp any more information from the book. However, the parts that talked about the power consuming me now made more sense.

Oanen finally brought me a burger and fries, which I nibbled on while reclined in bed. I must have dozed off because when I next woke, he was in bed with me, and we were both lying flat.

As soon as I shifted to a more comfortable position, he opened his eyes and looked at me.

"Sorry. The spot on my back was hurting."

"It's okay. Just making sure you're not going anywhere."

"No. I think it'll be a day or two before I feel any wickedness again." I moved a little closer to him and rested my head on his shoulder.

He stroked my back, careful to avoid the raw patch.

"Good, but I still don't think I'll sleep very deeply tonight. Just in case."

I didn't have the same problem. I slept hard and woke grudgingly just before dawn when my bladder refused to be ignored any longer.

"Going to the bathroom," I whispered softly as I eased away from Oanen.

He made a sound of affirmation and rolled to his side, his breathing still soft and even. I wondered how long he'd stayed awake to keep an eye on me. It must have been a while because he was still in the same position when I returned.

Easing into bed so as not to disturb him, I settled next to him. His warmth soothed me, and I exhaled contentedly. However, I'd slept so much that I couldn't fall back to sleep. So I lay there thinking.

Why was it so easy for me to know what everyone else wanted me to do and so hard for me to know what I wanted? I knew exactly what I did not want to do. But what did I want?

I decided what I really wanted was to go about my life my own way and not the way the gods wanted me to go. That didn't mean I was unwilling to have a task or job. To be useful in some way. When I really thought about it, I liked the idea of being part of something bigger than myself. I just didn't want to feel cornered or manipulated into doing something I didn't want to do.

I mean, why make some of us crave flesh and then condemn us to hell for answering the craving? Was everything just a test to see how we exercised our free will? What about those impulses some of us couldn't control? I couldn't fight the way rage consumed me whenever anyone wicked was around. What was the point of my existence, then? Was I truly only here to hurt others?

My thoughts went round and round until the sun rose, and Oanen jerked awake. I smiled when he rolled over, searching for me.

"Morning," I said.

He exhaled when he saw I was where he'd left me, and I smiled wider.

"Worried you'd lost something, again?"

"You have no idea. How long have you been awake?"

I shrugged and tilted my head to look at the clock.

"Almost two hours, I think."

He gently tucked me close to him again, and his lips brushed over the column of my throat. My eyes rolled back in my head at the sensation.

"Mmm." I couldn't help the sound. Every time he touched me, it just got better.

He groaned and pressed another kiss to my skin before getting out of bed.

"Don't make sounds like that, Megan. I don't have the restraint."

I watched him walk to the bathroom, glad he couldn't see my stupid grin. I liked that I was his weakness.

While he showered, I went to the kitchen and poured myself a bowl of cereal. He reemerged with shorts riding low on his waist and tousled wet hair before I finished my breakfast. In that glance, I knew he was my weakness, too.

"So what time do you want to leave?" I asked.

"I don't know yet. It's up to you."

"What do you mean?" I asked. I didn't miss the way his gaze skimmed my exposed legs as I sat there in his shirt.

"You're the one who has to face your great-grandmother, and you're right that she might have a better answer than what your mom already gave you. I'm not going to push you to leave until you're ready."

"But what about when I start feeling things again?"

"This place is warded. Unlike the druid's house, the warding here will keep out sound and emotion. You're safe here for as long as you need."

"And as soon as I step outside, the collective wickedness of this city will bring me to my knees. It's better if we leave before I get my powers back. We don't have to go to St. Louis. We can go anywhere. Somewhere quiet." I realized the flaw in my thinking as soon as I said it. If I waited to go to St. Louis, I'd run into the same problem I was trying to avoid when leaving New York.

"Crap," I said under my breath.

"Why don't you try your mom again?" he suggested.

I snorted. "What for?"

"You know more now. You understand what she's talking about. Maybe this time you'll be able to get through to her about why you don't want to kill your great-grandma."

I sighed heavily. "Normal humans would never have this conversation. No one kills grandmas."

"I don't know. The humans made a Christmas song about it."

"That doesn't count. It was Santa."

I froze and looked at Oanen in wide-eyed shock.

"Is Santa real?"

Oanen threw his head back and laughed. The sound did things to my middle and made me wish I wasn't hurt.

He turned away, still chuckling.

"I'll get your phone," he said.

I finished eating and put my bowl in the sink before he returned. This time, he also had a pair of shorts for me to put on.

Smiling, I accepted the phone and set the shorts aside. I sat down again and crossed my legs to expose one thigh up to my hip. Gold started to appear in his gaze.

Letting that distract me, I dialed my mom's number.

"This better not be another call from New York," Mom answered.

"We need to meet and talk in person again."

"Why? Everything you need to know is in the book."

"Obviously it's not, or I wouldn't have four very large burns on my body. Two of them I blame on you."

"The note said to get your ass to St. Louis to kill your Grandma Irene. I gave a name and address. That's everything you needed, Megan. Now get your ass into your lover boy's car and get to your grandma."

Frustration clawed at me because I knew that even if my mom would shut up and listen for two seconds, she still wouldn't give a damn about how I felt about all of this.

"How does a mom just stop loving her only child? I hope I never have kids."

Without waiting for her reply, I hung up.

Oanen caught the phone when I threw it.

"Don't let your mom's poor parenting skills close the door on having your own kids," he said softly.

I cringed, realizing what I'd said.

The phone in his hand started ringing, and he looked down at it.

"It's your mom."

I shook my head. "No. It's Paxton. And I don't need to talk to her."

Instead of setting the phone down, he answered and put the call on speakerphone.

"Megan's listening," he said.

"I never stopped loving you, Megan," my mom said in a much calmer tone. "I'm telling you to get to your grandma to save you. You set your power free, but without wings, you can't use it. It'll burn you up. You need to get to your grandma."

"No. I'm not going to kill her just to save myself. It doesn't make sense. We punish the wicked. How is killing her not going to be wicked?"

"It will be. But it doesn't matter. That's how we're made. You have to kill her, Megan."

"Never."

The call went dead. I made a face and looked up at Oanen.

"I hate to say this, but I told you so. She's useless." I thrummed my fingers on the counter, trying to think of what I wanted to do next.

"The smartest move would be to get out of New York now," I said, mostly to myself. Then inspiration struck.

"My mom isn't the only one who knows things." I glanced at Oanen. "The guy who shall not be named also knows stuff. Maybe he knows something—"

"Stop right there. We are not tracking him down so you can ask him for advice. You seem to be forgetting that he stole you."

"He borrowed me to clear his name. And, he returned me unharmed."

"He didn't return you. He left you broken and burned in a pool of your own vomit."

"That pool wasn't there when he left."

"I don't care."

I huffed an aggravated sigh.

"Between your jealousy and my fear of killing my grandma, which one wins?" I asked.

Oanen's expression cracked.

"Fine. We'll check out his house tomorrow."

"Tomorrow? What's wrong with today?"

"I barely survived yesterday," Oanen said. "Give me some time to recover. I just want to keep you here where it's safe. Twenty-four hours of just us. That's all I'm asking."

"Okay, but you better be ready to entertain me. I don't do bored."

Gold crept back into his gaze.

"I'm sure I can think of something fun to do."

I woke with a stretch and a smile. True to his word, Oanen had kept me very entertained the day before. Coed showering was now my new favorite sport. He'd been careful not to touch anything that would hurt, which meant we hadn't done a whole heck of a lot. But what we had managed had been amazing.

When we ran out of warm water, there had been movies to entertain us. And lots of couch snuggling. I was glad he'd asked for twenty-four hours. We'd needed it.

I looked at the clock, saw it wasn't yet 6 a.m., and rolled over with a smile, ready to tell him he still had two hours left. My smile faded when I saw his spot was empty. I stretched out a hand and felt the sheets were already cold.

Getting out of bed, I went in search of him. However, the condo was empty except for me and a box of cereal that had been set out on the counter along with my phone. I picked up my phone and saw a message from Oanen and another from Eliana. I read Oanen's first.

I brought the phone out here so it wouldn't wake you. Went to find Zayn. I'll call when I have him, so you can talk to him on the phone. Stay in the condo.

I smiled slightly and debated whether or not to call him

out on forgetting our whole sticking together promise. I decided it wasn't worth it. I knew his reasons for leaving me behind. The condo was the safest place for me because of the spell to keep stuff out. Staying here also kept me a healthy distance away from the guy who stole me. This time, my grin widened at Oanen's jealousy. I'd never admit it, but it was cute when it made him protective. Just not when he got overbearing with it.

I opened the other message from Eliana.

My mom is free but not leaving.

Swearing softly, I dialed Eliana's number. She picked up right away, despite the time. But, that didn't necessarily mean anything. I wasn't even sure what day of the week it was anymore.

"What do you mean she's not leaving?" I asked. "Does she have a choice?"

"Apparently she does now," Eliana said.

"What does that mean?"

"Adira thinks she is seeing a positive change in me with my mom being present. She also thinks I look healthier. I don't look healthier; I look angrier. The Council obviously can't tell the difference. I think they're confusing me with you."

I laughed softly.

"Give them hell, then," I said.

"Oh, I plan to."

"So, other than your mom staying, how are things back home?"

"Not too bad. I found some brownies who were willing to take Piepen in. He was a little upset by it, but I think he's adjusting well. I'm planning on visiting him later today. And, Elbner is making great progress on your house. For being such a grumpy, unkempt thing, he sure has that place looking nice. He's even started scraping the loose paint off the outside.

"Wow. I'm impressed," I said. "He knows that it's winter, though, right?"

"It doesn't seem to bother him."

"Other than that, anything new?" I was dying to blatantly ask about Fenris but didn't want to tip my hand if she wasn't aware yet.

"Nothing worth talking about," she said quickly.

I smiled into the phone. If she wasn't ready to admit it, that was fine.

"How about you?" she asked. "Is it true that a druid was involved in the deaths?"

"Yes. That would be Zayn. He's not wicked, though. That much I could sense."

"Be careful around him, Megan. It's not safe to trust druids."

"It's not safe to trust most of us," I said.

"Isn't that the truth."

After we hung up, I poured myself a bowl of cereal and turned on the TV. I managed to waste an hour that way then went to take a shower. Getting clean just wasn't the same without Oanen's help. When I was done, I went back to the phone and checked for new messages. Nothing.

Deciding to be the needy girlfriend, I started a message to Oanen.

"Did you get lost with a GPS? Come and get me. We'll look for Zayn together."

I set the phone down and went back to try to find something on TV. Every few minutes, I would glance at my phone. It never buzzed, though.

Close to noon, I finally got a text. Only it wasn't from Oanen; it was from my mom.

Meet me at the Gizzard in 20.

I groaned. Oanen had the car. That meant walking the streets of New York. Although it wasn't that far, if I felt anything, I'd be screwed. However, now that Mom was finally willing to meet me, I didn't want to text back asking to reschedule.

After writing a quick note and putting it on the counter, I slipped my coat and boots on and left the condo. Thankfully, when I stepped out on the street, I didn't feel a thing. I was still blissfully numb from the last burn.

Keeping my hands in my pocket and my steps quick, I made it to the Gizzard in the allotted time. A tingle of magic rippled over my skin as I open the door to a quiet and empty interior. I frowned and checked my phone. It was exactly twenty minutes since Mom's message. I looked around, again, wondering where the hell she was.

The door that led to the back hall opened, and Mom stepped out. She looked me over and crossed her arms.

"Good. You're here. Now, you're going to listen."

"Me? I should have known you weren't ready to actually help."

I turned to leave.

"Oanen's been gone a long time, hasn't he?" she asked, stopping me cold. "When was the last time you heard from him?"

I turned slowly, a sinking ball of fear and fury forming in my stomach.

"What did you do?"

"Nothing a loving mother wouldn't do." She tossed me a phone, which I caught by reflex. "I gave you motivation, Megan."

I looked at the phone's screen and saw Oanen's red face glaring back at me.

"What did you do?" I repeated, my voice deadly calm.

Through the haze of my anger, I noted four small ovals on his jawline that looked redder than the rest.

"Did you burn him?"

"It was an unintentional side effect of taking him to your great-grandma's. Having the two of us that close together resulted in—"

I flew at my mother with a strangled cry, blind to reason or caution. With the back of her hand, she sent me flying across the room.

"Calm down. The picture is proof that he's alive and well enough."

I rolled to my feet and plucked a splinter of wood the size of a pencil from my bicep. It snagged on my jacket on the way out, but I barely noticed that or the blood that immediately started to trickle down my arm.

Focused on my mom, I stalked forward. Unlike the last time, I didn't rush her.

"Fighting me will resolve nothing," she said, watching me.

"No, but making you bleed will make me feel a hell of a lot better."

Mom's eyes flared bright orange as I drew closer.

"Megan Smith," she said in her fury voice.

I embraced my fury, or what was left of her, and moved fast enough to punch my mom square in the face. Her head barely moved.

"Paxton Smith," I said in my own fury voice. "Go screw yourself."

Her eyes grew brighter, and the heat of her anger started to melt the shell of my jacket. The wood floor beneath our feet crackled and blackened.

Scary fast, she reached out and gripped me by my throat.

"I will not lose you to your own stupidity. Get your ass to St. Louis, now, and save your boyfriend."

She pushed me hard, and I went flying backward again. Barely a second after I landed, I was back up on my feet, glaring in her direction. Smoke drifted in the air between us, a murky blue haze that would have made it hard to see if fire wasn't slowly consuming my mom.

As I watched, wings sprouted from her back, vibrant twin infernos that folded forward to wrap around her torso in a bold display of yellow and orange. I knew what I was seeing. Her true form. My future true form, clothed in the fires of hell.

Zayn's comment about us being like daughters to Hades seemed more likely, looking at Mom just then.

The fire wings covering her grew impossibly bright then winked out of existence, taking her with them.

I coughed out some smoke and looked down at the phone still in my hand. The screen had cracked during one of my falls. The fissure didn't stop me from seeing Oanen's beautiful, angry face. Or his burns. Rage poked at me again as I noticed how his shoulders seemed stretched back. The image didn't show why, but I knew she'd bound his arms behind him.

First, Mom took him then tied him to a tree. Now, she wanted me to go save him. Or what? I considered the implied consequence. My family was insane. Insane enough to kill the man who held my heart? Absolutely.

The floor beneath my feet started to smolder.

"Save my boyfriend?" I said softly. "They have no idea what they've unleashed."

CHAPTER FIFTEEN

IN THE SMOKE-FILLED ROOM OF THE GIZZARD, MY MIND RACED. Oanen had taken his car to find Zayn. How exactly was I supposed to get to St. Louis? It was a one-day trip if I had a car and could drive straight through without stopping. A bus would be twice that. And the way I was feeling, I'd hurt someone before the bus arrived there. I needed a car.

I could try calling the Council. Or maybe, Oanen's mom. However, I doubted she'd appreciate that all the secrecy and withheld information had resulted in her son being kidnapped. And, given that my mom and grandma were involved and the Council feared me, I also doubted they would involve themselves in our family squabble.

Ignoring the burning pain in my arm, the smoke that followed me each step toward the door, and my throbbing headache, I left the Gizzard. The cold winter wind tore the accumulating heat from around me and cleared my mind long enough for me to think of another option.

I knew someone else who might help me. Maybe.

I used a ride app on my phone to get a lift to Elizabeth Sias's address.

The house looked the same—complete with moving curtain to the right as I approached. I pounded on the door, not pretending this time.

"Elizabeth," I called. "I need his help."

The door jerked open, and Zayn's sister stared at me.

"He's not here."

I swore.

"Do you have a car?"

Her glaze flicked over my jacket.

"Do you know you're smoldering and a little bloody?"

"Do you have a car and a change of clothes?" I amended.

She hesitated for a moment.

"Please, Elizabeth. I'm not after Zayn. I spoke on his behalf. What's going on with me now has nothing to do with any of that. The guy I was with? Someone took him. And I have to get him back."

"Fine. Wait right here." She moved to turn away then looked at me again. "Don't try to come in."

"I remember what happens. I'll wait here."

I watched her disappear into the depths of the house and idly wondered if the magic barrier was keeping the heat in, because I wasn't feeling anything. I waited and ignored the occasional slow car that drove by.

Elizabeth returned several minutes later with a bag along with a set of keys. The bag she tossed to me. Then, she pressed the button on the fob, and a nice-looking car almost a block away beeped.

"I hope you can replace it if you wreck it," she said.

"I can't, but I know people I can make do it. So, you're covered."

She smiled slightly.

"Good luck, Megan. Zayn said you were pretty cool."

I nodded and left, heading for the car. When I reached it, I looked into the bag. Elizabeth and I weren't close to the same size. She had a lot more height on me. While the pants wouldn't work, the shirt and jacket would. I stripped down to my bra right there on the street. Someone catcalled.

"Do it again so I can rip your tongue out and watch you eat it," I said without turning.

No one else watching made a noise. But, I could feel them. I shouldn't have been able to. Not yet. At least, I didn't think I should have this soon.

Ignoring the urge to follow through on my threat, I ripped the whole sleeve off my old shirt and used it as a bandage before putting on the new top and jacket. As far as anyone driving past me would see, I looked completely respectable and not like someone who had almost started a building on fire.

I threw the bag and my dirty clothes in the back and got into the new sedan. I didn't know what druids did exactly, but Zayn seemed to be doing well for himself. Or maybe his sister was a kickass president of some company.

"Nope," I said starting the car. "Prisoner of her own home. Doubt that works well on a resume."

I punched in granny-dearest's address and pulled away from the curb as the map app found me the fastest route.

The dash clock said it was almost two. The map app said I'd arrive tomorrow just before sunrise. I gritted my teeth and pressed the gas pedal until I was going the mandatory five over and hoped that I wouldn't run into any trouble.

Eight hours and one fueling later, I reconsidered my definition of trouble as I downed a gas station espresso and an energy drink. My eyeballs felt like they were wrapped with sandpaper, which grew grittier the longer I tried keeping them open.

"This better work," I said tossing the empty can and cup to the passenger floor.

As tired as I was, I didn't want to stop for even a few hours of sleep. I could feel the annoyance growing under my skin and feared what delaying even a few more hours would do to me when I entered St. Louis.

However, twenty-five minutes later, I was pulled over to the shoulder, peeing in a ditch and still tired as hell. Only, in addition to all that, I couldn't stop shaking.

"Stupid caffeine. Stupid fury burnout."

I pulled up my pants and got back into the car just as my phone started to ring. It wasn't a number I recognized. In the past, that meant nothing but trouble, and my anger over what potential bullshit my mom or the Council was going to throw at me next had me burning through the caffeine as I answered.

"Hello."

"Megan? This is Elizabeth. Zayn gave me your number and told me to call. Can you pull over?"

I looked around at the dark stretch of road.

"I already am."

"Great. Just a minute." Her voice became muffled. "She's pulled over."

A bright, blinding light filled the car.

"What the hell?" I dropped my phone to rub my stinging eyes.

"Sorry, Megan," Zayn said from beside me. "I haven't mastered portals without the light flare, yet."

I blinked several times until I could see him.

"I didn't know druids could do portals."

"Most can't. I'm sorry it took me so long to join you. I had some things that needed my attention before I could break away for a few hours to help you."

"Help me?"

"Elizabeth said you needed my help." He reached down and

picked up my phone. “I have her. Thank you.” He hung up and handed it back to me.

“If you would be so kind, I’d prefer you delete that number.”

I rubbed my face tiredly, trying to stay focused on what he was saying.

“I just needed a car,” I said, “not you, personally.”

“To get Oanen back from your great-grandmother. I know.”

“Then why are you here? And, how do you know about Oanen?”

He tapped his ear.

“I listen to the whispers. And I’m here because I think you need more than just a car. You’re exhausted. Now, let’s do a fire drill so I can drive for a while.”

I willingly switched places with him, figuring I had a better chance of reaching my destination uninjured and faster if I did so.

“Oanen left to look for you,” I said, when Zayn pulled out onto the road.

“I know. Elizabeth told me. I wasn’t home at the time.”

I leaned my head against the seat and watched Zayn drive. He was handsome enough, but there was something about him that said stay away. I wondered if he was close to anyone outside of his sister.

“You don’t seem to be home very much,” I said conversationally. “Girlfriend? Boyfriend?”

He chuckled.

“Unattached and unavailable,” he said confirming my thoughts. “And, no, I’m not home often. I work a lot, and that’s why I worry about Elizabeth. So why was Oanen looking for me?”

“What? Something you don’t know?”

He flashed a grin at me.

"It's been known to happen on occasion."

"He was looking for you because of me. You seemed to know a lot about what I'm going through. Fourth generation and all that. I was hoping you'd know of a way for me to become a full fury without having to kill someone for it."

"Ah," he said.

I waited for more, but he remained silent.

"Ah? That's it?"

He grinned again.

"You're unique for a fury, Megan. Most of your kind embrace their natural impulses to seek out and punish the wicked."

"So I've been told." I sighed, and it turned into a yawn.

"Do you know why a fury must confront the oldest generation when she comes into her power?" he asked.

"No. And that's a good part of what's pissing me off about all of this. We do so much without ever understanding why? We're just good little trained sheep, going about our business."

He chuckled.

"I will never be able to see a fury without picturing a sheep, now. Furies kill each other because of their wickedness. The older the fury, the more wickedness she'll have. It's from punishing all the wicked in her lifetime."

"Whoa—whoa—whoa." I lifted my head from the seat. "Are you saying I'm going to get condemned to hell for doing what I was made to do?"

"Yes. But not like every other wicked being you send there. Furies are forgiven their wickedness the moment their wings are ripped from their back, stripping them of their power. They die mortal and have a special resting place in hell. A peaceful one to make up for their restless and angry lives on Earth."

We get peace. But only when we die?

"What the hell? None of this is in the *Book of Fury*."

"There's a Fury book?" he asked, glancing at me. "I'd love to read it."

I studied him for a moment. Given the secrecy in which all creatures guarded information about themselves, and the protection spells on the super-secret library back at the Academy, I knew I should say no. But, I'd also read the book cover to cover and knew it didn't contain much.

"I'll let you read it if you promise to add to it, too."

He waved his hand at me. "What I told you is just common knowledge."

"Not so common if I don't know it. What else do you know?" I asked, resting my head against the seat again. Sleep was tugging at me, but I didn't want to give in.

"Probably not as much as you'd like. I don't have an answer for your problem. My understanding is that you'll be overcome with rage when you face your great-grandmother. You'll rip her wings away, stripping her of her power, and condemn her to hell. And, in doing so, you'll claim your power."

"Because there can only be three furies," I said with frustration.

"Exactly. Now, tell me something I don't know."

"Furies can only have girls."

"Common knowledge," he said with a smirk.

"Oh yeah? Griffins can only have males."

"Also common knowledge."

I waited for him to connect the dots and knew he had when his smirk faded. He looked thoughtful for a moment.

"Hooking up with Oanen might cause you some trouble."

"Yeah, my mom already tried to talk me out of it. Save your breath."

"I'm not trying to talk you out of anything."

"Then what are you saying?"

"Nothing really," he said with a shrug. "Things that might upset the balance always interest me."

"What balance?" I asked.

"The balance the gods created."

"They're dead."

"Are they?"

"I like talking to you, Zayn. You're smart, and you're not an information hog. Don't start holding back now."

He grinned again, his face illuminating from the headlights of a passing car.

"I'm not holding back," he said. "I really don't know if the gods are dead or not. But if they aren't dead, where are they? Why are they suddenly taking a hands-off approach to the creatures they warred for?"

"Good question. I've been wondering that myself."

"Not many of us have an opportunity to see the inside of a god's realm. When you deliver your first soul, try looking around."

"And report back to you?"

"Nah. It'd be better if you didn't come looking for me after this. But maybe, sometime in the future, I'll stop by and say hi."

I snorted as that potential scene came to life in my head.

"Oh, you showing up on our front stoop will make Oanen so happy," I said.

"Am I detecting some sarcasm?"

"Well, you did leave me naked on a cement floor."

"With a blanket and my jacket. And I didn't look. Well, I did, but in a clinical way to make sure you were okay."

"Yeah, you might not want to ever mention that in front of Oanen." I paused for a moment, thinking of him. "I hope he's okay."

Zayn tapped the wheel with his thumb, deep in thought.

"Griffins are singularly focused on the wellbeing of their mates," he said.

"Don't I know it. And, also, common knowledge."

Zayn looked at me. There wasn't a hint of humor in his eyes.

"You don't understand. Oanen can't be near you when you're fighting her."

Realization hit me hard. Oanen would try to protect me. Not from grandma, but from doing something I would hate myself for. And in doing so, he'd be hurt. Or worse. I'd already seen what fury fire could do to him.

So whatever happened, when I got to grandma's house, I needed to make sure Oanen was gone first. That wasn't going to be easy.

"Thanks," I said softly. "You've helped me more than the people who were supposed to be my guardians and councilors."

"I'm glad. This world can be scary without the right information, skills, or friends." He reached over and set a hand on my shoulder. "If you'll allow me, I'd like to help you sleep. I'll keep you under until we reach her house. You'll wake more rested and ready to face her this way. But the choice is yours."

"Maybe in a little bit. There's something else I wanted to ask you."

He removed his hand.

"Ask away."

"How are you not wicked? There are very few people I've met who've been as clean as you. And they're clean because they're stuck in Uttira and don't do anything. But you're out here, doing things to earn enough money to buy a car like this for your sister."

He chuckled again.

"Thank you for noticing. And for confirming something I have suspected for a long while."

"What's that?"

"In all of our recorded history, and all of the myths and fables, there are many commonalities. Not just in those old faiths and beliefs but in the current ones. And one we have seen over and over again is the concept of redemption.

"I've done wicked things, Megan. But I've always sought to atone for them in some way."

"So you're not wicked because you what? Repented?" I asked, not sure I believed removing wickedness could be that easy.

"No. It's not about being sorry for what I've done. At least, not only that. I do a lot of magic. Not all of it is good. But, I keep track. A mental set of scales, if you will. When the bad starts getting close to the good, I do more good to tip the balance back in my favor."

I considered his words as I stared out the window and watched the stars.

"It all feels like we are set up to play this game. To entertain the gods, you know?"

"I know. Only they stopped watching a long time ago. And I think it's giving us a little bit more room to interpret the rules in our favor."

"And if they start paying attention again?" I asked, looking at him.

His expression didn't change when he answered.

"Then we're all screwed."

He gave me a side glance.

"Except for maybe you, daughter of Hades," he said with a slight smirk.

I smiled in return. Zayn was different. Like he said, neither good nor bad. Just Zayn.

"I think I'm ready for a dose of that Zaynatonin, now."

He reached out and set his hand on my shoulder.

"The things we do to protect those we love shouldn't tip the balance one way or another," he said. "But sometimes, they do. Please remember that when you deal with any wicked in the future."

Before I could ask what he meant, he said, "sleep."

And, I did.

A cramp in my neck woke me. With a small cry of pain, I grabbed the mutinying muscle and rubbed lightly as I opened my eyes. The car sat unmoving on the shoulder of some country road, and the driver's seat was empty.

Frowning, I sat up straighter and looked around. It was still dark out and not easy to see far in the moonlight. However, I couldn't see Zayn anywhere. I opened the door and got out to stretch.

"Zayn?" I called.

Nothing but a cool wind answered me.

I bent down and reached into the car for my phone, which was still on the center console so I could check the time.

The screen was open to a draft of a text message.

Sorry I had to leave. Things are complicated with Elizabeth, and my first priority is keeping her safe. I didn't abandon you, though. Hopefully, the steps I've taken to protect Oanen will keep him safe when you get there. Good luck. Zayn.

I was so pissed I almost threw my phone. Instead of getting me to Grandma's like he'd promised, he'd ditched me who knew where on the side of the road.

"Eliana was right. Never trust a druid."

It took me a moment to calm down and read the message again. Anger turned to worry. What steps had Zayn taken to protect Oanen?

Pulling up the map app on my GPS, I saw I still had another two hours to drive before I reached Grandma Irene's address. However, the route it wanted me to take sent me directly through the city. I knew better than to try that. I'd have to go around, which meant even more time before I could get to Oanen.

This time, I did throw my phone. Only, I made sure it landed on the front passenger seat. I slammed the door shut, and I stomped around the car to get in behind the wheel. When I started the engine, I saw Zayn had at least left me with a full tank of gas.

Spinning gravel, I took off from the shoulder and listened to the map app's directions.

It wasn't long before I realized I had another problem. I either needed to pull over again and use the ditch or find a gas station. A hungry rumble from my stomach made the decision even though I hated having another delay. According to my map, there was a gas station not far from where I was.

I followed the directions and pulled into a fairly quiet parking lot at the edge of a small town. Wisps of annoyance skimmed over my skin before worming their way underneath it. I wouldn't be able to stay long because douchey people all over the place couldn't just be good.

Growling in agitation, I opened my door and slammed it hard behind me. I cringed, remembering my promise to return the car whole.

"You've got this, Megan. Just breathe."

The door opened, and two teens stepped out. My skin heated, and my temper rose as I walked toward them. The first one had keys in her hand and glanced at me nervously. The second one was engrossed in her phone and barely paying any attention.

"What did you steal?" I demanded, stopping in front of them.

The one with the keys lifted her hands and looked ready to cry.

"I just paid for my gas. I didn't steal anything. I swear."

"Not you. You," I said, staring at the girl with the phone.

The girl with the keys turned on her.

"Did you seriously steal something, Heather?"

The girl looked up in surprise.

"What? No. I was reading the whole time."

"She was," her friend said. "That's all she really ever does."

I studied Heather for a moment. The wickedness didn't lie. She'd done something to break a human or non-human law often enough that I had an urge to hurt her.

"Did you pay for the book you're reading?" I asked.

"Um. No. I downloaded it for free."

"How?"

"I searched for places that had it for free. Usually forums where people share book files."

I rubbed a hand over my face and tried to keep my cool.

"When you're downloading books for free from sites that are posting non-authorized copies that are normally purchased elsewhere for a fee, that's called book piracy and it's stealing. How many books did you download?" The echo of my fury voice had crept into my words.

"One thousand two hundred and twenty-three." She blinked in confusion. "How did I know that?"

"And how much would a book cost if you bothered to buy it."

"Three or four dollars," she said.

"Can you do the math?"

She paled and nodded.

"You've stolen around four thousand dollars and you're

what? Only sixteen? I can't wait to see you in another ten years," I said, thinking of Zayn's scales. "You'll be wicked enough by then that I'll be able to do something about it."

I moved to step around them.

"I don't have a lot of money," she said like that made her actions acceptable.

"I don't have a lot of money, either. Does that mean I can walk in this store and just take what I want if the cashier's back is turned? No. You want free entertainment? Turn on the TV and watch the damn news. Stop stealing books."

I went inside without a backward glance and asked for the bathroom key. The attendant gave me a once-over before handing me a chunk of wood with a key attached.

"We have problems with people stealing the key," he said when I gave it a long look.

"Yeah. Seems to be a thing."

When I stepped outside again, the two girls were gone, and I was able to let myself into the restroom without incident. However, I would have been better off on the side of the road.

Shaking my head at the complete sanitary disregard of the previous toilet users, I wiped off the seat, lined it with toilet paper, and quickly did my business. I tried to touch as little as possible and washed twice before using my elbow to open the door on the way out. It wasn't easy.

When I went back inside, I tossed the key to the cashier.

"Someone needs to go out there and clean that place. It's disgusting."

"If you don't like it, don't use it."

My fingers twitched.

"Don't test me, Anthony," I said. "I'm not in the mood, and I know you've done something wicked, too."

He gave me a startled look.

"How do you know my name?"

I pointed at the name tag on his chest.

Walking away from him, I went to the refrigerator section, hoping for some kind of edible food. There wasn't anything there, but they did have some hot rollers with a taco roll looking thing spinning dryly. Suddenly, I was missing Uttira's healthy food options.

Shaking my head, I took one of the rolls and was about to step away when I was hit from behind with a blast of wicked. I swore under my breath.

Turning slowly, I watched a woman walk in. She was dressed nicely in slacks and a business-type top. Her lipstick and makeup were perfect as was her hair. Yet, the outside didn't matter. Not when I knew the inside was so rotten.

"Don't do it, Megan. Don't do it. Just walk out. You don't have time for this."

I took one step toward the cashier and hesitated as the woman asked for the bathroom key.

The answer to protecting Oanen was right in front of me. If I tried to send this woman to hell, I'd get another burn. I would also have my abilities muted and be unable to sense my grandma's wickedness.

On the flip side, I'd almost killed myself the last time. I thought of the picture of Oanen tied to a tree. Once again, I'd been left with a non- choice.

The woman walked out the door, and I quickly paid for my crappy breakfast and followed.

No one was in the parking lot to see me waiting outside the bathroom door. Or how I grabbed the blond business woman by the throat as soon as the door opened again.

Lifting her high, I embraced my anger.

"Mabel Cartwater, confess." The harsh echo of my words brought forth the woman's sobbing confession.

I listened to how she had repeatedly abused her toddler.

Broken wrist. Broken collarbone. Broken femur. All separate occasions. All explained away with childish antics. The worst part was that this sad excuse for a mother was already trying to figure out how to get rid of the kid for good.

Her own child. What was it with shitty moms?

"If this doesn't work," I said, "know that I'll be coming for you."

I let go of my fury power at the same time I squeezed hard.

CHAPTER SIXTEEN

WHEN I WOKE UP, I WAS ALONE ON THE BLACKTOP OUTSIDE THE restroom. There was no sign of the woman or her car. I swore softly. It didn't matter. I knew her name, and I knew, somehow, I would be seeing her again very soon. The wicked couldn't escape my fury.

Slowly, I got to my feet and winced at the new ache on the side of my neck. Using the key that was lying beside me, I let myself into the bathroom and saw a new burn. The ugly red patch would be impossible to hide.

Leaving the key in the door, I returned to my car. Driving wasn't easy. I had to pull over twice to throw up, and my head felt like it was going to burst. Eventually, I made it around St. Louis to the quiet country subdivisions on the outskirts.

Grandma's house was small compared to its neighbors, but it was well kept. Quaint. I pulled into the driveway and turned off the car.

A flutter of white on the front door caught my attention. Getting out, I tried to feel for any wickedness. Nothing. Relieved, I went to the door and discovered that the flutter of white was a note for me.

. . .

Megan,

Let yourself in. There are cookies on the counter. Make sure you have one and some milk before you come to the backyard.

Grandma Irene

I ripped the note from the door.

"What the hell?"

This did not seem like a note from a fury grandma who wanted to kick my ass. The thought made me pause. Never once had I considered if she actually did want to fight me. The book only said that I had to fight her. Maybe she knew I was coming because it was an inevitable thing, not because it was something she wanted. The thought made me frown as I reached for the knob and let myself in.

The scent of freshly baked cookies filled the air. Exactly the smell I would have associated with a normal grandma's house.

Before I made it more than two steps in the direction of the kitchen, I heard the faint sound of pounding. I stopped, tilted my head, and listened.

The sounds seemed to be coming from the hall to my left. I moved that direction, peeking in a bedroom, a bathroom, and then another bedroom. Every room was empty and nicely decorated. Warm and welcoming.

The last door on the left was closed. And from behind it, the banging continued. I hesitated with my hand on the knob. What if sweet, cookie-baking Grandma Irene wasn't in the backyard like the note said? What if this was a trap?

I took a step or two back from the door.

"Hello?" I called, mustering every ounce of fake innocence I possessed.

The banging stopped.

"Megan?" came a familiar, muffled voice from the other side.

"Oanen!" I rushed for the door and flung it open. Before I made it more than a step inside, Oanen had me in his arms. His wind-and-sky scent filled my nose as I inhaled deeply and held on tightly.

"I was so scared," I said. "Are you okay?"

I tried to pull back enough to see for myself, but he wouldn't let me go.

"I'm fine," he mumbled in the crook of my neck. Thankfully, the good side. I shivered at the feel of his breath on my skin.

"I'm so sorry, Megan."

"No. This isn't your fault."

He loosened his hold, and I turned my head to meet his blue gaze. I winced, taking in everything that had changed since I last saw him. The picture on his phone had been right. He had been burned, a look I was familiar with. His eyebrows were a little melted and scorched off. And the faint stink of burnt hair clung to him.

Despite my recent burn, I could feel my fury lift her head.

"What happened? How did my mom find you?" I asked.

"I was at Zayn's house, waiting for the druid to show, when I got a text from an unknown number. I'd given my number out to so many people when we were looking for Zayn that I didn't even think anything of it. The text said to go to the Gizzard. That Zayn was there."

"But he wasn't," I said, already knowing what he would say next.

"No. I can't believe I was so stupid. I walked right into it. Your mom was there, waiting for me. As soon as she touched me, there was a bright flash of light, and I was here in the backyard."

"She teleported?" Even after seeing her disappear in front of me, I had a hard time believing she could teleport. That someday, I would be able to do the same.

"Yeah. She told me to consider myself lucky. That most people who hitched a fury ride went straight to hell."

"And teleporting burned you?"

"No. This was an accident. Your mom had barely finished tying me to the tree out back when the door to the house burst open. Your grandma came marching out, and man was she pissed. She started yelling your mom's name and demanding confessions. Your mom started doing the same. These burns are from the two of them being that close to each other. They were both engulfed in flames. It was like that time next to the car. The only thing that saved me was the tree. Your mom had tied me to the side."

I studied his face and lightly touched the redder spots I had guessed were finger marks.

"And these?" I asked.

"Once your mom disappeared, your grandma came over and demanded to know who I was. I don't think she realized how hot she still was."

I smirked.

"So, you thought my great-grandma was hot?"

He groaned and set his forehead against mine.

"I missed you," he said softly.

"I missed you, too." I tipped my head to lightly kiss his lips. "But I need you to leave."

He made an angry sound and let go of me to gesture at the wall. There were dents the size of a chair in the wall around the door, the windows, even the ceiling. Given the chair that was on the bed, it made sense. No. Not really.

"Um, what were you doing?"

"Trying to break out of here." He ran his hand through his

hair and looked at me. "That druid is nothing but trouble, and I still wish you would have been able to send him to hell."

"Explain."

"That insane druid showed up here a few hours ago. I was still tied to the tree in the backyard. Grandma Irene was weeding her garden in the moonlight. She was keeping me company until you arrived."

"Stay on topic, Oanen. What about Zayn?"

"He walked right through her house and out the backdoor like he owned the place. If you think your eyes glow, you should see your grandma's. She had him by the throat before he could blink. And, he calmly informed her that he wasn't trespassing; he was sent to protect Megan's mate."

Oanen reached out and threaded his fingers through mine.

"When your grandma asked who I was, I said I was a close friend. After your mom's reaction about us being together, I wasn't sure telling your grandma more would be wise."

"Yet, you lied to her? What were you thinking?"

"It wasn't a lie. I think I'm one of your closest friends. Aren't I?"

I melted a little and smiled up at him.

"After that shower together, I can't say no."

He frowned slightly.

"I really hope that doesn't mean you plan to shower with all your close friends."

I shrugged indifferently and watched the gold flecks creep into his eyes.

"Are you purposely provoking me?"

"Yes." I smiled sweetly, and he sighed.

"Once your grandma heard that I was your unconsummated mate, things changed. Zayn negotiated a contract with her. I'm locked in this room, unable to leave because of the druid's spell, until you claim your power."

"I don't understand. Why would my grandma agree to that?"

"That's what you don't understand? One, I don't understand what the hell Zayn was doing here. Two, I don't understand why, with all his power, he would lock me in this room instead of just taking me somewhere else. Because I know damn well he can teleport."

"He came to protect you because I asked for his help. The spell will ensure that you stay out of my fight with my grandma. And, I'm pretty sure he couldn't take you without tipping the scales to his wickedness."

I removed my hand from Oanen's and gently kissed his lips. When I pulled back, his golden eyes watched me closely. I saw the moment he caught sight of the new burn.

"Megan, what did you do?"

He reached for me, and I quickly stepped back into the hall.

"Wish me luck," I whispered.

"Megan!" He ran for the opening, hit nothing, and went flying backward. The door slammed shut on its own before he landed.

With a heavy heart, I went to the kitchen, grabbed a cookie, and looked out the window above the sink. The fenced-in yard was large, an acre at least. To the right, near the back, was a single old tree, it's craggy branches barren. To the left was the remnants of this year's garden. The brown, withered plants partially hid the woman bent over in their midst.

I couldn't see exactly what she was doing, but it looked like she was pulling out plants. She held a long handle for something. A support, given her age? Or perhaps a weapon for when I showed up?

The space from the house to the tree was charred. The dry winter grass hadn't stood a chance against whatever happened between my mom and Grandma Irene. I wondered if the same would happen when I stepped outside the door.

I bit into the cookie, wishing I didn't have to test my theories about grandma wanting to fight, wishing there'd been another answer.

"Worthless *Book of Fury*," I murmured, moving toward the back door.

Grandma Irene looked up at the sound of the hinge creaking. An orange light immediately flared to life in her eyes. I felt no fear. No annoyance or anger, either.

"Megan?" she called.

"Yeah. It's me." I walked toward the tree, slow and calm, as she straightened. She wore a long, knit sweater. Something that looked worn and comfortable—over a pair of tan slacks.

"It's a bit late in the year for weeding, isn't it?" I asked. "I mean, I've never gardened, but I would have thought the weeding happened when things were growing."

The orange light flickered in her eyes and went out. Without a word, she set her hoe aside and made her way through the brittle rows to leave her patch of earth. She didn't come closer to me, though. She waited on the normal brown grass, just on the edge of the burnt patch.

I kept walking until about fifteen feet separated us. Close enough to see the true brown color of her eyes and the thick white twist of hair peeking from the back of her head.

With the tree to my right and the house to my left, I faced her and waited for what would happen next.

Her gaze swept me head to toe, lingering on the exposed burn on my neck.

"How many burns do you have, sweetie?" she asked, sounding incredibly kind and loving. It wasn't something I was used to hearing from a motherly figure anymore.

"Five," I said.

"Is the one on your neck the freshest?"

"Yeah. I did it just before coming here. Maybe two hours ago."

Pity filled her gaze.

"On purpose?" she asked.

"Of course."

"Oh, honey," she said sadly. "You're going to burn yourself out trying to fight what you are."

"So I've been told. Repeatedly." I looked around the yard and then at the cookie I still held in my hand. "This is really good, by the way."

"It's a neighbor's recipe that I got a long time ago. Around the great depression."

I looked at the cookie again.

"Wow. That's pretty old."

"Watch it." There was no real anger in her warning. "I was older than you then."

My eyes widened in surprise.

"You've aged really well."

"You have no idea. But you will. You know your boy can't leave that room until you do what needs doing, right?"

"Yeah. I know. That complicates things."

"How so?"

"I don't want to kill you. I don't want to kill anyone just so I can live."

"You're old enough to know that just because you want something, doesn't mean you can have it." She said it sternly but not unkindly. "Like that boy inside."

A flicker of anger burst to life in my belly.

"Don't," I said.

Her eyes sparked orange in response to my warning tone. She didn't look angry, though.

"I knew it wouldn't last long," she said. "Not when you're

this close to me. I have dealt out punishments and delivered the wicked to hell for too long for you not to sense it. It's who we are. What we're made for. And that's why you need to let the boy go when we're done here. He's not right for you."

"You don't know that."

"I do. Our kind can only have girls. His kind can only have boys. Furies and griffins aren't meant to mix. And trust me when I say you want the next generation to be born. You won't want to punish the wicked forever."

Every word she spoke against my relationship with Oanen burrowed further under my skin and fueled the ball of anger growing in my middle.

"There has to be another way," I said stubbornly.

"Of course there is. Sleep with a human. They're very fertile and easy to leave."

The idea of being with someone other than Oanen ripped at my insides. We had already begun our bond. We were committed on a level I didn't fully understand. Even now, I could feel his worry and fear for me. And his love. What she was suggesting would be cheating.

I fisted my hands against her irreverent proposal and struggled to maintain control over my actions and thoughts.

"I meant there has to be another way to gain my power. A way that doesn't involve killing you. It isn't fair to punish you for something you couldn't stop yourself from doing. The gods made you this way. And, I'll hate myself for continuing their unjust system."

"I understand. I've hated myself for over one hundred years, now. I wish you could be spared that. But you can't. Now, if you want your winged friend freed, you better stop trying to deny what you're feeling and do what you're meant to do."

"No," I said through clenched teeth.

"Oh? You don't care about him? Well, that's a good thing

because he hasn't had anything to eat or drink since he's gotten here."

The rage grew.

"I know you're baiting me," I said, trying to deny the anger.

"No, this is baiting you." She smiled, a curl of her lips that held no humor. "I knew I would burn your boy when I touched him."

I couldn't stop the fury consuming me, and once the wrong done to Oanen brought it to life, I could feel every bit of wickedness coming from the old woman standing across from me. The need to punish her consumed me.

"Irene Firestorm, hell awaits you," I said, my double-edged voice rattling the branches of the scorched tree.

"Come take your birthright, fledgling. If you think you're able." She lifted her arms slightly. Flames ignited at her fingertips and slowly spread up her arms and over her shoulders to catch at her back.

Like when I'd faced my mother, I could feel the heat as wings burst forth from her back. These weren't the tiny wings I'd seen in the picture of myself at the lake but huge, beautiful wings that danced with the flames of hell.

The grass at the old fury's feet started to smoke. To me, the white wisps acted like cannon fire for our fight to start.

The rage inside me demanded that I scream my anger and launch myself at her. I shook with the need to hurt her. To rip her wings from her back. To make her bleed in retribution for her actions.

In my mind, I could see the countless wicked she'd punished and delivered to hell. The image of her face was burned further into my mind with each trip to the underworld.

My steps slowed.

There was no joy in her expression. Resolution. Anger. Impatience. So many other emotions. But never any joy.

"Don't fight it, Megan. It will kill you."

I focused on my grandmother's blazing eyes and saw the same thing now. So many emotions. Most of all, pity.

I couldn't stop my forward movement. I couldn't hold back the rage as I reached her or the tears that began a slow trek down my face.

"My poor fledgling," Irene said, opening her arms wider.

I walked right into them and let her wrap me in a hug even as I reached for her wings.

"Do what you must," she whispered in my ear.

Gripping the base of her right wing I pulled hard. She gasped, but didn't try to hurt me in return. Instead, she comforted me, running a hand over the back of my head.

"Good girl," she said, her words raspy with pain.

The wing shrunk in my hand, the power piercing my palm and filling me with its heady weight. I didn't just hunger for more. My fury needed it. I could feel how broken I was now. All the burns on my skin weren't just burns but holes in my existence. The power was working to fill them. To fix me. Without the other wing, I would die.

Knowing that, even with my need to hurt her still consuming me, I fought against myself as I reached for the other wing. I shook in her arms.

"Shh, now. It's almost over," she said.

"It will never be over," I said as I gripped her remaining wings. "I will never forgive the gods for forcing this on me."

I pulled hard, stripping her of her remaining power.

She slumped against me, and suddenly I was the one supporting her. I barely noticed her weight.

Hate and power consumed me. A new fire seared through my veins, ripping me apart and rebuilding me into something infinitely stronger than what I had been. Twin infernos sprouted from my back and grew into wings large enough to wrap around us.

In the cocoon of their flames, I could feel a pull, something urging me to allow the earth to swallow me whole. But, I ignored it, unwilling to let it distract me from the thought filling my mind. Eras. The incubus from the Roost, who had been harassing Zoe and Kelsey. He'd been wicked but his crimes petty, not wicked enough to send him to hell.

I remembered my words to him. *Make amends and cleanse your slate.*

I'd gone the other way with the girl at the gas station. I'd told her I couldn't wait for a few more years for her theft.

The druid had been right. Our deeds were being weighed on a scale that only a few could sense. Tip the scale, and go to hell. But, who decided what deeds went on each side of the scale? I realized it wasn't who but what. Our laws and rules determined the wicked.

And just like that, the view of my world shifted.

CHAPTER SEVENTEEN

I RELEASED MY HOLD ON MY GRANDMOTHER AND LET HER SLUMP TO the ground. She looked up at me with her dull brown eyes. Sweat beaded her forehead, and her pale skin was starting to redden. Yet, I saw no fear in her gaze.

"Irene Firestorm, you are condemned to a mortal life and are assured your peaceful resting place in hell."

She struggled to her feet, and I yearned to comfort her like she'd comforted me. Instead, I took several healthy steps back from her.

"But it is not your time," I said, my rage vanishing.

The back door banged open and Oanen came running out.

I held up my hand.

"Wait. Give me a minute to cool off," I said.

He stopped, his gaze shifting to my grandma who was looking at me with shock.

"What have you done?" she asked.

"Exactly what I was supposed to do."

"No, you were supposed to deliver me to hell to seal your power."

"I do not need to be told the laws set forth by humans and non-humans, alike, because I know them the moment they are created or changed. They are in me. They are who I am as much as I am hell's judge, jury, and executioner. And, I can interpret them as I choose.

"To obtain my power, I must strip it from the first living generation. To seal my newly acquired power, a wicked soul must be delivered to hell. There is nothing written that says that soul must be yours or that you must die when I strip you of power."

Knowing I was cooler, I went to the woman who'd welcomed me with cookies then provoked me to spare me.

"As a human, you've done nothing wicked. Your slate is wiped clean. Your remaining days are your own."

"But, the soul, Megan."

I smiled, my mind already seeking the soul I needed.

"Will you keep an eye on Oanen for me? He tends to go missing when I'm not at his side."

She nodded once, and I let the image of the woman from the gas station fill my mind. Her perfect hair, her pristine makeup, her nice clothes, and her foul, foul soul. As my wings sprouted and wrapped around me, I saw her clearly. Not because of a memory, but because I could see what she was doing at that exact moment. She was driving her car on a road in the city. I could feel her thoughts and knew what she was planning. She'd waited for her husband to drop their son off at daycare, and now she was on her way to pick him up again. The boy would die.

I listened to the pull of the earth and let myself sink into the darkness. I had form, but nothing else around me did. One moment, it felt like I was falling in a void; the next, I was rising. All the while, the woman, where she was and what she was doing, never left my mind. I could feel myself drawing closer to her. A moment before the darkness disappeared, instinct had me squatting down into a sitting position.

My sudden appearance in her passenger seat startled a shriek from her. She jerked the wheel and sent the car careening into a tree. It was a big tree, and she'd been in a hurry to end her son's life.

I listened to every snap of bone as the metal crunched. I flew forward too, the airbags cushioning any blow, not that I needed it. I was officially a favored daughter of hell, now. Very little could touch me.

When the car settled, I looked at the woman. Her head slowly turned toward me. Vessels had burst in her eyes.

"I take no joy in condemning you," I said. "But by doing so, I have saved a life and maintained my balance."

A rattling breath escaped her as I reached forward. Like the void I had used to get to her, she seemed to lose substance. I could see a soft blue-white glow radiating inside of her. It extended in an oval from her head to her heart, the center of it at the base of her throat. I grabbed the glow in my fist and let my wings close around us.

The same sensation of being pulled downward filled me but more strongly this time. I fell into the void, the soul still in my grasp. The woman looked at me with a mix of terror and anger in her eyes. If not for the way my fingers lingered within the illusion of her neck, I would have thought she was alive.

The heat of my wings stayed wrapped around me as we plunged downward. Outside their flaming protection, the temperature dropped until we slowed.

Below me, the darkness began to fade to reveal a vast expanse of black ice, underlit by the faint flicker of blue flame. The soul jerked in my grasp, a wisp of nothing that had no real strength.

Her gaze drifted from mine to look at the world around us,

and I did the same. To the left, a land covered in snow and mountains and storms. To the right, a golden flame lit the top of a towered fortress at the bottom of another tall mountain.

As soon as I saw the flame, I knew that was where I was meant to go.

I opened my wings and soared in that direction. My wings didn't flap to propel me forward; thought moved me. With incredible speed, I crossed the black ice and reached a black, rocky shore, seemingly devoid of life.

Far below, rivers of glowing orange and red twined through the rock in a meandering path toward the fortress. At first, I thought the streams were molten lava. Then, I heard the faint screaming and looked closer. Souls, twisted and tortured, writhed in channels of fire and blood. Like the soul I now carried, they all had form.

The sight of them didn't bother me. I knew every soul in those hell rivers had earned its place. But that wasn't where this soul belonged. There was a place for every level of wicked. The streams were for the worst. And this one wasn't the worst.

A rumble came from the side of the fortress. Something white moved against the black. And, as I neared, I could have sworn it was a man in a robe, pushing a boulder uphill. However, I was too far away to be sure.

The soul and I flew over the streams to the fortress, itself. The dark spires were silent and unwelcoming. None stood out more so than the others, yet I knew just where to go. After reaching my destination, I entered through a window, tucking in my wings to land lightly on my feet. The barren entry point, lit by torches, was as cold and dank as the hall leading from it.

With the soul at my side, thanks to my steady grip, I led her to a door. Everything I'd done so far had been instinctual. A knowing of rightness. And, now, I knew I was almost done. Instead of opening the door, I pushed the soul toward it. She struggled, her hands traveling through my arms even though I could grip her by the base of her throat. She passed through the wooden barrier as if it didn't exist. I released my hold and withdrew my empty hand.

Soul delivered. A ripple of ease shook my still visible wings, and I felt complete. Whole and healthy.

A scrape of noise down the hall drew my attention. In the flicker of torchlight, a pale specter leaned against the stone and stared at me. She looked like Ashlyn's doppelganger right out of the Grecian era, based on her flowing white dress. She lifted a hand and pointed at me, her lips moving. Like the soul I just delivered, no sound came out of her mouth.

I felt the tug again, pulling me upward, telling me not to linger. Turning on my heel, I retraced my steps down the hall and jumped out of the window. My wings expanded, and I soared upward into the void once more.

Oanen filled my thoughts, and I found myself in Grandma's backyard once more. My wings disappeared, and I looked around at the destruction of her yard. Most of the plants on the outside of her garden had burned away to ash.

The back door creaked.

"Don't you worry about any of that, Megan. Come inside and have another cookie."

I glanced at my great-grandmother, a woman I didn't really know. Yet, she'd given me so much in a brief period of time. And, it wasn't only her power that she'd given. She'd given me more understanding and comfort than anyone else I could remember, outside of Oanen and Eliana.

"Thank you," I said, moving toward her. "I hope you'll still be able to garden next year."

"I will. That ash will make the soil richer." She paused until I was closer to the door.

"What did you think of it?"

"Hell?"

"Yes."

"I guess it's just what I thought it should be. Cold, dark, depressing."

"Only the part furies visit," she replied.

"There's more?"

She smiled. "There's a lot you still don't know. And, now, there's someone who can tell you about it. If you'd like."

"I would. You have no idea how much."

"I might," she said with a small smile. "Would you like to stay for lunch?"

She opened the door and motioned me inside. The sight of Oanen pacing the kitchen while speaking on the phone prevented me from answering her.

"The answer hasn't changed. Megan said she didn't sense his wickedness, and I trust her." Seeing me, he paused his pacing. I walked up to him, kissed him lightly on the lips and stole the phone.

I put it on speaker just in time to hear Adira's reply.

"While he may not be wicked yet, he could become wicked. The kind of magic that requires souls can be dangerous, Oanen. He needs to be found and brought in for questioning."

"That's your decision," I said. "However, Oanen and I will not be the ones tracking him down."

"Respectfully, Fury, Oanen accepted a position as enforcer for the Council."

Irene waved her hands to gain my attention and mouthed, "use the voice."

"Accepting such a role," Adira said, "means he must heed the direction given by the Council to—"

"Enough," I said sharply. It wasn't the double fury voice, just the annoyed Megan voice. I shrugged at Irene at the same time Adira started speaking again.

"We acknowledge that you were unable to sense his wickedness, but that doesn't absolve us of our obligation to determine what he is planning to do with all that life energy."

Irene reached over and tapped the base of my throat.

"There," she said softly.

"From now until the end of time, Oanen belongs to me," I said, my voice ringing with the full power of a fury. "Any task he chooses to perform on behalf of the Council, he does with me at his side. And since I have spent time with Zayn Sias and have found him to be completely without any trace of wickedness, I will not waste my time tracking him down. Casting spells with life energy is not against the laws of Mantirum or mankind. Your persistence in finding the druid seems unusually driven. I think, perhaps, I would like to question you about that as well as your insistence in naming Nicolette Barchim guilty of a crime she was proven not to have committed."

Grandma Irene laughed silently beside Oanen, who watched me with his steady golden gaze. However, no indication of what Adira was thinking or feeling came from the other end of the call for several long moments.

"We understand your warning," she said finally. "Congratulations on your ascension, Fury."

"Thanks, Adira," I said in my normal voice. "We'll see you soon."

She started stammering, and with a wide grin on my face, I hung up on her.

"That felt so good," I said. "I think she might be peeing herself right now."

"You know they're going to try to find reasons to keep you out of Uttira," Oanen said.

"And they won't be able to," Grandma Irene said. "We've been using that house to raise our young for a very long time."

"That was a really cool trick, by the way," I said. "The only time I've ever been able to use that voice is when I was angry."

"Stick around, and I'll teach you plenty more cool tricks. Some, your mom might not even know."

"I'd like that very much."

We helped Grandma Irene prepare a simple lunch of sandwiches then spent the next few hours getting to know each other. She was a fount of knowledge as she guided me in the responsibilities of my new role and how I would now be perceived by the rest of the world.

"Speaking of perception, I think it's about time you called your mother," she said.

I made a face.

"I'm not sure I'm ready to talk to her yet. She took Oanen."

"And I burned him," Grandma said with a shrug. "We both did what we needed to do in order to help you become what you are."

This time, hearing it didn't send me into a rage because I really did believe her.

"You, maybe. But, Mom was pretty clear in her opinion of my relationship with Oanen."

Grandma nodded slowly and moved the plate of cookies in my direction.

"So was I," she said.

"And now?"

She glanced at Oanen, winking at him.

"I can see that a simple break isn't possible. And a complex one could be detrimental to a fury who just acquired her powers. What happens next is up to the gods. I only hope, for your sake, there will be future generations because you won't want to deliver souls forever."

I didn't think making occasional trips to hell would be so bad if it meant an eternity with Oanen.

"And what about Mom," I asked. "Is she going to try to take him again?"

"No. She won't risk going anywhere near you now." She paused with a frown. "Well, maybe she won't. You've proven that two furies can be in the same place and not kill each other. However, you may not want to test that theory, again."

It made me a little sad that I might not ever see my mom again. And suddenly, I understood why she'd deserted me.

"She was sensing my powers, wasn't she? Just before she left me in Uttira," I said.

"She held out longer than any mother before her. She loved you very much."

I took the phone from the table, and both Grandma Irene and Oanen excused themselves.

Knowing Mom hadn't just ditched me for no reason made dialing harder. Nerves made my hands sweaty. I remembered every shitty feeling I'd had toward her. Not once had I really thought of all the meals she'd made me before she'd left, the clean laundry that had just magically appeared in my drawers or all the times she had stuck up for me at school when I'd been caught fighting. Granted, it hadn't felt like that at the time, but I could see it now.

The phone rang twice before she picked up.

"Is it done?" she asked.

"I've delivered my first soul to hell and sealed my power."

She exhaled heavily.

"I'm so proud of you, baby."

The words touched me deeply since I now understood how much she meant them.

"Thanks, Mom."

"Now, you need to ditch the boy. I know it'll be hard but—"

"No, Mom. I won't leave him."

"Megan," she said with warning.

"There's something you should know. I didn't kill Grandma Irene."

"What?" Shock quieted her next word. "Impossible."

"Maybe for some. I guess I just saw things a little differently. She's mortal now. But if you can't believe that her deeds as a fury are the faults of the gods, you should probably stay away from her. Just in case."

She hesitated a moment.

"I promise not to make any plans to say hello. She's earned her remaining days of peace. But, finding a way around sending her to hell doesn't change your need to leave the griffin boy."

"Are you sure?" I asked. "Sparing Grandma was supposed to be impossible. Who's to say a relationship with a griffin needs to be thought of the same way? Has anyone actually tried it?"

Mom was quiet.

"If it's a mistake, let me make it," I said. "I just want to know that you'll leave him alone."

She chuckled softly.

"You're a full fury now. I know better than to meddle in person." She paused for a moment. "Will you call me again? Let me know how things are going?"

"I'll call you daily if you want."

"I'd like that very much."

I hung up smiling and turned to find Oanen just behind me.

"I could feel your worry," he said. "And then your joy."

"We need to talk more about how this feelings thing works."

He nodded slowly.

"We'll have plenty of time tonight. Are you ready to go back to the condo?"

"Almost. First, we need to return the car I borrowed."

Saying goodbye to Grandma Irene was bittersweet. She made me promise that I'd pop in whenever I needed advice or information.

"I know you can use the phone," she said. "But I missed out on a lifetime of having family. I want to see you as much as I can, now. And with your wings, you can be here in a blink, so there's no excuse."

And that turned into a quick lesson on how I could travel from place to place through the void, which wasn't actually a void but the entrance of the underworld that connected to everywhere.

I pulled to a stop in front of Elizabeth Sias' house and killed the engine. The car, as promised, was in the same pristine condition that it had been when I'd borrowed it.

"We're here," I said softly, looking over at Oanen.

We'd opted to take turns driving instead of stopping for a room somewhere. He'd driven most of the way, only letting me take the wheel a few hours before.

When he heard my voice, he sat up and rubbed a hand over his hair.

"I'm going to return the keys, then we can go," I said.

"How are we getting back to the condo from here?" he asked.

"Your choice. You can fly us or I can," I said with a grin before getting out.

It was just after dawn, but I hoped Elizabeth would be up.

The street was quiet as I let myself through the gate and up to the house. A prickle of awareness tickled the back of my neck, and I looked around. It felt like I was being watched, but I didn't see anything. And, either gaining my wings had toned down the volume on my wicked sensor, or there were less of them around.

The curtain moved, distracting me from my thoughts.

I smiled and went up to the door to knock softly. It opened a moment later.

Elizabeth looked over my shoulder.

"You found him," she said.

"I did. And I'm returning your car in one piece as promised."

I held out the keys. She shook her head.

"Toss them to me."

I did.

"I also have a message," I said quickly. "The Council wants to question Zayn. I let them know that Oanen and I wouldn't be involved in that. But, I wouldn't put it past them to send someone else. Zayn should make himself scarce for a while. Will you tell him?"

She nodded.

"Thanks for the car, and tell your brother thanks for his help," I said, turning away.

"And thank you for yours," she said before closing the door.

Oanen waited for me on the sidewalk.

"Ready?" I asked.

CHAPTER EIGHTEEN

"I've been ready for a long time," Oanen said, his eyes golden. "I think you can get us home faster."

My stomach did a happy twist, and I reached for his hand. Traveling through the void was almost instantaneous now that I knew how to focus.

As soon as we appeared in the condo, I released him. Every nerve ending was tingling, and it had nothing to do with our trip through hell's gate and everything to do with how Oanen was looking at me now.

"I love you, Oanen Quill," I said.

His gaze heated further.

"I don't know about you, but I could use a shower," he said.

Images of the last time we took a shower together flitted through my head.

"Are you sure you're not hungry first?" I asked.

"Oh, I'm hungry," he said.

I knew what he meant, and a moment's nervousness claimed me before I realized how pointless it was. All the time I'd hesitated and held myself back from him had almost cost us a life together.

I gave Oanen a soft smile and removed my jacket. He echoed the move and tossed his on the couch.

"Interested in a movie?" I asked, kicking off my shoes.

"Only if you are," he said, doing the same thing.

My pulse started to pick up speed.

"Maybe. It's hard to decide what I want to do now that we're back and I'm not tired, or hurt, or distracted."

I walked toward him and was thrilled at the sight of his pupils dilating.

"I heard there are some impressive views in New York. Maybe we should go sightseeing," I said.

Setting my hands on his shoulders, I stood on my toes to brush my lips against his. He groaned and started encircling me in his arms. I quickly twisted out of his grasp.

He didn't move to chase me but watched me hungrily as I backed toward the bedroom.

"Although, it is early. And not all the attractions might be ready for viewing. I think you were right the first time," I turned so I could watch where I was walking.

"I'm going to go take a shower," I said over my shoulder. "Know any best friends who might want to join me?"

I squealed when I was picked up and tossed over his shoulder.

"I love teasing-Megan," he said, stroking a hand over my butt.

"Then you're really going to love today."

Wrapped in Oanen's arms, I idly trailed my fingers over his pectorals and circled his nipple. Images of what we'd done repeatedly over the past few hours, flitted through my mind and rekindled the fire that burned inside of me only for Oanen.

"If you keep thinking like that, we're never going to leave this place. And, you need to eat."

I grinned and let the images keep playing in my mind until I found myself on my back, pinned under a very eager Oanen.

He kissed me hard then stared down at me.

"Thank you for finally saying yes," he said.

"Thank you for breaking the world's record for fastest trip to the store."

He grinned at me. "I promised no babies, and I meant it. You're all I want, Megan. Now and forever."

His love for me filled my mind.

"And if I want babies later?" I asked, growing more comfortable with the plural form of the hypothetical.

"Then, I'll want them, too."

"And you're okay practicing until then?" I wriggled under him enticingly. He groaned and playfully dropped down on me, his weight enough to smother a human but not me.

"Feed me." His words were muffled by the mattress.

I laughed and poked him in the ribs.

"I know you're only saying that because you heard my stomach growl."

He lifted himself and grinned down at me. A real smile, full and true. Not only did I see his humor, I felt it all the way down to my toes.

"You're right," he said. "And, I can't help it. This need to care for you is…"

"Awful? Stifling? Nauseating?"

"Too new and thrilling," he said. "You're mine, Megan. Finally. And I'm doing everything I can to make sure you never regret that."

He kissed me again then rolled off me and stood beside the bed.

I couldn't help but openly stare.

"Sightseeing?" he asked.

"Yep. New York sure has a lot to boast about."

He held out a hand.

"Let's shower and decide where we want to eat. We can go anywhere now, thanks to my amazing, slightly ornery, but completely adorable mate."

"Honestly, I'm ready to get home," I said. "I want to find out what's going on with Fenris and Eliana." I sat up quickly. "Crap. I forgot to call Eliana."

Ignoring the naked golden god at my side, I grabbed my phone from the nightstand and dialed Eliana.

"Hey, Megan," she answered.

"Hey. Sorry I didn't call sooner. It's been crazy."

Oanen trailed a finger down my arm, a reminder of how that "crazy" had ended.

"I heard," Eliana said with a light laugh. "You ruffled some feathers with your Oanen-is-mine speech."

I grinned. "Good. They need to stop toying with people."

"Agreed."

"Good news, though. Oanen and I are heading back to Uttira today." I bit my lip as I remembered something. "As soon as we find his car," I asked.

"Um, you might want to rethink that," she said.

"What? Finding his car?"

"No. Coming back to Uttira."

"Don't you love me anymore?" I tried to say it jokingly but couldn't ignore the insecurity I was feeling.

"Like crazy," she said. "And that's why I want you to go somewhere else for a while. Somewhere romantic and amazing where you and Oanen can do all the new couple things you're probably already doing. When you get it out of your system, you can come back."

I was quiet for a moment, feeling a little hurt.

"You're afraid of being around us," I said.

"Yes and no. I'd be fine with one of you at a time. But, wanting you to stay away has more to do with my mom. New couples are too tempting. You give off too much energy."

"You mean sexual energy." I loved finally being with Oanen, but I missed Eliana, too. It felt like I'd unintentionally picked between the two of them.

"Yes," Eliana said. "That. And with Mom being pregnant, I just don't want to worry about you."

I looked at Oanen, who was watching me closely.

"How long do we need to stay away?" I asked.

"Mom's due in five months, but I don't think it'll take that long for your new, um…lust to wear off."

Five months? I had hated being trapped in Uttira. Yet, now that I was free to come and go, Eliana was telling me I shouldn't. I couldn't imagine staying away from her for that long.

Oanen motioned for the phone, and I handed it over.

"Eliana, Megan needs to see you as much as you need to see her. We'll stay away for two weeks. Then we're coming home." His golden eyes pinned me, and he handed back the phone.

I quickly put it to my ear.

"Eliana?" I said.

"Yep, I'm still here. I'm glad the bossy griffin is officially in your hands," she said. "It'll be weird not having a male protectively hovering all the time, but I'm sure I'll manage."

I tried biting my lip again while fighting not to say something. But, my meddling, happily mated self couldn't control herself.

"You never know. There might be someone lurking in the shadows, waiting to take up that mantle."

She snorted.

"I hope not. I'll see you in two weeks," she said. "Hopefully, Mom will have lost interest in what Uttira has to offer by then and go back to New York."

I smiled, already anticipating the Fenris and Eliana details I would get when I saw her next.

"I'll see you in two weeks," I said.

EPILOGUE

WITH A CRITICAL EYE, I CONSIDERED THE HOUSE.

"What do you think?" Oanen called from his position on the roof. A pair of shorts hung low around his hips. It didn't matter how much time had passed, he looked tempting as hell.

"I think you need to get down from there and give me a foot rub."

He grinned, tossed the paintbrush he held into the can beside him, and jumped from the roof. Landing with his usual grace, he strode toward me so he could set his hands on my rounded belly.

"The baby being a troublemaker again?"

"No. I just wanted you to hold me."

Oanen kissed me then slipped his arms around me so we stood looking at our newly painted house. I would miss the obnoxious rainbow colors that had decorated it, but it was time to move on and grow up. The soft buttercream color definitely made the house look less crazy and more welcoming.

"Things will be different for this next generation," he said, tightening his hold just a smidge.

"I know." We'd talked at length before taking this next step.

"If this baby is a girl, she'll be raised knowing exactly what she is."

The newly rewritten *Book of Fury* would be her bedtime story. And when her anger started, she would live with her Auntie Eliana instead of being left alone. Not a day would go by where she would question my love for her. Well, not more than a week.

"And, if it's a boy," I said, "I'll build a coop."

Oanen chuckled behind me and pressed a kiss to my temple. Despite his outward affection, I could feel the worry that he was trying so hard to hide from me.

"I don't regret this decision," I said, twisting in his arms to look up at him. He had barely aged a day. Neither of us had.

It'd taken me a while to understand my Grandma Irene's words about needing the next generation. Watching all of our friends age, while time stood still for us, had been eye opening. As much as I worried about the gender, I didn't fear having a baby. Not anymore.

"If this one's not a girl, we'll try again," Oanen said.

"And again? And again? And again?" I asked playfully.

"I'm willing to sacrifice my evenings until we get it right." The husky note in his voice made me shiver.

"Except tonight," I said. "Our friends will be here in a few hours. You have paint to clean up, and I have a dinner to make."

"Get to it, woman," he said with a playful swat to my butt. "First one done gets a foot rub."

I bolted for the house. It was probably more of a waddled hustle, but I worked with what I had.

However, instead of going to the kitchen, I went to the study and pulled the new and improved *Book of Fury* from the shelf. It was much thicker than its predecessor and was filled with not only my handwriting, but Grandma Irene's, Grandma Grace's, and my mom's as well.

I thought of Grandma Irene, who had recently passed away. I

missed her terribly, but thanks to her, I had a relationship with the other two furies. A long distance one, but I'd take it. And also, thanks to Grandma Irene, I had hope for my own future and that of my future daughter's.

I opened the book and read a passage I'd written for the next generation.

While it's true there can only be three Furies, it's not necessary to kill the elder generation. It is only necessary to strip her of her power by ripping off her wings. It won't be easy to stop there. You'll want to condemn her to hell for her crimes against the wicked. But remember not to hold her at fault. It is the gods who made us the way we are. And while we can control some of our impulses, others cannot be refused.

Embrace who you are and take your power when you're ready. Remember that you will not age until you do. You will watch the lives of your friends move with time but you will remain standing still until you bring forth the next generation of fury.

I closed the book and placed it on the shelf. The gods made us, gave us our gifts, and left us to make our own choices. And, I'd made mine. I had no regrets.

"Megan?" Oanen called, the back-door slamming. "I think I won."

"Does that mean I don't get a foot rub?" I asked, coming out of the office.

He gave me a wry grin.

"It means I help with dinner, and you get a foot rub afterward."

I smiled at him.

Nope. I didn't have a regret in the world.

Thank you for reading *Fury Freed,* the conclusion to the *Of Fates and Furies* series. Want to know more about what's going on with Eliana and Fenris? You're in luck! The *By Kiss and Claw* series is already underway. Keep reading for a little peek from Fenris' point of view or skip straight to *The Howl,* book 1.

BONUS SCENE

Fenris...

I walked around Megan's house, inhaling deeply. It'd barely been an hour since she and Oanen had left and a little more than that since Eliana's departure. Not enough time to lose either of their scent trails this far out of town.

I focused on Eliana's sweet scent and followed it from the driveway to the backdoor. A hunger surged forward. A need to touch. To taste. I clenched my fists, tired of just inhaling her. If only she were here.

The urge to howl my frustration rose, stifling common sense. But only for a moment. I exhaled slowly and reminded myself why I couldn't give into any of my urges. Eliana wasn't ready. She needed more time.

When she finally did run from me, I needed it to be because she wanted me to chase her, not because she was afraid.

I pulled my phone from my pocket and sent a text.

First security sweep done. Megan's car is still here and unmaimed.

While Megan's abandonment caused me some serious issues

—how was I going to get my Eliana fix now?—there was a silver lining. I now had a valid reason to stay in contact with Eliana.

A message appeared as I stared at my phone.

They just left. Of course her car is still fine.

An intense satisfaction coursed through me reading her words, and I paced Megan's snow dusted lawn as I responded.

It doesn't hurt to be cautious. How's your car?

My car is fine. Go home, Fenris.

I'll see you Monday.

I waited for a minute, and when nothing came through, I smiled and pocketed my phone. I hadn't really expected her to respond.

Patience and a plan would get me what I desperately wanted. Good thing I had both. It wouldn't be much longer before Eliana was begging me to howl and chase her through the woods.

Whistling a jaunty tune, I stripped from my clothes, bundled them together, and shifted.

It was time to put my plan in motion.

Want more Eliana and Fenris?
Check out The Howl, now available!

AUTHOR'S NOTE

What a ride! I loved embarking on a new world and hope you enjoyed it enough to want more. Megan was so kickass to write, and Eliana's story is going to be epic as well.

It took over 900 hours to write this trilogy! Yep, that's a lot of hours. It's crazy the amount of time an author can spend creating the stories you love. But can you imagine working your job for 900 hours and not getting paid by your employer? It would suck sweaty monkey balls.

While I do occasionally run discounts on my books to entice new readers, please never download my books from sites offering them for free when they are otherwise paid books. It's called book piracy and hurts the literary economy more than you know. Mainly the authors.

If you're strapped for cash, the legal and most beneficial way to support any author you love, is to go to your local library and request they add a book (or a million) to their digital lending library. Libraries usually get discounts, so they rarely say no!

So, in summary, I love you for reading, but I'll love you even more if you're reading a legal copy that fairly compensates the author for the time spent writing.

And please, if you loved this series, don't forget to let me and other readers know by leaving a review on the retailer site of your choice.

Happy reading!

Melissa

Of Fates and Furies

Join the Academy!

Book 1: Fury Frayed

Raised to believe she's human, Megan must discover the truth about who and what she is to stop a murderer after her mom abandons her in Uttira, a town filled with mythological creatures posing as humans.

Book 2: Fury Focused

With a new boyfriend and new responsibilities, Megan's life is more complicated than ever. As new abilities start to emerge, she must learn to control them or risk never being able to leave Uttira again.

Book 3: Fury Freed

Discovering the Book of Fury forces Megan down a path she never thought she'd travel. It's a race against time to discover a way to obtain her powers without sacrificing who she's become and those she loves.

BY KISS AND CLAW

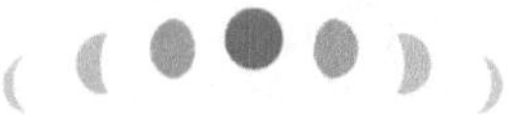

Run with the wolves!

BOOK 1: THE HOWL

A young succubus struggles to accept what she is and how she must feed in this hilarious yet emotional paranormal coming of age story filled with love, lust, and a brownie too horny to trust.

BOOK 2: THE HUNT

Eliana lost her chance at a peaceful life the moment her mom returned to Uttira and vowed to help her overcome her feeding disorder. Seeking to escape the pressure, she retreats to a cabin in the woods, but something is stalking her. Whatever beast is out there is about to become the hunted, because Eliana's had enough playing by everyone else's rules.

BOOK 3: THE HUNGER

Eliana has the one thing she thought she'd never have. Fenris. But in order to keep him, she'll need to unleash the last piece of herself that she's been hiding and fully embrace all that she is. And, the world will fall on its knees when she's done.

Book 1: Hope(less)

With her abilities, Gabby discovers the existence of werewolves and others like her. She is the spark that ignites an inescapable fate for six uniquely gifted women, a fate that will claim her life and her heart.

Book 2: (Mis)fortune

Tormented by her predictions, Michelle escapes from the creatures who seek to use her only to run straight into the arms of another beast. However, this one isn't what he seems, and with his help, she might be able to free herself forever.

Book 3: (Un)wise

Bethi, the keeper of past lives, fights the truth of who she is and what she needs to do when one of the werewolves finds her. But there's no hiding from her destiny. She is the key to bring them all together.

Book 4: (Un)bidden

Charlene has more power than she knows and all the strength that the werewolves need. And if she decides the werewolves are worth saving, she'll need to claim one of them as her own.

Book 5: (Dis)conent

An emotional syphon, Isabelle deals the best way she can – with her fists. When a werewolf comes crashing through friend's bar, Isabelle is forced into a game she doesn't want to play with new friends she doesn't really like.

Book 6: (Sur)real

Olivia is blind, yet sees. What she sees, she keeps to herself as he father plots for control. She does her own plotting, working with forces that only she understands. Her time is running out to save her sisters and the world.

Join the heroes!

Book 1: Clay's Hope

A werewolf more comfortable in his fur than his skin, Clay only thinks he knows what it means to be human. Until he meets Gabby, his unique human Mate. The Claiming rules have changed and learning has never been harder...

Book 2: Emmitt's Treasure

The story of finding my Mate starts like a bad bar joke–a woman walked into a diner. If only the punch line made it better. But it doesn't. She's running and scared and keeping a secret. One of my kind, a werewolf, had kept her prisoner for years. What he did is unforgivable. What I'll do when I find him will be far worse.

Book 3: Luke's Dream

Luke's been kicked in the teeth by fate enough to know: nice guys finish last. Yet, he still finds himself driving across the country to look for someone because Gabby asked him to. It's his one last nice deed. Afterward, he's going Mate hunting and nothing will stop him from Claiming what's his.

Book 4: Thomas' Heart

Thomas vows no human would go unpunished for the destruction of his world. His mission to rid the north of every one of them comes to a halt when he meets Charlene. He wants her, but can't have her. She's unique. And she's changing everything.

Book 5: Carlos' Peace

My earliest memory holds a secret that haunts me. Driven not to repeat the mistake of my past, I've molded myself to become what's needed, a protector of my race. But even that might be taken from me.

www.ingramcontent.com/pod-product-compliance
Lightning Source LLC
LaVergne TN
LVHW041050080826
845145LV00007B/1521